William Henry Wills

Old Leaves

Gathered from Household Words

William Henry Wills

Old Leaves
Gathered from Household Words

ISBN/EAN: 9783337395698

Printed in Europe, USA, Canada, Australia, Japan

Cover: Foto ©Andreas Hilbeck / pixelio.de

More available books at **www.hansebooks.com**

OLD LEAVES:

GATHERED FROM HOUSEHOLD WORDS.

BY

W. HENRY WILLS.

NEW YORK:
HARPER & BROTHERS,
FRANKLIN SQUARE.

1860.

TO

THE OTHER HAND,

WHOSE MASTERLY TOUCHES GAVE TO THE OLD LEAVES HERE FRESHLY

GATHERED, THEIR BRIGHTEST TINTS, THEY ARE AFFECTIONATELY

INSCRIBED.

CONTENTS.

OLD LEAVES.

VALENTINE'S DAY AT THE POST-OFFICE.

MARCH 30, 1850.

LATE in the afternoon of the 14th of February last past, an individual who bore not the smallest resemblance to a despairing lover, nor, indeed, to a lover in any state of mind, was seen to drop into the box of a Fleet-street receiving-house two letters folded in flaming covers. He did not look round to see if he were observed, but walked boldly into the shop with a third epistle, and deposited thereon one penny. Considering the suspicious appearance of this document—for its envelope was green—he retired from the counter with extraordinary *nonchalance*, and coolly walked on toward Ludgate-hill.

Long paces soon brought him to St. Martin's-le-Grand; for he strode like a man who had an imminent appointment. Sure enough, under the clock of the General Post-office, he joined another, who eagerly asked,

"Have you done it?"

The answer was, "I have!"

"Very well. Let us now watch the result."

Most people are aware that the Great National Post-office in St. Martin's-le-Grand is divided into halves by a passage, whose sides are perforated with what is called the "Window Department." Here huge slits gape for letters, whole sashes yawn for newspapers, or wooden panes open for clerks to frame their large faces, like giant visages in the slides of a Magic Lantern; and to answer inquiries, or receive unstamped paid letters. The southern side is devoted to the London District Post, and the northern to what still continues to be called

---

☞ Portions of the papers distinguished throughout the volume by this mark are by another hand.

the "Inland Department," although foreign, colonial, and other outlandish correspondence now passes through it. It was with the London District Branch that the two gentlemen first appeared to have business.

Having been led through a maze of offices and passages more or less dark, they found themselves—like knights-errant in a fairy tale—"in an enormous hall, illumined by myriads of lights." Without being exactly transformed into statues, or stricken fast asleep, the occupants of this hall (whose name was Legion) appeared to be in an enchanted state of idleness. Among a wilderness of long tables, and of desks not unlike those on which buttermen perform their active parts of leger-demain in making "pats"—only these desks were covered with black cloth—they were reading books, talking together, wandering about, lying down, or drinking coffee—apparently quite unused to doing any work, and not at all expectant of ever having anything to do, but die.

In a few minutes, and without any preparation, a great stir began at one end of this hall, and a long train of private performers, in the highest state of excitement, poured in, getting up, on an immense scale, the first scene in the "Miller and his Men." Each had a sack on his back; each bent under its weight; and the bare sight of these sacks, as if by magic, changed all the readers, all the talkers, all the wanderers, all the liers-down, all the coffee-drinkers, into a colony of human ants.

For the sacks were great sheepskin bags of letters tumbling in from the receiving-houses. Anon they looked like whole flocks suddenly struck all of a heap, ready for slaughter; for a ruthless individual stood at a table, with sleeves tucked up and knife in hand, who rapidly cut their throats, dived into their insides, abstracted their contents, and finally skinned them. "For every letter we leave behind," said the bag-opener, in answer to an inquiry, "we are fined half-a-crown. That's why we turn them inside out."

The mysterious visitors closely scrutinised the letters that were disgorged. These were *from* all parts of London *to* all parts of London and to the provinces and to the far-off quarters of the globe. An acute postman might guess the broad tenor of their contents by their covers;—business letters are in big envelopes, official letters in long ones, and lawyers' letters in none at all; the tinted and lace-bordered mean Valentines, the black-bordered tell of grief, and the radiant with white enamel announce marriage.   When the despatch of the Fleet-street receiving-house appeared the visitors tracked it, and the operations of the clerk who separated the three bundles of which it consisted were closely followed.   With the prying curiosity which now only began to show itself, one of the intruders took a copy of the bill which accompanied the letters.   It set forth in three lines that there were so many "Stamped," so many "Prepaid," and so many "Unpaid."

The clerk counted the stamped letters like lightning, and a flash of red gleaming past showed the inquirers that one of their epistles was safe.   Suddenly the motion was stopped; the official had instinctively detected that one letter was insufficiently adorned with the Queen's profile, and he weighed and taxed it double in a twinkling.   Having proved the number of stamped letters to be exactly as per account rendered, he went on checking off the prepaid, turning up the sender's green missive in the process.   He then dealt with the unpaid, amongst which the lookers-on perceived their yellow one. The cash column was computed and cast in a single thought, and a short-hand mark, signifying "quite correct," dismissed the Fleet-street bill upon a file, for the leisurely scrutiny of the Receiver-General's office.   All the other letters, and all the other bills of all the other receiving-houses, were going through the same routine at all the other tables; and these performances are repeated ten times in every day, all the year round, Sundays excepted.

"You perceived," said one of the two friends, "that in the rapid process of counting our stamped letter gleamed past like a meteor, whilst our money-paid and unpaid epistles remained long enough under observation for a careful reading of the superscriptions."

"That delay," said an intelligent official, "is occasioned because the latter are unstamped.   Such letters cause a great complication of trouble, wholly avoided by the use of Queen's heads.   Every officer through whose hands they pass—from the receiving-house-keeper to the carriers who deliver them at their destinations—has to give and take a cash account of each. If the public would put stamps on all letters, it would save us, and therefore itself, some thousands a year."

"What are the proportions of the stamped to the prepaid and unpaid letters which pass through all the post-offices during the year?"

"We can tell within a very near approximation to correctness: 337,500,000 passed through the post-offices of the United Kingdom during last year, and to every 100 of them about 50 had stamps; 46 were prepaid with pennies; and only 4 were committed to the box unpaid."*

While one of the visitors was receiving this information, the other had followed his variegated letters to the next process; which was that of stamping on the sealed face, in red ink, the date and hour of despatch. The letters are ranged in a long row, like a pack of cards thrown across a table, and so fast does the stamper's hand move, that he can mark 6000 in an hour. While defacing the Queen's heads on the other side, he counts as he thumps, till he enumerates fifty, when he dodges his stamp on one side to put his black mark on a piece of plain paper. All these memoranda are afterwards collected by the president, who reckoning fifty letters to every black mark, gets a near approximation to the number that have passed through the office.†

Feb. 14th, 1850.	Paid.	Unpaid.		Stamped.	Total.
	1d.	1d.	2d.		
Collections.					
8 o'clock.	6,872	52	1,216	20,082	28,222
10 "	6,212	19	607	13,629	20,467
12 "	7,069	36	612	15,240	22,957
1 "	2,989	17	277	6,395	9,678
2 "	6,520	39	535	13,696	20,790
3 "	2,456	36	328	6,909	9,729
4 "	4,873	36	375	13,478	13,478
5 "	3,340	28	317	8,207	11,892
6 "	9,300	129	958	27,950	38,337
8 "	3,903	32	812	6,650	11,487
	53,284	424	6,037	132,236	187,037

* Since 1850 the number of letters has increased by more than one half, and now exceeds five hundred millions: equal on an average to eighteen letters to every man, woman and child in the United Kingdom.

† Much of this work is now (1859) performed by machinery.

It was by this means that our friends obtained the foregoing account of the number of district letters that passed through this office on St. Valentine's Day.

To this total are to be added 6000 "bye" letters—or those which passed from village to village within the suburban limits of the district post without reaching the chief office—and 100,000 destined for the provinces and places beyond sea, which were transferred to the Inland Department. The grand total for the day, therefore, rose to nearly 300,000. Thus the sacrifices to the fane of St. Valentine—consisting of hearts, darts, Cupid peeping out of paper-roses, Hymen embowered in hot-pressed embossing, swains in very blue coats and nymphs in very opaque muslin, coarse caricatures and tender verses—caused an augmentation to the revenue on this anniversary equal to about 70,000 missives; 123,000 being the usual daily average for district and "byes" during the month of February. This increase, being peculiar to cross and district posts, does not so much affect the Inland-office, for lovers and sweethearts are generally neighbours. The entire correspondence of the three kingdoms is augmented on each St. Valentine's Day to the extent of about 400,000 letters.

"Is it possible?" exclaimed one of the visitors, regarding the piles of epistles on the numerous tables "that this mass of letters can be arranged and sent away to their respective addresses in time to receive the next collection, which will arrive in less than an hour?"

"Quite," replied an obliging informant; "I'll tell you how we do it. We have divided London into seventeen sections.* There they are, you perceive." He then pointed to the tables with pigeon-holes numbered from one to seventeen; one marked "blind," with a nineteenth labelled "general." It was explained that the proper arrangement of the letters in these compartments constitutes the first sorting. They are then sorted into subdivisions; then into districts, and finally handed over to the letter-carriers, who, in another room, arrange them for their own convenience into "walks." As the visitors looked round they perceived their coloured envelopes—which were all addressed to Scotland, suddenly emerge from a chaotic heap,

---

* The overgrown metropolis is now divided into ten post towns; each town receiving and despatching its letters at its own head-quarters, independently of the other.

and lodged in the division marked "general," as magically as
a conjuror causes any card you may choose to fly out of the
whole pack. "These letters," remarked the expositor, "being
for the country, will be presently passed into the Inland-office
through a tunnel under the hall. "The 'blind' letters have
superscriptions which the sorters cannot decipher, and are sent
to the 'blind' table, where a gentleman presides, to whom,
from the extreme sharpness of his vision, we give the *lucus à
non lucendo* name of the 'blind clerk.' You will have a specimen of his powers presently."

While this dialogue was going on there was a general abatement of the noise of stamping and shuffling letters ; and, when
the visitors looked round, the place had relapsed into its former
tranquillity. It was scarcely credible that from 30,000 to
40,000 letters had been received, stamped, counted, sorted, and
sent away in so short a time. "A judicious division of labour,"
remarked one of our friends, "must work these miracles."

"Yes, sir," was the reply of an official. "There are from
1200 to 1700 of us to do the work of the district post alone.
When it was removed from Gerrard-street to this building
there was not a quarter of that number. For instance—then,
three carriers sufficed for the Paddington district ; but, by the
despatch you have just seen completed, we have sent off 2000
letters to that single locality by the hands of twenty-five
carriers."

"The increase is attributable to the penny system ?" interrogated one of our inquiring friends.

"Entirely."

The questioner then referred to a Parliamentary paper of
which he had obtained possession. It showed him the history
of general postal increase since the era of dear distance rates.
In 1839—under the old system—the number of letters which
passed through the post was 76 millions. In 1840 came the
uniform penny, and for that year the number was 162 millions,
or an increase of 93 millions, equal to 123 per cent. That was
the grand start ; afterwards the rate of increase subsided from
36 per cent. in 1841, to 16 per cent. in 1842 and 1843. In 1845,
and the three following years, the increase was respectively,
39, 37, and 30 per cent. Then succeeded a sudden drop ; perhaps the culminating point in the rate of increase had been at-

tained. The Post-office is, however, a thermometer of commerce: during the depressing year 1848, the number of letters increased no more than 9 per cent. But last year 337,500,000 epistles passed through the office, being an augmentation of 8,500,000 upon the preceding year, or 11 per cent. of progressive increase. Another Parliamentary document shows, that, although the business is now four and a half times more than it was in 1839, the expense of doing it has only doubled. In the former year the cost of the establishment was not quite 690,000*l.*; in 1849 it was about 1,400,000*l.**

While one visitor was poring over these documents, the other deliberately watched the coloured envelopes. They were, with about 2000 other General Post letters, put into boxes and taken to the tunnel to be conveyed into the Inland-office upon a horizontal band worked by a wheel. The two friends now took leave of the District Department to follow the objects of their pursuit.

It was a quarter before six o'clock when they crossed the Hall—six being the latest hour at which newspapers can be posted without fee.

It was then just drizzling newspapers. The great window of that department being thrown open, the first black fringe of a thunder-cloud of newspapers impending over the Post-office was discharging itself fitfully—now in large drops, now in little; now in sudden plumps, now stopping altogether. By degrees it began to rain hard; by fast degrees the storm came on harder and harder, until it blew, rained, hailed, snowed, newspapers. A fountain of newspapers played in at the window. Water-spouts of newspapers broke from enormous sacks, and engulphed the men inside. A prodigious main of newspapers, at the Newspaper River Head, seemed to be turned on, threatening destruction to the miserable Post-office. The Post-office was so full already, that the window foamed at the mouth with newspapers. Newspapers flew out like froth, and were tumbled in again by the bystanders. All the boys in London seemed to have gone mad, and to be besieging the Post-office with newspapers. Now and then there was a girl; now and then a woman; now and then a weak old man: but

* In 1858 it was 1,926,100*l.*, but the gross revenue has risen to more than three millions sterling.

as the minute hand of the clock crept near to six, such a torrent of boys, and such a torrent of newspapers came tumbling in together pell-mell, head over heels, one above another, that the giddy head looking on chiefly wondered why the boys springing over one another's heads, and flying the garter into the Post-office with the enthusiasm of the corps of acrobats at M. Franconi's, didn't post themselves nightly, along with the newspapers, and get delivered all over the world.

Suddenly it struck six. Shut, Sesame! Perfectly still weather. Nobody there. No token of the late storm—Not a soul, too late!

But what a chaos within! Men up to their knees in newspapers on great platforms; men gardening among newspapers with rakes; men digging and delving among newspapers as if a new description of rock had been blasted into those fragments; men going up and down a gigantic trap—an ascending and descending-room worked by a steam-engine—still taking with them nothing but newspapers. All the history of the time, all the chronicled births, deaths, and marriages, all the crimes, all the accidents, all the vanities, all the changes, all the realities, of all the civilised earth, heaped up, parcelled out, carried about, knocked down, cut, shuffled, dealt, played, gathered up again, and passed from hand to hand, in an apparently interminable and hopeless confusion, but really in a system of admirable order, certainty, and simplicity, pursued six nights every week, all through the rolling year. Which of us, after this, shall find fault with the rather more extensive system of good and evil, when we don't quite understand it at a glance; or set the stars right in their spheres?

The friends were informed that 70,000,000 newspapers pass through all the post-offices every year. Upwards of 80,000,000 newspaper stamps are distributed annually from the Stamp-office;* but, most of the London papers are conveyed into the country by early trains. On the other hand, frequently the same paper passes through the post several times, which accounts for the small excess of 10,000,000 stamps issued over

* The newspaper stamp being no longer compulsory, the number is greatly reduced. As the privilege, however, of transmission and retransmission for a single payment can still be obtained by means of this stamp, about thirty millions of newspaper stamps are still issued every year.

papers posted. In weight, 187 tons of paper and print pass up and down the ingenious "lift" every week, and thence to the uttermost corners of the earth—from Blackfriars to Botany Bay, from the Strand to Chusan.

As to the rooms, revealed through gratings in the well, traversed by the ascending and descending-room, and walked in by the visitors afterwards,—those enormous chambers, each with its hundreds of sorters busy over their hundreds of thousands of letters—those despatching places of a business that has the look of being eternal and never to be disposed of or cleared away—those silent receptacles of countless millions of passionate words, for ever pouring through them like a Niagara of language, and leaving not a drop behind—what description could present them? But when a sorter goes home from these places to his bed, does he dream of letters? When he has a fever (sorters *must* have fevers sometimes), does he never find the Welsh letters getting into the Scotch divisions, and the London letters going to Jericho? When he gets a glass too much, does he see no double letters mis-sorting themselves unaccountably? When he is very ill, do no dead letters stare him in the face? And yonder dark, mysterious, ground-glass balcony high up in the wall, not unlike a church organ without the pipes—the screen from whence an unseen eye watches the sorters who are listening to temptation—when he has a nightmare, does he never dream of *that?*

Then that enormous table upon which the public shoot their letters through the window-slits—do the four men who sit at it never fancy themselves playing at whist, gathering up an enormous pack of red aces, with here and there a many-hued Valentine to stand for a Court card? Their duty is termed "facing," or turning the ace-like seals downwards, ready for stamping.

The system of stamping, sorting, and arranging, is precisely similar to that in the District Branch; and, by his recently acquired knowledge of it, the person who posted the coloured letters was able to trace them through every stage, till they were tied up ready to be "bagged," and sent away. While thus employed, his companion made the following observations:

In an opposite side of the enormous apartment, a good space

and a few officials are devoted to repairing the carelessness of
the public, which is, in amount and extent, scarcely credible.
Upon an average, 300 letters per day pass through the General
Post-office totally unfastened; chiefly in consequence of the
use of what stationers are pleased to call " adhesive" envelopes.
Many are virgin ones, without either seal or direction; and not
a few contain money. In Sir Francis Freeling's time, the sum
of 5000*l.* in Bank-notes was found in a " blank." It was not
till after some trouble that the sender was traced, and the cash
restored to him. Not long since, an humble post-mistress of
an obscure Welsh post-town, unable to decipher the address
on a letter, perceived, on examining it, the folds of several
Bank-notes protruding from a torn edge of the envelope. She
securely re-enclosed it to the secretary of the Post-office in
St. Martin's-le-Grand; who found the contents to be 1500*l.*,
and the superscription too much even for the hieroglyphic
powers of the " blind clerk." Eventually the enclosures found
their true destination.

It is estimated that there lies, from time to time, in the
Dead-Letter-office, undergoing the process of finding owners,
some 11,000*l.* annually, in cash alone. In July, 1847, for
instance—only a two months' accumulation—the post-haste of
4658 letters, all containing property, was arrested by the bad
superscriptions of the writers. They were consigned—after
a searching inquest upon each by that efficient coroner, the
" blind clerk"—to the Post-office *Morgue.* There were Bank-
notes of the value of 1010*l.*, and money-orders for 407*l.* 12s.
But most of these ill-directed letters contained coin in small
sums, amounting to 310*l.* 9s. 7d. On the 17th of July, 1847,
there were lying in the Dead-Letter-office bills of exchange
for the immense sum of 40,410*l.* 5s. 7d.

" I assure you," said a gentleman high in this department,
" it is scarcely possible to take up a handful of letters without
finding one with coin in it, despite the facilities afforded by the
money-order system. All this is very distressing to us. The
temptation it throws in the way of sorters, carriers, and other
humble *employés* is greater than they ought to be subjected
to. Seventy men have been discharged for dishonesty from
the District-office alone during the past two years."

"But the public do use the Money-Order-office extensively?"

This question was startlingly answered by reference to a Parliamentary return, which showed that there were issued in England and Wales alone, during the year which ended on the 5th of January, 1849, 3,468,823 Post-office orders for sums amounting to the enormous aggregate of 6,861,803*l*.*

Taking up a thin card-board box of artificial flowers, which had been shaken into the form of an irregular rhomboid, under the pressure of several pounds' weight of letters and newspapers, a sub-president remarked : "The faith the public have in us is extraordinary. Here is an article which is designed to go safely to Dublin ; yet not one single precaution, except this thin piece of twine, is taken by the sender to ensure its preservation. Here, again, is a pair of white satin shoes, fast losing their colour from friction with damp newspapers and the edges of books. The other day the toe of a similar packet protruded from its very thin casing, and the stamper not being able to stop his hand in time, ornamented it, in vividly blue ink, with the words, 'York, Feb. 1, 1850, D.' You will see by this Parliamentary return of the articles found in the Dead-Letter-office what curious things are trusted to our care."

The obliging gentleman then produced the document. Its lists showed, amongst other articles,—tooth-picks, tooth-files, fishing-flies, an eye-glass, brad-awls, portraits, miniatures, a whistle, corkscrews, a silver watch, a pair of spurs, a bridle, a soldier's discharge and sailors' register tickets, samples of hops and corn, a Greek MS., silver spoons, gold thread, dinner, theatre, and pawn tickets, boxes of pills, shirts, nightcaps, razors, all sorts of knitting and lace, "dolls' things," and a vast variety of other articles, that would puzzle ingenuity to conjecture.

"Besides carelessness, we have to contend against ignorance," was remarked as the visitors were introduced to the "blind" table, and to the hawk-eyed gentleman who presides at it. "He is provided, you perceive, with a small library of local and general Dictionaries, Court Guides, Army, Navy,

* The number of Post-office orders issued in England and Wales last year (1858) was upwards of five millions six hundred thousand, amounting in money value to more than ten millions eight hundred thousand pounds sterling. For the whole kingdom the number of orders was more than six millions six hundred thousand, and the aggregate money amount exceeded twelve millions six hundred thousand pounds sterling

and Clergy Lists; and much he needs them, as will be seen by these fac-similes." Several transcripts of curiously addressed letters were then produced. " Where would you or I have sent a letter

certainly not to its proper destination, which turned out to be the Amphitrite, Valparaiso, or elsewhere. Who but our friend here would have found out that another boy in Her Majesty's naval service, said to be on board

> *H. M. Steem Friegkt*
> *Vultur Uncon or els ware,*

belonged to the Steam Frigate Vulture, at Hong-Kong? Few would think that

> *Mr. Weston,*
> *Osburn Cottage,*
> *Ilawait*

was a neighbour of Her Majesty, and lived at Osborne Cottage, Isle of Wight."

The following additional epistolary puzzles were then read, amidst, as reporters say, "loud laughter:"

> *Mr. Laurence*
> *New Land*
> *Ivicum* (High Wycombe).

> *W. Stratton*
> *Commonly*
> *Ceald teapot*
> (We presume as a total abstinence man.)
> *Weelin* (Welwyn).

Thom Hoodless
3 *St. Ann Ct*
Searhoo Skur (Soho Square).

The ingenious orthographies *Ratlifhaivai* and *Ratlef Fieway* went straight to the proper parties in Ratcliffe Highway; but it is a wonder how—

Mr. Dick
Bishop Cans
ner the Wises

got his letter, considering that his place of abode was near Devizes.

For the next specimen of spelling there is some excuse. " In England," says a French traveller, " what they write 'Greenwich,' they pronounce 'Greenitch,' and I am not quite sure that when they set down 'Solomon,' they do not pronounce it 'Nebuchadnezzar.' " " I much question," continued one of the amateur Post-office inspectors, " if either of us had never seen the name of the place to which the following superscription applies, that we should not have spelt it nearly similarly to the correspondent of—

Peter Robertson
2 Compney 7 Batilian
Rolyl Artirian
Owilige
England.

" Although the writer's ear misled him grievously in the other words, he has recorded the sound into which we render *Woolwich* with curious correctness."

"Innocent simplicity balks us as much as ignorance," remarked the head of the hieroglyphic department. " Here are one or two specimens of it :

To Mr. Michl
Darcy
In the town of
England.

" A schoolboy sends from Salisbury,

To My Uncle Jon
In London.

" Another addressed the highest personage in the realm—
no doubt on particular business—as

Miss

Queene Victoria

of England."

While this amusement was going forward, the bustle in the
adjoining rooms had reached its climax. It was approaching
eight o'clock, and the " Miller and his Men" above stairs were
delivering their sacks from the mouth of the ever-revolving
mill at an incessant rate. These, filled nearly to choking with
newspapers, were dragged to the tables, which the brass label
fastened to the corner of each bag marked as its own, to have
the letters inserted. Our friends rushed to where they saw
"Edinburgh" painted up on the walls, and there they beheld
their yellow, green, and red letters in separate packets, though
destined for the same place; just as they had come in at first
from Fleet-street. The bundles were popped in a trice into
the Edinburgh bag, which was sealed and sent away. Exactly
the same thing was happening to every bundle of letters, and
to every bag on the premises.

The clock now struck eight, and the two visitors looked
round in astonishment. Had they been guests at the ball in
" Cinderella," when *that* clock struck they would not have been
more astonished; for hardly less rapidly did the fancy dresses
of the postmen disappear, and the lights grow dim. This is
the most striking peculiarity of the extraordinary establishment. Everything is done on military principles to minute
time. The drill and subdivision of duties are so perfect that
the alternations throughout the day are high pressure and
sudden collapse. At five minutes before eight the enormous
offices were glaring with light and crowded with men; at ten
minutes after eight the glass slipper had fallen off, and there
was hardly a light or a living being visible.

"Perhaps, however," it was remarked, as our friends were
leaving the building, "an invisible individual is now stealthily watching behind the ground glass screen. Only the other
day he detected from it a sorter secreting 140 sovereigns."

It is a deplorable thing that such a place of observation should
be necessary; but it is hardly less deplorable—and this should

be most earnestly impressed upon the reader—that the public, now possessed of such conveniences for remitting money, by means of Post-office Orders and Registered Letters, should lightly throw temptation in the way of these clerks by enclosing actual coin. No man can say that, placed in such circumstances from day to day, he could be steadfast. Many may hope they would be, and believe it; but none can be sure. It is in the power, however, of every conscientious and reflecting mind to make quite sure that it has no part in this class of crimes. The prevention for this one great source of misery is made easy to the public hand, and it is the public's bounden duty to adopt it. They who do not, cannot be blameless.

Such is the substance of information obtained by our friends before they took leave of the mighty heart of the postal system of this country.

In conclusion, they beg to be understood that their experimental letters were *not* Valentines.

II.

THE GHOST OF THE LATE MR. JAMES BARBER.

A YARN ASHORE.

APRIL 20, 1850.

"'LUCK!' nonsense. There is no such thing as luck. Life is not a game of chance any more than chess is. If you lose, you have no one to blame but yourself."

This was said by a young lieutenant in the Royal Navy to a middle-aged midshipman, his elder brother.

"Do you mean to say that luck had nothing to do with Dandy Bobbin passing for lieutenant, and my being turned back?" was the rejoinder.

"Bobbin, though a dandy, is a good seaman, and—and——" The speaker looked another way, and hesitated.

"I am *not*, you would say—if you had courage. But I say I am, and a better seaman than Bobbin."

"Practically, perhaps, for you are ten years older in the service. But it was in the theoretical part of seamanship—which is equally important—that you broke down before the examiners," continued the young officer. "You never *would* study."

"I'll tell you what it is, Master Ferdinand," said the elderly middy, roughly, "I don't think this is the correct sort of conversation to be going on between two brothers after a five years' separation."

The young lieutenant laid his hand on his brother's arm, and entreated him to take what he said in good part.

"Well, well!" rejoined the middy, with a half-forced laugh. "Take care what you are about, or, by Jove, I'll inform against you."

"What for?"

"Why, for preaching without a license.—Besides, you were once as bad as you pretend I am."

"I own it with sorrow; but I was warned in time by the wretched end of poor James Barber."

"End?" echoed the elder brother, starting back as he pushed his glass along the table. "You don't mean to say Jovial Jimmy, as we used to call him; once my messmate in the brig Rollock, is——?"

"Yes, I do."

"What! dead?"

"Yes."

"Why, it was one of our great delights, when in harbour and on shore, to 'go the rounds'—as he called it—with Jovial Jimmy. He understood life from stem to stern—from truck to keel. He knew everybody, from the First Lord downwards. I have seen him recognised by *the* Duke one minute, and the next pick up with a strolling player, and familiarly treat him at a tavern. He once took me to a quadrille party at the Duchess of Durrington's, where he seemed to know and be known to everybody present, and then adjourn to the Cider Cellars, where he was equally intimate with the comic singer. Though a favorite among the aristocracy, he was equally welcome in less exclusive societies. He was 'Brother,' 'Past Master,' 'Warden,' 'Noble Grand,' or 'President' of all sorts of Lodges and Fraternities, and was a member of the Rag and Famish in Bond-street. Uncommonly knowing was Jimmy in all sorts of club and fashionable gossip. He knew who gave the best dinners, and was always invited to the best balls.

When he betted upon a horse-race everybody backed him. He could hum all the fashionable songs, and was the fourth man who could dance the polka when it was first imported. Then he was as profound in bottle stout, Welsh rabbits, Burton ale, devilled kidneys, and bowls of Bishop, as he was in Roman punch, French cookery, and Italian singers. Afloat, he was the soul of fun:—he got up all our private theatricals, told all the best stories, and gave imitations that made even the purser laugh."

"An extent and variety of accomplishments," said Lieutenant Fid, "which had the precise effect of blasting his prospects in life. He was, as you remember, at last dismissed the service for drunkenness and incompetency."

"When did you see him last?" ·

"What, *alive?*" inquired Ferdinand Fid, changing countenance.

"Of course! Surely you do not mean to insinuate that you have seen his ghost!"

The lieutenant was silent. His brother took a deep draught of his favorite mixture—equal portions of rum and water—and hinted the expediency of immediately confiding the story to the Marines; for *he* declined to credit it. He then ventured another recommendation, which was that Ferdinand should throw the impotent tipple he was then imbibing "over the side of the Ship"—which meant the tavern of that name in Greenwich, at the open bow-window of which they were then sitting—and clear his intellects by something stronger.

"I can afford to be laughed at," said the younger Fid, "because I have gained immeasurably by the delusion, if it be one; but if ever there was a ghost, I have seen the ghost of James Barber. I, like yourself and he, was nearly ruined by love of amusement and intemperance, when he—or whatever else it might have been—came to my aid."

"Let us hear. I see I am 'in' for a ghost story."

"Well; it was eighteen forty-one when I came home in the Arrow with despatches from the coast of Africa; you were lying in the Tagus in the Bobstay. Ours, you know, was rather a thirsty station. A man inclined for it comes home from the Slaving Coasts with a determination to make

2

up his lee way. I did mine with a vengeance. As usual, I looked up 'Jovial James.' "

"It wasn't easy to find him."

"I did find him, though. He had by that time got tired of his more aristocratic friends. Respectability was too slow for him, so I found him presiding over the Philanthropic Raspers, at the Union Jack. He received me with open arms, and took me, as you say, the 'rounds.' I can't recal that week's dissipation without a shudder. We rushed about from ball to tavern, from theatre to supper-room, from club to gin-palace, as if our lives depended on losing not a moment. We had not time to walk; so we galloped about in cabs. On the fourth night, when I was beginning to feel knocked up, and tired of the same songs, the same quadrilles, the bad whisky, the suffocating tobacco-smoke, and the morning's certain and desperate penalties, I remarked to Jimmy that it was a miracle how he had managed to weather it for so many years. 'What a hardship you would think it,' I added, 'if you were *obliged* to go the same weary round from one year's end to another.' "

"What did he say to that?" asked Philip.

"Why, I never him saw him so taken aback. He looked quite fiercely at me, and replied, 'I *am* obliged!' "

"How did he make that out?"

"He had tippled and dissipated his constitution into such a state that use had become second nature. Excitement was his natural condition, and he dared not let himself down to flat sobriety for fear of a total collapse, and of dropping down like shot in the water.

The midshipman had his glass in his hand, but forebore to taste it. "Well, what then?"

"The 'rounds' lasted two nights longer. I was fairly beaten. Cast-iron could not have stood it. I was prostrated in bed with fever—and worse."

"Well, well, you need not enlarge upon that," replied Phil Fid, raising his glass toward his lips, but again thinking better of it; "I heard how bad you were from Seton, who shaved your head."

"I had scarcely recovered when the Arrow was ordered back, and I made a vow."

"Took the pledge?"

"No!" replied the lieutenant. "I determined to work more and play less. We had a capital naval instructor aboard, and our commander was as good an officer as ever trod the deck. I studied—a little too hard, perhaps, and I was laid up again. The Arrow was, as usual, as good as her name, and we shot across to Jamaica in five weeks. One evening, as we were lying in Kingston harbour, Seton, who had come over to join the Commodore as full surgeon, told me what he had never ventured to divulge before."

"What was that?" asked Philip.

"Why, that, on the very day I left London, James Barber died of a frightful attack of *delirium tremens !*"

"Poor Jimmy!" said the elder Fid, sorrowfully, taking a deep pull of consolation out of his rummer. "Little did I think, while singing some of your best songs off Belem Castle, in the Tagus, that I had seen you for the last time!"

"*I* hadn't seen him for the last time," returned the lieutenant, awfully.

Philip assumed a careless air, and said, "Go on."

"We were ordered home in eighteen forty-five, and paid off in January. I went to Portsmouth; was examined, and passed as lieutenant."

This allusion to his brother's higher rank made poor Philip look rather blank.

"On being confirmed at the Admiralty," continued Ferdinand, "I had to give a dinner to the Arrows; which I did at the Salopian, Charing-cross. In the excess of my joy at promotion, my determination of temperance and avoidance of what is called 'society' was swamped. I kept it up once more; I went the 'rounds,' and accepted all the dinner, supper, and ball invitations I could get, invariably ending each morning in one of the old haunts of dissipation. Old associations with James Barber returned, and like causes produced like effects. One morning while mooning home, I began to feel the same wild confusion as had previously commenced my dreadful malady."

"Ah! a little touched in the top-hamper."

"It was just daylight. Thinking to cool myself, I jumped into a wherry to get pulled down here to Greenwich."

"Of course you were not quite sober."

"Don't ask! I do not like even to allude to my sensations, for fear of recalling them. My brain seemed in a flame. The boat appeared to be going at the rate of twenty miles an hour. Fast as we were cleaving the current, I heard my name distinctly called out. I reconnoitered, but, at first, could see nobody. I looked over the gunwale on one side, and felt something touch me from the other. A chill crept through me. I turned round and saw——"

"Whom?" asked the midshipman, holding his breath.

"What seemed to be James Barber. I summoned courage to speak. 'Hallo! some mistake!'

"'Not at all,' it replied. 'I'm Jovial Jimmy. Don't be frightened. I'm harmless.'

"'But——'

"'I know what you are going to say,' interrupted the intruder. 'Seton did not deceive you—I am only an occasional visitor *up here*.'

"This brought me up with a round turn, and I had sense enough to wish my friend would vanish as he came. 'Where shall we land you?' I asked.

"'Oh, anywhere—it don't matter. I have got to be out every night and all night; and the nights are plaguey long just now.'

"I could not muster a word.

"'Ferd Fid,' continued the voice, which now seemed about fifty fathoms deep; and, fast as we were dropping down the stream, the boat gave a heel to starboard, as if she had been broadsided by a tremendous wave—'Ferd Fid, you recollect how I used to kill time; how I sang, drank, smoked, danced, and supped all night long, and then slept and soda-watered all day? You remember what a happy fellow I seemed. Fools like yourself thought I was happy; but I say again, I wasn't,' growled the voice, letting itself down a few fathoms deeper. 'Often and often I would have given the world to have been a market-gardener or a dealer in chickweed while roaring "He is a jolly good fellow," and "We won't go home till morning!" as I came away with a group from some tavern into Covent Garden-market. But I'm punished fearfully for my sins now. What do you think I have got to do every night of my—never mind—what do you think is now marked out as my dreadful punishment?'

" ' To walk the earth, I suppose,' said I.

" ' No.'

" ' To paddle about in the Thames from sunset to sunrise ?'

" ' Worse. Ha! ha!' His laugh sounded like a cracked gong. 'I only wish my doom *was* merely to be a mud-lark. No, no, I am condemned to rush about from one evening party and public-house to another. At the former I am bound for a certain term on each night to dance all the quadrilles, and a few of the polkas and waltzes, with clumsy partners; and then I have to eat stale pastry and tough poultry before I am let off from *that* place. After, I am hounded on to some cellar or singing place to listen to "Hail, smiling morn." "Mynheer Van Dunk," "The monks of old," "Happy land," imitation of the London actors, and to be bored for hours by improvisatores and ventriloquists at a judge-and-jury club after the trials are over. I must also smoke a dozen of cigars, knowing—as in my present condition I must know—what they are made of. The whole to end on each night with unlimited brandy (British), and eternal intoxication. Oh, F. F., be warned! be warned! Keep up your resolution, and don't do it again. When afloat, drink nothing stronger than purser's tea. When ashore be temperate in your pleasures; don't turn night into day; don't exchange wholesome amusement for rabid debauchery; robust health for disease and——well, I won't mention that either. When afloat, study your profession, and don't get cashiered and cold-shouldered as I was. Promise me—nay, you must swear!'

"At this word I thought I heard a gurgling sound in the water.

" ' If I can get six solemn pledges before the season's over, I'm only to go these horrid rounds during one more session of Parliament. *Will* you swear?' again urged the voice, with persuasive agony.

"I was just able to comply.

" ' Ten thousand thanks!' were the next words I heard; 'I'm off; for there is a pint of stale ale, a tainted chop, and a glass of bad brandy-and-water overdue yet, and I must devour them at the Shades.' We were then close to the Thames Tunnel. 'Don't let the waterman pull to shore; I can get there without troubling him.'

"I remember no more. When sensation returned, I was in bed, in this very house, The Ship, a shade worse than I had been from the previous attack."

"That," said Philip, who had left his tumbler untasted, "must have been when you had your head shaved for the second time."

"Exactly so."

"And you really believed it was Jovial James's ghost?" inquired Fid, earnestly.

"Would it be rational to doubt it?"

Philip rose and paced the room in deep thought. He cast two or three earnest looks at his brother, and a few longing looks at his glass. In the course of his cogitation, he groaned out more than once an apostrophe to poor "James Barber." At length he declared his mind was made up.

"Ferd!" he said, "I told you a while ago to throw your lemonade over the side of the ship. Don't! Souse out my grog instead."

The lieutenant did as he was bid.

"And now," said Fid the elder, "ring for soda water; for one must drink *something*."

Last year it was my own good fortune to sail with Mr. Philip Fid in the Bombottle (74). He is not exactly a teetotaller: but he never drinks spirits, and will not touch wine unmixed with water, for fear of its interfering with his studies; at which he is, with the assistance of the naval instructor (who is also our chaplain), very assiduous. He is our first mate, and the smartest officer in the ship. Seton is our surgeon.

One day, after a cheerful ward-room dinner, while we were at anchor in the bay of Cadiz, the conversation turned upon Jovial Jimmy's apparition, which had become the best authenticated ghost in Her Majesty's service. On that occasion Seton undertook to explain the mystery upon medical principles.

"The fact is," he said, "what the commander of the Arrow saw (Ferdinand had by this time got commissioned in his old ship) was a spectrum, produced by that morbid condition of the brain, which is brought on by the immoderate use of stimulants, and by dissipation. We call it Transient Monomania.

I could show you dozens of such ghosts in the books, if you only had patience while I turned them up."

I haven't; for I hate explained ghost stories. I am consoled by the conviction that not a soul except Seton and the chaplain had his faith one atom shaken in the reality of Jovial Jimmy's *post-mortem* appearance to Fid the younger.

Ghost or no ghost, however, the story had had the effect of converting Philip Fid from one of the most intemperate and inattentive to one of the soberest and most zealous of Her Majesty's officers.   May his promotion be speedy!

III.

THE TROUBLED WATER QUESTION.

APRIL 13, 1850.

MY excellent and eloquent friend, Lyttleton, of Pump-court, Temple, barrister-at-law, disturbed me on a damp morning at the end of last month, to bespeak my company to a meeting at which he intended to hold forth. "It is," he said, "the Great Water Supply Congress, which assembles to-morrow."

"Do you know anything of the subject?"

"A vast deal both practically and theoretically. Practically, I pay for my little box in the Regent's Park, twice the price for water our friend Fielding is charged; and both supplies are derived from the same Company. Yet his is a mansion, mine is a cottage; his rent more than doubles mine in amount, and his family trebles mine in number. So much for the consistency and exactions of an irresponsible monopoly. Practically, again, there are occasions when my cisterns are without water. So much for deficient supply."

"Is your water bad?"

"Not absolutely unwholesome; but I have drunk better."

"Now then, Theoretically."

"Theoretically, I learn from piles of Reports—a blue mountain of Parliamentary inquiry instituted in the years 1810, 1821, 1827, 1828, 1834, 1840, and 1845—from a cloud of prospectuses issued by embryo Water Companies; from a host of pamphlets *pro* and *con.*, and from the reports of the Board of

Health, that the great element of suction and cleanliness is supplied by nine water companies all linked together to form a giant monopoly;* and that, in consequence, the charge for water is in some instances excessive; that six of these companies draw their water from the filthy Thames; and the same number, including those which use the Lea and New River water, have no system of filtration—hence it is unwholesome: that in short, the public of the metropolis are the victims of dear, insufficient, and dirty water. Like Tantalus of old they are denied much of the great element of life, although it flows within reach of their parched and thirsty lips. And by whom? By that many-headed Cerberus—that nine gentlemen in one— the great monopolist Water Company combination of London. Unless, therefore, we bestir ourselves in the great cause for which this numerous, enlightened, and respectable meeting have assembled here this day——"

"You forget; you have only two listeners at present— myself and my spaniel. I can suggest a more profitable morning's amusement than a rehearsal of your speech."

"What?"

"Your theoretical knowledge is, I doubt not, very comprehensive and varied. But second-hand information is not to be trusted. Every statement of fact, like every story, gains something in exaggeration, or loses something in accuracy by repetition from book to book, or from book to mouth."

"Granted. What do you suggest?"

"Ocular demonstration. Let us at once visit the works of one of the Companies. I am sure they will let us in at the Grand Junction, for I have already been over their premises."

"A capital notion."

The preliminaries—consisting of the hasty bundling up of Mr. Lyttleton's notes for the morrow's oration, and the hire of a Hansom cab—were adjusted in a few minutes.

The order to drive to Kew Bridge was obeyed in capital style; for, in three-quarters of an hour, we were deposited on the towing-path on the Surrey side of the Thames, opposite the

---

* A tenth company, The Plumstead and Woolwich, has since been established; but, as the business of the Hampstead Waterworks has been absorbed by the New River Company, the number of water companies virtually remains the same as it was when this paper was written.

King of Hanover's house, and a short distance west of Kew Bridge.

"Here," I explained, "is the spot whence the Grand Junction Company derive their water. In the bed of the river is an enormous culvert pipe laid parallel to this path. Its mouth, open towards Richmond, is barred across with a grating, to intercept stray fish, murdered kittens, or vegetable impurities, and it admits nothing into the pipe but fluids, except now and then a small flounder, or an erratic eel. The culvert then takes a bend round the edge of the islet opposite to us; burrows beneath the Brentford-road, and delivers its contents into a well under that tall chimney and taller iron 'stand-pipe' which you see on the other side of the river."

"And is *this* the stuff I have to pay four pounds ten a year for?" exclaimed Mr. Lyttleton, contemplating the opaque fluid, part of which was then making its way into the cisterns of Her Majesty's lieges.

"Certainly; but it is purified first. We will now cross the bridge to the Works."

Those who make prandial expeditions to Richmond must have noticed, at the beginning of Old Brentford, a little beyond where they turn over Kew Bridge, a tall, thin column that shoots up into the air like a titanic sixpenny trumpet, or an iron mast unable to support itself, and requiring four smaller, thinner, and not much shorter props to keep it upright. This, with the engine and engine-houses, is all they can see of the Grand Junction Waterworks from the road. It is only when one gets inside that the whole extent of the aquatic apparatus is revealed.

Determined to follow the water from the Thames till it began its travels to London, we went straight to the well, and called for a glass of water. Our hosts—who had received our visit without hesitation—supplied us. "That," remarked one of them, as he held the half-filled tumbler up to the light, "is precisely the state of the water as emptied from the Thames into the well."

It looked like a dose of weak magnesia, or the deceitful London liquid sold under the name of milk.

"The analysis of Professor Brande," said Lyttleton, "gives to every gallon of Thames water taken from Kew Bridge 19·2

parts of solid matter; but the water, I apprehend, in which
he experimented must have been taken from the river on a
serener occasion than this.   To-day's rain appears to give, in
this specimen, a much larger proportion of solids to fluids than
his estimate.

"In this impure state," one of the engineers told us, "the
water is pumped by steam power into the reservoirs, to which
you will please to follow me."

Passing out of the building and climbing a sloping bank,
we now saw before us an expanse of water covering three and
a half acres, but divided into two sections.   Into the larger
the pump first delivers the water, that so much of the impurity as will form sediment may be precipitated.   It then
slowly glides through a small opening into the lesser section,
which is a huge filter.

"The impurities of water," said the barrister, assuming
an oratorical attitude, "are of two kinds; first, such as are
mechanically suspended—say earth, chalk, sand, clay, dead
vegetation, or decomposed dogs; and secondly, such as are
dissolved or chemically combined—like salt, sugar, or alkali.
Separation in the one case is easy; in the other it involves a
chemical process. If you throw a pinch of sand into a tumbler
of water and stir it about, you produce a turbid mixture; but,
to render the fluid clear again, you have only to adopt the
easy plan of letting it alone; for, on setting the tumbler down
for a while, the particles, being heavier than the water, fall to
the bottom, leaving the liquid translucent.   This is what is
happening in the larger section of the reservoir to the chalky
water of which we drank.   I think I am correct?" asked the
speaker, angling for a single "cheer" from the Engineer.

"Quite so," replied that gentleman.

"Provided the water could remain at rest long enough—
which the insatiable maw of the modern Babylon does not
allow," continued the honourable orator, "this mode of
cleansing would be effectual.   In proof of which I may only
allude to Nature's mode of depuration, as shown in lakes—
that of Geneva for instance.   The waters of the Rhône enter
that expansive reservoir from the Valais in a very muddy
condition; yet, after reposing in the lake, they issue at
Geneva as clear as crystal.   But so incessant is the London

demand, that scarcely any time can be afforded for the impurities of the Thames, the Lea, or the New River to separate themselves from the water by a mere deposition."

"True," interjected one of the superintendents. "It is for that reason that our water is passed, afterwards, into the filtering bed, which is four feet thick."

"How do you make up this enormous bed?"

"Thus," was the answer, "First, a surface of fine sand; second, a stratum of shells; third, a layer of garden gravel; and fourth, a base of coarse gravel. The water, after passing through this bed, falls through a number of ducts into cisterns, whence it is pumped up so as to commence its travels to town through the conduit pipe."

We were returning to the engine-house, when Lyttleton asked the Engineer, "Does your experience generally, enable you to say that water, as supplied by the nine companies, is reasonably pure?"

"Upon the whole, yes," was the answer.

"Indeed!" ejaculated the orator, sharply. "If that be true," he whispered to me, in a rueful tone, "I shall be cut out of one of the best points in my speech."

"Of course," continued the Engineer, "purity entirely depends upon the source, and the means of cleansing."

"Then, as to the source—how many companies take their supplies from the Thames, near to, and after it has received the contents of, the common sewers?"

"No water is taken from the Thames below Chelsea, except that of the Lambeth Company, which is supplied from between Waterloo and Hungerford Bridges; an objectionable source, which they have obtained an act to change to Thames Ditton. The Chelsea Waterworks have a most efficient system of filtration; as also have the Southwark and Vauxhall Company; both draw their water from between the Red House Battersea and Chelsea Hospital. The other companies do not filter.* The West Middlesex sucks up some of Father Thames as he passes Barnes Terrace. Except the lowest of these sources, Thames water is nearly as pure as any other rivers."

"Perhaps it is," was the answer; "but the unwholesome-

---

* The Metropolis Water Act, passed two years after this paper was written, obliged every company to filter the water it supplies.

ness arises from contamination received during its course; we don't object to the 'Thames,' but to its 'tributaries,' such as the black contents of common sewers, and the refuse of gut, glue, soap, and other nauseous manufactures; to say nothing of animal and vegetable offal, of which the river is the sole receptacle. Brande shows that, while the solid matter contained in the river at Teddington is 17·4, that which the water has contracted when it flows past Westminster is 24·4, and the City of London, 28·0."

"But," said the Engineer, "these adulterations are only mechanically suspended in the fluid, and are, as you shall see presently, totally separated from it by our mode of filtration."

"Which brings us to your second point, as to efficient cleansing; you admit that without filtration this is impossible, and also that only three companies filter; the deduction, therefore, is, that two-thirds of the water supplied to Londoners is insufficiently cleansed. This, indeed, is not a mere inference; we know it from a fact, we see it in our ewers, we taste it out of our carafes."

"But this does not wholly arise from the inefficient filtration of the six companies," returned an officer of this Company, "the public is much to blame—though, when agitating against an abuse, it never thinks of blaming itself. Half the dirt, dust, and animalculæ found at table are introduced after the water has been delivered to the houses. Impurity of all sorts finds its way into out-door cisterns, even when covered, and few of them, open or closed, are often enough cleansed. In some neighbourhoods water-butts are always uncovered, and hardly ever cleaned out. The water is foul, and the companies are blamed."

"The blame belongs to the system," said the barrister. "Domestic reservoirs are not only an evil but an unnecessary expense. Besides filth, they cause waste and deficient supply. They should be abolished; for continuous supply is the real remedy. Let the pipes be always full, and the water would be always ready, always fresh, and could never acquire new impurities. Still, despite all you say, I am bound to conclude that although one-third of the water may arrive in the domestic cisterns of the metropolis in a polluted state, the other two-thirds does not." Mr. L. then inscribed this calculation in his note-book, whispering to me that his pet " dirty water point" would come out even stronger than he had expected.

We had now returned to one of the engine-rooms.

" You have tasted the water before, I now present you with some of it after, filtration," said the Chief Engineer, handing us a tumbler. " This is exactly the condition in which we deliver it to our customers."

It was clear to the eye, and to the taste innocuous; but Lyttleton (who, I should mention, occasionally turns on power-streams of oratory at Temperance meetings, and is a judge of the article) complained that the liquid wanted flavour."

" In other words, then, it wants *impurity*," replied one of our cicerones, " for perfectly pure water is quite tasteless. Indeed, water may be too pure. Distilled water which contains no salt, is insipid, and tends to indigestion. It is a wise provision of Nature, that water should contain a greater or less quantity of foreign ingredients; for without these water is dangerous to drink. It never fails to take up from the atmosphere a certain proportion of carbonic acid gas, and, when passing through lead pipes, it imbibes enough carbonate of lead to constitute poison. Dr. Christison mentions several severe cases of 'lead,' or 'painter's' colic, which arose chiefly in country houses to which water (only too pure) was supplied from springs through lead pipes. The most remarkable case was that at Claremont, where the ex-king of the French and several members of his family were nearly poisoned by pure spring water conveyed to the mansion through lead pipes."

" Mercy !" I exclaimed, with all the energy of despair that a mere water-drinker is capable of, " if river water be unwholesome, and pure water poison, what *is* to become of every temperance pledgee ?"

The Engineer relieved me : " Chemists," he stated, " have agreed that a water containing from eight to ten grains of sulphate of magnesia or soda, to the imperial gallon, is best suited for alimentary, lavatory, and other domestic purposes."

We were now introduced to the great engine. Imagine an enormous see-saw, with a steam-engine at one end, and a pump at the other. Fancy this " beam," some ten yards long, and 28 tons in weight, moving on a pivot in the middle, the ends

of which show a circumference greater than the crown of the
biggest hat ever worn. See, with what earnest deliberation
the "see" or engine, pulls up the "saw," or balance-box of the
pump, which then comes down upon the water-trap with the
ferocious *aplomb* of 49 tons, sending 400 gallons of water in
one tremendous squirt nearly the twentieth part of a mile
high;—that is, to the top of the stand-pipe, or sixpenny
trumpet.

"We have a smaller engine which 'does' 150 gallons per
stroke," remarked our informant: "each performs 11 strokes,
forces up 4400 gallons of water per minute, and thus our
average delivery per diem throughout the year is from four to
five million gallons."

"Now," said my companion, sharpening his pencil, "to go
into the question of supply." He then unfolded his pocket
soufflet, and brought out a calculation, of quantities derived,
he said, from Parliametary returns and other authorities more
or less reliable :

	Galls. daily.
New River Company	20,000,000
Chelsea Company . , ...	3,250,000
West Middlesex Company	3,650,000
Grand Junction Company	3,500,000
East London Company	7,000,000
South Lambeth Company	2,500,000
South London Company and Southwark Company .	3,000,000
Hampstead Company	400,000
Kent Company	1,200,000
Artesian Wells	8,000,000
Land-spring Pumps	3,000,000
"Catch" rain water (say)	1,000,000

Making a total quantity supplied daily to London, from
    all sources, of 56,500,000*

"An abundant supply," said an Engineer eagerly, "for as
the present population of the metropolis is estimated at
2,336,000, the total affords about 24 gallons of water per day,
for every man, woman, and child."

"Admitted," rejoined Lyttleton; "but we have to deal

* The good effects of wholesome agitation is well exemplified by its results on the
supply of water to London. In 1856 (to which year the latest report applies), water was
propelled into 328,500 of the 340,000 houses included within the Registrar-General's district, at the rate of eighty-one millions of gallons per day. Greater purity and more continuous service have also been attained.

with large deductions; first, nearly half this quantity runs to
waste, chiefly in consequence of the intermittent system. I
live in a small house with proportionately small cisterns, which
are filled no more than three times a week; now, as my neighbours have larger houses and larger reservoirs, the water when
turned on runs for as long a time into my small, as it does into
their capacious cisterns, and consequently, if my stop-taps be
in the least out of order, a greater quantity descends the waste
pipe than remains behind. This is universally the case in similar circumstances."

"*We* supply water daily, Sundays excepted," remarked the
Engineer.

"Then you are wiser than your neighbours. But every inconvenience and nearly all the waste, would be saved by the
adoption of the continuous system of supply. Secondly, a
large quantity of water is consumed by cattle, breweries, baths,
public institutions; for putting out fires, and for laying dust.
The lieges of London have only, therefore, to divide between
them some 10 gallons of water each per day; and, as it is
generally admitted that a sixth part of their inhabitants are
without water at all, the division must be most unequally
made. That such is the fact is shown by your own figures—
your customers get 25 gallons each per day, or more than
double their share. For this excess, some in poorer districts
get none at all."

"That is no fault of the existing companies. As sellers of
an article, they are but too happy to get as many customers
for it as possible; but poor tenants cannot, and their landlords
will not, afford to buy water of us. If the companies were to
make the outlay necessary to connect the houses with their
mains, they would have no legal power to recover the money
so expended: nor indeed is it clear, that were they inclined
to run the risk, the parties would avail themselves of it. In
one instance, the Southwark and Vauxhall Company offered
to construct a tank which would give continuous supply to a
a block of 100 small houses, at the rate of 50 gallons per diem
to each, if the proprietor would pay an additional rate sufficient to yield 5 per cent. on the outlay, such additional rate
not exceeding one halfpenny per week for each house; but
the offer was declined."

"That is an extreme case of cheapness on the one side, and of stupidity on the other," said the barrister. "Other landlords will not turn on water for their tenants, because of the expense; not only of the 'plant,' in the first instance, but of the after water-rent. I find, by the account rendered to the House of Commons in 1814, that the South London Company (since incorporated with the Southwark, as the 'Southwark and Vauxhall,'—the very company you mention) charged considerably less than any other. The return shows that while they obtained only 15s. per 1000 hogsheads, the West Middlesex (the highest) exacted 48s. 6d. for the same quantity; consequently, had the houses of the foolish landlord who refused one halfpenny per week for water, stood in northwestern instead of southern London, he would have had to pay more than treble, or a fraction above three-halfpence per week."

"Allowing for difference of level," I remarked, "and other interferences with the cheap delivery of water; the disparity in the charges of the different companies, and even by the same company to different customers, is unaccountable: they are guided by no principle. You have mentioned the extreme points of the scale of rates; the remaining companies charged at the time you mention, respectively per 1000 hogsheads, 17s., 17s. 2d., 21s., 28s., 29s., and 45s. The only companies whose charges are limited by act of Parliament are the Grand Junction, the East London, the Southwark and Vauxhall, and the Lambeth. The others exact precisely what they please."

"And," interposed Lyttleton, "there is no redress: the only appeal we, the taxed, have, is to our taxers, and the monopoly is so tight that—as is my case—although your next-door neighbour is supplied from a cheaper company, you are not allowed to change."

"The companies were obliged to combine, to save themselves from ruin and the public from extreme inconvenience," said our informant; "during the competition, streets were torn up, traffic was stopped, and confusion was worse confounded in the district where the opposition raged."

"But what happened when the war ceased and the general peace was concluded?" said Lyttleton. "To show how ill some of the companies managed their affairs, I could cite some laughable cases. When the combination commenced, some of them forgot to stop off their mains, and supplied water to customers whom they had previously turned over to their quondam rivals; so that one company gave the water, and the other pocketed the rent. This, in some instances, went on for years."

Here the subject branched off into other topics. It is worthy of notice that the conversation was carried on by the side of the enormous Cornish engine, that was driving 4400 gallons per minute 218 feet high.

"It is marvellous," I remarked, "that so much power can be exercised with so little noise and vibration."

"That's owing to the patent valves in the pump," said the stoker.

Taking a last look at the monster, we went outside to view the stand-pipe. Being, we were told, 218 feet high, it tops the Monument in Fish-street-hill by 16 feet. Within is performed the last stroke of hydraulic art which is needed; for Nature does the rest. The water sent up through the middle or thickest of the tubes, falls over into the open mouths of the smaller ones (which most people mistake for supports), descends through all four at once into the conduit-pipe, and travels of its own accord leisurely to London. In obedience to the law of levels, it rises without further trouble to the tops of the tallest houses on the highest spots in the Company's district. In its way it fills a large reservoir on Campden-hill. The iron conduit-pipe ends at Poland-street, Oxford-street, and is 7½ miles long.*

Our inspection was now terminated. We took a parting glass of water with our intelligent and communicative hosts, and returned to town.

I firmly believe that the success of Lyttleton's speech at the great meeting next day, was very much owing to this visit. The room was crowded in every part. His tone was moderate. He avoided the extravagant exaggerations of the more fiery order of water spouters. Neither was he too tame; he was not—as Moore said of a Tory orator—like an

> awkward thing of wood,
> Which up and down its clumsy arm doth move;
> And only spout, and spout, and spout away,
> In one weak, washy, everlasting flood;

* The aggregate length of all the mains and branch pipes buried under the streets of London, exclusive of the private service-pipes, in 1856, was 2086 miles.

but he came out capitally in the hard, argumentative style.
His oration bristled with logic and statistics.

Sipping inspiration out of a tumbler filled with the flowing
subject of discussion, Mr. Lyttleton commenced by declaring
his conviction that the water supplied to the metropolis was,
generally speaking, bad in quality, extravagantly dear, and,
from excessive waste, deficient in quantity. In order to remedy
those defects an efficient control was essential. Continuous
supply, filtration, and a uniform scale of rates must be enforced.
Some of the companies were pocketing enormous dividends,
and was it a fair argument to retort that they are now being
reimbursed for periods of no dividend at all? Are we of
the present day to be mulcted to cover losses occasioned because the early career of some of these companies was marked
by the ignorance, imprudence, and reckless extravagance, which
he (Mr. Lyttleton) could prove it was? If our wine merchant,
or coal merchant, or baker, began business badly and with loss,
would he be tolerated, if, when he grew wiser and more prosperous, he tried to exact large prices to cover the consequences
of his previous mismanagement? Mr. Lyttleton apprehended
not. With this branch of the question the important subjects
of distribution and supply were intimately connected. It had
been ascertained that a vast proportion of the poor had no
water in their houses. Why? Partly because it was too dear;
but partly, he (the learned speaker) was bound to say, from
the parsimony of landlords. He had pointed out a remedy
for the first evil; for the second he would propose that every
house owner should be bound to introduce pipes into every
house. The law was stringent on him as to sewers and party-
walls, and why should not water be forced on him also? In
dealing with the whole question of supply, Mr. Lyttleton
could not agree with those who stated that the delivery of
it was deficient. A moderate calculation estimated the quantity
running through the underground network of London pipes at
56,000,000 of gallons per day. Waste (of which there is a
prodigious amount), steam-engines, cattle, public baths, and
other supplies deducted, left more than 10 gallons per diem
per head for the whole population—that is supposing these
gallons were equitably distributed; but they are not,—the
rich get an excess, and the poor get none at all. He was

not prepared to say that 10 or 20 gallons per head daily were sufficient for all the purposes of life in this or any other city, great or small; but this he would say, that under proper management the existing supply might be made ample for present wants;—whether for the requirements of augmenting population and increased cleanliness we need not discuss now. What was wanted at this time was a better distribution rather than a greater supply; but what was wanted most of all was united action and one governing body. Without this, confusion, extravagance, and waste would inevitably continue.

Mr. Lyttleton wound up with a peroration that elicited very general applause. "Although we must," he said, "establish an efficient control over the existing means of water supply, we must neither wholly despise nor neglect them, nor blindly rush into new and ruinous schemes. We must remove the onus of payment from the poorer tenants to their landlords, and into whatever central directing power the Waterworks of this great city shall pass," concluded the learned orator, with energetic unction, "our motto must be ' continuous supply, uniform rates, and universal filtration !' "*

IV.

A CORONER'S INQUEST.

APRIL 27, 1850.

IF there appeared a paragraph in the newspapers, stating that her Majesty's representative, the Lord Chief Justice of the Queen's Bench, had held a solemn Court in the parlour of the Magpie and Stump, the reader would rightly conceive that the Crown and dignity of our Sovereign Lady had suffered some derogation. Yet an equal abasement daily takes place without exciting especial wonder. The subordinates of the Lord Chief Justice of the Queen's Bench (the Premier Coroner of all England) habitually preside at pot-houses; yet they are no less delegates of Royalty—as the name of their office im-

---

* Many of the improvements suggested by Mr. Lyttleton have been since effected by the liberal outlay of more than two millions and a quarter of money, by the various companies.

plies*—than the ermined dignitary himself, when surrounded
with all the pomp and circumstances of Glorious Law at Westminster. This is quite characteristic of our thoroughly commercial nation. An action about a money debt is tried in an imposing manner in a spacious edifice, and with only too great. an
excess of formality; but, for an inquest into the sacrifice of a
mere human life, "the worst inn's worst room" is deemed
good enough. In order rightly to determine whether Jones
owes Smith five pounds ten, the Goddess of Justice is surrounded with the most imposing insignia, and worshipped in
an appropriate temple: but, when she is invoked to decide
why a human spirit,

> Unhousel'd, disappointed, unanel'd,
> No reckoning made, is sent to its account
> With all its imperfections on its head,

she is thrust into the Hole in the Wall, the Bag o' Nails, or
the parlour of the Two Spies.

We were attracted, a few weeks since, to the Old Drury
Tavern, in Vinegar-yard, Drury-lane. Having made our way
to a small parlour, we perceived the Majesty of England, per-
sonated by a tall man, with his hat on, sitting at the head of a
table, and surrounded by what might have seemed the other
members of a Free-and-Easy: only that the cigars and spirits
and water had not yet come in. There was nothing official to
be seen but a few pens, a sheet or two of paper, an inkstand,
and a parish beadle.

The Coroner was holding a friendly conversation with some
of the jury, the beadle, and the gentlemen of the press, respecting the inferiority of the accommodation afforded by the Vinegar-yard house of entertainment; and, considering the number
of persons present, and the accessions expected from more
jurymen, more parochial officers, and more witnesses, the subject was suggested naturally enough: for the private apartment of the landlord—which had been appropriated as the
temporary Court, was of exceedingly moderate dimensions.

Here then, to a back parlour of the Old Drury Tavern, Vinegar-yard, Drury-lane, London, the Queen's representative was

---

* It is derived from à corond (from the crown), because the coroner, says Coke, "hath
conusance in some pleas which are called *placita coronæ*."

consigned—by no fault of his own, but from that of a system
of which he is not a promoter, but a victim—to institute one
of the most important inquiries which the law of England pre-
scribes. A human being had been prematurely sent into
eternity, and the coroner was called upon, amidst several implements of conviviality, the steam of gin and the smell of
tobacco-smoke, "to inquire in this manner: that is, to wit, if
they [the witnesses] know where the person was slain, whether
it were in any house, field, bed, tavern, or company, and who
were there; who are culpable, either of the act, or of the force;
and who were present, either men or women, and of what age
soever they be, if they can speak or have any discretion; and
how many soever be found culpable they shall be taken and
delivered to the sheriff, and shall be committed to the gaol."
So runs the clause of the act of Parliament, by which the
coroner and jury were now assembled. It is the second statute
of the fourth year of Edward I., and is the identical law which
is discussed by the gravediggers in Hamlet.

The pleasant colloquy concerning the size of the room ended
in a resolution to adjourn the Court to the Two Spies, in a
neighbouring alley. But, before it was carried into effect—
time appearing to be as valuable as space, and the rest of the
jurors having dropped in—the Coroner at once administered
the oath to the foreman, with a Bible supplied from the bar.
The other jurors were rapidly sworn in batches, upon the Old
Drury Bible, under an abridged dispensation by the beadle.

"Now, then, gentlemen," said the Coroner, "we'll view the
body."

Not without alacrity, the entire company left their confined
quarters to breathe the air of Vinegar-yard. The subject of
inquiry lay at a baker's shop, "a few doors round the corner,"
—to use the topographical formula of the parish officer—and
thither he ushered us. A few of the window-shutters of the
shop were up; but, in all other respects there was as little to
indicate a house of death as there was to show it to be a house
of mourning. If the journeyman had not been standing at the
end of the counter in his holiday coat, it would have seemed
as if business was going on as usual. There was the same display of tarts, the same heaps of biscuits, the same supply of
loaves, the same ranges of flour in paper bags, as may be ob-

served in ordinary bakers' shops on ordinary occasions. Yet the mistress of this shop lay dead only a few paces within, and its master was in gaol on suspicion of having murdered her.

Through a parlour, and a passage with a bed and a sink in it, the jury were shown into a small kitchen. Here, on a mahogany dining-table, lay the dead wife covered with a dirty sheet. To describe the spectacle which presented itself when the beadle, with business-like immobility, turned down the covering, does not happily fall within our present object. There were evidences of continued ill-usage from blows and kicks, not to be beheld without strong indignation.

"The cause of death," said the beadle—*his* mind was quite made up—"is on the back. It's covered with bruises: but I suppose you won't want to see that, gentlemen."

By no means. Everybody had seen enough; being surrounded by whatever could increase distress and engender disgust. The apartment was so confined that the table left only room for the jurors to edge round it one by one; and it was hardly possible to do this without actual contact with the head or feet of the corpse. A gridiron and other black utensils were hanging against the wall, and could only be escaped by the exercise on the part of the spectators of great ingenuity. This and the bed-place indicated squalid poverty; but the scene was changed in the parlour. There, appearances were at least kept up. It was filled with decent furniture—even elegancies. There were a pianoforte and a couple of portraits.

These strange evidences of refinement only brought out the squalor, smallness, and unfitness for any part of a judicial inquiry of the inner apartments, into more glaring relief. Surely so important a function as that of a Coroner and his jury should not be conducted amidst such a scene! Besides other obvious objections, is there no danger in keeping corpses in confined apartments, and in close neighbourhoods? The smell was "close" and insanitary, and the first man who entered the den where the body lay, opened the window. Two children, the offspring of the victim and the accused, lived in these apartments; and above stairs the house was crowded with lodgers, to all of whom any sort of infection would have proved disastrous. They were living almost within the jaws of Death. It is terrible to reflect that every disease happening among the myriads of the population a little lower in circumstances than this baker, deals around it its proportion of destruction to the living from the same causes. True, that had it been impossible to retain the body on the spot where death occurred—as chances when several persons live in the same room—it would have been removed. But where? To the tap-room of a public-house.

There is another objection—all-powerful in the eyes of a lawyer; who recognises as a first necessity that the jurors should have no opportunity of communicating with witnesses, except when before the Court. But here the melancholy honours of the baker's shop and parlour were performed by the two persons from whose evidence the cause of death was to be chiefly elicited;—the journeyman and a female relative of the deceased, who were in the house when the last blows were dealt, and when the woman died. They did the honours of the house to the fifteen jurymen who were presently to receive their testimony; and there was nothing to prevent the witnesses from telling their own story privately in their own way, to any one or to half a dozen of the inquest, and thus to give a premature bent to opinions, the materials for forming which ought to be reserved for the public Court. Many examples can be supplied in illustration of this evil. Some years ago an old woman in the most wretched part of Westminster was found dead in her bed—strangled. When the Coroner and jury went to view the body, they were ushered into it by a young relative who lived with the deceased. This girl gave her version there and then of the death. When the Court reassembled, she was—chiefly, it was understood, in consequence of what had previously passed—examined as first and principal witness; and upon her evidence the verdict arrived at was "Temporary Insanity." The case, however, subsequently passed through more formal judicial ordeals, and the result was that the Coroner's prime witness was hanged for the *murder* of the old woman. We must have it distinctly understood that not the faintest shade of parallel exists between the two cases. We bring them together solely to illustrate the evils of a system.

On passing into the baker's parlour dumb witnesses pre-

sented themselves, which — properly or improperly — must
have had their effect on the promoters of the inquiry. The
piano indicated hours formerly spent, and thoughts once in-
dulged, which, when imagined by minds fresh from the appalling reality in the squalid kitchen, must have excited new
throes of indignation towards the accused, and new pity for
the victim. One portrait was that of the bruised and crushed
corpse herself. When it was painted she must have been
comely; now no feature of hers could be recognised as ever
having been human. Then, she was cleanly and neatly
dressed, and, if the pictured smile might be trusted, happy;
now, she lay amidst dirt, trodden down by lingering misery.
The other was a likeness of her husband. Had words of love
ever passed between the originals of those painted effigies?
Had they ever courted? It seemed that one of the jurors
was inwardly asking some such question while gazing at the
portraits, for he was strongly affected.

We all at length made our way to the Two Spies in White-
Hart-yard, Brydges-street. The accommodation afforded was
a little more spacious than that of the Old Drury; but the
delegated Majesty of the Crown had no dignity imparted to
it from the Coroner's figure being brought out in relief by a
clothes-horse and tablecloth which were, during the inquiry,
placed behind him to serve as a fire-screen. Neither did the
case of stuffed birds, the sampler of Moses in the bulrushes,
the sporting prints, the picture of the Licensed Victuallers'
School, or the portraits of the rubicund host and of his "good
lady," tend to impress the minds of the jury, witnesses, or
spectators, with that awe for the supremacy of the Law which
a court of justice is expected to inspire.

The circumstances as detailed by the witnesses are already
familiar to the readers of newspapers; but from the insecutive
manner in which the evidence was produced under the roof
of the Two Spies, it is difficult to frame a coherent narrative
from it. The husband had for several years exercised great
harshness towards his wife. Boxing her ears and kicking her
were among his "habits." On the Friday previous to her
death, the journeyman had been, as usual, "bolted down" in
the bakehouse for the night (such, he said, is the custom in
the trade), and from eleven o'clock till three in the morning

he heard a great noise overhead as of two persons quarrelling, and of one person dragging the other across the floor. There were cries of distress from the deceased woman. Another witness—a second cousin of the wife—called on Saturday afternoon. She found the wife in a pitiable state from ill-usage and want of rest. Her left ear and all that part of the head were much bruised. The husband was told how much she was injured, but he did not appear to take any notice of it. A trait of the dread in which the woman lived of the man was here mentioned; she asked the witness to ask her husband to allow her to lie down. She dared not lie down without his leave; nor prefer so reasonable a request herself, although she had been up, being brutally beaten, all the previous night. He refused. The cousin sat down to dinner with the wretched couple; only for the purpose of placing herself between them to prevent further violence; for she had dined. The cousin remained until half-past three o'clock, and during that interval the husband frequently boxed his wife's ears as hard as he could; and once kicked her with great force. Her usual remonstrance was, "Man alive, don't touch me." The same visitor returned in the evening, and she, with the journeyman, saw another brutal attack; some minutes after which the victim fell, as if in a fit. She was assisted into an inner room, sank down, and never rose again. She lay till the following Sunday morning in a state of insensibility, and no attempt had been made to procure surgical assistance. A medical practitioner at last was summoned, gave no hope, and the poor creature died on Monday morning. The post-mortem examination, described by the surgeon, revealed the cause of death in the blows at the side of the head. That, and the back of the neck, he said, were like "beefsteaks when beaten by cooks."

A lawyer would have felt especially fidgety while these facts were being elicited. The questions were put in an undecided, rambling manner, and were so interrupted by half-made remarks from the jurors and other persons in the room, that it was a wonder how the report of the proceedings which appeared in the morning newspapers, could have been cleared of the chaff from which it was winnowed. One or two circumstances occurred during this time which tended to throw

over the whole affair the air of an ill-played farce. At an
interesting point of the evidence the door was opened, and a
scream from a female voice announced, "Please, sir, the beadle's wanted!" There were four persons sitting on a horse-
hair sofa close behind some of the jury, with whom more than
once they entered into conversation, doubtless about the case
in hand. The way in which the Coroner took notice of this
breach of every jurisprudential rule, was extremely characteristic: he said, in effect, that there was, perhaps, no actual
harm in it, but it *might* be objected to—the parties conversing might be relatives of the accused. In fact, he mildly insinuated that such unprivileged communications might warp
the jurymen's judgment—merely that!

After the Coroner had summed up, the jury returned a verdict of manslaughter against the husband. The Queen's representative then retired, and so did the jury and the beadle; a
little extra business was done at the bar of the Two Spies, and
to use a reporter's pet phrase, "the proceedings terminated."

It is far from our desire, in describing this particular inquest,
in any way to disparage—supposing anything we have said can
be construed into disparagement—any person or persons concerned in it directly or remotely. Our wish is to point out
the exceeding looseness, informality, and difficulty of ensuring
sound judgment, which the system occasions. We were told
by a competent authority that the proceedings at the Old
Drury and Two Spies taverns, formed an orderly and superior
specimen of their class.

There is a mischief of some gravity, which we have yet to
notice. The essential check upon all judicial or private dere-
liction is publicity, and publicity gained through the press in
all cases which require it; but the existing system gives the
Coroner the power of excluding reporters. He can, if he
pleases, make a Star-chamber of his Court, hold it in a private
house, and conduct it in secret. Instances—though not many
—can be adduced of this having been actually done. Here
opens a door to another abuse;—it is known that a certain
few among newspaper hangers-on—persons only connected
with the press by the precarious and slender tenure of "a pen-
ny-a-line"—find it profitable to attend inquests, not for legitimate purposes (for their "copy" is seldom inserted by editors),

but to obtain money from relatives and others interested in
the deceased, for what they are pleased to call "suppressing"
their reports. This generally happens in cases having no public interest whatever, and which would not, under any circumstances, be reported; for we can with confidence say that
whenever the public interests are at stake, once before the editors of any London Journal, and supplied by an accredited
reporter, suppression is impossible. It happens again occasionally that, from the suddenness with which the Coroner is
summoned, and the slovenly manner in which his office is performed, an inquest that ought to have been made public has
wholly escaped the knowledge of newspaper reporters.

We now proceed to suggest a remedy for the inherent vices
of " Crowner's quests."

In the report of the Board of Health on intramural inter-
ments, upon which a bill now before Parliament is founded, it
is proposed to erect in convenient parts of London eight reception-houses for the dead, previous to interment in the cemeteries to be established. This will remove the mortal remains from that immediate and fatal contact—fatal morally as
well as physically—which is compulsory among the poorer
classes under the existing system of sepulture. It appears
that, of the deaths which take place in the metropolis, in upwards of 20,000 instances, the corpse must be kept, during
the interval between the death and the interment, in the same
room in which the surviving members of the family live and
sleep; while of the eight thousand deaths every year from
epidemic diseases, by far the greater part happen under the
circumstances here described.

If, from these causes, the necessity for dead-houses is so
great when no inquest is necessary, how much stronger is it
when the services of the Coroner are requisite? The reason
given for the peripatetic nature of the office, is the assumed
necessity of the jury seeing the bodies on the spot and in the
circumstances of death. But that such a necessity is unreal was
proved on the inquest we have been detailing, by the fact of
the remains having been lifted from the bed where life ceased
to a table, and having been previously opened by the surgeons.
Surely, removal to a wholesome and convenient reception-
house, would not disturb such appearances as may be pre-

sumed to form evidence. As it is, the only place among the poor in which medical men can perform the important duty of examination by post-mortem dissection, is a room crowded with inmates, or the tap-room of the nearest tavern.

To preserve, then, a degree of order, dignity, and solemnity equal at least to that which is maintained to try an action for forty shillings, and to prevent the possibility of any private dealings, we would urge that a suitable Coroner's Court-house be attached to each of the proposed reception-houses. With such accommodation, the Coroner could perform his office in a manner worthy of a delegate of the Crown.

☞ V.

THE HEART OF MID-LONDON.

MAY 4, 1850.

IT was with singular pride that Mr. Thomas Bovington of Long Hornets, Bucks, viewed his first "lot" of fat bullocks as they filed their way out of his stock-yard towards the nearest station of the North Western Railway. They were so sleek, so well fed, and so well behaved, that they turned out of their stalls with the solemn sobriety of animals attending their own funeral. Except a few capers cut by a lively West Highlander, they sauntered along like beasts who had never had a care in their lives. For how were they to know that the tips of their horns pointed to that bourne from whence few bovine travellers return—Smithfield? Smithfield, the Heart of Mid-London, the flower of the capital—the true, original, London-Pride, always in full bloom! A merciful ignorance blinded them to the fact that, the master who had fed and pampered them with indulgent industry—who had administered their food out of the scientific dietaries of Liebig; who had built their sheds after the manner of Huxtable; who had stalled and herded them in imitation of Pusey; who had littered them out of "Stevens's Book of the Farm"—was about, with equal care and attention to their comfort, to have them converted into cash, and then into beef.

This was Mr. Bovington's first transaction in bullocks.

Since his retirement from Northampton (where he made a small fortune by tanning the hides he now so assiduously filled out), he had devoted his time, his capital, and his energy to stock-farming. His sheep had always sold well; so well, indeed, that he had out-stocked the local markets; and, on the previous morning, had driven off a threescore flock to the same destination and on the same tragic errand, as that of his oxen. His success in the production of mutton had given him courage: he had, therefore, soared to beef.

Mr. Bovington had several hours to spare before the passenger-train, in which he intended to follow his cattle, was due. Like a thrifty man, he spent a part of it over his stock-book, to settle finally at what figure he could afford to sell. He was an admirable book-keeper; he could tell to an ounce how much oil-cake each ox had devoured, to a root how many beets; and, to a wisp, how much straw had been used for litter. The acreage of pasture was, also, minutely calculated. The result was, that Mr. Bovington could find in an instant the cost price of each stone of the flesh that had just departed of its own motion towards the shambles.

To a mercenary mind; to a man whose whole soul is ground down to considerations of mere profit; the result of Mr. Bovington's comparison of the cost with the present market prices, would have been extremely unsatisfactory. What he had produced at about 3s. 9d. per stone, he found by the Mark-lane Express was "dull at 3s. 6d., sinking the offal." Neither had the season been favourable for sheep—at least, not for *his* sheep—and by them, too, he would be a loser. But what of that? Mr. Bovington's object was less profit than fame. Being a beginner, he wanted to establish a first-class character in the market; and, that obtained, it would be time enough to turn his attention to the economics of feeding and breeding. With what pride would he hear the praises of those astute critics, the London butchers, as they walked round and round, pinching and punching each particular ox, enumerating his various good points, and contrasting it with the meaner, leaner stock of the mere practical graziers! With what confidence he could command the top price, and with what certainty he could maintain it for his "lots" in future!

Mr. Bovington was as merciful as he was above immediate

gain. He could not trust the stock he had nurtured and fed, to the uncontrolled dominion of drovers. Though hurried to their doom, he would take care that they should be killed "comfortably." He considered this as a sacred duty, else he —who was a pattern to the parish—would not have thus employed himself on a Sunday. As he took his ticket at the station, the chimes for evening service had just struck out. His conscience smote him. As his eye roved over the peaceful glades of Long Hornets, on which the evening sun was lowering his beams, he contrasted the holy Sabbath calm with the scene of excitement into which he was voluntarily plunging himself. As a kind of salve to his troubled mind he determined to pay extra care and attention to the comfort of his cattle.

His consignment was to remain, till Smithfield market opened at eleven o'clock on the Sunday night, at the Islington lairs. Thither Mr. Bovington repaired—on landing at the Easton Station—in a very fast cab. On his way, he calculated what the cost would be of all the fodder, all the water, and all the attendance, which his sheep and oxen would have received during their temporary sojourn. The first question he put, therefore, to the driver on arriving at the lairs, was:

"What's to pay?"

"Wot for?"

"Why," replied the amateur grazier, "for the feed of my sheep."

"Feed!" repeated the man with staring wonder, "who ever heerd of feedin' markit sheep? Why, they'll be killed to-morrow or Tuesday, won't they?"

"If sold."

"Well, they'll never want no more wittles, will they?"

"But they have had nothing since Saturday!"

"What on it! Sheep as comes to Smithfield *never* has no feed, has they?"

"Nor water either?" said Mr. Bovington.

"*I* should think not!" replied the drover.

As he spoke, he drove the point of his goad into the backs of each of a shorn flock that happened to be passing. He had no business with them; but it was a way he had.

With sorrowful eyes, Mr. Bovington sought out his own

sheep. Poor things! They lay closely packed, with their tongues out, panting for suction; for they were too weak to bleat. He would have given any money to relieve them; but relief no money could buy.

Mr. Bovington was glad to find his bullocks in better plight. To them, fodder and drink had been sparingly supplied, but they were wedged in so tightly that they had hardly room to breathe. Their good looks—which had cost him so much oil-cake and anxiety—would be quite gone before they got to Smithfield.

"It ain't o' no use a fretting," said the master drover; "your'n ain't no worse off nor t'others. What you've got to do, is, to git to bed, and meet me in the market at four." Naming a certain corner.

"Well," said Mr. Bovington, seeing there was no help for it, "let it be so; but I trust you will take care to get my lots driven down by humane drovers."

Mr. Whelter, the master drover, assented, in a manner that showed he had not the remotest idea what a humane driver was; nor where the article was to be found.

Mr. Bovington could get no ease in his inn, that night, and went his way towards the market, long before the time appointed. Before he came within sight of Smithfield, a din as of a noisy Pandemonium filled his ears. The shouting of some of the drovers, the shrill whistle of others, the barking of dogs, the bleating of sheep, and the lowing of cattle, were the natural expressions of a crowded market; but, added to these, were other sounds, which made Mr. Bovington shudder; something between the pattering of a tremendous hailstorm, and the noise of ten thousand games of single-stick played, all at once, in bloody earnest.

To get the bullocks into their allotted stands an incessant punishing and torturing of the miserable animals—a sticking of prongs into the tender part of their feet, and a twisting of their tails to make the whole spine teem with pain—was going on; and this seemed as much a part of the market, as the stones in its pavement. Across their horns, across their hocks, across their haunches, Mr. Bovington saw the heavy blows rain thick and fast, let him look where he would.

Obdurate heads of oxen, bent down in mute agony; bellowing heads of oxen lifted up, snorting out smoke and slaver; ferocious men, cursing and swearing, and belabouring oxen; made the place a panorama of cruelty and suffering. By every avenue of access to the market, more oxen were pouring in: bellowing, in the confusion, and under the falling blows, as if all the church-organs in the world were wretched instruments —all there—and all being tuned together. Mixed up with these oxen, were great flocks of sheep, whose respective drovers were in agonies of mind to prevent their being intermingled in the dire confusion; and who raved, shouted, screamed, swore, whooped, whistled, danced like savages; and, brandishing their cudgels, laid about them most remorselessly. All this was being done, in a deep red glare of burning torches, which were in themselves a strong addition to the horrors of the scene; for the men who were arranging the sheep and lambs in their miserably confined pens, and forcing them to their destination through alleys of the most preposterously small dimensions, constantly dropped gouts of the blazing pitch upon the miserable creatures' backs; and to smell the singeing and burning, and to see the poor things shrinking from this roasting, inspired a sickness, a disgust, a pity and an indignation, almost insupportable. To reflect that the gate of St. Bartholomew's Hospital was in the midst of this devilry, and that such a monument of years of sympathy for human pain should stand there, jostling this disgraceful record of years of disregard of brute endurance—to look up at the faint lights in the windows of the houses where the people were asleep, and to think that some of them had been to Public Prayers that Sunday, and had typified the Divine love and gentleness, by the panting, footsore creature, burnt, beaten, and needlessly tormented there, that night, by thousands— suggested truths so inconsistent and so shocking, that the Market of the Capital of the World seemed a ghastly and blasphemous Nightmare.

"Does this happen *every* Monday morning?" asked the horror-stricken denizen of Long Hornets, of a respectable-looking man.

"This?" repeated the stranger. "Bless you! This is nothing to what it is sometimes." He then turned to a passing drover, who was vainly trying to get some fifty sheep through a pen-alley calculated for the easy passage of twenty. "How many are spoke for to-night, Ned?"

"How many? Why, five-and-twenty thousand sheep, and forty-one hundred beasts."

"Ah! no more than an ordinary market," said Mr. Bovington's new friend; yet you see and hear what's now going on to wedge these numbers in. And it stands to reason if you've got to jam together a fourth more animals than there is space for, there *must* be cruelty."

"How much legitimate accommodation is there?" asked Mr. Bovington.

"There are pens for two-and-twenty thousand sheep, and they can tie up twenty-seven hundred beasts. Well! you hear; room has already been 'spoken for,' or bespoken, for three thousand more sheep and fourteen hundred more cattle than there is proper space for."

"What becomes of the surplus?"

"The beasts are formed, in the thoroughfares and in the outskirts of the market, into what we call 'off droves;' and the sheep wait outside, anywhere, till they can get in."

Here the conversation was interrupted by a sudden increase in the demoniacal noises. Opposite the speakers, was a row of panting oxen, each fastened by a slip-noose to a rail, as closely as their heads could be jammed together. Some more were being tied up, and one creature had just escaped. Instantly a dozen hoarse voices yelled:

"Out! out! out!"

The cry was echoed by a dozen others.

"Out! out! out!"

A wild hunt followed, every human hound shouting "Out! out! out!" as he ran. Then, the luckless truant being overtaken, was heard a shower of blows on its back, horns, and sides. The concentrated punishment of two dozen drovers' sticks made the bull too glad to resume its original station. It was then tied up, so tightly, that the swelled tongue protruded. That the poor brute should be rendered powerless for motion for some time to come, it was "hocked,"—that is to say, tremendous blows were inflicted on its hind legs till it was completely hobbled.

Mr. Bovington was glad that it was not one of his bul-

3*

locks. "Are *many* strangled by these tight nooses?" he asked.

"A good many in the course of the year, I should say. All the rails are full now, and the off-droves are beginning."

The battle raged faster and more furious than ever. To make the most of the room, they were forming "ring-droves;" that is, punishing the animals till a certain number had turned all their heads together to form the inside of a circle—which at last they did, to avoid the blows inflicted on them. After every imaginable torment had been practised, to get them into the right position, a stray head would occasionally protrude— where a tail should be—on the outside of the ring. Tremendous blows were then repeated on the nose, neck, and horns, till the tortured animal could turn; and when he succeeded, the goad was "jobbed" into his flanks till he could wedge himself in, so as to form his own proper radius of the dense circle. Mr. Bovington's blood ran cold as he witnessed the cruelty necessary for these evolutions.

"I have often seen their haunches streaming with blood before they could get into the ring," said Mr. Bovington's companion. "Why, a friend of mine, a tanner at Kenilworth, was actually obliged to leave off buying hides that came out of this market, because they were covered with holes that had been bored in the live animals by the Smithfield drovers. He called these skins Smithfield Cullenders."

"Cruel wretches!"

"Well," said the stranger, thoughtfully, "I can't blame *them*. I have known them forty years——"

"You are a salesman?"

"I *was;* but they worried me out of the market, for trying to get it removed, and for giving evidence against it before Parliament."

Mr. Brumpton, the ousted salesman, did a little fattening, now, on a few acres near London; and came occasionally to Smithfield to buy and sell in a small way: just, in fact, as Mr. Bovington had begun to do.

"Well," he continued, "I can't lay all the blame on the drovers. If they have got one hundred beasts to wedge into a space only big enough for seventy, what can they do? Even the labour their cruelty costs themselves is terrible. I have often seen seen drovers' men lying on the steps of doors, quite exhausted. None of them ever live long."

" How many are there ?"

" About nine hundred and fifty—licensed."

A deafening hullabaloo rose again. A new ring-drove was being begun, close by. Bovington threw up his hands in horror when he saw that some of his cherished cattle were to become members of it. The lively West Highlander was struggling fiercely against his fate; but in vain: he was goaded, beaten, and worried till forced into the ring.

Bovington hastened to the appointed corner to expostulate with Mr. Whelton.

" How can *I* help it !" was that individual's consolation. " I spoke for all your beasts ; but there was only room for seven on 'em to be tied up; so the rest on 'em is in off-droves. Where else *can* they be ?"

" And my sheep ?"

" Couldn't get none on 'em in. They're a waiting in the Ram yard till the sales empties some of the pens. You'll find 'em in the first floor."

" What ! Up stairs ?"

" Ah, in the one-pair back."

Mr. Bovington elbowed his way to the Ram Inn, to confirm by his eyes what he could not believe with his ears. Sure enough he found his favourite New Leicesters a whole flight of stairs above ground. How they had ever been got up, or how they were ever to be got down, surpassed his ingenuity to conjecture.

At length there was pen-room. When Mr. Bovington's little flock were got into the market, they met, and were mixed with, the sold flocks that were going out. Confusion was now worse confounded. The beating, the goading, the hustling, the shouting; the bleating of the sheep; the short, sharp, snarling of the dogs; above all, the stentorian oaths and imprecations of the drovers—no unaided human imagination could picture. Several flocks were intermixed in a manner that made correct separation seem impossible ; but, while Mr. Bovington shuddered at all this cruelty and wickedness— solely produced by want of space, and by the previous driving through the streets—he could not help admiring the instinct

of the sheep-dogs and the ingenuity of the men in lessening
the confusion: the former watching intently their masters'
faces for orders, and flying over the backs of the moving floor
of wool to execute them.

"Go for 'em, Bob!"

Like lightning the dog belonging to the drover of Bovington's sheep dashed over their backs, and he beheld the ear of
a favourite wether between his teeth. By some magic, however, this significant style of ear-wigging directed the sheep
into the alley that led to the empty pens; and the others were
pushed, punched, goaded, and thrashed, till each score was
jammed into the small enclosures, as tight as figs in a drum.

"They seem a nice lot," said Mr. Brumpton, who had followed the new seller; "but how is it possible for the best
butcher in London to tell what they are in a wedge like this?
Can he know how they will cut up after the punishment they
have had? Impossible: and what's the consequence? Why,
he will deduct ten or fifteen per cent. from your price for
bruised meat. It is the same with bullocks."

Mr. Bovington, at this hint, reverted to his herd of cattle
with a fresh pang. Crammed, rammed, and jammed as they
were between raw-boned Lincolnshires and half-fed Herefords,
how could his customers see and appreciate the fine " points"
of his fancy stock? He had worked for Fame; yet, however
loud her blast, who could hear it above the crushing din of
Smithfield?

Mr. Bovington having returned to the rendezvous, sat on
the edge of an old grindstone nailed against a cutler's door-
post, in profound rumination. He was at a dead-lock. He
could not sell all his stock, and he could not withdraw it; for
it was so fearfully deteriorated from the treatment it had got,
that he felt sure the recovery of many of his sheep and some
of his oxen would be impossible. The best thing he could
wish for them was speedy death; and, for himself, sales at
any price.

His reflections were interrupted by the pleasing information
that, although some of his beasts that were tied up had been
sold at the top price, only a few of those in the off-droves
could find customers at the second, because the butchers

could not get to see them. "And you see they *will* have the pull of the market, if they can get it."

Mr. Bovington looked unutterable despair, and told the salesman emphatically to SELL.

"It don't matter to him," said Brumpton, who was again at poor Bovington's elbow, "what the animals fetch. Sold for much or sold for little, the salesman's profit don't vary—4s. a head for beasts, and from 10s. to 13s. a score for sheep, at whatever price he sells. That's the system here, and it don't improve the profits of the grazier. Why should *he* care what you get, or what you lose?"

Towards the close of the market, Mr. Bovington perceived, that if it cost the animals intense torture to be got into their allotted places, it took unmitigated brutality to get them out again. The breaking up of a ring-drove might have made a treat for Nero; but honest Mr. Bovington had had enough. He retired from the arena of innumerable bull-fights in a state of mind in which disgust very much preponderated over personal disappointment.

Mr. Brumpton and he determined to breakfast together, at the Catherine Wheel, in St. John-street.

"What remedy do you propose for these horrors?" asked our dejected friend.

"A market in the suburbs," was the answer.

"But look at the rapidity with which London spreads. How long will you guarantee that any site you may select will remain ' out of town?' "

"Ah, that's the difficulty," said Brumpton. "In 1808, it was proposed to remove the market to the ' open fields'— Clerkenwell-fields; but, twenty years afterwards, there was not a blade of grass to be seen near the place. It was covered with bricks and mortar. Rahere-street—in the midst of a dense neighborhood—now stands on the very spot that was suggested. Again, only last year a field between Camden-town and Holloway was proposed; but since then, houses have been built up to the very hedge that encloses it."*

"What is to be done, then?"

"I'll tell you what I think would be best. Let a good site

* One of the most splendid cattle-markets in the world has been since built on the spot thus indicated, nevertheless.

be fixed upon; and don't rest contented with that. Fence off
a certain space around it with appropriate approaches. Let
these be kept sacred from innovating bricks. Deal with a new
cattle-market as the Board of Health proposes to deal with
cemeteries. Isolate it. Allow of no buildings, except for
market purposes—of no encroachments whatever—either upon
the area itself or its new approaches."

Mr. Bovington was about to hazard a remark about abat-
toirs, when deafening cries again rose in Smithfield-bars.

"Mad bull! mad bull! mad bull!"

"Mad bull! mad bull!" was echoed from the uttermost
ends of St. John-street.

Bovington looked out of window. A black ox was tearing
furiously along the pavement. Women were screaming and
rushing into shops, children scrambling out of the road, other
children tumbling over them, men hiding themselves in door-
ways, boys in ecstasies, drovers, as mad as the bull, tearing
after him, sheep getting under the wheels of cabs, carts, and
waggons, dogs half choking themselves with worrying the
wool off their backs, pigs obstinately connecting themselves
with a hearse and funeral, other oxen looking into public-
houses—everybody and everything disorganised, no sort of
animal able to go where it wanted or was wanted; nothing in
its right place; everything wrong everywhere; all the town
in a brain fever because of this infernal market!

The mad bull was Mr. Bovington's own West Highlander.
He was quite prepared for it. When he saw the harried
beast going round the corner, and at the same moment beheld
a nursemaid, a baby, and a baked potato-can, fly into the air
in opposite directions, he was horrified; but not surprised.
He followed the crowd tearing after his West Highlander,
down St. John-street, through Jerusalem-passage, along Clerk-
enwell-green, up a hill, and down an alley. He passed two
disabled apple-women, a fractured shop-front, an old man
being put into a cab and taken to the hospital. At last, he
traced the favourite of his herds into a back parlour in Liquor-
pond-street, into which he had violently intruded through a
tripe-shop, and where he was being slaughtered for his own
peace and for the safety of the neighborhood; but not at all
to the satisfaction of an invalid who had leaped out of a turn-

up bedstead, into the little yard behind. The carcase of the West Highlander was sold to a butcher for a sum which paid about half of what was demanded from its owner, from the different victims of its fury, for compensation.

Mr. Bovington returned to Long Hornets a wiser, though certainly not (commercially speaking) a better man. His adventures in Smithfield had made a large hole in a 50*l.* note.

Some of his oxen were returned unsold. Two came back with the "foot disease," and the rest did not recover their value for six months.

Mr. Bovington has never tried Smithfield again. He regards it as a place accursed. In distant Reigns, he says, it was an odious spot, associated with cruelty, fanaticism, wickedness, and torture; and in these later days it is worthy of its ancient reputation. It is a doomed, but a proper and consistent stronghold (according to Mr. Bovington) of prejudice, ignorance, cupidity, and stupidity:

> On some fond breast its parting soul relies,
> Some pious alderman its fame admires;
> Ev'n from its tomb, the voice of Suff'ring cries,
> Ev'n in its ashes live its wonted Fires!

☞ VI.

A POPULAR DELUSION.

JUNE 1, 1850.

VICTIMISED by a deceptive idea originating in "The Complete Angler," and industriously perpetuated by a numerous proprietary of punts, public-houses, and eel-pies, the London disciples of Izaak Walton usually seek for sport in the upper regions of the Thames. They resort to Shepperton, or Ditton, or Twickenham, or Richmond. Chiefly, it would seem, as a wholesome exercise of the greatest Christian virtue; for recent experience proves that anglers who soar above sticklebats, and are not content with occasional nibbles from starving gudgeons, or frequent entanglements of writhing eels, mostly return to their homes and families with their baskets innocent of scales as the backs of their own hands.

If, as may be safely asserted, the aim, end, and purpose of
all fishing is fish, the tenacity with which this idea is clung to
is amazing, when we reflect that there exists, below bridge, a
particular spot, more convenient, more accessible, and affording quite as good accommodation as any of the above-bridge
fishing stations, and which abounds at particular states of the
tide, at particular times of the day, and at no particular seasons of the year, but all the year round, in fish of every sort,
size, species, and condition, from the cod down to the sprat;
from a salmon to a shrimp; from turbots to Thames flounders.
Neither is there a single member of any one of these enormous families of fishes that may not be captured with the
smallest possible expenditure of Patience.   And although the
bait necessary for that purpose (a white bait manufactured of
metal at an establishment on the Tower Hill bank of the Thames)
is unfortunately not always procurable by every class of her
Majesty's subjects; yet it is so eagerly caught at, that with a
moderate supply, the least expert may be sure of filling his
fish-basket after a very short morning's sport.

To partake of all the advantages offered by this famed spot,
it is necessary to rise betimes.   Our own fishing excursion
commenced at about four o'clock on a Monday morning.   The
rain that was falling did not much matter; for the margin of
the Thames to which we were bound is well sheltered.   With
a small basket, and the waistcoat pocket primed with the
proper sort of bait; with no other rod than a walking-stick,
and no fly whatever (except one upon four wheels), we arrived at the great fish focus; which, we may as well mention,
is situated on the Middlesex shore of the Thames at a short
distance below London Bridge, close to the Custom House,
and has been known from time immemorial as BILLINSGATE.

The ancient reputation of this collection of sheds and stalls
had prepared us for scenes of confusion and for volubility of
abuse, which have ever been associated with those whose special business is with fish since the times of the Tritons.   It
was, therefore, with very great surprise that we walked unmo-
lested through that portion of the precinct set aside as the
market.   We went straight to the river's edge, rod in hand,
without having had once occasion to use it as a weapon, and
without hearing one word that might not have been uttered

in the Queen's drawing-room on a court day. No crowding, no elbowing, no screaming, no fighting : no ungenteel nick-names, no foul-mouthed females hurling anathemas and piscine offal at one another; no rude requests to descend suddenly down to the uttermost depth the human mind is capable of conceiving; no wish expressed that we might be inflated very tight; no criticisms on the quality of our hat, nor inquiries of the address of our hatter; no impertinent questions as to our present stock of soap, as to our mother, or her mangle; no injunctions to flare up on the strength of that lady's money; nothing whatever, in short, calculated to sustain the ancient reputation of Billingsgate.

We sauntered down to the dumb-barge which forms a temporary landing-place while a better one is being built. There we beheld a couple of clippers, quite as trim as any revenue-cutter; over the sides of which were being handed all sorts of fish : cod, soles, whitings, plaice, John Dorys, mackerel; some neatly packed in baskets. That nothing should be wanting utterly to subvert conventional notions of Billingsgate, the or · der, quietness, and system with which these cutters were emptied, and their cargoes taken to the stalls, could not be exceeded.

This office is performed by fellowship-porters. Being responsible individuals, they prevent fraud, they say. Formerly a set of scamps, called laggers, "conveyed" the fish; but they used to drop some of the best sort softly into the stream, and pick them up (and pocket them) at low water. An idea may be formed of the profits of their dishonesty from the fact that laggers offered seven shillings a day to be employed, instead of demanding the wages of labour. When a salesman had one or two hundred turbots consigned to him, a lagger would give the hint to an accomplice, who would quickly substitute several small fish for the same number of the largest size; a species of fraud which the salesman had it not in his power to detect; for it did not diminish the tally.

As we have a minute or two to wait on the Billingsgate punt before the market opens, let us trace the history of a fish from the sea to the salesman's stall. Suppose him to be a turbot hauled with a hundred other captives early on Monday afternoon on board one of the Barking fishing fleet moored on a bank some twenty miles off Dover. He is no sooner taken on board than he is transhipped in a row-boat, with thousands of his flat companions, into a clipper, which is being fast filled from other vessels of the fleet. When the clipper's cargo is complete, she sets sail for the mouth of the Thames; and, on entering it, is met by a tug steamer, which tows her up to Billingsgate early on Tuesday morning, bringing our turbot *alive*—for he has been put into a tank in the hold of the clipper. · He is sold as soon as landed, and finds his way to table in the neighbourhood of the Mansion House or Belgrave-square, some four-and twenty-hours after he has been sporting in the sea not less than a hundred and fifty miles off.

Enormous accessions in the supply of fish to the London market have been effected, first by the employment of clippers as carrier-boats (instead of each fishing-boat bringing its own cargo to market), and secondly, by the use of steam-tugs for towing the transit-craft up the river. In the old time a south-westerly wind deprived all London of fish. While it prevailed, the boats, which usually took shelter in Holy or East Haven on the Essex shore, waited for a change of wind, till the fish became odoriferous. The cargo was then thrown overboard, and the boats returned on another fishing voyage.

The Thames was, at that time, the only highway by which fish was brought to Billingsgate; but the old losses and delays are again obviated by another mode of acceleration. Our turbot is brought at waggon pace compared with the more perishable mackerel. The Eddystone lighthouse is not far short of three hundred miles from Thames-street. Between it and the Plymouth Breakwater lie some hundreds of fishing boats, plying their trawl-nets. A shoal of mackerel, which may be measured by the mile, find their way among them, and several thousands do not find their way out again. They are captured, hauled on board, shovelled into a clipper, and, while she stands briskly in for shore, busy hands on board are packing the fish in baskets. Thousands of these baskets are landed in time for the mail train, rattle their way by railroad to Paddington, and, by seven o'clock on the following morning—that is, in sixteen hours from the moment of their last swim in the ocean—are in a London fishmonger's taxed-cart on their road to the domestic gridiron or fish-kettle.

No distance appears to be too great from which to bring fish to Billingsgate. Salmon, packed in long boxes, between layers of ice, come daily both by rail and river in enormous quantities from the remotest rivers of Ireland, of Scotland, and even from Norway. So considerable an item is ice in the fishmonger's trade, that a large proprietor at Barking has an ice-well capable of stowing eight hundred tons. Another in the same line of business has contracted with the Surrey Canal Company for all the ice generated on their waters.

As we cogitate concerning these " great facts" on the dumb-barge, and while the baskets and boxes are being systematic-ally landed, the clock strikes five. Another bell—the only noisy appurtenance of Billingsgate — stunningly announces that the market is open. The landing of fish proceeds some-what faster, and fishmongers, from all parts of London, and from many parts of the provinces—from Oxford, Cambridge, Reading, Windsor, even from Boulogne—group themselves round the stalls of the salesmen. The choicest fish are rapidly sold by Dutch auction, and taken to the buyers' carts outside the market.

Nothing can exceed the gentlemanly manner in which the action is conducted ; the mode of doing business at Christie and Manson's not excepted. The salesman, with his flannel apron protecting his fashionable attire from scaly contact, is seen—behold him yonder !—seated behind his stall enjoying a mild Havannah, with an appearance of sublime indifference to all around him. Presently, his porter deposits a " lot" of fish between him and an eager group of buyers. He puts down his cigar and mounts his rostrum.

" What shall we say, gentlemen, for this score of cod ? Shall we say seven shillings apiece ?"

No answer.

" Six ?"

Perfect silence. The auctioneer gives pause for considera-tion, and takes a whiff at his Havannah. Time is, however, precious where fish is concerned, and he is not long in abating another shilling.

" A crown ?"

" Done !" exclaims Mr. Jollins of Pimlico.

" Five pounds, if you please ?" demands the seller. A note

is handed over, and the twenty cod are hoisted into Mr. Jollins's cart, which stands in Thames-street, before a second lot is quite disposed of.

This mild proceeding is going on all over the market. On looking to see if the remotest relic of such a being as a fish-fag is to be seen, we observe a gentlemen who, though girded with the flannel uniform of the craft, has so fashionable a surtout, so elegant a neckerchief, and such a luxuriance of moustache, that we mistake him for an officer in her Majesty's Life Guards, selling fish by way of—what in Billingsgate used to be called—a "jolly lark." Inquiry proves, however, that he is the accredited consignee of one of the largest fishing fleets sailing out of the Thames.

We are bound to confess that the high tone of refinement which had hitherto been so well supported, became, in a little while, slightly depressed. As the legislature of the British empire consists of Crown, Lords, and Commons, so also the executive of Billingsgate is composed of three estates: first, of the Lord Mayor (principal secretary of skate, &c., Mr. Goldham); secondly, of an aristocracy; and, thirdly, of a commonality, of salesmen. The latter—called in ancient Billingsgate *Bummarees*, in modern ditto, "Retailers"—are middlemen between the smaller fishmonger and the high salesmen aristocracy. These purchase the various sorts of fish, and arrange them in small assorted parcels to suit the convenience of suburban fishmongers, or of those peripatetic tradesmen, to whom was formerly applied the (in Billingsgate) obsolete term almost of "Costermonger." Their transactions were not concluded under the influence of those strict rules of etiquette which governed the earlier dealings of the morning. Indeed, we detected the proprietor of a very respectable-looking donkey answering a civil inquiry from a retailer as to what he was "looking for" with

"Not you; but another donkey!"

It is right, however, to add, in justice to the reputation of a locality which has been so long and so relentlessly regarded as the head-quarters of vituperation, that a friend of the offender asked him solemnly *if he remembered were he wos;* and if he warn't ashamed of his-self for going and bringing his Cheek into that 'ere markit!

Connected with the perambulating purveyors, there is a subject of very great importance ; namely, cheap food for the poor. Despite constant revelations of want amounting to starvation ; although the low dietaries of most workhouses, and some prisons, are very often complained of; yet the old Celtic prejudice against fish still exists in great force in humble life. Few poor persons will eat fish when they can get meat; many prefer gruel, and some no food at all. Wholesome and nutritious fish are now sold at prices not above the means of the poorest persons ; yet, so small is the demand, that the itinerant vender—through whom what little that is sold reaches the poorer consumer—makes it a matter of indifference, when he starts from home, whether his venture for the day shall be fish or vegetables. It is true that his first visit is to Billingsgate ; but if he find things, as regards price or kind, not to his taste, he adjourns to speculate in Covent Garden. He has, therefore, no regular market for what might most beneficially become a staple article. During the fruit season, he sells little or no fish; because he finds dealings with the " Garden" more profitable than dealings at the " Gate."

Not long since a large quantity of wholesome fish of various sorts was left upon the hands of the market superintendent. By the advice of the Lord Mayor, it was forwarded for consumption to Giltspur-street Compter. The prisoners actually refused to eat it, and accompanied their refusal with a jocose allusion to the want of a proper accompaniment of sauce.

Among the stronger instances of the popular aversion to this kind of food we may mention that in 1812 one of the members of the Committee for the Relief of the Manufacturing Poor, agreed with some fishermen to take from ten to twenty thousand mackerel a day, at a penny apiece; a price at which the fishermen said they could afford to supply the London market, to any extent, were they sure of a regular sale. On the 15th June, 1812, upwards of seventeen thousand mackerel, delivered at the stipulated price, were sent to Spitalfields, and sold to the working weavers at the original cost of a penny apiece. Though purchased with great avidity by the inhabitants of that district, it soon appeared that Spitalfields alone would not be equal to the consumption of the vast quantities of mackerel which daily poured into the market; they were, therefore, sent for distribution, at the same rate, in other parts of the town; workhouses and other public establishments were also served, and the supply increased to such a degree, that five hundred thousand mackerel arrived and were sold in one day. This cheap and benevolent supply was eagerly absorbed while the distress lasted; but, as soon as trade revived, the demand fell off, and finally ceased altogether.

Is this aversion to fish unconquerable? If it be not, what an enormous augmentation of wholesome food might be procured to relieve the increasing wants of the humble and needy. All the time the above experiment was tried, only a small portion of the coast was available for the supply of the densest inland populations of this island. Now, there is scarcely a creek or an estuary from which fish cannot be rapidly transported, however great the distance.

Compared with the present boundless means of supply, and the powers of rapid transit, fish is inordinately dear. But this is solely the fault of the public. The demand is too inconsiderable to call forth any great and, therefore, economical system. The voyager, per steam, between the Thames and Scotland, or between London and Cork, cannot fail to wonder when he sees, as he surely will see, on a warm, calm day, square miles of haddocks, mackerel, pilchards, herrings, and other shoaling fish; and when he remembers that he has left on shore thousands of human beings pining for food. These enormous shoals approach the land, too, on purpose to be caught. In the History of British Fishes, Mr. Yarrell says, "The law of Nature which obliges mackerel and many others to visit the shallower water of the shores at a particular season, appears to be one of those wise and beautiful provisions of the Creator by which not only is the species perpetuated with the greatest certainty, but a large portion of the parent animals are thus brought within the reach of man, who, but for the action of this law, would be deprived of many of those species most valuable to him as food. For the mackerel dispersed over the immense surface of the deep, no effective fishery could be carried on; but approaching the shore as they do from all directions, and roving along the coast collected in immense shoals, millions are caught, which yet form but a very small portion compared with the myriads that escape." The fecundity of some of the species is marvellous. It has been ascertained that the roe of the cod-fish contains from six to nine millions of eggs.

Nor are river fish less abundant. Mr. Yarrell says, that two persons once calculated from actual observation that from sixteen to eighteen hundred of the delicate ingredients for Twickenham pies passed a given point of the Thames in one minute of time; an average of more than one hundred thousand per hour. And this *eel-fare*, as it is called, is going on incessantly for more than two months. The king of fish is equally prolific, and quite as easily captured. The choicest salmon that appears in Billingsgate are from the river Bann, near Coleraine. We found it eighteenpence per pound at Billingsgate; yet it is recorded that fourteen hundred and fifty salmon were taken in that river at one drag of a single net.

The appetite for fish is, as it would seem, an acquired taste; but it would be of enormous advantage if any means could be devised for encouraging the consumption of this description of food. In order to commence the experiment, we would suggest the regular introduction of fish into workhouses and prison dietaries. Formerly, such a measure was not practicable during the whole of the year, but with a trifling outlay, such a system of supply might be organised as would ensure freshness and constancy.

The proprietor of the handsome donkey, who led us into this statistical reverie, informed us—and he was corroborated by his friend—that the only certainty was the red-herring and periwinkle trade; but then the competition was so very great " *I* don't know how it is," he observed, " but people 'll buy salt things with all the wirtue dried out on 'em, but——"

" That's because they has a relish," interrupted the Mentor.

" But fresh fish," renewed the old gentleman, with a glance of displeasure at being interrupted; " fresh fish—all alive, as we cries 'em—fresh fish, mind you!—they can't abear!"

We also learnt from these gentlemen that the professors of the Hebrew faith were the only constant fish-eaters.

" And wy ?" continued the councillor; " cos when they eats
fish, they thinks they're a fasting !"

This reminding us that we were actually fasting, we compli-
mented our friend on his donkey (which he assured us was a
" Moke" of the reg'lar Tantivy breed), and having completed
the filling of our basket, were about to return home to breakfast, with an excellent appetite, and a high respect for the
manners of modern fishmongers, when he hailed us easily with,
" Halloa, you sir !"

We went back.

" I tell you wot," he said, jerking his thumb over his shoulder, in the direction of the Market Tavern,—" but p'raps you
have though."

" Have what ?" said we.

" Dined at Simpson's, the Fish Hord'n'ry," said he.

" Never," said we.

" Do it !" said he. " You go and have a cut-out at Simpson's
at four o'clock in the afternoon (wen me and my old ooman is
a going to take our tea, with a winkle or wot not), and you'll
come out as bright as a star, and as sleek as this here Moke."

We thanked him for his hint towards the improvement of
our personal appearance, which was a little dilapidated at that
hour of the morning, and were so much impressed by the possibility of rivalling the Moke, that we returned at four o'clock
in the afternoon, and climbed up to the first floor of Mr.
Simpson's house.

A glance at the clock assured us that Mr. Simpson was a
genius. He kept it back ten minutes, to give stragglers a
last chance. Already, the long table down the whole length
of the long low room was nearly full, and people were sitting
at a side table, looking out through windows, like stern-win-
dows aboard ship, at flapping sails, and rigging. The host
was in the chair, with a wooden hammer ready to his hand;
and five several gentlemen, much excited by hunger and
haste, who had run us down on the stairs, had leaped into
seats, and were menacing expected turbots with their knives.

We slipped into a vacant chair by a gentleman from the
Eastern Counties, who immediately informed us that Sir
Robert Peel was all wrong, and the agricultural interest
blown to shivers. This gentleman had little pieces of stick-

ing-plaster stuck all over him, and we thought his discontent had broken out in an eruption, until he informed us that he had been "going it all last week" with some ruined friends of his who were also in town, and that "champagne and claret always had that effect upon him."

On our left hand, was an undertaker from Whitechapel. "Here's a bill," says he; "this General Interment! What's to become of my old hands who haven't been what you may call rightly sober these twenty years? Ain't there *any* religious feeling in the country?"

The company had come, like the fish, from various distances. There was a respectable Jew provision-merchant from Hamburg, over the way. Next him, an old man with sunken jaws that were always in motion, like a gutta-percha mouth that was being continually squeezed. He had come from York. Hard by, a very large smooth-faced old gentleman, in an immense ribbed satin waistcoat, out of Devonshire, attended by a pink nephew who was walking the London Hospitals. Lower down was a wooden leg that had brought the person it belonged to all the way from Canada. Two "parties," as the waiter called them, who had been with a tasting-order to the Docks, and were a little scared about the eyes, belonged to Doncaster. Pints of stout and porter were handed round, agreeably to their respective orders. Everybody took his own pint pot to himself, and seemed suspicious of his neighbour. As the minute hand of the clock approached a quarter past four, the gentleman from the Eastern Counties whispered us, that if the country held out for another year, it was as much as he expected.

Suddenly a fine salmon sparkled and twinkled like a silver harlequin before Mr. Simpson. A goodly dish of soles was set on lower down; then, in quick succession, appeared flounders, fried eels, stewed eels, cod-fish, melted butter, lobster-sauce, potatoes. Savoury steams curled and curled about the company's heads, and toyed with the company's noses. Mr. Simpson hammered on the table. Grace!

For one silent moment, Mr. Simpson gazed upon the salmon as if he were the salmon's admiring father, and then fell upon him, and helped twenty people without winking. Five or six flushed waiters hurried to and fro, and played cymbals with

4

the plates; the company rattled an accompaniment of knives and forks; the fish were no more, in a twinkling. Boiled beef, mutton, and a huge dish of steaks, were soon disposed of in a like manner. Small glasses of brandy round, were gone, ere one could say it lightened. Cheese melted away. Crusts dissolved into air. Mr. Simpson was gay. He knew the worst the company could do. He saw it done, twice every day. Again he hammered on the table. Grace!

Then, the cloth, the plates, the salt-cellars, the knives and forks, the glasses and pewter-pots, being all that the guests had not eaten or drunk, were cleared; bunches of pipes were laid upon the table; and everybody ordered what he liked to drink, or went his way. Mr. Simpson's punch, in wicked tumblers of immense dimensions, was the most in favour. Mr. Simpson himself consorted with a company of generous spirits —connected with a Brewery, perhaps—and smoked a mild cigar. The large gentleman out of Devonshire: so large now, that he was obliged to move his chair back, to give his satin waistcoat play: ordered a small pint bottle of port, passed it to the pink nephew, and disparaged punch. The nephew dutifully concurred, but looked at the undertaker's glass, out of the corner of his eye, as if he could have reconciled himself to punch, too, under pressure, on a desert island. The "parties" from the Docks took rum-and-water, and wandered in their conversation. He of the Eastern Counties took cold gin-and-water for a change, and for the purification of his blood. Deep in the oiled depths of the old-fashioned table, a reflexion of every man's face appeared below him, beaming. Many pipes were lighted, the windows were opened at top, and a fragrant cloud enwrapped the company, as if they were all being carried upward together. The undertaker laughed monstrously at a joke, and the agriculturist thought the country might go on, say ten years, with good luck.

Eighteenpence a-head had done it all—the drink, and smoke, and civil attendance, excepted—and again this was Billingsgate! Verily, there is "an ancient and fish-like smell" about our popular opinions sometimes; and our hereditary exaltations and depressions of some things would bear revision!

VII.

THE GOLDEN CITY.

JUNE 29, 1850.

" THE fitful flame of Young Romance,'' fed by the Arabian Nights' Entertainments, Fairy tales and Heathen Mythologies; Genii and Magicians; towns springing up, ready-built, out of deserts; cities paved with gold; the Happy Valley of Rasselas; the territories of Oberon and Titania; Robert Owen's New Harmony; the land of Cockaigne; Gulliver's Travels; Peter Wilkins; legends of beggars made kings, and mendicants millionnaires; Sinbad the Sailor, Baron Munchausen, Law of Laurieston, Major Longbow, Colonel Crocket, and the Poyais loan; illimitable exaggeration; undaunted lying; the most rampant schemes of the wildest speculators; the most gorgeous visions of the maddest poet; the airiest castle of Utopian lunacy—any one of these, and all of them put together, do not exceed the wonders of California.

The story of the magic growth of San Francisco would have defied belief, had it not literally grown up under the " eyes of Europe." When the returns were made to the United States authorities in 1831, it contained three hundred and seventy-one individuals, and very few more resided in it up to the discovery of gold at Sutter's Mill, in the Sacramento River. Even in April, 1840, we learn from a credible eye-witness, that there were only from thirty to forty houses in San Francisco; and that the population was so small, that so many as twenty-five persons could never be seen out of doors at one time. There now lie before us two prints; one of San Francisco, taken in November, 1848, soon after the discovery was made, and another exactly a year afterwards. In the first, we are able to count twenty-six huts and other dwellings dotted about at uneven distances, and four small ships in the harbour. In the second, the habitations are countless. The hollow, upon which the city partly stands, presents a bird's-eye view of roofs, packed closely together; while the sides of the surrounding hills are thickly strewed with tents and temporary dwellings. On every side are buildings of all kinds, begun or half-finished, but the greater part of them mere canvas sheds, open in front, and displaying all sorts of signs, in all languages. Great quantities of goods are piled up in the open air, for want of a place to store them. The streets are full of people, hurrying to and fro, and of as diverse and bizarre a character as the houses: Yankees of every possible variety, native Californians in *sarapes* and sombreros, Chilians, Sonorians, Kanakas from Hawaii, Chinese with long tails, Malays and others in whose embrowned and bearded visages it is impossible to recognise any especial nationality. In the midst is the plaza, now dignified by the name of Portsmouth-square. It lies on the slope of the hill; and, from a high pole in front of a long one-story building, used as the Custom House, the American flag is flying. On the lower side is the Parker House Hotel. The Bay of San Francisco is black with the hulls of ships, and a thick forest of masts intercepts the landscapes of the opposite coast and the islet of Yerba Buena. Flags of all nations flutter in the breeze, and the smoke of three steamers is borne away on its wings in dense wreaths.—The first picture is a rough outline of stagnation and poverty, the other is one of activity and wealth in glowing colours.

"Verily," says the correspondent of a Boston paper, "the place was in itself a marvel. To say that it was daily enlarged by from twenty to thirty houses may not sound very remarkable after all the stories that have been told; yet this, for a country which imported both lumber and houses, and where labour was then ten dollars a day, is an extraordinary growth. The rapidity with which a ready-made house is put up and inhabited, strikes the stranger in San Francisco as little short of magic. He walks over an open lot in his before-breakfast stroll—the next morning, a house complete, with a family inside, blocks up his way. He goes down to the bay and looks out on the shipping—two or three days afterwards a row of storehouses, staring him in the face, intercepts the view."

An intelligent traveller from the United States has recorded his impressions of this marvellous spot, as he saw it in August, 1849:

"The restless, feverish tide of life in that little spot, and the thought that what I then saw and was yet to see will here-after fill one of the most marvellous pages of all history, rendered it singularly impressive. The feeling was not decreased on talking that evening with some of the old residents (that is of six months' standing), and hearing their several experiences. Every new comer in San Francisco is overtaken with a sense of complete bewilderment. The mind, however it may be prepared for an astonishing condition of affairs, cannot immediately push aside its old instincts of value and ideas of business, letting all past experiences go for nought and casting all its faculties for action, intercourse with its fellows, or advancement in any path of ambition, into shapes which it never before imagined. As in the turn of the dissolving views, there is a period when it wears neither the old nor the new phase, but the vanishing images of the one and the growing perceptions of the other are blended in painful and misty confusion. One knows not whether he is awake or in some wonderful dream. Never have I had so much difficulty in establishing, satisfactorily to my own senses, the reality of what I saw and heard."*

The same gentleman, after an absence in the interior of four months, gives a notion of the rapidity with which the city grew, in the following terms:

"Of all the marvellous phases of the history of the Present, the growth of San Francisco is the one which will most tax the belief of the Future. Its parallel was never known, and shall never be beheld again. I speak only of what I saw with my own eyes. When I landed there, a little more than four months before, I found a scattering town of tents and canvas houses, with a show of frame buildings on one or two streets, and a population of about six thousand. Now, on my last visit, I saw around me an actual metropolis, displaying street after street of well-built edifices, filled with an active and enterprising people, and exhibiting every mark of permanent commercial prosperity. Then, the town was limited to the curve of the bay fronting the anchorage and bottoms of the hills. Now it stretched to the topmost heights, followed the shore around point after point, and sending back a long arm through a gap in the hills, took hold of the Golden Gate, and was building its warehouses on the open strait and almost fronting the blue horizon of the Pacific. Then the gold-seek-

* Eldorado, by Bayard Taylor, correspondent to the Tribune newspaper.

ing sojourner lodged in muslin rooms and canvas garrets, with
a philosophic lack of furniture, and ate his simple though substantial fare from pine boards. Now, lofty hotels, gaudy
with verandahs and balconies, were met with in all quarters,
furnished with home luxury, and aristocratic restaurants presented daily their long bills of fare, rich with the choicest
technicalities of the Parisian cuisine. Then, vessels were
coming in day after day, to lie deserted and useless at their
anchorage. Now scarce a day is passed, but some cluster of
sails, bound *outward* through the Golden Gate, took their way
to all the corners of the Pacific. Like the magic seed of the
Indian juggler, which grew, blossomed, and bore fruit before
the eyes of his spectators, San Francisco seemed to have accomplished in a day the growth of half a century."

In San Francisco, everything is reversed. The operations
of trade are exactly opposite to those of older communities.
There the rule is scarcity of money and abundance of labour,
produce, and manufactures; here cash overflows out of every
pocket, and the necessaries of existence will not pour in fast
enough. Mr. Taylor tells us, that "a curious result of the
extraordinary abundance of gold and the facility with which
fortunes were acquired, struck me at the first glance. All
business was transacted on so extensive a scale that the ordinary habits of solicitation and compliance on the one hand,
and stubborn cheapening on the other, seemed to be entirely
forgotten. You enter a shop to buy something; the owner
eyes you with perfect indifference, waiting for you to state
your want: if you object to the price, you are at liberty to
leave, for you need not expect to get it cheaper; he evidently
cares little whether you buy it or not. One who has been
some time in the country will lay down the money, without
wasting words. The only exception I found to this rule was
that of a sharp-faced Down-Easter just opening his stock, who
was much distressed when his clerk charged me seventy-five
cents for a coil of rope, instead of one dollar. This disregard
for all the petty arts of money-making was really a refreshing
feature of society. Another equally agreeable trait was the
punctuality with which debts were paid, and the general confidence which men were obliged to place, perforce, in each
other's honesty. Perhaps this latter fact was owing, in part,

to the impossibility of protecting wealth, and consequent dependence on an honourable regard for the rights of others."

While this gentleman was in San Francisco, an instance of the fairy-like manner in which fortunes are accumulated, came under his observation. A citizen of San Francisco died insolvent to the amount of forty-one thousand dollars the previous autumn. His administrators were delayed in settling his affairs, and his real estate advanced so rapidly in value meantime, that after his debts were paid, his heirs derived a yearly income from it of forty thousand dollars!

The fable of a city paved with gold is realised in San Francisco. Mr. Taylor reports: "Walking through the town, I was quite amazed to find a dozen persons busily employed in the street before the United States Hotel, digging up the earth with knives and crumbling it in their hands. They were actual gold hunters, who obtained in this way about five dollars a day. After blowing the fine dirt carefully in their hands, a few specks of gold were left, which they placed in a piece of white paper. A number of children were engaged in the same business, picking out the fine grains by applying to them the head of a pin, moistened in their mouths. I was told of a small boy having taken home fourteen dollars as the result of one day's labour. On climbing the hill to the Post-office I observed in places, where the wind had swept away the sand, several glittering dots of the real metal, but, like the Irishman who kicked the dollar out of his way, concluded to wait till I should reach the heap. The presence of gold in the streets was probably occasioned by the leakings from the miners' bags and the sweepings from stores; though it may also be, to a slight extent, native in the earth, particles having been found in the clay thrown up from a deep well."

The prices paid for labour were at that time equally romantic. The carman of one firm (Messrs. Mellus, Howard, and Co.) drew a salary of twelve hundred a year; and it was no uncommon thing for such persons to be paid from fifteen to twenty dollars, or between three and four pounds sterling per day. Servants were paid from forty to eighty pounds per month. Since this time (August, 1849), however, wages had fallen; the laborers for the rougher kind of work could—poor fellows—get no more than something above the pay of a Lieu-

tenant Colonel in the British army, or about four hundred per
annum. The scarcity of labour is best illustrated by the cost
of washing, which was one pound twelve shillings per dozen.
It was therefore found cheaper to put out washing to the an-
tipodes; and to this day, San Francisco shirts are washed and
" got up" in China and the Sandwich Islands. So many hundred dozens of dirty, and so many hundred dozens of washed,
linen form the part of every outward and inward cargo to and
from the Golden City.

The profits upon merchandise about the time we are writing
of, may be judged of by one little transaction recorded by
Mr. Taylor. " Many passengers," he writes, " began speculation at the moment of landing. The most ingenious and successful operation was made by a gentleman of New York, who
took out fifteen hundred copies of the Tribune and other papers, which he disposed of in two hours, at one dollar apiece!
Hearing of this, I bethought me of about a dozen papers which
I had used to fill up crevices in packing my valise. There was
a newspaper merchant at the corner of the City Hotel, and to
him I proposed the sale of them, asking him to name a price.
' I shall want to make a good profit on the retail price,' said
he, ' and can't give more than ten dollars for the lot.' I was
satisfied with the wholesale price, which was a gain of just
four thousand per cent."

The prices of food are enormous, and, unhappily, so are the
appetites; " for two months after my arrival," says a respectable authority, " my sensations were like those of a famished
wolf;" yet the first glance at the tariff of a San Francisco bill
of fare is calculated to turn the keenest European stomach.
" Where shall we dine to-day?" asked Mr. Taylor during his
visit. " The restaurants display their signs invitingly on all
sides; we have choice of the United States, Tortoni's, the
Alhambra, and many other equally classic resorts, but Del-
monico's, like its distinguished original in New York, has the
highest prices and the greatest variety of dishes. We go
down Kearney-street to a two-story wooden house at the corner of Jackson-street. The lower story is a market; the walls
are garnished with quarters of beef and mutton; a huge pile of
Sandwich Island squashes fills one corner, and several cab-
bage heads, valued at two dollars each, show themselves in

the window. We enter a little door at the end of the building, ascend a dark, narrow flight of steps, and find ourselves in a long, low room, with ceiling and walls of white muslin, and a floor covered with oil-cloth. There are about twenty tables disposed in two rows, all of them so well filled that we had some difficulty in finding places. Taking up the written bill of fare, we find such items as the following:

SOUPS.

	Dol.	Cents.
Mock Turtle . . . : . . .	0	75
St. Julien	1	00

FISH.

Boiled Salmon Trout, Anchovy Sauce . .	1	75

BOILED.

Leg of Mutton, Caper Sauce	1	00
Corned Beef, Cabbage	1	00
Ham and Tongues	0	75

ENTRÉES.

Fillet of Beef, Mushroom Sauce . . .	1	75
Veal Cutlets, breaded	1	00
Mutton Chop	1	00
Lobster Salad	2	00
Sirloin of Venison	1	50
Baked Maccaroni	0	75
Beef Tongue, Sauce piquant . . .	1	00

So that, with but a moderate appetite, the dinner will cost us five dollars, if we are at all epicurean in our tastes. There are cries of 'Steward!' from all parts of the room—the word 'Waiter' is not considered sufficiently respectful, seeing that the waiter may have been a lawyer or a merchant's clerk a few months before. The dishes look very small as they are placed on the table, but they are skilfully cooked, and are very palatable to men that have ridden in from the diggings."

Lodging was equally extravagant. A bedroom in an hotel, 50*l*. per month, and a sleeping berth or "bunk"—one of fifty in the same apartment—1*l*. 4s. per week. Social intercourse is almost unknown. There are no females, and men have no better resource than gambling, which is carried on to an extent, and with a desperate energy, hardly conceivable. "Gambling," says a private correspondent, whose letter, dated April 20, 1850, now lies before us, "is carried on here with a bold and open front, so as to alarm and astonish one. Thousands and thousands change hands nightly. Go in, for instance, to a place called Parker House, which is a splendid mansion, fitted up as well as any hotel in England; step into the front room, and you see five or six Monte, Roulette, and other gaming-tables, each having a bank of nearly half a bushel of gold and silver, piled up in the centre. That the excitement shall not be wholly devoid of diversion, the Muses lend their aid, and a band plays constantly to crowded rooms! Step into the next building, called 'El Dorado,' and there a similar scene is presented, and which is repeated, on a smaller scale, all over the town. The gamblers seem to control the town, but of course their days must be numbered. Fortunes are made or lost daily. People gamble with a freedom and recklessness which you can never dream of. Young men who come here must at all times resist gaming, or it must eventually end in their ruin: the same with drinking, as there is much of it here."

The variety of habits, manners, tastes, and prejudices, occasioned by the confluence in one spot of almost every variety of the human species, is another bar to a speedy deposit of all these floating and opposite elements into a compact and well assimilated community. "Here," writes the same gentleman, "we see the character and habits of the English, Irish, Scotch, German, Pole, French, Spaniard, and almost every other nation of Europe. Then you have the South American, the Australian, the Chilian; and finally, the force of this golden mania has dissolved the chain that has hitherto bound China in national solitude, and she has now come forth, like an anchorite from his cell, to join this varied mass of golden speculators. Here we see in miniature just what is done in the large cities of other countries; we have some of our luxuries from the United States and the tropics, butter from Oregon, and for the most part California, Upper and Lower, furnishes us with our beef, &c. The streets are all bustle, as you may imagine, in a place now of nearly thirty thousand inhabitants, independent of a small world of floating population."

Not the smallest wonder, however, presented in this region, is the rapid manner in which social order was shaped out of the human chaos. When a new placer or "gulch" was discovered, the first thing done was to elect officers and extend the area of order. The result was, that in a district five hundred miles long, and inhabited by one hundred thousand people—who had neither government, regular laws, rules, military or civil protection, nor even locks or bolts, and a great part of whom possessed wealth enough to tempt the vicious and depraved —there was as much security to life and property as in any part of the Union, and as small a proportion of crime. The capacity of a people for self-government was never so triumphantly illustrated. Never, perhaps, was there a community formed of more unpropitious elements; yet from all this seeming chaos grew a harmony beyond what the most sanguine apostle of Progress could have expected. Indeed, there is nothing more remarkable connected with the capital of El Dorado, than the centre point it has become.

The story of Cadmus, who sowed dragon's teeth, and harvested armed men, who became the builders of cities; the confusion of tongues at the tower of Babel; and the beautiful allegory of the lion lying down with the lamb; are all types of San Francisco. The first, of its sudden rise; the second, of the varieties of the genus Man it has congregated; and the third, of the extremes of those varieties, which range from the Polynesian savage to the most civilised individuals that Europe can produce. It is a coincidence well worthy of note, that, besides the intense attraction possessed from its gold, Upper or New California is of all other places the best adapted, from its geographical position, to become a rendezvous for all nations of the earth, and that the Bay of San Francisco is one of the best and most convenient for shipping throughout the western margin of the American continent. It is precisely the locality required to make a constant communication across the Pacific Ocean with the coasts of China, Japan, and the Eastern Archipelago, commercially practicable. Its situation is that which would have been selected from choice for a concentration of delegates from the uttermost ends of the earth. If the Chinese, the Malay, the Ladrone, or the Sandwich Islander had wished to meet his Saxon or Celtic brother on a

matter of mutual business, he would—deciding geographically
—have selected California as the spot of assembly. The attractive powers of gold could not, therefore, have struck forth
over the world from a better point than in and around San
Francisco, both for the interests of commerce and for those
of human intercourse.

The practical question respecting the Golden City remains
yet to be touched. Does it offer wholesome inducements for
emigration? On this subject we can do no more than quote
the opinions of the intelligent and enterprising gentleman, to
whose private letter we have already referred:—"This, I
should say, is the best country in the world for an active, enterprising, steady young man, provided he can keep his health,
as the climate, without due precaution, is not a healthy one.
In the summer season, the weather is pleasantly warm from
morning till noon, then it is windy till evening, and dusty, and
then becomes so cold as to require an over-coat. This weather
lasts to October, when the wind gets round to the south-west.
It is dry, warm, and pleasant now (April). This and the rainy
season are the pleasantest and warmest here. Thousands, on
arriving, fall victims to the prevailing disease of dysentery.
On the latter account, therefore, I should not advise, or be
the indirect means of inducing, any one to make the adventure here, because it is impossible to foresee or calculate
whether or not he can stand the climate and inconveniences
of this country; and, if so, he is sure to be exposed to a miserable and too often neglected sickness, and ending in a miserable death. I have not been ill myself so far, as my general
health has been extremely good, and I never looked so well
as now. The climate seems to operate injuriously on bilious
habits; but to those who can stand it, it is decidedly pleas-
anter than England. Fires are never necessary. Out of
doors, at night, a great-coat is required, but in the house it is
always warm. The whole and only question, with a man
making up his mind to locate in California, should be in regard
to his health. Business of all descriptions is better here than
in any other part of the world, and he who perseveres is sure
to succeed.

"There are various opinions afloat in regard to the fertility
of the soil, some holding that there are productive valleys in

the interior which would supply sufficient sustenance for home consumption; others assert the reverse. Certain it is, however, that in many parts of the interior, the climate is delightful, but owing to the long continued dry season, I have doubts as to her ever raising a sufficient supply of vegetable necessaries of life: our market is now supplied from the Sandwich Islands ánd Oregon.

"As to gold mining, it is altogether a lottery; one man may make a large amount daily, another will but just live. There is an inexhaustible quantity of gold, however, but with many it is inconceivably hard to get, as the operations are so many, and health so very precarious, that it is a mere chance matter if you succeed in getting a large sum speedily. It seems a question, whether it would not be advisable for the American Government to work the mines ultimately.

"California must 'go-ahead:' the east will pour through the country her immense commerce into the States, and the mines will last for ages. Finally, I would now say to my friends, that, if you are inclined to come to this country, upon this my report of it, you must, to succeed, attend to my warnings as to drinking and gambling, and to my precautions against climate."

☞ VIII.

THE OLD LADY IN THREADNEEDLE-STREET.

JULY 6, 1850.

PERHAPS there is no Old Lady who has attained to such great distinction in the world, as this highly respectable female. Even the Old Lady who lived on a hill, and who, if she's not gone, lives there still; or that other Old Lady, who lived in a shoe, and had so many children she didn't know what to do—are unknown to fame, compared with the Old Lady of Threadneedle-street. In all parts of the civilised earth the imaginations of men, women, and children figure this tremendous Old Lady of Threadneedle-street in some rich shape or other. Throughout the length and breadth of England, old ladies dote upon her; young ladies smile upon her; old gentlemen make much of her, young gentlemen woo her;

everybody courts the smiles, and dreads the coldness, of the powerful Old Lady in Threadneedle-street. Even prelates have been said to be fond of her; and Ministers of State to have been unable to resist her attractions. She is next to omnipotent in the three great events of human life. In spite of the old saw, far fewer marriages are made in Heaven, than with an eye to Threadneedle-street. To be born in the good graces of the Old Lady of Threadneedle-street, is to be born to fortune: to die in her good books, is to leave a far better inheritance, as the world goes, than the " grinning honour that Sir Walter hath," in Westminster Abbey. And there she is for ever in Threadneedle-street, another name for wealth and thrift, threading her golden-eyed needle all the year round.

This Old Lady, when she first set up, carried on business in Grocers' Hall, Poultry; but in 1732 she quarrelled with her landlords about a renewal of her lease, and built a mansion of her own in Threadneedle-street. She reared her new abode on the site of the house and garden of a former director of her affairs, Sir John Houblon. This was a modest structure, dignified by having a statue of William the Third placed before it; but not the more imposing from being at the end of an arched court, densely surrounded with habitations, and abutting on the churchyard of St. Christopher le Stocks.

But now, behold her, a prosperous gentlewoman in the hundred and fifty-seventh year of her age; "the oldest inhabitant" of Threadneedle-street! There never was such an insatiable Old Lady for business. She has gradually enlarged her premises, until she has spread them over four acres; confiscating to her own use not only the parish church of St. Christopher, but the whole of the parish itself.

We count it among the great events of our young existence, that we had, some days since, the honour of visiting the Old Lady. It was not without an emotion of awe that we passed her Porter's Lodge. The porter himself, blazoned in royal scarlet and gold lace, is an adumbration of her dignity and wealth. His cocked-hat advertises her stable antiquity as plainly as if there was written up, in imitation of some of her lesser neighbours, " established in 1694." This foreshadowing became reality when we passed through the Hall—the tellers' hall. A sensation of unbounded riches penetrated every sense, except, alas! that of touch.

The music of golden thousands clattered in the ear, as they jingled on the counters until its last echos were strangled in the puckers of tightened money-bags, or died under the clasps of purses. Wherever the eye turned, it rested on money; money of every possible variety; money in all shapes; money of all colours. There was yellow money, white money, brown money; gold money, silver money, copper money; paper money, pen and ink money. Money was wheeled about in trucks; money was carried about in bags; money was scavengered about with shovels. Thousands of sovereigns were jerked hither and thither from hand to hand—grave games of pitch and toss were played with staid solemnity; piles of bank-notes—competent to buy whole German dukedoms and Italian principalities—hustled to and fro with as much indifference as if they were (as they had been) old rags.

This Hall of the Old Lady's overpowered us with a sense of wealth; oppressed us with a golden dream of Riches. From this vision an instinctive appeal to our own pockets, and a few miserable shillings, awakened us to Reality. When thus aroused we were in one of the Old Lady's snug, elegant, waiting-rooms, which is luxuriously Turkey-carpeted, and adorned with two excellent portraits of two ancient cashiers; regarding one of whom the public were warned:

> Sham Abraham you may,
> I've often heard say,
> But you mustn't sham "Abraham Newland."

There are several conference-rooms for gentlemen who require a little private conversation with the Old Lady—perhaps on the subject of discounts.

It is no light thing to send in one's card to the Foster-Mother of British commerce; the Soul of the State; "the Sun," according to Sir Francis Baring, around which the agriculture, trade and finance of this country revolves; the mighty heart of active capital, through whose arteries and veins flows the entire circulating medium of this great country. It was not, therefore, without agitation that we were ushered from the waiting-room, into that celebrated private apartment of

the Old Lady of Threadneedle-street—the Parlour—the Bank
Parlour, the inmost mystery—the *cella* of the great Temple of
Riches.

The ordinary associations called up by the notion of an old
lady's comfortable parlour, were not fulfilled by this visit.
There is no domestic snugness, no easy-chair, no cat, no parrot,
no japanned bellows, no portrait of the Princess Charlotte
and Prince Leopold in the Royal Box at Drury Lane Theatre;
no kettle-holder, no worsted rug for the urn, no brass footman
for the buttered toast, in the parlour in Threadneedle-street.
On the contrary, the room is extensive—supported by pillars;
is of grand and true proportions; and embellished with architectural ornaments in the best taste. It has a long table for
the confidential managers of the Old Lady's affairs (she calls
these gentlemen her Directors) to sit at; and usually, a side
table fittingly supplied with a ready-laid lunch.

The Old Lady's "Drawing" Room is as unlike—but then
she is such a peculiar Old Lady!—any ordinary Drawing-
room as need be. It has hardly any furniture, but desks,
stools, and books. It is of immense proportions, and has no
carpet. The vast amount of visitors the Old Lady receives
between nine and four every day, would make lattice-work in
one forenoon of the stoutest carpet ever manufactured. Everybody who comes into the Old Lady's Drawing-room delivers
his credentials to her gentlemen-ushers, who are quick in examining the same, and exact in the observance of all points of
form. So highly-prized, however, is a presentation (on any
grand scale) to the Old Lady's Drawing-room, notwithstand-
ing its plainness, that there is no instance of a Drawing-room
at Court being more sought after. Indeed, it has become a
kind of proverb that the way to Court often lies through the
Old Lady's apartments, and some suppose that the Court
Sticks are of gold and silver in compliment to her.

As to the individual appearance of the Old Lady herself,
we are authorized to state that the portrait of a Lady (accompanied by eleven balls on a sprig, and a beehive) which appears
in the upper left-hand corner of all the old Bank of England
Notes, is NOT the portrait of *the* Lady. She invariably wears
a cap of silver paper, with her yellow hair gathered carefully
underneath. When she carries any defensive or offensive

weapon, it is not a lance, but a pen; and her modesty would on no account permit her to appear in such loose drapery as is worn by the party in question—who we understand is depicted as a warning to the youthful merchants of this country to avoid the fate of George Barnwell.

In truth, like the Delphian mystery, SHE of Threadneedle-street is invisible, and delivers her oracles through her high priests. As Herodotus got his information from the priests in Egypt, so did we learn all we know about the Bank from the great officers of the Myth of Threadneedle-street. All of them are remarkable for great intelligence and good humour, particularly one MR. MATTHEW MARSHALL; for whom the Old Lady is supposed to have a sneaking kindness, as she is continually promising to pay him the most stupendous amounts of money. From what these gentlemen told us, we are prepared unhesitatingly to affirm in the teeth of the assertions of Plutarch, and Pliny, and Justin, that although Crœsus might have been well enough to do in the world in his day, he was but a pettifogger compared with the Great Lady of St. Christopher le Stocks. The Lydian king never employed nine hundred clerks, or accommodated eight hundred of them under one roof; and if he could have done either, he would have been utterly unable to muster one hundred and thirty thousand pounds a year to pay them. He never had bullion in his cellars, at any one time, to the value of sixteen millions and a half sterling, as our Old Lady has lately averaged; nor " other securities"—much more marketable than the precious stones Crœsus showed to Solon—to the amount of thirty millions. Besides, *all* his capital was " dead weight;" that in Threadneedle-street is active, and is represented by an average paper currency of twenty millions per annum.

After this statement of facts, we trust that modern poets when they want a hyperbole for wealth will cease to cite Crœsus, and draw their future inspirations from the shrine and cellars of the Temple opposite the Auction Mart; or, as the late Mr. George Robins designated it when professionally occupied, "The Great House over the way."

When we withdrew from the inmost fane of this Temple, we were ushered by the priest, who superintends the manufacture of the mysterious Deity's oracles, into those recesses of her Temple in which these are made. Here we perceived, that, besides carrying on the ordinary operations of banking, the Old Lady is an extensive printer, engraver, bookbinder, and publisher. She maintains a steam-engine to drive letter-press and copper-plate printing machines, besides the other machinery which is employed in various operations, from making thousand pound notes to weighing single sovereigns. It is not until you see three steam-printing machines—such as we use for this publication—and hear that they are constantly revolving, to produce, at so many thousand sheets per hour, the printed forms necessary for the accurate account-keeping of this great Central Establishment and its twelve provincial branches, that you are fully impressed with the magnitude of the Old Lady's transactions. In this one department no fewer than three hundred account books are printed, ruled, bound, and used every week. During that short time they are filled with MS. by the eight hundred subordinates and their chiefs. By way of contrast we saw the single ledger which sufficed to post up the daily transactions of the Old Lady on her first establishment in business. It is no larger than that of a small tradesman, and served to contain a record of the year's accounts. Until within the last few years, visitors to the Bullion-office were shown the old box into which the books of the Bank were put every night for safety during the Old Lady's early career. This receptacle is no bigger than a seaman's chest. A spacious fire-proof room is now nightly filled with each day's accounts, and they descend to it by means of a great hydraulic trap in the Drawing-office; the mountain of calculation when collected being too huge to be moved by human agency.

These works are, of course, only produced for private reference; but the Old Lady's publishing business is as extensive as it is profitable and peculiar. Although her works are the reverse of heavy or erudite—being "flimsy" to a proverb—yet the eagerness with which they are sought by the public, surpasses that displayed for the production of the greatest geniuses who ever enlightened the world: she is, therefore, called upon to print enormous numbers of each edition,—generally one hundred thousand copies; and reprints of equally large impressions are demanded, six or seven times a year.

She is protected by a stringent copyright; in virtue of which piracy is felony, and was, until 1831, punished with death. The very paper is copyright, and to imitate even that entails transportation. Indeed, its merits entitle it to every protection, for it is a very superior article. It is so thin that each sheet, before it is sized, weighs only eighteen grains; and so strong, that, when sized and doubled, a single sheet is capable of suspending a weight of fifty-six pounds.

The literature of these popular prints is concise to terseness. A certain individual, duly accredited by the Old Lady, whose autograph appears in one corner, promises to pay to the before-mentioned Mr. Matthew Marshall, or bearer on demand, a certain sum, for the Governor and Company of the Bank of England. There is a date and a number: for the Old Lady's sheets are published in Numbers; but, unlike other periodicals, no two copies of hers are alike. Each has a set of numerals, shown on no other.—It must not be supposed from the utter absence of rhetoric in this Great Woman's literature, that it is devoid of ornament. On the contrary, it is illustrated by eminent artists: the illustrations consisting of the waves of a water-mark made in the paper; a large black block, with the statement in white letters of the sum which is promised to be paid; and the portrait referred to in a former part of this account of the Wonderful Old Lady.

She makes it a practice to print thirty thousand copies of these works daily. Everything possible is done by machinery, —engraving, printing, numbering; but we refrain from entering into further details of this portion of the Old Lady's Household here, as we are preparing a review of her valuable works, which shall shortly appear, in the form of a History of a Bank-note. The publication department is so admirably conducted, that a record of each individual piece of paper launched on the ocean of public favour is kept, and its history traced till its return; for another peculiarity of the Old Lady's establishment is, that every impression put forth comes back— with few exceptions—in process of time to her shelves; where it is kept for ten years, and then burnt. This great house is, therefore, a huge circulating library. The daily average number of notes brought back into the Old Lady's lap—examined to detect forgeries; defaced; entered upon the record

made when they were issued; and so stored away that they
can be reproduced at any given half-hour for ten years to
come,—is twenty-five thousand. On the day of our visit there
came in twenty-eight thousand and seventy-four of her picturesque pieces of paper, representing one million one thousand
two hundred and seventy pounds sterling, to be dealt with as
above, preparatory to their decennial slumber on her library
shelves.

The apartment in which the notes are kept *previous* to issue,
is the Old Lady's Store-room. There is no jam, there are no
pickles, no preserves, no gallipots, no stoneware jars, no spices,
no anything of that sort, in the Store-room of the Wonderful
Old Lady. You might die of hunger in it. Your sweet tooth
would decay and tumble out, before it could find the least
gratification in the Old Lady's Store-room. There was a
mouse found there once, but it was dead, and nothing but
skin and bone. It is a grim room, fitted up all round with
great iron safes. They look as if they might be the Old
Lady's ovens, never heated. But they are very warm, in the
City sense; for when the Old Lady's two storekeepers have, each
with his own key, unlocked his own one of the double locks
attached to each, and opened the door, Mr. Matthew Marshall
gives you to hold a little bundle of paper, value two millions
sterling; and, clutching it with a strange tingling, you feel
disposed to knock Mr. Matthew Marshall down, and, like a
patriotic Frenchman, to descend into the streets.

No tyro need be told that these notes are representatives of
weightier value, and were invented partly to supersede the
necessity of carrying about ponderous parcels of precious
metal. Hence—to treat of it soberly—four paper parcels
taken out, and placed in our hands—consisting of four reams
of Bank-notes ready for issue, and not much more bulky than
a thick octavo volume—though they represent gold of the
weight of *two tons*, and of the value of two millions of pounds
sterling, yet weigh not quite one pound avoirdupois each, or
nearly four pounds together. The value in gold of what we
could convey away in a couple of side pockets (if simply permitted by the dear Old Lady in Threadneedle-street, without
proceeding to extremities upon the person of the Chief
Cashier) would have required, but for her admirable publica-

tions, two of Barclay and Perkins's strongest horses to draw.*

We have already made mention of the Old Lady's Lodge, Hall, Parlour, Store-room, and Drawing-room. Her Cellars are not less curious. In these she keeps neither wine, nor beer, nor wood, nor coal. They are devoted solely to the reception of the precious metals.

They are like the caves of Treasures in the Arabian Nights; the common Lamp that shows them becomes a Wonderful Lamp in Mr. Marshall's hands, and Mr. Marshall becomes a Genie. Yet only by the power of association; for they are very respectable arched cellars that would make dry skittle-grounds, and have nothing rare about them but their glittering contents. One vault is full of what might be barrels of oysters—if it were not the Russian Loan. Another is rich here and there with piles of gold bars, set crosswise, like sandwiches at supper, or rich biscuits in a confectioner's shop. Another has a moonlight air from the presence of so much silver. Dusky avenues branch off, where gold and silver amicably bide their time in cool retreats, not looking at all mischievous here, or anxious to play the Devil with their souls. Oh, for such cellars at home! "Look out for your young master half a dozen bars of the ten bin." "Let me have a wedge of the old crusted." "Another Million before we part—only one Million more, to finish with!" The Temperance Cause would make but slow way, as to such cellars, we have a shrewd suspicion!

Beauty of colour is here associated with worth. One of those brilliant bars of gold weighs 16 pounds troy, and its value is eight hundred pounds sterling. A pile of these, lying in a dark corner — like neglected cheese, or bars of yellow soap—and which might be contained in an ordinary tea-chest, is worth two hundred and ten thousand pounds. Fortune herself transmuted into metal seems to repose at our feet. Yet this is only an *eightieth* part of the wealth contained in the Old Lady's cellars.

The future history of this metal is explained in three sen-

---

* One thousand sovereigns weigh twenty-one pounds, and five hundred and twelve Bank-notes weigh exactly one pound.

tences; it is coined at the Mint, distributed to the public, worn by friction (or "sweated" by Jews) till it becomes light. What happens to it then we shall see.

By a seldom failing law of monetary attraction nearly every species of cash, "hard" or soft, metallic or paper, finds its way some time or other back to the extraordinary Old Lady of Threadneedle-street. All the sovereigns returned from the banking-houses are consigned to a secluded cellar; and, when you enter it, you will possibly fancy yourself on the premises of a clockmaker who works by steam. Your attention is speedily concentrated to a small brass box not larger than an eight-day pendule, the works of which are impelled by steam. This is a self-acting weighing-machine, which with unerring precision tells which sovereigns are of standard weight, and which are light, and of its own accord separates the one from the other. Imagine a long trough or spout—half a tube that has been split into two sections—of such a semi-circumference as holds sovereigns edgeways, and of sufficient length to allow of two hundred of them to rest in that position one against another. The trough thus charged, is fixed slopingly upon the machine, over a little table as big as the plate of an ordinary sovereign-balance. The coin nearest to the Lilliputian platform drops upon it, being pushed forward by the weight of those behind. Its own weight presses the table down; but how far down? Upon that hangs the whole merit and discriminating power of the machine. At the back, and on each side of this small table, two little hammers move by steam backwards and forwards at different elevations. If the sovereign be full weight, down sinks the table too low for the higher hammer to hit it; but the lower one strikes the edge, and off the sovereign tumbles into a receiver to the left. The table pops up again, receives, perhaps, a light sovereign, and the higher hammer having always first strike, knocks it into a receiver to the right, time enough to escape its colleague, which, when it comes forward, has nothing to hit, and returns to allow the table to be elevated again. In this way the reputation of thirty-three sovereigns is established or destroyed every minute. The light weights are taken to a clipping machine, slit at the rate of two hundred a minute, weighed in a lump, the balance of deficiency charged to the banker from whom they were received, and sent to the Mint to be re-coined. Those which have passed muster are reissued to the public. The inventor of this beautiful little detector was Mr. Cotton, a former governor. The comparatively few sovereigns brought in by the general public are weighed in ordinary scales by the tellers. The average loss upon each light coin, on an average of thirty-five thousand taken in 1843, was twopence three-farthings.

The business of the "Great House" is divided into two branches; the issue and the banking department. The latter has increased so rapidly of late years, that the last addition the Old Lady was constrained to make to her house was the immense Drawing-room aforesaid, for her customers and their payees to draw cash on checks and to make deposits. Under this noble-apartment is the Strong Room, containing private property, supposed to be of enormous value. It is placed there for safety by the constituents of the Bank, and is concealed in tin boxes, on which the owners' names are legibly painted. The descent into this stronghold—by means of the hydraulic trap we have spoken of—is so eminently theatrical, that we believe the Head of the Department, on going down with the books, is invariably required to strike an attitude, and to laugh in three sepulchral syllables; while the various clerks above express surprise and consternation.

Besides private customers, everybody knows that our Old Lady does all the banking business for the British Government. She pays the interest to each Stockholder in the National Debt, receives certain portions of the revenue, &c. A separate set of offices is necessary, to keep all such accounts, and these Stock Offices contain the most varied and extensive collection of autographs extant. Those whom Fortune entitles to dividends, must, by themselves or by their agents, sign the Stock books. The last signature of Handel, the composer, and that upon which Henry Fauntleroy was condemned and executed, are among the foremost of these lions.

Here, standing in a great long building of divers stories, looking dimly upward through iron gratings, and dimly downward through iron gratings, and into musty chambers diverging into the walls on either hand, you may muse upon the National Debt. All the sheep that ever came out of

Northamptonshire, seem to have yielded up their skins to
furnish the registers in which its accounts are kept. Sweating
and wasting in this vast silent library, like manuscripts in a
mouldy old convent, are the records of the Dividends that
are, and have been, and of the Dividends unclaimed. Some
men would sell their fathers into slavery, to have the rum-
maging of these old volumes. Some, who would let the Tree
of Knowledge wither while they lay contemptuously at its
feet, would bestir themselves to pluck at these leaves, like
shipwrecked mariners. These are the books to profit by.

This is the place for X. Y. Z. to hear of something to his
advantage in. This is the land of Mr. Joseph Ady's dreams.
This is the dusty fountain whence those wondrous paragraphs
occasionally flow into the papers, disclosing how a labouring
thatcher has come into a hundred thousand pounds—a long,
long way to come—and gone out of his wits—not half so far
to go. Oh, wonderful Old Lady! threading the needle with
the golden eye all through the labyrinth of the National
Debt, and hiding it in such dry haystacks as are rotting here!

With all her wealth, and all her power, and all her business,
and all her responsibilities, she is not a purse-proud Old Lady;
but a dear, kind, liberal, benevolent Old Lady; so particularly
considerate to her servants, that the meanest of them never
speaks of her otherwise than with affection. Though her
domestic rules are uncommonly strict; though she is very
severe upon " mistakes," be they ever so unintentional; though
till lately she made her in-door servants keep good hours, and
would not allow a lock to be turned or a bolt to be drawn after
eleven at night, even to admit her dearly beloved Matthew
Marshall himself—yet she exercises a tender and maternal
care over her family of eight hundred strong. To benefit
the junior branches, she has recently set aside a spacious room,
and the sum of five hundred pounds, to form a library. With
this handsome capital at starting, and eight shillings a year
subscribed by the youngsters, an excellent collection of books
will soon be formed. Here, from three till eight o'clock every
lawful day, the subscribers can assemble for recreation or
study; or, if they prefer it, they can take books to their
homes. A member of the Committee of Management attends
in turn during the specified hours—a self-imposed duty, in the

highest degree creditable to, but no more than is to be expected from, the stewards of a Good Mistress; who, when any of her servants become superannuated, soothes declining age with a pension. The last published return states the number of pensioners at one hundred and ninety-three; each of whom received on an average 161*l*., or an aggregate of upwards of 31,000*l*. per annum.

Her kindness is not unrequited. Whenever anything ails her, the assiduous attention of her people is only equalled by her own bounty to them. When dangerously ill of the Panic in 1825, and the outflow of her circulating medium was so violent that she was in danger of bleeding to death, some of her upper servants never left her for a fortnight. At the crisis of her disorder, on a memorable Saturday night (December the seventeenth), her Deputy-Governor—who even then had not seen his own children for a week—reached Downing-street "reeling with fatigue," and was just able to call out to the King's Ministers—then anxiously deliberating on the dear Old Lady's case—that she was out of danger! Another of her managing men lost his life in his anxiety for her safety, during the burning of the Royal Exchange, in January, 1838. When the fire broke out, the cold was intense; and although he had but just recovered from an attack of the gout, he rushed to the rescue of his beloved Old Mistress, saw everything done that could be done for her safety, and died from his exertions. Although the Old Lady is now more hale and hearty than ever, two of the Senior Clerks sit up in turn every night, to watch over her; in which duty they are assisted by a company of Foot Guards.

The kind Old Lady of Threadneedle-street has, in short, managed to attach her dependents to her by the strongest of ties—that of love. So pleased are some with her service, that when even temporarily resting from it, they feel miserable. A late Chief Cashier never solicited but one holiday, and that for only a fortnight. In three days he returned, expressing his extreme disgust with every sort of recreation except that afforded him by the Old Lady's business. The last words of another old servant when on his death-bed, were, "Oh, that I could only die on the Bank steps!"

5

IX.

THE MODERN SCIENCE OF THIEF-TAKING.

JULY 13, 1850.

IF thieving be an Art, thief-taking is a Science. All the thief's ingenuty; all his knowledge of human nature; all his courage; all his coolness; all his imperturbable powers of face; all his nice discrimination in reading countenances; all his manual and digital dexterity; all his fertility in expedients, and promptitude in acting upon them; all his Protean clever-ness of disguise; all his capability of counterfeiting every sort and condition of distress; together with a great deal more than his patience, and the additional qualification, integrity, go to make a high class Detective Policeman.

If an urchin picks your poctet, or a bungling "artist" steals your watch so that you find him out in an instant, it is easy enough for any private in any of the seventeen divisions of London Police to obey your panting demand to "Stop thief!" But, for the detection and punishment of the impostors who wheedle money out of your pocket; who cheat you with your eyes open; who clear every vestige of plate out of your pantry while your servant is on the stairs; who set up imposing ware-houses, and ease you of large parcels of goods; who steal your acceptances, and swindle you out of your horse, a superior order of police is requisite.

To each division of the Metropolitan Police Force is at-tached two officers, who are denominated Detectives. The staff or head-quarters, consists of six sergeants and two inspec-tors. Thus the Detective Police, of which we hear so much, consists of only forty-two individuals, whose duty it is to wear no uniform, and to perform the most difficult operations of their craft. They have not only to counteract the machina-tions of every sort of rascal whose only means of existence is avowed rascality, but to clear up family mysteries, the investi-gation of which demands the utmost delicacy and tact.

Your wife discovers on retiring for the night, that her drawers are void; her toilette-table is bare; except the orna-ments she now wears, her beauty is as unadorned as that of a

Quakeress: not a thing is left; all the fond tokens you gave her when her pre-nuptial lover, are gone; your own miniature, with its setting of gold and brilliants; her late mother's diamonds; the bracelets "dear papa" presented on her last birthday; the top of every bottle in the dressing-case brought from Paris by Uncle John, at the risk of his life, in February, 1848 (being gold), are off—but the bottles (being glass) remain. Every valuable is swept away with the most discriminating villany; for no other thing in the chamber has been touched; not a chair has been moved; the costly pendule on the chimney-piece still ticks; the entire apartment is as neat and trim as when it had received the last finishing touch of the housemaid's duster. The entire establishment runs frantically up-stairs and down stairs; and finally congregates in my Lady's Chamber. Nobody knows anything whatever about it; yet everybody offers a suggestion, although they have not an idea "who ever did it." The housemaid bursts into tears; the cook declares she thinks she is going into hysterics; and at last you suggest sending for the Police; which is taken as a suspicion of, an insult on, the whole assembled household, and they descend into the lower regions of the house in the sulks.

X 49 arrives. His face betrays sheepishness, combined with mystery. He turns his bull's-eye into every corner of the passage, and upon every countenance on the premises. He examines all the locks, bolts, and bars, bestowing extra diligence on those which enclosed the stolen treasure.. These he declares have been "Wiolated;" thus concisely intimating, without quoting Pope, that there has been more than one "Rape of the Lock." He then notes the non-disturbance of other valuables; takes you solemnly aside, darkens his lantern, and asks, in a mysterious whisper, if you suspect any of your servants, which implies that *he* does. He then examines the upper bedrooms; and, in the room of the female servants he discovers the least valuable of the rings and a cast-off silver toothpick, between the mattresses. You have every confidence in your maids; but what *can* you think? You suggest their safe custody; but your wife intercedes, and the policeman would prefer speaking to his inspector before he locks anybody up.

Had the whole matter remained in the hands of X 49, it is possible that your whole troubles would have lasted till now. A train of legal proceedings—actions for defamation of character and suits for damages—would have followed, costing more than the value of the jewels, together with the entire execration of all your neighbours and every private friend of your domestics. But, happily, the Inspector promptly sends a plain, earnest-looking man, who announces himself as one of the two Detectives of the X division. He settles the whole matter in ten minutes. His examination is ended in five. As a connoisseur can determine the painter of a picture at the first glance, or a wine-taster the precise vintage of a sherry by the merest sip; so the Detective at once pounces upon the authors of the work of art under consideration, by the style of performance; if not upon the precise executant, upon the "school" to which he belongs. Having finished the toilette branch of the inquiry, he takes a short view of the parapet of your house, and makes an equally cursory investigation of the attic window fastenings. His mind is made up, and most likely he will address you in these words:

"All right, sir. This is done by one of the 'Dancing School!'"

"Impossible!" exclaims your plundered partner. "Why, our children go to Monsieur Pettitoes, of No. 81, and I assure you he is a highly respectable professor. As to his pupils, I——"

The Detective smiles and interrupts. "Dancers," he tells her, "is a name given to the sort of burglar by whom you have been robbed; and every branch of the thieving profession is divided into gangs, which are termed 'Schools.' From No. 42 to the end of the street the houses are unfinished. The thief made his way to the top of one of these, and crawled to your garret——"

"But we are twenty houses distant, and why did he not favour one of my neighbours?" you ask.

"Either their uppermost stories are not so practicable, or the ladies have not such valuable jewels."

"But how did the thieves know that?"

"By watching and inquiry. This affair may have been in preparation for more than a month. Your house has been

watched: your habits have been ascertained. They have
found out when you dine—how long you remain in the dining-
room. A day is selected ; while you are busy dining, and
your servants busy waiting on you, the thing is done. Previously, many journeys have been made over the roofs, to find
out the best means of entering your house. The attic is
chosen ; the robber gets in, and creeps noiselessly, or ' dances'
into the place to be robbed."

"Is there *any* chance of recovering our property ?" you
ask, anxiously, seeing the whole matter at a glance.

"I hope so. I have sent some brother officers to watch
the Fences' houses."

"Fences ?"

"Fences," explains the Detective, in reply to your innocent
wife's inquiry, "are purchasers of stolen goods. Your jewels
will soon be forced out of their settings, and the gold melted."

A suppressed scream.

"We shall see, if, at this unusual hour of the night, there
is any bustle in or near any of these places.; if any smoke is
coming out of any one of their furnaces, where the melting
takes place. *I* shall go and seek out the precise ' garretteer'
—that's another name these plunderers give themselves —
whom I suspect. By his trying to 'sell' your domestics by
placing the ring and toothpick in their bed, I think I know
the man."

The next morning, you find all these suppositions verified.
The Detective calls, and obliges you, at breakfast (after a
sleepless night), with a complete list of the stolen articles, and
produces some of them for identification. In three months,
your wife gets nearly every article back, except some of the
gold; her damsels' innocence is fully established ; and the
thief is taken from his ' school' to spend a long holiday in a
penal colony.

This is a mere common-place transaction, compared with
the achievements of the staff of the little army of Detective
policemen at head-quarters. Sometimes they are called upon
to investigate robberies so executed, that no human ingenuity
appears, to ordinary observers, capable of finding the thief.
The robber has left no trail ; not a trace. Every clue seems
cut off; but the experience of a Detective guides him into

tracks invisible to other eyes. Not long since, a trunk was rifled at a fashionable hotel. The theft was so managed, that no suspicion could rest on any one. The Detective sergeant who had been sent for, fairly owned, after making a minute examination, that he could afford no hope of elucidating the mystery. As he was leaving the bedroom, however, in which the plundered portmanteau stood, he picked up an ordinary shirt-button from the carpet. He silently compared it with those on the shirts which the thief had left behind in the trunk. It did not match them. He said nothing, but hung about the hotel for the rest of the day. Had he been narrowly watched, he would have been set down for an eccentric critic of linen. He was looking out for a shirt-front or wristband without a button. His search was long and patient; but at length it was rewarded. One of the inmates in the house showed a deficiency in his dress, which no one but a Detective would have noticed. He looked as narrowly as he dared at the pattern of the remaining buttons. It corresponded with that of the little tell-tale he had picked up. He went deeper into the subject, got a trace of some of the stolen property, ascertained a connexion between it and the suspected person, confronted him with the owner of the trunk, and finally succeeded in convicting him of the theft. At another hotel-robbery, the blade of a knife, broken in the lock of a portmanteau, formed the clue. The Detective employed in that case was for some time indefatigable in seeking out knives with broken blades. At length he found one belonging to an under-waiter, who proved to be the thief.

The swell-mob—the London branch of which is said to consist of from one hundred and fifty to two hundred members—demand the greatest amount of vigilance to detect. They hold the first place in the "profession."

Their cleverness consists in evading the law. The most expert are seldom taken. One of them, named Mo. Clark, had an iniquitous career of a quarter of a century, and never was captured during that time. He died a "prosperous gentleman" at Boulogne; whither he had retired to live on his savings; which he had invested in house property. An old man named White lived unharmed to the age of eighty; but he had not been prudent, and existed on the contributions of

the "mob," till his old acquaintances were taken away, either
by transportation or death, and the new race did not recognise his claims to their bounty. He died in a workhouse.
The average run of liberty which one of this class counts upon
is four years.

The gains of some of the swell-mob are great. They can
always command capital to execute any special scheme. Their
travelling expenses are large; for their harvests are great
public occasions, whether in town or country. As an example of their profits, the exploits of four of them at the Liverpool Cattle Show some seven years ago may be mentioned.
The London Detective police did not attend, but one of them
waylaid the rogues at the Euston Station. After an attendance of four days, the gentlemen he was looking for appeared,
handsomely attired, the occupants of first-class carriages. The
Detective, in the quietest manner possible, stopped their luggage; they entreated him to treat them like "gentlemen."
He did so, and took them into a private room, where they
were so good as to offer him fifty pounds to let them go. He
declined, and overhauled their booty; it consisted of several
gold pins, watches (some of great value), chains and rings,
silver snuff-boxes, and bank-notes of the value of one hundred
pounds! Eventually, however, as owners could not be found
for some of the property, and some others would not prose-
cute, they escaped with a light punishment.

To counteract the plans of the swell-mob, two of the sergeants of the Detective Police make it their business to know
every one of them personally. The consequence is, that the
appearance of either of these officers upon any scene of operations is a bar to anything or anybody being "done." This is
an excellent characteristic of the Detectives, for they thus become as well a Preventive Police. We will give an illustration :

You are at the Oxford commemoration. As you descend
the broad stairs of the Roebuck to dine, you overtake, on the
landing, a gentleman of foreign aspect and elegant attire. The
variegated pattern of his waistcoat, the jetty gloss of his boots,
and the exceeding whiteness of his gloves—one of which he
crushes in his somewhat delicate hand—convince you that he
is going to the grand ball, to be given that evening at Merton.
The glance he gives you while passing, is sharp, but compre-

hensive; and, if his eye does rest upon any one part of your
person and its accessories more than another, it is upon the
gold watch which you have just taken out to see if dinner be
"due." As you step aside to make room for him, he acknowl-
edges the courtesy with "Par-r-r-don," in the richest Parisian
gros parle, and, a smile so full of intelligence and courtesy,
that you hope he speaks English, for you set him down as an
agreeable fellow, and mentally determine that if he dines in
the Coffee-room, you will have a chat with him.

On the mat at the stair-foot there stands a plain, honest-
looking fellow, with nothing formidable in his appearance, or
dreadful in his countenance; but the effect of this apparition
on your friend in perspective is remarkable. The poor little
fellow raises himself on his toes, as if he had been suddenly
overbalanced by a bullet; his cheek pales, and his lip quivers,
as he endeavours ineffectually to suppress the word "*coquin!*"
He knows it is too late to turn back (he would, if he could),
for the man's eye is upon him. There is no help for it, and he
speaks first; but in a whisper. All you can overhear is spoken
by the latter, who says he insists on Monsieur withdrawing
his "School" by the seven o'clock train.

You imagine him to be some poor French teacher in difficulties; captured, alas, by a bailiff. They leave the inn together, perhaps for a sponging house. So acute is your pity,
that you think of rushing after them, and offering bail. You
are, however, very hungry, and, at this moment, the waiter
announces that dinner is on the table.

In the opposite box there are covers for four, but only three
convives. They seem quiet men: not gentlemen, decidedly,
but well enough behaved.

"What has become of Monsieur?" asks one. None of them
can answer.

"Shall we wait any longer for him?"

"Oh no. Waiter—Dinner!"

By their manner, you imagine that the style of the Roebuck
is a "cut above them." They have not been much used to
plate. The silver forks are so curiously heavy, that one of the
men, in a dallying sort of way, balances a prong across his
fingers, while the chasing of the castors engages the attention
of a second. This is all done while they talk. When the fish

is brought, the third casts a careless glance or two at the
dish-cover; and, when the waiter has gone for the sauce, he
taps it with his nails, and says inquiringly to his friend across
the table, "Silver?"

The waiter brings the cold punch, and the party begin to
enjoy themselves. They do not drink much, but they mix
their drinks rather injudiciously. They take sherry upon cold
punch, and champagne upon that, dashing in a little port and
bottled stout between. They are getting merry, not to say
jolly; but not at all inebriated. The amateur of silver dish-
covers has told a capital story, and his friends are revelling in
a hearty laugh, when a man appears at the end of the table.
You never saw such a change as he causes, when he places
his knuckles on the edge of the table, and looks at the diners
seriatim. You can only compare it to the courtiers of Beauty
suddenly struck sleepy. The loud laugh is so instantaneously
turned to silent consternation, that you now most impressively understand the meaning of the term "dumbfoundered."
The mysterious stranger makes some inquiry about "any
cash?"

The answer is "Plenty."

"All square with the landlord, then?" asks the inflexible
voice which—to my astonishment—put the Frenchman to the
torture.

"To a penny," the reply.

"*Quite* square?" continues the querist, taking with his busy
eye a rapid inventory of the plate.

A pause.

"Have you done anything to-day?" he continues.

"Not a thing."

Some more is said in a low tone; but you again distinguish
the word "school," and "seven o'clock train." They are too
old to be the Frenchman's pupils; perhaps they are his assistants. Surely they are not all the victims of the same *capias*
and the same officer.

By this time the landlord, looking very nervous, arrives
with his bill: then comes the head waiter; who clears the
table, carefully counting the forks. The reckoning is paid,
and the trio steal out of the room with the man of mystery
behind them, like sheep driven to the shambles.

You follow to the railway station, and there you see the Frenchman, who complains bitterly of being "sold for noting" by his enemy. The other three utter a confirmative groan. In spite of the omnipotence of their persevering follower, your curiosity impels you to address him. You take a turn on the platform together, and he explains the whole mystery. "The fact is," he begins, "I am Sergeant Witchem, of the Detective Police."

"And your four victims are —— ?"

"Members of a crack school of swell-mobsmen."

"What do you mean by 'school?' "

"Gang. There is a variety of gangs: that is to say, of men who 'work' together, who play into one another's hands. These gentlemen hold the first rank, both for skill and enterprise; and, had they been allowed to remain, would have brought back a considerable booty. Their chief is the Frenchman."

"Why do they obey your orders so passively?"

"Because they are sure that if I were to take them into custody—which I could do, knowing what they are—and present them to a magistrate, they would all be committed to prison for a month, as rogues and vagabonds."

"They prefer, then, to have lost no inconsiderable capital in dress and dinner, and their chances of booty at the Oxford Commemoration, to being laid up in gaol."

"Exactly so."

The bell rings, and all five go off into the same carriage to London.

A similar circumstance happened when the Queen went to Dublin. The mere appearance of one of the Detective officers before a "school" which had transported itself in the Royal train, spoilt their speculation; for they all found it more advantageous to return to England in the same steamer with the officer, than to remain with the certainty of being put in prison for fourteen or twenty-eight days as rogues and vagabonds.

So thoroughly well acquainted with these men are the Detective officers we speak of, that they frequently tell what they have been about by the expression of their eyes and their general manner. This process is aptly termed "reckoning them up." Some days ago, two skilful officers were walking

along the Strand on other business, when they saw two of the
best dressed and best mannered of the gang enter a jeweller's
shop. They waited till they came out, and, on scrutinising
them, were convinced, by a certain conscious look which they
betrayed, that they had stolen something. They followed
them, and, in a few minutes, that something was passed from
one to the other. The officers were convinced, challenged
them with the theft, and succeeded in eventually convicting
them of stealing two gold eye-glasses, and several jewelled
rings. "The eye," said our informant, "is the great detector.
We can tell in a crowd what a swell-mobsman is about by the
expression of his eye."

It is supposed that the number of persons who make a
trade of thieving in London is not more than six thousand; of
these, nearly two hundred are first-class thieves or swell-mobsmen; six hundred macemen, and trade swindlers, bill-swind-
lers, and dog-stealers; about forty burglars, dancers, garret-
teers, and other adepts with the skeleton-keys. The rest are
pickpockets, gonophs—mostly young thieves who sneak into
areas and rob tills—and other pilferers.

X.

REVIEW OF A POPULAR PUBLICATION.

JULY 27, 1850.

THE BANK NOTE. *Oblong Octavo,* London, 1850. *The Governor and Company of the Bank of England. Price, from Five to One Thousand
Pounds.*

THE object of this popular but expensive pocket companion,
is not wholly dissimilar from that of its clever and cheaper
contemporary Notes and Queries. As the latter is a "medium
of intercommunication for literary men," so the former is a
medium of intercommunication for commercial men; and
surely there is no note with which so many queries are constantly connected as the Bank Note. Nothing in existence is
so assiduously inquired for; nothing in nature so perseveringly
sought.

For, in whatever light we view it; to whatever test we

bring it; whether we read it backwards or forwards, from
left to right, or from right to left; or whether we make it a
transparency to prove its genuineness and worth, who can
deny that the Bank Note is a most valuable work?—a publication, in short, without which no gentleman can pretend to
be complete?

Few can rise from a critical examination of the literary contents of this narrow sheet, without being forcibly struck with
the power, combined with the exquisite fineness of the writing.
Its terse logic strikes conviction at once. It dispels all
doubts, and relieves all objections. There is a concentrated
conciseness; a downright, direct, straightforward, coming to
the point, which would be wisely imitated in contemporaneous
literature. Here we have no circumlocution, no discursive
pedantry, no smell of the lamp; the figures, though wholly
derived from the East, being Arabic numerals, are distinct and
full of purpose. If the writing abounds in flourishes—which it
does—these are not rhetorical, but boldly graphic: struck with
a nervous decision of style, which, instead of obscuring the text
and meaning, convinces the reader that he who traced them
when promising to pay the sum of five, ten, twenty, thirty,
forty, fifty, one hundred, or a thousand pounds, means that he
will pay it to bearer on demand, honestly and instantly.

Although intended for utility, the dulcet is not wholly overlooked; and the graces of art bend over this much-prized
publication. The effigy of Britannia is no slavish reproduction of the P. R. B. or any other school. That commanding
figure sits upon her scroll of state utterly and inimitably
unique. Neither, if judged by the golden rule of our greatest
bard, is the work wholly deficient in another charm. As we
have explained, its words are few: brevity is the soul of wit.
We fearlessly put it to the dullest sense of humour, whether
a Bank Note (say for a hundred) is not the best joke possible
—except a Bank Note for a thousand.

A critical analysis of a work of this importance cannot be
complete without going deeply into the subject. Reviewing
is, alas, too often mere surface-work; for seldom do we find
the critic going below the superficies, or extending his scrutiny beyond the letter-press. We shall, however, set an example of profundity, and, having discharged our duty to the face

of the Bank Note, shall proceed to penetrate below it: having analysed the print, we shall now speak of the paper.

The late Mr. Cobbett, to express his idea of the intrinsic worthlessness of these sheets, was wont to designate Bank Notes as "Rags." It may, indeed, be said of them that, "Rags they were, and to tinder they return;" for they are born of shreds of linen, and, ten years after death are converted in bonfires into the finest of known tinder. It may be considered a curious fact by those who wear shirts, and a painful, because hopeless one, by those who make them, that the refuse or cuttings of linen is, with a slight admixture of cotton, the pabulum or pulp of Bank Note Paper. Machinery has intruded itself into this branch of paper-making. The pulp is kept so well mixed in a large vat, that the fibrous material presents the appearance of a huge caldron of milk. Into this the paper-maker dips his mould, which is a fine wire sieve, having round its edge a slight mahogany frame called the "Deckel," which confines the pulp to the dimensions of the mould. This dip is a feat of dexterity, for on it depends the thickness and evenness of the sheet of paper. The watermark, or, more properly, the wire-mark, is obtained by twisting wires to the desired form or design, and stitching them on the face of the mould; therefore the design is above the level face of the mould, by the thickness of the wires it is composed of. Hence, the pulp in settling down on the mould, must of necessity be thinner on the wire design than on other parts of the sheet. When the water has run off through the sieve-like face of the mould, the new-born sheet of paper is "couched:" the mould is gently but firmly pressed upon a blanket, to which the spongy sheet clings. Sizing is a subsequent process, and, when dry, the water-mark is plainly discernible, being, of course, transparent where the substance is thinnest. The paper is then dried, and made up into reams of five hundred sheets each, ready for press. The water-mark in the notes of the Bank of England is secured to that establishment by a special act of Parliament. Imitation of anything whatever connected with a Bank Note is an extremely unsafe experiment.

This curious sort of paper is unique. There is nothing like it in the world of sheets. Tested by the touch, it gives out a crisp, crackling, sharp music, which resounds from no other quires. To the eye it shows a colour belonging neither to blue-wove, nor yellow-wove, nor cream-laid: but a white, like no other white, either in paper or pulp. The three rough fringy edges are called the "deckeled" edges, being the natural boundary of the pulp when first moulded: the fourth is left smooth by the knife, which eventually cuts the two notes in twain. This paper is so thin that, when printed, there is much difficulty in making erasures; yet it is so strong that a "water-leaf" (a leaf before the application of size) will support thirty-six pounds; and, with the addition of one grain of size, will hold half a hundred-weight, without tearing; yet the quantity of fibre of which it consists, is no more than eighteen grains and a half.

The general design of the Bank Note is remarkably plain—steel plates are engraved in a manner somewhat analogous to that employed in the Mint for the production of the coin, except that heavy pressure is used instead of a blow. The form of the Note is divided into four or five sections, each engraved on steel dies, which are hardened. Steel rollers, or mills, are obtained from these dies, and each portion of the Note is impressed on a steel plate to be printed from by the mills until the whole is complete.

By means of an ingenious machine, the engraving on the plates when worn by long printing is repaired by the same mills, and thus perfect identity of form is permanently secured. The merits of this system are due to the late Mr. Oldham, and the many improvements introduced not only into this, but into the printing department, are the work of his son and successor, Mr. Thomas Oldham, the present chief engraver to the Bank of England. The plate—always with a pair of notes upon it—is now ready for the press; for it contains all the literary part of the work, except the date, the number, and the cashier's signature.

Before passing through the press, all paper must be damped that it may readily absorb ink; and Bank Note paper is not exempt from this law; but the process by which it is complied with is an ingenious exception to the ordinary modes. The sheets are put into an iron chamber which is exhausted of air; water is then admitted, and forces itself through every pore at the rate of thirty thousand sheets, or double notes, per minute.

In a long gallery that looks like a chamber of the Inquisition with self-acting racks, stands a row of plate-printing presses worked by steam. Every time a sheet passes through them they emit a soft "click" like a ship's capstan creaking in a whisper. By this sound they announce to all whom it may concern that they have printed two Bank Notes. They are tell-tales, and keep no secrets; for, not content with stating the fact aloud, each press moves an index of numerals at the end of the room; so that the chief of the department can see at any hour of the day how many each press has printed. To take an impression of a Note plate " on the sly," is therefore impossible. By a clever invention of Mr. Oldham the impression returns to the printer when made, instead of remaining on the opposite side of the press, after it has passed through the rollers, as of old. The plates are heated, for inking, over steam boxes instead of charcoal fires.

When five hundred sheets, or one thousand notes have been printed, they are placed in a tray which is inserted in a sort of shelf-trap that shuts up with a spring. No after-abstraction can, therefore, take place. One such repository is over the index appertaining to each press; and, at the end of the day, it can at once be seen whether the number of sheets corresponds with the numerals of the tell-tale. Any sort of mistake can thus be readily detected. The average number of " promises to pay" printed per diem is thirty thousand.

As we cannot allow the dot over an *i*, or the cross of a *t* to escape the focus of our critical microscope, we now proceed to apply it to the Bank Ink. This is made from the charred husks of Rhenish grapes after their juice has been expressed and bottled for exportation to the dinner-tables of half the world. When mixed with pure linseed oil, carefully prepared by boiling and burning, the vinous refuse produces a species of blacks so tenacious that they obstinately refuse to be emancipated from the paper when once enslaved to it by the press. It is so intensely nigritious that, compared with it, all other blacks are musty browns.

The note is, when plate-printed, two processes distant from negotiable; the first being the numbering and dating—and here we must point out the grand distinction which exists between the publication which we have the satisfaction of stating, now lies before us (it is only a " Five") and ordinary prints. When the types for this miscellany, for instance, are once set up, every copy struck off from them by the press is precisely similar. On the contrary, of those emitted from the Bank presses *no two are alike.* They differ either in date, in number, or in denomination. This difference constitutes a grand system of check, extending over every stage of every Bank Note's career : a system which records the completion and issue of each note, tracks it through its public adventures, recognises it when it returns to the Bank from among hundreds of thousands of companions, and finally enables the proper officers to pounce upon it, in case of inquiry, at any official half-hour for ten years after it has returned in fulfilment of its "promise to pay." A threat to explain what must appear so complicated a plan, may seem to the reader like a threat of prolixity. But he may read on in security; the system is as simple as the alphabet.

Understand, then, that the dates of Bank Notes are arbitrary, and bear no reference to the day of issue. At the beginning of the official year (February) the Directors settle what dates each of the eleven denominations of Bank Notes shall be during the ensuing twelve months, taking care to apportion to each sort of note a separate date. The table of dates is then handed to the proper officer, who prints accordingly. The five-pound note which now rejoices our eyes is, for example, dated February the 2nd, 1850 ; we therefore know that there is no genuine note in existence, for any other sum, which bears that date ; and if a note for ten, twenty, fifty, or a hundred, having "2nd Feb., 1850," upon it were to be offered to us or to a Bank Clerk, we or he would, without a shadow of further evidence, impound it as a forgery.

Now, as to the numbering :—It is a rule that of every date and denomination, one hundred thousand Notes—no more and no less—shall be completed and issued at one time. We know, therefore, that our solitary five is one of a hundred thousand other fives, each bearing a different number—from 1*

---

* To prevent fraudulent additions of numerals, less than five figures are never used. When units, tens, &c., are required, they are preceded by ciphers. "One" is therefore expressed on a Bank Note thus:—"00001."

to 100,000—but all dated 2nd Feb., 1850. The numbers
are printed on each Note by means of a letter-press, the types
of which change with each pull of the press. For the first
Note, the press is set at "00001," and when that is printed,
the "1," by the mere act of impression, retires to make room
for "2," which leaves its mark on the next Note, and so on
up to "100,000." The system has been applied to the stamping of railway tickets. The date being required for the whole
series, is of course immovable. After this has been done, the
autograph of a cashier is only requisite to render the Note
worth the value inscribed on it in gold.

While the printers are at work, manufacturing each series
of Notes, the account-book makers are getting up a series of
ledgers so exactly to correspond, that the books of themselves,
without the stroke of a pen, are a record of the existence of
the Note. The book in which the birth of our own especial
and particular "Five" is registered, is legibly inscribed,

"Fives, Feb. 2, 1850."

When you open a page, you find it to consist of a series of
horizontal and perpendicular lines, like the pattern of a pair
of shepherd's plaid inexpressibles, variegated with columns of
numerals; these figures running on regularly from No. 1, on
the top of the first page, to No. 100,000 at the bottom of the
last. Therefore, the mere existence of that book, with its arbitrary date and series of numbers, corresponding to the like
series of Notes, is a sufficient record of the existence and issue
of the latter. The return of each Note after its public travels
is recorded in the square opposite to its number. Each page
of the book contains two hundred squares and numbers; consequently, whatever number a Note may bear, the Clerk who
has to register its safe return from a long round of public circulation, knows at once on which page of the book to pounce
for its own proper and particular square. In that he inserts
the date of its return—not at full length, but in cypher. "S"
in red ink means 1850, and the months are indicated by one
of the letters of the word AMBIDEXTROUS, with the date in
numerals. Our only, and therefore favorite five is numbered
31177. Should it chance to finish its travels in the Account-
ant's Office on the 6th of August next, it will be narrowly in-

spected (for fear of forgery) and defaced—a Clerk will then turn at once to the book lettered " Fives, Feb. 2," and so exactly will he know which to open, and where the square numbered 31177 is situated, that he could point to it blindfold. He will write in it " 6 t," which means 6th August; that being the eighth month in the year, and " t" the eighth letter in the chosen word.

The intermediate history of Bank Notes is soon told. Nineteen-twentieths are issued to Bankers or known houses of business. If Glynn's or Smith's, or any other banking firm, require a hundred ten-pound Notes, the Clerk who issues them makes a memorandum showing the number of the Notes so issued, and the name of the party to whom they have been handed—an easy process, because Notes being new,* are always given out in regular series, and the first and last Note that makes the sum required need only be recorded. Most Bankers make similar memoranda when notes pass out of their hands; and the public, as each note circulates among them, frequently sign the name of the last holder. When an unknown person presents a Note for gold at the Bank of England, he is required to write his name and address on it, and if the sum be very large, it is not paid without inquiry. By these expedients, a stolen, lost, or forged Note can often be traced from hand to hand up to its birth.

The average periods which each denomination of London Notes remain in circulation is shown by the following table :

£5	72·7 days.		£50	38·8 days.
10	77·0 ,,		100	29·4 ,,
20	57·4 ,,		200	12·7 ,,
30	18·9 ,,		300	10·6 ,,
40	13·7 ,,		500	11·8 ,,
	£1000	11·1		

The exceptions to these averages are few, and, therefore, remarkable. On the 27th of September, 1845, a fifty-pound Note was presented bearing date 20th January, 1743. Another for ten pounds, issued on the 19th November, 1762, was not paid till the 20th April, 1843. There is a legend extant, of the eccentric possessor of a thousand-pound Note, who kept it framed and glazed for a series of years, preferring to feast

† The Bank ceased to reissue its Notes since 1835.

his eyes on it, to putting the amount it represented out at interest. It was converted into gold, however, without a day's loss of time by his heir on his demise. Stolen and lost Notes .are long absenteees. The former usually make their appearance soon after some great horse-race, or other sporting event altered or disguised so as to deceive Bankers, to whom the Bank of England furnishes a list of the numbers and dates of stolen Notes.

Mr. Francis, in his History of the Bank of England, tells a curious story about a Bank post-bill, which was detained during thirty years from presentation and payment. It happened in the year 1740: "One of the Directors, a very rich man, had occasion for 30,000*l*., which he was to pay as the price of an estate he had just bought; to facilitate the matter, he carried the sum with him to the Bank and obtained for it a Bank bill. On his return home, he was suddenly called out upon particular business; he threw the Note carelessly on the chimney, but when he came back a few minutes afterwards to lock it up, it was not to be found. No one had entered the room; he could not therefore suspect any person. At last, after much ineffectual search, he was persuaded that it had fallen from the chimney into the fire. The Director went to acquaint his colleagues with his misfortune; and as he was known to be a perfectly honourable man he was readily believed. It was only about four-and-twenty hours from the time that he had deposited his money; they thought, therefore, that it would be hard to refuse his request for a second bill. He received it upon giving an obligation to restore the first bill, if it should ever be found, or to pay the money himself, if it should be presented by any stranger. About thirty years afterwards (the Director having been long dead, and his heirs in possession of his fortune), an unknown person presented the lost bill at the Bank, and demanded payment. It was in vain that they mentioned to this person the transaction by which that bill was annulled; he would not listen to it; he maintained that it had come to him from abroad, and insisted upon immediate payment. The Note was payable to bearer; and the thirty thousand pounds were paid him. The heirs of the Director refused restitution; and the Bank was obliged to sustain the loss. It was discovered afterwards that an

architect, having purchased the Director's house, had taken it
down, in order to build another upon the same spot, had found
the Note in a crevice of the chimney, and made his discovery
an engine for robbing the Bank."

Carelessness, equal to that here recorded, is not at all uncommon, and gives the Bank enormous profit, against which
the loss of a mere thirty thousand pounds is but a trifle.
Bank Notes have been known to light pipes, to wrap up snuff,
to be used as curl-papers; and British tars, mad with rum and
prize-money, have not unfrequently, in time of war, eaten
them as sandwiches between bread-and-butter. In the forty
years between the years 1792 and 1832 there were outstanding
Notes (presumed to have been lost or destroyed) amounting
to one million three hundred and thirty odd thousand pounds;
every shilling of which was clear profit to the Bank. .

The superannuation, death, and burial of a Bank of England
Note is a story soon told. The returned Notes, or promises
performed, are kept for ten years in "The Library," and then
burnt in an iron cage in one of the Bank yards.

A few words on the history and general appearance of the
Bank of England Note will conclude our criticism.

The strong principle to ensure the detection of forgery is
uniformity; hence, from the very first Note issued by the
Bank, to that, the merits of which we are now discussing, the
same general design has been preserved,—only that the execution has been from time to time improved; except, we are
bound to add, that of the signatures, some of which are still
as illegible as ever.* During the great coinage crisis in the
reign of William the Third, Notes were granted in the form
of Bank post-bills,—that is, not nominally to a member of the
establishment, but really to the party applying for them, and
for any sum he might require. If it suited his convenience,
he presented his Note several times, drawing such lesser
sums as he might require; precisely as if it were a letter
of credit, after the manner of the Sailor mentioned in the
latest edition of Joe Miller. Jack, somehow or other, got
possession of a fifty-pound Note; the sum was so dazzlingly
enormous that he had not the heart, on presenting it for pay-

---

* Recently an act of Parliament was obtained to permit fac-similes of the signing
officers' handwriting to be *printed* on the note.

ment, to demand the whole sum at once, for fear of breaking the Bank. So, leaning confidentially over the counter, he whispered to the cashier, that he wouldn't be hard upon 'em. As it was all the same to him, he would take five sovereigns now, and the rest at so much a week. A specimen of one of the earliest Bank Notes, preserved in the Bank, shows that the holder took the amount as Jack proposed;—by instalments. It was granted to Mr. Thomas Powell, on the 19th of December, 1699, for five hundred and fifty-five pounds. His first draft was one hundred and thirty-one pounds, ten shillings, and one penny; the second "in gould," three hundred and sixty; the third, sixty-three pounds, nine shillings, and eleven-pence, when the note was retained by the Bank as having been fully honoured.

XI.

THE RAILWAY WONDERS OF LAST YEAR.

August 17, 1850.

WHEN, in his dazzling document the preposterous "promoter" of the first Railway certified the forthcoming goods transit at six times the amount his most sanguine "traffic-taker" could conscientiously compute; when he quadrupled the boldest calculations of the expected number of passengers; when, in short, he projected his prognostics beyond the widest bounds of probability, and then added a few cyphers at the end of each sum, to make "round numbers"—he was not so mad as to believe that he lied in the least like truth. Mad as he was *not*, he never could have supposed that an after-time would come when his lying prospectus would be pronounced as far short of, as he had endeavoured to make it exceed, the Truth. But that time has arrived.

Let us suppose a friend of his, a far-seeing prophet, reading, by the aid of magnifying glasses, a proof of the pet prospectus; let us figure the statistical prophet assuring its author that, twenty years thence, his immeasurable exaggerations would be out-exaggerated by what should actually come to pass; that his brazen bait to catch share-jobbers would shrink, when placed beside the Railway records of eighteen hundred and forty-nine, into a puny, minimised, under-statement. How he would have laughed! How immediately his mind would have reverted from the sanguine seer to the terminus of flighty intellects known as Bedlam. With what remarkable unction he would have exclaimed: "What! Do you mean to say I have not laid it on thick enough? Why, look here!" and he turns to the latest of the Stamp-office stage-coach returns: "Do you mean to tell me—now that coach-travelling has arrived at perfection, and that the wonderful average of coach passengers is six millions a year—that, instead of quadrupling the number of travellers who are likely to use my line, I ought to multiply them by a hundred? Why, you may as well try to persuade me that I ought to promise for our locomotives twenty, instead of fifteen, miles an hour; which—Heaven forgive me—I have had the courage to set down. If I were to romance at that rate, we should not sell a share."

And our would-be Major Longbow would have had reason for the faith that was in him. In his highest flights he dared not exceed too violently the statistics of G. R. Porter, or have added too high a premium on the expectations of George Stephenson. The former calculated that, up to the end of 1834 when not a hundred miles of Railway were open, the annual average of persons who travelled by coach was about two millions, each going over one hundred and eighty miles of ground in the year.* Supposing each individual performed that distance in three journeys, the whole number of *persons* must have multiplied themselves into six millions of *passengers*. As to speed, Mr. George Stephenson said at a dinner-party given to him at Newcastle in 1844, that when he planned the Liverpool and Manchester line, the directors entreated him, when they went to Parliament, not to talk of going at a faster rate than ten miles an hour, or he "would put a cross upon the concern." Mr. George Stephenson *did* talk of fifteen miles an hour, and some of the Committee asked if he were not mad! A Mr. Nicholas Wood delivered himself in a pamphlet as follows: "It is far from my wish to promulgate to the world that the ridiculous expectations, or rather *professions*, of the *enthusiastic speculatist* will be realized, and that we

* "Porter's Progress of the Nation," vol. ii. p. 22.

shall see engines travelling at the rate of twelve, sixteen, eighteen, twenty miles an hour. Nothing could do more harm towards their general adoption and improvement than the promulgation of such NONSENSE!"

It would seem, then, that the Longbow of the aboriginal prospectuses was only too modest in his estimate as to passengers and speed. A few years must have made him utterly ashamed of his modesty. How disgusted he must have felt with his timid prelusions, even when 1843 arrived! That year revealed travellers' tales which exceeded his early romances by what Major Longbow himself would have called "an everlasting long chalk." Within that year, seventy railroads, constructed at an outlay of sixty millions sterling, conveyed twenty-five millions of passengers three hundred and thirty millions of miles, at an average cost of one penny three-farthings per mile, and an average speed of twenty-four miles per hour, with but one fatal accident.

But if our parent of railway proprietors were astonished at what happened in 1843, with what inconceivable amazement he must peruse the details of 1849? We should like to see the expression of his countenance while conning the report of Her Majesty's Commissioners of Railways for last year.

From this record of scarcely credible statistics, it appears that, at the end of 1849, there were, in Great Britain and Ireland, five thousand five hundred and ninety-six miles of railway in active operation; upwards of four thousand five hundred and fifty-six of which are in England, eight hundred and forty-six in Scotland, and four hundred and ninety-four in Ireland. Besides this, the number of miles which have been authorised by Parliament, and still remain to be finished, is six thousand and thirty; so that, if all the lines were completed, the three kingdoms would be intersected by a network of railroad measuring twelve thousand miles;* but of this there is only a remote probability, the number of miles in course of active construction being no more than one thousand five hundred, so that by the end of the present year it is calculated that the length of finished and operative railway may be about seven thousand four hundred miles, or as many

* So many railway schemes have been since abandoned, that, in June, 1858, no more than nine thousand three hundred and twenty-three miles of railway were in operation.

as lie between Great Britain and the Cape of Good Hope, with a thousand miles to spare. The number of persons employed on the 30th of June, 1849, in the operative railways, was fifty-four thousand ; on the unopened lines, one hundred and four thousand.

When the schemer of the infancy of the giant railway system turns to the passenger account for the year 1849, he declares he is fairly " knocked over." He finds that the railway passengers are put down at *sixty-three million eight hundred thousand ;* nearly three times the number returned for 1843, and *a hundred times* as many as took to the road in the days of stage-coaches. The passengers of 1849 actually double the sum of the entire population of the three kingdoms.*

The statement of capital which the six thousand miles now being hourly travelled over represents, will require the reader to draw a long breath ;—it is one hundred and ninety-seven and a half millions of pounds sterling.† Add to this the cash being disbursed for the lines in progress, the total rises to two hundred and twenty millions. The average cost of each mile of railway, including engines, carriages, stations, &c. (technically called " plant"), is thirty-three thousand pounds.

Has this outlay proved remunerative ? The Commissioners tell us, that the gross receipts from all the railways in 1849 amounted to eleven millions eight hundred and six thousand pounds ; from which, if the working expenses be deducted at the rate of forty-three per cent. (being about an average taken from the published statements of a number of the principal companies), there remains a net available profit of about six millions seven hundred and twenty-nine thousand four hundred and twenty pounds to pay the holders of property valued at one hundred and ninety-seven millions and a half; or at the rate, within a fraction, of three and a half per cent. Here our parent of railway prospectuses chuckles. He promised twenty per cent. per annum.

In short, in everything except the dividends, our scheming

* Although the length of railway lines has been not quite doubled since this article was written, the number of passengers has much more than doubled. In the year which ended in June, 1858, they transmitted one hundred and thirty-nine millions of passengers from place to place: about two hundred and fifty times the number formerly travelling by stage-coaches, and equal (within a fraction) to the entire population of the United Kingdom multiplied by six !

† The corresponding figures for 1858 were 325,375,507*l.*

friend finds that recent fact has outstripped his early fictions. He told the nervous old ladies and shaky half-pay officers on his projected line, that Railways were quite as safe as stage-coaches. What say the grave records of 1849 ? The lives of five passengers were lost during that year, and those by one accident—a cause, of course, beyond the control of the victims ; eighteen more casualties took place, for which the sufferers had themselves alone to blame. Five lives lost by official mismanagement, out of sixty-four millions of risks, is no very outrageous proportion ;* especially when we reflect that, taking as a basis the calculations of 1843, the number of miles travelled over per rail during last year, may be set down at eight hundred and forty-five millions ; or *nine times the distance between the earth and the sun.*

Such are the Railway wonders of the year of grace one thousand eight hundred and forty-nine.

XII.

TWO CHAPTERS ON BANK-NOTE FORGERIES.

SEPTEMBER 7, 1850.

I.

IN the month of August, 1757, a gentleman living in the neighbourhood of Lincoln's Inn fields, named Bliss, advertised for a clerk. There were, as was usual even at that time, many applicants ; but a young man of twenty-six, named Richard William Vaughan, was selected. His manners were so winning, and his demeanour so much that of a gentleman (he belonged, indeed, to a good county family in Staffordshire, and had been a student at Pembroke Hall, Oxford), that Mr. Bliss at once engaged him. Nor had he occasion, during the time the new clerk served him, to repent the step. Vaughan was so diligent, intelligent, and steady, that not even when it transpired that he was, commercially speaking, "under a cloud," did his master lessen confidence in him. Some in-

---

* Applying the doctrine of chances to the statistics of accidents for 1858, it would appear that the odds are 5,353, 603 to one that a passenger loses his life on commencing a journey ; and 832,304 to one that he meets with personal injury.

quiry into his antecedents showed that he had, while at College, been extravagant; that his friends had removed him
thence; set him up in Stafford as a wholesale linendraper,
with a branch establishment in Aldersgate-street, London;
that he had failed, and that there was some difficulty about
his certificate. But so well did he excuse his early failings
and account for his misfortunes, that his employer did not
check the regard he felt growing towards him. Their intercourse was not merely that of master and servant. Vaughan
was a frequent guest at Bliss's table; by-and-by a daily visitor
to his wife, and—to his ward.

Miss Bliss was a young lady of some attractions, not the
smallest of which was a handsome fortune. Young Vaughan
made the most of his opportunities. He was well-looking,
well-informed, dressed well, and made love well, for he won
the young lady's heart. The guardian was not flinty hearted,
and acted like a sensible man of the world. "It was not," he
said on a subsequent and painful occasion, " till I learned from
the servants and observed by the girl's behaviour that she
greatly approved Richard Vaughan, that I consented; but, I
did so, with the condition that he should make it appear that
he could maintain her. I had no doubt of his character as a
servant, and I knew his family were respectable. His brother
is an eminent attorney." Vaughan boasted that his mother
(his father was dead) was willing to reinstate him in business
with a thousand pounds; five hundred of which was to be
settled upon Miss Bliss for her separate use.

So far all went on prosperously. Providing Richard Vaughan
could attain a position satisfactory to the Blisses, the marriage
was to take place in the Easter week following, which the
Calendar tells us happened early in April, 1758. With this
understanding, he left Mr. Bliss's service, to push his fortune.

Months passed on, and Vaughan appears to have made no
way in the world. He had not even obtained his bankrupt's
certificate. His visits to his affianced were frequent, and his
protestations passionate; but he had effected nothing substantial towards a happy union. Miss Bliss's guardian grew
impatient; and, although there is no evidence to prove that
the young lady's affection for Vaughan was otherwise than
deep and sincere, yet even she began to lose confidence in

him. His excuses were evasive, and not always true. The
time fixed for the wedding was fast approaching; and Vaughan
saw that something must be done to restore the young lady's
confidence.

About three weeks before the appointed Easter Tuesday,
Vaughan went to his mistress in high spirits. All was right:
his certificate was to be granted in a day or two; his family
had come forward with the money, and he was to continue the
Aldersgate business he had previously carried on as a branch
of the Stafford trade. The capital he had waited so long for,
was at length forthcoming. In fact, here were two hundred
and forty pounds of the five hundred he was to settle on his
beloved. Vaughan then produced twelve twenty-pound notes;
Miss Bliss could scarcely believe her eyes. She examined
them. The paper, she remarked, seemed rather thicker than
usual. "Oh," said Vaughan, "all Bank-bills are not alike."
The girl was naturally much pleased. She would hasten to
apprise Mistress Bliss of the good news.

Not for the world! So far from letting any living soul
know he had placed so much money in her hands, Vaughan
exacted an oath of secrecy from her, and sealed the notes up
in a parcel with his own seal; making her swear that she
would on no account open it till after their marriage.

Some days after, that is, "on the twenty-second of March"
(1758), we are describing the scene in Mr. Bliss's own words:
"I was sitting with my wife by the fireside. The prisoner
and the girl were sitting in the same room—which was a
small one—and although they whispered, I could distinguish
that Vaughan was very urgent to have something returned
which he had previously given to her. She refused, and
Vaughan went away in an angry mood. I then studied the
girl's face, and saw that it expressed much dissatisfaction.
Presently a tear broke out. I then spoke, and insisted on
knowing the dispute. She refused to tell, and I told her that
until she did, I would not see her. The next day I asked the
same question of Vaughan; he hesitated. 'Oh!' I said, 'I
dare say it is some ten or twelve pound matter—something
to buy a wedding bauble with.' He answered that it was
much more than that, it was near three hundred pounds!
'But why all this secrecy?' I said; and he answered it was

not proper for people to know he had so much money till his certificate was signed. I then asked him to what intent he had left the notes with the young lady? He said, as I had of late suspected him, he designed to give her a proof of his affection and truth. I said, 'You have demanded them in such a way that it must be construed as an abatement of your affection towards her.'" Vaughan was again exceedingly urgent in asking back the packet; but Bliss remembering his many evasions, and supposing this was a trick, declined advising his niece to restore the parcel without proper consideration. The very next day it was discovered that the notes were counterfeits.

This occasioned stricter inquiries into Vaughan's previous career. It turned out that he bore the character in his native place of a dissipated and not very scrupulous person. The intention of his mother to assist him was an entire fabrication, and he had given Miss Bliss the forged notes solely for the purpose of deceiving her. Meanwhile the forgeries became known to the authorities, and he was arrested. By what means, does not clearly appear. The "Annual Register" says that one of the engravers gave information; but we find nothing in the newspapers of the time to support that statement; neither was it corroborated at Vaughan's trial.

When Vaughan was arrested he thrust a piece of paper into his mouth, and began to chew it violently. It was, however, rescued, and proved to be one of the forged notes; fourteen of them were found on his person, and when his lodgings were searched twenty more were discovered.

Vaughan was tried at the Old Bailey on the 7th of April, before Lord Mansfield. The manner of the forgery was detailed minutely at the trial: On the first of March (about a week before he gave the twelve notes to the young lady), Vaughan called on Mr. John Corbould, an engraver, and gave an order for a promissory note to be engraved with these words:

"No. ———.

    "I promise to pay to ————, or Bearer, ——,
London ——."

There was to be a Britannia in the corner. When it was

done, Mr. Sneed (that was the *alias* Vaughan adopted) came
again, but objected to the execution of the work. The Britannia was not good, and the words " I promise" were too near
the edge of the plate. Another plate was in consequence engraved, and, on the fourth of March, Vaughan took it away.
He immediately repaired to a printer, and had forty-eight impressions taken on thin paper, provided by himself. Meanwhile, he had ordered, on the same morning, of Mr. Charles
Fourdrinier, another engraver, a second plate, with what he
called " a direction," in the words, " For the Governor and
Company of the Bank of England." This was done, and
about a week later he brought some paper, each sheet " folded
up," said the witness, " very curiously, so that I could not see
what was in them. I was going to take the papers from him,
but he said he must go up-stairs with me, and see them worked
off himself. I took him up-stairs; he would not let me have
them out of his hands. I took a sponge and wetted them,
and put them one by one on the plate in order for printing
them. After my boy had done two or three of them, I went
down stairs, and my boy worked the rest off, and the prisoner
came down stairs and paid me."

Here the Court pertinently asked, " What imagination had
you when a man thus came to you to print on secret paper,
' the Governor and Company of the Bank of England ?' "

The engraver's reply was: " I then did not suspect anything. But I shall take care for the future." As this was the
first Bank of England note forgery that was ever perpetrated,
the engraver was held excused.

It may be mentioned as an evidence of the delicacy of the
newspaper reporters, that, in their account of the trial, Miss
Bliss's name is not mentioned. Her designation is " a young
lady." We subjoin the notes of her evidence:

" A young lady (sworn). The prisoner delivered me some
bills; these are the same (producing twelve counterfeit Bank-
notes sealed up in a cover, for twenty pounds each); said they
were Bank bills. I said they were thicker paper—he said all
bills are not alike. I was to keep them till after we were
married. He put them into my hands to show he put confidence in me, and desired me not to show them to anybody;
sealed them up with his own seal, and obliged me by an oath

not to discover them to anybody. And I did not till he had discovered them himself. He was to settle so much in Stock on me."

Vaughan urged in his defence that his sole object was to deceive his affianced, and that he intended to destroy all the notes after his marriage. But it had been proved that the prisoner had asked one John Ballingar to change first one, and then twenty of the notes; but which that person was unable to do. Besides, had his sole object been to dazzle Miss Bliss with his fictitious wealth, he would most probably have entrusted more, if not all the notes, to her keeping.

He was found guilty, and passed the day that had been fixed for his wedding as a condemned criminal.

On the 11th May, 1758, Richard William Vaughan was executed at Tyburn. By his side, on the same gallows, there was another forger: William Boodgere, a military officer, who had forged a draft on an army agent named Calcroft.

The gallows may seem hard measure to have meted out to Vaughan, when it is considered that none of his notes were negotiated and no person suffered by his fraud. Not one of the forty-eight notes, except the twelve delivered to Miss Bliss, had been out of his possession. The imitation must have been very clumsily executed, and detection would have instantly followed any attempts to pass the counterfeits. There was no endeavour to copy the style of engraving on a real Bank-note. That was left to the engraver; and as each sheet passed through the press twice, the words added at the second printing, "For the Governor and Company of the Bank of England," could have fallen into their proper place on any one of the sheets, only by a miracle. But what would have made the forgery clear to even a superficial observer was the singular omission of the second "n" in the word England.*

The criticism on Vaughan's note of a Bank clerk examined on the trial was: "There is some resemblance to be sure; but this note" (that upon which the prisoner was tried) "is numbered thirteen thousand eight hundred and forty, and we never reach so high a number." Besides, there was no water-mark in the paper.

* Bad orthography was by no means uncommon in the most important documents at that period; the days of the week, in the old day-books of the Bank of England itself, are spelt in a variety of ways.

Vaughan was greatly commiserated. But despite the un-skilfulness of the forgery, and the insignificant consequences. which followed it, the crime was considered of too dangerous a character not to be marked, from its very novelty, with ex-emplary punishment. Hanging created at that time no remorse in the public mind, and it was thought necessary to set up Vaughan as a warning to all future Bank-note forgers. For-gery differs from other crimes not less in the magnitude of the spoil it may obtain, and of the injury it inflicts, than in the facilities for its accomplishment. The common thief finds a limit to his depredations in the bulkiness of his booty, which is generally confined to such property as he can carry about his person; the swindler raises insuperable and defeating obstacles to his frauds if the amount he seeks to obtain is so inconsiderable as to awaken close vigilance or inquiry. To carry their projects to any very profitable extent, these crim-inals are reduced to the hazardous necessity of acting in concert, and thus infinitely increasing the risks of detection. But the forger need have no accomplice; he is burdened with no bulky and suspicious property; he needs no receiver to dispose of his spoil. The skill of his own individual right hand can command thousands; often without detection, and oftener with such rapidity as to enable him to baffle the pursuit of justice.

It was a long time before Vaughan's rude attempt was im-proved upon; but in the same year (1758), another depart-ment of the crime was commenced with perfect success: namely, an ingenious alteration, for fraudulent purposes, of real Bank-notes. A few months after Vaughan's execution, one of the northern mails was stopped and robbed by a high-wayman; several Bank-notes were comprised in the spoil, and the robber, setting up with these as a gentleman, went boldly to the Hatfield post-office, ordered a chase and four, rattled away down the road, and changed a note at every change of horses. The robbery was, of course, soon made known, and the numbers and dates of the stolen notes were advertised as having been stopped at the Bank. To the genius of a high-wayman this offered but a small obstacle, and this gentleman-thief changed all the figures " 1 " of the notes remaining in his possession into " 4's." These notes passed currently enough;

but, on reaching the Bank, the alteration was detected, and the last holder was refused payment. As that person had given a valuable consideration for the note, he brought an action for the recovery of the amount; and it was ruled by the Lord Chief Justice, that "any person giving a valuable consideration for a Bank-note, payable to bearer, in a fair course of business, has an understood right to receive the money at the Bank."

It took a quarter of a century to bring the art of forging Bank-notes to perfection. In 1779, this was nearly attained by an ingenious man named Mathison, a watchmaker, from the matrimonial village of Gretna Green. Having learnt the arts of engraving and of simulating signatures from a dissipated engraver, he tried his hand at the notes of the Darlington Bank; but, with the confidence of skill, was not cautious in passing them, was suspected, and a warrant issued for his arrest. He absconded to Edinburgh. Scorning to let his talent lie idle, he favoured the Scottish public with many spurious Royal Bank of Scotland notes, and regularly forged his way through Glasgow (where he operated with success) to London. At the end of February he established himself and his sister (whom he kept ignorant of his crimes) in handsome lodgings in the Strand, opposite Arundel-street. Having procured a twenty-pound note from the Bank of England itself, he obtained from a brazier two pieces of copper cut exactly to the proper size. These he prepared and polished himself. One he appears to have used for the engraved writing, and the other for imitating the water-mark. His industry was so great that by the 12th of March he had printed a sufficient supply of notes. He then set out on his travels; buying articles in one place and selling them in another. A pair of shoe-buckles he purchased in Coventry, by the aid of which he was eventually convicted, were traced to Edinburgh.

Mathison no sooner returned to London, than he applied to the Bank for fresh notes. Indeed, he became so frequent a lounger about the offices, that he made acquaintance, under the name of Maxwell, of some of the clerks. On the 24th of March he looked in to have a couple of notes "made out" to him (all Bank-notes were, in fact, Bank post-bills at that time) for cash. At the same time seven thousand guineas were paid

in from the Excise-office in notes, one of which was " scrupled."
Mathison looked at it, and, although standing at a distance,
pronounced it to be a good one.   How did he know so well?
From that moment he was suspected.

It happened that during his next visit, one of his own notes
came to the counter to be changed.   The teller saw that it
was spurious, and roundly challenged " Mr. Maxwell" with
some knowledge of the innumerable forgeries which were now
becoming common talk.   The accused expressed indignation
at being suspected; but his countenance denoted guilt.   Yet
he was allowed to go away.   Alarmed, Mathison determined
to leave England, and made preparations for departure.

Stronger suspicions were soon confirmed, and, early the
next morning, the teller was informed that his friend Maxwell,
as he was jokingly called, had just been met passing up Cornhill with a bundle.   The teller instantly posted after him, and
overtaking him, pretended he had made a mistake of half a
guinea which he had paid to Mathison the day before.   " That
could soon be settled," he said, " here is a guinea."   The
clerk declined to take that sum, and induced the forger to return with him to the Bank.   He was given into custody, and
the contents of his bundle examined.   There were some
clothes, a pair of pistols, two hundred guineas in gold, some
real Bank-notes, some engraving, and several watchmaking
tools.   Nothing could, however, be brought forward to substantiate the charge before Sir John Fielding, and Mathison
was sent to a public-house in the neighbourhood of the court,
while the magistrate and the Bank solicitor consulted about
restoring the bundle, and setting the suspected forger at liberty.   No doubt he would have escaped, but for his own folly.
The seat he took in the box of the tavern parlour was next to
a window.   Complaining of a want of air, he opened it.   He
diverted the officer's attention by a stratagem, gave a sudden
spring and jumped out.   This act confirmed every suspicion;
and when recaptured, and asked why he tried to escape, his
only excuse was that it was his humour.   " Then," replied Sir
John Fielding, " it is my humour to commit you."   At his
trial, the Bank-note which he had changed at Coventry to pay
for the shoe-buckles was the means of convicting him, and he
was hanged at Tyburn.

Mathison was a genius in his criminal way; but a greater genius than he appeared in 1786. In that year, so considerable was the circulation of spurious paper-money, that it appeared as if some unknown power had set up a bank of its own. False notes were issued, and readily passed current, in hundreds and thousands. These were not to be distinguished from the genuine paper of Threadneedle-street. Indeed, when one was presented there in due course, so complete were all its parts; so masterly the engraving; so correct the signatures; so skillful the water-mark, that it was promptly paid. From that period forged paper continued to be presented almost daily, especially at the time of lottery drawing. Consultations were held with -the police. Plans were laid to help detection. Every effort was made to trace the forger. Clarke, the best detective of his day, went, like a sleuth-hound, on the track; for in those days, "blood-money" rewarded success. Up to a certain point there was little difficulty; but beyond that point, consummate árt defied the ingenuity of the officer. In whatever way the notes came, the train of discovery always paused at the lottery-offices. Advertisements, offering large rewards were circulated; but the unknown forger baffled detection.

While this base paper was in full currency, there appeared an advertisement in the Daily Advertiser for a servant. A young man, who had been in the employment of a musical instrument maker, wrote an answer to it. The next day he was called upon by a coachman, and informed that the advertiser was waiting in a coach to see him, The young man was desired to enter the conveyance, where he beheld a person with something of the appearance of a foreigner, sixty or seventy years old, apparently troubled with the gout. A camlet surtout was buttoned round his person, and even over his mouth; a large patch was placed over his left eye; and nearly every part of his face was concealed. He affected much infirmity. He had a faint hectic cough; and invariably presented the patched side of his countenance to the view of the servant. After some conversation—in the course of which he represented himself as Mr. Brank, of 29, Titchfield-street, Oxford-street, guardian to a young nobleman of great fortune—the engagement was concluded. Brank frequently inveighed against his whimsical ward for his love of speculating in lottery tickets; which, he told the new servant it would be his principal duty to purchase. Brank kept his face muffled, whenever he had occasion to give orders to his servant. In a day or two, he handed the latter a forty and a twenty pound Bank-note; and directed him to buy lottery-tickets at separate offices. The youth fulfilled his instructions; and, at the moment he was returning, was suddenly called by his employer from the other side of the street, congratulated on his rapidity, and then told to go to various other offices in the neighbourhood of the Royal Exchange, and to purchase more shares. Four hundred pounds in Bank of England notes were handed him, and the wishes of the mysterious Mr. Brank were satisfactorily fulfilled. These scenes were continually enacted. Notes to a large amount were thus circulated; lottery-tickets were purchased; and Mr. Brank—always in a coach, with his face concealed—was ever ready on the spot to receive them. At last the servant's suspicions were aroused; but, had he known that from the period he left his master to purchase the tickets, one female figure accompanied all his movements; that when he entered the offices, it waited at the door, peered cautiously in at the window, hovered around him like a shadow, watched him carefully, and never left him until once more he was in the company of his employer—those suspicions would have been greatly increased.

At last the Bank obtained a clue, and the servant was taken into custody. The directors imagined that they had secured the wholesale forger; that the flood of base notes which had inundated that establishment would at length be dammed up at its source. Their hopes proved fallacious, and it was found that "Old Patch" (as the mysterious forger was, from the servant's description, nicknamed) had been sufficiently clever to baffle the Bank Directors. The house in Titchfield-street was searched; but Mr. Brank had deserted it, and not a trace of a single implement of forgery could be found.

Some little knowledge of "Old Patch's" proceedings was, however, obtained. It appeared that he carried on his paper coining entirely by himself; his only confidant being his mistress. He was his own engraver, his own ink-maker; his own paper-maker; and, with a private press, he worked his own

notes; counterfeiting the signatures of the cashiers with his
own hand.   But these discoveries had no effect; for Old Patch
had set up a press elsewhere.   Although his secret continued
as impenetrable, his notes became as plentiful as ever.   Five
years of unbounded prosperity ought to have satisfied him;
but it did not do so.   His genius was of that insatiable order
which demands new excitements, and a constant succession of
new flights.   The following is from a newspaper of 1786:

"On the 17th of December, ten pounds was paid into the
Bank, for which the clerk, as usual, gave a ticket to receive a
Bank-note of equal value.   This ticket ought to have been
carried immediately to the cashier, instead of which the bearer
took it home, and curiously added an 0 to the original sum,
and returning, presented it so altered to the cashier, for which
he received a note of one hundred pounds.   In the evening,
the clerks found a deficiency in the accounts; and on examining the tickets of the day, not only that but two others were
discovered to have been obtained in the same manner.   In the
one, the figure 1 was altered to 4, and in another to 5, by
which the artist received, upon the whole, nearly one thousand
pounds."

To that princely felony, Old Patch added smaller misde-
meanours, which one would think was far beneath his notice;
except to prove to himself and his mistress the unbounded
facility of his genius for fraud.

At that period the affluent public were saddled with a tax
on plate; and many experiments were made to evade it.
Among others, one was tried by a Mr. Charles Price, a stock-
jobber and lottery-office keeper, which, for a time, puzzled the
tax-gatherer.   Mr. Charles Price lived in great style, gave
splendid dinners, and did everything on the grandest scale.
Yet Mr. Charles Price had no plate.   The authorities could
not find so much as a silver spoon on his magnificent premises.
He was too cunning to possess plate: he borrowed it.   For
one of his sumptuous entertainments, he hired the plate of a
silversmith in Cornhill, and left the value in Bank-notes as
security for its safe return.   One of these notes proved to be
a forgery.   Mr. Charles Price was sent to; but Mr. Charles
Price was not to be found at that particular juncture.   Although this excited no surprise—for he was often absent from

his office for short periods—yet in due course, and, as a formal matter of business, an officer was sent to find him, and to ask his explanation regarding the false note. After tracing a man whom he had strong notions was Mr. Charles Price through countless lodgings and innumerable disguises, the officer (to use his own expression) "nabbed" that gentleman. But, as Mr. Clark observed, his prisoner and his prisoner's lady were, even then, "too many" for him; for although he lost not a moment in trying to secure the forging implements after he had discovered that Mr. Charles Price, and Mr. Brank, and Old Patch, were three gentlemen in one, he found that the lady had destroyed every vestige of the forging implements. Not the point of a graver, not a spot of ink, not a shred of silver-paper, not a scrap of anybody's handwriting, could be found. Despite, however, this paucity of evidence to convict him, Mr. Charles Price had not the courage to face a jury, and eventually saved the judicature much trouble and expense, by hanging himself in Bridewell.

The success of Old Patch has never been surpassed; and even after the darkest era in the history of Bank forgeries—which dates from the suspension of cash payments, in February 1797—"Old Patch" was still remembered as the Cæsar of Forgers.

☞ II.

SEPTEMBER 21, 1850.

IN the history of crime, as in all other histories, there is one great epoch by which minor dates are arranged and defined. In a list of remarkable events, one remarkable event more remarkable than the last, is the standard around which all smaller circumstances are grouped. Whatever happens in Mohammedan annals, is set down as having occurred so many years after the flight of the Prophet; in the records of London commerce a great fraud or a great failure is mentioned as having come to light so many months after the execution of Fauntleroy or the flight of Rowland Stephenson.* Sporting

* Unfortunately such helps to the chronology of crime are overshadowed by the more recent frauds of the Robsons, Redpaths, and Windle Coles.

men date from remarkable struggles for the Derby prize; and
refer to 1840 as "Bloomsbury's year." The highwayman of
old dated from Dick Turpin's last appearance on the fatal
stage at Tyburn turnpike. In like manner, the standard epoch
in the annals of Bank-note Forgery, is the year 1797, when (on
the 25th of February) one-pound notes were put into circulation instead of golden guineas.

At that time the Bank of England note was no better in
appearance—had not improved as a work of art—since the
days of Vaughan, Mathison, and Old Patch; it was just as
easily imitated, and, with increased skill and experience, the
chances of successful forgery were increased a thousand-fold.

Up to 1793 no notes had been issued even for sums so small
as five pounds. Consequently all the Bank paper then in use,
passed through the hands and under the eyes of the affluent
and educated, who could more readily distinguish the false
from the true. During the fourteen years which preceded the
non-golden and small-note era, there were only three capital
convictions for the crime. When, however, the Bank of England notes became "common and popular," a prodigious quantity was also made "base," and many persons were hanged for
passing them.

To a vast number of the humbler orders, Bank-notes were
a rarity and a "sight." Many had never seen such a thing
before they were called upon, for the first time, to take one or
two pound notes in exchange for small merchandise, or their
own labour. How were they to judge? How were they to
tell a good, from a spurious note?—especially when it happened that the officers of the Bank themselves were occasionally mistaken. There cannot be much doubt that where one
graphic rascal was found out, ten escaped. They went on
enjoying their winter treats to the play; their summer excur-
sions to the suburban tea-gardens; their fashionable lounges
at Tunbridge Wells, Bath, Margate, and Ramsgate; doing
business with wonderful unconcern. These usually expensive,
but to them profitable enjoyments, were continually coming
to light at the trials of the lesser rogues who undertook the
issue department. The fraternity and sisterhood of utterers
played many parts, and were banded in strict compact with
the forgers. Some were turned loose into fairs and markets,

in all sorts of disguises. Farmers who could hardly distinguish a field of wheat from a field of barley: butchers who never wielded more deadly weapons than two-pronged forks; country boys with Cockney accents, bought gingerbread, and treated their so-called sweethearts with ribbons and muslins, all by the interchange of false notes. The better mannered disguised themselves as ladies and gentlemen, paid their losings at cards or hazard, or their tavern bills, their milliners, and coachmakers, in motley money composed of part real and part base Bank paper. Some went about in the cloak of the Samaritan, and generously subscribed to charities wherever they saw a chance of changing a bad "five" for three or four good "ones." Ladies of sweet disposition went about doing good among the poor. They personally inquired into distress, relieved it by sending out a daughter or a son to a neighbouring shop for change; and, leaving five shillings for present necessities, walked off with fifteen. So openly was forgery carried on, that whoever chose to turn utterer found no difficulty in getting a stock-in-trade to commence with. No travelling gentleman's pocket or valise was considered complete without a few forged notes wherewith to turn aside the muzzle of a loaded pistol when stopped on the king's highway. This offence against the laws of the road, however, soon became too common, and wayfarers, thus interrupted, had to pledge their sacred words of honour that their notes were the genuine promises of Abraham Newland, and that their watches were not from the factory of Mr. Pinchbeck.

With temptations so strong, it is no wonder that the forgers' trade flourished, with only an occasional check from the strong arm of the law. It followed, therefore, that from the issue of the small notes in February, 1797, to the end of 1817—twenty years—there were eight hundred and seventy prosecutions connected with Bank-note Forgery, in which there were only one hundred and sixty acquittals, and upwards of three hundred executions. The year 1818 brought this crime to its culminating point. In the first three months there were no fewer than one hundred and twenty-eight prosecutions by the Bank; and, by the end of that year, two-and-thirty individuals had been hanged for Note Forgery. So far from this appalling series of examples having any effect in checking the progress of the crime, it is proved that at, and after that very time, base notes were poured into the Bank at the rate of *a hundred a day.*

The enormous number of undetected forgeries afloat, may be estimated by the fact, that from the 1st of January, 1812, to the 10th of April, 1818, one hundred and thirty-one thousand three hundred and thirty-one pieces of paper were ornamented by the Bank officers with the word "forged"—upwards of one hundred and seven thousand of them having been one pound counterfeits.

Intrinsically it would appear from an Hibernian view of the case, that bad notes were, with the trifling drawback of not having been manufactured at the Bank, quite as good as good ones. So accurately did some of them resemble the authorised engraving of the Bank, that it was next to impossible to distinguish the false from the true. Countless instances, showing rather the skill of the forger than want of vigilance in Bank officials, could be cited. Respectable persons were constantly taken into custody on a charge of uttering forgeries, imprisoned for days and then liberated; a close scrutiny, proving that the accusations arose out of genuine notes. In September, 1818, Mr. A. Burnett, of Portsmouth, had a note, which had passed through his hands, returned to him from the Bank of England with the base mark upon it. Satisfied of its genuineness, he re-enclosed it to the cashier, and demanded payment. By return of post he received the following letter :

"BANK OF ENGLAND, 16 *Sept.* 1818.

"Sir,—I have to acknowledge your letter to Mr. Hase, of the 13th inst. enclosing a one-pound note, and, in answer thereto, I beg leave to acquaint you, that, on inspection, it appears to be a genuine note of the Bank of England; I therefore, agreeably to your request, enclose you one of the like value, No. 26,276, dated 22nd August, 1818.

"I am exceedingly sorry, Sir, that such an unusual oversight should have occurred to give you so much trouble, which I trust your candour will induce you to excuse when I assure you that the unfortunate mistake has arisen entirely out of the hurry and multiplicity of business.

"I am, Sir, your most obedient servant,

"A. Burnett, Esq.   "J. RIPPON.
"7 Bellevue-terrace, Southsea, near Portsmouth."

A more extraordinary case is on record. A note was traced to the possession of a tradesman, which had been pronounced by the Bank Inspectors to have been forged. The man would not give it up, and was taken before a magistrate, charged with "having a note in his possession, well knowing it to be forged." He was committed to prison, but was afterwards released on producing bail. He was not called on to appear again ; and, at the expiration of twelve months (having kept the note all that time), he brought an action against the Bank for false imprisonment. On the trial the note was proved to be genuine, and the plaintiff was awarded damages of one hundred pounds.

It is an awful fact that three hundred and thirty human lives should have been sacrificed in twenty-one years ; but when we relate a circumstance which admits the merest probability that some—even one—of those lives may have been sacrificed in innocence, the consideration becomes appalling :

Some time after the frequency of the crime had, in other respects, subsided, there was a sort of bloody assize at Haverfordwest, in Wales. Several prisoners were tried for forging and uttering, and thirteen were convicted ; chiefly on the evidence of Mr. Christmas, a Bank Inspector, who swore positively, in one case, that the document named in the indictment "was not an impression from a Bank of England plate ; was not printed on the paper with the ink or water-mark of the Bank ; neither was it in the handwriting of the signing clerk." Upon this testimony the prisoner, together with twelve participators in similar crimes, was condemned to be hanged.

The morning after the trial, Mr. Christmas was leaving his lodging in the assize town, when an acquaintance stepped up and asked him, as a friend, to give his opinion on a note he had that morning received. It was a bright day ; Mr. Christmas put on his spectacles, and carefully scrutinised the document in a business-like and leisurely manner. He pronounced it to be forged. The gentleman, a little chagrined, brought it away with him to London. It is not a little singular that he happened to know Mr. Burnett, of Portsmouth, whom he accidentally met, and to whom he showed the same note. Mr. Burnett was evidently a proficient judge of Bank-notes. He said nothing, but slipping his hand into one pocket, handed to the astonished gentleman full change, and put the note into another. "It cannot be a good note," exclaimed the latter,

" for my friend Christmas told me at Haverfordwest that it is
a forgery !" Mr. Burnett had backed his opinion to the
amount of twenty shillings, and declined to retract it ; but to
make quite sure, appealed to Mr. Henry Hase, Abraham Newland's successor, who referred the matter to Mr. Christmas's
co-inspectors at the Bank of England. These gentlemen offi-
cially pronounced it to be a good note ; yet, upon the evidence
of Mr. Christmas (who had condemned it) as regards other
notes, the thirteen human beings at Haverfordwest were
trembling at the foot of the gallows. It was promptly and
cogently argued that, as Mr. Christmas's judgment had failed
him in the deliberate examination of one note, it might also
err as to others, and the convicts were respited.

Bad notes were occasionally pronounced to be genuine by
the Bank. Early in January, 1818, a well-dressed woman
entered the shop of Mr. James Hammond, of Bishopsgate-
street Without, and having purchased three pounds' worth of
goods, tendered in payment a ten-pound note. There was
something hesitating and odd in her manner ; and, although
Mr. Hammond could see nothing the matter with the note,
yet he was ungallant enough to suspect that all was not right.
He hoped she was not in a hurry, for he had no change ; he
must send to a neighbor for it. He immediately despatched
his shopman to the most affluent of all his neighbours—The
Old Lady in Threadneedle-street. The delay occasioned the
customer to remark, " I suppose he is gone to the Bank ?"
Mr. Hammond having answered in the affirmative, engaged
his customer in conversation, and they freely discussed the
current topics of the day ; till the young man returned with
ten one-pound Bank of England notes. Mr. Hammond felt a
little remorse at having suspected his patroness ; who departed
with her purchases with the utmost despatch. She had not
been gone half an hour before two gentlemen hastened into
the shop ; one was the Bank clerk who had changed the note.
He begged Mr. Hammond would be good enough to give him
another for it. "Why ?" asked the puzzled shopkeeper.
" Why, sir," replied the distressed clerk, " it is forged !" Of
course his request was not complied with. The clerk declared
that his dismissal was highly probable ; but Mr. Hammond
was inexorable.

The arguments in favour of death punishments never fail so signally as when brought to the test of the scaffold and its effect on Bank Forgeries. Although from twenty to thirty persons were put to death in one year, the gallows was never deprived of an equal share of prey during the next. As long as simulated notes could be passed with ease and detected with difficulty, the Old Bailey had no terrors for clever engravers and dexterous imitators of the hieroglyphic autographs of the Bank of England signers.

Public alarm at the prevalence of forgeries, and the difficulty of knowing them as such, rose to such a height in 1819, that a committee was appointed by the Government to inquire into the best means of prevention. One hundred and eighty projects were submitted. They mostly consisted of expensive and intricate designs. But none were adopted, for the obvious reason that ever so indifferent and easily executed an imitation of an elaborate note deceives an uneducated eye; as had been abundantly proved in the instance of the Irish "black note." The Bank of England had not been indifferent or idle on the subject, for it had spent some hundred thousand pounds in projects for inimitable notes. Not long before the Commission was appointed, they were on the eve of adopting an ingenious and costly mechanism for printing a note so precisely alike on both sides as to appear as one impression, when one of the Bank printers imitated it exactly, by the simple contrivance of two plates and a hinge. This may serve as a test of the value of the remaining one hundred and seventy-nine other projects.

Neither the gallows, nor expensive and elaborate works of art, having been found effectual in preventing forgery, the true expedient for at least lessening the crime was adopted in 1821: the issue of small notes was wholly discontinued, and sovereigns were brought into circulation. The forger's trade was nearly annihilated. Criminal returns inform us that, during the nine years after the resumption of gold currency the number of convictions for offences having reference to the Bank of England notes were less than one hundred, and the executions only eight. This clinches the argument against the efficacy of the gallows. In 1830 death punishments were repealed for all minor offences; and, although the cases of

Bank-note Forgeries slightly increased for a time, yet there is no reason to suppose that they are greater now than they were between 1821 and 1830.

At present Bank forgeries are not numerous. One of the latest was that of the twenty-pound note, of which about sixty specimens found their way into the Bank. It was well executed in Belgium by foreigners, and the impressions were passed among the Change-agents in various towns in France and the Netherlands. The speculation did not succeed; for the notes got into the Bank a little too soon to profit the schemers much.

The most considerable frauds now perpetrated are not forgeries; but are done upon the highwayman's plan mentioned in our first chapter. To give currency to stolen or lost notes which have been stopped at the Bank (lists of which are supplied to every banker in town and country), the numbers and dates are fraudulently altered. Some years since, a gentleman, who had been receiving a large sum of money at the Bank, was robbed of it in an omnibus. The notes gradually came in. All were altered. On the Monday (3d June) after the last "Derby Day," amid the *twenty-five thousand* pieces of paper that were examined by the Bank Inspectors, there was one note for five hundred pounds, dated 12th March, 1848, and numbered 32409, which suddenly arrested the inspector's rapid examination of the pile. He scrutinised it for a minute, and pronounced it "altered." On the next day, that same note, with a perfect one for five hundred pounds, was shown to the writer of this paper with an intimation of the fact. He looks at every letter; he traces every line; follows every flourish; he holds both up to the light; he follows the undulations of the water-mark. He confesses that he cannot pronounce decisively; but he believes, from a slight "goutiness" in the fine stroke of the figure 4, that No. 32409 is the forgery. So indeed it was. Yet the Bank Inspector had picked it out from the hundred genuine notes as instantaneously as if it had been printed with green ink upon cardboard.

This then, O gentlemen forgers and sporting note alterers, is the kind of odds which is against you! A minute investigation of the note assured us of your exceeding skill and inge-

nuity; but it also convinced us of the superiority of the detective ordeal which you have to blind and to pass. In this
instance you had dexterously put the additional marks to the
1, in 32409, to make it into a 4. To hide the scraping out of
the top or serif of the figure 1—to make the angle from which
to draw the fine line of the 4—you had artfully inserted with
a pen the figures "16*l.* 16" as if that sum had been received
from a person bearing a name that you had written above.
You had with extraordinary neatness cut out the "6" from
1846, and filled up the hole with an 8 abstracted from some
note of lesser value. You had fitted it with remarkable precision; only you had not got the 8 quite upright enough to
pass the shrewd glance of the Bank Inspector.

We have seen a one-pound note made up of refuse pieces of
a hundred other Bank-notes, and pasted on a piece of paper
(like a note that had been accidentally torn), so as to present
an entire and passable whole.

To alter with a pen a 1 into a 4 is an easy task—to cut out
the numeral from the *date* in one note and insert it into another,
needs only a tyro in paper-cutting; but to change the special
number by which each note is distinguished, is a feat only
second in impossibility to trumping every court-card of every
suit six times running in a rubber of whist. Yet we have seen
a note so cleverly altered by this expedient, that it was actually paid by the Bank cashiers. If the reader will take a
Bank-note out of his purse, and examine its "number," he will
at once appreciate the combination of chances required to find,
on any other note, any other figure that shall displace any one
of the numerals so as to avoid detection. The number of every
Bank-note is printed twice on one line—first, on the word "I
promise," secondly, on the words, "or bearer." Sometimes
the figures cover the whole of those words; sometimes they
only partly obscure them. No. 99066 now lies before us.
Suppose we wish to substitute the "0" of another note for the
first "9" of the one now under our eye; we see that the "9"
covers a little bit of the "P," and intersects in three places
the "r," in "Promise." Now, to give this alteration the
smallest chance, we must look through hundreds of other
notes till we find an "0" which not only covers a part of the
"P" and intersects the "r" in three places, but in precisely

the same places as the " 9" on our note does; else the strokes
of those letters would not meet when the " 0" was let in,
and instant detection would ensue. But even then the job
would only be half done. The second initial " 9" stands upon
the " or" in " or bearer," and we should have to investigate
several hundred more notes to find an " 0" that intersected
that little word exactly in the same manner, and then let it in
with such mathematical nicety, that not the hundredth part
of a hair's breadth of the transferred paper should fail to
range with the word " bearer," and the rest of the letters and
figures on the altered note; to say nothing of hiding the joints
in the paper. This is the triumph of ambidexterity; it is a
species of patchwork far beyond the most sublime achievements of " Old Patch" himself.

Time has proved that the steady perseverance of the Bank
in gradually improving its original note—and thus preserving
those most essential qualities, simplicity and uniformity—has
been a better preventive to forgery than any one of the hundreds of plans, pictures, engine-turning, chemicals, and colours,
which have been forced upon the Directors' notice. Whole-
note forgery is nearly extinct.

The lives of Eminent Forgers need only wait for a single
addendum. Only one man is left who can claim superiority
over Mathison or Old Patch, and that gentleman was, unfortunately for the Bank of England, born too late to trip up
their heels. He can do everything with a note that the
patchers, and alterers, and simulators, can do, and a great
deal more. Flimsy as a Bank note is to a proverb, he can
split it into three perfect continuous, flat, and even leaves.
He has forged more than one design sent into the Bank as an
infallible preventive to forgery. You may, if you like, lend
him a hundred-pound note : he will undertake to discharge
every trace of ink from it, and return it to you perfectly un-
injured and a perfect blank. We are not quite sure, if you
were to burn a Bank-note and hand him the black cinders,
that he would not bleach it, and join it, and conjure it back
again into a very good-looking, payable piece of currency.
But we *are* sure of the truth of the following story, which we
have from our friend the transcendent forger referred to ; and

who is no other than the chief of the Engraving and Engineering department of the Bank of England.*

Some years ago—in the days of the thirty-shilling notes—a certain Irishman saved up the sum of eighty-seven pounds ten, in notes of the Bank of Ireland. As a sure means of securing this valuable property, he put it in the foot of an old stocking, and buried it in his garden, where bank note paper couldn't fail to keep dry, and to come out, when wanted, in the best preservation.

After leaving his treasure in this excellent place of deposit for some months, it occurred to the depositor to take a look at it, and see how it was getting on. He found the stocking-foot apparently full of the fragments of mildew and broken mushrooms. No other shadow of a shade of eighty-seven pounds ten.

In the midst of his despair, the man had the sense not to disturb the ashes of his property. He took the stocking-foot in his hand, posted off to the Bank in Dublin, entered it one morning as soon as it was opened, and, staring at the clerk with a most extraordinary absence of all expression in his face, said:

"Ah, look at that, sir! Can ye do anything for me?"

"What do you call this?" said the clerk.

"Eighty-sivin pound tin, praise the Lord, as I'm a sinner! Ohone! There was a twinty as was paid to me by Mr. Phalim O'Dowd, sir, and a tin as was changed by Pat Reilly, and a five as was owen by Tim; and Ted Connor, ses he to ould Phillips—

"Well! Never mind old Phillips. You have done it, my friend!"

"Oh Lord, sir, and it's done it I have, most com-plate! Oh, good luck to you, sir, can you do nothing for me?"

"I don't know what's to be done with such a mess as this. Tell me, first of all, what you put in the stocking, you unfortunate blunderer?"

"Oh yes, sir, and tell you true as if it was the last word I had to spake entirely, and the Lord be good to you, and Ted

---

* Mr. Oldham, who unhappily died not long after this narrative was first published.

Connor ses he to ould Phillips, regarden the five as was owen
by Tim, and not includen of the tin which was changed by
Pat Reilly——"

"You didn't put Pat Reilly or ould Phillips into the stocking, did you?"

"Is it Pat or ould Phillips as was ever the valy of eighty-
sivin pound tin, lost and gone, and includen the five as was
owen by Tim, and Ted Connor——"

"Then tell me what you *did* put in the stocking, and let
me take it down. And then hold your tongue, if you can,
and go your way, and come back to-morrow."

The particulars of the notes were taken, without any reference to ould Phillips: who could not, however, by any means,
be kept out of the story; and the man departed. When he
was gone, the stocking-foot was shown to the Chief Engraver
of the notes, who said that if anybody could settle the business, his son could. And he proposed that the particulars of
the notes should not be communicated to his son, who was
then employed in his department of the Bank, but should be
put away under lock and key; and that if his son's ingenuity
should enable him to discover from these ashes what notes had
really been put in the stocking, and the two lists should tally,
the man should be paid the lost amount. To this prudent
proposal the Bank of Ireland readily assented; being extremely anxious that the man should not be a loser; but, of
course, deeming it essential to be protected from imposition.

The son readily undertook the delicate commission proposed
to him. He detached the fragments from the stocking with
the utmost care, on the fine point of a penknife; laid the
whole gently in a basin of warm water; and presently saw
them, to his delight, begin to unfold and expand like flowers.
By-and-by, he began to "tease them" with very light touches
of a camel's-hair pencil, and so, by little and little, and by the
most delicate use of the warm water, the camel's-hair pencil,
and the penknife, got the various morsels separate before him,
and began to piece them together. The first piece laid down
was faintly recognisable by a practised eye as a bit of the left-
hand bottom corner of a twenty-pound note; then came a bit
of a five; then of a ten; then more bits of a twenty; then more
bits of a five and ten; then, another left-hand bottom corner of

a twenty—so there were two twenties!—and so on, until, to the admiration and astonishment of the whole Bank, he noted down the exact amount deposited in the stocking, and the exact notes of which it had been composed. Upon this, as he wished to see and divert himself with the man on his return— he provided himself with a bundle of corresponding new, clean, rustling notes, and awaited his arrival.

He came exactly as before, with the same blank staring face, and the same inquiry, "Can you do anything for me, sir?"

"Well," said our friend, "I don't know. Maybe I *can* do something. But I have taken a great deal of pains, and lost a great deal of time, and I want to know what you mean to give me!"

"Is it give sir? Thin, is there anything I wouldn't give for my eighty-sivin pound tin, sir; and its murdered I am by ould Phillips."

"Never mind him; there were two twenties, were there not?"

"Oh, holy mother, sir, there was! Two most illigant twenties! and Ted Connor—and Phalim—which Reilly——"

He faultered and stopped, as our friend, with much ostentatious rustling of the crisp paper, produced a new twenty, and then the other twenty, and then a ten, and then a five, and so forth. Meanwhile, the man, occasionally murmuring an exclamation of surprise, or a protestation of gratitude, but gradually becoming vague and remote in the latter as the notes reappeared, looked on, staring, evidently inclined to believe that they were the real lost notes, reproduced in that state by some chemical process. At last they were all told out, and in his pocket, and he still stood staring and muttering, "Oh, holy mother, only to think of it! Sir, it's bound to you for ever that I am!"—but more vaguely and remotely now than before.

"Well," said our friend, "What do you propose to give me for this?"

After staring and rubbing his chin for some time longer, he replied with the unexpected question:

"Do you like bacon?"

"Very much," said our friend.

7

"Thin it's a side as I'll bring your honour to-morrow morn-ing, and a bucket of new milk—and ould Phillips——"

"Come," said our friend, glancing at a notable shillelagh the man had under his arm, "let me undeceive you. I don't want anything of you, and I am very glad you have got your money back. But I suppose you'd stand by me, now, if I wanted a boy to help me in any little skirmish?"

They were standing by a window on the top story of the Bank, commanding a court-yard, where a sentry was on duty. To our friend's amazement, the man dashed out of the room without speaking one word, suddenly appeared in the court-yard, performed a war-dance round this astonished soldier—who was a modest young recruit—made the shillelagh flutter, like a wooden butterfly, round his musket, round his bayonet, round his head, round his body, round his arms, inside and outside his legs, advanced and retired, rattled it all round him like a fire-work, looked up at the window, cried out with a high leap in the air, "Whooroo! Thry me!"—vanished—and never was beheld at the Bank again from that time forth.

XIII.

A SUBURBAN ROMANCE.

DECEMBER 14, 1850.

WHEN I became an incumbent of the parochial district of St. Barnabas, Copenhagen-lanes, I lodged in Peppermint-place. Peppermint-place was then creeping its way into the fields, with the apparent determination not to stop till it had reached Highgate. The march of brick and mortar had pushed on two ranks of houses, in all conditions, from snug finish to cheerless rooflessness. I went to take rooms in number one, on a drizzling afternoon. My landlord assured me, while ex-tending his arm out of a back window over a landscape in the last stage of damp decay, that the situation was " uncommon cheerful." It displayed a few dismantled garden allotments; a superannuated summer-house despondently lying against a deserted pigsty; bunches of drooping hollyhocks broken down by the weight of their misfortunes; patches of cabbages and other greens sicklied o'er with the pale cast of lime ; and tulips struggling up out of beds, between brick-bats, in agonies of strangulation. This uncommonly cheerful situation was finished by a background of damp and ragged hedge ; the next mouthful of the green and patient Country to be swallowed by the dense, insatiate Town.

The chief attraction from my sitting-room in front of the house was a clayey slough, in which a succession of brick-carts was continually stuck during all the working hours of the day ; yet the boundary to this prospect was far from uninviting. Several of the opposite houses were finished and inhabited. The neatest and prettiest of them was that immediately facing my room. If window-curtains were ever made of woven snow, that must have been the material of those at the first-floor window of the modest habitation. There was so much taste in the disposition of the crocuses and snowdrops in the window-sill ; such pleasure taken in concealing the wires of the bird-cage in branches of geranium and intertwined primroses, that I was reminded of one of those charming little cottage windows which belong to a French landscape. Nor was this impression weakened when I occasionally espied — but very seldom — between the rows of bobfringe that dangled merrily from the curtains, the face of a lovely brunette, framed in bandeaux of jet hair, and illuminated by a pair of piercing black eyes.

What busy eyes they were! Though I seldom saw *them*, I could see what they were doing all day long ; for, although everything being dark, but the curtains, as if to correspond to them (their owner was in mourning), I could observe how the little lady in black employed herself behind the film of white muslin. She was incessantly bending over a frame, and I could guess, from the motion of the arm nearest the window, that she embroidered, or did something of that sort, all day long. Now and then the hand appeared to move higher than the frame, and I supposed, from the angle of the elbow, that she was pressing it against her over-wrought eyes. Poor girl! No wonder if they ached ; for, from morning till evening, every day, except Sundays, during all that cold and cheerless spring, she was to be seen busily at work. Except on Sunday mornings—I suppose to go to church—she never went abroad ; and no other living soul was ever observed in her room.

In the course of months, my observations of the captivating
SILHOUETTE—so I had nicknamed the little black profile—
were more frequent than polite. The little gauze of mystery
which half-veiled her, piqued my curiosity; and I could safely
indulge in it, as my draperies were much less aërial than hers.
Though the east wind blew with continued intensity, and it
was quite an effort to leave one's fireside, she was never during
daylight away from her window. Sometimes I could distinguish that she paused, leant her head on her hand, and gazed
earnestly directly under where I sat. Then, as if suddenly
caught in the act, she would turn like lightning to her frame,
and the little black arm would move up and down with greater
rapidity. There was a curious coincidence connected with
these fits of abstraction and starts of work: they happened
inversely to the proceedings of my clever young landlord below (inlayer, carver, and cabinet-maker); for, during the moments of my Silhouette's fascination, his saw, his chisel, his
plane, or hammer were in full and noisy operation; and it was
exactly at the instant that either of these tools was laid down
and the sound ceased, that my little lady resumed her work.
I was convinced one morning that this coincidence was no
mere fancy. Friend Bevil was making sharp, short, lively
strokes with his plane. The damsel opposite tracing an embroidery pattern against the glass. The tracing goes on well
enough for a while; but, presently, the left hand is lifted to
the little head, the tip of the elbow rests against the window-
frame, the tracing no longer hangs against the glass by the
point of the pencil, and the black eyes pour their rays straight
into the window below me. The shavings are still being
turned off merrily; but, hark!—the plane suddenly stops!—
and see! the piquant little artist has vanished from the window.
Presently the planing is continued with a slow and pensive
regularity that makes me feel quite low-spirited.

Although mine was a pastoral as well as an ecclesiastical
charge of the St. Barnabas district, and I was bound to watch
over my flock, yet it may be said that such close scrutiny of
my neighbours as that which I have confessed to, was scarcely
dignified; but it must be remembered that what I have here
brought together in a short space was spread over several
months. The arduous duties of a new district did not admit

of much idle window gazing. My church was only a temporary one, and I made it my business to call, in succession, on
my parishioners; not only to make myself personally acquainted with each, but to invite them all to worship. I began this
mission at home; for, although my landlord's mother was a
regular attendant at church, the son never once made his appearance within its walls.

Old Mrs. Bevil was a large lady of painfully timid temper-
ament, whose existence was passed in one of the sunken
kitchens, and whose mission on earth was apparently to cook
glue for the shop, vouchsafing any of the time to be spared
between the steaming of the pots, in attendance upon me.
One Saturday morning I expressed my regret to her that so
excellent and industrious a son should appear to be negligent
to his Sabbath duties.

"He is n't!" said Mrs. Bevil, sidling towards the door, and
feeling, with a hand outstretched behind her, for the handle.

I should mention that Mrs. Bevil was so much "put out"
when spoken to by any one above her in station, that, when
you showed symptoms of engaging her in talk, she winced
and made artful efforts to escape.

"What church does he go to?"

"French Protestant, sir."

"Indeed! then he is conversant with the French language?"

Mrs. Bevil had by this time found the door-knob, and had
turned it. Her confusion was so great that her face—never
very pale—glowed like a live coal.

"Of course," I repeated, "as your son attends a French
place of worship, he understands French?"

In the midst of her bewilderment Mrs. Bevil stammered,

"Yes, sir—French polishing."

I then asked, perhaps rather too abruptly (for I tried to help
laughing) if she knew anything of the mysterious young woman opposite?

Mrs. Bevil curtseyed herself backwards into the opening of
the door, and having felt that retreat was practicable, she said
"Please, sir; no, sir;" and vanished with the rapidity of a
large mouse let out of a cage.

It was not difficult to guess why young Bevil preferred the
French church to my own. I had never doubted that the

charming embroideress opposite was a foreigner. She worshipped in a language she understood best; and her admirer —more in obedience to his silent passion than his spiritual professions—followed her thither to worship *her*. On expatiating to him one day, however, on the sinfulness of Sabbath-breaking, he partially disarmed me by owning that he had been assiduously learning French in order to understand, and join in the service. I made not the slightest allusion to the Silhouette; for I saw, from his nervous and blushing manner, it was too deep an affair with him to be lightly touched. I ascertained that, although he saw his adored daily, and followed her weekly to church, he had never had courage to speak to her, nor to address her in any way whatever.

My interest in this case deepened daily. I pitied young Bevil. Supposing, after he had proceeded to the extremity of avowed courtship, his idol should prove a wicked little French coquette, and jilt him? Such a presentiment did not want foundation. Although the summer had arrived—and warmer, more congenial weather, I never remember—the Silhouette disappeared entirely from behind the fairy curtains. During all the cold weather, when she must have shivered while sitting there, she was never absent; but now, when the window is the only endurable part of the room, she is utterly invisible. Is she skilfully manœuvering Love's sensitive telegraph, conscious that she has secured her victim; and now, after the manner of finished coquettes, she leaves him to the throes of despair. Or, does she doubt the truth and ardency of his love, as expressed by his silent watchings of her window, and by his regular church-goings; and does she disappear from his longing, loving looks to lure him quickly to the overt-act —a verbal declaration? If the latter, her tactics will fail. Young Bevil's passion is not a mere flash of romance; it is earnest and practical. He does not stand idly gazing, and sighing, and hoping, and despairing. The more he loves the harder he works. Until he has placed himself in a position to speak to her with confidence as to the future, he will be silent.

Here I am probably asked, how could I know all this? I answer;—from substantial evidence. When one sees a man running a race, it is certain that there is, far or near, a goal.

Young Bevil raced manfully, and the winning-post he kept in view was matrimony. Early and late his tools were in use. When I first took his lodgings, they were scantily furnished; but the rooms were rapidly filling; evidently not for *my* use and pleasure. The capacious tea-caddy, curiously inlaid and splendidly mounted, did not signify much to me; neither was I ever likely to require the Gothic work-table that I found one evening slid, as if by accident into a recess; and to what earthly use could a bachelor in lodgings put that frame on swivels, studded all round with cribbage-pegs? Every addition to the apartments was of the feminine gender. I looked upon these novelties as so many notices to quit; for I did not doubt that the rooms were being quietly prepared for a cherished occupant. This supposition was confirmed, when, curiosity prompting me to examine the work-table, I saw, exquisitely inlaid in cypher on the inside of the lid, the word " Manette."

All this while, the Silhouette remained obstinately invisible. For a few Sundays she continued to go to church; but, so thickly veiled, that a sight of her face was impossible. Still he followed; but refrained from speaking. The time had not come. He would not offer his rough but honest hand while yet without a home to which it could lead her.

Poor Bevil had soon to live on not only in silent, but in sightless despair; the little black profile ceased to appear not only behind her snowy transparencies, but bodily on Sundays. From this time Bevil's intelligent, but sad and thoughtful features struck me with pity. I could not but see during my daily gossip with him in passing through the shop, that he was staking his very existence on a cast, which might turn up a deadly blank.

On one occasion, my hopes revived for him. It was towards the close of a lovely summer's day. The whiteness of the gossamer curtains made them dazzle in the sun. The figure in black approached; and, after a hesitating interval, appeared in distinct outline close behind the gauze. All this while, the sharp cuts of Bevil's chisel were audible in busy succession under me. The Silhouette's eyes only, appeared just above the short curtain, darting a long, devouring gaze upon the toiler: they were red. The chisel goes on chipping

away, without one intermission. I would give a quarter's
stipend if Bevil would only be idle for a second, and look up;
for, as the gazer strains her eyes upon him, tears pour out of
them, and sparkle in the sun like falling diamonds. Presently
she disappears. With this anguish, whatever its immediate
cause, I felt certain that Bevil was connected.

"Surely this mystery is not impenetrable. I will unravel
it." Accordingly, next morning I took our opposite neighbours out of the regular order of my visits, called, and questioned the woman who rented the house. I learnt that the
girl's name *was* Manette. She was an orphan: her father, a
French teacher, had died recently in an hospital. Her embroidery was fetched and carried to and from the warehouse
by my informant's husband. Her industry was extraordinary,
and she earned a comfortable subsistence. Lately, she had
been ill; something that had altered her face; for she had
taken to concealing it. I asked to see her; but was told she
admitted no person whatever into her room.

My inquiries, therefore, darkened rather than cleared up
the mystery. As I left the house, I observed that my landlord had been watching. He looked wistfully into my face as
I passed him on the door-step, and I answered his appeal by
desiring him to follow me to my room.

A short conversation proved that all my observations and
deductions had been correctly made. He owned everything.
It was painful to see a fine, muscular, handsome man, suffused
with the shame—honest shame though it was—trembling with
the weakness we only expect in young and tender girls. I
reasoned with him. I showed him the full risk he ran in nur-
turing so perfect an ideal out of a mere image. I pointed out
the uselessness of his self-imposed penance. She might be all
he thought her; she might be everything the reverse. How
could he know without some acquaintanceship? It would be
madness to give rashly a pledge of matrimony without some
probation.

In the end he promised to try and see Manette the following
day; and, descending to his shop, worked away harder than
ever.

Even now I see Bevil as, next morning, he stands at the
door opposite. His lips quiver; but his brow expresses a firm

but anxious purpose. The woman who admits him tells him something which surprises and disappoints him. Manette, for the first time for a month, has gone out.—The next day was Sunday, and the lover abstained from intruding himself. On the Monday he had as little success. In the evening he consulted me as to what he had better do. Should he write?

I advised him by no means to commit himself in that way; and offered, if he would wait, to use the influence of my cloth to obtain an interview for him. When the morning came, Bevil desired to accompany me. He would, he said, go himself; but would feel comforted and fortified by my presence.

Accordingly we sallied forth across the road at noon the next morning. I would not wait to hear the answer of the landlady; but, pushing by the driver of a spring-cart that had just stopped at the house, went straight up to Manette's door. Bevil followed. I knocked. No answer. Not a sound within. I knocked again, and quietly called her by name. Utter silence. I then tried the door; it yielded, and we entered.

The picture of neatness and prettiness which I had drawn as existing behind the dainty muslin curtains was not realised. It was reversed. The room was in the greatest confusion, and was untenanted. "Why you see, sir," said the woman of the house who had ushered the carter up behind us, Madamselle went away the first thing yesterday morning. She was so weak, that she could hardly get into the cab as took her away. She sold her bits of things to the broker (you'll have to get the sofa-bed out o' window, Mr. Bracket), and never give us no notice in a regular way (now mind the walls with them saucepans!), leastways not a week's; but my husband never went for to charge her, poor thing, for she was so very petickler: she paid as punctual as the Monday morning cum."

"Has she left her present address?" I asked.

"O dear no, quit contra-ry. Says she to me, says she—leastways as well as I could understand her French brogue, and she had her han'kercher a kivering of her face—Mrs. Blinkinson," says she, "don't," says she, "answer no questions as may be asked about me. I am a going," says she, "to where I hope nobody may find me out." And then she

pulled the street door to, and I never see no more of her—
and never shall."

I looked at Bevil. He gazed round the room slowly,
vacantly. The bird was lying at the bottom of its cage—
dead. The flowers, no longer tended, were drooping. He
stretched forth his trembling hand, and plucked a geranium.
He then turned, and, without speaking, descended the stairs.
With unsteady gait he entered his own house.

For more than a week I missed the sounds from below.
Bevil had shut himself up in his bedroom. His mother now,
instead of tending him with glue-pots, was constantly on the
stairs with broths, and coffee, and tea, and other sloppy sustenance; but her son would partake of them but very sparingly.
I determined to rouse him, and advised that, as he would not
or could not work, an active search after the lost damsel was
better than stolid, inactive grief. This did rouse him, and he
followed my advice.

Weary days and weary weeks were spent in the search.
The cunning Silhouette eluded him like an *Ombre Chinoise*.
Bevil first addressed himself to the shop for which Manette
had worked. The master of it said that he never saw Manette
but once, and then she came with specimens of her embroidery,
to get work. It was so good that he had employed her ever
since, and was both surprised and chagrined at her sudden
desertion. He had, through her landlord, offered her a good
salary to work at his house, and had hoped she would have
accepted it. Her strange disappearance was therefore the
more unaccountable.

The clergyman of the French church, when Bevil sought
him, was as surprised as her lover, at Manette's absence from
service and communion. In the latter he said she was a
regular and deeply impressed partaker. He could give no
information. Neither could the officers of the hospital, where
the girl's father had died in the winter, give him comfort.

"There is nothing for it," I told him one day, "but time
and work."

Bevil did, after a time, resume his work; but his tools were
taken up and laid down with a slow, intermittent apathy,
which showed that the heart and the hands did not go together.

Work, on the contrary, grew so fast on *my* hands, that I hardly had time for sleep. My successor to the curacy I had left in Southwark was taken ill, and, besides my own duty, I had volunteered to do a part of his. This occasionally consisted in administering consolation and prayer to the inmates of one of the Borough hospitals.

During one of my visits to the female ward, I was attracted by a few words which fell from the clinical lecturer who was addressing a knot of pupils standing at the bed on a case of tumour of the face. He had, in fact (warming with his subject), glided from details of the operation which had been performed and of the after-treatment, to an involuntary allusion on the beauty of the patient, which the consequences of the disease and its remedy tended to impair. I got a peep at the damsel between the shoulders of a couple of medical students, and saw just above the bedclothes (which were held up with extreme care to conceal the lower part of the face) a pair of familiar black eyes. They quite thrilled through me. The students were dismissed; and I overheard a sweet voice ask something of the surgeon.

"Don't let it trouble you for one instant," said Mr. Fleam, as he left the bedside; "it will hardly be visible, and, in a week, you will be as well—and almost as pretty—as ever."

I looked again. Those piercing black eyes met mine pointblank. The little head was instantly concealed under the bedclothes.

But that was enough. I felt convinced that Manette was found.

About a month from that date there was joy at No. 1 Peppermint-place. It is November: on one side of my fireplace sit Bevil and Manette. Old Mrs. Bevil has gradually pushed her chair back to the window; and, bit by bit, has nibbled, in her nervous hand, folds of the curtain, until she is completely hidden behind it in that comfortable obscurity in which she alone delights. They had assembled to hear a lecture from me.

"Personal vanity," I began, with all the solemnity to be invoked in the presence of a pair of eyes, which sparkled so brightly with joy, that it seemed impossible for their mistres to school and temper them for the occasion—"the vanity of mere personal comliness had nearly wrecked the happiness of both of you. Because you, Manette, were afflicted with a disease that distorted, for a time, that which you seemed to cherish more than your worldly welfare—your beauty—you sold your worldly goods and deserted your home and means of subsistence, rather than the deformity should be seen by one whom you secretly loved. Had you no confidence in the attractions which never fade, that you depended solely upon those which, despite all your efforts, will assuredly pass away?"

"*Non,*" said Manette, lifting her eyelids with a sort of timid courage. "He love me only for my face—he 'ad nevare spoken. When he saw and loved my face, it was *comme il faut. Eh, bien!* if he 'ad seen my face when it was horrib' disfiguré, would he not have hate me? *Oui.*"

The end of this, like that of most other romances, was marriage. With marriage, as is well known, all mysteries vanish. Manette's story was this: Her father was a political refugee from the storm of 1848; he had been a staunch Orleanist Deputy in the French Chamber, and had to fly, with his daughter, for his life. In England he taught his native tongue as a means of livelihood, till overtaken by illness. Then Manette practised an accomplishment she was proficient in with so much success, that she supported her father till his death. She knew the time would come when the family property they possessed near Bordeaux would be restored, and she did not wish to let her situation be known; hence, she kept herself a recluse till her terrible sufferings and disappointment drove her to the hospital.

I was not allowed the honor of officiating: the minister of the French Protestant Chapel having been preferred. Of course I was obliged to remove to another lodging.

Passing the shop the other day, I was surprised to find another name over the door. The owner of it told me that Mr. Bevil had gone to live in France, in order to superintend his wife's estate on the Garonne. It appeared, then, that my piquant Silhouette had regained her patrimony. The next holiday I get I shall certainly pay her and her husband a visit.

XIV.

RAILWAY WAIFS AND STRAYS.

DECEMBER 28, 1850.

GENTLEMEN who will look out of the windows of railway carriages to see "what's the matter," and get their hats blown off and left behind at the rate of fifty miles an hour; third-class young Ladies who will hold parasols over their complexions on windy days, and let them go ballooning down the line at hurricane pace; Dandies who won't look after their own luggage, but leave everything to "those fellows," the porters, and so lose it; Wives who will terminate their journeys at the terminus in their husbands' arms, regardless of their "trifles from Tunbridge" packed up in pretty baskets; Commercial Travellers who forget their samples; Young Gents who rush away without their canes, and Old Gents who fuss off without their pocket pistols; Aunts who leave behind their umbrellas; Nieces oblivious of their patterns;—in short, everybody who misses, or forgets, or leaves behind, or mislays anything on a railway, may consider it nearly as safe as if they had not been stupid, or careless, or in too great a hurry, or forgetful;—and have a much better chance of finding it than if they had lost it at home.

To the terminus of most railways is attached what the French would call an *administration* or *service*, consisting of a warehouse and staff of clerks and porters, for the deposit and restoration of the lost or left behind. These, for variety and value, would put to shame the dazzling and heterogeneous treasures of Don Rolando's Cave. Inspecting one of these offices some time since, the writer had occasion to describe the scene in the following terms:

A visit to this depository would repay a philosopher. He might readily guess at the owners from the articles—they are so thoroughly characteristic. Some of the single articles are in themselves idiosyncracies; whilst many of the bundles tie up unwritten histories, and journals of travel. There was one which we had the curiosity to inspect, that belonged, there can be not the smallest doubt, to a courier or a valet. It was

formed by a silk handkerchief tied by the corners, in one of
the ends of which were secured about sixpennyworth of Italian
halfpence. Its contents proved to be pretty nearly as follows:
A pair of hair-brushes; a chart and tariff of fares of the Austrian Lloyd's Steam-Boats Company; a small jar of preserved
meat beside a pot of bear's-grease, to give it a flavour; a play-
bill of the San Scala Theatre, where the owner had, it would
seem, the pleasure of hearing Donizetti's new opera of "La
Regna del Golconda;" a case of toothpicks, a Prussian bill for
post-horses, a comb, a half-nibbled pipe of maccaroni, and a
screw of tobacco, the savour of which imparted the predomi-
nating smell to the entire bundle.

From this pleasing amalgamation, an experienced tourist
might have traced a complete *carte du voyage*. It presented
a map of the owner's route, which began in an English per-
fumer's shop—for the hair-brushes and bear's-grease were of
British manufacture—was continued through Italy to the office
of the Austrian Lloyd's in Vienna, and back to the Dover
terminus by way of Prussia.

Before we pry into the next parcel, we must make an apology
for breaking the sacred confidence of a lady's basket; but the
breach was irresistible. There it stood, a straw-bonnet-like
receptacle bound with red leather, having a close-shutting flap
and no button—which is our apology. Within we found a
pair of ladies' shoes, the neat covering of as pretty a foot as
ever stepped out of a carriage—railway or family—wrapped
up in a quarto leaf of a popular religious periodical. Beside
them lay, *horresco referens!* a pint bottle, which emitted an
odor neither of Rose-water, nor of Eau-de-Cologne, but of
very excellent Geneva. Could there have been, however, any
doubt as to the nature of the spirit, it would have been cleared
up at the bottom of the basket, where there lay a wine-glass
without a foot. On whom shall we fix the ownership of this
treasure? Shall it be a muddling duenna, entrusted with her
lovely mistress's shoes, or—a more probable conjecture—a
"serious" lady slightly addicted to gin?

Our old friend, Mrs. Gamp, was as plain on one of the shelves
as if she stood before us. She was personified by a cotton
umbrella, with a tremendous horn-head, and a pair of pattens
as tall and as clumsy as Dutch horse-shoes. Beside these was

stretched at full length a well-folded, well-brushed, precise-looking silk umbrella, very seedy at the edges, with a dingy ivory knob, the property, we infer, of an elderly bachelor of limited income. Slim umbrellas, of foreign extraction, in polished leather cases, stood beside family concerns which would answer for pic-nic tents, having convenient wires to hang up the ladies' bonnets. There were some with comic handles carved to resemble Punch and Tim Bobbin, grimly contrasting with ivory Death's-heads. The umbrella shelf, in short, is a collection of silk, gingham, and whalebone characters, as palpable as those of Theophrastus or La Bruyère.

Commend us, however, to the hat-shelf; for nothing can exceed the heterogeneous jumble of rank, station, character, and indicative morality which that conglomeration presents. Here, a dissipated-looking four-and-nine leans its battered side against the prim shovel of a church dignitary; there, a highly-polished Parisian silk hat is smashed under the weight of a carter's slouch. On one side, the torn brim of a broad straw strays into the open crown of a bran new beaver. Some bear the crushing marks of the wheels of a luggage-train, or the impression of the moistened clay of an embankment; others are neat, trimly brushed, and show how carefully they have been hung up in the first-class carriage while the owner inducted his caput into a Templar or foraging cap, and how he carelessly left it behind. Boys' and men's, quakers' and soldiers', carters' and lords', clergymen's and sporting-men's are all ranged side by side, or thrown together higgledy-piggledy, topsy-turvy, in such a confusion that, should an applicant endeavour to comply with the clerk's suggestion to "Choose your own, sir," he would be in very great danger of committing petty larceny, and find his head under somebody else's hat. If, however, these head-casings were arranged according to their owners' probable rank in life, they would plainly indicate their wearers' station and mode of travelling. There would be first-class hats, consisting of sporting, clerical, military, and best beavers—second-class, all neat and well brushed —and third-class, carters', carpenters', valets', and hay-makers'.

Over and above articles left behind by mistake, some are impounded, and consist of forced deposits exacted in satisfaction of unpaid fares. A gentleman has forgotten to provide himself with the cash necessary for the beginning of every railroad journey. In such cases the majesty of the law, clothed in green, institutes prompt proceedings, and, suing out a peremptory *fieri facias* (or legal spontaneous combustion), puts in an immediate execution on the debtor's movables, and distrains on the spot, in a sufficient amount to cover the debt and costs. Such deposits generally consist of walking-sticks of various sizes and values, pocket-handkerchiefs, whips, and workmen's tools. Odd mixtures are made in this way. One insolvent traveller was deprived of a twelve-rowel ladder; another, a doctor's boy (who had, perhaps, dissipated his master's money in hardbake), had nothing left to offer to the ruthless cashiers but a few bottles of physic. And there they stand, labelled with the usual directions to be taken every three hours, in far more harmlessness than if they had reached their destinations.

As evidence of carelessness these deposits are scarcely credible. We were shown purses innumerable, all containing money, sometimes as much as from ten to fifty pounds, jewellery of every sort and description, from whole suites to single rings and breast-pins; all left behind in carriages. It is difficult to imagine how it is that the losers *can* get quit of some of the articles without carrying carelessness and forgetfulness to an extraordinary point of ingenuity. A glove, a shawl, a handkerchief, or a walking-stick are readily left behind; and so to umbrellas, to be lost would seem to be one of the functions they are manufactured to fulfil; but how a ring, which must cost some trouble to remove from the finger; a watch which, when a question of time has been decided, it is usual to return to the pocket—can be left in a railway carriage, is not easily to be comprehended.

The most astonishing kind of property to leave behind, at a railway station, is mentioned in an advertisement, which appeared in the newspapers, dated Swindon, April 27th, 1844. It gave notice, "that a pair of bright bay carriage-horses, about sixteen hands high, with black switch tails and manes," had been left there in the name of Hibbert; and notice was given, that unless the horses were claimed on or before the 12th day of May, they would be sold to pay expenses. Accordingly on that day they *were* sold.

The lost luggage warehouse, of another railway—that at the North-Western Railway terminus—has been cleverly sketched by Sir Francis Head. It consists " of," he says, " a large pitch-dark subterranean vaulted chamber, warmed by hot-air iron pipes, in which are deposited the flock of lost sheep, or without metaphor, the lost luggage of the last two years. Suspended from the roof, there hangs horizontally in this chamber a gas-pipe about eight feet long, and as soon as the brilliant burners at each end were lighted, the scene was really astounding. It would be infinitely easier to say what there is not than what there is in the forty compartments, like great wine-bins, in which all this lost property is arranged. One is choke-full of men's hats, another of parasols, umbrellas, and sticks of every possible description. One would think that all the ladies' reticules on earth were deposited in a third. How many little smelling-bottles—how many little embroidered pocket-handkerchiefs—how many little musty eatables and comfortable drinkables—how many little bills, important little notes, and other very small secrets each may have contained, we felt that we would not for the world have ascertained ; but when we gazed at the enormous quantity of red cloaks, red shawls, red tartan plaids, and red scarfs, piled up in one corner, it was, we own, impossible to help reflecting that surely English ladies of all ages, who wear red cloaks, &c., must in some mysterious way or other be powerfully affected by the whine of compressed air, by the sudden ringing of a bell, by the sight of their friends—in short, by the various conflicting emotions that disturb the human heart on arriving at the up-terminus of the Euston Station ; for else how, we gravely asked ourselves, could we possibly account for the extraordinary red heap before us ? Of course there were plenty of carpet-bags, gun-cases, portmanteaus, writing-desks, books, bibles, cigar-cases, &c., but there were a few articles that certainly we were not prepared to meet with, and which but too clearly proved that the extraordinary terminus-excitement which had so suddenly caused so many virtuous ladies to elope from their red shawls—in short, to be all of a sudden not only in a ' bustle' behind, but all over—had equally affected men of all sorts and conditions. One gentleman had left behind him a pair of leather hunting-breeches !

another his boot-jack! A soldier of the Twenty-second Regiment had left his knapsack containing his kit! Another soldier, of the Tenth, poor fellow, had left his scarlet regimental coat! But what astonished us above all was, that some honest Scotchman, probably in the ecstasy of suddenly seeing among the crowd the face of his faithful Jeanie, had actually left behind him the best portion of his bagpipes!"

The trouble which is bestowed by the railway companies to cause the restitution of lost property is incalculable. Not long ago, a young lady lost a portmanteau from the rest of her luggage—a pardonable oversight, for she was a bride starting on the honeymoon trip. The bridegroom—never on such occasions an accountable being—had not noticed the misfortune. When the loss was discovered and application made respecting it, the lady spoke positively of having seen it at the station whence they started; then again at a station where they had to change carriages; she saw it also when they left the railway. She was also certain that it was amongst the rest of the "things" when they again started; but when they arrived at their destination, it was missing. It contained a new riding-habit, value fifteen pounds. The search that was instituted for this portmanteau recalled that of Telemachus for Ulysses; the railway officials sent one of their clerks with a *carte blanche*, to trace the bride's journey to the end of the last mile, till some tidings of the strayed trunk could be traced. He went to every station, to every coach-office in connexion with every station, to every town, to every hotel, and to every lodging that the happy couple had visited. His expenses actually amounted to fifteen pounds. He came back without success. At length the treasure was found; but where?—At the by-station on another line, whence the bride had started from home, on the previous morning, a maiden. Yet she had positively declared without doubt or reservation, that she had "with her own eyes" seen the trunk on the previous stages of her tour. This can only be accounted for by the peculiar flustration of the young lady just plunged into the vortex of matrimony. The husband paid the whole of the cost.

In further illustration of the pains taken to return missing property by the railway company, we may revert to Sir Francis Head, on the North-Western:—A ledger, entitled "Luggage

Inquiry Book," is kept, and if the articles therein inquired after have not been brought in by the searcher, copies of the description are forwarded to each of the offices where lost luggage is kept; for by the company's orders all luggage found between Wolverton and London is without delay forwarded to the latter station, all between Wolverton and Birmingham to Birmingham, and so on. "It is possible, however, that the above orders may not have been attended to, and therefore, as a last resource, the Superintendent of the Lost Luggage Office at Euston Station writes to three hundred and ten stations on forty-two lines of rail to inquire after a lost article, be it ever so small, and if it be at none of these stations, a letter is then addressed to the owner, informing him that his lost property *is not on the railway*."

We are sorry to find that the public do not always show themselves so conscientious as the companies. The authorities are, as carriers, liable—under certain circumstances—to make good the losses of their customers; and in some cases articles are no sooner missing than an apparent eagerness to turn them into cash is displayed. A demand for payment is sent. The managers demur; and, ask for particulars; then arrives a long list of contents. The value to the highest possible amount is set upon every describable thing; and, after many *pros* and *cons*, a settlement is generally made upon a very reduced scale of charges. One such demand was sent in the other day by an elderly lady and her sister, who said they had lost a box of apparel. They set the contents down at thirty pounds prime cost. Upon the eve of payment of a sum something approaching to this demand, the box was recovered, and five pounds proved to be the utmost value of it, with all it contained. In another instance, a gentleman of property lost a leather hat-case, containing "very valuable articles," but did not, in his modesty, name their exact worth in money. For some time the search was fruitless, and a heavy drag upon the treasury was anticipated—when, at the eleventh hour, the hat-case was "washed ashore" as the wreckers would say, and the value of the inside did not prove so much as that of the outside—the price of a second-hand hat-box.

On the North-Western Railway, luggage left behind at the stations is kept for two days, and if, during that time, no one calls for it, it is, if it be *properly addressed* (a proviso which should impress all travellers with the advantage of legible labels), forwarded to its owner. Should there be no address, it is kept for a month, and then opened to find a clue to the possessor. Some time ago the superintendent, on breaking open a locked leather hat-box, found in it, under the hat, sixty-five pounds in Bank of England notes, with one or two private letters, which enabled him to restore the money to the owner; who, it turned out, had been so positive that he had left his hat-box at an hotel at Birmingham, that he had made no inquiry for it at the railway office.

Lastly, should no clue whatever be found to ownership, the property is kept about two years, and has hitherto been sold by auction in the large coach-factory to the company's servants—a portion of the proceeds being handed over to the sick-fund for persons who have been hurt in the service, and the remainder to " the Friendly Society" among the men. It having, however, been ascertained that a few of the railway men who had spare cash purchased the greater portion of these articles, it has been determined henceforward to sell the whole of this property by auction exclusively to the public; and, as the company's servants are not allowed to be purchasers, they can no longer derive any benefit whatever from lost property.

The quantity and value of property thus remaining, even after passing through the two days' and two months' test, is almost incredible; and while it surprises, it may amuse the reader to glance over a list of the two years' accumulations but very recently submitted to public auction.

Umbrellas, 243; Parasols, 168; Walking-sticks, 173; various sorts of Men's Attire, 508 articles; Men's Caps, 129; Women's Attire, 301 articles; Respirators, 2; Pocket Handkerchiefs, 302; Clogs and Pattens, 28; Travelling-bags, 63; Gloves, 366; Brushes, 47; Combs, 17; Books, 135; Sample Cases, 5; Card Cases, 7; Cushions, 20; Baskets, 50; Whips, 14; Fishing-rods, 6; One Cricket-bat; Birdcages, 3; Small Casks, 2; Beds, 3; One Bundle of Horn; One Iron Wheel; Boxes, 8; Purses, 14; Cigar-cases, 7; Snuff-boxes, 5; Smelling-bottles, 8; Pocket-knives, 10; Scissors, 7; Razors, 4; One Paper-knife; Bracelets, 4; Brooches, 26; Shawl and Scarf Pins, 17; Necklaces, 4; Gold Rings, 2; One Gold Toothpick; One Gold Eye-glass; Gold Pencil-cases, 3; One Gold Chain and Seals; Pairs of Spectacles, 20; Silver Pencil-cases, 4; Studs, 5; One Lever Watch Cap; One Fusee Box; Flask Bottles, 3; One Opera-glass.

It has been calculated that only about forty per cent. of railway waifs and strays remain unowned, and come to the hammer. From the above list, therefore—that of only one trunk line—the enormous amount of property that is continually left behind may be calculated.

These facts show, that while the public is excessively heedless, railway officials are curiously careful.

XV.

THE PRIVATE HISTORY OF THE PALACE OF GLASS.
JANUARY 18, 1851.

On New Year's Day in the year 1837, a traveller was proceeding in a native boat, on a difficult exploration up the river Berbice in Demerara, when, on arriving at a point where the river expanded and formed a currentless basin, his attention was attracted to the southern margin of the lake by an extraordinary object. He caused his crew to paddle quickly towards it. The nearer he approached, the higher his curiosity rose. Though an accomplished botanist, and especially familiar with the flora of South America, he had never seen anything like it before. It was a Titanic water-plant, in size and shape unlike any other known plant. "I felt as a botanist," says Sir Robert Schomburgh, "and felt myself rewarded! All calamities were forgotten. A gigantic leaf, from five to six feet in diameter, salver-shaped, with a broad rim, of a light green above, and a vivid crimson below, rested upon the water! Quite in character with the wonderful leaf was the luxuriant flower, consisting of an immense number of petals, passing in alternate tints from pure white to rose and pink. The smooth water was covered with blossoms, and as I rowed from one to the other, I always observed something new to admire.

Such flowers Polyphemus must have gathered for Galatea's nosegay; but Sir Robert Schomburgh, not content with mere flowers, dug up whole plants; and sent first them, and afterwards seeds, to England, where the magnificent lily was named the "Victoria Regia." After some unsuccessful attempts, the task of forcing it to blossom in an artificial climate, was con-

fided to Mr. Paxton, the celebrated horticulturist of the Duke
of Devonshire's celebrated Chatsworth.

Mr. Paxton is not a mere academic *savant*. *His* Alma
Mater is Nature. When the Victoria Regia was to be flow-
ered, Mr. Paxton determined to imitate Nature closely enough
to make that innocent offspring of the Great Mother fancy itself back again in the broad waters and under the burning
heats of British Guiana. He deceived the roots by imbedding
them in a hillock of burned loam and peat; he deluded the
great lubberly leaves by letting them float in a tank, to
which he communicated, by means of a little wheel, the gentle ripple of their own broad, deep river. He coaxed the
flower into bloom by manufacturing a Berbician climate in a
tiny South America, under a glass case.

With that glass-case our history properly begins. In imitation of a philosophic French Cook, who began a chapter on
stewed-apples with an essay on the Creation, we have thought
it wise to start with the parentage and gestation, before proceeding to the birth and development of the Great Giant in
Hyde Park. The first parent of the most extensive building
in Europe was the largest known floral structure in the world.
Although, co-relatively, they differ as widely as the popular
disparity of St. Paul's and a China orange; yet the one proceeded from the other, as consequently as oaks grow from
acorns.

Mr. Paxton had already effected many improvements in
horticultural buildings; the workmanship of which has always
been unnecessarily massive. With the conviction that glass
houses are not Egyptian tombs built for darkness and eternity,
he set about making them lighter than of old, both as regards
actinism and architecture. He discarded all ponderous and
opaque materials. He pared away all clumsy sash-bars, whose
broad shadows robbed plants of the sun's light and heat during
the best parts of the day; he abolished dirty and leaking
overlaps, by using large panes, and inserting them in wooden
grooves, rendered water-tight by a sparing use of putty.
Lastly, finding that, into the ordinary sloping roof, the sun-
beams enter at an indirect and unprofitable angle, Mr. Paxton
invented a horizontal glazing composed of angular ridges, the
glass presenting itself to the sun's rays so as to admit them to

the plants in a straight line at almost any time of day; but especially early and late.

In a green-house constructed with some of these improvements, and acclimated as we have already explained, a Victoria Regia was planted on the tenth of August, 1849. So well had everything been prepared for its reception, that it flourished as vigorously as if it had been restored to its native soil and climate. Its growth and development were astonishingly rapid; for on the ninth of November a flower was produced, one yard in circumference. In little more than a month, the first seeds ripened; some of them were tilled, and, on the sixteenth of February succeeding, young plants made their appearance. Success, however, brought a fresh embarrassment. The extraordinary lily obeyed Nature's law of development with such unexpected rapidity, that it outgrew its home in little more than a month. It therefore set Mr. Paxton a problem to solve, the formula of which was something like this:—Given, an exotic growing in a green-house at the rate of six hundred and forty-seven square inches of circumference per diem: required, in three months, a new house of dimensions proper for its maturity.

Mr. Paxton went to work; and, combining all his improvements in constructing green-houses with his special inventions for maturing the Victoria Regia, he soon produced the Q. E. D., in the shape of a novel and elegant conservatory, sixty feet long by forty broad. This building became the immediate precursor of the gigantic structure in Hyde Park,—*why*, necessitates a short explanation.

Among the many desiderata required for every kind of habitation—whether for plants or princes, for a pine-house or a palace, for the Victoria Regia, or for the enormous glass-case under which to collect the products of All Nations,—the most imperative conditions, after stability, are, facilities for drainage and for ventilation; another, though scarcely subordinate proviso, is economy. The man who can construct houses which shall repel external humidity, and allow of a constant and gentle change of atmosphere at any controllable temperature, and at the lowest cost consistent with durability, is, of course, the prince of builders. To be economical, he must necessarily so manage, that each of his materials shall perform as many different functions as it is possible for it to perform effectually. If he build walls which answer for warmth and strength only, if he add gutters for drainage, and if he call in Dr. Reid for ventilation, he may, probably, build a good habitation, but it will certainly be costly, perhaps clumsy; and will turn out a very long job. Mr. Paxton, when he set about the new Victoria Regia house — guided by previous study and experience, and forced into new expedients by the peculiarities of the extraordinary tenant he was building for— had become a better economist. The result is, as shown in his latest effort—the great Building—that his walls and foundations are not simply walls and foundations, but ventilators and drains as well. His roofs are not simply roofs; but, besides being the most extensive of known skylights, are light and heat adjusters. His sash-bars not only hold the glass together, but are self-supporting, and his rafters form drains for both sides of the glass,—for draining off internal, as well as external moisture, the tops of the girders being conduits also. His floors are dust-traps, and aid in ventilation. Lastly, his whole building is, while in course of construction, its own scaffolding. Thus he saves time as well as money.

The Victoria Regia house, which combines most of the advantages above detailed, was finished in several weeks less time, and cost considerably less money, than the slenderest old-fashioned conservatory that has ever been built.

While Mr. Paxton was busy with this novel and model garden-house, a hot war was raging in London about the site for the new building for exhibiting specimens of the Art and Industry of all nations in 1851. Mr. Paxton is a reader of the "Times," and perused with sympathising interest its fiercely urged objections against the invasion of Hyde Park by armies of excavators, bricklayers, blacksmiths, and timber-fellers. The picture daily drawn of the tearing-up of fashionable roads by the carting of more bricks and mortar, for a *temporary* edifice, than the eternal Pyramids of Ghizeh consist of; the cutting down from one side of Rotten-row of its most cherished ornaments, the trees; the uncertainty of miles of brickwork being put together in time for sufficient consolidation to bear the weight of the tremendous iron dome designed to rest upon it; the impossibility of the entire mass of mortar and plaster duly drying; all this, though occasionally overdrawn and ex aggerated, presented a black perspective, which the means and appliances of the Victoria Regia conservatory would, thought its architect, considerably lighten. Every new thunder bolt from the newspaper *Tonans*, strengthened this notion in the projector's mind. All that was wanted, was a great many great lily-houses joined together. A multiplication of hands and of materials could be readily commanded, and no struc ture could be raised so quickly and so cheaply. The prome naders and neighbours of Hyde Park would be relieved of the incessant " click—click " of bricklayers' trowels, the madden ing noise of the blacksmiths' riveting hammers, and have per fect immunity from the hourly transit of bricks and scaffold poles. The proposed edifice could be constructed at Birming ham, at Dudley, and at Thames Bank, brought home to Hyde Park ready-made, and put up like a bedstead. As to the trees: for a couple of hundred pounds Mr. Paxton would transplant them, and bring them back again at the end of the Industrial fair without injuring a single twig. And here we may remark, in passing, that, according to Horace Walpole, Mr. Paxton is half a century before his time in his huge trans planting operations. In August, 1748, the Twickenham Pro phet wrote to his Cousin Conway, as a piece of extravagant fun—" I lament living in so barbarous an age, when we are come to so little perfection in gardening. I am persuaded that, a hundred and fifty years hence, it will be as common to remove oaks a hundred and fifty years old, as it is now to transplant tulip roots."

However, Mr. Paxton *could* do without moving the vene rable wood " on the shortest notice," as if it had been con verted into household furniture before its time. If the Park authorities preferred, he would clap the trees, all standing, under his great glass-case.

But, alas! feasible as the plan appeared, it was not to be thought of. The fiat of the Building Committee had gone forth. The competition of architectural skill invited by the authorities had not produced one available design. The first exhibition of the Industry of the Architects of all Nations had been pronounced a failure; and the fact of the

8

Building Committee having invited tenders for the construction of a design of its own, shut out fresh competitors.

One day, however—it was Friday, the fourteenth of June—Mr. Paxton happened to be in the House of Commons conversing on this subject with Mr. Ellis, a member of it, who accompanied him to the Board of Trade to see what could be done. Then, nothing could be done; for Mr. Paxton (who is one of the busiest men in England—whose very leisure would kill a man of fashion with hard work) was off immediately to keep a special appointment at the tubular bridge over the Menai. After his journey, the next morning, the conversation with his friend, the M. P., was clenched by another and more than usually powerful burst of thunder in that day's issue from Blackfriars. Mr. Paxton's mind was made up; "and," said the Duke of Devonshire, at a recent public meeting at Bakewell, "I never knew Mr. Paxton resolve to undertake what he did not fully accomplish." To have engagements for every day in the week in different parts of England and Ireland, together with the management of the estates at Chatsworth, did not much matter; there was still time to be found for concocting the plans and details of a few score square acres of building. Tuesday morning, the eighteenth of June, found Mr. Paxton at Derby, seated, as Chairman of the Works and Ways Committee of the Midland Railway, to try an offending pointsman. This was the first *leisure* moment he had been able to secure since he resolved to plan the great building. At the end of the table stood the culprit; and, upon it, before the Chairman, was invitingly spread a virgin sheet of blotting-paper. As each witness delivered his evidence, Mr. Paxton appeared to be taking notes; and, when the case closed, one of his colleagues turned specially to him, saying,

"As you seem to have noted down the whole of the evidence, we will take the decision from you."

"The truth is," whispered the Chairman, "I know all about this affair already, having accidentally learned every particular last night. *This*," he continued, holding up the paper, "is a design for the Great Industrial Building to be erected in Hyde Park."

The pointsman was let off with a fine, and, before evening the blotting-paper plan had found its way into Mr. Paxton's

office at Chatsworth. By the help of that gentleman's ordinary assistants, elevations, sections, working details, and speci-
fications were completed in ten days.

When Mr. Paxton made his next appearance at the Derby
station, he had the complete plans under his arm. There was
not a minute to spare, for the train was on the point of starting, and the Royal Commissioners met the next morning ; so,
taking his dinner in his pocket, he entered a carriage. Here,
to his extreme satisfaction, he found one of the greatest and
most influential engineers of the day—a member, moreover,
of the Royal Commission—who was going to London by the
same train.

"This is extraordinarily lucky !" he exclaimed; "for I want
you to look over a few plans and a specification of mine."

Accordingly the plans were unrolled. "There they are,"
said the impromptu architect; "look them over, and see if
they will do for the great Building for eighteen hundred and
fifty-one !"

"For what ?" asked the engineer, looking at his friend with
the serio-comic surprise of incredulity.

"I am serious."

"But you are too late ; the whole thing is settled and decided."

"Well, just see what you think of them. I am very hungry, and if you will run them over while I eat my dinner I'll
not speak a word."

"Neither will I disturb *you*, for I *must* light a cigar ;" and
in spite of every regulation in that case made and provided,
the engineer began to smoke.

There was a dead taciturnity; the Royal Commissioner
went over the plans slowly and carefully; their originator narrowly watching their effect on his mind. It was an anxious
moment for the one ; for, upon the opinion of the other, no
little depended. At first there was not much to augur from.
The drawings were scanned with no more than business-like
attention. No word of commendation was uttered ; no sign
of pleasure or surprise appeared. The smoke rose in regular
wreaths; but, presently, it grew fainter and more intermittent,
and by-and-by the cigar went out; yet the suction was continued as vigorously as ever. The projector's hopes rose ; his

friend's attention was evidently drawn into a vortex, for he
went on during twenty minutes, pulling away at the effete
weed, quite unconscious that it was extinguished. At length
gathering the unrolled papers up in a bundle, he threw them
into the opposite seat, exclaiming—" Wonderful!—a thousand
times better than anything that has been brought before us!
What a pity they were not prepared earlier!"

" Will you lay them before the Royal Commission ?"

"I will."

The value of this promise and of the favourable expression
of opinion which would doubtless accompany its performance,
will be best understood when we divulge to the reader (without, we trust, any breach of confidence) that the gentleman
who made it was Mr. Robert Stephenson.

The next day fills a melancholy page in English history. It
was Saturday, the twenty-ninth of June. The Royal Commission met, headed by Prince Albert. After the regular business of the Board was over, the Prince and Sir Robert Peel
retired to one of the bay-windows, and were some time engaged in earnest conversation. Mr. Stephenson's time was
precious, for he had an appointment elsewhere. He was, in
short, obliged to depart without an opportunity of placing
Mr. Paxton's plans before his colleagues and the Prince. He
delegated that office, however, to an able hand, Mr. Scott
Russell, one of the Secretaries of the Commission.

Both Prince Albert and Sir Robert Peel gave great attention to the drawings, and the Prince signified his wish that
Mr. Paxton should wait upon him at Buckingham Palace, to
explain the details. Sir Robert Peel greatly admired the design for its unity and simplicity; remarking with pleasure,
that, if it were accepted, it would occasion the first great operation in glass since the introduction of his own new tariff.
Alas! this was the latest connected remark which that great
statesman was destined to utter. He almost immediately left
Westminster Palace on horseback for an airing, was thrown
on Constitution Hill, and three days afterwards ceased to exist.

The Paxton scheme was referred to the Building Committee;
which, in the regular routine of business, could not entertain
it, having rejected all the designs it had invited for competition, and having devised a plan of its own. Nothing daunted,

however, Mr. Paxton determined to appeal to a tribunal which
(to borrow the tag of most modern comedies) is "never
sought in vain;" namely, to the British public.   This he did
by the aid of the woodcuts and pages of the "London Illustrated News."   Never was an appeal more promptly or satisfactorily answered!   The practicability, the simplicity, and
beauty of the scheme convinced every member of the many-
headed court of appeal of its efficacy.

Meanwhile, the projector of the building waited on the
projector of the entire Exhibition, Prince Albert, on another
memorable morning—that of the Christening day of Prince
Patrick.   What passed need not be divulged; but the encouragement vouchsafed, added to the expression of public
opinion daily gathering strength, induced Mr. Paxton to decide
on procuring a tender to be sent in to the Building Committee
for his design.   He therefore went straight to Messrs. Fox
and Henderson, and these gentlemen immediately engaged to
prepare a tender.   It happened that the Building Committee
in their advertisement had invited the candidates for raising
their edifice, to suggest any improvements in it that may occur
to them.   This opened a crevice, into which Messrs. Fox and
Henderson were able to thrust their tender for Mr. Paxton's
plan.   Seeing at once it was, of all other plans, *the* plan—the
supreme desideratum—they tendered it as an "improvement"
on the Committee's design.

Here a new and formidable difficulty arose.   It was now
Saturday, and only a few days more were allowed for receiving
tenders.   Yet before an approximate estimate of expense
could be formed, the great glass manufacturers and iron-masters of the north had to be consulted.   This happened to be
dies mirabilis the third, for it was the identical Saturday on
which the Sunday postal question had reached its crisis; and
there was to be no delivery of letters next day!   But, in a
country of electric telegraphs and of indomitable energy,
time and difficulties are annihilated, and it is not the least of
the marvels wrought in connection with the great edifice,
that, by the aid of railway parcels and the electric telegraph,
not only did all the gentlemen summoned out of Warwick-
shire and Staffordshire appear on Monday morning at Messrs.
Fox and Henderson's office, in Spring-gardens, London, to

contribute their several estimates to the tender for the whole ; but, within a week, the contractors had prepared every detailed working drawing, and had calculated the cost of every pound of iron, of every inch of wood, and of every pane of glass.

There is no one circumstance in the history of the manufacturing enterprise of the English nation which places in so strong a light as this its boundless resources in materials, to say nothing of the arithmetical skill in computing at what cost, and in how short a time, those materials could be converted to a special purpose. What was done in those few days? Two persons in London, relying on the accuracy and good faith of certain iron-masters, glass-workers in the provinces, and of one master carpenter in London, bound themselves for a certain sum of money, and in the course of some four months, to cover eighteen acres of ground, with a building upwards of a third of a mile long (1851 feet—the exact date of the year), and some four hundred and fifty feet broad. To do this, the glass-maker promised to supply in the required time, nine hundred thousand square feet of glass, weighing more than four hundred tons, in separate panes, and these the largest that had ever been made of sheet glass : each being forty-nine inches long. The iron-master passed his word to cast in due time three thousand three hundred iron columns, varying from fourteen and a half feet to twenty feet in length ; thirty-four *miles* of guttering tube ; to join every individual column together under the ground ; to produce two thousand two hundred and twenty-four girders (some of them of wrought iron) ; besides eleven hundred and twenty-eight bearers for supporting galleries. The carpenter undertook to get ready within the specified period two hundred and five *miles* of sash bar ; flooring for an area of thirty-three millions of cubic feet ; besides enormous quantities of wooden walling, louvre work, and partition.*

It is not till we reflect on the vast sums of money involved in transactions of this magnitude, that we can form a notion of the great, almost ruinous, loss a trifling arithmetical error would have occasioned, and of the boundless confidence the contractors must have had in their resources and in the cor-

---

* The quantities and dimensions here quoted are those of the building as it now stands. They differ but slightly from Mr. Paxton's original specification.

rectness of their computations. But it was one great merit
in Mr. Paxton's original details of measurement that they
were contrived to facilitate calculation. Everything in the
great building is a dividend or multiple of *twenty-four*. The
internal columns are placed twenty-four feet apart, while the
external ones have no more than eight feet (a third of twenty-
four) of separation : while the distance between each of the
transept columns is three times twenty-four, or seventy-two
feet. This also is the width of the middle aisle of the building; the side aisles are forty-eight feet wide, and the galleries
and corridors twenty-four. Twenty-four feet is also the distance between each of the transverse gutters under the roof;
hence, the intervening bars, which are at once rafters and gutters, are, necessarily, twenty-four feet long.

There was little time for consideration, or for setting right
a single mistake, be it ever so disastrous. On the prescribed
day the tender was presented, with whatever imperfections it
might have had, duly and irredeemably sealed. But, after-
checkings have detected no material error. The result was,
that Messrs. Fox and Henderson's offer for erecting the Paxton edifice proved to be the lowest practicable tender that was
submitted to the Building Committee.

The public have long known what followed :—Mr. Paxton's
Glazed Palace was eventually chosen unanimously; not only
by the Building Committee but by the Royal Commission.
Some modifications were, however, adopted. It was decided
that the most revered of the trees were to be admitted into
the Industrial building; and the central transept—the apex
of whose curvilinear roof is one hundred and twelve feet from
the ground—was contrived by Mr. Paxton for their enclosure.
In August the space in Hyde Park was boarded in ; and the
first castings for the iron columns were delivered on the fourteenth of September. Yet, when these pages meet the reader's eye, the cheapest, most gigantic, and substantial structure
ever dreamt of, will be nearly ready for decoration.

If for nothing else, this tremendous pile of transparency is
astounding for its cheapness. It is actually less costly per
square foot than an agricultural barn or an Irish cabin. A
division of its superficies in cubic feet by the sums to be paid
for it, brings out the astonishing quotient, of little more than

one halfpenny (nine sixteenths of a penny) per cubic foot,
supposing it to be taken down and the materials returned to
the contractors when the Exhibition is over. Or, if it remain
a fixture, the rate of cost will be rather less than a penny and
and one twelfth of a penny per cubic foot. The ordinary expense of a barn is more than twice as much, or twopence-
halfpenny per foot. Here are the figures: The entire edifice
contains thirty-three millions of cubic feet. If borrowed
from the contractors and taken down, the sum to be paid
is seventy-nine thousand eight hundred pounds: if bought,
to become a winter garden, one hundred and fifty thousand
pounds.

The smallness of cost is due to the principle we have previously explained, of each component of the building being
endowed with more than one purpose. The six rows of columns are, as had been already said, not only props but drain-
pipes. They are hollow, and into them the glass roof will
deliver its collections of water. In the base of each column
is inserted a horizontal iron pipe to conduct the drainage into
sewers. These strong tubes serve also as foundation; they
are links that connect the whole of the three thousand three
hundred uprights together. At the top, each column is fastened to its opposite associate by a girder, run up by means
of a pole and pully in a few minutes; and, once fastened, no
other scaffolding is requisite for the roof which it supports.
Thus, by means of the iron pipes below, and the iron girders
above, the eighteen acres of structure is held from end to end
so compact and fast that it becomes an enormous hollow cube,
as immovable as if it were a solid cube dropped down near
Rotten-row by a gang of Titans.

The roofs—of which there are five, one to each side or cor-
ridor, the highest in the middle—play many parts. They are
windows, light and heat adjusters, rain conductors outside, and
condensed moisture ducts within. They are interminable rows
of roofing, so placed as to form in the aggregate a plane; in
other words, they are parallel rows of the letter $\vee$ done in
glass, in endless ridges "long drawn out," thus: $\vee\vee\vee$ The
apex of each "ridge" is a wooden sash bar, with notches on
either side for holding the sloping laths in which are fitted the
edges of the glass. The bottom, or "furrow" bar—otherwise

a rafter—is hollowed in the middle, to form a gutter, into which every drop of rain glides down from the glass, and passes through the transverse gutters into the hollow columns. These longitudinal gutters are formed at the tops of the girders; for the roof is self-supporting. This is not all: in converting a conservatory for plants into a resort for breathing beings, and a depôt for articles emphatically "to be kept dry;" internal as well as external moisture must be drawn off: the breath of myriads of visitors, condensed against the glass, would otherwise return in continual Scotch mists. That difficulty partly dictated the ∧-like form of the ceiling. Mr. Paxton ascertained that vapours ascending to glass inclined to a slope of one foot in two feet and a half, do not condense in separate drops and descend again, but slide down over the smooth surface. To receive them, therefore, he grooves each rafter under the inside of the glazing. Into these grooves the condensed breath of "all nations" will fall and be conveyed into the transverse gutters; thence through the columns into the jurisdiction of their honours the Commissioners of Sewers. We subjoin a section of the rafter, to show the "Paxton gutter," and to clench our explanation: A is the external gutter, B B the frames of the glass, C C the internal ducts. These ingenious rafters are cut out of solid wood, in a machine (invented by the inventor of all the rest), with incredible rapidity. In order that there may be a fall for the water to run off, each rafter is slightly curved; and, to correct warping, a rod of iron, with nuts and screws at each end, forms the string of the bow, so as to regulate its deflexion. For this ingenious expedient Mr. Paxton has taken out a patent.

We must now give proof that the floor is a ventilator, and a dust-trap. It is laid four feet above the sward of the park. A series of subterraneous lungs are thus provided, and air is admitted to them, by means of louvres, fixed in the outer walling of the building. These being made to open and shut like Venetian blinds, will admit much or little air, which gently passes through the seams of the open flooring, and circulates over the building. Finally, through the openings of the floor the daily accumulations of dust will be swept into

the space below by a machine, which Mr. Paxton has invented
for that purpose.

Enough has now been said to indicate rather than describe
how each part of the building "plays many parts," and how,
consequently, incalculable saving has been effected in time
and money. It is hardly necessary to repeat, that the interior
of the edifice is the most expansive covered space in the world.
That some idea may be formed of the excess of its capacity,
we may mention that the largest covered area in England is
believed to be that of the Ravenhead Glass Works, at St.
Helen's, in Lancashire; where the space roofed in is three
hundred and thirty-nine feet by one hundred and five feet, or
not one quarter so great as the section of Hyde Park which
Mr. Paxton has glazed over.

That a Palatial Exhibition building, providing a total exhibiting surface of twenty-two acres, and affording space for
nine miles of tables, shall have been put up in four months,
for less than a penny farthing a cubic foot, would in itself make
1851 famous in the history of enterprise, if nothing else were
to happen to stamp it as pre-eminently The Industrial Year.

☞ XVI.

PLATE GLASS.

FEBRUARY 1, 1851.

Two other gentlemen occupied the railway carriage, which,
on a gusty day in December, was conveying us towards Gravesend, *via* Blackwall. One wore spectacles, by the aid of which
he was perusing a small pocket edition of a favourite author.
No sound escaped his lips; yet, his under-jaw and his disen-
gaged hand moved with the solemn regularity of an orator
emitting periods of tremendous euphony. Presently, his delight exploded in a loud shutting up of the book and an enthusiastic appeal to us in favour of the writings of Dr. Samuel
Johnson. "What, for example, can be finer, gentlemen, than
his account of the origin of glass-making; in which, being a
drysalter, I take a particular interest. Let me read the passage to you!"

"But the noise of the train——"

" Sir, I can drown that."

The tone in which the Johnsonian "Sir" was let off, left no doubt of it. Though a small man, the reader was what his favourite writer would have denominated a Stentor, and what the modern school would call a Stunner. When he reopened the book and began to read, the words smote the ear, like the discharge of cannon. To give additional effect to the rounded periods, he waved his arm in the air at each turn of a sentence, as if it had been a circular saw. "Who," he recited, "when he saw the first sand or ashes, by a casual intenseness of heat, melted into a metalline form, rugged with excrescences, and clouded with impurities, would have imagined, that in this shapeless lump lay concealed so many conveniences of life, as would in time constitute a great part of the happiness of the world? Yet by some such fortuitous liquefaction was mankind taught to procure a body at once in a high degree solid and transparent, which might admit the light of the sun, and exclude the violence of the wind; which might extend the sight of the philosopher to new ranges of existence, and charm him at one time with the unbounded extent of the material creation, and at another with the endless subordination of animal life: and, what is yet of more importance, might supply the decays of nature, and succour old age with subsidiary sight. Thus was the first artificer in glass employed, though without his own knowledge or expectation. He was facilitating and prolonging the enjoyment of light, enlarging the avenues of science, and conferring the highest and most lasting pleasures; he was enabling the student to contemplate nature, and the beauty to behold herself. This passion for——"

" Blackwall, gents! Blackwall, ladies! Boat for Gravesend!" We should unquestionably have been favoured with the rest of the ninth number of the "Rambler" but for these announcements.

" There is one thing, however,' said the little man with the loud voice, as we walked from the platform to the pier, "which I *cannot* understand. What does the illustrious essayist mean by the 'fortuitous liquefaction' of the sand and ashes? Was glass found out by accident?"

Luckily, a ray of school-day classics enlightened a corner

of our memory, and we mentioned the well-known story, in Pliny, that some Phœnician merchants, carrying saltpetre to the mouth of the river Belus, went ashore ; and, placing some lumps of the cargo under their kettles to cook food, the heat of the fire fused the nitre, which ran among the sand of the shore.   The cooks finding this union to produce a translucent substance, discovered the art of making glass.

" That," said our other companion, holding his hat to prevent the wind from blowing it aboard the Gravesend steamer (which was not to start for ten minutes), " has been the stock tale of all writers on the subject, from Pliny down to Ure ; but, Sir Gardiner Wikinson has put it out of the power of future authors to repeat it.   That indefatigable haunter of Egyptian tombs discovered minute representations of glass-blowing, painted on tombs of the time of Orsirtasin the First, some sixteen hundred years before the date of Pliny's story. Indeed, a glass bead, bearing the name of a king who lived fifteen hundred years before Christ, was found in another tomb by Captain Henvey, the specific gravity of which is precisely that of English crown-glass.

" You seem to know all about it !" exclaimed the loud-voiced man.

" Being a director of a plate-glass company I have made it my business to learn all that books could teach me on the subject.".

" I should like to see glass made !" said the vociferous admirer of Dr. Johnson, " especially plate glass."

To this, the other replied, with steady politeness, " If your wish be very strong, and you have an hour to spare, I shall be happy to show you the works, to which I am going,—those of the Thames Plate Glass Company.   They are close by."

" The fact is," was the reply, " Mrs. Bossle (I'm sorry to say Mrs. Bossle is an invalid) expects me down to Gravesend to tea ; but an hour won't matter much."

" And you, sir ?" said the civil gentleman, addressing me.

My desire was equally strong, and the next hour equally my own ; for, as the friend, whom a negligent public had driven to emigration, was not to sail until the next morning, it did not much matter whether I took my last farewell of him at Gravesend early, or late, that evening.

Tracking our guide through dock gates, over narrow draw-bridges, along quays; now, dodging the rigging of ships; now, tripping over cables, made "taut" to rings; now, falling foul of warping-posts (for it was getting dusk); one minute, leaping over deserted timber; the next, doubling stray casks; the next, winding amongst the strangest ruins of dismantled steam-boats, for which a regular hospital seemed established in that desolate region of mud and water; then, emerging into dirty lanes, and turning the corners of roofless houses; we finished an exciting game of Follow my Leader, at a pair of tall gates. One of these, admitted us into the precincts of the southernmost of the six manufactories of plate glass existing in this country.

The first ingredient in the making of glass, to which we were introduced, was contained in a goodly row of barrels in full tap, marked with the esteemed brand of Truman, Hanbury, Buxton, & Co. It is the well-known fermented extract of malt and hops, which is, it seems, nearly as necessary to the production of good plate glass, as flint and soda. To liquefy the latter materials by means of fire, is, in truth, dry work; and our *cicerone* explained that seven pints per day, per man, of Messrs. Truman, Hanbury, Buxton, and Company's entire, has been found, after years of thirsty experience, to be absolutely necessary to moisten human clay, hourly baked at the mouths of blazing furnaces. These furnaces emit a heat more intense than the most perspiring imagination can conceive, or the staunchest thermometer indicate. An attempt to ascertain the degree of heat was once made: a pyrometer, or "fire-measurer," (a thermometer of the superlative degree), was applied to the throat of a furnace—for every furnace has its mouth, its throat, and its flaming tongues; but, the wretched instrument, after five minutes' scorching, made an expiring effort to mark *thirteen hundred degrees above boiling point*, cracked, was shivered into bits, and was finally swallowed up by the insatiable element whose proceedings it had presumptuously attempted to register.

Having, by this time, crossed a yard, we stood on the edge of a foul creek of the Thames, so horribly slimy that a crocodile, or an alligator, or any scaly monster of the Saurian period, seemed much more likely to be encountered in such

a neighbourhood than the beautiful substance that makes
our modern rooms so glittering and bright, our streets so
dazzling, and our windows at once so radiant and so
strong.

"In order to understand our process thoroughly," said the
obliging director of the seven acres of factory and the four
hundred operatives we had come to see, "we must begin with
the beginning. This," picking up from a heap a handful of
the finest of fine sand; the glittering pounce, in fact, with
which our forefathers spangled their writing, "is the basis of
all glass. It is the whitest, most highly pulverised flint sand
that can be procured. This comes from Lynn, on the coast
of Norfolk. Its mixture with the other materials is a secret,
even to us. We give the man who possesses it a handsome
salary for exercising his mystery."

"A secret!" cried Mr. Bossle. "Everybody, I thought,
knew—at least everybody in the drysaltery line knows—
what glass is made of. Why, I can repeat the recipe given
by Dr. Ure, from memory :—To every hundred parts of materials, there are of pure sand forty-three parts; soda twenty-
five and a half (by-the-by, we have some capital carbonate
coming forward *ex* Mary Anne, that we could let you have at
a low figure) ; quick-lime, four; nitre, one and a half; broken
glass, twenty-six. The Doctor calculates, if I remember
rightly, that of the whole, thirty parts of this compound run
to waste in fusing, so that seventy per cent. becomes, on an
average, glass."

"That is all very true," was the answer; "but our glass is,
we flatter ourselves, of a much better colour, and stands an-
nealing better, than that made from the ordinary admixture :
from which, however, ours differs but little—only, I think, in
the relative quantities. In that lies the secret."

Mr. Bossle expressed great anxiety to behold an individual
who was possessed of a secret worth several hundreds a year,
paid weekly. Romance invariably associates itself with mystery; and we are not quite sure from the awful way in which
Mr. Bossle dropped his voice to a soft whisper, that he did
not expect, on entering the chamber of pre-vitrified chemicals,
to find an individual clothed like the hermit in "Rasselas," or
mingling his "elements" with the wand of Hermes Trisme-

gistus. He looked as if he could hardly believe his spectacles, when he saw a plain, respectable-looking, indifferent-tempered man, not a whit more awe-inspiring—or more dusty—than a miller on a market-day.

We do not insinuate that Mr. Bossle endeavoured to "pluck out the heart of the mystery," though nothing seemed to escape the focus of his spectacles. But, although here lay, in separate heaps, the sand and soda and saltpetre and lime and *cullet*, or broken glass; while there, in a huge trough, those ingredients were mixed up (like "broken" in a confectioner's shop) ready to be pushed through a trap to fill the crucible or stomach of the furnace; yet, despite Mr. Bossle's sly investigations, and sonorous inquiries, he left the hall of "elements" as wise as he had entered.

Passing through a variety of places in which the trituration, purification, and cleaning of the materials were going on, we mounted to an upper story that reminded us of the yard in which the cunning Captain of the Forty Thieves, disguised as an Oil Merchant, stored his pretended merchandise. It was filled with rows and rows of great clay jars, something like barrels with their heads knocked out. Each had, instead of a hoop, an indented band round the middle, for the insertion of the iron gear by which they were, in due time, to be lifted into and out of the raging furnaces. There were two sizes; one about four feet deep, and three feet six inches in diameter, technically called "pots," and destined to receive the materials for their first sweltering. The smaller vessels (*cuvettes*) were of the same shape, but only two feet six inches deep, and two feet in diameter. These were the crucibles in which the vitreous compound was to be fired a second time, ready for casting. These vessels are *built*—for that is really the process; and it requires a twelvemonth to build one, so gradually must it settle and harden, and so slowly must it be pieced together, or the furnace would immediately destroy it—of Stourbridge clay, which is the purest and least silicious yet discovered.

"We have now seen," said Mr. Bossle, wiping his spectacles, and gathering himself up for a loud Johnsonian period, "the raw materials ready to be submitted to the action of the fire, and we have also beheld the vessels in which the vitrification is to take place. Let us therefore witness the actual liquefaction."

In obedience to this grandiloquent wish, we were shown into the hall of furnaces.

It was a sight indeed. A lofty and enormous hall, with windows in the high walls open to the rainy night. Down the centre, a fearful row of roaring furnaces, white-hot: to look at which, even through the chinks in the iron screens before them, and masked, seemed to scorch and splinter the very breath within one. At right angles to this hall, another; an immense building in itself, with unearthly-looking instruments hanging on the walls, and strewn about, as if for some diabolical cookery. In dark corners, where the furnaces redly glimmered on them, from time to time, knots of swarthy muscular men, with nets drawn over their faces, or hanging from their hats: confusedly grouped, wildly dressed, scarcely heard to mutter amidst the roaring of the fires, and mysteriously coming and going, like picturesque shadows, cast by the terrific glare. Such figures there must have been, once upon a time, in some such scene, ministering to the worship of fire, and feeding the altars of the cruel god with victims. Figures not dissimilar, alas! there have been, torturing and burning, even in Our Saviour's name. But, happily those bitter days are gone. The senseless world is tortured for the good of man, and made to take new forms in his service. Upon the rack, we stretch the ores and metals of the earth, and not the image of the Creator of all. These fires and figures are the agents of civilisation, and not of deadly persecution and black murder. Burn fires and welcome! making a light in England that shall not be quenched by all the monkish dreamers in the world!

We were aroused by a sensation like the sudden application of a hot mask to the countenance. As we instinctively placed a hand over our face to ascertain how much of the skin was peeling off, our cool informant announced that the furnace over against us had been opened to perform the *tréjetage*, or ladling of the liquid *pot au feu* from the large pots into the smaller ones. "I must premise," he said, "that one-third of the raw materials, as put together by our secret friend, is first thrown in; and, when that is melted, one-third more: on

that being fused, the last third is added. The mouth of the
furnace is then closed, and an enormous heat kept up by the
tiseur or stoker (all our terms are taken from the French),
during sixteen hours. That time having now elapsed in the
case of the flaming pot before you, the furnace is opened.
The man with the long ladle thrusts it, you perceive, into the
pot, takes out a ladleful, and, by the assistance of two companions, throws the vitrified dough upon an iron anvil. The
other two men turn it over and over, spread it upon the inverted flat-iron, and twitch out, with pliers, any speck of
impurity; it is tossed again into the ladle, and thrown into a
cuvette in another furnace. When the cuvettes are full, that
furnace is stopped up to maintain a roaring heat for another
eight hours; and, in the language of the men, 'the ceremony
is performed.' "

At this moment, the noise burst forth from the middle of the
enormous shed, of several beats of a gong: so loud that they
drowned the thundering inquiries with which Mr. Bossle was
teasing one of the "teasers." In an instant the men hastened
to a focus, like giants in a Christmas pantomime about to
perform some wonderful conjuration; and not a whisper was
heard.

"Ah!" exclaimed the director, "they are going to cast.
This way, gentlemen!"

The kitchen in which the Ogre threatened to cook Jack and
his seven brothers could not have been half so formidable an
apartment as the enormous cuisine into which we were led.
One end was occupied with a row of awful ovens; in the
midst, stood a stupendous iron table; and upon it lay a rolling-pin, so big that it could only be likened to half a dozen
garden-rollers joined together at their ends. Above, was an
iron crane or gallows to lift the enormous masses of red-hot
gruel, thick and slab, which were now to be brought from the
furnaces.

"Stand clear!" A huge basin, white with heat, approaches,
on an iron hurley; at one end of which sits, triumphant, a
salamander, in human form, to balance the Plutonian mass, as
it approaches on its wheeled car—playing with it—a game
of see-saw. It stops at the foot of the iron gallows. Mr.
Bossle approaches to see what it is, and discovers it to be a

cuvette filled with molten glass, glowing from the fiery furnace. What is that man doing with a glazed mask before his
face? " Why, if you will believe me," exclaimed Mr. Bossle,
in the tones of a speaking-trumpet (we are at a prudent distance), " he is ladling off the scum, as composedly as if it were
turtle-soup!" Mr. Bossle grows bold, and ventures a little
nearer. Rash man! His nose is assuredly scorched; he darts
back, and takes off his spectacles, to ascertain how much of
the frames are melted. The dreadful pot is lifted by the crane.
It is poised immediately over the table : a workman tilts it;
and out pours a cataract of molten opal which spreads itself,
deliberately, like infernal sweetstuff, over the iron table.
Though spilled and slopped about in a crowd of men, it
touches nobody. " And has touched nobody since last year,
when one poor fellow got the large shoes he wore filled with
white-hot glass." Then the great rolling-pin begins to "roll
it out."

But, those two men narrowly inspecting every inch of the
red-hot sheet as the roller approaches it—is their skin sala-
mandrine? Are their eyes fireproof?

They are looking, we are told, for any accidental impurity
that may be still intruding in the vitrification, and if they can
tear it out with their long pincers before the roller has passed
over it, they are rewarded. From the shape these specks as-
sume in being torn away, they are called " tears."

When the roller has passed over the table, it leaves a sheet
of red-hot glass, measuring some twelve feet by seven.

This translucent confection is pushed upon a flat wooden
platform on wheels—sparkling, as it touches the wood, like
innumerable diamonds—and is then run rapidly to an oven,
there to be baked or annealed. The bed or "sole" of this
carquèse is heated to a temperature exactly equal to that of
the glass; which is now so much cooled that you can stand within a yard or so of it without fear of scorching off your eyelashes.
The pot out of the furnace is cooled too, out in the rain, and
lies there, burst into a hundred pieces. It has been a good
one; for it has withstood the fire, seventy days.

So rapidly are all these casting operations performed, that,
from the moment when Mr. Bossle thought his spectacles
were melting off his nose, to the moment when the sheet of

glass is shut up in the oven, about five minutes only have elapsed! The operations are repeated, until the oven is full of glass plates.

When eight plates are put in to the *carquèse* it is closed up hermetically; for the tiniest current of cold air would crack the glass. The fire is allowed to go out of its own accord, and the cooling takes place so gradually, that it is not completed until eight days are over. When drawn forth, the glass is that "rough plate" which we see let into the doors of railway stations, and forming half-transparent floors in manufactories. To make it completely transparent for windows and looking-glasses, elaborate processes of grinding and polishing are requisite. They are three in number:—roughing down, smoothing, and polishing.

"I perceive," said Mr. Bossle, when he got to the roughing-down room, where steam machinery was violently agitating numerous plates of glass, one upon the other, "that the diamond cut diamond principle is adopted."

"Exactly: the under plate is fastened to a table by plaster of Paris, and the upper one—quite rough—is violently rubbed by machinery upon it, with water, sand, and other grinding powders between. The top plate is then fastened to a table, to rough down another first plate; for the under one is always the smoother."

Then comes the smoothing. Emery, of graduated degrees of fineness, is used for that purpose. "Until within the last month or so, smoothing could only be done by human labour. The human hand alone was capable of the requisite tenacity, to rub the slippery surfaces over each other; nay, so fine a sense of touch was requisite, that even a man's hand had scarcely sensitiveness enough for the work; hence females were, and still are, employed."

As our painstaking informant spoke, he pushed open a door, and we beheld a sight that made Mr. Bossle wipe his spectacles, and ourselves imagine for a moment that a scene from an Oriental Story-Book was magically revealed to us; so elegant and graceful were the attitudes into which a bevy of some fifty young women—many of them of fine forms and handsome features—were unceasingly throwing themselves. Now, with arms extended, they pushed the plates to one verge of the low tables, stretching their bodies as far as possible; then, drawing back, they stood erect, pulling the plate after them; then, in order to reach the opposite edge of the plane, they stretched themselves out again to an almost horizontal posture. The easy beauty of their movements, the glitter of the glass, the brilliancy of the gas-lights, the bright colours of most of the dresses, formed a *coup d'œil* which Mr. Bossle enjoyed a great deal more than Mrs. Bossle, had she been there, might have quite approved. The fairy scene is soon, however, to disappear. Mr. Blake, the ingenious manager of the works, has invented an artificial female hand, by means of which, in combination with peculiar machinery, glass smoothing can be done by steam.

The last process is "polishing." This art is practised in a spacious room glowing with red. Every corner of the busy interior is as rubicund as a dutch Dairy. The floor is red, the walls are red, the ceiling is red, the pillars are red, the machinery is very red. Red glass is attached, by red plaster of Paris, to red movable tables; red rubbers of red felt, heavily weighted with red leads, are driven rapidly over the red surface. Little red boys, redder than the reddest of Red Indians, are continually sprinkling on the reddened glass, the rouge (moistened crocus, peroxide of iron), which converts the scene of their operations into the most gigantic of known Rubrics.

When polished, the glass is taken away to be "examined." A body of vigilant scrutineers place each sheet between their own eyes and a strong light: wherever a scratch or flaw appears, they make a mark with a piece of wax. If removable, these flaws are polished out by hand. The glass is then ready for the operation, which enables "the beauty to behold herself." The spreading of the quicksilver at the back is, however, a separate process, accomplished elsewhere, and performed by a perfectly distinct body of workmen. It is a very simple art.

The manufacture of plate glass adds another to the thousand and one instances of the advantages of unrestricted and unfettered trade. The great demand occasioned by the immediate fall in price consequent upon the New Tariff, produced this effect on the Thames Plate Glass Works:—they now manufacture as much plate glass per week as was turned out

in the days of the Excise, in the same time, by all the works
in the country put together. The Excise incubi clogged the
operations of the workmen, and prevented every sort of improvement in the manufacture. They put their gauges into
the "metal" (or mixed materials) before it was put into the
pot. They overhauled the paste when it was taken out of the
fire, and they applied their foot-rules to the sheets after the
glass was annealed. The duty was collected during the various stages of manufacture half a dozen times, and amounted
to three hundred per cent. No improvement was according
to law, and the Exciseman put his veto upon every attempt
of the sort. In the old time, the mysterious mixer could not
have exercised his secret vocation for the benefit of his employers, and the demand for glass was so small that Mr.
Blake's admirable polishing machine would never have been
invented. Nor could plate-glass ever have been used for
transparent flooring, or for door panels, or for a hundred other
purposes, to which it is now advantageously and ornamentally
applied.

Thanking the courteous gentleman who had shown us over
the works, we left Mr. Bossle in close consultation with the
manager. As, in crossing the yard, we heard the word
"soda!" frequently thundered forth, we concluded that the
Johnsonian drysalter was endeavouring to complete some
transaction in that commodity, which he had previously
opened with the director. But, it is not in our power to report decisively on this head, for our attention was directed to
two concluding objects.

First, to a row of workmen—the same we had lately seen
among the fires and liquid glass—good-humouredly sitting
with perfect composure, on a log of timber, out in the cold
and wet, looking at the muddy creek, and drinking their beer,
as if there were no such thing as temperature known. Secondly, and lastly, to the narrow passages or caves underneath
the furnaces, into which the glowing cinders drop through
gratings. These looked, when we descended into them, like a
long Egyptian street on a dark night, with a fiery rain falling.
In warm divergent chambers and crevices, the boys employed
in the works love to hide and sleep, on cold nights. So slept
De Foe's hero, Colonel Jack, among the ashes of the glass-

house where *he* worked. And that, and the river together, made us think of ROBINSON CRUSOE the whole way home, and wonder what-all the English boys who have been since his time, and who are yet to be, would have done without him and his desert Island.

XVII.

THE INVITED INVASION.

FEBRUARY 8, 1851.

WHEN, O provincial or foreign visitor! you look down at mid-day upon Ludgate-street from the outer gallery of the dome of St. Paul's, you behold four currents of hats with a variegation of bonnets here and there (like flowers floating in an inky river), flanking two more streams of vehicles. These trails move in alternate rows eastward and westward without intermission and without end. Upon that gilded and giddy height, you get an idea of a dense population. It is there that you fully understand that two millions and a quarter of us are congregated upon this out-of-the-way corner of the earth, which is, on terrestrial globes, labelled "London." It is there that you smile at the stories of ancient Babylon and its fabulous census of Assyrians, and laugh the vaunted population of Pekin to scorn. It is there that, straining your eyes to the right and to the left, while circumambulating your airy perch, you feel some hesitation in descending; lest, there being no room even for your moderate corpus, you should be pushed aside like a straw in a torrent. Yet this traffic is not so great as that which passes under the ugly clock which protrudes from the elegant spire of Bow Church, like a mis-shapen tumour on the neck of a beauty. Into Cheapside are disgorged, not only the east-going thousands now passing under your eye; but an equal multitude from Holborn and Newgate-street. These concentrate and thicken at Bow Church—to be born within earshot of whose belfry constitutes a Cockney. Ethnologically, therefore, Bow Church is the centre of London.

You may, perhaps, suppose, O innocent provincial! that the moving manifestation of to-day is exceptional. Like the other

countryman, who waited at the threshold of Goldsmith's publisher (whose house is just below you) for half a day, and then
inquired " when the crowd would have done passing," you imagine that some extraordinary attraction has brought the people into the streets. But, be assured, you behold the ordinary
average. Hear the secretary of the City of London police on
the number of foot, omnibus, cab, carriage, and coach passengers who daily traverse the City thoroughfares :—During
every twenty-four hours throughout the year, he says, an average of one hundred and nineteen thousand six hundred and
two individuals pass Bow Church, and only a little more than
half of them are foot passengers, the rest being riders. In
the month of May, he adds, the number of persons who enter
the City daily, on foot and in carriages, is little less than four
hundred thousand persons. Two-thirds more than the entire
population of Edinburgh ; and four times greater than the
number of lieges who own the sway of the Grand-Duke of
Mecklenburg-Strelitz.

With these facts before you and the moving masses below
you, do you not tremble when told that from May next ensuing to September, the narrow necks of the swarming
thoroughfares will be throttled with one-third more passengers ?—not mere population, including the infantine, aged,
and disabled ; but sturdy, trudging, untiring sight-seeing
beaters of pavements and throngers of shop-fronts. You box
the compass on your elevated balcony, and see little or no
preparation for this Invited Invasion. The new Cannon-street
opening will hardly draw off much traffic from Cheapside ;
for, although the street may be ready in time, its attractions
will not have been put forth. There will be no shops ; it has
no public buildings ; nothing but London-stone to divert our
visitors from the highway to the Mansion House, the Bank,
the Royal Exchange, Gog and Magog, and the new Post-
office. Then, north-westward the new Farringdon-street
opening, which is to lead, some day or other, to Clerkenwell,
can scarcely be made worthy of foreign or provincial patronage
in time ; despite Sharp's-alley on the one side, and Field-lane
on the other. It follows, therefore, that from whatever quarter visitors may arrive in order to get at the great centres of
city attraction, they must pass Bow Church.

Come down, then, O half-frozen stranger! from your gusty place of contemplation, and battle with me to the Old Jewry, that we may look in at the City Police-office, and examine its returns on the matter a little more closely. We will glance over a " Report of the Number of Vehicles which passed Bow Church, Cheapside, between the hours of six P. M. on Thursday, the eighth day of August, and six P. M. on Friday, the ninth day of August, one thousand eight hundred and fifty; and the Number of Persons in and with the said vehicles. Also the Number of Foot Passengers who passed during the same time."

Here is the history of a City thoroughfare on an autumn day. 'Tis " post meridan half-past six." Most of the public' and merchants' offices are cleared of their clerks. The principals are at home, dining at the West-end, or are miles away at their villas; yet during the hour between six and seven, eight hundred and fifty-one vehicles, with three thousand three hundred and twenty-three persons riding in or guiding them, and four thousand and forty foot passengers (total seven thousand three hundred and sixty-three), have passed Bow Church. At eleven, when every retailer and every assistant has finished his day's work, the numbers have dropped off to three hundred and fifty-two vehicles and three thousand and seventeen persons. After bedtime the traffic subsides, though it never ceases. The hour between three and four in the morning, is that of the greatest repose; for then, only thirty-five wheeled carriages and one hundred and fifteen individuals pass the Church.

Circulation increases gradually from four o'clock until after breakfast-time. During the hour which ends on the stroke of nine, the numbers are—vehicles, four hundred and eleven; persons, three thousand nine hundred and fifty. Then, business begins in earnest; the public and merchants' offices are to be filled by ten, hence, for that hour, the figures are nearly doubled, standing thus :—carriages, nine hundred and twenty-nine; individuals, eight thousand and seventy-five. The culminating point of traffic is reached at noon, during the hour previous to which one thousand and eighty-two vehicles, and nine thousand eight hundred and fifty-five persons, stream through Cheapside. Then a subsidence takes place until between three and five in the afternoon. During the last of those hours upwards of a thousand carriages and eight thousand eight hundred and eighty individuals are crowding once more towards their houses, their villas, or their lodgings.

What, then, will be the condition of Cheapside, about twelve o'clock, on the eighth day of August, one thousand eight hundred and fifty-one? The lowest estimate we have seen (we do not pledge ourselves to put our trust in it) computes that there will be an extra million of people in the Metropolis, during the most part of the time that the Great Exhibition remains open. These would augment the passengers through the City's centre to *fifteen thousand ;* and, as the new comers will have to be fed with food carried from place to place on wheels, the passage of vehicles will be enormously increased. What they will do when they try to push through the Poultry, the Lord Mayor only knows!

Upon this, another consideration supervenes:—if there will be a deficiency of walking and riding room for the welcome invaders, how are they to be housed?

Although a great pressure of business is being forced upon house agents by persons living in more affluent neighbourhoods who hope to make harvests of profit from the influx of strangers, yet, such strangers as can afford good accommodation and high rents, will, we apprehend, form but a small minority. The majority of visitors will be of the artisan and humbler classes; yet, for such persons, has any temporary accommodation been planned, upon a comprehensive scale? Londoners in their own rank are not so circumstanced as to be able to turn out of their houses to oblige, even to their own profit, the coming strangers; neither are tents particularly well adapted for an English climate.

XVIII.

THE TYRANT OF MINNIGISSENGEN.

FEBRUARY 22, 1851.

" YOUR Serene Highness must not forget that the eyes of Europe are upon us!" exclaimed the Baron Von Rrobrecht, Prime Minister, Commander of the Forces, Privy Councillor, and Minister of Foreign Affairs of the principality of Hesse Minnigissengen.

"But, my dear Baron," returned the Prince, pointing out the passage, "my cousin's letter expressly states that his visit is to be without ceremony."

The Baron Von Rrobrecht proudly drew himself up to his full height. It being a court-day, he was in full dress; for the Reception—which lasted exactly eight minutes—was just over. The display upon the Baron's small round person, would have led a stranger to believe that, in him, were concentrated the highest honours of the greatest realm in Europe. His coat was stiff with embroidery; and, would have been, but for the dimming ravages of Time, gorgeous with gold; it was fastened at the waist with a rainbow of sashes, girdles, and lace; while a grotesque menagerie of honorific animals dangled at his breast. Having expanded his person to its utmost dimensions to give the greater impressiveness to his arguments, he proceeded to say: "Your Highness will permit me to observe, that, in this affair, your Highness's consequence and consideration, in the eyes of foreign courts, are in question. When I had the honour to be attached to the person of his Serene Highness the late Prince your beloved father, we were, under similar circumstances, accustomed to spare no expense."

"Very true; but you must not forget that under those similar circumstances you were obliged to pledge, to the Jews, the diamonds of her Serene Highness the late Princess my beloved mother."

"But, then," interrupted the First Minister, eagerly, "we enjoyed, amongst the neighbouring principalities, the reputation of being the most polished and elegant court in Germany. And," persisted the Baron, "to what did we owe your illustrious predecessor's marriage; which brought him a revenue of ten thousand florins. Why, to the magnificence of his court, when your august uncle visited it. Dazzled by his brilliant reception, the Grand-Duke of Saxe Kissankumagen bestowed on us his sister in marriage."

At the word "marriage" the Prince sighed, and said, abstractedly, "Well, Baron; receive my cousin as you think best:" then sighed again, and was soon plunged into a reverie.

"Nine of the palace servants must have new liveries," said

Rrobrecht, commencing his arrangements. "Your Serene Highness will excuse my absence. I must hasten to the tailor."

That announcement suddenly aroused the royal dreamer.

"To the tailor?" he echoed.

"To the tailor," repeated the functionary.

"Then I will accompany you."

Popularity was thought at that time—to the great discomfort of that thorough absolutist, the Baron Von Rrobrecht—to be a necessary policy of the crown of Hesse Minnigissengen. Revolution was stalking rapidly over Germany; and it was essential that the prince should become familiar with his people. This was not difficult; for his capital consisted of seventy-eight houses, and a population that did not exceed three hundred and two souls, ten per cent. of whom were babies in arms.

The tailor's house was, beyond contradiction, the prettiest dwelling in Minnigissenbourgh; it was approached by a quadruple row of acacias, which were then in full bloom. Under these trees his Serene Highness expressed his intention of taking "a turn," while his Prime Minister entered the house to negotiate the transaction in liveries.

"The business I have come upon is this," said Rrobrecht to Herr Hubert Oberschneider; "we require fifteen new state liveries, complete, by the end of the week."

"Impossible!" said the tailor, dryly.

"Nevertheless," rejoined the Baron, haughtily, "we must have them. His Serene Highness's cousin, his Royal Highness the Prince of Saxe Kissankumagen, is about to pay us a visit."

"*I*, too, am expecting a visitor," rejoined the tailor; "my nephew; and the two or three first days after his arrival are destined to merry-making. No work will be done."

"So!" exclaimed Rrobrecht, with severity. "These are the fruits of that excessive familiarity with which his Highness indulges his subjects. It renders them impertinent."

Mr. Oberschneider lit his pipe. "Baron Rrobrecht," he said, with great composure, "you have the option of giving the Prince's custom to any other tailor you please; I do not seek it; I do not even demand payment of my little bill of four hundred and odd florins. Thank Heaven, I am not in need of them at present. But," continued the tailor, "why do you require fifteen suits, since you have only nine domestics at the palace; one of whom is bedridden?"

"Because," replied Rrobrecht, "we are going, provisionally, to double the number of our retainers." As the tailor went on smoking his pipe, with an irreverent indifference which betokened obstinacy, the Baron found a mollifying tone expedient. "Come, good Master Hubert," he coaxed, "do this for the Prince, and we will not quarrel about price."

"I am hourly expecting my nephew," was the tailor's next remark. "He is coming from Paris after having completed his studies at Göttingen. He is a young man who, to judge by the money he has cost me, must be a wonderful genius. I cannot think of your fifteen suits; all that I can do is to lend his Highness *my* people's clothes. My nephew, I dare say, will not care about being received in grand liveries."

The Baron groaned inwardly. "I must," he thought, "lower our dignity before this miserable tailor's money-bags!" The Minister of State then tapped his snuff-box, and cogitated profoundly. At length he caught an idea. "You will change the collars and facings to our colour?" he asked.

"Willingly:" and Master Hubert held out his hand to the Baron, for the purpose of clinching the bargain. The latter, though deeply shocked at this familiarity, thought it better, under present circumstances, to swallow his resentment; and, exerting a gentle violence over his pride, he mildly shook the outstretched digits of the independent tailor.

"Ah!" thought Rrobrecht, as he proceeded to rejoin the Prince. "If I could only persuade his Highness to create some sort of income or property-tax, we should soon pull down the pride of these moneyed gentlemen."

As he advanced under the acacias, Rrobrecht discovered that the Prince was not alone. He was too discreet a courtier to interrupt a *tête-à-tête*, and bent his steps where numerous and pressing engagements required his presence. The sex and beauty of the Prince's companion explained, perhaps, the eagerness with which his Highness accompanied his Minister to the spot. He was long in quitting it. For more than an hour he and Albertina, the tailor's daughter, paced the avenue.

Early on the morning of the day appointed for their visitor's arrival, the Baron Von Rrobrecht, magnificently attired, and glittering in the effulgence of all his orders, presented for the Prince's signature a closely written parchment: it was the royal consent to the sale of a farm.

"The means are violent, I must admit," said Rrobrecht; "but, then, our peculiar position demands the sacrifice. We shall thus be enabled to receive your august cousin (although travelling in modest incognito) with proper pomp and splendour."

The Prince signed without reading.

About eleven o'clock in the forenoon, Rrobrecht again made his appearance, to announce that some peasants had seen a horseman of distinguished mien, but evidently travelling incognito, enter the inn at Zwéibrüken, on the frontiers—about a quarter of a league distant—having previously inquired his way to Minnigissenbourgh.

The Prince mounted his charger, and set off to meet the visitor, accompanied by Rrobrecht, the soldiery, and the band. To tell the truth, his Serene Highness was delighted at getting away from home for a short time, under whatever pretext; for, during the last two or three days, all had been at sixes and sevens in the palace. His own valet had been metamorphosed by the Baron into a sort of grand chamberlain. A horrible noise of hammering rendered the palace unbearable. All the old state-rooms had been furbished up with the furniture which but scantily garnished the private apartments.

As they approached the frontier, they beheld a cloud of dust. Rrobrecht drew up his forces in open order, and the band began to tune their instruments: but it was only the postman who trotted by without stopping. The Prince, it should be mentioned here, was an amateur, and, out of the seventy men of which his army consisted, forty-five were musicians. In a few minutes a denser cloud of dust appeared, and rapidly increased in volume and propinquity. Rrobrecht gave the signal, and the band struck up Spontini's *marche triomphale.*

Then there issued from the cloud a horse covered with foam. A figure was seated on it, clad precisely in the way in which a peasant would suppose noblemen go about. The costume was

ultra-fashionable and gaudy; consisting partly of the dress of
the German students, and partly of that of the young Parisian
exquisites of the day.

He halted. Rrobrecht, who had dismounted, walked
solemnly up to the side of the horse, and commenced reading
an address of welcome. The soldiery presented arms.

The new comer stood erect in his stirrups with surprise.
The Prince laughed. Rrobrecht had not got further in his
recitation than—"Penetrated with a sense of delight at the
honour conferred by your Royal Highness's presence, we
cordially——" when the horseman expressed a hope to the
Prince that the old gentleman was not a dangerous lunatic;
for a lunatic of some sort he assuredly thought him.

"This is all a mistake," said the Prince.

"I should think it was," asserted the stranger. "Don't
you know who I am, old fellow?"

These expressions assured the Baron that their utterer was
not his Royal Highness the Grand-Duke of Saxe Kissankumagen.

"I am Heinrich, nephew to Master Hubert Oberschneider
the tailor," continued the free-and-easy student. He then
cantered off, leaving the soldiery at "present arms;" the
band playing the march of triumph, and the Prince reeling
with laughter in his saddle.

The disgusted Lord High Chamberlain and Commander-in-
Cheif pocketed his address, and set his army in motion
towards home. On arriving at the palace, a letter was put
into the Prince's hand by the postman who had passed them
on the road, announcing that his cousin had been obliged to
change his route.

Everything was in readiness for the *fête* which was intended to dazzle and astound his Royal Highness the Grand-
Duke of Saxe Kissankumagen; and the Premier was in despair! The Prince, on the contrary, took no pains to conceal
his delight. "Baron," he said, "your talent for arranging
and managing a *fête* shall not be thrown away. The festival
shall still be held. You have my permision to command the
presence of every soul in the city." His Serene Highness
then sat down, and wrote an autograph letter to Mr. Oberschneider, inviting him, his daughter, and nephew, to dinner.

At this democratic proceeding, the Baron Von Rrobrecht trembled for the security of the throne of Hesse Minnigissengen. But the Prince was peremptory, and the state servant was obliged to obey.

The invitation set every member of the establishment near the acacias in an exceeding flutter, except Heinrich. That young gentleman, having imbibed the politics of the least respectable of the Parisian estaminets, told his uncle that he would never sit at the table of a "tyrant."

Oberschneider, who was tying on his whitest neckcloth at the glass, made a grimace expressive of the most condign ridicule; to which his nephew retorted that he—Hubert Oberschneider, tailor—was a worshipper of power, and a sycophant! The uncle—an easy-going, but shrewd man, who regularly read the papers, and knew what was going on in the world—said to his daughter, while escorting her to the palace, "The truth is, my dear, your cousin has got hold of those egregious notions which are so flattering to people who prefer amusement or idleness, to work. Property is robbery; restraint, tyranny; government, brigandage."

"How very odd!" said Albertina; who knew nothing of politics, and was thinking of the Prince.

The tailor went on, warming as his subject expanded. "Confounding such silly theories with the glorious acts of the true patriots, who have burst the bonds of royal chicanery in France, and of tyranny in some portions of this empire, Heinrich has, I fear, brought notions home to my shop which will unsettle the heads of all my journeymen."

"How very naughty of him!" said Albertina; because she felt it was necessary she must say something just then.

When they arrived at the palace, the Prince received them in the throne-room, with marked distinction. The Baron Rrobrecht grinned and bore it (like one of his own heraldic hyenas) with wonderful fortitude.

The dinner went off well; because the rain, which fell in torrents, could not spoil that. But the fireworks proved utterly uninflammable, the thunderstorm drowned the music, and nobody could dance on the lawn; yet Albertina was there, and the Prince was delighted. She wore his favorite colours —white with blue ribbons.

" Baron," said he that night after his guests had departed, " your *fête* was charming and amused me immensely. You may sell another farm to-morrow."

" Something must be done," returned the Prime Minister, who, to his other multifarious places, added that of Chancellor of the Exchequer ; " our coffers are exhausted, and two years' revenues have been already anticipated. Only one resource remains——"

" Which is——?" interrogated the Prince, as he folded up a piece of blue ribbon and put it inside his vest.

" Marriage !"

The Premier said this very solemnly. " You have a crowd of wealthy and noble cousins, out of which your Serene Highness might choose a wife—a rich wife."

The Prince yawned. He was tired. Would Von Rrobrecht ring for his valet ?

Many days had not elapsed since the grand *fête* at the palace in honour of the Prince who did not arrive, before old Hubert's fears about his nephew proved true to the letter. He had originally conceived the idea of getting up a match between Albertina and her cousin; but the young student's coarse and turbulent manners were in the highest degree displeasing to the girl, and Heinrich himself made no efforts to overcome her antipathy. He passed his time in the public-houses, uttering a variety of common-places to a pack of young fellows, as idle and ill-disposed as himself. He formed them into a Club, and explained to them his political creed. He spoke a great deal about Brutus, and a " bloated oligarchy ;" by which he meant the First Minister, who united in his own podgy little person all the aristocratic and oligarchical power of the state. He denounced the Prince merely as an incarnation of royalty, against which he made war in the abstract; but—because, perhaps, he found the roll of the Baron's name tell with effect in his harangues (for he had learned at Paris to revel in the canine letter), his enmity towards the Baron " R-r-r-r-robrecht" was relentless. Every misfortune that happened to anybody, he attributed to the Government ; otherwise to the bloated oligarchy ; otherwise to R-r-r-r-robrecht. The storm on the night of the *fête* he traced to the vengeance of Heaven on the atrocious vices, corruptions, and oppressions

. of the court. When Hans Hiccup the cobbler reduced himself to beggary by beer, and people would not trust him with their boots, Heinrich held him up as a martyr to political oppression, and demanded an organisation of labour. When Madame Maggschifter's baby took the small-pox, Heinrich had no manner of doubt that the infant had been infected by a secret emissary of Government. The Club spread the sentiments which their leader originated, and obtained the support of all the idlers in Minnigissenbourgh.

Yet, for a people ground down by all manner of social and political oppression, the Minnigissenbourghers did not seem to be an unhappy or discontented community. Each lived in the bosom of his family. In the evening, under the acacias or lime trees that overshadowed these miserable people's porches might be heard the cheerful song, with its accompaniment of flute or harpsicord; neither was the native hurdy-gurdy silent.

It happened about this time that a violent hailstorm did · some damage to the crops. This was an opportunity not to be lost. Heinrich and his acolytes spread themselves over the principality (this was soon done, and at a cost for travelling expenses quite nominal), bewailing the loss of the husband-men. They insinuated that one of the rights of the horticul-tural and agricultural interests was that of not having their glass broken, and their fields cut up by hail.

This doctrine soon became popular; for the most disagree-able of all human misfortunes are those which we are unable to lay at our neighbour's door. We would all of us rather be stoned almost to death by a man upon whom we can be re-venged than be ever so gently hit by an aërolite, for the fall of which no one is responsible. Urged on, therefore, by the Club, the farmers profited by the hailstorm to neglect paying their rent, and to utter loud complaints and woeful lamentations.

The consequence of such defalcation* was that the State Treasury became more and more impoverished; and Rro-brecht was obliged to discharge more servants, and sell two of the three horses which his royal master still possessed. Un-der these disagreeable circumstances, however, the Prince had his consolation. He practised new symphonies with his mu-sicians; he passed his time in angling, and in botanising expe-ditions into the woods, close to the dwelling of Master Hubert

Oberschneider; where, by some extraordinary confluence of circumstances, he had very frequently the pleasure (entirely by accident) of meeting Albertina.

One day the student Heinrich, mounted upon a table covered with pots of beer and drinking-horns, spoke thus to his followers, at what he was pleased to term a Monster Meeting. Thirty-seven malcontents were actually present:

"It is time, my friends, that a corrupt and bloated oligarchy should cease from battening upon our substance! It is cowardice that produces the insolence of kings! Let us rend asunder the chains that have too long held captive our beautiful fatherland. Let us break the yoke of tyranny! Let us proceed at once to the palace, where the tyrant gives himself up to impure delights, surrounded by Von R-r-r-r-robrecht and his ferocious satellites: let us reclaim our right and liberties, or perish in the attempt!"

By the time the peroration was finished, the crowd had increased to very nearly threescore.

While these affairs, big with the fate of Minnigissenbourgh, were passing at the *bierhaus*, the Prince was sauntering in his garden, plucking dead leaves from four favourite carnations, and angling for rhymes for a sonnet to Albertine's blue eyes. "Desires" and "fires" were just arranging themselves prettily at the ends of a couplet, when the conspirators, burning with beer and patriotism, arrived at the palace gates.

One of the ferocious satellites, of whom Heinrich had spoken, was then busily engaged in practising on the flute, his difficult part in the overture to Zauberflöte, which the band was to perform on the following day. This warrior (who was posted as a sentry while practising) permitted the revolters to pass, on their stating that they desired to speak to the Prince. But, as a preliminary precaution, he put down his flute, shouldered his firelock, dressed himself up in line with his sentry-box; and asked the invaders to be so good as to keep on the gravel-walks, and not to pluck the flowers.

The Prince, though a little surprised at this great gathering, turned his calm and indifferent countenance carelessly on the mob; and when he demanded what they wanted with him? no one had sufficient nerve to speak. They replied only by confused and almost unintelligible cries; amongst which, how-

ever might be detected a timid stuttering, which sounded like
"Down with the tyrant!"

The Prince smiled, and, in a voice which was clearly audible
above the whispered clamour of the disaffected, said :

"Let some one among you speak for the whole : for, if you
all speak in turns, it will take up too much time ; and, if altogether, you will not be intelligible."

At these words there was a dead silence. All recoiled a few
paces ; leaving by common assent to the student Heinrich the
right of explaining those grievances, of which none were exactly cognisant.

"We stand here," said Heinrich, "in the name of——"

"Pray don't stand!" interrupted the Prince, pointing to a
rustic chair.

"We come," continued the orator, not heeding the sarcas-
tic invitation, "to protest against abuses too long suffered.
We come in the name of the People!"

"My good friend," said the Prince. "My people are not
so numerous as to have need of delegates. Haven't they
spoken for themselves? Let them assemble to-morrow in the
inner court of the palace, and, if they wish it, we will have a
chat together."

"The people have no time to wait!" exclaimed the orator,
fiercely.

"Believe me, Monsier Heinrich, my calling of Prince is not
such a delightful profession that I should desire to exercise it
every day. I shall be a prince to-morrow ; to-day I am but
a private individual, very anxious respecting the fate of a
beautiful carnation of which I have just set a cutting. As a
private individual, therefore, I desire to be master in my own
house. So, my friends, be advised by me, and go home.
Above all things, do not tread upon my carnations.

Heinrich turned towards his friends. "Are you content,"
he said, "with the evasive, the ferocious irony, which has dictated the tyrant's words?"

"My worthy friend Heinrich," said the Prince quietly, "you
really *must* be so obliging as to leave my garden."

"I see," said Heinrich, "that the end of the career which
I have embraced, will bring me but a martyr's crown. Well, I
am ready to shed my blood for the People. Take my head!"

"Your head? What should I do with your head? It is
useless even to yourself," responded the Prince. "I shall expect my people to-morrow. I have some excellent beer; and
we will discuss that while we talk over our affairs. In case of
rain, there shall be an awning."

When the delegates had departed, the Prince made a
bouquet of his finest carnations for Albertina; and wrote to
remind her that she had promised to waltz with him on the
ensuing evening.

At daybreak next morning the band assembled at the
palace, for the final rehearsal of Beethoven's overture, which
was to be performed, for the first time in public, that
evening.

"What on earth can my people want with me?" thought
Richard; "and what unfortunate accident can have recalled
to their minds that I am a prince? However," he exclaimed to a servant, "rinse out some glasses for my people! Happy the sovereign who can thus hob-nob with his
subjects!"

At the appointed hour, an assemblage of about one hundred persons made their appearance at the palace. After
them came a second hundred, to see what the first hundred
were about; and finally, the whole of the remaining inhabitants of the capital who were capable of locomotion, brought
up the rear, anxious to ascertain the cause of the unaccustomed gathering.

"My friends, said his Serene Highness, "drink your beer
while it is fresh."

The people did as they were told.

When the barrels had to be tilted, the Prince asked his
people what they wanted? "Have I," he said, "ever interfered with your pleasures or your affairs? Do I even know
what you do, or how you pass your time?"

"Down with the tyrants!" said Heinrich.

"Down with the tyrants!" shouted the Club in cuckoo
chorus.

"Why is the Prince surrounded with guards?" demanded
Heinrich.

"I am surrounded by my musicians," replied the Prince;
"the rest of the soldiers are gone out to take a walk. Pray

be silent for one moment and listen to me:—I am not rich; but he among you, whoever he be, who has wished to partake of my soup or my beer, has he not ever been welcome?"

No one could deny this, therefore their leader went off into generalities.

"We desire," said Heinrich, "the liberty of the press."

"Yes, we desire the liberty of the press," repeated the Club.

"Well," replied the Prince, "buy a press if you want one. You have my full liberty to use it if you know how. But, alas, I am afraid that there are a great many of you who cannot read."

Something was then said about "dying for liberty and fatherland;" but, during the parley, Von Rrobrecht had succeeded in collecting the scattered forces, and now disposed them round the court-yard. "I beg to acquaint your Highness," said he, pompously, "that our troops hem in the rebels on all sides, and that they are now in our power."

"I am sorry to hear it," said Richard: "for what am I to do with rebels? I have no place to put them in. There is but one prison in Minnigissenbourgh, and that I converted long ago into an orangery. Dismiss the soldiers!"

"But if I might suggest to your Highness—your personal safety——"

"Pray don't alarm yourself about trifles, Baron, and do as I bid you."

"Treachery!" shouted Heinrich, as the soldiers moved.

"Treachery! echoed the Club.

"The palace of the tyrant is about to be reddened with the blood of patriots!" screamed Heinrich hoarsely.

But no denunciative enthusiasm was to be infused into the other patriots; too much of whose attentions were riveted on the Prince's beer. When they found the casks producing nothing but lees, they sauntered peaceably home.

After the signal failure of this "demonstration," all went on well for some time.

There being no Press, the liberty thereof could not be taken advantage of, and the pen supplied its place. Heinrich started a newspaper in manuscript, although never was a place so destitute of news as Minnigissenbourgh. However, despite few occurrences, leaders abounded. "R-r-r-r-robrecht," above all, was never spared; and the Prime Minister came one day to the Prince to request his permission to start a newspaper also.

"They have desired the liberty of the press," said his Highness; "that liberty is yours as well as theirs, and you may use it as you think proper."

Then began the great paper war between Rrobrecht and Heinrich. The rival journals appeared every morning. Heinrich expressed in every number his conviction that all princes were criminals; Rrobrecht inculcated that a sovereign's most trivial action was angelic. One day the Baron announced "that his Serene Highness was in excellent health and spirits; no addition was made to the illustrious dinner circle; and his Serene Highness ate French beans." On the next day, Heinrich's paper came out with, "How long will an enslaved people suffer Tyranny to eat French beans?" In the succeeding number of Rrobrecht's paper it was replied, "That the Prince's fondness for French beans showed his unflinching desire to encourage agriculture."

"To eat French beans," retorted Heinrich, in Number three, "is a bitter mockery of the people; who cannot afford even sour-krout."

One evening the Prince was walking under the lime trees; Albertina happened (accidentally, as usual) to be passing that way. She showed the rival papers to the Prince. He laughed heartily at Heinrich's denunciations, and commanded Rrobrecht to discontinue his "organ" altogether.

In the mean while, Prince Richard's affairs went from bad to worse, until they brought him to the condition of a gentleman in hopelessly embarrassed circumstances. He had hardly a florin to bless himself with. Retrenchment was imperative. Having communicated with certain potentates, he therefore assembled his army, and addressed his brave soldiery in the following terms:

"My friends, I have no longer the means of paying you. I have, accordingly, disposed of your services to a great power, who will lead you into Africa and glory. You will have double pay."

The Commissariat arrangements were neither extensive nor intricate; and the entire force was soon in heavy marching order (band included), with drums beating and colours flying. The departing army made its first halt, on its way to Africa, at Zwéibrüken, the head-quarters of beer.

René of Anjou has said, that a king without music is a crowned ass; and the Prince, after the departure of his brave band, became the most unhappy of monarchs. Albertina alone consoled him: but in a very short time she also took her departure, accompanied by a female attendant. The alleged reason for the journey was a visit to an old relation.

The loss of his farms, of his fortune, of his army, and even of his band, did not affect the Prince so much as the loss of Albertina; and the Prince placed in Rrobrecht's hands a letter addressed to his Serene Highness's uncle, in these terms:

"MY DEAR UNCLE,—I neither can, nor do I any longer desire to remain a Prince.

"When you receive this letter, I shall have taken my departure from my dominions. I abandon to you all my rights; requiring only at your hands, as a compensation for the same, a yearly pension of one thousand five hundred florins. I will let you know when you are to forward me my pension, and where. Keep Rrobrecht near your person: he is a good and loyal servant.

"I embrace you affectionately,
"RICHARD-AUGUSTUS-FREDERIC-ERNEST-
ALPHONSE-HANS-ALBERT."

The following morning, as soon as the rising sun had tinged with its first rosy beams the muslin curtains of his bed-room windows—silk curtains were used only in the throne-room—his Serene Highness sprang from his couch, dressed himself hastily, and proceeded to pack into a small valise his four most precious articles. To wit:

A small canvas bag containing thirty crowns.

A blue sash which had formerly encircled Albertina's waist.

Albertina's letters.

His own favourite flute.

This done, he glided down stairs, placed the valise upon his horse, mounted, and took his departure from Minnigissen-bourgh. When he had reached the outskirts of the town, he paused, looked round, and his eyes rested upon the acacias which overshadowed the tailor's dwelling. After a long gaze, he sighed and went his way.

His horse padded on steadily. Towards evening, he arrived at a little forest retreat, also surrounded by acacias, and fronted by a nicely-mown grass-plot dotted with several flower-beds, each containing a variety of carnations in full bloom.

He entered the cottage, and an aged domestic received him politely. He had scarcely sat down near the window, when he perceived, at a turning of the gravel walk, two ladies approaching. One of them was old, of a gentle and prepossessing countenance; the other was Albertina.

In a few words the ex-Prince put the ladies in possession of all that had occurred. "Albertina," said the Prince, "how sweet would be a life spent here with you! I cannot now demand your hand, after having been refused possession of it when I was a prince. Behold to-day my entire fortune!—— I have thirty ducats in my valise, and I am assured a pension of fifteen hundred florins a year."

"My Prince," said the aunt, "you have no cause for despair. Albertina loves you. Remain here. She shall come to see me every month; and, when I shall have been assured that your resolution of marrying her is not the result of a momentary enthusiasm; when I am convinced that you do not regret your palace and power, then we will arrange all for the best."

Richard could make no other reply than that of kissing the kind old lady's wrinkled hand.

When she presented to him, three months later, the little hand of Albertina, he exclaimed, as he pressed it to his lips, "Adieu, adieu, Hesse Minnigissengen; adieu the sad past! And yet blessings be upon it, if it has been the price of the future!"

The future was happiness both to him and to Albertina. As plain unostentatious man and wife, they both henceforth lived in the cottage part of the year, and in the finest seasons took pleasant tours to different parts of Europe.

The conclusion of the history of the great political movement which caused the ultimate downfall of the Tyrant of Hesse Minnigissengen, is soon told. By twelve o'clock on the day upon which the Prince fled there were eight princes of

Hesse Minnigissengen; the same evening there were thirty-two. On the following morning, the Prince's uncle—who had gladly accepted his nephew's offer—sent over to Minnigissenbourgh an armed force, consisting of a corporal and ten men. In the brief space of two hours, these troops, effectually and for ever, nipped the budding germs of the great Minnigissenbourgh revolt.*

XIX.

TEN MINUTES WITH HER MAJESTY.

MARCH 1, 1851.

In divulging the details of a distinguished honour, we are not, we hope and believe, committing any breach of court confidence. A desire to gratify the pardonable curiosity of all classes of the community respecting the person of our beloved Sovereign, will not, we feel sure, be construed harshly. We are, indeed, incapable of rudely bursting the golden bonds of Etiquette that doth hedge the throne.

To guard against the imputation of boasting of a higher privilege than that really extended to us, we think it right to mention at once, that the business which took us into the presence of the highest personage in the Realm, was not of a private nature.

The memorable morning was a bright one in February, the fourth of that month. The sky was cloudless; a brilliant sun gave to it that cheering character which—from the good fortune Her Majesty experiences whenever she appears publicly —has passed into a proverb, as "The Queen's Weather." The conveyance in which we were approaching the palace— that of Westminster—was suddenly stopped at Charing-cross. A great crowd had collected between that point and our destination. A long *queue* of carriages, of which our Hansom formed the last joint, had been brought to a stand; and when, after a time, we were permitted to move on, we perceived that not only the streets, but the fronts of the houses, were thickly lined. Individuals of every age, size, and condition, occupied

---

* A part of this story is derived from a sketch by Alphonse Karr.

the pavements. The houses were decorated with a bright
variegation of lovely faces, prettily framed in bewitching bonnets. Every window was filled; every balcony-crowded; even
the roofs of the public offices were tenanted. Head over head
appeared on the steps of doors; the owners of apple-stalls,
fitting them up as temporary standing-places, realised small
fortunes; and, on grades of seats protected by crimson awn-
ings and built over areas, reclined the beauty and chivalry of
eighteen hundred and fifty-one; recalling the days of the
" Tilt-yard," whose site they actually overlooked. The standing army of spectators gave the docile Life Guards and patient policemen but little trouble to keep the carriage-road
clear; for they passed the time pleasantly in viewing the procession of ladies and great officers of state slowly drawn along
on the same errand as ourselves.

The stopping of a hackney cabriolet at the entrance of that
portion of Her Majesty's Palace of Westminster which is devoted to the deliberations of the lords spiritual and temporal
in Parliament assembled, is not calculated to produce such
solemn impressions upon the attendant police and marshals'
men, as emblazoned panels drawn up, under the auspices of a
court coachman in a full-bottomed wig. On alighting, therefore, the only mark of attention we received, was from an
official, who, with the anxious look of one who thinks he has
encountered an intruder, demanded a sight of our credentials.
One glance at the signature of the Lord High Chamberlain in
the corner of our card, sufficed to dispel his anxiety; and,
with a bland smile of relief, he waved his truncheon towards
the staircase it was necessary for us to mount—the same
which, at no distant period of time, was to be pressed by the
feet of Royalty. In expectation of that event, more royal
subjects lined the avenues, and stood on the. stairs. In fact,
from the drawing-room door of Buckingham Palace, to the
foot of the throne in the House of Lords, an unbroken lane
of loving subjects ranged themselves to behold their Queen.

No one who enters the House of Lords for the first time
can suppress a certain emotion. As an assemblage of florid
ornament, as a specimen of gorgeous decoration, this chamber
is, perhaps, unsurpassed in the world; but whether the emotion be that of sober reverence for the high functions per-

formed in it, or a flash of exhilaration called up by a surpris-
ingly gaudy ball-room, it is not necessary to inquire. It must
be owned, however, that a ceiling blazing with gold, a floor of
burning red, a throne of burnished brass, and galleries en-
amelled with coloured mastics, can scarcely be consonant with
the important interests gravely discussed by the Peers of
Great Britain. Yet, at the performance of a state ceremony,
when the whole house is surrendered to a court pageantry
and proudly decked Beauty, the apartment is not inappro
priate.

When we entered, the Peeresses' gallery was untenanted ;
but a group of privileged ladies had already assembled upon
the back benches on each side of the floor. Both groups were
fast augmented by fresh arrivals, guided to seats by good-
natured ushers, in black silks and brass badges. The honest,
familiar pleasantry of the most active of these functionaries
would have astonished those who associate courts with nothing but stately formality. To one bevy of beauties he smilingly observes, " Ah ! you're on the Peers' benches—that will
never do. *This* way, if you please !" And the ladies flutter
after him to a back seat. "*Will* you sit a little closer ?" he
asks of several other ladies, regardless of the amplitude of
brocades and the probable crushing of satins. Frigid formality—for which the vulgar invariably give the aristocracy
credit—is not to be met with even in the House of Lords,
on the opening of Parliament : a buzz of conversation commences ; above which rises, now and then, the music of a merry
laugh. Presently a few peers, in their red and ermined robes,
drop in ; then an ambassador or two ; and conversation
becomes general. As the appointed hour approaches, the
House fills ; the Peeresses' gallery being the soonest occupied.

The picture of a peeress present to the imaginations of the
million, is that of a tall lady, with a long train, a diamond
stomacher, and jewelled hair glistening under an arch of ostrich
feathers. That is an Old School portrait. It is all altered
now. Only one arching plume could we espy ; not a single
train ; a display of precious stones far from overwhelming ;—
an array of costume, in short, of which the hackneyed epithet
" elegant simplicity," is the true expression. An ordinary
assemblage of ladies of middle rank at an evening party seen

by daylight, would present the same general appearance as
that displayed in the House of Lords on the opening of Parliament.

The hands of the clock move on. Bishops, lay peers, judges,
ambassadors, converse in knots on the vacant spaces around
the throne, the woolsack, and the clerks' table, and the hum
of gossip grows louder and louder. "There," to borrow a
sentence (not unworthy of a footman) from De Foe, "you see
blue and green ribbons sitting familiarly, and talking with the
same freedom as if they had left their quality and degrees of
distance at home." It is a huge *conversazione*. The even
tenor of the buzz, reverberating from every corner, is only
interrupted by the clanking of the spurs and accoutrements
of the military lords and the officers of the guard. The good-
tempered little gentleman in black, threads his way upon the
floor of the House with increased alacrity. More visitors and
less room! His entreaties to his fair charges to economise
sittings are redoubled. At length he has found the last visitor
a seat, and many eyes are turned towards the clock ;—the
hands have passed the figure " II."

A slight but sudden lull denotes that experienced ears have
distingushed, above the dulled roar of the crowd, the booming
of distant cannon. Her Majesty has started from Buckingham
Palace ; and her approach is gradually heralded by the dead-
ened sounds of successive salutes. Conversation ceases, and
a great fluttering ensues. Every peer finds his allotted place.
The Lord Chamberlain, the State Officers, the Gentlemen-at-
Arms, and other officials, retire into the Prince's chamber,
through doors on each side of the throne, to receive their mistress.

Now, there is not a sound. So sudden and dead a silence
in so dense a crowd—nine-tenths of which (may they forgive
us for adding !) are women—excites surprise. A pattering
noise comes from outside. It can hardly be rain, for the sun
floods the chamber with his light through the livid countenances and parti-hued figures of the glass kings and queens.
Hall ? No. What you hear from without are the wheels of
passing vehicles grinding their gritty way on the gravel. The
grinding increases, and then suddenly stops. You think you

can disguish a cheer, muffled by the thick walls. The Queen is alighting.

During a very few minutes all eyes are turned towards the little door on the right side of the throne. Silently—with no flourish of trumpets; without the faintest note of preparation—it opens. Two heralds appear; then two more; then the Lord Chamberlain; and next, the Queen herself and Prince Albert, attended by the Mistress of the Robes, and the great Officers of State, including the Lord Chancellor and the Duke of Wellington.

Every being in the House rises. The Queen—her hand in that of Prince Albert—mounts the steps of the throne, her train borne by two pages, and spread over the back of the state chair by the Duchess of Sutherland. She sits: then rises; and, with graceful gesture, bids the assembly to be seated also, and then sits again. The Prince reclines in the arm-chair on the left side of the throne.

The pause which ensues while the Usher of the Black Rod departs to summon the "Faithful Commons," would be painful, were we not occupied in taking a survey of the magnificent spectacle as it is now arranged. The Queen, richly, tastefully robed—her head-dress a tiara of diamonds, formed like a mural crown—pleasantly addresses a few whispers to the attendant Duchess. The Prince is not within speaking distance, and surveys the House in the glittering uniform and jack-boots of a Field Marshal. The Duke of Wellington holds erect the sword of state on one side of the Queen; on the other, the Marquis of Winchester displays the Cap of Maintenance, and beside him, upon the extended arms of the Marquis of Lansdowne, rest the cushion and the crown.

The sensation of beauty communicated through the eye when it drinks in an endless variety and exquisite groupings of colour, is that which predominates, on viewing the scene in the mass, from above. Two large patches of spectators, arrayed in every tint and texture of women's attire, are fringed by the red robes of the lay peers on the bottom benches, and tapered off on one side by the lawn sleeves of the bishops; while, in the Peeresses' gallery, similar hues are repeated—from the black silk of the mourner to the white satin of the bride. On the right of the throne, in the Ambassador's box,

is a more compact kaleidoscope of colours. The red Fez cap
of the Turkish envoy, and the sky-blue uniform of the Foreign
Minister of one of the Northern Courts, tell out conspicuously
from the rest. Opposite, on the left of the throne, a group of
Life Guards and Gentlemen-at-Arms make a gorgeous display
of scarlet and gold. The judges of the land, packed together
on the woolsack under their powdered wigs, look like a bed
of blooming cauliflowers.

This gorgeous still-life is suddenly and rudely animated by
disorderly sounds, like the opening of the pit door of a theatre, or the battering in of a house at a riot. The Speaker of
the House of Commons answers the summons of his liege lady
the Queen, as if he were a schoolmaster with a mob of unman-
nerly boys at his heels; and is propelled to the bar of the
House with the frantic fear of being knocked down and tram-
pled upon, by the rush of M. P.s. A transient cloud passes
over the Royal countenance; but it is rapidly succeeded by a
succession of smiles at the ludicrous efforts of a couple of
hundred of her eager Commons to squeeze themselves into
space enough for only a hundred. The account of a sufferer
in the scramble is amusing: "I happened," said Mr. Joseph
Hume, in his place in Parliament on the following evening,
"to be the twenty-fifth from the Speaker; but both sides of
the bar were so filled, that I neither saw the Queen, nor heard
her voice. I was knocked against a corner; my head was
knocked against a post, and I might have been much injured,
if a stout member, to whom I felt much obliged, had not come
to my assistance. (Hear, hear, and laughter.) It was no
laughing matter." Mr. Hume recollected, moreover, that on
a similar occasion, the coat of a member of the House who
now fills a high office abroad, had been torn, and that his
shoulder was dislocated.

Before the hubbub at the bar has quite subsided, the Lord
Chancellor, kneeling on the step of the throne, presents to the
Queen the manuscript of the speech. Its appearance is that of
a piece of music, so unskilfully stitched with ribbon to a cover,
that the royal reader is more than once interrupted by a difficulty in turning over the leaves. At the words, "My Lords
and Gentlemen," increased efforts are made at the bar towards

silence. The Queen pauses for an instant; but when she re-sumes, not a sound is heard but her voice.

In clear, fresh, distinct tones, Queen Victoria expresses her satisfaction at again meeting her Parliament. She continues to maintain relations of peace and amity with Foreign Powers. She is much gratified that the German Confederation and the Government of Denmark are putting an end to hostilities which threatened the Peace of Europe, and that the Government of Brazil has taken new and efficient measures to abolish the "atrocious" traffic in slaves. The "Gentlemen of the House of Commons" are assured, as usual, that the Estimates of the coming year have been framed with a due regard to economy and to the necessities of the public service. "My Lords and Gentlemen" are again addressed in terms of satis-faction at the prosperity of the country, with the exception of the owners and occupiers of land; but a hope is expressed that the prosperous condition of all other classes will eventually diminish even their difficulties.

Here there is a short pause. And the following sentences are read with a slight elevation of tone:

"The recent assumption of certain ecclesiastical titles conferred by a for-eign power, has excited strong feelings in this country, and large bodies of my subjects have presented addresses to me, expressing attachment to the Throne, and praying that such assumption should be resisted. I have assured them of my resolution to maintain the rights of my Crown, and the independence of the nation, against all encroachment, from whatever quarter it may proceed. I have, at the same time, expressed my earnest and firm determination, under God's blessing, to maintain unimpaired, the religious liberty which is so justly prized by the people of this country."

After announcing measures for the better administration of justice, and for the registry of deeds, a peroration closes the political brief. The cover is folded over; and the manuscript handed to the Lord Chancellor.

The elocution of the speech was perfect. Nature has com-bined in Queen Victoria's voice, sweetness, youthfulness, and fulness; and Art has taught her to deliver it with exceeding purity of tone, and without the smallest effort. Every sylla-ble, therefore, found its way into every sound pair of ears in the House; except those placed, unhappily like Mr. Joseph Hume, more than twenty-five removes from the Speaker—not of the speech—but of the House of Commons.

The music of the last words has scarcely passed into silence before the Queen rises, and bows to the spectators; who, also, rise in a body. Prince Albert hands her from the throne, and the short procession retires into the Prince's chamber in the same order as it entered. This ends the ceremony which has lasted but very little more than ten minutes. In a few minutes the House of Lords is left to the sole occupation of the dapper gentleman in black.

We have heard a great deal of the powers of the Press, and have experienced the wonders of the electric telegraph; but those who had the privilege of spending ten minutes with Her Majesty, in opening Parliament, must have been a little startled on reaching Whitehall, to be offered an evening newspaper containing the Queen's speech; the last sentence of which from the Queen's lips had hardly died on the ear. Wonder, too, would be increased by the recollection that although the Reporters' gallery was filled, not one of the Gentlemen of the Press had taken a note. By what magic, then, could the speech have been so quickly printed?

Everybody knows that the "Queen's Speech" does not deserve its name. It is not the Queen's; nor is it a speech;—it is a *document*. The First Minister sketches it, subsequent Cabinet Councils reduce it to shape, and it is then submitted to Her Majesty. When returned with her approval, the speech is divulged (at a ministerial dinner) to the non-cabinet members of the administration. Thus the mere topics of the manifesto ooze out at the Clubs the night before the speech is spoken. But it is the actual text which the public is eager for; and, that no time may be lost, emissaries from the London evening papers appear at the Treasury about the time Her Majesty is preparing her toilette, at Buckingham Palace, for the ceremony. The moment the first gun announces that the procession is in motion, the evening paper envoys are obliged with copies of the document; and before the Queen has done speaking in the House her words are in type.

Formerly the Gentlemen of the Press were locked in a room in the Treasury till the *cortège* was on its way back. Some years ago an escape was made from this official durance, which caused some amusement. The editor of the Government paper in Dublin was most anxious to start for Liverpool by one o'clock, to catch the packet for Dublin. The speech was handed to him some time before that hour, and the key was turned upon him as usual. Presently the clerks and messengers were alarmed by frantic cries of "Fire!" They opened the door: the room was filled with smoke. The editor, in the confusion, made his escape, leaving the frightened clerks to extinguish the harmless sheet of brown paper he had intentionally ignited.

We, of the present day, improve on the Irish editor's plan. His was a fire escape; our's are lightning conductors. It is at such a time as this, that the wonders of the Electric Telegraph become startlingly apparent. The City of Edinburgh is about four hundred miles from Buckingham Palace. While the state procession is wending its slow way back from Westminster, the wires are charged; and—marvellous fact!—at the same moment that Her Majesty is alighting at the steps of the Marble Hall, several of her lieges in the Scottish capital are beginning to read her speech; which has taken no more than fifteen minutes to transmit. She dines at Windsor; and before the banquet is over, the text, *verbatim et literatim*, of what she had uttered at a quarter-past two, has reached Dublin. Before the royal family has retired to rest, the speech is published in every principal town in the kingdom. In these cases there had been no anticipation; for, the speech has been read off at the London Telegraph station from the evening papers.

XX.

TO CLERGYMEN (AND OTHERS) IN DIFFICULTIES.

MARCH 22, 1851

THE family of the Reverend Carmichael Crample, perpetual curate of Crookenden, Hunts, is seated at breakfast. Mrs. Crample is blandly declining the request of Master Shirley Crample for more sugar to his milk-and-water; Miss Crample is reading the day-old copy of The Times, which the vicar is so good as to send regularly from London; and Miss Emilia Crample is spreading butter over Master Charles James Cram-

10

ple's bread, with fairy-like thinness, while the reverend head of the family notices, through the glass door leading upon the lawn, the approach of a figure, which gives him some disquietude.

"It is only poor Mr. Slicer the butcher, my dear," says Mrs. Crample. "He is very civil and patient; for his is only a balance since last Christmas: it is a call from Mr. Plumley which I dread most; for he has had no money from us since this time twelvemonth."   •

Mr. Slicer is shown into the study; to which the reverend gentleman, humbled and abashed, creeps unwillingly from the parlour. The butcher, equally embarrassed, stammers out something about having a large bill to meet on Thursday; and, if quite convenient—well, he hopes Mr. Crample will oblige him with at least something on account. The clergyman pleads poverty, and begs a little time. Slicer has not the heart to say more; but, brushing his hat very frequently with his sleeve, trusts Mr. Crample won't forget him as soon as——

"Mr. Plumley, sir!" says the servant, announcing the grocer; of whose visitation Mrs. Crample had expressed her apprehensions. Meanwhile the butcher, having brought his hat up to a brilliant polish, proceeds to put it to its proper use, and returns towards his shop.

"It's no use, sir," exclaims Plumley, after Mr. Crample has swiftly, but noiselessly shut the study door. "It's no use talking any more about it. I owe a duty to my wife and family, and I owe a sum of money to Gampling and Co., my wholesale house. Their traveller worrits my life out. I'm a poor man—I am an uncommon poor man, with a large family."

"So am I," falters Mr. Crample, timidly.

"Well," rejoins Mr. Plumley, "if I had tithes coming in, sir, besides a stipend, I should say I was *not* a poor man. That's what I should say. Why, they tell me the tithes of this parish is worth seven-teen hundred a year."

"The *great* tithes," replies Mr. Crample, with eagerness; "but, they are the dues of my principal, the Reverend Dr. Recumber. Mine are only the small tithes, and I assure you they do not amount to one hundred a year. The additional complement I receive from the vicar is very small."

These mild statements have the effect of diverting Mr.

Plumley's wrath from the curate to the vicar; of whom, oddly enough, he, a parochial man (Mr. Plumley is "sidesman" for this year), has scarcely before heard. Presently he breaks out into a strong expression of the "shame" it is that the man who does all the work should have so little of the pay.

"I beg you will not imagine that the doctor is unkind or unmindful of us," says the timid curate; "for instance, he sends us the Times newspaper every day gratis—and that, merely on condition of our forwarding it by every mail to his cousin in India."

"Kind you call it! The Times newspaper don't help you to pay your butcher, or," adds the shopkeeper with emphasis, "or your grocer, does it?"

"Why no," continues the clergyman, looking as if that fact had never before occurred to him. "I am indeed most grieved that I am unable to meet your demand; but, Emilia's long illness, and a disappointment Jane has had in getting a situation as governess, have thrown me back; still I——" Here the poor curate stops. He is about to add a hope; but, his conscience tells him that he ought not to lead his creditor astray.

The despondent manner in which he drops his voice, touches Plumley's heart. Plumley feels he has been blunt, and re- pents. He, too, lowers his voice, hopes he has n't said any- thing hurtful to Mr. C.'s feelings; but Gampling and Co.'s traveller worrits men out o' their lives! "I *know*," he adds a little louder, "that if you had it you'd pay it; but what I say is this;—it's a burning shame that you have not got it!"

Mr. Plumley entered the house with the firm determination that not another ounce of tea should be supplied to the family on credit, until his bill was paid. But, as he passes the kitch- en door to go out, he cannot look the servant in the face with- out saying, "Well, Mary Anne; any orders this morning?"

Before Mary Anne can inquire of her mistress, her master has returned to the parlour. He is the picture of despair. Mrs. Crample has much ado to keep up spirits enough to cheer him. The younger children retire, and a consultation begins as to what can be done to obtain some respite from their difficulties, and pay bills off by instalments. "If," says the head of the house, "I could only anticipate a sufficient sum from my stipend and pay it back at intervals, I could relieve these poor, patient tradesmen!"

Jane, who has read every advertisement for governesses in The Times twice over, here ventures to suggest that nothing could be easier. "Look here, papa," she remarks, pointing to the front page of the Supplement. "A gentleman named N. G., evidently very rich, who dates from Cecil-street, Strand, London, addresses himself particularly to clergymen; for the advertisement is headed, 'To CLERGYMEN (AND OTHERS) IN DIFFICULTIES.' He says he is prepared to advance, by way of loan, any sum of money, from ten, to ten thousand pounds, on personal security."

The curate takes the newspaper from his daughter, and studies the notification carefully, over and over again. He cannot exactly make out the signification of "personal security." Mr. Carmichael Crample is a profound Greek scholar. In mathematics and theology he brought away high honours from college. He can dissect a Pindaric ode, or construe a crabbed passage from any of the Latin Fathers better than his bishop. But, of the ordinary transactions of life he is as innocent as his own baby. He does not know the meaning of "personal security;" but in order to learn, there will be no harm in inquiring. He will ask N. G. Mr. Crample is sure that N. G. must be a benevolent millionaire, who is fond of doing good generally, and who will give a prompt and clear answer.

Mr. Crample immediately indites an epistle to Cecil-street, Strand, London, to go by the next post. It gives a candid statement of his wants and wishes (viz. fifty pounds immediately). It also sets forth his income, to show that he would be able to repay the loan punctually by instalments. He concludes with a request that N. G. will be kind enough to explain the exact nature of the security required.

By the very next return of post there came an answer. The curate opened it with a trembling hand; and, having first glanced it over silently, repeated it aloud to his anxious wife, in a voice faltering with joy. It ran thus:

"REV. SIR,—Yours of yesterday came duly to hand. Though we seldom negotiate with parties for small transactions; yet, under circumstances, are not averse.

" Our system of doing business is always to ascertain the perfect respectability of parties before we undertake commissions, &c., and are happy to state that, as a matter of business, we have made the necessary inquiry, and find your living to be as you state.

" Time being, no doubt, an object, we enclose a Bill of Exchange, viz.:— fifty pounds, at two months; renewable, if not quite convenient for you to meet, in whole or part. You have merely to sign your name under the word ' accepted' written across thereof, and remit to us; with post-office order for our charge for searches (as per account below), stamp, &c., and we will forward you the amount, less discount and commission, immediately.

" We are,

" ST. JOHN CLARE, THOMPSON, AND CO.

		£.	s.	d.
"*Mem*. No. 985423. Stamp		0	3	6
Drawing Bill		0	6	8
Inquiries, Searches at Somerset House, Consulting Clergy-List, &c., &c.		2	2	0
		2	12	2"

For two pounds twelve shillings and twopence, the Crample family, it seemed, could be released from their embarrassments; but, two pounds odd were as much at their command, as two thousand pounds. A family committee of ways and means was held to plan how the little sum could be raised. Could anything be disposed of? Alas! the inventory of their entire possessions was called up, without much effort of memory, in Mrs. Crample's mind; and object by object was discussed, and truly pronounced indispensable. At last, Jane suggested that her father should write again, to propose that, in addition to " commission and discount," the ready-money charges should be deducted from the sum to be lent. On this advice Mr. Crample immediately acted.

On the second morning came another letter from Messrs. St. John Clare, Thompson, and Company. "Nothing," said Mr. Crample, with a smile, " could be kinder than these gentlemen; and I really marvel how, being utter strangers, they can be so considerate. They cheerfully agree to my last proposal. All I have to do, is, to put my signature to a new document they have sent me, on which the amount is changed from pounds to guineas, and return it by post."

The villagers of Crookenden had, of late, seen almost as little of their perpetual curate as of their vicar; and when he did go abroad, he appeared dejected and unhappy. The very day, however, on which he sent off the accepted bill, a change came over him. He went out. He patted all the children on the head; he looked in at the school; he promised a little girl who read the list of hard names in the Genealogical Chapter of Numbers without a mistake, that he would very soon present her with a sixpence. He even called upon Plumley, and had a chat with Mrs. P.; in the course of which, he expressed his regret that "Jane had not been so generous a godmother to *her* Jane as he could have wished, but soon, he hoped——"

Mrs. Plumley interrupted him by begging he wouldn't mention that.

"And not only that," Mr. Crample continued, looking pointedly towards the grocer, " but other obligations we are under to our kind neighbours, we hope in a short period to a—(hem!)—liquidate."

The butcher was not at home when Mr. Crample called; but, Mr. Crample left an ambiguous message, implying that his next interview with Mr. Slicer should be more agreeable than the last one was.

Mrs. Crample employed herself in making out a list of the household liabilities, and apportioning the coming cash, in various sums, to each creditor. In fact, every possible preparation was made in time for its arrival; and, on the morning when it was expected, nothing was wanted to the renovated prosperity of the Crample establishment—but the money.

The next morning, alas! the postman passed the window! Shirley was sent after him. Was he *sure* there was no letter for papa?

"None!"

The morning after, and the next, it was the same. Could the bill have miscarried?

On the fifth day, Mr. Crample wrote again, inquiring if his last letter had reached Messrs. St. John Clare, Thompson, and Company. With hungry patience, he paused for a reply during another week. Poor Mrs. Crample was, meantime, obliged to turn the screw of economy tighter and tighter, until the pinch reached even the younger branches. Shirley had to drink his milk-and-water without any sugar whatever; and

Charles James was reduced to dry bread. Their dress, too, was so shabby they could not appear at church.

Innumerable were the excuses for Messrs. St. John Clare, Thompson, and Company, with which Crample amused himself. Perhaps the entire firm had gone out of town, and would send the money when they returned; possibly, their capital had suddenly got "locked up" (he derived this expression from an indigo broker, to whose son he had been tutor, but had not the remotest idea of its meaning), and somebody had mislaid the key. Suddenly it struck him that he might not have addressed his letters legibly enough for post-office deciphering—a very common fault of college-bred men. He therefore wrote once more; and, in a clear round text that might have served for a sign, directed his letter to " Messrs. St. John Clare, Thompson, and Company, Cecil-street, Strand, London."

In a few days the letter was returned to the writer, with the following inscription: " Gone away; not known where."

" Ah !" said the reverend victim, when he showed this to his wife : " I now feel sure that the whole matter is a hoax. Peradventure Messrs. Thompson and Co. are a fiction—some young college bloods, perhaps, who just put these advertisements into the papers for fun !"

Two months have passed. Breakfast, such as it is, has been removed. Plumley and Slicer both appear; they know that yesterday their pastor received his quarter's stipend. They have dropped in, to ascertain to what extent he is prepared to liquidate the balances upon their once little, now large accounts. They have scarcely opened the glass door to go away, when the post-man appears. The parson seizes a letter eagerly; it is directed in a strange, stiff, business hand. Would his visitors wait till he reads the first line? He breaks the seal, and the words " St. John Clare, Thompson, and Co." gladdened his eyes. He turns to his creditors. He hints that Plumley's patience and the butcher's long-suffering will now be rewarded. He turns the leaf with the greatest care, lest the bank-note or cheque on the neighbouring bank may drop out. Pleased with a confused and nervously murmured promise of speedy payment, coupled with the word " remit-

tance," the creditors retire joyfully. Crample has now time
and composure to examine the letter with care.

Not the vestige of a bank-note or bank paper of any kind!
He feels that he is not strong enough to peruse the epistle by
himself, and desires the presence of his wife and eldest daughter. Thus reinforced, he reads; and the following words
grow dim before his eyes:

"The Rev. Carmichael Crample,
　"Crookenden Vicarage, Hunts.

"*Clifford's Inn.*

"SIR,—Unless the amount of the dishonoured bill (fifty pounds), drawn by
Messrs. St. John Clare, Thompson, and Co., and accepted by you, be paid
forthwith (together with interest and costs), I am instructed by the present
holder thereof, Oloman l'Evy, Esq., to inform you that legal proceedings will
be commenced against you without further notice.

"We are, Sir, your obedient servants,
　"WRINKLE AND CLIP."

The trio are silent. Each looks at the other for an explanation of the meaning of the extraordinary application. The
reverend gentleman, having earnestly applied this dumb cate-
chism first to his wife and then to his daughter, turns his abstracted look upon the backs of books; and, staring intently at
his St. Ignatius, asks it aloud "how he could be expected to
pay a debt he has never incurred, while a great many debts
which, alas! he honestly owes, he is unable to liquidate?" St.
Ignatius is, of course, not communicative. By this time, the
full scope and effect of the villany has revealed itself to Jane.

"It is all my doing!" she exclaims, weeping—"all my
doing!"

"Your doing?" repeat Mr. and Mrs. Crample both at once.

"Yes! It was I who suggested that papa should write to
those wicked men; and ruin has come of it!"

The kind old man takes his daughter's hand, and says all he
can think of to soothe her. He assures her, in his simplicity,
that there is, without any manner of doubt, some mistake.
He will write to Mr. Wrinkle, or, better perhaps, to Mr.
l'Evy—probably a French gentleman—and explain to him
that, from some oversight on the part of Messrs. Thompson
and Co., he never was favoured with a shilling of the money;
and that, consequently, they will at once perceive he is not

their debtor, Mrs. Crample proposes that, to make assurance doubly sure, an additional letter be forwarded to Messrs. Thompson and Co., to their old address in Cecil-street, Strand, London, with a memorandum requesting the postman to inquire whither they have removed to; and then to be good enough to take it without delay to their new residence.

Jane, after reperusing Wrinkle and Clip's letter, and considering for a moment, weeps afresh, despite every effort to repress her grief. Without being able to disentangle the affair, she feels a distinct conviction that her father has been caught in meshes, spread in the newspapers, by a gang of swindlers. Her advice is, that her father lose no time in laying the whole case, in person, before his patron.

Poor Mr. Crample recoils at the thought. He will never have sufficient courage. Besides, the Reverend Dr. Recumber, vicar of Crookenden, and rector of No Souls, City, lives in London; and how is the expense of a journey thither to be borne?

"And then the exposure!" hinted Mrs. Crample.

"Exposure, anything, is better than ruin!" urged Jane, turning to her mother; "I feel convinced that the wretches will put papa in prison, unless he gets proper advice how to act. Dr. Recumber will, perhaps, know some solicitor who will tell him how to defend himself from these bad people. Besides, being chaplain to the Duke of Lammersley, he will have great influence in London."

"But who is to do duty in my absence?" asks the curate, rubbing his eyes like a man awakening out of one dream to be drawn into another.

"Doubtless the Doctor will recommend some friend of his!"

The next morning, the Reverend Carmichael Crample was seen in a second-class carriage, duly booked for London; paying the expenses of his journey out of the quarter's scanty stipend, which his careful wife had been, for previous days and weeks, calculating and contriving, to spread over the largest possible surface of debt.

With trembling knees and a palsied knock at the great Belgravian door, Mr. Crample announced his arrival to the portentous pluralist. The Honourable Mrs. Recumber (daughter of the Earl of Pompton) passed him on the stairs on her way

10*

to the Opera; and he was ushered into the drawing-room by
a powdered footman. The splendour to which Mr. Crample
was here suddenly introduced, bewildered him. Scarcely an
article upon which his wondering eyes fell, whose value would
not have paid the whole of his Crookenden creditors, and have
left a handsome surplus to liquidate the dreadful acceptance.
The vicar—a large, pompous man—received his curate with
bland surprise. He inquired, in a flute-like voice, after each
member of his family, seriatim, with great apparent interest,
and the husband and father was quite touched. When Mr.
Crample explained the object of his visit, the Doctor was
greatly shocked, and then said he was "deeply grieved."
He assured his curate that he was in the hands of swindlers:
he advised him by all means to pay the money at once without
any further delay or discussion; and thus save himelf endless
vexation and certain exposure. It was much better to put
up with the first loss. Going to law with such scoundrels was
not only unsatisfactory, but, in the end, expensive.

Poor Mr. Crample felt precisely like the sick pauper, when
a fashionable physician prescribed him chicken broth and carriage exercise. He stuttered out something about not having
the ability to pay, and expressed—more audibly—a wish that
Dr. Recumber would recommend him to a respectable solicitor.

"Well, my dear sir, if you *will* be rash, nothing," said he
Doctor, "would give me greater pleasure.

The bell was rung; another floury footman brought in a
silver standish and a mother-o'-pearl writing-case. The letter
was penned, and the curate, with a profusion of thanks,
backed himself out of the apartment. The next morning, at
the earliest business hour, he presented it.

Mr. Blindle, of the firm of Blindle and Blob, received Dr.
Recumber's epistle with reverential awe; for the agency of
the Doctor's property was worth five hundred a year to "the
office." Mr. Blindle produced a pair of scissors; and, instead
of profanely tearing open the letter, carefully cut away she
coat-of-arms, not to disfigure it with the slightest crack. Had
he lived in Pekin, and not in Furnival's Inn, he would have
burnt incense before the revered document.

The nature of Mr. Crample's business, however, produced
a considerable change in Mr. Blindle's mind.

"This!" said Mr. Blindle, "is a case rather for the Police, than for Common-Law practice. You are at the mercy of a gang of bill-stealers. I presume the transaction began by your answering an advertisement in The Times newspaper, headed, 'To Clergymen (and others) in Difficulties?'"

Mr. Crample breathed forth "Yes!" with the wonderment of a mystified peasant replying to a conjuror.

"Exactly; and no doubt they have already proceeded against you; for Wrinkle and Clip are what we call in the profession 'no-quarter men.' However, if you will leave the papers with me, I will send one of our clerks to Clifford's Inn, to see what can be done. Good morning Mr. Crample!" Mr. Blindle's time was worth about sixty shillings an hour, and he could not afford to waste many minutes on a clergyman in difficulties. Having bowed Mr. Crample out, he thrust half his head into the clerks' office, and exclaimed, "Peggs!— look over this gentleman's papers, and try whether you can do anything with Wrinkle and Clip!" He then shut himself in again.

Mr. Peggs turned over the letters (Mr. Crample had carefully folded and docketed every one of them); and, having without much ado, recapitulated everything that had happened to Mr. Crample, concluded with the query, "Ain't I right, sir?"

"Wonderfully correct!" said Mr. Crample, holding up his hands in amazement. He had previously made up his mind that the fatal bill transaction was one of a most extraordinary and unheard-of character, the like of which had never happened before. By what divination had the wonderful attorney and his amazing clerk come to a knowledge of the minutest circumstances? "Bless you, sir," said the latter, "all bill-stealing cases are as like one another as two new ha'-pence."

The interview in Clifford's Inn was short and decisive. Mr. Peggs went in alone. He pushed open a faded green-baize door, which shut upon him like a rat-trap; and addressed himself to a dirty man, behind a row of rails, who answered to the name of Clip. A dirtier individual at a side-desk, took a slip of parchment from a pigeon-hole, and began to rub a dirty roll of cloth over it.

Mr. Peggs stated his business:

"Come to pay?" asked Clip.

"Oh no; merely to see about an arrangement!" said Peggs.

"Debt and costs in full im-mediately are the only terms," rejoined Clip.

"It's a clear case of bill-stealing," Peggs remarked loudly and boldly.

"My client is an innocent holder," replied Clip.

"Very!" said Peggs, ironically.

"You accept service for defendant?" inquired Clip.

"We do," responded Peggs.

"You do? Then, Smudge—go it!" said Clip to his clerk; and before Mr. Peggs was out of the trap, Mr. Smudge had made him the bearer of a parchment command to Carmichael Crample, clerk, to appear before our Lady the Queen, at Westminster, to answer Olomon l'Evy, upon promises, &c.

Meantime, the clergyman had paced the flags of Clifford's Inn passage, his mind torn between anxiety and hope. Despite all that had been told him, he flattered himself that Messrs. Wrinkle and Clip would rectify the "mistake," when they were fully convinced that he had not received the money they had applied to him for. Peggs appeared, and he hastily joined him, with the sanguine inquiry,

"Are they convinced of the error? Will they forego——"

"Nothing."

"Peradventure they will wait?"

"Not five minutes," replied Peggs. "They have commenced their action already. Here is a copy of the writ. When they declare, we shall plead—our defence is, no consideration, and fraud, eh?".

Mr. Crample gave a stupified assent. Peggs walked to the end of Fetter-lane with the bewildered defendant, and then, wishing him good day, cast him adrift on the ocean of London, without rudder or compass.

Mr. Crample having slept upon his misfortunes in a musty bed at a dirty inn, Hope, as is her wont in such cases, returned to him with undiminished brightness. All would be right. Messrs. Blindle and Blob would, doubtless, do all that was necessary; and he would return home to await the result.

The curate dreams on; and the Crookenden creditors wait with exemplary patience. Sugar and butter are banned the parsonage; domestic prayers, read by Jane, have been established on Sundays for the benefit of the younger branches, and for the want of Sunday clothes. At length the day of trial arrives, and the defendant takes another expensive journey to London. He smilingly paces Westminster Hall; for he feels confident of a verdict in the cause of l'Evy v. Crample, clerk. He knows that great efforts have been made by Blindle and Blob to secure that issue; for, on making a modest application to Dr. Recumber to guarantee their costs, the Doctor had declined; and, as Oloman l'Evy was reputed to be wealthy, a verdict for the defendant was a matter of moment to "the office." One favourable circumstance had occurred: Messrs. St. John Clare, Thompson, and Company, had been found guilty at the Central Criminal Court, in the single name of Higgs (but with an appendix of six aliases), in respect of another bill of exchange; across which, he (the firm) had accidentally written a wrong name.

The matter of l'Evy v. Crample, clerk, did not occupy her Majesty, sitting by proxy in her Court of Common Pleas, much time.

The plaintiff's counsel, in opening the case, made a playful allusion to the misfortune of Messrs. St. John Clare, Thompson and Company (*alias* Higgs); but, indignantly repudiated any connexion, on the part of his unimpeachable client, with that atrocious convict. The acceptance had, he asserted, passed through several hands; and plaintiff, who was a highly respectable wine and cigar merchant at the West-end—had, in an evil hour, discounted it.

The only witness called to support these statements was the plaintiff's clerk. That young gentleman simply swore that he saw the money paid to the "party" whose name appeared as the last of the indorsers. In his cross-examination, he said yes, he *was* Mr. Oloman l'Evy's nephew. His duties as clerk were very light, for the plaintiff had no regular office nor wine cellar, and bought his cigars, like any other gentleman—when he wanted to smoke. The "party" for whom the bill was discounted was his (witness's) father, who was Mrs. l'Evy's brother. Knew Higgs, otherwise St. John Clare, Thompson,

and Company. Was no relation whatever to Higgs—at least,
would not have been, if plaintiff had not married his (witness's)
aunt, and if Higgs had not been Mrs. l'Evy's son by a former
husband—which he was. But what had that to do with it?

As the counsel for the defence could not prove a negative;
—that the defendent never had received a farthing of consideration for his bill, he relied upon his eloquence in denouncing
the transaction as a wicked fraud, and on the facts elicited in
the cross-examination of the plaintiff's witness.—The judge,
however, summed up with the simple remark that, although
the evidence in support of the plaintiff's case was of an extremely suspicious character; yet, no direct testimony had
been adduced on behalf of the defendant to rebut it—and the
jury returned a verdict for the plaintiff.

That day week was passed by the Rev. Carmichael Crample
in the receiving ward of Whitecross-street prison. The hope
which had buoyed him up even to the last, had now fled.
Thoughts of his parish, his home, and the dear ones there
lamenting, overcame him. He sat in the darkest corner of the
dismal apartment, and wept.

The condition of affairs at Crookenden will be best understood from the following letter, written by the Honourable
and Reverend Kenrick Speckle, B. A. (youngest son of the
Earl of Pompton), whom Dr. Recumber had sent down to do
duty while Crample was going through the Insolvent Court.
The letter was addressed to Sir Richard Rumble, Bart., Baliol
College, Oxford.

"Parsonage, Crookenden, Hunts.

"MY DEAR DICK,—Here's a go!—Old Drizzle, who is keeping the best
living in our family warm for me till I can complete my title for orders, is at
death's door; and I shall not become due for full orders for another twelvemonth. Even if he hold out three months longer (and I'm game to lay a
thousand to twenty he doesn't), I shall be bowled out.

"I was packed off from Town by my aged brother-in-law, Recumber,
under the plea that I can read for my title, down here, as well as anywhere
else; and do him a service at the same time. The fact is, the regular Crookenden Curate has gone up for a six weeks' whitewash. Our old friend and
usurer l'Evy is the executioner.

"Instead of a parsonage, this is more like the Valley of the Shadow, &c.
The weeping and wailing and gnashing of teeth, are indescribable. The
hostess—a limp lady, with a faded face—cries all breakfast-time; and when
I ask the second daughter for an egg she bursts into tears. The two little

boys blubber over their milk-and-water, and Molly, the servant, never comes into one's presence without whimpering. The very tradesmen are melancholy. I ordered, and *paid for* (what d'ye think of that?) a quarter of a hundred-weight of the best almond hard-bake, for distribution amongst the parochial juveniles, yesterday. They sucked every ounce of it in the dumps.

"I don't think there is a smile to be had, for love or money, in the whole parish; and if I did not contrive a chat, now and then, with the eldest daughter of the house of Crample, I should abscond. It is martyrdom to be here. She (Jane Crample, I mean) has wonderful sense—and only rising nineteen. She sings much better than Miss Huskeye, our Oxford *prima donna*. Indeed, all the sense and talent of the family seem centred in her. Five feet five and a half, I should say, splendidly proportioned, and a wonderful complexion. She puts the best face on things, and keeps her spirits up, like a little heroine. I had a gossip with her last night, alone, and she spoke so sensibly of her father's affairs, that——But I'm boring you, Dick.

"I will tell you what I wish you would do! Just ride over to the governor, and hint that, if old Drizzle should pop off, a month or two too soon, Jane's father would be a capital warming-pan for me. The living is worth eight hundred a year, and would save the dear old boy from the Insolvent Court.

"Yours ever,

" KEN. SPECKLE."

Not only did Sir Richard ride over to the Earl of Pompton and make the suggestion; but it actually had to be put in force in less than a week; for, as Dr. Drizzle died next day, no time was to be lost.

When Mr. Oloman l'Evy saw the appointment of Crample to the new living in the newspapers, he instantly posted off to Whitecross-street. He expressed intense commiseration for the curate's sufferings, and told Mr. Crample he was willing to release him on his own personal security:—another bill at two months, for nearly double the amount of debt and costs. Could anything be fairer? Peggs nipped the transaction in the bud. He happened to come down at the same time, paid the money by his master's orders (B. and B. took only ten per cent. upon such transactions); and the clergyman, no longer in difficulties, went down by express train to lighten the hearts and dry the eyes, not only of his dearest and nearest, but of the whole parish. Slicer, Plumley, and the rest, had not to wait long for the amount of their respective bills; and the charity-girl not only got her sixpence, but as many other sixpences for distribution among her schoolfellows as made capitalists, for one whole evening, of the entire school.

At the end of the year, it turned out that Mr. Crample had not been a mere warming-pan for his new patron's son. A conviction slowly crept over that young gentleman's mind that the Church was not exactly his vocation. He found the Army (into which he "bought") the very thing for him. Mr. Crample, therefore, got the living for life.

The latest intelligence of the Crample family reports Miss Crample to be a guest at Pompton Castle. Captain Speckle is in India with his regiment. It is said that he and Jane correspond.

"To Clergymen (and others) in Difficulties" still heads an advertisement inserted in various newspapers; and, as Mr. Oloman l'Evy has lately set up his carriage, there is little doubt that "our system of doing business" flourishes, in spite of exposure, and the forced exile of Higgs, *alias* St. John Clare, Thompson, and Company.*

☞ XXI.

SPITALFIELDS.

APRIL 5, 1851.

HAVE you any distinct idea of Spitalfields? A general notion, no doubt, you have—an impression made up of squalid streets lying, like narrow black trenches, somewhere about London—towards the East, perhaps—where sallow, unshorn weavers who have nothing to do, prowl languidly about, or lean against posts, or sit brooding on door-steps, and occasionally crowd together to petition Parliament or the Queen to prohibit the importation of French silks: the petition logically answered by our gracious Queen with a Drawing-room or a Court Ball, where all the great ladies wear dresses of Spitalfields manufacture. Then the weavers dine for a day or two, and, the ball over, they relapse into prowling about the streets, leaning against posts, and brooding on door-steps. If your occupation in town or country ever obliges you to travel by the Eastern Counties Railway, you may connect with this impression a great many pigeons; for, you may remember, as

* The outline of this story was suggested by facts derived from a correspondent.

you rattled along above the dirty streets, pigeon-hutches and pigeon-traps abounded on the tops of the poor dwellings; it being a natural aspiration of the inhabitants to connect themselves with any living creatures that could take a flight into fresh air. The smoky little bowers of scarlet-runners that you may have sometimes seen on the house-tops among the pigeons, may have suggested to your fancy—I pay you the poor compliment of supposing it to be a vagrant fancy, like my own—abortions of the bean-stalk that led Jack to fortune: by the slender twigs of which, the Jacks of Spitalfields will never, never climb to where the giant keeps his money.

Will you come to Spitalfields?

Turning eastward out of the most bustling part of Bishopsgate, we suddenly lose the noise that has been resounding in our ears, and fade into the quiet churchyard of the Priory of St. Mary, Spital, otherwise "Domus Dei et Beatæ Mariæ, extra Bishopsgate, in the Parish of St. Botolph." Its modern name is Spital-square. Cells and cloisters were, at an early date, replaced by substantial burgher houses, which, since the Revocation of the Edict of Nantes, in 1685, have been chiefly the depositories of the silk manufacture introduced into London by the French Huguenots, who flew from the perfidy of Louis the Fourteenth. Much of the old quiet cloistered air still lingers in the place.

The house to which we are bound, stands at an angle with the spot where the Pulpit-cross was anciently planted; whence, on every Easter Monday and Tuesday, the Spital sermons were preached in presence of the Lord Mayor and Corporation of London, and children of Christ's Hospital. We cross the many-cornered "square" and enter a sort of gateway.

Along a narrow passage, up a dark stair, through a crazy door, into a room not very light, not very large, not in the least splendid; with queer corners and quaint carvings, and massive chimney-pieces; with tall cupboards, prim doors, and squat counters with deep dumpy drawers; with desks behind thin rails, with aisles between thick towers of papered-up packages, out of whose ends flash all the colours of the rainbow; where all is as quiet as a playhouse at daybreak, or a church at midnight; where, in truth, there is nobody to make a noise, except one well-dressed man, one attendant porter, and one remarkably fine male cat, admiring, before the fire, the ends of his silky paws; where the door, as we enter, shuts with a deep, dull, muffled sound, that is more startling than a noise; where there is less bustle than at a Quakers' meeting, and less business going on than in a Government office. The painfully neat man threads the mazes of the piles, and desks, and cupboards, and counters, to greet us, and to assure us, in reply to our apology, that we have *not* made any mistake whatever, and that we are in the silk warehouse we were seeking: a warehouse in which, we have ·previously been informed, by one whose word we never before doubted, that there is "turned over" an annual average of one hundred thousand pounds of good and lawful money of Great Britain.

We may now tell our informant, frankly, that, looking round upon the evidences of stagnation which presented themselves we uttterly disbelieved his statement. Our faith, however, soon returns. Somebody mounts the stairs, and enters the apartment with the deliberate air of a man who has nothing whatever to do but to walk about in a beautifully brushed hat, and a stock of amazing satin; to crush his gloves tightly between his hands, and to call on his friends, to ask them—as this gentleman asked our friend—how he is getting on; and whether he has been down "yonder" lately (a jerk eastward of the glossy hat); and if he hasn't, whether he intends going down next Sunday, because, if he does, he (the visitor) means to go too, and will take him down in his "trap." He then, in a parenthetical, postscriptum sort of way, alludes to certain "assorted Glacés," and indicates the pile of silks he means, by the merest motion of his ring finger. "The figure is——?" says he.

"Two and seven," replies the vendor; "how many pieces shall I put aside?"

"Well—fifty. By-the-by, have you heard?"—Mr. Broadelle (our friend) has *not* heard, and the visitor proceeds to announce, from unimpeachable authority, that the match between Mr. Crumpley of Howell's, and Miss Lammy of Swan's is to come off at last: in fact, next Thursday. Cordial "good-by;" graceful elevation of the well-polished hat to myself; and departure of, as Mr. Broadelle informs us, one of his best customers.

" Customer ?"

" Yes ? You heard ? He has just bought fifty pieces of silk of various or ' assorted' colours."

" At two shillings and sevenpence per yard ?"

" Just so. And there are eighty-four yards in a piece."

Our organs of calculation, already wound up, are instantly set a-going. The result brought out when these phrenological works have run down, is, that this short, easy, jaunty gossip began and ended a transaction involving the sum of five hundred and forty-two pounds ten shillings. No haggling about price; no puffing of quality on one side, no depreciation of it on the other. The silks are not even looked at. How is this ?"

" Our trade," says our friend, in explanation, "has been reduced to a system that enables us to transact business with the fewest possible words, and in the easiest possible way. The gentleman who has just left, is Messrs. Treacy and McIntyre's silk-buyer. That department of their establishment is handed over to his management as unrestrictedly and unreservedly as if the whole concern were his own. In like manner the different branches of large houses—such as the cotton, woollen, hosiery, small wares branches—are placed under the control of similar buyers. At the end of every half year, an account is taken of the stewardship of each of these heads of department; and, if his particular branch has not flourished, should the stock on hand be large and unsaleable, the Buyer is called to account, and his situation jeopardised. The partners, of course, know the capabilities and peculiarities of their trade, and can tell, on investigation, how and why the Buyer has been at fault. If, on the contrary, the Buyer has narrowly watched the public taste, and fed it successfully; if he has been vigilant in getting early possession of the most attractive patterns, or in pouncing on cheap markets (by taking advantage, for instance, of the embarrassments of a " shaky" manufacturer or a French revolution; for he scours the country at home and abroad in all directions), and if his department come out at the six-monthly settlement with marked profit, his salary is possibly raised. Should this success be repeated, he is usually taken into the firm as a partner."

"But *no* judgment was exercised in the bargain just made. The Buyer did not even look at your goods."

"That is the result of previous study and experience. It is the art that conceals art. He need not examine the goods. He has learned the characteristics of our dyes to a shade, and the qualities of our fabrics to a thread."

"Then, as to price. I suppose your friend is lounging about in various other Spitalfields warehouses at this moment. Perhaps by this time he has run his firm into debt for a few thousand pounds more?"

"Very likely."

"Well; suppose a neighbour of yours were to offer him the same sort of silks as those he has just chosen here, for less money, could he not—as no writing has passed between you —be off his bargain with you?"

"Too late. The thing is done, and cannot be undone," answers Mr. Broadelle, made a little serious by the bare notion of such a breach of faith. "Our bargain is as tight as if it had been written on parchment and attested by a dozen witnesses. His very existence as a Buyer, and mine as a Manufacturer, depend upon the scrupulous performance of the contract. I shall send in the silks this afternoon. And I feel as certain of a cheque for the cash, at our periodical settlement, as I do of death and quarter-day."

Mr. Broadelle brings to my notice from quaint cupboards and unnoticed drawers, stores of gorgeous satins, velvets, lutestrings, brocades, damasks, and other silk fabrics, the whole worth a sum of money so enormous that I cannot reconcile it with the poignant cry of poverty which is often sent forth from this quarter of the metropolis.

What says Mr. Broadelle to it? He says this:

"Although most masters make this locality their headquarters, and employ the neighbouring weavers, yet they nearly all have factories in the provinces: chiefly in Lancashire: and most of these goods are the produce of their provincial looms. The Spitalfields weaver of plain silks and velvets keeps up a hopeless contest against the machinery and cheaper labour in use elsewhere, and struggles against overwhelming odds. Will you step round and see a family engaged in this desperate encounter?"

"Is there no remedy?" we ask, as we go out together.

"A very simple one. In the country—say in Suffolk, where we have a hand-weaving factory—food is cheaper and better; both food for the stomach, and food for the lungs."

"The air is better; so less money, you think, would be spent in drink than is spent in Spitalfields?"

"Undoubtedly. Fancy yourself stewed up in a stifling room all day; imagine the lassitude into which your whole frame would collapse after fourteen hours' mere inhalation of a stale, bad atmosphere—to say nothing of fourteen hours' monotonous work in addition; and consider what stern self-denial it would require to refrain from some stimulant—a glass of bad gin, perhaps—if you could get it. On the other hand, think of the fresh air which plays around country looms, and which, being exhilarating in itself, is the best possible substitute for gin."

"I have heard that the atmosphere of London is also detrimental to the manufacture of silk. Is that so?"

"Why sir," replies Mr. Broadelle, stopping short, and speaking like a deeply injured man, "the two days' fog we had in December last, was a dead loss to me of one hundred pounds. The blacks (London genuine particular) got into the white satins, despite the best precautions of the workpeople, and put them into an ugly, foxy, unsaleable half-mourning, sir. They would not even take a dye, decently. I had to send down, express, to our Suffolk branch to supply the deficiency; and the white satins, woven there on the same days, came up as white as driven snow."

Considering that both the worker and the work are deteriorated by an obstinate tenure of the present dense and unfit site, it seems wonderful that the weavers themselves are not as anxious to remove from a noxious and unprofitable neighborhood, as their well-wishers can be to effect their removal. From fourteen to seventeen thousand looms are contained in from eleven to twelve thousand houses—although, at the time at which we write, not more than from nine to ten thousand of them are at work. The average number of houses per acre in the parish is seventeen; and the average per acre for all London being no more than five houses and one-fifth of a house, Spitalfields contains the densest population, perhaps,

existing. Within its small boundaries, not less than eighty-
five thousand human beings are huddled. "They are," says
Mr. Broadelle, "so interlaced, and bound together, by debt,
marriage, and prejudice, that, despite many inducements to
remove to the country establishments of the masters they
already serve, they drag on a miserable existence in their
present abodes. Spitalfields was the Necropolis of Roman
London; the Registrar-General's returns show that it is now
the grave of modern Manufacturing London. The average
mortality is higher in this Metropolitan district than in any
other."

And what strange streets they are, Mr. Broadelle! These
high gaunt houses, all window on the upper story, and that
window all small diamond panes, are like the houses in some
foreign town, and have no trace of London in them—except
its soot, which is, indeed, a large exception. It is as if the
Huguenots had brought their streets along with them, and
dropped them down here. And what a number of strange
shops, that seem to be open for no earthly reason, having nothing to sell! A few halfpenny bundles of firewood, a few
halfpenny kites, halfpenny battledores, and farthing shuttle-
cocks, form quite an extensive stock in trade here. Eatables
are so important in themselves, that there is no need to set
them off. Be the loaves never so coarse in texture, and never
so unattractively jumbled together in the baker's dirty window, they *are* loaves, and that is the main thing. Liver,
lights, and sheep's-heads, freckled sausages, and strong black
puddings, are sufficiently enticing without decoration. The
mouths of Spitalfields will water for them, howsoever raw and
ugly they be. Is its intellectual appetite sharp-set, I wonder,
for that wolfish literature of highly-coloured show-bill and
rampant wood-cut, filling the little shop-window over the way,
and covering half the house? Do the poor weavers, by the
dim light of their lamps, unravel those villanous fabrics, and
nourish their careworn hearts on the last strainings of the
foulest filth of France?

"I can't say," replies Mr. Broadelle; "we have but little
intercourse with them in their domestic lives. They are
rather jealous and suspicious. We have tried Mechanic's
Institutions, but they have not come to much."

" Is there any school here ?"

" Yes. Here it is."

An old house, hastily adapted to the purpose, with too much darkness in it and too little air, but no want of scholars. An infant school on the ground floor, where the infants are, as usual, drowsily rubbing their noses, or poking their forefingers into the features of other infants on exploratory surveys. Intermediate schools above. At the top of all, in a large, long, light room—occupying the width of two dwelling-houses, as the room made for the weaving, in the old style of building does—the " ragged school."

" Heaven send that all these boys may not grow up to be weavers here, Mr. Broadelle, nor all these girls grow up to marry them !"

" We don't increase much, now," he says. " We go for soldiers, or we go to sea, or we take to something else, or we emigrate, perhaps."

Now, for a sample of the parents of these children. Can you find us a man and wife who should be in Lancashire, or Suffolk, or anywhere rather than here ? Nothing easier to find in Spitalfields. Enter by this doorway.

Up a dark narrow winding public stair, such as are numerous in Lyons or in the wynds and closes of the old town of Edinburgh, and into a room where there are four looms ; one idle, three at work.

A wan, thin, eager-eyed man, weaving in his shirt and trousers, stops the jarring of his loom. He is the master of the place. Not an Irishman himself, but of Irish descent.

" Good day !"

" Good day !" Passing his hand over his rough chin, and feeling his lean throat.

" We are walking through Spitalfields, being interested in the place. Will you allow us to look at your work ?"

" Oh ! certainly."

" It is very beautiful. Black velvet ?"

" Yes. Every time I throw the shuttle, I cut out this wire, as you see, and put it in again—so !" Jarring and clashing at the loom, and glancing at us with his eager eyes.

" It is slow work."

" Very slow." With a hard dry cough, and the glance.

" And hard work."

" Very hard." With the cough again.

After a while, he once more stops, perceiving that we really are interested, and says, laying his hand upon his hollow breast, and speaking in an unusually loud voice, being used to speak through the clashing of the loom :

" It tries the chest, you see, leaning for'ard like this for fifteen or sixteen hours at a stretch."

" Do you work so long at a time ?"

" Glad to do it when I can get it to do. A day's work like that, is worth a matter of three shillings."

" Eighteen shillings a week."

" Ah ! But it ain't always eighteen shillings a week. I don't always get it, remember ! One week with another, I hardly get more than ten, or ten-and-six."

" Is this Mr. Broadelle's loom ?"

" Yes. This is. So is that one there ;" the idle one.

" And that, where the man is working ?"

" That's another party's. The young man working at it pays me a shilling a week for leave to work here. That's a shilling, you know, off my rent of half-a-crown. It's rather a large room."

" Is that your wife at the other loom ?"

" That's my wife. She's making a commoner sort of work, for bonnets and that."

Again his loom clashes and jars, and he leans forward over his toil. In the window by him, is a singing-bird in a little cage, which trolls its song, and seems to think the loom an instrument of music. The window, tightly closed, commands a maze of chimney-pots, and tiles, and gables. Among them, the ineffectual sun, faintly contending with the rain and mist, is going down. A yellow ray of light crossing the weaver's eager eyes and hollow white face, makes a shape something like a pike-head on the floor.

The room is unwholesome, close, and dirty. Through one part of it the staircase comes up in a bulk, and roughly partitions off a corner. In that corner are the bedstead and the fireplace, a table, a chair or two, a kettle, a tub of water, a little crockery. The looms claim all the superior space and have it. Like grim enchanters who provide the family with their scant food, they must be propitiated with the best accommodation. They bestride the room, and pitilessly squeeze the children—this heavy, watery-headed baby carried in the arms of its staggering little brother, for example—into corners. The children sleep at night between the legs of the monsters, who deafen their first cries with their whirr and rattle, and who roar the same tune to them when they die.

Come to the mother's loom.

"Have you any other children besides these?"

"I have had eight. I have six alive."

"Did we see any of them, just now, at the——"

"Ragged School? O yes! You saw four of mine at the Ragged School."

She looks up, quite bright about it—has a mother's pride in it—is not ashamed of the name: she, working for her bread, not begging it—not in the least.

She has stopped her loom for the moment. So has her husband. So has the young man.

"Weaver's children are born in the weaver's room," says the husband, with a nod at the bedstead. "Nursed there, brought up there—sick or well—and die there."

To which, the clash and jar of all three looms—the wife's, the husband's, and the young man's, as they go again—make a chorus.

"This man's work, now, Mr. Broadelle—he can't hear us apart here, in this noise?"—

"Oh no!"

—"requires but little skill?"

"Very little skill. He is doing now exactly what his grandfather did. Nothing would induce him to use a simple improvement (the 'fly shuttle') to prevent that contraction of the chest of which he complains. Nothing would turn him aside from his old ways. It is the old custom to work at home, in a crowded room, instead of in a factory. *I* couldn't change it, if I were to try."

Good Heaven, is the house falling! Is there an earthquake in Spitalfields! Has a volcano burst out in the heart of London! What is this appalling rush and tremble?

It is only the railroad.

The arches of the railroad span the house; the wires of the

11

•

electric telegraph stretch over the confined scene of his daily
life; the engines fly past him on their errands, and outstrip
the birds; and what can the man of prejudice and usage hope
for, but to be overthrown and flúng into oblivion! Look to
it, gentlemen of precedent and custom, standing, daintily opposed to progress, in the bag-wigs and embroidered coats of
another generation, you may learn from the weaver in his
shirt and trousers.

There we leave him in the dark, about to kindle at the poor
fire the lamp that hangs upon his loom, to help him on his
labouring way into the night. The sun has gone down, the
reflexion has vanished from the floor. There is nothing in the
gloom but his eager eyes, made hungrier by the sight of our
small present; the dark shapes of his fellow-workers mingling
with their stopped looms; the mute bird in its little cage,
duskily expressed against the window; and the watery-headed
baby crooning in a corner God knows where.

We are again in the streets.

"The fluctuations in the silk trade, and, consequently, in
the condition of the Spitalfields weaver," says our friend,
"are sudden and unforeseen; for they depend upon a variety
of uncontrollable causes. Let us take, for example, the past
four or five years."

"But does that period afford a fair average of the condition
of the trade? Were not the fluctuations extreme, then?"

"They were. In 1846 the price of raw silk was very low.
The manufacturers bought all they could, and worked up all
they bought. Not a hand was idle: not a loom at rest.
Enormous stocks soon accumulated, silk became dearer; but
in May 1847, there came a sudden stop."

"Was it not, at that time, that the last loud cry of distress
arose from Spitalfields, and that public meetings were held for
finding means of.'redress?'"

"It was. The stagnation was prolonged by a dispute, in
which the silk manufacturers and wholesale dealers were involved with the large retail houses. It got the name of the
'short measure question.' The retailers claimed from us
thirty-seven inches to every yard. The autumn trade was
completely crippled by this discussion; which did not end till
the breaking out of the French Revolution in February, 1848.

West-end and wholesale buyers rushed over to Paris and Lyons, in regiments, and with unlimited capital. They bought for almost any price they chose to offer. This cut two ways; although wholesale and retail houses brought home great parcels of manufactured articles, we also bought raw silk, in France, from fifteen to twenty per cent. below the lowest price I ever knew it. What do you think, sir, of the finest French organzine for a guinea a pound?"

"You don't say so!" we exclaimed; not knowing whether organzine silk ought to be one guinea, or ten guineas a pound; or whether an ounce of raw silk, meant a piece of woven silk, or a yard.

"Such a price as this enabled us to set some of our looms at work for stock, and, during 1849, the French goods being exhausted, ours came into play. Indeed, during that year the British manufacturer was in a position to defy competition."

"The French had not recovered themselves?"

"Not only that; but we had bought nearly all their raw silk, and they were actually obliged to buy raw silk back from us at advances of from twenty to fifty per cent.! From that time prices advanced here, and work kept on increasing, so that, during most of last year, Spitalfields was busy."

"A glut of stock has been again the consequence."

"Yes; and what with that and the advancing price of raw silk, I have within the last fortnight been compelled to discharge one hundred hands."

Spitalfields, however, has its bright side. As yet, machinery has not been taught to turn artist, or to guide the shuttle through the intricate niceties of the Jacquard loom, so as to execute designs. Figured and brocaded silks must still be done by hands, and those hands must be skilful.

"Our silks," Mr Broadelle tells us, "have never been inferior, in quality, to those of our foreign rivals; but, we have always been beaten in taste. In the stolid assiduous painstaking motion of the hand and treadle, the English weaver is unsurpassed; but, he has seldom exercised his fancy. Until lately, therefore, few designs originated in this country. We silk-manufacturers, like the Dramatic Authors' Society, have been content to take our novelties from the French."

"You say, 'until lately.' Has the 'English manufacturer improved in that respect?"

"Decidedly. Schools of Design have done something; the encouragement given by masters to those who make available patterns, has done something too; but, the great improver of the English silk trade was the last French revolution."

"How?"

"That political disaster brought the manufacturers of France to a dead-lock. During the whole of 1849 the English markets were stocked with the most splendid fashions that ever came into it. As we could not sell a yard of our manufacture, we had plenty of leisure to examine the different foreign goods minutely. So rich a variety had never fallen under our observation, and never before had such a flood of light been thrown on the manufactures of our greatest rivals. We profited by it. More important improvements have been effected in the fabric of fancy silk goods since 1848, than were made, down to that time, since the days of Jacquard."

"This shows the value of national intercourse, Mr. Broadelle. Will the Great Exhibition do much service in this way?"

"I have no doubt it will. But, we are now at the door of a figure-weaver; and you will compare a visit to him with our last visit."

We knock at the door of a cheerful little house, extremely clean. We are introduced into a parlour, where a young artist sits at work with crayons and water-colours. He is a student of the School of Design. He is at work on a new pattern for a table-cover. He has learnt to paint in oil. He has painted the portraits of his sisters—and of some one who I suspect is not a sister, but who may be

> "A nearer one
> Yet and a dearer one,"

and they decorate the room. He has painted groups of flowers. He shows us one that was in last year's Exhibition of the Royal Academy. He shows us another that he means to finish in good time to send to the next Exhibition. He does these things over and above his regular work. He don't mind work—gets up early. There are cheap casts prettily arranged about the room, and it has a little collection of cheap books of a good sort in it. The intrinsic worth of every simple article of furniture or embellishment is enhanced a hundred-fold (as it always may be) by neatness and order. Is father at home? Yes, and will be glad to see the visitors. Pray walk up!

The young artist shows us the way to the top of the house, apologising cheerfully for the ladder staircase by which we mount at last. In a bright clean room, as pure as soap and water, scrubbing, and fresh air, can make it, we find a sister whose portrait is down stairs—we are able to claim her instantly for the original, to the general satisfaction. We find also, father, who is working at his Jacquard loom, making a pretty pattern of cravat, in blue upon a black ground. He is as cordial, sensible, intelligent a man, as any one would wish to know. He has a reason for everything he says, and everything he does. He is learned in sanitary matters among other necessary knowledge, and says the first thing you have to do, is, to make your place wholesome, or you can't expect to work heartily. Wholesome it is, as his own pleasant face, and the pleasant faces of his children well brought up. He has made various improvements in his own loom; he has made an improvement in his daughter's who works near him, which prevents her having to contract her chest although she is doing very ordinary work. Industry, contentment, sense, and self-respect, are the hopeful characteristics of everything animate and inanimate in this little house. If the veritable summer light were shining, and the veritable summer air were rustling, in it, which the young artist has tried to get into the sketches of green glades from Epping Forest that hang near father's loom, and can be seen by father while he is at work, it could not be more cheering to our hearts, oppressed with what we have left.

I meant to have had a talk with our good friend Mr. Broadelle, respecting a cruel persistence in one inflexible principle which gave the New Poor Law a particular severity in its application to Spitalfieds, a few years back, but which I hope may have been amended. Work in the stone-yard was the test of all able-bodied applicants for relief. Now, the weaver's hands are soft and delicate, and *must be so* for his work. No matter. The weaver wanting relief, must work in the stone-

yard with the rest. So, the Union blistered his hands before
it relieved him, and incapaciated him from doing his work
when he could get it.

But, let us leave Spitalfields with an agreeable impression,
and be thankful that we can.

☞ XXII.

THE METROPOLITAN PROTECTIVES.

APRIL 26, 1851.

NERVOUS old ladies, dyspeptic half-pay officers, suspicious
quidnuncs, plot-dreading diplomatists, and grudging rate-
payers, all having the fear of the forthcoming Industrial Invasion before their eyes, are becoming anxious respecting the
adequate efficiency of the London Police. Horrible rumours
are finding their way into the clubs; prophecies are permeating the tea-parties of suburban dowagers of mischief and
confusion, the most insignificant result whereof is to be (of
course) the overthrow of the British Constitution. Comprehensive conspiracies are being hatched in certain back parlours behind Mr. Cantelo's Chicken Establishment in Leicester-
square. A complicated web of machination is being spun—
we have it on the authority of a noble peer—against the
integrity of the Austrian Empire, at a small coffee-shop in
Soho. Prussia is being menaced by twenty-four determined
Poles and Honveds in the attics of a cheap *restaurateur* in the
Haymarket. Lots are being cast for the assassin of Louis
Napoleon, in the inner parlours of various cigar shops.
America, as we learn from that mighty lever of the civilised
world, the New York Weekly Herald, is of opinion that the
time bids fair for a descent of Red Republicans on Manchester. The English policemen have been tampered with, and
are suborned. Mr. Justice Maule can't find one anywhere.
In short, the peace of the entire continent of Europe may be
considered as already gone. When the various conspiracies
now on foot are ripe, the armies of the disaffected of all nations will land at the British ports under pretence of "assist-
ing" at the Great Glass show, and be privately and confiden-
tislly drilled in secret *Champs de Mars*, armed with weapons

stealthily abstracted from the Tower of London: while the Metropolitan Police and the Guards, both horse and foot, will fraternise, and (to a man) pretend to be fast asleep.

Neither have our quaking prophets omitted to fortell minor disasters. Gangs of burglars from the counties of Surrey, Sussex, and Lancashire, are also to fraternise with their brethren in London, and to "rifle, rob, and plunder," as uninterruptedly, as if every man's house were a Castle of Andalusia. Pickpockets—not in single spies but in whole battalions—are to arrive from Paris and Vienna, and are to fall into compact organisation (through the medium of interpreters) with the united swell-mobs of London, Liverpool, and Manchester.

In short, it would appear that no words can express our fearful condition, so well, as Mr. Croaker's in "The Good Natured Man." "I am so frightened," says he, "that I scarce know whether I sit, stand, or go. Perhaps at this moment I am treading on lighted matches, blazing brimstone, and barrels of gunpowder. They are preparing to blow me up into the clouds. Murder! We shall be all burnt in our beds!"

To the end that the prophets and their disciples may rest quietly in *their* beds, we have benevolently abandoned our own bed for some three nights or so, in order to report the results of personal inquiry into the condition and system of the Protective Police of the Metropolis. If our details of the patience, promptitude, order, vigilance, zeal, and judgment, which watch over the peace of the huge Babylon when she sleeps, do not dispel the fears of the most apprehensive, we shall have quitted our pillow, and plied our pen in vain. But we have no such distrust.

Although the Metropolitan Police Force consists of nineteen superintendents, one hundred and twenty-four inspectors, five hundred and eighty-five sergeants, and four thousand seven hundred and ninety-seven constables, doing duty at twenty-five stations; yet, so uniform is the order of proceeding in all, and so fairly can the description of what is done at one station be taken as a specimen of what is done at the others, that, without further preface, we shall take the reader into custody, and convey him at once to the police station in Bow-street, Covent-garden.

A policeman keeping watch and ward at the wicket gives us admission, and we proceed down a long passage into an outer room, where there is a barrack bedstead, on which we observe Police-constable Clark, newly relieved, asleep, and snoring portentously—a little exhausted, perhaps, by nine hours' constant walking on his beat. In the right-hand corner of this room—which is a bare room like a guard-house without the drums and muskets—is a dock, or space railed off for prisoners: opposite, a window breast-high at which an Inspector always presides day and night to hear charges. Passing by a corner door into his office on the other side of this window, we find it much like any other office—inky, dull, and quiet; papers stuck against the walls; perfect library of old charges on shelves overhead; stools and desks; a hall porter's chair, little used; gas-lights; fire; sober clock. At one desk stands a policeman, duly coated and caped, looking stiffly over his glazed stock at a handbill he is copying. Two Inspectors sit near, working away at a great rate with noisy pens that sound like little rattles.

The clock points a quarter before nine. One of the Inspectors takes under his arm a slate, the night's muster-roll, and an orderly book. He proceeds to the Yard. The gas jet, shining from the office through its window, and a couple of street lamps, indistinctly light the place.

The inspecting officer notifies his presence in the yard by the sound of the word " attention !" and about seventy white faces, peering out above half a dozen parallel lines of dark great-coat, fall into military ranks. A sergeant from each section comes forward to form the staff of the commanding officer. The roll is called over, and certain men are told off as a Reserve, to remain at the station for any exigencies that may arise. The book is then opened, and the Inspector reads aloud a series of warnings. P. C. John Jones, J., No. 202, was discovered drunk on duty on such a day, and dismissed the force. Sergeant Jenkins did not report that a robbery had been complained of in such a street, and is suspended for a month. The whole division are then enlightened as to the names, addresses, ages, and heights, of all persons who have been " missing" from the radius of fifteen miles from Charing-cross (the police definition of the Metropolis) since the previous night; as to the colour of their hair, eyes, and clothes; as to the cut of their coats, the fashion and material of their gowns, the shape of their hats or bonnets, the make of their boots. So minute and definite are all these personal descriptions, that a P. C. (the official ellipsis for Police Constable) must be very sleepy, or dull of observation, if, in the event of his meeting with any of these missing individuals, he does not put them in train of restoration. Lost articles of property are then enumerated and described with equal exactness. The same routine is being performed, at the same moment, at the head of every police regiment or division in the Metropolis, and how any thing or person *can* be lost in London, is a problem. Among the trifles enumerated as " found," are a horse and cart, a small dog, a brooch, a baby, and a firkin of butter.

Emotion is no part of a policeman's duty. If felt it must be suppressed : he listens as stolidly to the following account of the baby, as to the history of the horse and cart, the little dog, the brooch, and the butter.

S. DIVISION. Found, at Eight and a quarter, P. M., on the 2nd instant, by [a gentleman named], of Bayham-street, Camden-town, on the step of his door, the body of a new-born Infant, tied up in a Holland Bag. Had on a Calico Bedgown and Muslin Cap, trimmed with Satin Ribbon. Also a Note, stating," "Any one who finds this precious burden, pay him the last duties which a Mother—much in distress and trouble of mind—is unable to do. May the blessing of God be on you !"

The book is closed. The mother " much in distress and trouble of mind," is shut up with it ; and the Inspector proceeds to make his inspection. He marches past each rank. The men, one by one produce their kit; consisting of lantern, rattle and staff. He sees that each man is clean and properly provided for the duties of the night. Returning to his former station amidst the sergeants, he gives the word " Close up !"

The men now form a compact body, and the sergeants take their stand at the head of their respective ranks. But, before this efficient body of troops deploy to their various beats, they are addressed by the superior officer much as a colonel harangues his regiment before going into action. The Inspector's speech is sharp, short, and pithily delivered :

" Now, men, be careful in your examination of empty houses.

11*

See that the doors are fast. If not, search for any persons un-
lawfully concealed therein.   Number nineteen section will
allow no destitute parties to herd together under the Adelphi
arches.   Section number twenty-four will be very particular in
insisting on all gentlemen's carriages [it is an Opera night]
keeping the rank, close to the kerb-stone. Caution the coachmen
not to leave their horses. Be sure and look sharp after flower-
girls. Offering flowers for sale is a pretence. The girls are
either beggars or thieves; but be cautious. The chief thing
is the empty houses; thieves get from them into the adjoining
premises, and then there's a burglary.—'Tention, to the left
face, march!"

The sections march off in Indian file, and the Inspector returns to his office by one door, while the half dozen " reserves"
go into the outer room by another. The Inspector now buttons
on his great-coat ; and, after supper, will visit every beat in
the division, to see that the men are at their duties. The other
Inspector remains, to take the charges.

A small man, who gives his name, Mr. Spills (or for whom
that name will do in this place as well as another), presents
himself at the half-open window to complain of a gentleman
now present, who is stricken in years, bald, well dressed, staid
in countenance, respectable in appearance, and exceedingly
drunk. He gazes at his accuser from behind the dock, with
lacklustre penitence, as that gentleman elaborates his griev-
ance to the patient inspector ; who, out of a tangle of digres-
sions and inuendoes dashed with sparkling scraps of club-room
oratory, extracts—not without difficulty—the substance of the
complaint, and reduces it to a charge of " drunk and disorderly." The culprit, it seems, not half an hour ago—purely
by accident — found his way into Craven-street, Strand.
Though there are upwards of forty doors in Craven-street, he
would kick, and thump, and batter the complainant's door.
No other door would do. The complainant don't know why;'
the delinquent don't know why; nobody knows why. No
entreaty, no expostulation, no threat, could induce him to
transfer his favours to any other door in the neighbourhood.
He was a perfect stranger to Mr. Spills; yet, when Mr. Spills
presented himself at the gate of his castle in answer to the

thundering summons, the prisoner insisting on finishing the evening at the domestic supper-table of the Spills family. Finally, the prisoner emphasised his claim on Mr. Spill's hospitality by striking Mr. Spills on the mouth. This led to his being immediately handed over to the custody of a P. C.

The defendant answers the usual questions as to the name and condition, with a drowsy indifference peculiar to the muddle. But, when the Inspector asked his age, a faint ray of his spirit shines through him. What is that to the police? Have they anything to do with the census? They may lock him up, fine him, put him in gaol, work him on the treadmill, if they like. All this is in their power; he knows the law well enough, sir; but they can't make him tell his age—and he won't—won't do it, sir!—At length, after having been mildly pressed, and cross-examined, and coaxed, he passes his fingers through the few grey hairs that fringe his bald head, and suddenly roars:

" Well then :—Five-and-twenty !"

All the policemen laugh. The prisoner—but now triumphant in his retort—checks himself, endeavours to stand erect, and surveys them with defiance.

" Have you anything about you, you would like us to take care of?" This is the usual apology for searching a drunken prisoner: searches cannot be enforced except in cases of felony.

Before the prisoner can answer, one of the Reserves eases him of his property. Had his adventures been produced in print, they could scarcely have been better described than by the following articles: a penknife, an empty sandwich-box, a bunch of keys, a bird's-eye handkerchief, a sovereign, fivepence in halfpence, a toothpick, and a pocket-book. From his neck is drawn a watch-guard, cut through. *No* watch.

When he is sober, he will be questioned as to his loss; a description of the watch, with its maker's name and number will be extracted from him; this will be sent round to every station; and, by this time to-morrow night, every pawnbroker in the Metropolis will be asked whether such a watch has been offered as a pledge? Most probably the watch will be recovered and restored before he has time to get tipsy again— and then, he will probably lose it again.

" " When shall I have to appear before the magistrate," asks the prosecutor.

"At ten o'clock to-morrow morning,"—and so ends that case.

There is no peace for the Inspector. During the twenty-four hours he is on duty, his window is constantly framing some new picture. For some minutes, a brown face with bright black eyes has been peering impatiently from under a quantity of tangled black hair and a straw hat, behind Mr. Spills. It now advances to the window.

" Have you got e'er a gipsy woman here, sir ?"

" No gipsy woman to-night." As if one were always expected.

" Thank'ee, sir :" and the querist retires to repeat this new reading of " Shepherds, I have lost my love," at every other station-house, till he finds her—and bails her.

Most of the constables who have been relieved from duty by the nine o'clock men have now dropped in, and are detailing anything worthy of a report to their respective sergeants. The sergeants enter these occurrences on a printed form. Only one is presented now :

" P. C. 67 reports that, at 5¼ P. M., a boy, named Philip Isaac, was knocked down, in Bow-street, by a horse belonging to Mr. Parks, a Newsvender. He was taken to Charing + Hospital, and sent home, slightly bruised."

The Inspector has not time to file this document before an earnest-looking man comes to the window. Something has happened which evidently causes him more pain than resentment.

" I am afraid we have been robbed. My name is Parker, of the firm of Parker and Tide, Upholsterers. This afternoon at three o'clock, our clerk handed to a young man who is our collector (he is only nineteen), about ninety-six pounds, to take to the bank. He ought to have been back in about fifteen minutes; but he had n't come back at six o'clock. I went to the bank to see if the cash had been paid in, and it had not."

" Be good enough to describe his person and dress, sir" says the Inspector, taking out a printed form called a " Route."

These are minutely detailed and recorded. " Has he any friends or relatives in London ?"

The applicant replies by describing the residence and condition of the youth's father and uncle. The Inspector orders "Ninety-two" (one of the Reserve) to go with the gentleman, "and see what he can make of it." The misguided delinquent's chance of escape will be lessened every minute. Not only will his usual haunts be visited in the course of the night by Ninety-two; but his description will be known, before morning, by *every* police-officer on duty. This Route—which is now being copied by a Reserve into a book—will be passed on, presently, to the next station. There, it will again be copied; passed on to the next; copied; forwarded—and so on until it shall have made the circuit of all the metropolitan stations. In the morning, that description will be read to the men going on duty. "Long neck, light hair, brown clothes, low-crowned hat," and so on.

A member of the E division throws a paper on the window-sill, touches his hat, exclaims, "Route, sir!" and departs.

The Routes are coming in all night long. A lady has lost her purse in an omnibus. Here is a description of the supposed thief—a woman who sat next to the lady—and here are the dates and numbers of the bank-notes, inscribed on the paper with exactness. On the back, is an entry of the hour at which the paper was received at, and sent away from, every station to which it has yet been. A Reserve is called in to book the memorandum; and in a quarter of an hour he is off with it to the station next on the Route. Not only are these notices read to the men at each relief, but the most important of them are inserted in the Police Gazette, the especial literary organ of the Force, which is edited by one of its members.

A well-dressed youth, about eighteen years of age, now leans over the window to bring himself as near to the Inspector as possible. He whispers in a broad Scotch accent :

"I am destitute. I came up from Scotland to find one Saunders M'Alpine, and I *can't* find him, and I have spent all my money. I have not a farthing left. I want a night's lodging."

"Reserve!" The Inspector wastes no words in a case like this.

" Sir."

" Go over to the relieving officer and ask him to give this young man a night in the casual ward."

The policeman and the half-shamed suppliant go out to-gether.

"That is a genuine tale," remarks the Inspector.

"Evidently a fortune-seeking young Scotchman," we ventured to conjecture, "who has come to London upon too slight an invitation, and with too slender a purse. He has an honest face, and won't know want long. He may die Lord Mayor."

The Inspector is not sanguine in such cases. "He *may*," he says.

There is a great commotion in the outer office. Looking through the window, we see a stout bustling woman who announces herself as complainant, three female witnesses, and two policemen. This solemn procession moves towards the window; yet we look in vain for a prisoner. The prisoner is in truth invisible on the floor of the dock, so one of his guards is ordered to mount him on a bench. He is a handsome, dirty, curly-headed boy about the age of seven, though he says he is nine. The prosecutrix makes her charge.

"Last Sunday, sir (if you please, sir, I keep a cigar and sta-tioner's shop), this here little creetur breaks one of my windows, and the moment after, I loses a box of paints——"

"Value?" asks the Inspector, already entering the charge, after one sharp look at the child.

"Value, sir? Well, I'll say eightpence. Well, sir, to-night again, just before shutting up, I hears another pane go smash. I looks out, and I sees this same little creetur a running away. I runs after him, and hands him over to the police."

The child does not exhibit the smallest sign of fear or sorrow. He does not even whimper. He tells his name and address, when asked them, in a straightforward business-like manner, as if he were quite used to the whole proceeding. He is locked up; and the prosecutrix is desired to appear before the Magistrate in the morning to substantiate her charge.

"A child so young, a professional thief!"

"Ah! these are the most distressing cases we have to deal with. The number of children brought here, either as prisoners or as having been lost, is from five to six thousand per annum. Juvenile crime and its forerunner—the neglect of children by their parents—is still on the increase. That's the experience of the whole Force."

"If some place were provided at which neglected children could be made to pass their time, instead of in the market and streets—say in industrial schools provided by the nation —juvenile delinquency would very much decrease——?"

"I believe, sir (and I speak the sentiments of many experienced officers in the Force), that it would be much lessened, and that the expense of such establishments would be saved in a very short time out of the police and county rates. Let alone morality altogether."

And the Inspector resumes his writing. For a little while we are left to think to the ticking of the clock.

There are six hundred and fifty-six gentlemen in the English House of Commons assembling in London. There is not one of those gentlemen who may not, in one week, if he choose, acquire as dismal a knowledge of the Hell upon earth in which he lives, in regard of these children, as this Inspector has—as we have—as no man can by possibility shut out, who will walk this town with open eyes observant of what is crying to God in the streets. If we were one of those six hundred and fifty-six, and had the courage to declare that we know the day must come when these children must be taken, by the strong hand, out of our shameful public ways, and must be rescued—when the State must (no will, or will not, in the case, but must) take up neglected and ignorant children wheresoever they are found, severely punishing the parents when they can be found, too, and forcing them, if they have any means of existence, to contribute something towards the reclamation of their offspring, but never again entrusting them with the duties they have abandoned; if we were to say this, and were to add that as the day must come, it cannot come too soon, and had best come now—Red Tape would arise against us in ten thousand shapes of virtuous opposition, and cocks would crow, and donkeys would bray, and owls would hoot, and strangers would be espied, and houses would be counted out, and we should be satisfactorily put down. Meanwhile, in Aberdeen, the horror has risen to that height, that against the law, the authorities have by force swept their streets clear of these unchristian objects, and have, to the

utmost extent of their illegal power, successfully done this
very thing. Do none of the six hundred and fifty-six know
of it—do none of them look into it—do none of them lay
down their newspapers when they read of a baby sentenced
for the third, fourth, fifth, sixth, seventh time to imprisonment
and whipping, and ask themselves the question, "Is there any
earthly thing this child can do when this new sentence is fulfilled, but steal again, and be again imprisoned and again
flogged, until, a precocious human devil, it is shipped away to
corrupt a new world?" Do none of the six hundred and
fifty-six, care to walk from Charing-cross to Whitechapel—to
look into Wentworth-street—to stray into the lanes of Westminster—to go into a prison almost within the shadow of their
own Victoria Tower—to see with their eyes and hear with
their ears what such childhood is, and what escape it has from
being what it is? Well! Red Tape is easier, and tells for
more in blue books, and will give you a committee five years
long if you like, to inquire whether the wind ever blows, or
the rain ever falls—and then you can talk about it and do
nothing.

Our meditations are suddenly interrupted.

"Here's a pretty business!" cries a pale man in a breathless
hurry, at the window. "Somebody has been tampering with
my door-lock!"

"How do you mean, sir?"

"Why, I live round the corner, and I had been to the
play, and I left my door on the lock (it's a Chubb!), and
I come back, and the lock won't act. It has been tampered with. There either are, or have been, thieves in the
place!"

"Reserve!"

"Sir!"

"Take another man with you, and a couple of ladders, and
see to this gentleman's house."

A sallow anxious little man rushes in.

"Oh! you haven't seen anything of such a thing as a black
and tan spaniel, have you?"

"Is it a spaniel dog we have got in the yard?" the Inspector
inquires of the gaoler.

"No, sir, it's a brown tarrier."

O! It can't be my dog then. A brown tarrier? O! Good night, gentlemen! Thank you!"

"Good night, sir."

The Reserve just now despatched with the other man and the two ladders, returns, gruff-voiced and a little disgusted.

"Well? what's up round the corner?"

"Nothing the matter with the lock, sir. I opened it with the key directly!"

We fall into a doze before the fire. Only one little rattle of a pen is springing now, for the other Inspector has put on his great-coat and gone out, to make the round of his beat and look after his men. We become aware in our sleep of a scuffling on the pavement outside. It approaches, and becomes noisy and hollow on the boarded floor within. We again repair to the window.

A very ill-looking woman in the dock. A very stupid little gentleman, very much overcome with liquor, and with his head extremely towzled, endeavouring to make out the meaning of two immovable Policemen, and indistinctly muttering a desire to know "war it's awr abow."

"Well?" says the Inspector, possessed of the case in a look.

"I was on duty, sir, in Lincoln's Inn-fields just now," says one of the Policemen, "when I see this gent——"

Here, "this gent," with an air of great dignity, again observes, "Mirrer Insperrer, I requesherknow war it's awr ABOW."

"We'll hear you presently, sir. Go on!"

—"when I see this gent, in conversation again the railings with this woman. I requested him to move on, and observed his watch-guard hanging loose out of his pocket. 'You've lost your watch,' I said. Then I turned to her. 'And you've got it,' I said. 'I an't,' she said. Then she said, turning to him, 'You know you've been in company with many others to-night, flower-girls, and a lot more.' 'I shall take *you*,' I said, 'anyhow.' Then I turned my lantern on her, and saw this silver watch, with the glass broke, lying behind her on the stones. Then I took her into custody, and the other constable brought the gent along."

"Gaoler!" says the Inspector.

"Sir!"

"Keep your eye on her. Take care she don't make away with anything—and send for Mrs. Green."

The accused sits in a corner of the dock, quite composed, with her arms under her dirty shawl, and says nothing. The Inspector folds a charge-sheet, and dips his pen in the ink.

"Now, sir, your name, if you please?"

"Ba—a."

"*That* can't be your name, sir. What name does he say, Constable?"

The second Constable "seriously inclines his ear;" the gent being a short man, and the second constable a tall one. "He says his name's Bat, sir." (Getting at it after a good deal of trouble.)

"Where do you live, Mr. Bat?"

"Lamber."

"And what are you?—what business are you, Mr. Bat?"

"Fesher," says Mr. Bat, again collecting dignity.

"Profession, is it? Very good, sir. What's your profession?"

"Solirrer," returns Mr. Bat.

"Solicitor, of Lambeth. Have you lost anything besides your watch, sir?"

"I am nor aware—lost—any—arrickle—prorrery," says Mr. Bat.

The Inspector has been looking at the watch.

"What do you value this watch at, sir?"

"Ten pound," says Mr. Bat, with unexpected promptitude.

"Hardly worth so much as that, I should think?"

"Five pound five," says Mr. Bat. "I doro how much. I'm not par-TICK-ler" (this word costs Mr. Bat a tremendous effort) "abow the war. It's not my war. It's a frez of my."

"If it belongs to a friend of yours, you wouldn't like to lose it, I suppose?"

"I doro," says Mr. Bat; "I'm nor any ways par-TICK-ler abow the war. It's a frez of my;" which he afterwards repeats at intervals, scores of times. Always as an entirely novel idea.

Inspector writes. Brings charge-sheet to window. Reads same to Mr. Bat.

" You charge this woman, sir"—her name, age, and address have been previously taken—"with robbing you of your watch. I won't trouble you to sign the sheet, as you are not in good writing order. You'll have to be here this morning— it's now two—at a quarter before ten.

"Never get up till har par," says Mr. Bat, with decision.

" You'll have to be here this morning," repeats the Inspector, placidly, " at a quarter before ten. If you don't come, we shall have to send for you, and that might be unpleasant. Stay a bit. Now, look here. I have written it down. 'Mr. Bat to be in Bow-street, quarter before ten.' Or I'll even say, to make it easier to you, a quarter past. There! 'Quarter past ten.' Now, let me fold this up and put it in your pocket; and when your landlady, or whoever it is at home, finds it there, she'll take care to call you."

All of which is elaborately done for Mr. Bat. A Constable who has skilfully taken a writ out of the unconscious Mr. Bat's pocket in the mean time, and has discovered from the endorsement that he has given his name and address correctly, receives instructions to put Mr. Bat into a cab and send him home.

" And, Constable," says the Inspector to the first man, musing over the watch as he speaks, " do you go back to Lincoln's Inn-fields, and look about, and you'll find, somewhere, the little silver pin belonging to the handle. She has done it in the usual way, and twisted the pin right out."

" What mawrer is it ?" says Mr. Bat, staggering back again, " T'morrow mawrer ?"

" Not to-morrow morning. This morning."

" *This* mawrer ?" says Mr. Bat. " How can it be this mawrer ? *War* is this aur abow ?"

As there is no present probability of his discovering " what it is all about," he is conveyed to his cab; and a very indignant matron with a very livid face, a trembling lip, and a violently heaving breast, presents herself.

" Which I wishes to complain immediate of Pleesemen forty-two and fifty-three and insists on the charge being took; and that I will substantiate before the magistrates to-morrow morning, and what is more will prove and which is saying a great deal sir!"

"You needn't be in a passion, you know, here, ma'am. Everything will be done correct."

"Which I *am* not in a passion sir and everythink shall be done correct, if you please!" drawing herself up with a look designed to freeze the whole division. "I make a charge immediate," very rapidly, "against Pleesemen forty-two and fifty-three, and insists on the charge being took."

"I can't take it till I know what it is," returns the patient Inspector, leaning on the window-sill, and making no hopeless effort, as yet, to write it down. "How was it, ma'am?"

"This is how it were sir. I were standing at the door of my own 'ouse."

"Where is your house, ma'am?"

"*Where* is my house, sir?" with the freezing look.

"Yes, ma'am. Is it in the Strand, for instance?"

"No, sir," with indignant triumph. "It is *not* in the Strand!"

"Where then, ma'am?"

"Where then, sir?" with severe sarcasm. "I *ope* it is in Doory-lane."

"In Drury-lane. And what is your name, ma'am?"

"*My* name, sir?" with inconceivable scorn. "My name is Megby."

"Mrs. Megby?"

"Sir, I *ope* so!" with the previous sarcasm. Then, very rapidly, "I keep a coffee-house, as I will substantiate to-morrow morning and what is more will prove and that is saying a great deal." Then, still more rapidly, "I wish to make a charge immediate against Pleesemen forty-two and fifty-three!"

"Well, ma'am, be so good as make it."

"I were standing at my door," falling of a sudden into a genteel and impressive slowness, "in conversation with a friend, a gentleman from the country, which his name is Henery Lupvitch, *Es*-quire——"

"Is he here, ma'am?"

'No, sir," with surpassing scorn. "He is *not* here!"

" Well, ma'am ?"

" With Henery Lupvitch, *Es*-quire, and which I had just been hissuing directions to two of my servants, when here come between us a couple of female persons which I know to be the commonest dirt, and pushed against me."

" Both of them pushed against you ?"

" No, sir," with scorn and triumph, " they did *not! One* of 'em pushed against me." A dead stoppage, expressive of implacable gentility.

" Well, ma'am—did you say anything then ?"

" I ask your parding. Did I which, sir ?" As compelling herself to fortitude under great provocation.

"Did you say anything?"

" I *ope* I did. I says, how dare you do that, ma'am ?"

Stoppage again. Expressive of a severe desire that those words be instantly taken down.

" You said how dare you do that ?"

" ' Nobody,' continuing to quote with a lofty and abstracted effort of memory, ' never interfered with you.' She replies, ' That's nothink to you, ma'am. Never you mind.' "

Another pause, expressive of the same desire as before. Much incensed at nothing resulting.

" She then turns back between me and Henery Lupvitch, *Es*-quire, and commits an assault upon me, which I am not a acquisition and will not endoor, or what is more submit to."

What Mrs. Megby means by the particular expression that she is not an acquisition, does not appear; but she turns more livid, and not only her lip but her whole frame trembles as she solemnly repeats, " I am not an acquisition."

" Well, ma'am. Then forty-two and fifty-three came up——"

" No, they did *not*, sir; nothink of the sort !—I called them up."

" And you said ?"

" Sir ?" with tremendous calmness.

" You said—— ?"

" *I made the observation,*" with strong emphasis and exactness, " I give this person in charge for assaulting of me. Forty-two says, ' O you're not hurt. Don't make a disturbance here.' Fifty-three likewise declines to take the charge. Which," with greater rapidity than ever, " is the two pleesemen I am here to appear against; and will be here at nine to-morrow morning, or at height if needful, or at sivin—hany hour—and as a ouseholder demanding the present charge to be regularly hentered against pleesçmen respectually numbered forty-two and fifty-three, which shall be substantiated by day or night or morning—which is more—for I am not a acquisition, and what those pleesemen done, sir, they shall answer!"

The Inspector—whose patience is not in the least affected—being now possessed of the charge, reduces it to a formal accusation against two P. C.s for neglect of duty, and gravely records it in Mrs. Megby's own words—with such fidelity that, at the end of every sentence when it is read over, Mrs. Megby, comparatively softened, repeats, " Yes, sir, which it is correct!" and afterwards signs, as if her name were not half long enough for her great revenge.

On the removal of Mrs. Megby's person, Mr. Bat, to our great amazement, is revealed behind her.

"I say! Is it t'morrow mawrer?" asks Mr. Bat, in confidence.

"He has got out of the cab," says the Inspector, whom nothing surprises, and will be brought in, in custody, presently! No. This morning! Why don't you go home?"

" *This* mawrer!" says Mr. Bat, profoundly reflecting. " How car it be *this* mawrer? It must be yesterday mawrer."

" You had better make the best of your way home, sir," says the Inspector.

"No offence is interrer," says Mr. Bat. I happened to be passing this dirrertion—when—saw door open—kaymin. It's a frez of my—I am nor——" he is quite unequal to the word particular now, so he concludes with "you no war I me!—I am aw ri! I shall be here in the mawrer!" and stumbles out again.

The watch stealer, who has been removed, is now brought back. Mrs. Green (the searcher) reports to have found upon her some halfpence, two pawnbroker's duplicates, and a comb. All produced.

"Very good. You can lock her up now, gaoler.—What does she say?"

"She says, can she have her comb, sir?"

"Oh yes. She can have her comb. Take it!" And away

she goes to the cells, a dirty unwholesome object, designing, no doubt, to comb herself out for the magisterial presence in the morning.

"O! Please, sir, you have got two French ladies here, in brown shot silk?" says a woman with a basket. (We have changed the scene to the Vine-street station-house, but its general arrangement is just the same.)

"Yes."

"Will you send 'em in this fowl and bread for supper, please?"

"They shall have it. Hand it in."

"Thank'ee, sir. Good night, sir."

The Inspector has eyed the woman, and now eyes the fowl. He turns it up, opens it neatly with his knife, takes out a little bottle of brandy artfully concealed within it, puts the brandy on a shelf as confiscated, and sends in the rest of the supper.

What is this very neat new trunk in a corner, carefully corded? It is here on a charge of "drunk and incapable." It was found in Piccadilly to-night (with a young woman sitting on it), and is full of good clothes, evidently belonging to a domestic servant. Those clothes will be rags soon, and the drunken woman will die of gin, or be drowned in the river.

We are dozing by the fire again, and it is past three o'clock, when the stillness (only invaded at intervals by the head voices of the two French ladies talking in their cell—no other prisoners seem to be awake) is broken by the complaints of a woman and the cries of a child. The outer door opens noisily, and the complaints and the cries come nearer, and come into the dock.

"What's this?" says the Inspector, putting up the window. "Don't cry there, don't cry!"

A rough-headed miserable little boy of four or five years old stops in his crying and looks frightened.

"This woman," says a wet constable, glistening in the gas-light, "has been making a disturbance in the street for hours, on and off. She says she wants relief. I have warned her off my beat over and over again, sir; but it's of no use. She took at last to rousing the whole neighbourhood."

" You hear what the constable says. What did you do that
for ?"

" Because I want relief, sir."

" If you want relief, why don't you go to the relieving-
officer ?"

" I've been, sir, God knows; but I couldn't get any. I
haven't been under a blessed roof for three nights; but have
been prowling the streets the whole night long, sir. And I
can't do it any more, sir. And my husband has been dead
these eight months, sir. And I've nobody to help me to a
shelter or a bit of bread, God knows !"

" You haven't been drinking, have you ?"

" Drinking, sir ? Me, sir ?"

" I am afraid you have. Is that your own child ?"

" O yes, sir, he's my child ?"

" He hasn't been with you in the streets three nights, has
he ?"

" No, sir. A friend took him in for me, sir; but couldn't
afford to keep him any longer, sir, and turned him on my hands
this afternoon, sir."

" You didn't fetch him away yourself, to have him to beg
with, I suppose ?"

" O no, sir ! Heaven knows I didn't, sir !"

" Well !" writing on a slip of paper, " I shall send the child
to the workhouse until the morning, and keep you here. And
then, if your story is true, you can tell it to the magistrate,
and it will be inquired into."

" Very well, sir. And God knows I'll be thankful to have
it inquired into !"

" Reserve !"

" Sir !"

" Take this child to the workhouse. Here's the order. You
go along with this man, my little fellow, and they'll put you in
a nice warm bed, and give you some breakfast in the morning. There's a good boy !"

The wretched urchin parts from his mother without a look,
and trots contentedly away with the constable. There would
be no very strong ties to break here if the constable were
taking him to an industrial school. Our honourable friend
the member for Red Tape voted for breaking stronger ties

than these in workhouses once upon a time. And we seem faintly to remember that he glorified himself upon that measure very much!

We shift the scene to Southwark. It is much the same. We return to Bow-street. Still the same. Excellent method carefully administered, vigilant in all respects, except this main one :—prevention of ignorance, remedy for unnatural neglect of children, punishment of wicked parents, interposition of the State, as a measure of human policy, if not of human pity and accountability, at the very source of crime.

Our Inspectors hold that drunkenness as a source of crime is in the ratio of two to one greater than any other cause. We doubt if they make due allowance for the cases in which it is the consequence or companion of crime, and not the cause; but, we do not doubt its extensive influence as a cause alone. Of the seven thousand and eighteen charges entered in the books of Bow-street station during 1850, at least half are against persons of both sexes, for being " drunk and incapable." If offences be included which have been indirectly instigated by intoxication, the proportion rises to at least seventy-five per cent. As a proof of this, it can be demonstrated from the books at head-quarters (Scotland-yard) that there was a great and sudden diminution of charges after the wise measure of shutting up public-houses at twelve oclock on Saturday nights.

Towards five o'clock the number of cases falls off, and the business of the station dwindles down to charges against a few drunken women. We have seen enough, and we retire.

We have not wearied the reader, whom we now discharge, with more than a small part of our experience; we have not related how the two respectable tradesmen, " happening" to get drunk at " the house they used," first fought with one another, then " dropped into" a policeman; as a witness related in evidence, until admonished by his Inspector concerning the Queen's English : nor how one young person resident near Covent-garden, reproached another young person in a loud tone of voice at three o'clock in the morning, with being a " shilling minx"—nor how that young person retorted that, allowing herself, for the sake of argument, to be a minx, she must yet prefer a claim to be a pound minx rather than a

12

shilling one, and so they fell to fighting and were taken into
custody—nor how the first minx, piteously declaring that she
had "left her place without a bit of key," was consoled, before having the police-key turned upon herself, by the despatch of a trusty constable to secure her goods and chattels
from pillage: nor how the two smiths taken up for "larking"
on an extensive scale, were sorely solicitous about a "centre-
punch" which one of them had in his pocket; and which, on
being searched (according to custom) for knives, they expected never to see more: nor how the drunken gentleman
of independent property—who being too drunk to be allowed
to buy a railway ticket, and being most properly refused,
most improperly "dropped into" the railway authorities—
complained to us, visiting his cell, that he was locked up on a
foul charge at which humanity revolted, and was not allowed
to send for bail, and was *this* the Bill of Rights?

We have seen that an incessant system of communication,
day and night, is kept up between every station of the Force;
we have seen, not only crime speedily detected, but distress
quickly relieved; we have seen regard paid to every application, whether it be an inquiry after a gipsy woman, or a black
and tan spaniel, or a frivolous complaint against a constable;
we have seen that everything that occurs is written down, to
be forwarded to head-quarters; we have seen an extraordinary degree of patience habitually exercised in listening to
prolix details, in relieving the kernel of a case from its intricate and impenetrable husk; we have seen how impossible it
is for anything of a serious, of even an unusual, nature to
happen without being reported; and that, if reported, additional force can be immediately supplied from each station:
where from twenty to thirty men are always collected while
off duty. We have seen that the whole system is well, intel-
ligently, zealously worked; and we have seen, finally, that
the addition of a few extra men will be all-sufficient for any
exigencies which may arise from the coming influx of visitors.

Believe us, nervous old lady, dyspeptic half-pay suspicious
quidnunc, plot-dreading diplomatist, you may sleep in peace!
As for you, trembling ratepayer, it is not to be doubted that,
after what you have read here, you will continue to pay your
eightpence in the pound without a grudge.

And if, either you nervous old lady, or you dyspeptic half-pay, or you suspicious qiudnunc, or you plot-dreading diplomatist, or you ungrudging ratepayer, have ever seen or heard, or read of, a vast city which a solitary watcher might traverse in the dead of night as he may traverse London, you are far wiser than we. It is daybreak on this third morning of our vigil—on, it may be, the three thousandth morning of our seeing the pale dawn in these hushed and solemn streets. Sleep in peace! If you have children in your houses, wake to think of, and to act for, the doomed childhood that encircles you out of doors, from the rising up of the sun unto the going down of the stars, and sleep in greater peace. There is matter enough for real dread there. It is a higher cause than the cause of any rotten government on the continent of Europe, that, trembling, hears the-Marseillaise in every whisper, and dreads a barricade in every gathering of men!

☞ XXIII.

EPSOM.

JUNE 7, 1851.

A STRAGGLING street, plenty of inns, a pond, a pump, and a magnificent brick tower, make up—with a few more touches not necessary to be given here—the picture of the metropolis of English racing, and the fountain of Epsom salts. For three hundred and sixty-four days in the year a cannon-ball might be fired from one end of Epsom to the other without endangering human life. On the three hundred and sixty-fifth, a population surges and rolls, and scrambles through the place, that would people a colony. That one exceptional day is the Derby day.

Believing in the dictum of the Universal Spelling Book that the "horse is a noble animal;" that he is nowhere so noble, so well bred, so handsome, so tractable, so intelligent, so well cared for, and so well appreciated, as in this country; that, in consequence of the national fondness for races his breed has been improved until he has attained his present excellency—believing all this, we think it quite possible to do him justice,

without defiling the subject with any allusion to the knavery
to which he innocently gives rise. Those who practise it are
his vulgar parasites; for the owners of race-horses number
among them the highest and most honourable names in the
country.

Financially, the subject is not unworthy of notice. Racers
give employment to thousands. According to Captain Rous,
there are upwards of two hundred thorough-bred stallions, and
one thousand one hundred brood mares, which produce about
eight hundred and thirty foals annually; of these there are
generally three in the first class of race-horses, seven in the
second class; and they descend gradually in the scale to the
amount of four hundred and eighty, one half of which never
catch the judge's eye; the remainder are either not trained,
or are found unworthy of training for the Course, at an early
period.

The number of race-courses is one hundred and eleven; of
which three are in Ireland, and six in Scotland.

It is Monday—the Monday before the Derby Day, and a
railway takes us, in less than an hour, from London Bridge to
the capital of the racing world, close to the abode of its Great
Man, who is—need we add ?—the Clerk of the Epsom Course.
It is, necessarily, one of the best houses in the place; being—
honour to literature !—a flourishing bookseller's shop. We are
presented to the official. He kindly conducts us to the Downs,
to show how the horses are temporarily stabled; to initiate us
into some of the mysteries of the "field;" to reveal to us the
private life of a race-horse.

We arrive at a neat farm-house, with more outbuildings
than is usually seen appended to so modest a homestead. A
sturdy, well-mannered, purpose-like man, presents himself.
He has a Yorkshire accent. A few words pass between him
and the Clerk of the Course, in which we hear the latter as-
severate with much emphasis that we are, in a sporting sense,
quite artless—we rather think "green," was the exact expression—that we never bet a shilling, and are quite incapable, even if willing, to take advantage of any information, or
of any inspection vouchsafed to us. Mr. Filbert (the trainer)
hesitates no longer. He moves his hat with honest politeness ;
bids us follow him, and lays his finger on the latch of a stable.

The trainer opens the door with one hand; and, with a gentleman-like wave of the other, would give us the precedence. We hesitate. We would rather not go in first. We acknowledge an enthusiastic admiration of the race-horse; but at the very mention of a thorough-bred, the animal described in the Book of Job prances before our mind's eye: "The glory of his nostril is terrible. He mocketh at fear and is not affrighted. He swalloweth the ground with the fierceness of his rage." To enjoy, therefore, a fine racer—not as one does a work of art—we like the point of sight to be the point of distance. The safest point, in case of accident (say, for instance, a sudden striking out of the hinder hoofs), we hold to be the vanishing point—a point by no means attainable on the inside of that contracted kind of stable known as a "loose box."

The trainer mistakes our fears for modesty. We boldly step forward to the outer edge of the threshold, but uncomfortably close to the hinder-quarters of Pollybus, a "favourite" for the Derby. When we perceive that he has neither bit nor curb; nor bridle, nor halter; that he is being "rubbed down" by a small boy, after having taken his gallops; that there is nothing on earth—except the small boy—to prevent his kicking, or plunging, or biting, or butting his visitors to death; we breathe rather thickly. When the trainer exclaims, " Shut the door, Sam!" and the little groom does his master's bidding, and boxes us up, we desire to be breathing the fresh air of the Downs again.

"Bless you, sir!" says our good-tempered informant, when he sees us shrink away from Pollybus, changing sides at a signal from his cleaner; "these horses" (we look round, and perceive, with a tremor, the heels of another high-mettled racer protruding from an adjoining stall), "these horses are as quiet as you are; and—I say it without offence—just as well behaved. It is quite laughable to hear the notions of people who are not used to them. They are the gentlest and most tractable creeturs. Then, as to shape and symmetry, is there anything like them?"

We acknowledge that Pretty Perth—the mare in the adjoining box—could hardly be surpassed for beauty.

"Ah, *can* you wonder at noblemen and gentlemen laying out their twenty and thirty thousand a year on them?"

" So much ?"

" Why, my gov'nor's stud costs us five-and-twenty thousand a year, one year with another.—There's an eye, sir !"

The large, prominent, but mild optics of Pretty Perth are at this moment turned full upon us. Nothing, certainly, can be gentler than the expression which beams from them. She is " taking," as Mr. Filbert is pleased to say, " measure of us. She does not stare vulgarly, or peer upon us a half-bred indifference ; but, having duly and deliberately satisfied her mind respecting our external appearance, allows her attention to be leisurely diverted to some oats with which the boy has just supplied the manger.

" It is all a mistake," continues Mr. Filbert, commenting on certain vulgar errors respecting race-horses; " thorough-breds are not nearly so rampagious as mongrels and half-breds. The two horses in this stall are gentlefolks, with as good blood in their veins as the best nobleman in the land. They would be just as backward in doing anything unworthy of a lady or gentleman, as any lord or lady in St. James's—such as kicking, or rearing, or shying, or biting. The pedigree of every horse that starts in any great race, is to be traced as regularly up to James the First's Arabian, or to Cromwell's White Turk, or to the Darley or Godolphin barbs, as your great English families are to the Conqueror. The worst thing they will do, is running away now and then with their jockeys. And what's that? Why, only the animal's animal spirit running away with *him*. They are not," adds Mr. Filbert, with a merry twinkle in his eye, " the only young bloods that are fond of going too fast."

Could a racer go too fast? Mr. Filbert gives a jolly negative, and remarks that it is all owing to high feeding and fine air; " for, mind you, horses get much better air to breathe than men do, and more of it."

All this while the two boys are sibilating lustily while rubbing and polishing the coats of their horses ; which are as soft as velvet, and much smoother. When the little grooms come to the fetlock and pastern, the chamois-leather they have been using is discarded as too coarse and rough, and they rub away down to the hoofs with their sleek and plump hands. Every wish they express, either in words or by signs, is cheerfully obeyed by the horse. The terms the quadruped seems to be on with the small biped, are those of the most easy and intimate friendship. The two thoroughly understand one another. We feel ashamed of our mistrust of so much docility, and leave the stable with less awe of a race-horse than we entered it.

"And now, Mr. Filbert, one delicate question—What security is there against these horses being drugged, so that they may lose a race?"

Mr. Filbert halts, places his legs apart, and his arms akimbo, and throws into his reply a severe significance, mildly tinged with indignation. He commences with saying, "I'll tell you where it is:—there is a deal more said about foul play and horses going amiss, than there need be."

"Then the boys are never heavily bribed?"

"Heavily bribed!" Mr. Filbert contracts his eyes, but sharpens up their expression, to look the suspicion down. "Bribed!—it mayn't be hard to bribe a man, but it's not so easy to bribe a boy. What's the use of a hundred-pound note to a child of ten or twelve year old? Try him with a pen'north of apples or a slice of pudding, and you have a better chance; though I would not give you the price of a sugar-stick for it. Nine out of ten of these lads would not have a hair of their horse's tail ruffled if they could help it; much more any such harm as drugs or downright poison. The boy and the horse are so fond of one another, that some racing stables are regular happy families of boys and horses."

"How does this happen?"

"When the foal is first born, it is turned loose into the paddock; and if the mother don't give enough milk, a cow makes up the deficiency. He scampers about in this way for about a year: then he is 'taken up;' that is, bitted, and backed by a 'dumb-jockey'—a cross of wood with a bridle made for the purpose. When he has got a little used to that, we try him with a speaking jockey—a child some seven or eight years old, who has been born, like the colt, in the stables. From that time till the horse retires from the turf, the two are inseparable. They eat, drink, sleep, go out and come in together. Under the directions of the trainer, the boy tells the horse what to do, and he does it; for he knows that he is indebted

to the boy for everything he gets. When he is hungry, it is
the boy that gives him his corn; when he is thirsty, the boy
hands him his water; if he gets a stone in his foot, the boy
picks it out. By the time the colt is old enough to run, he
and the boy have got to like one another so well that they fret
to be away from one another. As for bribing! Why, you
may as well try to bribe the horse to poison the boy, as the
boy to let the horse be injured."

"But the thing *has* happened, Mr. Filbert?"

"Not so much as is talked about. Sometimes a likely foal
is sent to a training stable, and cracked up as something wonderful. He is entered to run. On trial, he turns out to be
next to nothing; and the backers, to save their reputation,
put it about, that the horse was played tricks with. There is
hardly a great race but you hear something about horses going
amiss by foul play."

"Do many of these boys become jockeys?"

"Mostly. Some of them are jockeys already, and ride
'their own' horses, as they call them. Here comes one."

A miniature man, with a horsewhip neatly twisted round
the crop or handle, opens the gate.

"Well, Tommy, how are you, Tommy?"

"Well, sir, bobbish. Fine day, Mr. Filbert."

Although Mr. Filbert tells us in a whisper that Tommy is
only twelve next birthday, Tommy looks as if he had entered
far into his teens. His dress is deceptive. Light trousers
terminating in buttons, laced shoes, long striped waistcoat,
a cut-away coat, a coloured cravat, a collar to which juveniles aspire under the name of "stick-ups," and a Paris
silk hat.

"Let's see, Tommy; what stakes did you win last?"

Tommy flicks, with the end of his whip-crop, a speck of dirt
from the toe of his "off" shoe, and replies carelessly, "The
Great Northamptonshire upon Valentine. But then, I have
won a many smaller stakes, you know, Mr. Filbert."

Are there many jockeys so young as Tommy?

"Not many so young," says Tommy, tying a knot in his
whip-thong, "but a good many smaller." Tommy then walks
across the straw-yard to speak to some stable friend he has
come to see.

"That boy will be worth money before he's a man," says Mr. Filbert. "It is no uncommon thing for a master to give a lad like that a hundred pound when he wins a race. As he can't spend it in hardbake, or ginger-beer, or marbles (the young rogue *does*, occasionally, get rid of a pound or two in cigars), he saves it. I have known a racing-stable lad begin the world at twenty, with from three to four thousand pound."

Tommy is hopping back over the straw, as if he had forgotten something. "O, I beg your pardon for not asking before," he says, "but—how does Mrs. Filbert find herself?"

"Quite well, thank you, Tommy." Tommy says he is glad to hear it, and walks back.

Our interview with Mr. Filbert is finished, and we pace towards the race-course with its indefatigable clerk. Presently, he points to a huge white object that rears its leaden roof on the apex of the highest of the "Downs." It is the Grand Stand. It is so extensive, so strong, and so complete, that it seems built for eternity, instead of for busy use during one day in the year, and for smaller requisition during three others. Its stability is equal to St. Paul's or the Memnonian Temple. Our cicerone tells us that he pays as rent, and in subscriptions to stakes to be run for, nearly two thousand pounds per annum for that stand. Expecting an unusually great concourse of visitors this year, he has erected a new wing, extended the betting enclosure, and fitted up two apartments for the exclusive use of ladies.

Let us go into the basement. First into the weighing-house, where the jockeys "come to scale" after each race. We then inspect the offices for the Clerk of the Course himself; wine-cellars, beer-cellars, larders, sculleries, and kitchens, all as gigantically appointed, and as copiously furnished, as if they formed part of an Ogre's Castle. To furnish the refreshment-saloon, the Grand Stand has in store two thousand four hundred tumblers, one thousand two hundred wine-glasses, three thousand plates and dishes, and several of the most elegant vases we have seen out of the Glass Palace, decorated with artificial flowers. An exciting odour of cookery meets us on our descent. Rows of spits are turning rows of joints before

12*

blazing walls of fire. Cooks are trussing fowls; confectioners
are making jellies; kitchen-maids are plucking pigeons; crates
of boiled tongues are being garnished on dishes. One hundred
and thirty legs of lamb, sixty-five saddles of lamb, and one
hundred and thirty shoulders of lamb; in short, a flock of
sixty-five lambs have to be roasted, and dished, and garnished
by the Derby Day. Twenty rounds of beef, four hundred
lobsters, one hundred and fifty tongues, twenty fillets of veal,
one hundred sirloins of beef, five hundred spring chickens,
three hundred and fifty pigeon-pies; a countless number of
quartern loaves, and an incredible quantity of ham; eight
hundred eggs. Besides the eggs, the forests of lettuces, the
acres of cress, and beds of radishes, which will have to be
chopped up; the gallons of "dressing" that will have to be
poured out, will be best estimated by a memorandum from
the chief of that department to the *chef de cuisine*, which
happened, accidentally, to fall under our notice: "Pray don't
forget a large tub and a birch-broom for mixing the salad!"

We are preparing to ascend, when we hear the familiar
sound of a printing machine. The Grand Stand, like the
kingdom of China, is self-supporting. It scorns foreign aid;
even for printing the Racing Lists. This is the source of the
innumerable cards with which hawkers persecute the sporting
world on its way to the Derby, from the Elephant and Castle
to the Grand Stand. "Dorling's list! Dorling's correct list!
with the names of the horses, and colours of the riders!"

We step out upon the lawn; in the midst is the betting-
ring, where sums of money of fabulous amounts change hands.
The following salutary notice, respecting too numerous a class
of characters, is printed on the admission card:

"The Lessee of the Epsom Grand Stand hereby gives notice that no person guilty of any malpractices, or notoriously in default in respect of stakes,
forfeits, or bets lost upon horse-racing, will be admitted within the Grand
Stand or its enclosure during any race meetings at Epsom; and if any such
person should gain admittance therein or thereupon, he will be expelled, upon
his presence being pointed out to the Stewards for the time being, or to the
Clerk of the Course."

The first floor is entirely occupied with a refreshment-room
and a police court. Summary justice is the law of the Grand
Stand. Two magistrates sit during the races. Is a pick-

pocket detected, a thimble-rigger caught, a policeman assaulted? The delinquent is brought round to the Grand Stand, to be convicted, sentenced, and imprisoned in as short a time as it takes to run a mile race.

The sloping roof is covered with lead, in steps; the spectator from that point has a bird's-eye view of the entire proceedings, and of the surrounding country, which is beautifully picturesque. When the foreground of the picture is brightened and broken by the vast multitude that assembles here upon the Derby Day, it presents a whole which has no parallel in the world.

On that great occasion, an unused spectator might imagine that all London turned out. There is little perceptible difference in the bustle of its crowded streets; but all the roads leading to Epsom Downs are so thronged and blocked by every description of carriage that it is marvellous to consider how, when, and where, they were all made—out of what possible wealth they are all maintained—and by what laws the supply of horses is kept equal to the demand. Near the favourite bridges, and at various leading points of the leading roads, clusters of people post themselves by nine o'clock, to see the Derby people pass. Then come flitting by, barouches, phaetons, broughams, gigs, four-wheeled chaises, four-in-hands, Hansom cabs, cabs of lesser note, chaise-carts, donkey-carts, tilted vans made arborescent with green boughs and carrying no end of people, and a cask of beer,—equestrians, pedestrians, horse-dealers, gentlemen, notabilities, and swindlers, by tens of thousands—gradually thickening and accumulating, until, at last, a mile short of the turnpike, they become wedged together, and are very slowly filtered through layers of policemen, mounted and a-foot, until, one by one, they pass the gate and skurry down the hill beyond. The most singular combinations occur in these turnpike stoppages and presses. Four-in-hand leaders look affectionately over the shoulders of ladies, in bright shawls, perched in gigs; poles of carriages appear, uninvited, in the midst of social parties in phaetons; little, fast, short-stepping ponies run up carriage-wheels before they can be stopped, and hold on behind like footmen. Now, the gentleman who is unaccustomed to public driving, gets into astonishing perplexities. Now, the Hansom cab whisks craf-

tily in and out, and seems occasionally to fly over a waggon
or so. Now, the postboy on a jibbing or a shying horse,
curses the evil hour of his birth, and is ingloriously assisted
by the shabby ostler out of place, who is walking down with
seven shabby companions more or less equine, open to the
various chances of the road. Now, the air is fresh, and the
dust flies thick and fast. Now, the canvas booths upon the
course are seen to glisten and flutter in the distance. Now,
the adventurous vehicles make cuts across, and get into ruts
and gravel-pits. Now, the heather in bloom is like a field of
gold, and the roar of voices is like a wind. Now, we leave
the hard road and go smoothly rolling over the soft green
turf, attended by an army of importunate worshippers in red
jackets and stable jackets, who make a very Juggernaut-car
of our equipage, and now breathlessly call us My Lord, and
now, Your Honour. Now, we pass the outer settlements of
tents where pots and kettles are—where gipsy children are—.
where airy stabling is—where tares for horses may be bought
—where water, water, water, is proclaimed—where the Tumbler in an old pea-coat, with a spangled fillet round his head,
eats oysters, while his wife takes care of the golden globes,
and the knives, and also of the starry little boy, their son, who
lives principally upside-down. Now, we pay our one pound
at the barrier, and go faster on, still Juggernaut-wise, attended by our devotees, until at last we are drawn, and
rounded, and backed, and sidled, and cursed, and compli-
mented, and vociferated, into a station on the hill opposite the
Grand Stand, where we presently find ourselves on foot, much
bewildered, waited on by five respectful persons, who *will*
brush us all at once.

" Well, to be sure, there never was such a Derby Day as
this present Derby Day! Never, to be sure, were there so
many carriages, so many fours, so many twos, so many ones,
so many horsemen, so many people who have come down by
" rail," so many fine ladies in so many broughams, so many of
Fortnum and Mason's hampers, so much ice and champagne!
If I were on the turf, and had a horse to enter for the Derby,
I would call that horse Fortnum and Mason, convinced that
with that name he would beat the field. Public opinion would
bring him in somehow. Look where I will—in some connex-

ion with the carriages—made fast upon the top, or occupying
the box, or tied up behind, or dangling below, or peeping out
of window—I see Fortnum and Mason. And now, Heavens!
all the hampers fly wide open, and the green Downs burst into
a blossom of lobster-salad!

As if the great Trafalgar signal had been suddenly displayed
from the top of the Grand Stand, every man proceeds to do
his duty. The weaker spirits, who were ashamed to set the
great example, follow it instantly, and all around me there are
table-cloths, pies, chickens, hams, tongues, rolls, lettuces, radishes, shell-fish, broad-bottomed bottles, clinking glasses, and
carriages turned inside out. Amidst the hum of voices a bell
rings. What's that? What's the matter? They are clearing the course. Never mind. Try the pigeon-pie. A roar.
What's the matter? It's only the dog upon the course. Is
that all? Glass of wine. Another roar. What's that? It's
only the man who wants to cross the course, and is intercepted
and brought back. Is that all? I wonder whether it is always the same dog and the same man, year after year! A
great roar. What's the matter? By Jupiter they are going
to start.

A deeper hum and a louder roar. Everybody standing on
Fortnum and Mason. Now they're off! No. *Now* they're
off! No. *Now* they're off! No. *Now* they are! Yes!

There they go! Here they come! Where? Keep your
eye on Tattenham Corner, and you'll see 'em coming round in
half a minute. Good gracious, look at the Grand Stand, piled
up with human beings to the top, and at the wonderful effect
of changing light as all their faces and uncovered heads turn
suddenly this way! Here they are! Who is? The horses!
Where? Here they come! Green first. No: Red first. No:
Blue first. No: the Favourite first! Who says so? Look!
Hurrah! Hurrah! All over. Glorious race. Favorite wins!
Two hundred thousand pounds lost and won. You don't say
so? Pass the pie!

Now, the pigeons fly away with the news. Now, every one
dismounts from the top of Fortnum and Mason, and falls to
work with greater earnestness than before, on carriage boxes,
sides, tops, wheels, steps, roofs, and rumbles. Now, the living
stream upon the course, damned for a little while at one point,

is released, and spreads like parti-colored grain. Now, the
roof of the Grand Stand is deserted. Now, rings are formed
upon the course, where strong men stand in pyramids on one
another's heads; where the Highland lady dances; where the
Devonshire Lad sets-to with the Bantam; where the Tumbler
throws the golden globes about, with the starry little boy tied
round him in a knot.

Now, all the variety of human riddles who propound themselves on race-courses, come about the carriages, to be guessed.
Now, the gipsy woman, with the flashing red or yellow handkerchief about her head, and the strange silvery-hoarse voice,
appears, My pretty gentleman, to tell your fortin, sir; for you
have a merry eye, my gentleman, and surprises is in store for
you, connected with a dark lady as loves you better than you
love a kiss in a dark corner when the moon's a-shining; for
you have a lively 'art my gentleman, and you shall know her
secret thoughts, and the first and last letters of her name, my
pretty gentleman, if you will cross your poor gipsy's hand with
a little bit of silver, for the luck of the fortin as the gipsy will
read true, from the lines of your hand, my gentleman, both as
to what is past, and present and to come. Now, the Ethio-
pians, looking unutterably hideous in the sunlight, play old
banjoes and bones, on which no man could perform ten years
ago, but which, it seems, any man may play now, if he will
only blacken his face, put on a crisp wig, a white waistcoat
and wristbands, a large white tie, and give his mind to it.
Now, the sickly-looking ventriloquist, with an anxious face
(and always with a wife in a shawl), teaches the alphabet to
the puppet pupil, whom he takes out of his pocket. Now,
my sporting gentlemen, you may ring the Bull, the Bull, the
Bull; you may ring the Bull! Now, try your luck at the
knock-em-downs, my Noble Swells—twelve heaves for sixpence, and a pincushion in the centre, worth ten times the
money! Now, the Noble Swells take five shillings' worth of
" heaves," and carry off a halfpenny wooden pear in triumph.
Now, it hails, as it always does hail, formidable wooden trun-
cheons round the heads, bodies, and shins of the proprietors
of the said knock-em-downs, whom nothing hurts. Now, in-
scrutable creatures in smock frocks, beg for bottles. Now, a
coarse vagabond, or idiot, or a compound of the two, never

beheld by mortal off a race-course, minces about, with ample skirts and a tattered parasol, counterfeiting a woman. Now, a shabby man, with an overhanging forehead, and a slinking eye, produces a small board, and invites your attention to something novel and curious—three thimbles and one little pea—with a one, two, three,—and a two, three, one,—and a one—and a two—in the middle—right hand, left hand—go you any bet from a crown to five sovereigns you don't lift the thimble the pea's under! Now, another gentleman (with a stick) much interested in the experiment, will "go" two sovereigns that he does lift the thimble, provided strictly that the shabby man holds his hand still, and don't touch 'em again. Now, the bet's made, and the gentleman with the stick lifts obviously the wrong thimble, and loses. Now, it is as clear as day to an innocent bystander, that the loser must have won if he had not blindly lifted the wrong thimble—in which he is strongly confirmed by another gentleman with a stick, also much interested, who proposes to "go him" halves—a friendly sovereign to *his* sovereign—against the bank. Now, the innocent agrees, and loses ;—and so the world turns round bringing innocents with it in abundance, though the three confederates are wretched actors, and could live by no other trade if they couldn't do it better.

Now, there is another bell, and another clearing of the course, and another dog, and another man, and another race. Now, there are all these things all over again. Now, down among the carriage-wheels and poles, a scrubby growth of drunken post-boys and the like has sprung into existence, like weeds among the many-coloured flowers of fine ladies in broughams, and so forth. Now, the drinking-booths are all full, and tobacco-smoke is abroad, and an extremely civil gentleman confidentially proposes roulette. And now, faces begin to be jaded, and horses are harnessed, and wherever the old grey-headed beggerman goes, he gets among traces and splinter-bars, and is roared at.

So, now, we are on the road again, going home. Now, there are longer stoppages than in the morning ; for we are a dense mass of men and women, wheels, horses and dust. Now, all the houses on the road seem to be turned inside out, like the carriages on the course, and the people belonging to the houses, like the people belonging to the carriages, occupy stations which they never occupy at another time—on leads, on house-tops, on outbuildings, at windows, in balconies, in door-ways, in gardens. Schools are drawn out to see the company go by. The academies for young gentlemen favour us with dried peas; the Establishments for Young Ladies (into which sanctuaries many wooden pears are pitched), with bright eyes. We become sentimental, and wish we could marry Clapham. The crowd thickens on both sides of the road. All London appears to have come out to see us. It is like a triumphant entry—except that, on the whole, we rather amuse than impress, the populace. There are little love-scenes among the chesnut-trees by the roadside—young gentlemen in gardens resentful of glances at young ladies from coach-tops—other young gentlemen in other gardens, whose arms, encircling young ladies, seem to be trained like the vines. There are good family pictures—stout fathers and jolly mothers—rosy cheeks squeezed in between the rails—and infinitesimal jockeys winning in canters on walking-sticks. There are smart maid-servants among the grooms at stable-doors, where Cook looms large and glowing. There is plenty of smoking and drinking among the tilted vans and at the public-houses, and some singing; but general order and good-humour. So, we leave the gardens and come into the streets, and if we there encounter a few ruffians throwing flour and chalk about, we know them for the dregs and refuse of a fine, trustworthy people, deserving of all confidence and honour.

And now we are at home again—far from absolutely certain of the name of the winner of the Derby—knowing nothing whatever about any other race of the day—still tenderly affected by the beauty of Clapham—and thoughtful over the ashes of Fortnum and Mason.

XXIV.

THE GREAT BAR IN THE HARBOUR OF LONDON.

JULY 26, 1851.

THESE lines, when they meet your eye, Mr. Swallow, will astonish you. When you arrive at the Hotel des Bains, on an evening early in the present month, too late for the *table d'hôte :* when, on that account, you were denied access to the *salon à manger*, although you told the attendant you were dying of hunger: when the waiter shrugged a very good imitation of despair, and said in his native language that he was desolated, but that it was defended for the too tardy to disturb the convives who were already served ; but that, if you liked, he would command you a particular dinner in a particular chamber: when you indignantly refuse the latter offer, but accepted the former, calling in a menacing manner for pen, ink, and paper: when you retired and wrote a biting article (for the " Warrior for Peace," of which you are the distinguished Editor) against the entire population of Boulogne, with special reference to the infamous treatment of English travellers at the hotels of the city: when, in the midst of our denunciating perorations, you joyfully threw down the pen at the waiter's announcement that " Monsieur is served :" when you snatched up your article, rushed into the saloon, and found it adorned with the ruins of a dessert : when you found a place cleared for you behind six strawberries on an enormous dish, the rinds of two melons, a few " lady's fingers," and a Turk's caftan (in sponge cake) very much the worse for wear: when, as the various courses of the dinner-over-again which the few remaining guests were doomed to behold were brought in succession, you devour them in an uncommunicative solitude, as if you and the waiter were the only two individuals left in Naure, and as if the whole world were bounded by the edges of your plate: when, as you dallied with your *maccaroni au gratin*, and sipped your Medoc, the acidity of your visage gradually relaxed, and you deigned to stutter a few foreign words to the waiter; who, because he thought that they were meant to be French words answered you in broken English: when you ordered him to wake you in time for the London boat the next morning, and to pack up for exportation, half a dozen of the best cognac: when you lighted your cigar with your annihilating manuscript, retired, and visited several shops in the Rue de l'Ecu, to make a variety of purchases: and when, finally, you retired to chamber number twenty-one for the night, you little thought, Mr. Swallow, that a mysterious being dogged every step you took, heard every word you uttered, witnessed every bargain you made. Perhaps he was a detective policeman who mistook you for a St. Albans elector. Possibly, he was a disguised tide-waiter, watching to see what amount of fraud you contemplated, on that amiable department of the British Government—her Majesty's Customs.

In the morning, Mr. Swallow, disregarding the early announcement that *l'eau chaude* was at your door, you overslept yourself.

It was considerably past six; the boat was to start in half an hour, and your carpet-bag would not close by any means you had at command: no sort of squeezing, nor punching, nor thrusting, nor jamming, nor ramming, nor stamping: no attempt to distend its sides by pulling it on like a tight boot: no frantic jumping upon it from high chairs to flatten it: no kind of dexterity in coaxing shaving-tackle into bunged-up corners, in fitting hair-brushes into slippers, or wrapping up bottles of Eau-de-Cologne in a night-shirt: no crushing of your finest linen: no smashing of satin cravats: no artful insertion of fancy waistcoats between the leaves of your writing-case: no ruthless rolling up of your dress-coat to the resemblance of a black pudding: no stratagem, no force succeeded. The jaws of your carpet-bag with its one double tooth grinned open defiance, and would not on any terms become a locked jaw. You looked around in despair: a bottle of Maraschino, a dozen of gloves, a new pair of boots, and a "Guide to French Conversation," still lay on your toilette-table under an unavailing sentence of transportation. The clock of St. Gudule chimed the half hour; and protracted exile on a foreign shore presented itself horridly as your destiny. Captain Tune, of the "City of Paris," advertised that he would leave the wharf at seven A.M., precisely; and you knew that Time and Tune wait for no man.

It was the present writer, Mr. Swallow, who passed you on

the stairs when, giving up all hope, you abandoned your unfastened effects to the porter. You were telling him, in your
own original mode of uttering the language of the nation, to
lock the carpet-bag in number twenty-one. With a matter-
of-course coolness that implied the mere shooting of an easy
bolt, you treacherously transferred to him a task you had
found impossible, and descended to breakfast.—It was I who
translated your desires to the proper officer to whom you were
applying on the port for your permit to leave the country of
your three weeks' adoption: it was my hat which was knocked
off upon the deck of the steamer, when, just as the paddles
were making their first revolution, the hotel porter flung your
bursting bag triumphantly into the vessel. My eye was upon
you when you ostentatiously superintended the stowage of the
luggage belonging to the elegant widow who breakfasted with
us at the Hôtel des Bains; and I observed all your subsequent
attentions to that stately beauty; who, you artfully learnt,
was travelling quite alone. My hands were ready when, yield-
ing to the influence of a sudden lurch, you nearly poured a
bubbling glass of brandy and soda-water over her dress. It
was to me you remarked, as she passed us to descend into the
cabin, that she reminded you of the portraits of the late Mrs.
Siddons, only that she was a great deal handsomer.

You may remember, Mr. Swallow, that the boat was very
full. The passengers were mostly foreigners, whose destination was chiefly Hyde Park. A few, however, had special engagements; which, from their numerous and anxious inquiries
of Captain Tune as to when they would probably reach London, appeared to be of a pressing nature. It was no less conventional than true (as I think you remarked) that the London
alderman who was escorting his niece from a Capécure board-
ing-school had an appointment to dine in Westbournia at six;
the Frenchman in the green shooting-jacket and gaiters—
whose slouched hat shaded the swarthiest complexion and
thickest moustaches in the boat, and who reminded us of
Caspar and a sporting tour—was pledged, he said, to be in
Leicester-square at six and a half hours, on a matter of supreme importance. (I thought there was nothing in your
suspicion, Swallow, that he alluded to one of the promised
back-street conspiracies which have never yet broken out into

a blazing revolution, as it was cunningly foretold they would,
by certain nervous politicians as a sure result of '51.) Your
Mrs. Siddons was desirous, as you adroitly extracted from
her, of reaching her mother, who was alarmingly ill in Essex,
that night. The contractor for conveying the twenty-eight
ladies and gentlemen from Paris to London and back at so
much a head, had ordered a splendid repast to be prepared
for them in Ann-street, Soho, at seven precisely. You, Swallow, were in great anxiety to fulfil with your usual zeal your
critical duties for the " Warrior for Peace," by being in time
for the overture of Thalberg's new opera at Her Majesty's
Theatre. The young fellow with the pretty sister *said* he
wished very much to get down to Cambridge by the half-past
six o'clock train. All these anxious querists would have been
made happy by the captain's confident answer that they would
assuredly be abreast of Nicholson's Wharf at half-past four,
had not the alderman followed him about, and tagged on to
the end of each of his replies:

" But then there's the Custom House !"

The jolly skipper looked very blank, and shook his head till
the gold lace in his cap glistened in the sun like a portentous
meteor; he added, assentingly, " I can't answer for the Baggage Warehouse ! Who can ?"

" *I* can," thundered a gruff comforter ;—it was the alderman. "The last time I went to France I travelled from
Tooley-street to Folkestone harbour (seventy-six miles)in exactly"—here he exhibited a huge stop-watch—" one hundred
and sixty-nine minutes, forty seconds : on my return by long
sea it took me and my baggage two hours and five minutes to
pass from this very boat to the Thames-street side of the Baggage Warehouse."

Why, Swallow, were alarm and disgust so powerfully depicted in your countenance when you heard these facts ? Did
the six bottles of brandy sit heavily on your soul ? Were the
Maraschino, and the boots, and the lavender-water, and the
gloves excoriating your conscience ? No, Swallow, I will not
do you the injustice of any such supposition. You intended,
I feel certain, to declare them for duty, and to pay. You
shrank from the idea of sneaking ashore, a timid or even a
bold smuggler ; it was, I sincerely believe, your intention from

the first to tread the gangway with the honest independence of a British tax-payer. It was not the money—it was the time you grudged. The dread of being too late for the opening of Thalberg's opera, and that alone, distorted your countenance.

It is a pity, Swallow, that the consolations you were pouring into the widow's ear on the probability of her long detention at the Custom House all that day, prevented you from benefiting by a conversation which Caspar and several of his compatriots were carrying on with the Contractor. It took place as we passed the Nore. The mention of the Custom House suggested the subject of passports; which some of them manifestly did not know were unnecessary in this free country. One gentleman—his friends called him *Monsieur le Docteur*—drew near to you both, and became glowingly eloquent (for a woman *must* grace a French orator's auditory) on the freedom liberality, magnanimity, and hospitality of this great nation. Alas! his warm panegyric was suddenly chilled—his budding rhetoric rudely blighted :—The boat stopped, and there skipped on board from the port of Gravesend a couple of Custom House Officers.

I must say it was very apt of you to improve this untoward circumstance by reciting to your Siddons Don Juan's reception in this country on Shooter's Hill :

> "'And here,' he cried, 'is Freedom's chosen station ;
> Here peals the people's voice, nor can entomb it
> Racks, prisons, inquisitions; resurrection
> Awaits it, each new meeting or election.

> "'Here are chaste wives, pure lives; here people pay
> But what they please; and if that things be dear,
> 'Tis only that they love to throw away
> Their cash, to show how much they have a year.
> Here laws are all inviolate ; none lay
> Traps for the traveller; every highway's clear :
> He—' he was interrupted by a knife,
> With,—' * * *' your money or your life !' "

Neither do I think that, in answering the doctor's inquiries as to the necessity for these tide-waiters, you put their intrusion in too strong a light when you declared that their presence tacitly pronounced every individual on board, from the engine-boy at the hatchway to the Earl, to be a suspected smuggler.

But see, Swallow, we are off the Custom House Quay. The official clock attests to the captain's perfect accuracy :—it is exactly half-past four. Look alive, Swallow; you will have enough to do. Besides your brandy, and your widow, and your other articles of value, you have undertaken to "clear" the lady's luggage. "The City of Paris" has entered the City of London, and is lashed alongside Nicholson's Wharf. With all your alacrity, you are not quick enough; for, while you are investigating the names and addresses on the various portmanteaux and bags, your widow shows you one of her three boxes dangling mast-high in the air, being craned into Mr. Nicholson's premises. Before this box has touched the threshold of the huge hole in the wall that is neither a window nor a door, half a dozen unseen hands have nearly relieved it of its contents. The rapidity with which all this is done gives everybody hopes. The alderman anticipates being seated at six with his soup before him : the widow flutters with the hope of being yet able to see her invalid mother before morning; the Cantab does not despair of reaching his rooms in " Maudlin :" and you would bet even with Caspar or any other sporting gentleman present, that you will reach your stall in time to hear Thalberg's first chords. You are wrong. The odds are ten to one against you, Swallow.

Everything had gone on swimmingly up to the moment that the doom of office was inflicted upon us. Captain Tune had rattled us over from Boulogne in nine hours; his crew had unstowed some three or four hundred packages of baggage, and the wharfinger had swung it into the warehouse with magic rapidity. Nothing remained for us but to walk home, if the Custom House had not set its seal upon further progress. A Custom House officer arrested us seriatim as we attempted to leave the vessel. Any sort of bundle, or basket, or parcel, was peeped into or routed about by a pair of by no means spotless hands—*perhaps ;* for, as often as not, according to the caprice of the officer, it was passed untouched, almost unnoticed. You asked me to take ashore the widow's reticule. It was bulky. Bottles evidently predominated. The lady told us it was medicine. The officer—there was only one searching officer to some two hundred passengers—merely felt the bottom of the bag; discovered bottles; took my word that they contained medicine, and I passed on. The bag was big enough to conceal a fortune of lace, watches, or jewels : medicine *may* have meant Eau-de-Cologne, or brandy. If the duty of the searcher be to search, why were some molested and others allowed to go free ?

Your answer was excellent, Swallow. You said, " Because one man cannot do the work of ten; he cannot fight against such tremendous odds as two hundred to one; and because the whole affair is a stupid farce."

" But a farce, though not amusing, may be well acted," was, you will recollect, my rejoinder. " Yet this is only the first scene."

The next expedient of Her Majesty's Government to impart to foreign visitors *viâ* the Thames a favourable impression of England and the English, is to herd them together under the flattering designation of " aliens," and to oblige them and their fellow-travellers to mount to the Baggage Warehouse by means of a flight of exterior ladders, some part of which is exposed to whatever cold, wind, or sunshine, may happen to be raging. These stairs are not exceedingly well adapted for ladies, for other reasons than their steepness. Although your Mrs. Siddons would, in her sylph-like days, have made light of the ascent, yet the assistance you so gallantly afforded to her matured figure was not merely complimentary aid. The thanks she panted when you gracefully seated her on the hard bench of the dark, long, low, hot, reeking waiting-room, were evidently sincere.

When all the passengers had been slowly emptied out of the steamer, and had ascended to this house of detention, the " aliens" were penned up in one corner, to give their names, and to receive from two clerks their " certificates of arrival." In complaining to you and to our fellow-victims of a suffocating sensation, the alderman was by no means singular. You were, luckily, near the only practicable window; but my end of the room was in a stifling condition, and the supplications for air were general. Even the stalwart Caspar gasped as if he were breathing the sulphurs of the magic circle. There were general cries of " How long is this to last ?"

"When are we to get our luggage?"

"When your name is called," replied the porter, holding the door hermetically close. The alderman produced his stopwatch. "We landed," he remarked, "at ten minutes to five o'clock—it is now a quarter past five, and not a single name has been demanded!"

At length even the doorkeeper's patience was exhausted; and, in a fit of despair, he opened the door. A crowd immediately jammed itself between the sides. The affrighted porter had undammed a sluice. He rushed to the foot of the first flight of steps. He held on by the two banisters like grim death, and opposed his broad back to the torrent. Ladies screamed; men exclaimed "Shame!" Presently, the confusion confounded itself; for the crowd became so tightly wedged into the doorway and on the stairs, that it could not make any sort of demonstration either by speech or action. I pitied you, Swallow, most especially. You had nobly resolved to fight your way to the van in search of the widow's luggage; and a creeping shiver came over me when I beheld your round little form rasped and grated against the brick wall like a stray nutmeg.

About this time a theory was propounded by a nervous clerk (who was protected by an iron barrier in a doorway on the first landing opposite to the crowd), that all those who had single packages were to be served first. The individuals who immediately announced that each had travelled from the Continent with a single trunk, were curiously numerous. But they might as well have boasted of cart-loads of luggage; because, except three ladies of seven-package power, and the Contractor for the twenty-eight from Paris (an old stager), not a soul, whether of single pretensions or not, could gain entrance to the warehouse in which the baggage awaited inspection. The single-to-do fiction was therefore exploded, and the calling of names commenced. At twenty-four minutes to six (the alderman is my authority for this precise datum) the fortunate owner of the name of "Roots" was asked for. Mr. Roots, planted in a remote recess of the waiting-room, answered the call in a tone of good-humoured mockery. Mr. Roots had as much chance of wedging himself through the crowd, as you, my poor Swallow, had of grating yourself through the brick wall. At this moment, the Contractor, in a foaming state, appeared on a platform of the warehouse, and frantically invoked Monsieur le Docteur : Monsieur le Docteur was delaying the luggage of all the other members of the Contract, because he had not delivered up his keys. Would any one find Monsieur le Docteur, and entreat Monsieur le Docteur to pitch over his keys? Monsieur le Docteur, although invisible, managed to make himself heard. A statement—proceeding, apparently, from a few inches of sharp red nose thrust tightly through a couple of closely-wedged shoulders in the crowd, but really from the medical gentleman behind it—was heard to the effect that his (Monsieur le Docteur's) keys were indeed on his person, but that he was quite unable to get his hand into his own pocket without special permission of his co-constituents of the mob ; who, with the best will in the world, could not, by any means in their power, contrive to accord it.

Time wore on. Several persons had been summoned by name ; but, as they were unable to appear in person by reason of the crowd, the individuals nearest to the barrier and the beadle were admitted, regardless of any other rule than that of first come, first served ; consequently, two very rude and very strong Frenchmen made their way in by coarsely pushing aside the Cantab's sister and two ladies from their own country.

It would be tedious to narrate all that happened to me at the back of the crowd, while you, Swallow, suffered in the front. At last, I struggled my way into the place of search, where I was glad to find that you had not been much ground away ; and that a stratagem which I overheard you divulging to the widow, succeeded in gaining her admission also.

I appeal to you, Swallow, whether this third scene of the farce did not present a contrast to that which was just over. Here, in the Baggage Warehouse itself—in the actual receipt of Custom—the ventilation and deliberation were supreme. A fine view of the river, seen through one of the open windows, was being calmly enjoyed by a portly person, of considerable official pretensions. A clerk, writing the reverse of a running-hand, sat at a desk ; another (who seemed, by the jaunty style in which he wore his hat, to be a chance visitor

from some other department of the Customs) leaned lazily
against the desk, enjoying the proceedings of the baffled,
heated, ladies and gentlemen who had escaped from the
crowd, and who were anxiously threading the confused maze
of passengers' effects strewed on the floor, to find their own.
A third was criticising, with an easy air, a couple of lace collars belonging to the Cantab's sister. The scene was made
complete by two or three porters, whose deliberate mode of
opening carpet-bags, boxes, and trunks, showed that it was
not their fate to be hurried in their passage through this life.

You were wrong, Swallow, in venting so much indignation
when the search of Mrs. Siddons's largest box was in progress. What was the use of talking about "prying impertinence" to the man who would insist upon untying the strings
of both the lady's new bonnets, to see that they were not
lined with kid gloves or stuffed with perfumery or cambric
handkerchiefs or silk dresses? Why threaten to report him
for routing, and crushing, and creasing her cherished collars
and cuffs? And did you think it possible to reach the soul
of a Custom House searcher, by accusing that gentleman of
"infamous tyranny" when, despite your *protégée's* entreaties
(which, I admit, melted into tears; and in them I find your
excuse), he insisted upon seizing and confiscating two packs
of soiled French playing-cards, which the importer had, she
said, been specially commissioned to bring over for her
mother, whose only recreation left in the world was whist,
and whose infirmities prevented her from using the thick cards
manufactured here? *He* could not help that. Being unable
to perceive the accrediting ace of spades, what could he do?
He must show his employers that he searched *some* of the
packages.

No, Swallow, you wasted both breath and temper. It was
when the same person contented himself with thrusting his
arm half way down one side of Mrs. Siddons's carpet-bag, and
"passing" it instanter, that you ought to have reproved him.
Why were the contents of that lady's box turned topsy-turvy,
and the bag left unexamined? If a discretion be allowed to
subordinate officers, should it not be rationally exercised?
Why did this man confiscate a paltry pack of cards, which
the owner had a great wish to retain, and allow her the

chance of defrauding the revenue of hundreds? If no discretion be vested in these executives, and it be the law that
the contents of all baggage be examined, why is it not all examined?

Why? I'll tell you, Swallow;—because in this era of railways, and steamboats, and journeys to Paris in one day, and
voyages to New York and back in a month: in these times,
when an enormous glass palace can be built in seven months,
and messages are daily delivered and answered by electric
telegraph from one end of the island to the other in seven
minutes, the public won't wait! Listen, Mr. Swallow, to the
clamour that is still going on outside, on the stairs we have
just left; do you think if each of the five officials did his duty
rigidly, and examined every article minutely, that, somewhere
about half-past ten or eleven at night, the door of the Baggage
Warehouse would not be battered down by an injured and
impatient public? Deal in denunciation as strongly as a
gentleman dare, in the article you threaten to publish in the
Warrior for Peace, but, pray, do not pour the vials of your
inky wrath upon the unhappy five whom the Commissioners
of the Customs set to do the work of a dozen; and who
dawdle over their duty out of a hopeless despair of doing it
even passably. Why blame these men for the incompetency
of their superiors; who, if they have brains to organise, have
not industry to carry out one of a half-dozen plans that a child
would invent for the quick despatch of passengers' luggage?
Could not an efficient staff of searchers board the steamer at
Gravesend, and examine the packages on the voyage thence?
Could not an officer be stationed, on the vessel arriving, at
each of three or four gangways—instead of one officer at one
gangway—and allow no personal luggage to be landed which
did not display the Custom House seal? Or, failing this, could
not the two tide-waiters who already embark, and whose hard
fate it is to pace the deck in pleasant converse during the up-
Thames voyage, be set to arrange the list of passengers' names
handed to him by the captain, in alphabetical order? Then,
could not the warehouse at the wharf be divided off in compartments (from A to D;" from "E to K;" and so on
throughout the whole alphabet), like the Dividend Office at
the Bank of England, like all the Railway Stations in France,

and the Great Western Railway at Paddington? Could not
each passenger walk straight to the place of his initials, and
there expose it to the scrutineers, and have done with it? Or
does a system of corresponding numbers—one set for luggage,
and the other for passengers—demand too high an effort of
contrivance for Custom genius to aspire to? I modestly made
these suggestions to you, Swallow, with the assurance that you
are at liberty to make any public use of them you may think
proper.

While I dissent from some of your proceedings, I must say
you deserve high commendation for the masterly manner in
which you concealed your impatience, when the porter, who
had expressed his intention of opening your case of brandy,
stood by in idleness waiting for "his book," which clerk number three was making up. You would have enjoyed with a
keener relish his conversation relative to the proper mode of
nailing up bottles, and the probability of your importing
Eau-de-Cologne under the name of brandy to escape the
higher duty, if you had not felt that the residuary of your
fellow-travellers were still clamouring outside for admittance.
This conviction prevented you also from deriving all the
amusement which another official would, under other circumstances, have afforded you, when, coming forward with one
hand in his trousers-pocket, he took up with the other one
of your bottles; shook it, timed the appearance and subsidence of the bead, and pronounced your importation
"very weak;" but still brandy. On paying the duty, you
murmured at the unnecessary length of time the transaction
had occupied; but I could prove to you that had your box
arrived as merchandise instead of baggage; or, had you
been in greater haste than you were, and had left an agent
to clear your effects, the operation would have occupied
two days' dodging backwards and forwards, from one office
to another.

I could see that it was a great relief to you when you
safely handed the widow and her luggage into a cab. The
alderman was consulting his watch. "It is now," he said,
"seventeen minutes to seven o'clock, and we landed at ten
minutes to five. Consequently we have been detained by
these——" (you know that a hungry alderman is an angry

alderman) "Custom House people two hours all but seven minutes."

I must say I heard you repeat your intention to expose publicly the treatment we had all received with pleasure; because this is the treatment which everybody receives who lands from abroad in London, and has been receiving, to my knowledge, for the last twenty years. I trust you will indulge the public with a sound, temperate, and practical paper on the subject, in an early number of the Warrior for Peace. Pray point out that while the vexatious system of levying Customs duty on passengers' baggage lasts (which assuredly will not be long),* it ought to be effected in a decent, orderly, and systematic manner. You will not, I hope, take it amiss when I own that I have ventured to address these lines to you in order to refresh your recollection of our wrongs, and to suggest what might, if tried, prove remedies. Permit me humbly to add, that if anything I have mentioned be thought worthy of a place in your excellent journal, I shall feel very much flattered.

☞ XXV.

MY UNCLE.

DECEMBER 6, 1851.

It is neither in family pride, nor in a gush of gratitude for obligations in the nature of debts paid, or fortune inherited or expected; but it is after profound contemplation, and with the light of Tooke's Pantheon, Lempriere, and the Biographie Universelle, beaming from my book-shelves, that I persist in the conviction that My Uncle is a very remarkable, and a truly great man.

Osymandes, the Egyptian conqueror (vulgarly called Sesostris), was a great man. Julius Cæsar was a great man; so (in spite of the Quarterly Review) was the late Napoleon Bonaparte. His Royal Highness the Duke of York, Bishop of

---

* This was a rash prophecy. The Baggage Warehouse Bar in the Harbour of London is still, in 1859, as obstructive as ever. A writer in a recent impression of The Times, declares that "there is one instance on private record of a respectable nobleman from Russia, who landed at St. Katharine's Docks early in the morning, and did not arrive at the Clarendon, to which he had directed his cabman, till late at night."

Osnaburgh, and Commander-in-Chief of the British Forces, was a great man. Mr. William Cobbett, the implacable foe of tyrants, turnpike-keepers, bank-notes, and The Times newspaper, was another great man. Mr. Nathan Meyer Rothschild was also a great man. But My Uncle is a concentration of all the different sorts of greatness by which these great men were severally distinguished : he was born great ; he has had greatness thrust upon him ; he has achieved greatness.

That My Uncle was born great, his family-tree will attest. The roots of his genealogy strike deeply into the earliest traditions of the Western World ; but, turning to the East, I have discovered that My Uncle, gunpowder, the mariner's compass, the art of printing, and the treadmill equally owe their origin to China. I now follow a respectable Chinese historiographer. Some time after *Yan* (Heaven) was separated from *Yin* (Earth), and when Pwan-koo (who reigned forty-five thousand years) ruled the earth from its core and centre, to wit, the Flowery Land, My Uncle's ancestors were prosperous gentlemen. They have continued to flourish with unabated prosperity down to the present date, under the enlightened Tao-Kwang.

In regard to the first appearance of his family in Europe, My Uncle is fond of asserting that Charlemagne was in early life, a cadet of the transplanted branch of his ancestry; but, I confess that none of the authorities I have consulted support him in that pardonable boast. The most I have been able to do for My Uncle in this wise, has been to trace his more immediate European progenitor to a physician who established a lucrative medical practice, somewhere about the beginning of the thirteenth century, at Florence, in Tuscan Italy. As this physician left an ample fortune, his grateful successors took their name from his profession—a name which illuminates the page of history, and gives lustre to the annals of Art—MEDICI. The offshoots of this illustrious race removed, early in the fifteenth century, to Milan, took to trade, and were called, indifferently, when they travelled, " Lombards." It must be understood that these Lombards did not all retain the family name. But the heraldic insignia of the Medici, derived from their ancestor's calling, they have rigidly preserved, unto the present hour. No change of country ; no vicissitude of trade ;

no commercial crisis; no persecution; no prosperity; has induced My Uncle's family to abandon their arms. Whether trading in Lombardy in the Middle Ages; or giving their name, at a later period, to a London street; or finally distributed, as we now find them, amidst the necessitous populations of modern cities; the simple blazonry of the Medici, still denotes the abiding-places of My Uncle's race. Heraldically speaking, it consists of three giant boluses, or, pendant, opposed—two to one.

How did my Uncle achieve greatness? By cultivating the common-place virtue of minding his own business. This virtue My Uncle has always possessed in a degree the more remarkable, considering the temptations continually presented to him of intermeddling with the affairs of others. Although the daily depositary of commercial and pecuniary confidences, so little does he abuse the trust reposed in him, that he never was known to divulge the secrets of a single client. While he seems to be a most mysterious old gentleman, My Uncle's mystery really consists in the art of minding his own business.

In London alone My Uncle conducts upwards of four hundred establishments, each trading on a capital varying from two thousand to fourteen thousand pounds. His gross metropolitan principal is two millions and a quarter sterling; not to mention an ever-flowing and constantly-accumulating interest, averaging from fifteen to twenty per cent. per annum. Without taking into the present calculation his provincial business, the aggregate of My Uncle's immense variety of separate transactions in London alone during the year 1849 was twenty-four millions; the average at each of his places of business, sixty thousand. My Uncle's affairs are publicly recognised as of the most important description. Acts of Parliament have been passed, expressly for his guidance and protection. He has a Fire and Life Assurance office of his own; and a weekly newspaper solely devoted to his business. This commercial point of greatness is the more extraordinary, from its having been obtained by means of a description of dealing by which almost every other man is certain to lose. To buy, and to sell, and to live by the profit, generally requires no uncommon capacity; but to live, as My Uncle lives, by lending, demands a superlative order of talents.

Although My Uncle is, in a small way on a large scale, a
banker; yet he is a banker whose operations are of a much
more complicated character than those now carried on in
Lombard-street. The deposits upon which he issues his paper
are more varied, and demand a wider range of judgment than
the ordinary banker need to exercise. He is obliged to possess an expanded practical knowledge of the value of securities, ranging over every portable article in existence. Here
is one of My Uncle's notes:

This document, which is partly a voucher, partly a deposit
note (and, like all deposit notes, negotiable only to a limited
extent), is the result of a transaction by which a portion of
the passive capital of Mr. Charles de Montague has been temporarily turned into active capital. Some demand for money
has been made upon Mr. de Montague, which he has been
unable to meet *in* money. He therefore has recourse to My
Uncle, who takes his watch and appendages as security for an
advance of forty shillings; on condition that Mr. de Montague
shall, before the expiration of twelve months, return the said
forty shillings together with interest at the rate of eightpence
per month. Should Mr. de Montague not redeem his pledge
before the specified period of twelve months is completed, then
it is competent for My Uncle (after a further delay of three
months) to sell the pledge by public auction, and to abstract
from the proceeds the principal and interest; but, supposing

the amount realised by such sale be greater than the principal and interest, then it is in the power of Mr. de Montague to demand the balance from My Uncle. Should, on the other hand, Mr. de Montague's watch and appendages fetch less than the principal and interest, My Uncle must abide by the loss.

This transaction is the model of every other in which My Uncle engages. It is essentially a banking transaction. The deposit branch of his establishments, instead of receiving money on customers' account, takes in property: the issue department is solely conducted by means of specie. My Uncle's bills are, as I have said, merely deposit notes, redeemable within twelve months after date. What the Bank of England is to Her Majesty's Government; what Smith Payne, and Jones Lloyd, are to the City magnates; what Coutts and Company, and Drummonds are to the nobility and gentry; that My Uncle is to the De Montagues, the artisans, the labourers, and the poor generally. Take the case of Phelim O'Shea, bricklayer's labourer. A strike, a wet week, or a defaulting brickmaker, has thrown Phelim O'Shea temporarily out of employment, and his stock of cash is inadequate to meet his current expenses. Yet, although without money, he is not without means. He has a coat—a loose blue coat, long in the cuffs, with a swallow-tail, and brass buttons rubbed black in the centre. He converts that coat into a bank deposit, and My Uncle advances him a sum of money, which enables him to meet contingent demands, until conciliation, fine weather, or plenty of bricks shall set him up again. In like manner, Mrs. Lavers, the charwoman, is short of shillings; but she has a fender; also her neighbour the washer-woman has no money at all, but is, thanks to My Uncle, a capitalist while she possesses a flat-iron. Biddle, the bootcloser, has been rather idle during the early part of the week, and is proportionately pressed for time at the end of it. He works as hard as he can all Saturday, yet he has finished his job only in time to be too late to take it home ; for at nine his employer's premises are closed. Money he must have; so he takes some of the boots to My Uncle; and, on Monday, redeems them with the money he has been paid for the rest of them. The operation by which money is raised upon the coat, the fender, and the flat-iron, or the new boots,

is usually described as " pawnbroking ;" and My Uncle is (not
to mince the matter) called a pawnbroker.

My Uncle's office—or we can afford to say, shop, for My
Uncle has not the least desire to sink it—in a poor neighbourhood, is a remarkable scene. It is so particularly on a Saturday
night. The reader who should trudge with me, following the
Eastern index of the church weathercocks, to My Uncle's in
the region of the Commercial-road, on a Saturday night, would
find another sort of interest going on there, besides the interest My Uncle is empowered by law to take. He (for the
reader is of an arbitrary gender, according to the cases wisely
cited in the old school grammar, where it instanced, " as we
say of the sun, he is setting ; or of a ship " she sails well")—he
would find My Uncle's full of company. He would find the
little private boxes in the shop, with bolts inside the doors—
supposed to be designed for bashful clients, coyly emulous of
solitude—crowded with miscellaneous customers ; the public
portion of the shop no less so. He would find three-fourths
of these attendants on My Uncle to be Nieces—women prolific in children, to judge from the babies present, and from other
powerful symptoms. Inquiring of My Uncle of what class
these mostly were, he would be answered, " Wives of labourers in the Docks." Hereupon his thoughts would probably
go wandering down long ranges of warehouses, and wharfs,
and cellarage, working at windlasses and cranes, at logs of
wood, at bales, at sacks, at casks, at rum and sugar, until he
is brought back to My Uncle's by a Plump ! close to him as
he stood behind the counter, and the tumbling out of the wall
of half a dozen bundles. Then, remembering that popular
figure of speech, The Spout, he would inquire of My Uncle
whether those bundles had been up the Spout, and were now
coming down ? To which My Uncle, with a forbearing smile,
as one who could not expect him to be otherwise than innocent of the proprieties of the trade, would mildly make reply,
" It *is* called the Spout, but *we* call it the Well."

Then, his eyes would follow the bundles from the Spout to
the counter, admiring to see how they were whisked away,
and tossed intuitively, label upwards, by brisk jugglers of
shopmen. " Now, then, Flathers !" " Here !" " How many,
Mrs. Flathers ?" " Six !" " Only three down yet." (Those

three would be laid aside, and Mrs. Flathers would resign herself to more waiting.) "Bailey, how many?" "One." A rapid pen-and-ink sum would be worked by the shopman on the back of the ticket. "Eighteenpence halfpenny." Bailey would know it well beforehand—would have the exact amount ready—would depart with a bald infant son in arms (one red sock missing), and make room for Dennet.

Dennet, slatternly and aged seventeen, would produce a gown. The shopman, opening it with sleight of hand, would know it at a glance. "A shilling." "Eighteenpence." "Can't be." "Say one and three." "Impossible." Gown slapped, thrown up, tossed over—wrapped and pinned as tight as a ship's block! Ticket and duplicate made out, sixpence and halfpence jerked from the till like water. All right! "Now, Mrs. Jolly, what are *you* waiting for?" "My husband's rule. I think it's behind you, Charles. Do give it me, that's a good soul, and let me go, for I've got marketing to do, and supper besides!"—"This it?"—"That's it, Charles!" Another rapid calculation. "Eighteenpence three farthings." Change for a shilling at a blow. Mrs. Jolly gone, and somebody come into the genteeler portion of the shop, supposed to be set aside for purchasers of articles exposed for sale.—"About that table-cloth this morning." "Oh!"

Then, My Uncle in person would present himself, and confront a middle-aged matron of respectable appearance, accompanied by a poor-looking girl, half servant-girl, and half companion. "This," My Uncle would say, pointing to the latter and addressing the former, "is the young woman who offered a very long tablecloth in pledge this morning,"—which My Uncle would produce whilst speaking. "Yes, sir," the repectable-looking woman would reply. "This is the young person. And it is my property."—"She said," My Uncle would quietly proceed, "that it was her sister's property, and that her sister sent her."—"Yes, sir, it is quite correct, she did."—"Well! but you know," My Uncle would retort, glancing confidentially at the two, "you are *not* her sister?" "No, sir, I am not; I confess I am not. But a person don't wish to mention the exact truth when reduced to these necessities, and such was the instructions that I giv' her. I am aware that it is not, strictly speaking, right fur to pervert the truth, and I am sorry for it now, since it has caused me a deal of trouble, and forced me to come a good distance."—"I am sorry too, both to have stopped the tablecloth, and to have put you to any inconvenience," My Uncle would return, "but we are obliged to be cautious. Her account was not satisfactory, though not so unsatisfactory as to justify me in detaining her—and it's such a very long tablecloth! It might be a ship's tablecloth, for instance, not honestly come by, especially as the marking in the corner was illegible!" "So it might, sir, and I don't complain."—"Besides," My Uncle would proceed, "it's too long a tablecloth for any table that *you* have in your house, you know?" "Certainly it is, sir, but I used to keep a public house. I kept the Fox and Grapes at Bow, for several years, and that tablecloth was used in the business." Then, My Uncle, reassured by his ears, as well as by his eyes, would roll it up, and say that he was glad to lend the matron the money that she wanted "on it;" and the affair would be completed to the satisfaction of all parties.

The reader of the arbitrary gender would observe, perhaps, as the matron and the servant left the shop, another matron enter by the same genteel door, accompanied, to his thinking (though, of course, he is anything but suspicious) by a doubtful-looking little Niece, of thirteen years or so—doubtful as a Niece, because of her very strong resemblance to her Aunt. A plump little, comfortable, pippin-cheeked Aunt, mighty softspoken, and wrapped-up to her chubby chin in reputable furs. He would observe them come in, with a mincing pretence of inquiring on what terms the purchase of a great-coat near the door could be effected—so, gradually, and without abatement of gentility, approach the counter, and slide into a shopman's hand (the immediate link of communication between Aunt and Shopman, being Niece) two duplicates for silver spoons. To the inquiry, "Do you wish to take 'em out?" he would observe Aunt's neck bend, swan-like, in the affirmative, while Niece as the more artless spirit, said openly, "Please!" The strangeness of Aunt in such a place; her timid surprise, repressed by a continual effort; the expressive appeal of her gentility to the chivalrous feelings of the shopman; the mysterious gathering of her furs about her chin; the delicate way

in which, when Niece has the spoons all safe, Aunt bends forward, to say in a fluttered whisper, as she draws her glove
upon her short plump hand, "that there is a fish-slice which
she will probably require to redeem on Monday, and will the
forenoon be a good time for coming unobserved?" would not
be lost upon him. But it is a thousand to one that he would
be amused by this elaboration, because perfectly convinced
that Aunt and Niece are quite as intimate with Mr. Uncle as
Mrs. Flathers herself is—just then going out, with her six
bundles.

In Mrs. Flathers and the general customers, he would find
no pretence of shyness, either with My Uncle or with one another. In the intervals of not ungracious expostulations with
"Charles" or "William," to "see if that shawl's down yet!"
they would gossip about their husbands, and their families,
and Mrs. Walker's having come better through it than they
had thought she would, after Walker's treatment of her—as
they might at any other place of assemblage. Their children,
too: whether so young as to be taking their regular meals at
My Uncle's, or to be staring at the gas and sucking their
fists: or so old as to be, stood down in corners to poke their
fingers into one another's eyes; would be found quite at home.
Of little old men and women of an older growth, yet, very
knowing, and very observant of all the business done, there
would be no want. Men would be found (especially married
men) a little out of place—rather awkward and shy—something hustled by the women—and sensible of its being better
to leave such ordinary domestic affairs as pawnbroking to
them. Girls from ten to fifteen would be seen highly to
cherish this privilege, and to fly at boys of corresponding years
like tigresses.

The transactions to be contemplated at My Uncle's on such
an occasion would be of a singular and various nature. This
woman would be "taking out" a sheet and a child's petticoat,
pawned in the morning of that very day—most likely to provide her husband's dinner. That man would be redeeming a
saw, which has been in My Uncle's keeping, hundreds of times
—which is constantly passing in and out of his possession.
And this, not because the man is a drunkard or an idler, but
because he is a poor jobbing carpenter, without a penny of

moneyed capital: who, when he has a small job in hand, and
has done the sawing part of it and wants the nails and glue to
finish it, pawns the saw to provide them, until he is paid and
can redeem it.   Endless cases of this kind the reader would
encounter.   But he would see no pawning of "The Society's
Bibles," which My Uncle refuses to receive, as possessions the
poor do not usually acquire on terms that involve a right to
dispose of them for money; and he would see no drunkenness
—for My Uncle flatly refuses to deal with men or women in a
state of intoxication.

We would then survey My Uncle's stores or pledges up-
stairs, binned exactly like wine, and kept with as much order.
Giving him a lamp in a lantern, as a necessary precaution
against fire, and carrying one myself, I would show him floor
above floor of these storerooms; "the well" communicating
with each; and a boy, with another lantern and sundry duplicates, going about, searching for the bundles to which the
latter refer.   He should see how the seven shilling coats are
all binned together in order of date; how the ten shilling
coats are all binned together; the fifteen shilling coats, the
pound coats.   So with the shawls, so with the gowns, so with
the petticoats, so with the trousers, so with the shirts, so with
the waistcoats.   And he should witness the surprising facility
with which My Uncle can find in his great stock the least
article that he wants.   As to miscellaneous pledges, he should
see plenty of them, although in a poor neighbourhood, common wearing apparel is the staple pawn.   He should see some
(but not many) beds, plenty of spades and flat-irons, alleys of
clocks.   He should roam among China figures, landscapes,
fire-arms, fire-irons, portraits, mathematical instruments, instruments of navigation, boots, shoes, umbrellas, fenders,
fishing-rods, saddles and bridles, fiddles, books, key-bugles,
and hearth rugs.

Finally, he should come down stairs again, and have a talk
with My Uncle.   Then he should learn how poor people, in
buying articles of sale from that part of My Uncle's mansion
in which such things are displayed, habitually ask what such a
thing would fetch if it were offered in pawn; and frequently
confess that they are influenced in their choice by their
"handiness" in that regard.   How this strange forethought

is conspicuous in costermongers and fishwomen; the former often wearing great squab brooches as convenient pledges, and the latter massive silver rings.

Also, what wonderful things are offered in pawn. How a child's caul is frequently offered. How Bank of England notes have been pawned for security's sake; especially by hop-pickers, who have no settled home. How gamblers have a superstitious idea that pawnbrokers' money is lucky, and therefore pawn bank-notes in order to get pawnbrokers' gold to stake. How a thousand-pound note was once pawned by a gambler at a shop near Charing-Cross.

Further. How a German nobleman took to a pawnbroker at the West-end of London, only three years ago, his wife's patent of Spanish nobility. How the whole stock of an apothecary's shop, including pills, perfumery, draughts, bottles, ointments, counters, desks, pestles, mortars, scales, and infinitesimal weights, was once pawned and remained unredeemed for two years; when it was taken out of pawn to be started in business in a fashionable neighbourhood. How there have been included among pawnbrokers' pledges such extraordinary articles as an immense dancing-booth, well known at fairs and races; live parrots; several hundred weight of human hair; a travelling carriage complete; a horse and chaise; and some twelve thousand pounds' worth (from one place in one year) of manufactured silk. How a thousand pounds was not long since lent on Manchester goods, which it took My Uncle and assistants four days to examine. But most of these loans were not strictly pawnbroking transactions; being beyond the limits set by the pawnbroking Act of Parliament, and being effected under private agreement.

Likewise, how My Uncle, besides the ordinary risks of his calling, occasionally suffers from mistakes, not of his own commission, as in the following case. One Saturday night, a clergyman of the Church of England having been dining with a friend (which phrase we use in a perfectly innocent and literal sense), found himself walking home in a heavy rain with no money in his pocket, and no one at his chambers of whom to borrow any when he got home. In this difficulty, he stepped into My Uncle's, and there deposited his great coat. About a month afterwards, he called to redeem it; but, on its being produced, most positively denied that that coat was his. Being a gentleman of undoubted respectability, his assurance was readily believed; some unaccountable mistake was supposed to have arisen at My Uncle's, and he received a full and proper compensation for his loss. Within a short time afterwards, two gentlemen called upon My Uncle, to remind him of the circumstance, to repay the money, and to inform him that it had since transpired, that the clergyman (then dead) had taken from his friend's house a coat that was not his own, and had never discovered his error.

My Uncle's business is by no means confined to the poorer classes. To support our third proposition concerning him— namely, that he has had greatness thrust upon him—it is only necessary to mention that he is in the ordinary habit of dealing with the upper classes of society. Such transactions are not so numerous as his dealings with the humbler orders, but they involve nearly as much capital. Neither are they so profitable; because, for every loan above two guineas, the charge for interest is only threepence per month. Moreover, the pressure of pecuniary circumstances does not drive the better class of borrowers to pledge and redeem so frequently as the poorer; and thus to pay interest upon short terms. My Uncle numbers among his more aristocratic customers, clergymen, barristers, baronets, and noblemen. He has *some* peers; also editors, wholesale-warehousemen, painters, and musicians on his books. He confesses that the most business is brought to him by Irish members of Parliament. Contrary to popular prejudice, My Uncle flourishes when trade is brisk and times are prosperous; for then, people not in a very large way of business, yet giving credit, have most need of ready-money capital.

My Uncle is an active and skilful tradesman, who conducts the details of his business, and keeps his books, on quite a model system. There is a prejudice against him; and his calling may (as other callings may, incidentally) furnish the reckless and dissipated with means of carrying on their career. But, no social system can be framed with an exclusive reference to its dregs; and it is a fair question whether My Uncle be not, to some striving people, a real convenience and an absolute necessity. Those who have plenty of money, abundance of credit, or as much discount as they want, will probably say, No. But they may not be qualified to sit upon the Jury.

There is a popular idea that My Uncle grinds the faces of the poor. It is indisputable that his business is placed under very stringent restrictions; that it requires him to do a great deal for a halfpenny; and that it does not return greater profits than many other trades. My Uncle is accused of lending too little on the pledges he receives; but he can have no motive for so doing, as he speculates on the receipts of interest: and the more principal he can safely lend, the more interest he hopes to gain. Moreover, there is individual competition in his business, as in all other businesses.

There is only one Quaker in My Uncle's family. With this last scrap of the history of My Uncle's race, I am mute.

☞ XXVI.

A CURIOUS DANCE ROUND A CURIOUS TREE.
JANUARY 17, 1852.

ON the 13th of January, 1750—when the corn that grew near Moorfields was ground on the top of Windmill Hill, "Fensbury;" when Bethlehem Hospital was "a dry walk for loiterers," and a show; when lunatics were chained, naked, in rows of cages that flanked a promenade, and were wondered and jeered at through iron bars by London loungers—Sir Thomas Ladbroke the banker, Bonnel Thornton the wit, and half a dozen other gentlemen, met together to found a new asylum for the insane. Towards this object they put down, one guinea each. In a year from that time, the windmill had been given to the winds, and on its ancient site, there stood a hospital for the gratuitous treatment of the insane poor.

With the benevolence which thus originated an additional madhouse, was mixed, as was usual in that age, a curious degree of unconscious cruelty. Coercion for the outward man, and rabid physicking for the inward man, were then the specifics for lunacy. Chains, straw, filthy solitude, darkness, and starvation; jalap, syrup of buckthorn, tartarised antimony, and ipecacuanha administered every spring and fall in fabulous doses to every patient, whether well or ill; spinning in whirligigs, corporal punishment, gagging, "continued intoxication;" nothing was too wildly extravagant, nothing too monstrously cruel to be prescribed by mad-doctors. It was their mono-mania; and, under its influence, the directors of Lunatic Asylums acted. In other respects these physicians were grave men, of mild dispositions, and—in their ample-flapped, ample-cuffed coats, with a certain gravity and air of state in the skirts; with their large buttons and gold-headed canes, their hair-powder and ruffles—were men of benevolent aspects. Imagine one of them turning back his lace and tightening his wig to supply a maniac who *would* keep his mouth shut, with food or physic. He employed a flat oval ring, with a handle to it. "The head being placed between the knees of the operator, the patient, blinded and properly secured, an oppor-tunity is watched. When he opens his mouth to speak, the instrument is thrust in and allows the food or medicine to be introduced without difficulty. A sternutatory of any kind" (say a pepper-castor of cayenne, or half an ounce of rappee) "always forces the mouth open, in spite of the patient's deter-mination to keep it shut." "In cases of great fury and violence," says the amiable practitioner from whom I quote, "the patient should be kept in a dark room, confined by one leg, with metallic manacles on the wrist; the skin being less liable to be injured,"—here the Good Doctor becomes espe-cially considerate and mild,—"the skin being less liable to be injured by the friction of polished metal than by that of linen or cotton.

These practitioners of old, would seem to have been, with-out knowing it, early homœopathists; their motto must have been, *Similia similibus curantur;* they believed that the most violent and certain means of driving a man mad, were the only hopeful means of restoring him to reason. The in-side of the new hospital, therefore, even when, in 1782, it was removed, under the name of "Saint Luke's," from Wind-mill Hill to its present site in the Old street-road, must have appeared, to the least irrational new patient, like a collection of chambers of horrors. What sane person indeed, seeing, on his entrance into any place, gyves and manacles (however highly polished) yawning for his ankles and wrists; swings dangling in the air, to spin him round like an impaled cock-

chafer; gags and strait-waistcoats ready at a moment's notice
to muzzle and bind him; would be likely to retain the perfect
command of his senses?   Even now, an outside view of Saint
Luke's Hospital is gloomy enough; and, when on that cold,
misty, cheerless afternoon which followed Christmas Day, I
looked up at the high walls, and saw, grimly peering over
them, its upper stories and dismal little iron-bound windows,
I did not ring the porter's bell (albeit I was only a visitor, and
free to go, if I would, without ringing it at all) in the most
cheerful frame of mind.

How came I, it may be asked, on the day after Christmas
Day, of all days in the year, to be hovering outside Saint
Luke's, after dark, when I might have betaken myself to that
jocund world of Pantomime, where there is no affliction or
calamity that leaves the least impression? where a man may
tumble into the broken ice, or dive into the kitchen fire, and
only be the droller for the accident; where babies may be
knocked about and sat upon, or choked with gravy spoons, in
the process of feeding, and yet no Coroner be wanted, nor
anybody made uncomfortable; where workmen may fall from
the top of a house to the bottom, or even from the bottom
of a house to the top, and sustain no injury to the brain,
need no hospital, leave no young children; where every one,
in short, is so superior to all the accidents of life, though
encountering them at every turn, that I suspect this to be the
secret (though many persons may not present it to themselves)
of the general enjoyment which an audience of vulnerable
spectators, liable to pain and sorrow, find in this class of
entertainment.

Not long before the Christmas Night in question, I had
been told of a patient in Saint Luke's, a woman of great
strength and energy, who had been driven mad by an infuri-
ated ox in the streets—an inconvenience not in itself worth
mentioning, for which the inhabitants of London are frequently
indebted to their inestimable Corporation. She seized the
creature literally by the horns, and so, as long as limb and life
were in peril, vigorously held him; but, the danger over, she
lost her senses, and became one of the most ungovernable of
the inmates of the asylum.   Why was I there to see this poor
creature, when I might have seen a Pantomimic woman gored

to any extent by a Pantomimic ox, at any height of ferocity, and have gone home to bed with the comforting assurance that she had rather enjoyed it than otherwise?

The reason of my choice was this. I had received a notification that on that night there would be, in Saint Luke's, "a Christmas Tree for the Patients." And further, that the "usual fortnightly dancing" would take place before the distribution of the gifts upon the tree. So there I was, in the street, looking about for a knocker and finding none.

There was a line of hackney cabriolets by the dead wall; some of the drivers, asleep; some, vigilant; some, with their legs not inexpressive of "Boxing," sticking out of the open doors of their vehicles, while their bodies were reposing on the straw within. There were flaming gas-lights, oranges, oysters, paper lanterns, butchers and grocers, bakers and public-houses, over the way; there were omnibuses rattling by; there were ballad-singers, street cries, street passengers, street beggars, and street music; there were cheap theatres within call, which you would do better to be at some pains to improve, my worthy friends, than to shut up—for, if you will not have them with your own consent at their best, you may be sure that you *must* have them, without it, at their worst; there were wretched little chapels too, where the officiating prophets certainly were not inspired with grammar; there were homes, great and small, by the hundred thousand, east, west, north, and south; all the busy ripple of sane life (or of life, as sane as it ever is) came murmuring on from far away, and broke against the blank walls of the Madhouse, like a sea upon a desert shore.

Abandoning further search for the non-existent knocker, I discovered and rang the bell, and gained admission into Saint Luke's—through a stone court-yard and a hall, adorned with wreaths of holly and like seasonable garniture. I felt disposed to wonder how it looked to patients when they were first received, and whether they distorted it to their own wild fancies or left it a matter of fact. But, as there was time for a walk through the building before the festivities began, I discarded idle speculation and followed my leader.

Into a long, long gallery: on one side a few windows; on the other a great many doors leading to sleeping cells. Dead silence—not utter solitude; for, outside the iron cage enclosing the fireplace between two of the windows, stood a motionless woman. The fire cast a red glare upon the walls, upon the ceiling, and upon the floor, polished by the daily friction of many feet. At the end of the gallery, the common sitting-room. Seated on benches around another caged fireplace, several women: all silent, except one. She, sewing a mad sort of seam, and scolding some imaginary person. (Taciturnity is a symptom of nearly every kind of mania, unless under pressure of excitement. Although the whole lives of some patients are passed together in the same apartment, they are passed in solitude; there is no solitude more complete.) Forms and tables, the only furniture. Nothing in the rooms to remind their inmates of the world outside. No domestic articles to occupy, to interest, or to entice the mind away from its malady. Utter vacuity. Except the scolding woman sewing a purposeless seam, every patient in the room either silently looking at the fire, or silently looking on the ground—or rather through the ground, and at Heaven knows what, beyond.

It was a relief to come to a workroom; with coloured prints over the mantel shelf, and china shepherdesses upon it; furnished also with tables, a carpet, stuffed chairs, and an open fire. I observed a great difference between the demeanour of the occupants of this apartment and that of the inmates of the other room. They were neither so listless nor so sad. Although they did not, while I was present, speak much, they worked with earnestness and diligence. A few noticed my going away, and returned my parting salutation. In a niche—not in a room—but at one end of a cheerless gallery—stood a piano-forte, with a few ragged music-leaves upon the desk. Of course, the music was turned upside down.

Several such galleries on the "female side;" all exactly alike. One, set apart for "boarders" who are incurable; and, towards whose maintenance their friends are required to pay a small weekly sum. The experience of this asylum did not differ, I found, from that of similar establishments, in proving that insanity is more prevalent among women than among men. Of the eighteen thousand seven hundred and fifty-nine inmates, St. Luke's Hospital has received in the century of its

existence, eleven thousand one hundred and sixty-two have
been women, and seven thousand five hundred and eighty-
seven, meh. Female servants are, as is well known, more
frequently afflicted with lunacy than any other class of persons. The table, published in the Director's Report, of the
condition in life of the one hundred and seven female inmates
admitted in 1850, sets forth that while, under the vague description of "wife of labourer" there were only nine admis-
sions, and under the equally indefinite term "housekeeper,"
no more than six, there were of women servants, twenty-four.

I passed into one of the galleries on the male side. Three
men, engaged at a game of bagatelle; another patient kneeling against the wall apparently in deep prayer; two, walking
rapidly up and-down the long gallery arm-in-arm, but, as
usual, without speaking together; a handsome young man
deriving intense gratification from the motion of his fingers as
he played with them in the air; two men standing like pillars
before the fire-cage; another man, with a newspaper under
his arm, walking with great rapidity from one end of the cor-
ridor to the other, as if engaged in some important mission
which admitted of not a moment's delay. The only furniture
in the common sitting-room not peculiar to a prison or a
lunatic asylum of the old school, was a newspaper, which was
being read by a demented publican. The same oppressive
silence—except when the publican complained, in tones of the
bitterest satire, of one of the keepers, or (said the publican)
"attendant, as I suppose I must call him." The same listless
vacuity here, as in the room occupied by the female patients.
Despite the large amount of cures effected in the hospital
(upwards of sixty-nine per cent. during the past year, testify-
ing to the general efficacy of the treatment pursued in it), I
think that, if the system of finding inmates employment, so
successful in other hospitals, were introduced into Saint Luke's,
the proportion of cures would be much greater. Appended
to the latest report of the charity is a table of the weights of
the new comers, compared with the weights of the same individuals when discharged. From this, it appears that their
inactivity occasions a rapid accumulation of flesh. Of thirty
patients, whose average residence in the hospital extended
over eleven weeks, twenty-nine had gained at the average

rate of more than one pound per week, each. This can hardly be a gain of health.

On the walls of some of the sleeping cells were the marks of what looked like small alcoves, that had been removed. These indicated the places to which the chairs, which patients were made to sit in for indefinite periods, were, in the good old times, nailed. A couple of these chairs have been preserved in a lumber-room, and are hideous curiosities indeed. As high as the seat, are boxes to enclose the legs, which used to be shut in with spring bolts. The thighs were locked down by a strong cross-board, which also served as a table. The back of this cramping prison is so constructed that the victim could only use his arms and hands in a forward direction; not backward or sideways.

Each sleeping cell has two articles of furniture—a bed and a stool; the latter serving instead of a wardrobe. Many of the patients sleep in single-bedded rooms; but the larger cells are occupied by four inmates. The bedding is comfortable, and the clothing ample. On one bed-place the clothes were folded up, and the bedding had been removed. In its stead, was a small bundle, made up of a pair of boots, a waistcoat, and some stockings. "*That* poor fellow," said my conductor, "died last night—in a fit."

As I was looking at the marks in the walls of the galleries, of the posts to which the patients were formerly chained, sounds of music were heard from a distance. The ball had begun, and we hurried off in the direction of the music.

It was playing in another gallery—a brown sombre place, now brilliantly illuminated by a light at either end, adorned with holly. The staircase by which this gallery was approached, was curtained off at the top; and, near the curtain, the musicians were cheerfully engaged in getting all the vivacity that could be got, out of their two instruments. At one end were a number of mad men, at the other, a number of mad women, seated on forms. Two or three sets of quadrille dancers were arranged down the centre, and the ball was proceeding with great spirit, but with great decorum.

There were the patients usually to be found in all such asylums, among the dancers. There was the brisk, vain, pippin-faced little old lady, in a fantastic cap—proud of her foot and ankle ; there was the old-young woman, with the dishevelled long light hair, spare figure, and weird gentility ; there was the vacantly-laughing girl, requiring now and then a warning finger to admonish her ; there was the quiet young woman, almost well, and soon going out. For partners, there were the sturdy bull-necked thick-set little fellow who had tried to get away last week ; the wry-faced tailor, formerly suicidal, but much improved ; the suspicious patient with a countenance of gloom, wandering round and round strangers, furtively eyeing them behind from head to foot, and not indisposed to resent their intrusion. There was the man of happy silliness, pleased with everything. But the only chain that made any clatter was the Ladies' Chain, and there was no straiter waistcoat in company than the polka-garment of the old-young woman with the weird gentility, which was of a faded black satin, and languished through the dance with a lovelorn affability and condescension to the force of circumstances, in itself a faint reflection of all Bedlam.

Among those seated on the forms, the usual loss of social habits and the usual solitude in society, were again to be observed. It was very remarkable to see how they huddled together without communicating ; how some watched the dancing with lacklustre eyes, scarcely seeming to know what they watched ; how others rested weary heads on hands, and moped ; how others had the air of eternally expecting some miraculous visitor who never came, and looking out for some deliverances that never happened. The last figure of the set danced out, the women-dancers instantly returned to their station at one end of the gallery, the men-dancers repaired to *their* station at the other ; and all were shut up within themselves in a moment.

The dancers were not all patients. Among them, and dancing with right good will, were attendants male and female —pleasant-looking men, not at all realising the conventional idea of " keepers"—and pretty women, gracefully, though not at all inappropriately, dressed, and with looks and smiles as sparkling as one might hope to see in any dance in any place. Also, there were sundry bright young ladies who had helped to make the Christmas Tree ; and a few members of the resident officer's family ; and, shining above them all, and shining everywhere, his wife : whose clear head and strong heart Heaven inspired to have no Christmas-wish beyond this place, but to look upon it as her home, and on its inmates as her afflicted children.   And may I see as seasonable a sight as that gentle Christian lady every Christmas that I live, and leave its counterpart in as fair a form in many a nook and corner of the world, to shine, like a star in a dusk spot, through all the Christmases to come!

The tree was in a by-room by itself, not lighted yet, but presently to be displayed in all its glory.   The porter of the Institution, a brisk young fellow, with no end of dancing in him, now proclaimed a song.   The announcement being received with loud applause, one of the dancing sisterhood of attendants sang the song, which the musicians accompanied. It was very pretty, and we all applauded to the echo, and seemed (the mad part of us, I mean) to like our share in the applause prodigiously, and to take it as a capital point, that we were led by the popular porter.   It was so great a success that we very soon called for another song, and then we danced a country-dance (the porter perpetually going down the middle and up again with the weird gentility), until the quaint pictures of the Founders hanging in the adjacent committee-chamber, might have trembled in their frames.

The moment the dance was over, away the porter ran, not in the least out of breath, to help light up the tree. Presently it stood in the centre of its room, growing out of the floor, a blaze of light and glitter ; blossoming in that place (as the story goes of the American aloe) for the first time in a hundred years.   O shades of Mad Doctors with laced ruffles and powdered wigs, O shades of patients who went mad in the only good old times to be mad or sane in, and who were therefore physicked, whirligigged, chained, handcuffed, beaten, cramped, and tortured, look from

"Wherever in your sightless substances,
  You wait"—

on this outlandish weed in the degenerate garden of Saint Luke's.

To one coming freshly from outer life, unused to such scenes, it was a very sad and touching spectacle, when the patients were admitted in a line, to pass round the lighted tree, and admire. I could not but remember with what happy, hopefully-flushed faces, the brilliant toy was associated in my usual knowledge of it, and compare them with the worn cheek, the listless stare, the dull eye raised for a moment and then confusedly dropped, the restless eagerness, the moody surprise, so different from the sweet expectancy and astonishment of children, that came in melancholy array before me. And when the sorrowful procession was closed by "Tommy," the favourite of the house, the harmless old man with a giggle and a chuckle and a nod for every one, I think I would have rather that Tommy had charged at the tree like a bull, than that Tommy had been, at once so childish and so dreadfully un-childlike.

We all went out into the gallery again after this survey, and the dazzling fruits of the tree were taken from their boughs, and distributed. The porter, an undeveloped genius in stage-management and mastership of ceremonies, was very active in the distribution, blew all the whistles, played all the trumpets, and nursed all the dolls. That done, we had a wonderful concluding dance, compounded of a country-dance and galopade, during which all the popular couples were honoured with a general clapping of hands, as they galoped down the middle; and the porter in particular was overwhelmed with plaudits. Finally, we had God Save the Queen, with the whole force of the company; solo parts by the female attendant with the pretty voice who had sung before; chorus led with loyal animation, by the porter. When I came away, the porter, surrounded by bearers of trays, and busy in the midst of the forms, was delivering out mugs and cake, like a banker dealing at a colossal round game. I dare say he was asleep before I got home; but I left him in that stage of social briskness which is usually described among people who are at large, as "beginning to spend the evening."

Now, there is doubtless a great deal that is mournfully affecting in such a sight. I close this little record of my visit with the statement that the fact is so, because I am not sure but that many people expect far too much. I have known some, after visiting the noblest of our institutions for this terrible calamity, express their disappointment at the many de-

plorable cases they had observed with pain, and hint that, after
all, the better system can do little. Something of what it can
do, and daily does, has been faintly shadowed forth, even in
this paper. Wonderful things have been done for the Blind,
and for the Deaf and Dumb; but, the utmost is necessarily far
inferior to the restoration of the senses of which they are deprived. To lighten the affliction of insanity by all human
means, is not to restore the greatest of the Divine gifts; and
those who devote themselves to the task do not pretend that
it is. They find their sustainment and reward in the substitu-
tion of humanity for brutality, kindness for maltreatment, peace
for raging fury; in the acquision of love instead of hatred;
and in the knowledge that, from such treatment, improvement, and hope of final restoration will come, if such hope be
possible. It may be little to have abolished from madhouses
all that is abolished, and to have substituted all that is substituted. Nevertheless, reader, if you can do a little in any good
direction—do it. It will be much some day.

☞ XXVII.

POST-OFFICE MONEY ORDERS.

MARCH 20, 1852.

IN 1792, when the true British sailor was stoutly preparing
to defy the French in various parts of the globe at thirty
shillings a month; and when British military valour was fighting Tippoo Saib, in India, at a shilling a day; it was felt as a
great hardship, that the affluent warriors of both services
could not transmit their surplus capital to their sweethearts
and wives, even from one part of the United Kingdom to another. Government—seeing the danger of allowing the savings of its servants to burn holes in their pockets—was good
enough to concoct a snug little job, by means of which such
pocket-conflagrations might be extinguished. The monopoly
of sending money from one place to another was conceded to
three gentlemen, in connexion with the Post-office. Their
terms were eightpence for every pound; but, if the sum exceeded two pounds, a stamp-duty of one shilling was levied

by Government, in addition. Five guineas was the highest
amount which could be thus remitted; and the charge for that
sum was four shillings and sixpence, or nearly five per cent.;
besides the price of the postage of the letter which contained
the advice—perhaps a shilling more.

Now, happily, the days of monopoly have passed, and Mr.
Rowland Hill does the same thing for the odd sixpence, with
an odd penny, at a profit to the Government;"* exclusive of
the gain derived from the enormous number of letters of advice which Post-office orders have created. When the privilege was extended from soldiers and sailors to the general
public, the three monopolists of the last century could divide
between them, on an average, no more than six hundred and
fifty pounds per annum. No longer ago than the year 1838,
the Money-order Office was absorbed into the Post-office; and,
although the charges were reduced to a commission of sixpence for sums not exceeding two pounds, and of one shilling
and sixpence for sums up to five pounds, a chief clerk and
two assistants were appointed to do all the business; and
did it, but at a loss to the department. People could not
afford to increase even the reduced charges for commission,
by the eightpenny and shilling postages, for their letters of
advice.

Penny Postage, therefore, is the parent of the gigantic
Money-order system, which now flourishes. In estimating the
advantages of that great stroke of economical, administrative,
and commercial sense, many of its less prominent agencies for
good are overlooked. The facilities it has afforded for epistolary intercommunication are so wonderful and self-evident,
that we who benefit by them are blinded to the hidden im-
pulses it has given to social improvement and to commerce.
Regarded only as the origin of the present Money-order
system, Penny Postage has occasioned the exercise of prudence, benevolence, and self-denial; it has, in many instances,
stopped the sufferings of want by timely remittances; and it
has quickened the under-currents of trade by effecting small
transactions easily and promptly. During the advent-year of
penny postage, the commission on Post-office orders was re-

* The profits of the Money-order Office during the year 1859, amounted to 26,000l.;
having been nearly trebled since 1851.

duced to threepence for sums not exceeding two pounds, and sixpence for sums not exceeding five pounds. In that year the number of orders granted in the United Kingdom was (in round numbers, which we shall use throughout, for the reader's greater convenience) one hundred and eighty-eight thousand, for an aggregate amount of three hundred and thirteen thousand pounds. Even this was a great advance on the business previously done at the old price; but what are the figures for the tenth year of penny postage? During the year 1850, the number of orders granted in the United Kingdom was four million four hundred and forty thousand, for amounts making up eight million four hundred and ninety-five thousand pounds;—only a million less than the yearly produce of the income and assessed taxes put together! This marvellous increase can, perhaps, be better appreciated by being seen through a diminished medium. In the first *month* of the penny postage (1840), the issue of orders was about ten thousand in number, for something over sixteen thousand pounds; but in the month of December, 1851, the number of orders issued was more than three hundred and ninety-seven thousand, for six hundred and ninety thousand pounds. That is to say, during that single month twice as many orders were taken out and paid for, as were issued and paid in 1840 during the whole *year.**

Of all the possessions vouchsafed to mankind, the most difficult to keep, is money. That difficulty first brought the Money-order Office into existence. It is because it relieves that difficulty in some degree, that the Money-order Office is now so extensively patronised. Formerly, when the young English provincial, or aspiring Scotchman, left his straitened home to seek his fortune in some distant town—and found it—the temptations that gleamed from his hoarded earnings often overcame him; and, instead of keeping them to remit, at some uncertain opportunity, to his struggling relations, he squandered them on his own pleasures. Now, that temptation is greatly lessened; he can send home his spare cash by the cheap, immediate, and safe agency of Post-office orders:

---

* These figures are now more than doubled. In the year 1858, six million seven hundred thousand money orders were issued for upwards of twelve million six hundred and fifty pounds sterling.

to be applied either in relieving the wants of the recipients, or to be prudently invested for himself. The amount of money which is passed to Ireland in this way is very great. It can be ascertained, approximately, by a comparison between the number of orders issued in England, and paid in Ireland, at ordinary times, and so issued and paid during the Irish invasion, at haymaking time. For instance, during the month of February, 1851 (the business during which month affords a fair monthly average), thirteen thousand orders were issued in England, and paid in Ireland with nineteen thousand pounds; but in the July following, thirty-three thousand English orders were presented in Ireland, in exchange for nearly thirty-three thousand pounds; being an excess over the transactions of February of nineteen thousand orders, and thirteen thousand eight hundred pounds. It would be a curious (but impossible) calculation which should show us how much of this large sum would have reached Ireland, under the respected ancient dispensation, when Irish haymakers hoarded their money;—after it had been hidden in holes and hedges; or screwed up in worsted stockings; or inserted in the linings of brimless hats. During the famine year (1847), the orders transmitted hence and paid in Ireland, exceed the average by one hundred and forty-three thousand, representing about one hundred and fifty thousand pounds. This shows how readily the poor will help the poor, when facilities for so doing are presented to them.—The Money-order Office accounts paint the character of Scotland for prudence, saving habits, and commercial activity in small matters, in glowing colours. With a population two-thirds less than Ireland, her absent sons and daughters sent home, for various purposes, in the year which ended on the 30th September, 1851, two hundred and fifty thousand pounds. During the same period, the Irish absentees and their commercial connexions in this country forwarded to Ireland very little more; namely, two hundred and ninety thousand pounds. The poverty of the Irish remitters is strikingly shown by the smallness of the average amounts. Less than one hundred and fourteen thousand orders were issued to send the two hundred and fifty thousand pounds to Scotland; while nearly double that number of orders were taken out to forward the two hundred and ninety thousand pounds to Ireland. The average amount of each remittance to Scotland was two pounds three shillings and fourpence; while the average of each order on Ireland was not quite one pound five shillings and sixpence. During the haymaking season, the average of each order on the Irish offices was only fourteen shillings and five farthings.

The Money-order system has opened up an enormous amount of small traffic. In many country places it has super-seded the pedlar, and has lessened the number and variety of those commissions with which any member of a country fam-ily is loaded, when he happens to be "going into town." Whatever articles may be required by private families, by small manufacturers, or by petty shopkeepers, can now be ordered at once from headquarters in a penny letter. The goods are sent, through various conveyances, by the town shopkeeper; and payment for them is made per Post-office orders. Thus, we find that in all the great centres of trade or manufactures, there is a great excess of orders paid, over orders granted. During the year ending on the thirteenth of last September, the excess of payments over receipts, in Birmingham, was ninety-five thousand pounds; in Liverpool, eight thousand pounds; in Manchester, thirty-six thousand five hundred pounds. By the medium of money orders and penny postage, the watchmaker at Cheltenham or Plymouth can as readily write for, pay for, and obtain by return of post from Birming-ham, any tool he may require, as if the maker were his neigh-bour in the next street. In places, therefore, where trade and manufactures are not the staple; where fashion resorts; or where—as in cathedral cities—pursy respectability vegetates, the excess is the other way. The year's transactions, at Chel-tenham, for example, leave a large balance of orders issued, over orders paid. It is found, in effect, that all small Money-order Offices issue more orders than they pay.

A great many Money-orders are taken out as answers to ad-vertisements. Tradesmen especially have widened the circles of their connexion in this way. The amount of tea, coffee, con-fectionary, books, jewellery, wearing apparel, and innumera-ble other articles, which advertising traders get paid for in Post-office orders, would be astounding, if it could be ascer-tained. Answers (in cash) to charitable appeals, and payment

of small debts, are also much facilitated by Post-office orders.
We mentioned in our account of "My Uncle," that bank-
notes were sometimes pawned for safety's sake. In like manner, hawkers, trampers, sailors, and other humble travellers,
take out money orders in one place, to be paid to themselves
in another.

The Central Money-order Office in which these remarkable
results have been ascertained, is in Aldersgate-street, London,
hard by the Post-office. It is a large establishment—large
enough to be a very considerable Post-office in itself—with
extensive cellerage branching off into interminable groves of
letters of advice, and receipts, all methodically arranged for
reference. The room in which the orders are issued and paid,
has a flavour of Lombard-street. and money. It has its long
banker's counter, where clerks sit behind iron gratings, with
their wooden bowls of cash, and their little scales for weighing
gold ; and vistas of pigeon-holes stretch out behind them—
which are not without their pigeons, as we shall presently see.
Here, from ten o'clock to four, keeping the swing-doors on the
swing all day, all sorts and conditions of people come and go.
Greasy butchers and salesmen from Newgate Market with
bits of suet in their hair, who loll, and lounge, and cool their
foreheads against the grating, like a good-humoured sort of
Bears ; sharp little clerks not long from school, who have
everything requisite and necessary in readiness ; older clerks
in shooting-coats, a little sobered down as to official zeal,
though possibly not yet as to Cigar Divans and Betting-offices ;
matrons who *will* go distractedly wrong, and whom no consideration, human or divine, will induce to declare in plain
words what they have come for ; people with small children
which they perch on edges of remote desks, where the children, supposing themselves to be for ever abandoned and lost,
present a piteous spectacle ; labouring men, merchants, half-
pay officers ; retired old gentlemen from trim gardens by the
New River, excessively impatient of being trodden on, and
very persistent as to the poking in of their written demands
with tops of canes and handles of umbrellas. The clerks in
this office ought to rival the lamented Sir Charles Bell in their
knowledge of the expression of the hand. The varieties of
hands that hover about the grating, and are thrust through

the little doorways in it, are a continual study for them—or would be, if they had any time to spare, which assuredly they have not. The coarse-grained hand which seems all thumb and knuckle, and no nail, and which takes up money or puts it down with such an odd, clumsy, lumbering touch ; the retail trader's hand which chinks it up and tosses it over with a bounce ; the housewife's hand which has a lingering propensity to keep some of it back, and to drive a bargain by not paying in the last shilling or so of the sum for which her order is obtained ; the quick, the slow, the coarse, the fine, the sensitive and dull, the ready and unready ; they are always at the grating all day long. Hovering behind the owners of these hands, observant of the various transactions in which they engage, is a tall constable (rather potential with the matrons and widows on account of his portly aspect), who assists the bewildered female public ; explains the nature of the printed forms put ready to be filled up, for the quicker issuing of orders and the greater exactness as to names ; and has an eye on the Unready one, as he knots his money up in a pocket-handkerchief, or crams it into a greasy pocket-book. If you have any bad money by you, be careful not to bring it here ! The portly constable will whisk you into a back office before you can say Jack Robinson ; will snip your bad half-crown or five shilling piece in half, directly ; and (at the best) after searching inquiry, will fold the pieces in a note of your name and address, and consign them to a bundle of similar trophies for evermore !

A prosaic place enough at first sight, the Money-order Office is ; but, when we went there to look about us, the walls seemed presently to turn to burnished gold, the clock to go upon a thousand jewels : the clerks to be the ministers of Fortune, dispensing wisdom, riches, beauty, to the human race. For, if you want to know what you are fit for (true wisdom in itself), will not a money order for five shillings in favour of the gentleman who pierces you through and through if you only show him your handwriting, settle it beyond a doubt ! If you seek that one efficient receipt for curls, eyebrows, whiskers, sparkling eyes, and general bloom, can it not be yours to-morrow, through this wonderful establishment ! If you want to acquire, for seven-and-sixpence sterling, that light

14*

and elegant accomplishment which will enable you to realise from two to twenty pounds per week, during the whole remainder of your natural life, have you anything to do but to take your money order out and send it to the great philanthropist, whose modesty is equal to his merit, and who lives retired behind initials! Or, if your tastes be sporting tastes, and you would prefer to realise a handsome competence on the turf, is not "The Kiddy's Tip" (for the small charge of a crown, and a per-centage on your winnings) to be had by the next post, on remittance to the Kiddy from this place; and has not the Kiddy ever been The Lucky One; and does he not refer with pride to that eventful day when he cautioned his kind patrons to beware of Stagger's lot; and is not the Kiddy absolutely sure that he can pick the winner from the field, this time, and lead the sporting gents who honour him with their confidence to wealth and laurels!

All these people, we found, on sober inquiry, in common with a host of quacks and fortune-tellers, really do use the office, and really do receive large sums of money from the unlucky pigeons, the records of whose folly pass into the pigeon-holes. We were shown a circular, which has been very extensively disseminated in the provinces. It explains (with patterns of the article produced) a pretended patent for the manufacture of a fabric in universal demand. It promises to each subscriber for one share, price five shillings (to be sent, of course, per money order), not a paltry return of three or four hundred per cent.; but a good round income. "Subscribers," we quote the precise words of the printed bait, "will, for every five shillings they invest, realise from seventy-five to three hundred pounds sterling *per annum!*"—to be paid, it is politely stated in another part of the prospectus, quarterly. Now, rational people will say that the wild extravagance of such a promise, exceeding all possible gullibility, would be its own defeat. The said rational people, however, will be (as they sometimes are) in error. Credulity has no bounds. It is a fact, that since the issue of that golden circular, the Post-office authorities have paid to its concoctor—not hundreds but thousands of pounds. Post-office orders have poured in from believers in impossible profit, at such a rate, that three hundred pounds were handed over to the successful schemer in the course of one single week! Could Clairvoyance get a postman's place, and read the sealed letters as well as deliver them, what insane credence, what impossible hope, what glowing cupidity would be revealed in the wrappers to those particular Post-office orders! Perhaps a clergyman writes to inquire whether the first quarter's produce of his five shillings enclosed (on the before mentioned scale of productiveness), is likely to become due about September? because, at the beginning of that month, "he has a little bill of exchange to take up!" So, a lady, writing in August, wishes to open a school in December: and does the gentleman think that, by that time, her five shillings will grow into—say even fifty pounds? The next letter may show (mesmerically) the inmost soul—and the five shillings—of a young gentleman, who is "loved and beloved," &c., and who wishes to know whether, if he take a house at Lady-day, the first instalment of the annual fortune will arrive in time for him to enshrine his idol in it with the requisite appliances for persons about to marry?

It is right, however, to observe, that the authorities, when they find themselves accidentally and innocently agents in carrying on such infamous schemes, take advantage of any informality to withhold the payment, and restore the orders to the deluded senders.

This sort of mystification is even more surprising than that under which certain uneducated individuals (Irish) have been known to stagger. The belief has more than once been manifested at a Money-order Office window, that the mere payment of the commission would be sufficient to procure an order for five pounds; the form of paying in the five pounds being deemed purely optional. An Irish gentlemen who had left his hod at the door, recently applied in Aldersgate-street for an order for five pounds on a Tipperary post-office: for which he tendered (probably congratulating himself on having hit upon so good an investment) sixpence! It required a lengthened argument to prove to him that he would have to pay the five pounds into the office, before his friend could receive that small amount in Tipperary; and he went away, after all, evidently convinced that his not having this order was one of the personal wrongs of Ireland, and one of the particular injustices done to hereditary bondsmen only.

To pass from the Pigeons to the Pigeon-holes, it may be observed that, in the paying department, there are eleven hundred of the latter (Heaven knows how many of the former; they are incalculable), corresponding to the eleven hundred Money-order Offices spread all over England. The Scotch and Irish advices have pigeon-holes to themselves. When an order is presented, the clerk goes straight to the hole marked with the name of the town it has been issued from. If the order correspond in every respect with the advice, the cash is instantly paid.

The number of Money-order Offices in the United Kingdom is nearly seventeen hundred;* their accounts are dealt with, in Aldersgate-street, by one hundred and seventy-eight clerks. So promptly and accurately are these accounts posted up, that a balance of the whole kingdom as to money orders is struck daily; and by two o'clock, the state of each deputy's (or postmaster's) account can be accurately ascertained—what he owes, or what is due to him—up to the latest postal communication.

That the gigantic operations of the entire system may be seen at one view, we present an account of its transactions during the year which ended on thirty-first of last December: The number of orders issued in the United Kingdom during that time, was nearly four million seven hundred thousand, for money amounting to nearly nine millions sterling. The cash which changed hands by the intervention of the Post-office Money-order Office—in other words, the combined total of issues and payments of money-orders, in the United Kingdom, during the last year—was upwards of seventeen millions sterling; a sum more than equal to one-third of the whole official expenditure of this very expensive and rather official country. Every day, an interchange of small sums (each averaging in England and Wales no more than one pound eighteen shillings and ninepence) takes place in the United Kingdom by the agency of Money-order Offices, to the amount of upwards of fifty thousand pounds.

---

* There are now (1859) two thousand three hundred and sixty Money-order Offices spread over the United Kingdom.

The revenue of the Money-order Office exceeded its expenses, in the year 1851, by more than seven thousand pounds of profit. The same office, before the important improvements of the last few years had been effected, cost the country *a loss* of ten thousand six hundred pounds. Despite the prodigious increase in the business of the department, which we have pointed out, its efficiency has been doubled, and its cost almost halved. By superseding seventy-eight superfluous ledgers, the labour of sixty clerks has been saved ; by simply reducing the size of the money orders and advices, the expense of paper and print alone has been diminished by eleven hundred pounds per annum ; while the abolition of separate advices of each transaction has economised the number of letters by forty-six thousand, weekly. The upshot is, that these economical reforms have effected a saving in the Money-order Office, alone, equal to *seventeen thousand pounds per annum !*

☛ XXVIII.

A PLATED ARTICLE.

APRIL 24, 1852.

PUTTING up for the night in one of the chiefest towns of Staffordshire, I find it to be by no means a lively town. In fact, it is as dull and dead a town as any one could desire not to see. It seems as if its whole population might be imprisoned in its Railway Station. The Refreshment-Room at that Station is a vortex of dissipation compared with the extinct town inn, the Dodo, in the dull High-street.

Why High-street? Why not rather Low-street, Flat-street, Low-spirited-street, Used-up-street? Where are the people who belong to the High-street? Can they all be dispersed over the face of the country, seeking the unfortunate Strolling Manager who decamped from the mouldy little Theatre last week, in the beginning of his season (as his play-bills testify), repentantly resolved to bring him back, and feed him, and be entertained? Or, can they all be gathered to their fathers in the two old churchyards near to the High-street—retirement into which churchyards appears to be a

mere ceremony, there is so very little life outside their confines, and such small discernible difference between being
buried alive in the town, and buried dead in the town tombs?

Over the way, opposite to the staring blank bow-windows
of the Dodo, are a little iron-monger's shop, a little tailor's
shop (with a picture of the Fashions in the small window, and
a bandy-legged baby on the pavement staring at it)—a watchmaker's shop, where all the clocks and watches must be stopped,
I am sure, for they could never have the courage to go, with
the town in general, and the Dodo in particular, looking at
them. Shade of Miss Linwood, erst of Leicester-square, London, thou art welcome here, and thy retreat is fitly chosen!
I myself was one of the last visitors to that awful storehouse
of thy life's work, where an anchorite old man and woman
took my shilling with a solemn wonder, and conducted me to
a gloomy sepulchre of needlework dropping to pieces with
dust and age, and shrouded in twilight at high noon, left me
there, chilled, frightened, and alone. And now, in ghostly
letters on all the dead walls of this dead town, I read thy
honoured name, and find that thy Last Supper, worked in
Berlin Wool, invites inspection as a powerful excitement!

Where are the people who are bidden with so much cry to
this feast of little wool? Where are they? Who are they?
They are not the bandy-legged baby, studying the fashions in
the tailor's window. They are not the two earthy ploughmen
lounging outside the saddler's shop, in the stiff square where
the Town-hall stands, like a brick and mortar private on
parade. They are not the landlady of the Dodo in the empty
bar, whose eye had trouble in it and no welcome, when I asked
for dinner. They are not the turnkeys of the Town Gaol,
looking out of the gateway in their uniforms, as if they had
locked up all the balance (as my American friends would say)
of the inhabitants, and could now rest a little. They are not
the two dusty millers in the white mill down by the river,
where the great water-wheel goes heavily round and round,
like the monotonous days and nights in this forgotten place.
Then who are they, for there is no one else? No; this de-
ponent maketh oath and saith that there is no one else, save
and except the waiter at the Dodo, now laying the cloth. I
have paced the streets, and stared at the houses, and am come

back to the blank bow-window of the Dodo ; and the town clocks strike seven, and the reluctant echoes seem to cry, " Don't wake us !" and the bandy-legged baby has gone home to bed.

If the Dodo were only a gregarious bird—if it had only some confused idea of making a comfortable nest—I could hope to get through the hours between this and bedtime, without being consumed by devouring melancholy. But, the Dodo's habits are all wrong. It provides me with a trackless desert of sitting-room, with a chair for every day in the year, a table for every month, and a waste of sideboard where a lonely China vase pines in a corner for its mate long departed, and will never make a match with the candlestick in the opposite corner, if it live till Doomsday. The Dodo has nothing in the larder. Even now, I behold the Boots returning with my sole in a piece of paper ; and with that portion of my dinner, the Boots, perceiving me at the blank bow-window, slaps his leg as he comes across the road, pretending it is something else. The Dodo excludes the outer air. When I mount up to my bedroom, a smell of closeness and flue gets lazily up my nose like sleepy snuff. The loose little bits of carpet writhe under my tread, and take wormy shapes. I don't know the ridiculous man in the looking-glass, beyond having met him once or twice in a dish-cover—and I can never shave *him* to-morrow morning ! The Dodo is narrow-minded as to towels; expects me to wash on a freemason's apron without the trimming ; when I ask for soap, gives me a stony-hearted something white, with no more lather in it than the Elgin marbles. The Dodo has seen better days, and possesses interminable stables at the back—silent, grass-grown, broken-windowed, horseless.

This mournful bird can fry a sole, however, which is much. Can cook a steak, too, which is more. I wonder where it gets its Sherry ! If I were to send my pint of wine to some famous chemist to be analysed, what would it turn out to be made of? It tastes of pepper, sugar, bitter almonds, vinegar, warm knives, any flat drink, and a little brandy. Would it unman a Spanish exile by reminding him of his native land at all? I think not. If there really be any townspeople out of the churchyards, and if a caravan of them ever do dine, with a

bottle of wine per man, in this desert of the Dodo, it must
make good for the doctor next day!

Where was the waiter born? How did he come here?
Has he any hope of getting away from here? Does he ever
receive a letter, or take a ride upon the railway, or see anything
but the Dodo? Perhaps he has seen the Berlin Wool. He
appears to have a silent sorrow on him, and it may be that.
He clears the table; draws the dingy curtains of the great
bow-window, which so unwillingly consent to meet, that they
must be pinned together; leaves me by the fire with my pint
decanter, and a little thin funnel-shaped wine-glass, and a
plate of pale biscuits—in themselves engendering desperation.

No book, no newspaper! I left the Arabian Nights in the
railway carriage, and have nothing to read but Bradshaw, and
" that way madness lies." Remembering what prisoners and
shipwrecked mariners have done to exercise their minds in
solitude, I repeat the multiplication table, the pence table, and
the shilling table: which are all the tables I happen to know.
What if I write something? The Dodo keeps no pens but
steel pens; and those I always stick through the paper, and
can turn to no other account.

What am I to do? Even if I could have the bandy-legged
baby knocked up and brought here, I could offer him nothing
but sherry, and that would be the death of him. He would
never hold up his head again, if he touched it. I can't go to
bed, because I have conceived a mortal hatred for my bedroom; and I can't go away because there is no train for my
place of destination until morning. To burn the biscuits will
be but a fleeting joy; still it is a temporary relief, and here
they go on the fire! Shall I break the plate? First let me
look at the back, and see who made it. COPELAND.

Copeland! Stop a moment. Was it yesterday I visited
Copeland's works, and saw them making plates? In the confusion of travelling about it might be yesterday, or it might be
yesterday month; but I think it was yesterday. I appeal to
the plate. The plate says decidedly yesterday. I find the
plate, as I look at it, growing into a companion.

Don't you remember (says the plate) how you steamed
away yesterday morning, in the bright sun and the east wind,
along the valley of the sparkling Trent? Don't you recollect

the many kilns you flew past, looking like the bowels of gigantic tobacco pipes, cut short off from the stem and turned upside down?   And the fires—and the smokes—and the roads made with bits of crockery, as if all the plates and dishes in the civilized world had been Macadamized, expressly for the laming of all the horses?   Of course I do!

And don't you remember (says the plate) how you alighted at Stoke—a picturesque heap of houses, kilns, smoke, wharfs, canals and river, lying (as was most appropriate) in a basin—and how, after climbing up the sides of the basin to look at the prospect, you trundled down again at a walking-match pace, and straight proceeded to my father's, Copeland's, where the whole of my family, high and low, rich and poor, are turned out upon the world from our nursery and seminary, covering some fourteen acres of ground?   And don't you remember what we spring from: heaps of lumps of clay, partially prepared and cleaned in Devonshire and Dorsetshire, whence said clay principally comes—and hills of flint, without which we should want our ringing sound, and should never be musical?   And as to the flint, don't you recollect that it is first burnt in kilns, and is then laid under the four iron feet of a demon slave, subject to violent stamping fits, who when they come on, stamps away incessantly with his four iron legs, and would crush all the flint in the Isle of Thanet to powder, without leaving off?   And as to the clay, didn't they tell you how it is put into mills or teasers, and is sliced, and dug, and cut at, by endless knives, clogged and sticky, but persistent—and is pressed out of that machine, through a square trough, whose form it takes—and is cut off in square lumps and thrown into a vat, and there mixed with water, and beaten to a pulp by paddle-wheels—and is then run into a rough house, all rugged beams and ladders splashed with white—superintended by Grindoff the Miller in his working clothes—where it passes through no end of machinery-moved sieves also splashed with white, arranged in an ascending scale of fineness (some so fine that three hundred silk threads cross each other in a single square inch of their surface), and all in a violent state of ague with their teeth for ever chattering, and their bodies for ever shivering?   And as to the flint again, isn't it mashed and mollified and troubled and soothed, exactly as rags are in a paper-mill, until it is reduced to a pap so fine that it contains no atom of "grit" perceptible to the nicest taste? And as to the flint and the clay together, are they not, after all this, mixed in the proportion of five of clay to one of flint, and isn't the compound—known as "slip"—run into oblong troughs, where its superfluous moisture may evaporate; and finally, isn't it slapped and banged and beaten and patted and kneaded and wedged, and knocked about like butter, until it becomes a beautiful grey dough, ready for the potter's use?

In regard to the potter, popularly so called (says the plate), you don't mean to say you have forgotten that a workman called a Thrower is the man under whose hand this grey dough takes the shapes of the simpler household utensils as quickly as the eye can follow? You don't mean to say you cannot call him up before you, sitting, with his attendant woman, at his potter's wheel—a disc about the size of a dinner plate, revolving on two drums slowly or quickly as he wills—who made you a complete breakfast set for a bachelor, as a good-humoured little off-hand joke? You remember how he took up as much dough as he wanted, and, throwing it on his wheel, in a moment fashioned it into a teacup—caught up more clay and made a saucer—a larger dab and whirled it into a teapot—winked at a smaller dab and converted it into the lid of the teapot, accurately fitting by the measurement of his eye alone—coaxed a middle-sized dab for two seconds, broke it, turned it over at the rim, and made a milkpot—laughed, and turned out a slop-basin—coughed, and provided for the sugar? Neither, I think, are you oblivious of the newer mode of making various articles, but especially basins, according to which improvement a mould revolves instead of a disc? For you *must* remember (says the plate) how you saw the mould of a little basin spinning round and round, and how the workman smoothed and pressed a handful of dough upon it, and how with an instrument called a profile (a piece of wood, representing the profile of a basin's foot) he cleverly scraped and carved the ring which makes the base of any such basin, and then took the basin off the lathe like a doughey skull-cap to be dried, and afterwards (in what is called a green state) to be put into a second lathe, there to be finished and burnished with a steel burnisher? And as to moulding in general (says the plate),

it can't be necessary for me to remind you that all ornamental
articles, and indeed all articles not quite circular, are made in
moulds. For you must remember how you saw the vegetable dishes, for example, being made in moulds; and how the
handles of teacups, and the spouts of teapots, and the feet of
tureens, and so forth, are all made in little separate moulds,
and are each stuck on to the body corporate, of which it is
destined to form a part, with a stuff called "slag," as quickly
as you can recollect it. Further, you learnt—you know you
did—in the same visit, how the beautiful sculptures in the
delicate new material called Parian, are all constructed in
moulds; how, into that material, animal bones are ground up,
because the phosphate of lime contained in bones makes it
translucent; how everything is moulded, before going into the
fire, one-fourth larger than it is intended to come out of the
fire, because it shrinks in that proportion in the intense heat;
how, when a figure shrinks unequally, it is spoiled—emerging
from the furnace a mis-shapen birth: a big head and a little
body, or a little head and a big body, or a Quasimodo with
long arms and short legs, or a Miss Biffin with neither legs
nor arms worth mentioning!

And as to the Kilns, in which the firing takes place, and in
which some of the more precious articles are burnt repeatedly,
in various stages of their process towards completion—as to
the Kilns (says the plate, warming with the recollection), if
you don't remember THEM with a horrible interest, what did
you ever go to Copeland's for? When you stood inside of
one of those inverted bowls of a Pre-Adamite tobacco-pipe,
looking up at the blue sky through the open top far off, as you
might have looked up from a well, sunk under the centre of
the pavement of the Pantheon at Rome, had you the least idea
where you were? And when you found yourself surrounded,
in that dome-shaped cavern, by innumerable columns of an
unearthly order of architecture, supporting nothing, and
squeezed close together as if a pre-Adamite Samson had
taken a vast Hall in his arms and crushed it into the smallest
possible space, had you the least idea what they were? No
(says the plate), of course not! And when you found that
each of those pillars was a pile of ingeniously made vessels
of coarse clay—called Saggers—looking, when separate, like

raised-pies for the table of the mighty Giant Blunderbore, and now all full of various articles of pottery ranged in them in baking order, the bottom of each vessel serving for the cover of the one below, and the whole Kiln rapidly filling with these, tier upon tier, until the last workman should have barely room to crawl out, before the closing of the jagged aperture in the wall and the kindling of the gradual fire; did you not stand amazed to think that all the year round these dread chambers are heating, white hot—and cooling—and filling—and emptying—and being bricked up—and broken open—humanly speaking, for ever and ever? To be sure you did! And standing in one of those Kilns nearly full, and seeing a free crow shoot across the aperture a-top, and learning how the fire would wax hotter and hotter by slow degrees, and would cool similarly through a space of from forty to sixty hours, did no remembrance of the days when human clay was burnt, oppress you? Yes, I think so! I suspect that some fancy of a fiery haze and a shortening breath, and a growing heat, and a gasping prayer; and a figure in black interposing between you and the sky (as figures in black are very apt to do), and looking down, before it grew too hot to look and live, upon the Heretic in his edifying agony—I say I suspect (says the plate) that some such fancy was pretty strong upon you when you went out into the air, and blessed God for the bright spring day and the degenerate times!

After that, I needn't remind you what a relief it was to see the simplest process of ornamenting this "biscuit" (as it is called when baked) with brown circles and blue trees—converting it into the common crockeryware that is exported to Africa, and used in cottages at home. For (says the plate) I am well persuaded that you bear in mind how those particular jugs and mugs were once more set upon a lathe and put in motion; and how a man blew the brown colour (having a strong natural affinity with the material in that condition) on them from a blow-pipe as they twirled; and how his daughter, with a common brush, dropped blotches of blue upon them in the right places; and how, tilting the blotches upside down, she made them run into rude images of trees, and there an end.

And did'nt you see (says the plate) planted upon my own

brother that astounding blue willow, with knobbed and gnarled trunk, and foliage of blue ostrich feathers, which gives our family the title of "willow pattern?" And didn't you observe, transferred upon him at the same time, that blue bridge which spans nothing, growing out from the roots of the willow; and the three blue Chinese going over it into a blue temple, which has a fine crop of blue bushes sprouting out of the roof; and a blue boat sailing above them, the mast of which is burglariously sticking itself into the foundations of a blue villa, suspended sky-high, surmounted by a lump of blue rock, sky-higher, and a couple of billing blue birds, sky-highest— together with the rest of that amusing blue landscape, which has, in deference to our revered ancestors of the Cerulean Empire, and in defiance of every known law of perspective, adorned millions of our family ever since the days of platters? Didn't you inspect the copper-plate on which my pattern was deeply engraved? Didn't you perceive an impression of it taken in cobalt colour at a cylindrical press, upon a leaf of thin paper, streaming from a plunge-bath of soap and water? Wasn't the paper impression daintily spread, by a light-fingered damsel (you *know* you admired her!), over the surface of the plate, and the back of the paper rubbed prodigiously hard—with a long tight roll of flannel, tied up like a round of hung beef— without so much as ruffling the paper, wet as it was? Then (says the plate), was not the paper washed away with a sponge, and didn't there appear, set off upon the plate, *this* identical piece of Pre-Raphaelite blue distemper which you now behold?

Not to be denied! I had seen all this—and more. I had been shown, at Copeland's, patterns of beautiful design, in faultless perspective, which are causing the ugly old willow to wither out of public favour; and which, being quite as cheap, insinuate good wholesome natural art into the humblest households. When Mr. and Mrs. Sprat have satisfied their material tastes by that equal division of fat and lean which has made their *ménage* immortal; and have, after the elegant tradition, "licked the platter clean," they can—thanks to modern artists in clay—feast their intellectual tastes upon excellent delineations of natural objects.

This reflection prompts me to transfer my attention from

the blue plate to the forlorn but cheerfully painted vase on the sideboard. And surely (says the plate) you have not forgotten how the outlines of such groups of flowers as you see there, are printed, just as I was printed, and are afterwards shaded and filled in with metallic colours by women and girls? As to the aristocracy of our order, made of the finer clay—porcelain peers and peeresses;—the slabs, and panels, and table tops, and tazze; the endless nobility and gentry of dessert, breakfast, and tea services; the gemmed perfume-bottles, and scarlet and gold salvers; you saw that they were painted by artists, with metallic colours laid on with camel-hair pencils, and afterwards burnt in.

And talking of burning in (says the plate), didn't you find that every subject, from the willow-pattern to the landscape after Turner—having been framed upon clay or porcelain biscuit—has to be glazed? Of course, you saw the glaze—composed of various vitreous materials—laid over every article; and of course you witnessed the close imprisonment of each piece in saggers upon the separate system, enforced by means of fine-pointed earthenware stilts placed between the articles to prevent the slightest communication or contact. We had in my time—and I suppose it is the same now—fourteen hours firing to fix the glaze and to make it "run" all over us equally, so as to put a good shiny and unscratchable surface upon us. Doubtless, you observe that one sort of glaze—called printing-body—is burnt into the better sort of ware *before* it is printed. Upon this you saw some of the finest steel engravings transferred, to be fixed by an after glazing—didn't you? Why, of course you did!

Of course I did. I had seen and enjoyed everything that the plate recalled to me, and had beheld with admiration how the rotatory motion which keeps this ball of ours in its place in the scheme, with all its busy mites upon it, was necessary throughout the process, and could only be dispensed with in the fire. So, listening to the plate's reminders, and musing upon them, I got through the evening after all, and went to bed. I made but one sleep of it—for which I have no doubt I am also indebted to the plate—and left the lonely Dodo in the morning, quite at peace with it, before the bandy-legged baby was up.

XXIX.

FOR INDIA DIRECT.

MAY 1, 1852.

HALF-PAST six, on the twentieth of the month. Although, according to the calendar, Spring has commenced, a corroding morning mist rolls in acrimoniously between the crevices of the crazy cab, and bites its way straight to the bones of inner man. The fog is dense and brown. It so shrivels up the driver, that he is careful to occupy the smallest surface possible on his freezing perch; at the South-Western Railway Station, it has huddled together, for the sake of warmth and gossip, a knot of porters, who rapidly disentangle themselves to compete for any active employment that a carpet-bag may afford: it drives the money taker to the effeminacy of mittens, and he slides the cold change, singly, across the counter with the tips of his fingers: it slanders the countenances of the three ladies on the platform, with a suspicion of jaundice; and, when the eldest (with ringlets) ventures into the waiting-room and stands at the fire, her crisp, hoar-frosted curls thaw and descend about her boa—dank, straggling, and unlovely: it freezes the breath of the military officer in his moustaches, which stick out, stark as bristles: it stiffens the Mackintosh of the fox-hunter around his jack-boots and buckskins: it enters the very souls of all the passengers; for they are cross and uncommunicative. The disheveled lady returns to her friends, gazes silently on a heap of luggage, and weeps. The blazing red labels, marked CALCUTTA, communicate to all beholders but her, a factitious glow.

The bell has rung; the passengers are locked up in their locomotive cells. The puffy engine blows and pants impatiently; the distressed lady—giving vent to her emotion and again straightening her curls at the fire—is dragged across the platform between a porter and a strong-minded sister. She is thrust bodily into the carriage beside me. "Are you right, forward?" shouts the guard. "Yes!" shrieks the engine. We are off.

As this is the early passenger train for the conveyance of travellers for India to the end of their first stage, Southamp-

ton, I am curious to know which of my companions are on
their way to the far East. The sportsman is not attired for
the jungle; neither does the wife of the moustaches seem
very well provided—with a knitting-box—for a journey of ten
thousand miles. And, surely, the most useful adjuncts for the
overland route are not a bundle of swords, umbrellas, fishing-
rods, and walking-sticks; all the apparent travelling apparatus
belonging to the moustached lieutenant. To judge, also, from
the accompaniments of the young Scotch gentleman, he can
not be going to a very great distance—perhaps to Winchester
College. He passes, after much admiring scrutiny, the contents of three or four paper parcels into the pockets of his
paletôt; his only travelling bags. These consist of a cutty
pipe in a morocco case, a canister inscribed "Latakia," a
small poetical work entitled the "Stunning Warbler," a comprehensive claspknife like a pocket tool-chest, a compass,
a weighty watch-chain, a tiny spirit-case, a packet of steel
pens, an American revolver, a portable inkstand, and a bran
new prayer book. The individual opposite to me, whose
travelling appointments are complete from top to toe—and
whose valise, protruding from under his seat, very much cir-
cumscribes the lawful space for my legs—must be our only
India-bound companion. I'll ask him.

His reply is, "No, sir; I'm not bound for India, sir. I'm
going to Putney."

Somebody remarks that he has got into a train which does
not pass that village. He is not in the least disconcerted.

"Then, pray, ma'am, where are *you* going?" He addresses
the officer's wife. The lady looks up from her crochet, and
answers quietly:

"To Hong Kong."

The querist is utterly dumbfoundered.

At Kingston, the hunter bound for a "meet," at Hampton
Wick, and my *vis-à-vis* overshot, with his huge valise, far beyond Putney, leave the lieutenant and his wife to continue
their journey to China, the loosened curls to be blown by
wind and steam to Calcutta, and the young Scotchman from
Addiscombe (who is not going to Winchester) to be shot
across the globe to Koondooz, at the northern foot of the
Hindoo Koosh.

And, really now that I step on board the P. & O. S. N. Co.'s (technical ellipsis for Peninsular and Oriental Steam Naviga- tion Company's) good ship Bentinck, from Southampton dock, with no more ado than I stepped out of the railway carriage; now that I behold the spacious luxuriousness of the saloon, the domestic snugness of the sleeping berths which open into it, the lavish appointments of the steward's pantry; now that I observe the cow which is to deliver the daily milk, and the hencoops crowded with victims for the spit; now that I in- spect the kitchen apparatus (in what I ought nautically to call a "galley"), and observe the scientific galley-slaves, in snow- white uniforms, who manufacture dinners that emperors might long for; now that I see, hoisted in and stowed away, innume- rable hampers of champagne and soda-water: now that I am introduced to the Captain, whose dress and demeanour are those of a well-bred country gentleman doing the honours of a distinguished mansion; now that I reflect on all this, I quite understand the composed calmness, the trusting unprepared- ness, of the outward-bound. Why need travelling disturb the lightest of their every-day habits? Why should the soldier's wife suspend the knitting begun in her boudoir, merely be- cause the easy chair in which she sits is moving swiftly upon smooth iron rails; or because the sofa on which she reclines is gliding through the British Channel or the Indian Ocean? Do I exaggerate when I say that the Putney enterprise re- quired more personal provision? Perhaps the visitor knew that he would have to sleep in a damp villa; and perhaps he took care to stuff his valise with sheets which he could depend upon. Perhaps the maiden sister whose guest he is, not ap- proving of spirits, and not wearing Wellington boots, con- strained him to bring his own brandy and his own boot-jack. We, on board the Bentinck, need to bring nothing; we find every conceivable requirement that life in its highest state of pampered affluence can desire, in every grade of want between the extremes of a spare topmast and a cribbage-peg.

The passengers, therefore, who have already come on board are curiously unexcited. They have nothing to think of as to their voyage. Sentiment, indeed, be it ever so overflowing, cannot be conveniently exchanged in words; for the noise of the escaping steam would drown the loudest efforts of the human voice. Nothing of the pathos of a parting can I by the minutest scrutiny discover. The Scotch cadet—his panniers still laden—quaffs the soda and brandy with one of Her Majesty's midshipmen—a messmate of mine, who has come from Portsmouth to see his friend off—with as few of the tokens of parting glass as if he were leisurely crossing his native waters from the Granton Hotel to Burnt Island. He discourses on the prospects of the London Opera season with as much earnestness as if he had no other expectation than that of reclining in a Haymarket stall a fortnight hence, instead of being jolted on the back of a camel. The lady's maid, who is fitting up the little house in which her mistress and two children are going to live for the next fortnight, does her office as methodically as if she were still in Bryanston-square. The lieutenant's clever wife seems to have emptied her own and her husband's portmanteaux, which came down by last night's train, and has filled the ship's chests of drawers by magic; and see (the door of her berth is open), she is putting studs into the lieutenant's shirt, that it may be ready for him to dress for dinner. Nobody seems to do anything different here to what they do at home. Nobody is agitated; nobody is in a hurry; and, wonderful to add! nobody has left anything behind. The calm completeness of the whole ship, low and aloft, has even dried the tears of the sorrowing lady: the cold east wind, too, has tightened her curls.

One of the ship's officers delivers a short report to the Captain :—" High water, sir."

That is the signal for sailing. As I am here merely out of curiosity; being on my way to my own ship in Portsmouth dock (the Copperas, to which I was appointed, the day before yesterday, naval instructor) and have no wish to end my adventure at the mouth of the Nile, I step from the ship upon the wharf, to see the Bentinck get out of dock: an operation which, after scanning the breadth of the vessel, and measuring with my eye the narrow mouth of the harbour, I mentally pronounce to be within a hair's breadth of impossible ; the Southampton dock being shaped like a Bohemian decanter with its neck in the wrong place. When, in walking round its edge, I behold the Bentinck, with engines of five hundred and twenty horse power, and capacity for nearly two thousand tons ;

when I also notice the Euxine, the Madras, and three of the
Royal West India Mail Packet Company's steamers, all of vast
dimensions, lying in the dock, I regard them with the lively
curiosity of little boys looking at model mail-coaches inside
ounce phials, and wonder, like Peter Pindar's monarch in
reference to the apples in the dumplings, how they got there;
or, once there, how they are to be got out. Having reached
the neck of the broad bottle, I watch the Bentinck sway
round; and, obedient to her sluggish paddles, present her
handsome bows straight at the narrow outlet. I feel that the
problem will be immediately solved. There is great activity
in the bows of the ship, and the Captain stands on one of the
paddle-boxes, his surtout and eyeglass blown wildly about by
the wind. The pilot dances frantically from the bridge to the
other paddle-box; now directing the helmsman, now shouting hoarse orders to the engineer. Beside me and other idlers,
the P. and O. S. N. Co.'s admiral, or superintendent of vessels,
directs the shore operations. The monstrous marine locomotive must be warped out by means of a cable or " check," lying
coiled at my feet, one end of which is fastened to a Titanic
post. The Bentinck's cutwater is close upon us. The moment
is exciting. A rowboat, which is bringing a rope from the
ship to the shore, ruffles the admiral-superintendent's serenity.
He roars speaking-trumpet-wise, through his hands, "What
are you doing with that hawser? Send a line ashore for the
check." The vessel drifts nearer to the harbour wall: will
she strike? Excitement increases. "Bear a hand with the
line!" The smaller rope is pulled ashore in another boat; is
attached to the check, and is returned to the ship. "Send up
all hands upon deck; cook, firemen—everybody—to run out
the line!" Twenty men start up on the ship's deck like ap-
paritions, seize the rope all in a row, and run a mad race aft
with it, until the check is rove in and secured to the vessel.
"Go on easy!" The paddles revolve. Surely she will be
jammed in between the jaws of the narrow harbour's mouth.
I hold my breath. "Hoist the jib. Keep her head well off.
Bear a hand with the fenders!" The ship's bows scrape the
wall as they glide past it. " Port your helm—down with the
jib!" The check, tight as a fiddle-string, now holds the ship

to the post, and sways her head round into deep water. Cast
off the check !"

I breathe again. The mail-coach has been driven through
the neck of the phial: the Bentinck has found her way out ot
the wry-necked water-bottle, and is steaming off gallantly
through the broad Southampton Water.

As she recedes with the steady power which, in a fortnight,
will guide her into the harbour of Alexandria, I reflect on her
score of sisters—members of the Peninsular and Oriental
Steam Navigation Company family—immediately smile at Invasion, and defy the French. I communicate my sentiments
to the P. and O. admiral-superintendent. His responses
strengthen my defiant valour. He tells me, that the steam
navy belonging to his company alone, consists of twenty-four
vessels in active service, and six more in course of construction (including the Himalaya, which will be the largest steam-
boat in the world): total, thirty ships. To which I add, flat-
teringly, that his single fleet nearly equals the Imperial steam
navy of Russia; it is double that of Holland; the State steam
squadron of Brother Jonathan numbers only six more vessels; and the entire Danish flotilla, including sailing ships,
musters one less, or only twenty-nine. The number of persons employed, continues the P. and O. Admiral, afloat and
ashore, in the year 1851, was about two thousand three hundred persons. That (I add, telling him that I am a schoolmaster and am " up" in these matters), nearly equals the entire
military force of Saxe Altenbourg. The salaries paid to them
amounted to ninety-seven thousand pounds (says he). One-
third more (says I) than the cost of the Belgian navy for the
same year; and four times greater than the entire revenues of
the principality of Saxe Coburg. Four hundred colliers (he
continues) are employed in transporting English coal to the
different coaling stations between Southampton and Hong
Kong; some of them having to double the Cape of Good Hope.
The average yearly consumption of coal is one hundred and
thirty thousand tons; and the average cost per ton being
forty-two shillings, two hundred and seventy-three thousand
pounds per annum is spent to keep the steam up. Your dis-
bursements (I remark), for fuel and wages, fall very little short
of the payments for the Civil List of this country for the

year 1851. Yet (I begin to consider) there are other steam-
packet companies equally flourishing, and the combined fleets
of these powerful associations could show to our enemies, in
case of utmost need—how many steam-vessels at one view
averaging upwards of one thousand tons burden ? "Let us
see," replies the Admiral, "about seventy; besides smaller
steamers and swarms of colliers." "With complements of
how many thoroughly trained British tars?" I ask. "Quite"
(he answers) "eight thousand, not to mention the crews of
the coal-vessels." "Guns?" "Innumerable." A fig for the
French !

> Rule Britannia ! Britannia rules the waves,
> For Brit——

"Pray, don't sing here!" remonstrates my excellent informant.

"Here? Where?"

I looked round in amazement. Have I been bewitched?
or has the good, hearty, earnest Admiral Superintendent so
thoroughly interested me, that he has brought me ."here "
without my knowing it? I see dangling above me, stacked
around me, and strewed below me, so thickly that I am
obliged to mind where I tread. every sort of article that the
daintiest housewife could desire. I hear a steam-engine
driving circular saws, grindstones, and paint-mills. I smell
(and that loved fragrance restores my scattered senses) tar.
I am, it seems, in the P. and O. S. N. C.'s storehouse—a spacious piece of architecture just outside the Southampton dock-
gate. I am brought here to be plunged from my informant's
comprehensive statements, into the actual working of P. and
O. details. He leads me through forests of brushes of all
sorts, sizes, and descriptions; lakes of paint; more oil-cans
than would have concealed the Forty Thieves forty times
over; museums of pickles and jellies; stacks of spare spars;
mountains of sail-cloth; round towers of coiled rope; pyramids
of carpets and rugs; piles of blankets, counterpanes; show-
rooms of glass and crockery; warehouses crammed with cabin
stoves, cooking utensils, bundles of fire-irons, regiments of
coal-scuttles; floors of elegant chairs, tables, and drawers;
cabinet-work and upholstery enough to suggest the notion

that the P. and O. S. C.'s navy are always about to marry; artisans planing, glueing, and inlaying; six women, in deep mourning, sewing bed and table linen ("all widows of men who have died in the service," whispers my cicerone), or folding it into hot-air chambers; "for not a stitch goes aboard, sir"—I quote the head laundress—"without being aired, bone dry."

Once more in the dock, two objects present themselves at the same moment, which would occasion uneasiness to a less superstitious person than a sailor. In the offing I perceive the smoke of the Bentinck paying itself out in coils of black gossamer: passing across the wharf, in his habit as he lived when I last saw him on the paddle-box, walks the Captain! Has he flown from his own deck, now at least a couple of miles distant? or has he a twin-brother, who wears twin kid-gloves, a twin brown surtout, and a twin eyeglass? I have not time to ask. I am suddenly entangled in a maze of overland tin cases, overland trunks, and overland hat-boxes. I am hustled about by several overland officers, and bilious blacks in white turbans. A distracted overland female, dragging along two overland children, nearly sweeps me into the funnel of a small steamer moored upon the sinking tide, below the level of the wharf. Everything portable is being poured into that little steamer, in a thick strong stream. I try to get out of the way, and am instantly knocked aside by one of three enormous horse-boxes, which is being drawn (overland upon rails) from the railway station to the bewildering, busy, little steamer.

That is the Overland Mail.

I had long wished to see the Overland Mail. I never had a notion what the Overland Mail could be like; whether it was a coach, painted red, with a blazing royal arms, attended by a gold-laced guard; or a portable post-office, to be conveyed by rail and ship from the Waterloo station to India and China. But now, the entire broadside of the horse-box being let down, the Overland Mail bursts upon me like a trick in a pantomime. The huge van is suddenly transformed into a prodigious exaggeration of the sign of the Chequers on Portsmouth Hard, or the side wall of Harlequin's private residence; for it is a series of squares in blazing colours, filling up the horsebox from floor to roof. It is received with all befitting ceremony. Two gentlemen—attired in cocked hats (made, I think, of black court-plaster edged with faded lace) and surtout coats hitched up at the hips, like window-curtains, by the pommels of their swords—attended by the Southampton post-master, and a second ubiquitous officer of the Bentinck, solemnly draw forth pencils and printed forms, and order the gaudy squares to be separated. I find them to consist of wooden boxes, about two feet long by one foot deep, each distinguished by a separate colour, that its destination may at once be seen. Down a slide into the little steamer tumbles a red box. A porter shouts "Hong Kong!" Then comes a blue box—"Calcutta!" Buff—"Madras!" No paint— "Aden!" White—"Bombay!" Black (coffins for dead letters?)—"Ceylon!" At each of the one hundred and ninety announcements thus made, the cocked hats nod gracefully; not so much out of respect to her Majesty's mail-boxes, as to enable the gentlemen under them to record each colour in its proper column on the printed form. The mails are, in fact, given into their charge. These gentlemen are called "Admiralty Agents."

Presently (it is "post meridian, half-past one") amidst the tearing, frantic confusion, which is now come to a climax, I *am* swept bodily on board the little steamer. She is to take me out, it seems, to witness, positively and for the last time, the final departure of the Bentinck; which has been anchored in the Southampton Water to await the mails and late passengers; amongst whose luggage I have got bewilderingly entangled. Their last links with England are now irrevocably snapped. The Captain cannot again, under some pretence about "his papers," dash back from the Bentinck to his fireside for one more last word. Had the Admiralty Agent left his cocked hat on shore, no power on earth could have restored it to him this voyage. As we dart through the harbour's narrow mouth, blessings are wafted to us, from lines of parted friends on the outermost edges of the sea-wall. There is hardly time for our "Indians" to return these valedictions. Our little steamer shoots along like an arrow; for the Bentinck must start at two. Every point of the ten thousand four hundred miles which lie between Southampton and Hong Kong, is as rigidly timed as if it were a station upon a short line of railway. The accuracy and punctuality with which each single mile is performed out or home, operates upon thé punctual delivery of the mails in China or in London. The Bentinck *must*, therefore, start at two. How else will she be able to reach Gibraltar on the twenty-fifth (it is now the twentieth), Malta on the thirtieth, and Alexandria on the fourth of the following month? She must not detain, for a single hour, the canal boats which are to take her mails and passengers down to Cairo; or the camels and four-horse-carriages which are to effect their exodus out of Egypt. Another panting steamer will be waiting at the head of the Red Sea at Suez, and *must* steam off, bag and baggage, on the seventh, to the various ports between Egypt and China.*

Bump! We are alongside the Bentinck. Her port is crowded. Every hand is stretched forth to catch the first clutchable object out of the tiny tender, and to drag it into the ship. Things are whirled up out of the little steamer over one another in a cascade, like lumps shot up out of a volcano. A black trunk, a black nurse, a couple of mail boxes, a little boy, a birdcage, two or three more mail boxes, a military officer, a hamper of fish, mail boxes again, a dressing-case, a young lady, several baskets of ice, a bundle of hat boxes, a petty officer—the deck of the small vessel is cleared in no time, and every object, animate and inanimate, is mixed up and jumbled together upon the gangway.† The bustle is intense. Everything, including boxes of specie, seems endowed with locomotive power; and I am the more struck with the calm unconcern of my ringletted friend. I espy her at her cabin window, behind a jar of beautiful flowers, reading, with the settled, unruffled air of having lived there for the last twelvemonth. I am torn from contemplating her longer by being made into a sandwich (between a huge bread basket and

---

* The number of miles travelled by the Company's steamers during the year 1851, was 589,842, equal to more than twenty-three times the circumference of the globe, and equal also to 1,616 miles per day. During every minute of that year, an average of one mile and one-eighth of a mile was traversed by the Peninsular and Oriental Steam Navigation Company's steam power.

† The number of packages—independent of passengers' personal baggage, and Government mails—shipped to the various ports between Southampton and Hong-Kong, by this Company, in 1850, was twenty-five thousand six hundred. The number of passengers, in the same year, was nearly twenty thousand—thirteen thousand of whom were deck passengers, chiefly going to and fro on the Black Sea, or between the northern and southern ports of Spain—mostly labourers in harvest time.

a bag of biscuit), and gulped into the Bentinck, to be digested at leisure.

Suddenly, every hand in the ship is struck motionless; but every pair of legs runs as fast it can to the quarter deck. Two small elegant steamers have been reported within hail; and, above the second, the royal standard is displayed. The Queen is coming! She is on her way from Osborne.

The royal yacht, the bright little Fairy, trips along over the waves in the dazzling clear sunshine, and alters her course to pass close under us. The starboard bulwark of the Bentinck is beaded with passengers' heads. "Away aloft!" is the word. The ship's company dance into the shrouds, and stick to them; —a swarm of blue bottles. "Dip the colours!" The bunting makes its bow; for the Fairy is close under us:—Two men, with a Lieutenant in the fullest fig, at the wheel. A Lady in black seated at the cabin-door; two children beside her, looking at us with eager curiosity; the Captain, cocked-hat in hand, explaining all about us. Three dips of a parasol is the greeting from the Fairy, and three clear, distinct hearty English cheers were returned from the Bentinck.

In another minute, hardly without knowing it, I find myself again on the deck of the little tender. Two ladies are weeping beside me. An old man with white hair is waving one hand to a handsome cadet, and covering his eyes with the other. We move away. I am roused by more cheering, as the paddles of the Bentinck revolve. Good speed to her, and three times three!

☞ XXX.

RECEIVED, A BLANK CHILD.

MARCH 19, 1853.

THE blank day of blank, Received a blank child.

Within a few weeks, this official form, printed on a piece of parchment, happened to come in our way. Finding it to be associated with the histories of more than twenty thousand blank children, we were led into an inquiry concerning those little gaps in the decorous world. Their home and headquar-

15*

ters whence the document issues, is the Foundling Hospital, London.

This home of the blank children is by no means a blank place. It is a commodious roomy comfortable building, airily situated, though within advertisement distance of Temple Bar, which, as everybody knows, is precisely ten minutes' walk. It stands in its own grounds, cosily surveying its own shady arcades, its own turf, and its own high trees. It has an incredible fishpond behind it, no curious windows before it, and the wind (tempered to the shorn lambs within) is free to blow on either side of it. It preserves a warm, old fashioned, rich-relation kind of gravity, strongly indicative of Bank stock. Its confidential servants have comfortable places. Its large rooms are wainscoted with the names of benefactors, set forth in goodly order like the tables of the law. Its broad staircases, with balustrades such as elephants might construct if they took to the building arts, not only lead to long dining-rooms, long bedroom galleries, long lavatories, long school-rooms and lecture halls, for the blank children; but to other rooms, with listed doors and Turkey carpets, which the greatest English painters have lent their aid to adorn. In the halls of the blank children, the Guards for ever march to Finchley, under General HOGARTH. Deceased patrons come to life again under the hands of KNELLER, REYNOLDS, and GAINSBOROUGH. Nay, the good Duke of Cambridge himself, in full masonic paraphernalia, condescends to become a stupendous enigma over the chimney-piece of the smallest of the blank infants who can sit at dinner. Under the roof of the blank children the Royal Academy of Painting and Sculpture was originated. In the chapel of the blank children there is a noble organ, the gift of HANDEL; from whose great oratorio The Messiah—also his munificent contribution for their benefit—their hospital has received ten thousand pounds. There, too, the Church service is every Sunday performed at its best, with all the assistance of devotional music, yet free from the stage-playing of any ism, not forgetting schism. There, likewise, may be heard at this present time, if we may presume to say so, one of the least conventional, most sensible, naturally eloquent and earnest of preachers.

The knowledge of all these things accumulating in our mind

upon the receipt for that blank child on the blank day of
blank, induced us to look more curiously into the history of
the Foundling Hospital.

In or about the Christian year one thousand seven hundred
and twenty-two: a good old time, when England had had too
much to do, through all the good old times intervening since
the days of Pope Innocent the Third, to do anything whatever for Foundlings; in or about that year there dwelt in
London the gentle sea-captain, THOMAS CORAM. Although
the captain had made his fortune on the American plantations,
and had seen sights in his day, he came out of it all with a
tender heart; and this tender heart of Captain Coram was so
affected by seeing blank children, dead and alive, habitually
exposed by the wayside as he journeyed from Rotherhithe
(where he had set up his retreat, that he might keep a loving
eye on the river) to the Docks and Royal Exchange, and from
the Docks and Royal Exchange home to Rotherhithe again,
to receive the old shipmate who was generally coming to dinner, that he could not bear it. So, the Captain went to work
like a man who had gone down to the sea in ships, and knew
what work was. After conquering innumerable thorns and
brambles springing out into his path from that weedy virtue
which is always observed to flower in a wrong place when nobody wants to smell it, Captain Coram found that he had got
together subscriptions enough to begin a hospital for poor
foundlings, and to buy an estate of fifty-six acres—out in
Lamb's Conduit fields then—for five thousand five hundred
pounds. Little did the Captain think that the whole amount
of that purchase-money would ever come to be annually received back in rents; but so it is at this day.

Nineteen years after good Captain Coram's heart had been
so touched by the exposure of children, living, dying, and dead,
in his daily walks, one wing of the existing building was completed, and admission given to the first score of little blanks.
At that time, any person who brought a child was directed
"to come in at the outward door and ring a bell at the inward door, and not to go away until the child is returned
(diseased children were not admitted), or notice given of its
reception. But no questions whatever will be asked of any
person who brings a child, nor shall any servant of the house

presume to discover who such person is on pain of being discharged." It was further desired, that each child should have
some distinguishing mark or token by which it might be afterwards known, if necessary. Most of these tokens were small
coins, or parts of coins; sometimes, an old silk purse was substituted; sometimes, doggrel verses were pinned to the poor
baby's clothes; once a lottery ticket was so received. The
Hospital chronicles do not record that it turned up a prize—
the blank child was true to its designation.

As the Hospital became more extensively known, the numbers of applicants were enormous. The outward door was
besieged by women who fought and scratched their way to
the bell at the inward door; and in these disturbances, as in
all physical force proceedings, the strongest were successful.
To put a stop to such scenes, the little candidates were then
admitted by ballot.

In fifteen years' time from the opening of the Hospital, the
Governors found it necessary to apply to Parliament for assistance. It was conceded in such liberal measure, that it was
thought all comers could henceforth be received. Nursing
establishments were formed in various parts of the country, a
basket was hung outside the Hospital gate, and an advertisement publicly announced, that all children under the age of
two months tendered for admission would be received. The
result was, that on the 2d of June, 1756, the first day of such
indiscriminate reception, the basket at the gate was filled and
emptied one hundred and seventeen times. Fraudulent parish
officers, married women who were perfectly able to maintain
their offspring, parents of depraved and abandoned character
(unconsciously emulative of Jean Jacques Rousseau), basketed
their bodies by thousands. It is almost incredible, but none
the less true, that a new branch of the Carrier's trade was
commenced. Baby-carriers undertook to convey infants to
the all-embracing basket from distant parts of the country, at
so much per head. One man who had charge of five infants
in baskets, got drunk; and, falling asleep on a bleak common,
found when he awoke that three of the five were dead. Of
eight infants consigned to a country waggoner, seven died
before he got to London; the surviving child owing its life
solely to its mother, who followed the waggon on foot to save

it from starvation. Another man, established in business as a baby-carrier with a horse and a pair of panniers, was loud in his complaints of an opposition man, " who," said he, " is a taking the bread out of my mouth. Before he started, it was eight guineas·a trip per child from Yorkshire. Now, I've come down a third; next week I must come down another third; that's the way trades get ruined by over-competition." At the time when he made this representation, he had eight children in his panniers. Many of these amiable carriers stripped off such poor clothes as the children wore, and basketed them without a shred of covering. It is related among the Hospital legends, as a remarkable instance of change of fortune, that a few years ago a rich and aged banker applied to search the register of the establishment for such information as it might afford of his own origin, when all he could learn was, that he had been taken out of the basket stark naked. That was his whole previous history.

During the three years and ten months of the existence of this system, there were dropped into the hospital-basket fifteen thousand children; and so great was the difficulty of providing for such an enormous influx, and so little were the necessary precautions understood, that only four thousand four hundred of this large number lived to be apprenticed. So the practice was discontinued, and Heaven knows, with reason! It is melancholy to think of the regrets and anxieties of the gentle Captain Thomas Coram under all these failures, and more melancholy to know that he died a very old man, so reduced in circumstances as to be supported by subscription. But, though shipwrecked here, the tender-hearted captain gained a brighter shore, we will believe, where even foundlings who have never spoken a word on earth, possess their eloquence.

What genius originated the next idea, we have not discovered; but the Hospital being poor again, as well it might be, some bold spirit proposed that every child that should be mysteriously presented with a hundred pound note attached, should be received. The Governors adopted the inspiration with success; and this most reprehensible practice actually continued until the beginning of the present century. In January, 1801, it was abolished, and the existing rules of admission were substituted. What these are, may be best described through our own observation of the admission of two children who happened to be brought there by two mothers while we were inspecting the place.

Each of the mothers had previously rung the porter's bell to obtain a printed form of petition to the Governors for the admission of her child. No petition is allowed to be issued, except from the porter's lodge: no previous communication with any officer of the Hospital must have been held by the mother: the child must have been the first-born, and preference is given to cases in which some promise of marriage has been made to the mother, or some other deception practised upon her. She must never have lived with the father. The object of these restrictions (careful personal inquiry being made into all such points) is as much to effect the restoration of the mother to society, as to provide for her child.

The conditions having been favourably reported on, the two mothers had brought their children, and had received, filled up, the form we quoted at the commencement of this paper.

"Hospital for the Maintenance and Education of Exposed and Deserted Young Children. The blank day of blank, received a blank child. Blank, Secretary. Note—Let this be carefully kept, that it may be produced whenever an inquiry is made after the health of the child (which may be done on Mondays between the hours of ten and four), and also in case the child should be claimed."

Then they departed, and we saw the children.

One was a boy; the other, a girl. A parchment ticket inscribed with the figures 20,563 was sewn upon the shoulder-strap of the male infant, and a similar ticket was attached to the female infant, denoting that she was 20,564—so numerous were the babies who had been there before them. To meet these present babies, a couple of wholesome-looking wet-nurses had been summoned from one of the nursing districts in Kent, by whom they were immediately borne into the chapel to be baptised. Here, at the altar, we found awaiting them, the steward, the matron, the schoolmaster, and the head nurse—fit representatives of the provision made for their various wants —who were to be their sponsors. The right of baptism impressively performed by the chaplain, gave the children the additional identity of names.

These names have been a fruitful source of minor difficulty. At the baptism of the first twenty, there was present at the ceremony, a contemporary record states, "a fine appearance of person of quality: His Grace the Duke of Bedford, their Graces the Duke and Duchess of Richmond, the Countess of Pembroke, and several others, honouring the children with their names, and being their sponsors." Persons of quality not being free from a certain tendency to play at follow my leader, which is found to run in vulgar blood, the early registers of the Hospital swarm with the most aristocratic names in the land. When the peerage was exhausted, the names of historical celebrities were adopted; it therefore behoves a Mark Anthony Lowell, or an Editor of Notes and Queries, to take this circumstance into account in "making a note of" the pedigree of a modern Wickliffe, Latimer, Chaucer, Shakespeare, Milton, Bacon, Cromwell, Hampden, Hogarth, or Michael Angelo. Celebrated real names having, in process of time, been exhausted, the authorities had recourse to novels, and sent into the world, as serving-maids, innumerable Sophia Westerns, Clarissa Harlowes, and Flora Mac Ivors; innumerable hard-handed artisans as Tom Jones, Edward Waverley, Charles Grandison, and Humphrey Clinker. Then, the Governors were reduced to their own names, which they distributed with the greatest liberality, until some of their namesakes on growing up, occasioned inconvenience (and possibly scandal) by claiming kith and kin with them. The present practice is for the treasurer to issue lists of names for adoption; in which responsible duty he, no doubt, derives considerable comfort from the Post-Office London Directory.

The two babies were then borne off into Kent by their respective nurses (each of whom gave a receipt for a deserted young child) with little packets of clothes, a few sensible admonitions from the matron, and the following document:

"The Child blank, No. blank, is placed under your care by the Governors of the FOUNDLING HOSPITAL, and it is expected that you will pay such attention to the said Child as will be satisfactory to the Inspector. You will receive for the maintenance of the said Child Sixpence per day, which will be paid on the first day of each month according to the number of days in the month preceding.

"Should you rear the said Child to the end of the first year, and pay such

attention to it as shall be satisfactory to the Inspector, you will receive a gra-
tuity of Twenty-five Shillings at that period.

"For clothing the said Child (after the first year) you will receive allow-
ances as follows, viz.:

		£	s.	d.
Between the Second and Third Year		0	14	0
„ Third and Fourth Year		0	17	0
„ Fourth and Fifth Year		0	18	0

"For your trouble and expenses in coming to London for a Child you will
receive Two Shillings from the Inspector, your coach-hire being paid by the
Governors of the Hospital.

"You are to be particularly careful in preserving this parchment, which
you must return with the Child whenever it shall be sent up to the Hospital,
or removed from you, and it is especially required that you keep the *number*
of the Child always affixed to its person. If you neglect this, the Child will
be taken from you."

When they should be old enough to walk, these two children would be returned to the hospital, and placed in its
juvenile department.

Proceeding to visit the infant school, which was their future
destination, we found perhaps a hundred tiny boys and girls
seated in hollow squares on the floor, like flower-borders in a
garden; their teachers walking to and fro in the paths between, sowing little seeds of alphabet and multiplication table
broad-cast among them. The sudden appearance of the secretary and matron whom we accompanied, laid waste this little
garden, as if by magic. The young shoots started up with
their shrill hooray! twining round and sprouting out from the
legs and arms of the two officials with a very pleasant familiarity. Except a few Lilliputian pulls at our coat-tails; some
curiosity respecting our legs, evinced in pokes from short fingers, very near the ground; and the sudden abstraction of
our hat (with which an infant extinguished himself to his
great terror, evidently believing that he was lost to the world
for ever); but little notice was taken of our majestic presence.
Indeed it made no sensation at all.

One end of this apartment being occupied by a grade of
seats for the little inmates, is used as a convenient orchestra
for a band of wind instruments, consisting of the elder boys.
These young musicians, about thirty in number, now made
their appearance, and commenced the performance of some
difficult Italian music, executed with so much precision and

spirit, as amply to justify the expressions of commendation
and surprise, which we found in letters addressed to their
music-master by that admirable artist, Signor Costa, and by
Mr. Godfrey, one of the bandmasters of the Household troops.
The ophicleide was made to emit sounds of tremendous
volume and richness, by a boy hardly bigger than itself. The
body of sound emitted in passages of Handel's Hallelujah
chorus was no less full and sonorous than that we remember
to have heard produced by the stalwart lungs of Mr. Strutt's
band of blacksmiths at Belper.

A new supply of toys had just been brought into the room;
and, during the musical performance, the juvenile audience
were vigorously beating toy drums, blowing dumb horns and
soundless trumpets, marching regiments of wooden infantry,
balancing swinging cavalry, depopulating Noah's arks, starting miniature railway trains, and flourishing wooden swords.
They were all sensibly and comfortably clothed, and looked
healthy and happy. They were certainly under no undue
restraint. The only hush that came upon the cheerful little
uproar was when the chaplain entered. He came to take out
the first clarionet (and he laid his hand on the boy's shoulder
in a friendly manner which was very agreeable), who had attained the maximum age of fourteen, and was that day to be
apprenticed to a lithographic printer. They went away together for some talk about his future duties, and he would receive, in common with all the other foundlings when they go
out into the world, the following advice in print and
parchment:

"You are placed out Apprentice by the Governors of this Hospital. You
were taken into it very young, quite helpless, forsaken, poor, and deserted.
Out of Charity you have been fed, clothed, and instructed; which many have
wanted.

"You have been taught to fear God; to love him, to be honest, careful,
laborious, and diligent. As you hope for Success in this World, and Happiness in the next, you are to be mindful of what has been taught you. You
are to behave honestly, justly, soberly, and carefully, in everything, to everybody, and especially towards your Master and his Family; and to execute all
lawful commands with Industry, Cheerfulness, and good Manners.

"You may find many temptations to do wickedly, when you are in the
world; but by all means fly from them. Always speak the Truth. Though
you may have done a wrong thing, you will, by sincere Confession, more
easily obtain Forgiveness, than if by an obstinate Lie you make the fault the

greater, and thereby deserve a far greater Punishment. Lying is the beginning of every Thing that is bad; and a Person used to it is never believed, esteemed or trusted.

"Be not ashamed that you were bred in this Hospital. Own it: and say, that it was through the good Providence of Almighty God, that you were taken Care of. Bless him for it.

"Be constant in your Prayers, and going to Church; and avoid Gaming, Swearing, and all evil Discourses. By this means the Blessing of God will follow your honest Labours, and you may be happy; otherwise you will bring upon yourself Misery, Shame, and Want.

"Note.—At Easter of every year, upon producing a testimonial of good conduct for the previous twelve months to the satisfaction of the Committee, you will receive a pecuniary reward proportioned to the length of time you have been apprenticed, and at the termination of your Apprenticeship, upon producing a like testimonial for the whole term thereof, the further sum of Five Guineas, or such smaller sum as the Committee shall consider you entitled to."

Although we inspected the schoolrooms, the dormitories, the kitchen, the laundries, the pantries, the infirmary, and saw the four hundred boys and girls go through the ceremony of dining (a sort of military evolution in this asylum), and glanced at their school-life, we saw nothing so different from the best conducted charities in the general management, as to warrant our detaining the reader by describing them.

We thought, when the male pupils were summoned by trumpet to the playground to go through their military exercises—which they did, their drill master assured us confidentially, in a manner that would not disgrace the Foot Guards— we had traced the entire history of the connexion of a blank child with the hospital. But, as we were leaving the building, a decently dressed woman made her appearance from the lodge, to announce to the secretary that "Joe" had arrived at the Diggings; that Joe had sent her a ten pound-note, and expected to be able to transmit to the Institution a similar token of his regard in a very weeks; that in a short time Joe intended to remit enough money to take herself (this was Joe's wife), their son and their two daughters, over to join him; but their eldest daughter being of age, and having a will of her own, refused to promise to go to Joe, because of another promise of a tender description which she had made to a worthy young ivory turner whose name was *not* Joe. All of . which we heard with a growing curiosity to know who Joe was: more especially as Mrs. Joe was in a state of great excitement and joy about Joe.

The explanation of this little family history was, that out of a separate fund established in connexion with the Hospital, Joe, an old foundling—although he had left the hospital when very young to volunteer as a cabin-boy in Lord Nelson's fleet—had, in common with some others of his schoolfellows, been assisted through life with temporary loans of money, the latest of which loans had enabled Joe to seek another fortune (Joe, in the course of his career, had found and lost many fortunes) in Australia. This put us in an excellent humour for participating in the joy that there was over Joe. And we devoutly wished, and do wish, that Joe may find gold enough to provide for himself, Mrs. Joe, their son, their two daughters, and the ivory turner; and that with love and gold to spare for the gentle memory of Captain Thomas Coram, he may have this line to himself among the donors on the wall of the boys' dining-room,

JOE . . . . £500.

This home of the blank children is rich, and possibly has blemishes. But, from what we saw of it, we derived much satisfaction, and the good that is in it seems to us to have grown with its growth. Of the appearance, food, and lodging of the children, any of our readers may judge for themselves after morning service any Sunday.

We happen to have had our personal means of knowing that in one respect the Governors of this charity are a model to all others. That is, in holding themselves strictly aloof from any canvassing for an office connected with it, or a benefit derivable from it. Canvassing and electioneering are the disgrace of many public charities of this time; and, in all such cases, but particularly where the candidates are persons of education who have known a happier and better estate, we view the preliminary solicitation and humiliation as far outweighing the subsequent advantages, and believe there is something very rotten in the state of any Denmark that does not apply itself to find a better system for its government.

XXXI.

IDIOTS.

JUNE 4, 1853.

THE popular notion of an Idiot would probably be found to vary very little, essentially, in different places, hower modified by local circumstances. To the traveller in France or Italy the name recalls a vacant creature all in rags, gibbering and blinking in the sun with a distorted face, and led about, as a possession and a stock-in-trade, by some phenomenon of filth and ugliness in the form of an old woman. In association with Switzerland, it suggests a horrible being, seated at a châlet door (perhaps possessing sense enough to lead the way to a neighbouring waterfall), of stunted and misshapen form, with a pendulous excrescence dangling from his throat, like a great skin-bag with a weight in it. In the highlands of Scotland, or on the roads of Ireland, he becomes a red-haired Celt, rather more unreasonable than usual, plunging ferociously out of a mud cabin, and casting stones at the stranger's head. As a remembrance of our own childhood in an English country town, he is a shambling, knock-kneed man who was never a child, with an eager utterance of discordant sounds which he seemed to keep in his protruding forehead, a tongue too large for his mouth, and a dreadful pair of hands that wanted to ramble over everything—our own face included. But, in all these cases, the main idea of an idiot would be of a hopeless, irreclaimable, unimprovable being. And if he be further recalled as under restraint in a workhouse or lunatic asylum, he will still come upon the imagination as wallowing in the lowest depths of degradation and neglect: a miserable monster, whom nobody may put to death, but whom every one must wish dead, and be distressed to see alive.

Until within a few years, it was generally assumed, even by those who were not given to hasty assumptions, that because an idiot was, either wholly or in part, deficient in certain senses and instincts necessary, in combination with others, to the due performance of the ordinary functions of life—and because those senses and instincts could not be supplied—therefore nothing could be done for him, and he must always remain an object of pitiable isolation. But, a closer study of the subject has now demonstrated that the cultivation of such senses and instincts as the idiot is seen to possess, will, besides frequently developing others that are latent within him but obscured, so brighten those glimmering lights, as immensely to improve his condition, both with reference to himself and to society. Consequently there is no greater justification for abandoning him, in his degree, than for abandoning any other human creature.

This important truth, a conviction of which led to the establishment of Institutions for the care and education of idiots, received daily and hourly confirmation from the experience of those Institutions. We will lay some of their results before our readers, but will first beg to present the great leading distinction between Idiocy and Insanity as being:—that, in the Insane, certain faculties which once existed have become obliterated or impaired; and that, in Idiots, they either never existed or exist imperfectly. Dr. VOISIN in his learned French treatise, defines idiocy to be "that particular state in which the instincts of reproduction and preservation, the moral sentiments, and the intellectual and perceptive powers are never manifested, or that particular state in which the different essentials of our being are only imperfectly developed."

Dr. ABERCROMBIE, in his interesting book on the Intellectual Powers, has this passage on idiocy: "It is a simple torpor of the faculties, in the higher degrees amounting to total insensibility to every impression; and some remarkable facts are connected with the manner in which it arises without bodily disease. A man mentioned by Dr. Pinel, was so violently affected by some losses in trade, that he was deprived almost instantly of all his mental faculties. He did not take notice of anything; not even expressing a desire for food, but merely taking it when it was put into his mouth. A servant dressed him in the morning, and conducted him to a seat in his parlour, where he remained the whole day, with his body bent forward, and his eyes fixed on the floor. In this state he continued nearly five years, and then recovered completely and rather suddenly. The account which he afterwards gave of his condition during this period was, that his mind was entirely lost, and that it was only about two months before his final recovery, that he began to have sensations and thoughts of any kind. These at first served only to convey fears and apprehensions, especially in the night-time. Of perfect idiocy produced in the same manner by a moral cause, an affecting example is given by Pinel. Two young men, brothers, were carried off by the conscription, and, in the first action in which they were engaged, one of them was shot dead by the side of the other. The survivor was instantly struck with perfect idiocy. He was taken home to his father's house, where another brother was so affected by the sight of him, that he was seized in the same manner; and, in this state, they were both received into the Bicêtre. For the production of such an extraordinary result, it is not necessary that the mental impression should be of a painful description. Pinel mentions an engineer, who, on receiving a flattering letter from Robespierre respecting an improvment he had proposed in the construction of cannon, was struck motionless on the spot, and soon after conveyed to the Bicêtre in a state of complete idiocy." It may be questioned, we think, whether in all these cases there was not a strong predisposition to the melancholy state thus superinduced by circumstances, and it is to be observed that the general question of idiocy has received some light since Dr. Abercrombie's time.

It was not supposed until recently that a child who wanted the sense to feed itself, could ever be taught to write; or that one incapable of dressing or undressing, could ever learn arithmetic; yet, the faculties required for each of these two sets of operations are distinct, and this is known to be a mistake. Patients with natural instincts too weak to eat with decency, or to perform other daily functions properly, have been found to possess intellectual perceptions sufficiently strong to enable them to acquire one or more of the imitative and mechanical branches of art or science, with perfect success; and the cultivation of the best faculty has in nearly all cases improved the other faculties. Dr. Fodére (*Traité du goitre et du crétinisme*) had met, he says, with idiots gifted with especial talents for copying designs, for finding rhymes and for performing music. "I have known others," he adds, "put watches together and other pieces of mechanism; yet these individuals not only were unable to read books which treated of their arts, but were utterly incoherent when spoken to about them." At the Essex Hall Asylum for Idiots, near Colchester, there is a youth whose case, when first admitted, was looked upon as quite hopeless. He was deaf, incapable of articulating although not dumb, and appeared to have no sense of change of place or change of the circumstances surrounding him. Yet his tutors gradually found out that, like Dr. Fodére's mechanists, he had a latent power of construction. This being assiduously encouraged, he presently made a neat model of a ship, with nothing to copy it from, but the figure of a vessel printed on a cotton pocket-handkerchief. He is now the glazier and carpenter of the establishment, and does his work admirably. It is predicted of this once deaf and speechless creature, who now speaks and hears perfectly, that if he be placed under the roof of some carpenter and his wife, or on an estate, he will make a valuable journeyman, and be an amiable, gentle, and attached dependent. Another boy in the same asylum could do nothing at first but tailor's work. He has now acquired a passion for sewing on buttons. He always carries a bag, containing needles and thread, a thimble, and a large supply of buttons. Whenever a male visitor appears, this boy scrutinises the state of his buttons with the deepest interest. If he can only find a visitor with a loose button or with a button wanting, he is happy, and instantly sets to work to sew it on again with the greatest dexterity. The Reverend Mr. Sidney reports of this lad : " He was so anxious to exhibit his skill to me, that he wanted to cut off one of my buttons to show how well he could restore it ; but, luckily, I happened to observe one nearly off a boy's jacket, and he sewed it on as neatly and firmly as you could conceive."

The devoted and distinguished founder of the asylum on the Abendberg, in Switzerland, Dr. Guggenbühl—whose name has a peculiar attraction for us as being what an uneducated idiot might hit upon, in trying to say Jones—is inclined to think that no special aptitude is so frequently developed among idiots as one for mental arithmetic. It is remarkable that among these disordered intellects, order and numbers should often be, of all other accomplishments, the most readily acquired. A patient admitted into the Park House Asylum for idiots, at Highgate—at first useless and generally incapable—

was gradually trained to set out all the Sunday clothes for the rest of the inmates; and this duty (in which he is assisted by one or two of his schoolfellows) he directs and performs with curious exactness. There is a boy at Essex Hall who cleans and takes care of all the knives and forks; he counts them carefully at stated times, and if he misses one, never rests until he finds it. Several calculating boys are mentioned in the reports of the various asylums. They work out in their minds arithmetical problems of a by no means easy nature, that are put to them; but they are wholly unable to calculate on paper or slate, or to describe how they get at their results. Distinctive specialities belong to some idiots, so fine and curious as to be scarcely credible. A youth at the Highgate Asylum has the extraordinary gift of invariably knowing the time, within a minute or two, at any period of the day. On our asking him what o'clock it was, he instantly informed us; and he "went" better than our watch, though it is a watch of reputation. At Dr. Guggenbühl's establishment, there is a pupil who has never been able to acquire the correct pronunciation of his own native German language,- but who has learned to speak and to read French correctly, and who writes it very well. Another youth was brought into the same asylum, to whom for a long time it was impossible to teach the difference between various objects, however opposite; it is doubtful whether he knew any distinction between a flower and a table. At last, he identified a cat; and from that moment cats became the especial business and pleasure of his life. After continually playing with the cat belonging to the asylum, and with her kittens, he improved sufficiently to be taught to draw. He could draw nothing but cats, and can draw nothing but cats. He produces drawings of cats and kittens in every conceivable variety of attitude and frolic, with astonishing expression. And although he cannot get beyond cats, still, as he has advanced in cats, so he has advanced in his habits and in his general intelligence.

Changes of a remarkable nature have been effected in the external appearance of idiots by training and culture. Dr. Guggenbühl tells us of a little child brought to his establishment in a state "truly dreadful; the bodily organisation was that of a stunted, withered skeleton, covered with a livid, wrinkled, cold skin. Where there were some traces of muscles, elasticity•was wanting; the extremities were very small, the countenance deadly pale, the cheeks and forehead wrinkled, the eyes small and dark, and the whole expression of the face that of an old woman. In the spring, when fine weather adds to the favourable effect of the pure mountain air in the cure of these miserable children, she was brought to the Abendberg. The natural advantages of the situation were aided by the most careful medical treatment and diet. Although this poor creature had been gradually becoming more dwarf-like and deformed ever since her birth, she now advanced rapidly towards a perfect development. Three months worked a visible improvement; the muscles strengthened with her growth, the skin became elastic, and attained the usual degree of warmth, the wrinkles of the face vanished, the old-woman expression disappeared, and the pleasing traces of youth became apparent."

We presume that the bodily sensitiveness of this afflicted class is increased, as their deprivations are diminished. However this be, idiots often suffer less from physical pain than beings of a finer organisation. A boy, now at Highgate, was once found by his mother with a species of buckle thrust through his tongue. He had made this experiment merely to amuse himself, and testified no inconvenience whatever—was vain of the ornament, but not otherwise moved by it. Idiots are found below the average sensitiveness to the electric battery; and yet, so remarkable are the contradictions in their nature, they are invariably affected by thunder and lightning. The mere approach of a thunderstorm is observed to disorder the stomachs of a whole idiot asylum. They generally like music—bright colours almost always—and are remarkably susceptible to the influence of sunlight. Such things as they do, they do, as an established rule, best on a bright day, and worst on a dark one. In respect of mental pain, as of physical, they have their compensation. Separation from friends does not affect them much, grief and sorrow hold but slight dominion over them, and the contemplation of death does not distress them. They are very fond of attending prayers in a body. What dim religious impressions they connect with public worship, it is impossible to say, but the struggling soul would seem to have some instinctive aspirations towards its Maker.

The Institutions from which these facts are derived, are, as we have mentioned, of recent establishment. In eighteen hundred and twenty-eight M. FERRUS, Chief physician of the hospital for the Insane at Bicêtre, near Paris, selected from the eight hundred cases under his care, such as were idiots, and organised a school where, each morning, they were taught habits of order and industry, reading, writing, cyphering, and gymnastics. In eighteen hundred and thirty-one M. VALRET followed the example in the Salpetrière lunatic asylum for females of which he had charge. In eighteen hundred and thirty-nine Dr. Guggenbühl, then a young physician at Zurich, observed a poor Crétin muttering a prayer before a crucifix, not comprehending what he was doing. He was so deeply affected by this sight, that he entered a cottage near, for the purpose of ascertaining some particulars; and learned, from the mother of the Crétin, that she had taught him the prayer when he was a little child. Dr. Guggenbühl became convinced, from that time, that there was a dormant mind in the Crétins; and resolved to make them his peculiar study. He succeeded, by dint of great perseverance, in establishing the asylum already several times referred to, on the Abendberg above Interlaken, and three thousand feet above the level of the sea. This is above the level at which crétinism, so prevalent in Switzerland, is known to exist. The establishment has flourished under Dr. Guggenbühl's care; and he has travelled successfully into other countries to urge the foundation of other asylums. They were set on foot in various parts of Germany, in Sardinia, and in the United States, before they were thought of in England. But, in eighteen hundred and forty-six, some ladies in Bath, having read an account of Dr. Guggenbühl's efforts, established a school for Idiots in that city; which was, in eighteen hundred and fifty-one, removed to Belvedere, a more elevated and airy situation. At the end of the year eighteen hundred and forty-seven, Dr. ANDREW REED and Dr. CONOLLY excited public attention to the want of such an asylum in London, and so successfully, that they were soon enabled, by voluntary subscriptions, to take Park House, Highgate. The same society now holds Essex Hall, near Colchester, likewise. The first report thus graphically describes the opening of Park House :

"The first gathering of the idiotic family was a spectacle unique in itself, and sufficiently discouraging to the most re-solved, and not to be forgotten in after time by any. It was a period of distraction, disorder, and noise of the most un-natural character. Some had defective sight; most had defective or no utterance; most were lame in limb or muscle; and all were of weak or perverted mind. Some had been spoiled, some neglected, and some unconscious and inert. Some were screaming at the top of the voice; some making constant and involuntary noises from nervous irritation; and some, terrified at scorn and ill-treatment, hid themselves in a corner, from the face of man, as from the face of an enemy."

To this establishment we paid a visit within a few weeks of the present date. It is a fine detached house, beautifully situated at a considerable elevation above the metropolis—high ground is indispensable for the purpose—and looking down upon the spot where Richard Whittington heard the bells summon him to his glorious destiny of being thrice Lord Mayor of London. We found the schoolroom for male pupils —and full of pupils too—as quiet and orderly as any school-room we have ever seen. Writing was in progress, and the copies were clean, plain, and good. Drawing appeared to be the favourite pursuit. Barns, gables, gates, houses, walls, haystacks, churches, fences, and the usual compositions, were in many cases exceedingly well executed. One pupil was very proud of a pump—a portrait, as we conceived—with the legend "Stick no Bills," on it. Two young men—one, a curiously slow deep-voiced dark youth, and the other a round-shouldered healthy-looking fellow, rather overgrown and heavy—stood before a map of England, pointed out towns with a wand as they were named, and told what they were famous for—frequently correcting each other as the occasion arose; they also achieved some simple arithmetic. In a second room, likewise perfectly quiet and placid, were some little fellows busily plaiting straw of various colours. In a third, the whole male body turned out on parade, and were drilled by an old soldier; going through their exercise with such precision, that we were disposed to suggest the addition of an

Idiot Corps to the Militia. We found a workroom full of
girls, sewing, and making little fancy ornaments with beads
and parti-coloured strips; some of the faces among them were
extremely pretty, and gave little or no indication of the blank
within. We found rooms full of children of all ages, in the
keeping of female attendants, whose pleasant and patient
countenances were a strong assurance of their being well
selected, except in only one instance where we certainly
derived a less agreeable impression. We found a capital
gymnasium, which is of the first importance, as the mental
faculties of these poor creatures can only be approached by
strengthening their bodies and enlivening their spirits. There
was but one child in bed. Every room was airy, orderly, and
cheerful; and everybody seemed devoted heart and soul to
the good work in hand.

That class of persons, unhappily always too large a one for
this world, who are so desperately careful to receive no uncomfortable emotions from sad realities or pictures of sad realities,
that they become the incarnation of the demon selfishness, and
are, by their sickly letting-alone, the most intolerably mischievous people in the community, will probably exclaim, " O,
but all this must be excessively painful!" To which we reply,
that such an affliction, considered by itself, is very painful; but
that, considered with a rational reference to the alleviations
and improvements of which it is plainly susceptible under such
treatment, it ought to become the reverse of painful, and
ought to do the visitor good. Madam, you are a lady of very
fine feelings; you are very easily shocked; you " can't bear"
a great deal that a higher wisdom than yours would seem to
have contemplated your bearing when your little place was
allotted to you on this ball. This idiot child of thirteen, sitting
in its little chair before the fire—as to its bodily growth, a
child of six; as to its mental development, nothing—is an
odious sight to you. This idiot old man of eight, with the
extraordinarily small head, the paralytic gestures, and the half-
palsied fore-finger, eternally shaking before his hatchet face as
he chatters and chatters, disturbs you very much. But, madam,
it were worth while to inquire while the brazen head is yet
saying unto you " Time is!" how much of the putting away of
these unfortunates in past years, and how much of the putting

away of many kinds of unfortunates at any time, may be attributable to that same refinement which cannot endure to be told about them. And, madam, if I may make so bold, I will venture to submit whether such delicate persons as your ladyship may not be laying up a rather considerable stock of responsibility; and you will excuse my saying that I would not have so sensitive a heart in my bosom for the dignity of the whole corporation.

When we had made the tour of the establishment and had looked at the whole prospect without and within, not forgetting the pet birds, or the idiot woman who was so busy in carrying the dinners about and so delighted to be useful, we came back to the schoolroom, and had, with the assistance of the master's fiddle, The sea, the sea, in chorus, and likewise All's well! In the course of which latter piece our friend the deep-voiced boy got a chance well known to, and appreciated by, the amateurs of the last generation. Finally, several smoking-hot legs of mutton were served, and grace was said, and all set down to dinner with a self-restraint and decorum perfectly wonderful.

There cannot be a doubt that these Institutions are deserving of all encouragement and support. They are truly humane, and they also afford opportunities for a most interesting study which may prove exceedingly beneficial to mankind. The causes of idiocy are as yet imperfectly understood. Little is known of the origin of the disorder, beyond the facts that idiocy is sometimes developed during the progress of dentition, and that it would seem to be generally associated with mental suffering, fright, or anxiety, or with a latent want of power, in the mother. These causes, however, are complex, and difficult to trace. A woman with two idiot children happened to mention that her husband was a drunkard, and ill-used her. It was then supposed that their condition might be referable to his degraded habits and his treatment of his wife; but, on pursuing the inquiry, it appeared that these two children had been born in his sober and kind days, and that the subsequent children of his later life were healthy and sensible.

The funds of the society who maintain Park House and Essex Hall, are devoted in aid of the maintenance and education of idiots, for whom the parents pay a certain annual sum. This is an admirable means of helping those who help themselves, and who, as the subjects of a peculiar misfortune, have a pressing claim on such aid. But we hope, through the instrumentality of these establishments, to see the day, before long, when the pauper idiot will be similarly provided for, at the public expense. Then may some future Mr. COLLIER—if our friend in his zeal and diligence be destined to have any successor—find in some future annotated copy of SHAKESPEARE the following happy emendation:

> " A tale
> Told by an idiot, full of sound instruction,
> Signifying something."

XXXII.

A LEGAL FICTION.

JULY 21, 1855.

THERE is no fiction more wildly extravagant than some of the fictions of English law. Perversions of truth and nature, more grotesque than the griffins and dragons of old story-books, have, for ages, been poured forth out of the tubular curls and hoary records of that rusty institution. Some have been slowly and painfully worn away from stony bigotry by the droppings of common sense; but others remain, which no power of ridicule, no amount of conviction, no strength of reasoning, can overcome. Amongst them, few represent injustice pushed to the extreme of absurdity more vividly than that legal fiction, an English wife.

Neither statute law, nor equity law, can be brought to acknowledge that the Source of our being and of our best affections lives and breathes in that part of Great Britain called England. Law is totally blind to her existence within that limit. There are English daughters and sisters, English aunts and nieces, English widows, and even English mistresses. There are also English mothers—they having been recently brought within the range of the Great Owl's vision—but there are no English wives. The proclaiming of bans in an English church is a proclamation of female outlawry: a due notice that the woman is to be banned from the protection of the law. When she marries, she dies; being handed over to be buried in her husband's arms, or pounded and pummelled into the grave *with* his arms. Not only she herself, but every semblance of property she possesses, is handed over to her lord; unless she has previously passed it away to somebody else. In the curious eye of the law (which does not see her, but sees her natural or acquired rights plainly enough to deprive her of them) a wife—like a convict—cannot have or hold one iota of anything that has value. Even the clothes she wears at the altar, the ornaments with which her friends have decked her, the ring the bridegroom pretends to give her, belong to him from that time forward. The law does not forbid him to cut off the hair of her head, and to sell it to adorn the heads of other women. Time was, when her very children might be torn from her breast, without any fault on her part. There is one instance in which a husband did actually seize and carry away an infant, as his wife sat nursing it in her own mother's house. Another, in which the husband being himself in prison for debt, gave his wife's legitimate child to the woman he cohabited with. A third (in which the parties were of high rank), where the husband deserted his wife; claimed the baby born after his desertion; and left her to learn its death from the newspapers. In all these cases, the claim of the father was held to be indisputable. There was no law then to help the mother, as there is no law now to help the wife. It is only recently that this has been altered, so as to give a wife a partial power over her children.

Having nothing for herself, the wife can leave nothing to others : consequently, if she make a will, it is void; and if she made a will before marriage, that ceremony annuls it. She cannot legally claim her own earnings, whether she weed potatoes, or paint pictures, or mangle linen, or educate other people's children, or make shirts, or sing operas, or knit purses, or write poems. Every farthing she gains belongs to her husband; and, if the employer pay her without his sanction, he can compel a second payment to himself. The English wife cannot make a contract with her husband binding upon him; her signature to any bill, warrant, quittance, or obligation, is so much wasted ink. Any person may publicly vilify, libel,

cheat her—do, in short, any injury to her, out of the reach of
the criminal law—with impunity, if her husband refuse to pros-
ecute the offender. She must not leave her husband's house
under the cruellest persecution, and he may force her out of
any other house with, if he pleases, the aid of the police. If
she be accused of infidelity, and her alleged lover be sued for
pecuniary damages—in accordance with a chivalrous custom
of this country—she is allowed no voice in the proceedings,
although it is her reputation that is always the point in discussion. She cannot claim support as a matter of personal
right from her husband; for, although, nominally, he is bound
to maintain her, he is not bound to *her* to do so; he is only
bound to the country; and to see that she does not cumber
the parish. If parochial relief be denied her, because she has
help from friends, or for other sufficient reason, he need not
contribute a sixpence towards her support, however large the
fortune she may have brought him, and which he enjoys.

The short cut to the Gordian knot of miseries, Divorce, is
impossible either to wife or husband, unless the wife or husband, yearning for that release from misery, can command
several thousand pounds to obtain an act of Parliament. Even
if there be riches, the wife cannot divorce the husband, except
under circumstances of extreme atrocity—only four cases of
the kind having been successful in a century—although the
husband can divorce the wife. In lower life a respectable
tradesman was tried for bigamy, and convicted. The second
wife deposed that he had courted her for six years; had no
money with her; on the contrary, supplied her with money
since his apprehension; had always been very kind; and that
they had a child of his residing with them. The undivorced
wife was living with an omnibus man, and had been in a lunatic asylum. Mr. Russell Gurney, in deciding the case, observed, with truth, that "this was one of those unfortunate
cases, in which, in the present state of the law, if a man was
not possessed of wealth, he had no power to remedy his situation:" and knowing (as we do know), that if, instead of plain
Mr. Gray and obscure Mary Adams, these people had been
Lord Grayton and Lady Mary Eve, we should simply have
had "Grayton's Divorce Bill" going quietly through the
House of Lords, we cannot wonder if murmurs arise against

this wonderful system of legislation. Another case: A Mrs. Adsett claimed support from her husband, a gunmaker. The husband coolly informed the magistrate that he could not support her ; on the contrary, for some months she had supported him ; but she might come back to him if she chose to do so. The wife replied that he had a mistress, and she had three children. The magistrates remarked that they were very sorry, but the wife must go to the home provided for her, mistress or no mistress: the law of England not making that a ground of special protection to virtuous wives.

If anything could add to the ridicule and absurdity of this part of the law, it is the fact that, although it is law in England, it is not law in Scotland. In that country divorce is obtainable by a simple process, and is open to the appeal of either party. A wife accused of infidelity defends herself when her presumed paramour may be prosecuted: her property is protected; alimony is allotted to her ; and her clothes and "paraphernalia" cannot be seized by the husband.

What golden magic is there in the silver Tweed that, dividing the Scottish from the English matron, throws over the one the shield of the law, and overlooks the other as a legal fiction? The opponents to easy and equal divorce declare, with trembling voice and prophetic solemnity, that an assimulation of the law would be productive of the grossest immorality. Therefore, England is virtuous, and " Caledonia, stern and wild," a nursery of vice. "Everybody who has studied that hot-blooded nation, knows that, solely in consequence of its protection of women, it is a land dedicated to Cupid. Statues of Venus are set up in all the principal squares of Edinburgh. The marriage-tie is a mere true lovers' knot. The ladies who present themselves at Holyrood are triumphant Messalinas. And, on the decks of the emigrant vessels which crowd the harbour of Leith, groups of melancholy cast-off husbands may be seen, bidding reproachful farewell to that inhospitable country where they only exist to be repudiated!"* The Scotch ladies will deny their guilt. They will deny that the upper classes of their nation have proved themselves more immoral than the upper classes in England. They will prove,

---

* Letter to the Queen on Lord Chancellor Cranworth's Marriage and Divorce Bill. By the Hon. Mrs. Norton.

that in five years, only twenty Scottish couples have availed themselves of the privilege of divorce. In vain. The Lord Chancellor and the House of Peers have pronounced that, to permit women in England to enjoy the privileges accorded to women in Scotland, would be productive of the grossest immorality, of multitudinous divorce, and, finally (the burden of every protectionist Solomon's song), the ruin of the country.

The spirited letter to the Queen which we have here quoted —written by a lady whose statements of her own case include almost every moral wrong and deprivation, suffered in her own person, that a wife can be subjected to—ought to give such a stimulus to public opinion and sense of right, as will hasten the slow operations of law-making.*

XXXIII.

PARIS IMPROVED.

NOVEMBER 17, 1855.

THE citizens of London and the citizens of Paris can be compared and contrasted in almost the same terms as the cities themselves: the one sombre, heavy, large, continually expanding, seldom changing; the other bright, compact, open, lively, and trying to improve. The pace of City improvement in London is that of the overgrown alderman, or of his own beloved turtle. It takes a lustre to pull down and rebuild a house or two in Chancery-lane, a decade to reconstruct Cannon-street, and a lifetime to open out an entirely new thoroughfare in Farringdon-street. In our youth, a nest of rookeries was demolished on the Clerkenwell side of Holbornbridge, under pretence of continuing Farringdon-street to be an open route for the then projected Northern and Western Railways: we are now more than middle-aged, our second son has attained his majority, and Farringdon-street still stands where it did. It is neither longer nor broader than it was when Fleet-ditch ceased to be navigable for merchant ships, and

---

* The law has since been amended. The English wife is now recognised as a legal entity, and none of the disasters foretold by the prophets have come to pass. The country is not ruined; and although much pent-up matrimonial immorality, and wrong have been brought to light, the new law has neither encouraged nor increased them.

when Fleet-market flourished above that covered estuary. It is not a foot nearer to Bath, nor Liverpool, nor Berwick-upon-Tweed. The loose bricks; the unconsidered tiles; the rusty, dinted pots and kettles; the rugged mounds of filth; the slimy holes and puddles; the jagged profiles of torn down tenements; the empty coal-cellars; the carcasses of dead cats; the bones of other domestic animals, whose death and skeletonhood date three reigns back; the "temporary" posts and barriers decayed with age; and the stenches from Cowcross; all continue to seethe and breed pestilence in the hideous gap dug, very many years ago, out of the centre of this metropolis. Yet, during the time, there has been activity of another kind close by. Hundreds of dinners have been eaten; thousands of turtles have been slain; oceans of cold punch have washed them down; millions of money in coal-dues and corn-dues have been squandered and diverted from their legal purposes, into ever-running channels of gormandising and jobbery. Further off in the world, a vast amount of work has been done, of the kind which our citizens have wretchedly shirked. Within the territories of the United States and Canada, whole cities have been built, peopled, and organized, of not much smaller extent than the City of London proper. Leagues of ground have been covered with habitations in other parts of the globe, and called St. Francisco, Melbourne, Port Phillip, what you will. While our wise men of the East having been haggling about one little piece of open ground at the base of St. Paul's Cathedral, a considerable portion of the capital of the great French empire has been not only razed, but rebuilt; rebuilt with a degree of solidity not easily conceivable in this our city of bricks and stucco; and in a style of splendour which would have startled even the architectural poet, the late Mr. John Martin.

But Emperors are not Aldermen, and, since the tradition of Cadmus and the real magic of the gold districts, we know of no instance of rapid building to equal the recent transformations in Paris. In the three years during which this short work has been mainly in action, there have been swept away a great many narrow crooked streets, which reeked with open streams of fœtid refuse; which were without side-pavements—foot-passengers, horses, vehicles and filth, all mixing there in

continual confusion—which were seldom lighted by the sun
by day, in consequence of the height and close proximity of the
opposite houses, and which were but dimly lighted by night,
with miserable lamps slung across the road; which were densely
thronged from the cellars to the roofs, by a variety of inmates
whose salient characteristic was wicked squalor; into which
prudent people never ventured after sunset, and where impru-
dent people were frequently robbed and sometimes qualified
by the *coup de clef*, or some other sudden passport, for the
Morgue; nests, in short, of disquiet, disease, and iniquity.
Not only have entire neighbourhoods such as these, been
swept away wholesale, but every part of the city has been
more or less improved in detail.   Streets of moderate width
have had their narrow entrances enlarged; sharp turns have
been squared, and corner houses made to form double, instead
of single angles—so that these widened cross-roads are never
crowded, and seldom obstructed; projecting houses have been
forced back into line with the rest; convenient thoroughfares have been opened through blind blocks of buildings
which separate one quarter from another.   Yet, utility was
not the sole motive power which has executed these improvements.   The love of ornament and a passion for display,
always attributed to the French, have been brilliantly and
beautifully manifested; especially in the Rue de Rivoli and
the Boulevard de Sébastopol.   But above these, common
sense (the most uncommon sense known) proclaims itself from
every improved street and altered house.   An English architect, or a member of the City Improvements Committee with
any conscience or any observation, cannot walk through Paris
without feeling ashamed and humiliated.

"But, sir, we live in a free country: in a country where
private property is respected and private right a palladium.
France, sir, is a despotic country.   There, your house is not
your castle: you may have it pulled down about your ears at
a moment's notice, merely to promote public convenience.
Our government cannot, with one stroke of a pen or after a
one-sided discussion with civic authorities, depopulate a neighbourhood to have it built up again.   *We* must wait until capital has accumulated from the proper sources; until leases have
fallen in, and ground-landlords fallen out; until paving-boards

have been conciliated, and conflicting commissioners of sewers
are agreed; until acts of Parliament are battled through both
Houses, surveyors consulted, fees guaranteed to high-minded
architects, building contracts—wickedly paraphrased by the
vulgar as 'jobs'—solemnly sealed and legalised. Sir, the
boasted Parisian improvements have been made, I will venture
to say, at the single will of the Emperor, and against the several wills of thousands of ousted tenants and ruined landlords;
for despotism can do in ten minutes, what sober, constitutional
legality is obliged to be busy ten years about."

So says the honourable Deputy for the ward of St. Vitus's
Backlane; but that eminent and respected public nuisance is
in error. He will perhaps be surprised to hear, that not a jot
of private right was invaded in Paris; that every stone which
formerly stood on the area of improvement was paid full value
for, before a slate was removed or a pickaxe lifted; that every
owner and occupier was fairly compensated, not only for loss
and removal of property, but for damage done to his business—
compensated, too, not with the off-hand tyranny of "take that
or none;" but, in case of dispute, by juries selected from his
own class. If the worthy St. Vitus's Deputy could divest
himself of his London Corporation prejudices, and could inquire into the subject, he would perceive that nearly every
expedient, every administrative arrangement, every mode of
negotiation and adjustment between the authorities of the
city of Paris and the imperial government, is applicable to
the speedy improvement of his own or any other pent-up,
ill-planned, ill-governed city in these liberally governed dominions.

The nucleus of the Paris improvements is the Hotel de
Ville. Around it the first great shattering of vile streets took
place; and, in it, are performed the administrative and finan-
cial operations by which the wholesale changes are set in motion. The chief municipal authorities do all their work in this
gorgeous Guildhall, partly of their own free inspirations and
will, and partly under the direction of government. There,
the plans for changing some of the worst parts of the capital into palatial habitations are devised, deliberated on, and
adopted; thence, come out the loans for carrying on the work,
which capitalists eagerly "take up;" and there the work is

paid for when it is finished. As, however, it is thought possible that a body of gentlemen of equal status to the aldermen and common-councilmen of London, are not solely sufficient for deciding upon works of such magnitude, their proceedings have to be ratified by the *conseil des bâtiments civils*, or imperial board of works, a committee, composed of five of the most eminent French architects and eight non-professional colleagues, whose business is to report upon all plans respecting public structures. The sanction and co-operation of the minister of finance is also necessary to the monetary operations; because, as the construction of several public offices and other public works is included, a certain quota of expense is paid out of the imperial treasury. It must not be supposed that these and other excellent regulations were framed to direct this single outburst of architectural renovation; they are the law of the land, made and provided for all such cases, by the astonishingly far-seeing and comprehensive Code Napoléon—a code which Britain, though she *did* rise out of the azure main to the singing of Guardian Angels, has, in some respects, cause to envy.

It was originally intended that the vast alterations to be made in the map of Paris should occupy fifteen years; but the present Emperor had his reasons for ordering that they should be finished in five years; so that a considerable amount of capital had to be raised in a very short time. Fortunately the task of raising it was not difficult; for, as municipal tomfoolery and gluttony, are not the business of the Hôtel de Ville, a fund, applicable to the work, already existed in its coffers amounting to about sixty millions of francs. The credit of a corporation so flushed with ready money, is in itself a bank; and, when more money was wanted, an additional sum of fifty millions of francs was eagerly lent by capitalists. No sooner are proposals for a loan announced than the scrip rises to a high premium, and the competition for it is so strong, that ten millions more francs have been raised by lottery, upon the excess in premiums alone. Five millions of pounds sterling have therefore been raised since the year eighteen hundred and fifty-two, for buying up property to improve Paris, besides vast sums realised by old building materials and fittings. Two years more of well-spent and costly activity have yet to elapse, before the contemplated regeneration will be complete.

The doomed quarters having been marked out, notices to quit are served upon the occupiers. The bargain with each proprietor differs little, in the first instance, from that entered into between an ordinary buyer and seller. The municipality is willing to give so much; the vendor demands so much; if terms cannot at once be arranged, the dispute is referred to a compensation jury, composed of members of the council-general of the department of the Seine. Upon the whole, our inquiries led to the belief that the sums awarded are fair. Some cases of underpayment and hardship could, of course, be adduced on the one side, as well as instances of exorbitant demand on the other. There are, indeed, whispers, of tradesmen living in the line of projected improvement, who made out beforehand on their books, enormous transactions which only existed in their books, to mystify the jurors into extravagant payment for loss of trade by forced removal. Even lodgers are compensated by *indemnités locatives* according to the value of their holdings. Where one family in London is put to the rout by the demolition of a house, from four to five families are ejected in Paris, where the inhabitants are nearly all lodgers; each house being separated into tenements; and each floor containing a complete and distinct household.* The consequence of the sudden sweeping away of inhabitants, caused shelter to become uncommonly scarce. Enormous rents were, for a time, demanded, even for the merest garrets and the dampest cellars; and the poorer and industrious classes suffered intensely. Ejected families, in a most piteous plight, were seen in the streets, following the tumbrils or handcarts in which their household appliances were piled, unable to find a roof to cover them. Many were obliged to remain out of doors, in the midst of frost and snow, until the government caused certain waste places to be hutted, in which they gave the houseless shelter, free of charge. After a time, new houses were ready, and these inconveniences disappeared.

There are, it must be remarked, some circumstances which render these sudden changes in Paris much more easy than in

* In eighteen hundred and fifty-one, according to the Census, the average number of individuals living in each house in Paris was twenty-six. In eighteen hundred and seventeen the average was twenty-four inmates per house.

London. Hitherto, underground works have not cost much time there; and—although the ancient fosses surrounding the garrison were converted at an early period into main sewers, and a great straight sewer, running east and west under the city, was constructed in thirteen hundred and seventy—yet few of the houses are drained into them to this day. But, by a decree of the sixth of December, eighteen hundred and fifty-three, a system of tubular drainage into them, and into a new sewer running parallel to the Seine, on the south side, was established; ten years being allowed to the proprietors of house-property to cause the necessary connexion to be made. The main sewers will be eventually discharged into the Seine at a few miles below Paris; but, so far above tidal influence, that the sewage will be carried away. Not all the grand new streets and beautiful houses, nor the noble monuments and public buildings, will improve Paris so thoroughly as this measure. The abolition of cesspools centuries old, with which its foundations are honeycombed, and of the pestiferous *voiries* of Montfaucon and Bondy into which they have for ages been emptied, will increase the salubrity of the city beyond all calculation.

The ground cleared, at the expense already indicated, had to be covered; and the four thousand master builders who habitually find business in Paris—though taking upon themselves a fair share of such work as adding some half mile to the arcaded Rue de Rivoli, already one of the grandest streets in Europe—were not able to provide capital for realising all the gigantic projects demonstrated in the plans held out on paper. The universal remedy in such a case, a joint-stock company, instantly sprang into existence; and the covering of those acres of rugged waste known as the Place de Carrousel—with its noble triumphal arch and its tall, grim coffee-shop that stood for many years a solitary and shaky spectre of the past; with its second-hand book, curiosity, and stuffed-bird stalls; with its clamorous shoe-cleaners and politely importunate dealers in second-hand umbrellas, canes, and catalogues of the picture gallery—has been gorgeously accomplished by the Société des Immeubles de Rivoli assisted by the funds of the Société de Crédit Mobilier. The palace of the Louvre and the palace of the Tuileries—recently not much less than a quarter of a mile

apart—are now joined by galleries and arcades of great architectural beauty set with gateways and pavilions adorned with
caryatides and allegorical groups of the most elaborate design
and execution. The new edifices thus enclosing the Place de
Carrousel, comprise two inner squares, immense barracks, public offices, an extensive riding-school, stables, and great additions to the Tuileries palace itself. The same company have
also built, close by, the largest hotel in Europe. The Hôtel
du Louvre, standing opposite to the north face of these structures, in the Rue de Rivoli, covers more than an English acre
and a half of ground. It has eight hundred rooms; and presents as splendid a specimen of interior decoration and fur-
nishing as is known to exist. Four years ago, when the Place
de Carrousel was a void, this magnificent traveller's rest was
the site of several back streets.

It is needless to detail all that the Société des Immeubles de
Rivoli has effected; and, to those readers not thoroughly acquainted with Paris as it stood in eighteen hundred and fifty-
one, a description of the other improvements would be tedious. What has already been said will give a faint idea of the
power of capital and skill when energetically directed. What
capital, without well-directed skill, can effect they know pretty
well from experience at home. The architectural and struc-
tural achievements of Paris are on a much larger scale than
those of our Houses of Parliament, for instance, yet have taken
in proportion to the extent of the spaces covered, not a hundredth—perhaps (for we do not yet see the end of Westmin-
.ster Palace looming in the distance) not a thousandth part of
the time.

We must repeat, however, that building of the first class is
naturally an easier operation in France than in England. The
neighbourhood of Paris, the banks of the Loire, and other
large districts, abound with a soft, tractable stone of dazzling
whiteness, which cuts with a little more difficulty than wood;
hardening with age and exposure. Squared into cubes, and
moved with ease from its lightness, this material enables the
French mason to pile up his walls in half the time, and
with three times the solidity, that an English bricklayer can
raise his; the neatness and beauty of the work being necessarily very much greater. Even rough walls, built with small

unhewn stone (*limousinage*), are more rapidly raised than brick walls, and are often faced and dressed with the softer hewn stone. The new streets abound with the richest sculptured ornament; and this is chiefly executed after the shell has been run up: not delayed piecemeal in the sculptor's shed before being set in.

But, evil was foreseen in these rapid building performances themselves. Philosophers of the St. Vitus's Backlane school shrugged their shoulders, and predicted that the concentration of a prodigious number of workmen whose employment could last for only a certain time, would be a huge foundation for disturbance, when the work was done and the workmen discharged. These prophets knew nothing about the character and circumstances of the French mason and stone cutter; necessarily the largest body of operatives massed together in the capital. They had not read M. le Play's account of him in his prodigious (but not quite trustworthy) Monography of the Workmen of Europe. This author declares that the masons are, or have been—for they are deteriorating, he says, —models of prudence and sobriety. They travel up from La Creuse or La Haute Vienne, as the Irish haymaker visits England in summer, during la belle saison, and return to their homes when frost forbids work. There are at present about a hundred and fifty thousand stone-cutters and stone-setters in Paris, working with unflagging zeal, to earn from two francs and a half to five francs a day; to live after so much only of the communist principle as promotes economy; and to turn their faces finally homeward with light hearts and heavy purses after they have converted Paris into a stone and sculptured paradise. The masons never marry a Parisienne, and seldom contract unlawful unions. They live in large parties of twenty or thirty, called chambrées, in one room, for about thirty-eight francs each a month for board and lodging; and soon save enough money to marry a woman of their own country: and to buy a house, land, and cows. They then stay at home, and send their sons as emigrant masons to Paris in their stead. The stone-cutters are in two factions, or societies; one called the Children of Solomon; the other, the Children of Maître Jacques. These work together well enough, but do not live in anything like harmony. Whether the four hundred thou-

sand persons now engaged in the remaining branches of building and decorating, will devote their attention to barricades
by-and-by, becomes very doubtful when we know, that the ordinary absorption of labour in all the various building trades,
including masonry, usually keeps forty thousand operatives out
of mischief, in Paris alone.

We have said that the best kind of building is rapidly
accomplished in France; and only the best kind of building is, as a rule, tolerated. There, a house is not a lath and
plaster, or a brick-thick, shell. The self-contained pride of
being a respectable housekeeper (that is, very often, of inhab-
iting an expensive kennel "without lodgers," where every
sound in the kennels right and left is distinctly audible) does
not exist. The French, like the Scotch, live one above another,
under the same roof, in the separate floors of large houses;
thus economising space and money. In the principal streets,
the ground floor consists of a shop; then comes a mezzanine
floor, or entresol; then a suit of rooms, all on the same level,
which includes every convenience for a family; and so up and
up, to the highest floor. This last is usually divided into two
sets of apartments, for residents of humble means. Below, at
the end of a pretty tesselated passage beside the shop, there
is, at the foot of the stairs, a snug little glass-case or lodge,
Looking in, you will usually see a woman in a clean cap, knitting a stocking; a gilt pendule is certain to be ticking on the
chimney-piece; and a clean bed ensconced in an alcove. This
woman's husband—always dressed, in the morning, in a cap
and a coarse green apron—is one of the trustworthy and ser-
viceable class of domestic hall-keepers, or porters, for which
Paris is remarkable. He polishes the stairs, polishes the banisters, polishes everything he can lay his hands upon, and has
generally polished his own manners too. He is shrewd, steady,
observant, and can keep his own counsel withal. Every floor
pays him a small, fixed, monthly stipend; and he is the guardian genius of the whole house. You ask his wife on which floor
your friend lives, and she, the portress on duty, takes all sorts
of pains to make you understand her directions, if she sees
there be any dulness in your foreign apprehension. You ascend a flight of oak stairs (carefully, for the porter-husband
has polished every grain of the wood) by the help of a ban-

ister supported by bronzed and gilt rails.   Your friend's door
opened, admits you to a little hall, in which, when it is shut
after you, you feel as much isolated from the world as if you
were standing on the mat of the private residence of the honourable Deputy of St. Vitus's Backlane, near Camberwell-
green.   Little drawing-room, dining-room, study, nursery,
bedrooms, kitchen (and a backstair leading to it, for servants
and tradesmen), all furnished with an amount of sensible taste,
highly suggestive to all the Deputies in all Camberwell.   And
all—horrid idea!—over a shop.   Yet your friend may be an
English baronet or a foreign count, with thousands a year,
and with some capital horses in a stable close by.   Does Monsieur Viteplume, chef de Bureau at the office of the Minister
of the Interior, who lives in the floor above, or Madame
Bonnebonnet, the court milliner, who lives over him, or M.
Burin, the engraver, who resides nearer heaven by the alti-
tude of one story, or Jules Cordon, the journeyman boot-
maker, or Mademoiselle Fleurschâteau, who each inhabit the
attic apartments—ever interfere with the rich baronet or
with one another?   Never.   When the cobbler meets the
baronet or the government official, or madame or mademoiselle, on the stairs, he claims them as neighbours only by a
bow, and a "bon jour."

Even in the more private streets, few people occupy a whole
house.   There is generally a court-yard surrounded by apartments, with one common entrance.   Sometimes, houses are
clustered together round a larger court-yard, and called a cité.
In the poorer quarters, some of these cités swarmed to a
degree prejudicial to health; but their populations are now
distributed.

This mode of residence of course necessitates large houses.
There are no Prospect-places, Adeliza-terraces, or Paradise-
rows in Paris: no small, mean, slightly-built streets; but every
house is of sufficient dimensions to admit of architectural
display.   Even in the humblest parts of the town the houses
are lofty and substantial.

When the stipulated five years shall have elapsed, and the
contemplated improvements shall be completed, Paris will be
a marvel of improvement.   And London?   London will go
on talking for and against improvement for another half-

century or so, and will remain, as to its general ugliness, pretty much what it has been for the last ten or a dozen years. The Hôtel de Ville in Paris, and the Guildhall in London, are mightily expressive, in their vast differences, of the intelligence and spirit of the public bodies they represent. But then the corporation of Paris really expresses Paris itself, while the corporation of London expresses nothing but obsolete pretences.

XXXIV.

THE NINTH OF JUNE.

IN TEN CHAPTERS. CHAPTER THE FIRST.

JUNE 7, 1856.

IT amounted to an expostulation. A close four-wheeler for a gentleman like me, come down to Matlock Bath for the benefit of his health? Why, what fresh air could be got in a shut-up trap like that, he should like to know. No, no; a canter was the thing to suit my complaint; a canter on his old roan, that had carried—ay, and cured—many a gentleman that looked much more white about the gills than I did. She wasn't young, to be sure; but game as a three-year old, and uncommon quiet to drive *or* ride. The country for miles round was, as everybody knew, a sight of itself, and who could see it in a stifling fly?

To give full vent to his feelings, the job-master released the buttons from the gaping button-holes of his box-coat, and peeled off a fold or two of his bulbous cravat. I had not seen the whole of his face; for, as he had never looked up, I could only catch occasional glimpses of his forehead, as he smoothed down his hair with the flat of one hand, the rest of his features receding to a perspective of chin that lost itself on the depths of loosened neckcloth. He spoke very earnestly—not to me—but into his hat; which he held close under his mouth that it might catch every word as it dropped.

"But I am not a good horseman," I said, letting down my deficiencies in that respect as gently as possible. I had never mounted a horse above twenty times in my life, and had tumbled off twice.

"That won't matter," he replied. "I don't like to brag,"
he said, making circles on the crown of his hat with his fore-
finger; "but, if anybody can show a gentleman how to ride,
I can. When I left the army (I was in the Twelfth Hussars)
I was riding-master to Bokicker's riding-school at Brighton,
till I found an opening down here and took to the fly and job
trade." Looking up and taking a furtive, and I hope accurate, inspection of my figure, he added, "You're just the build
for horse-back, you are; and how you've kept yourself out of
the saddle all these years, is a wonder. But it's never too
late to begin." In answer to a word of mine about the danger
of the experiment, he said, "Look'ee here, sir—I'll ride the
grey pony that I let with the phaeton to ladies for paying
visits, and'll go with you. You shall mount the old mare;
and if she don't take you along as easy as a Bath-chair, my
name isn't Tom Hockle."

"I may depend upon your word that the creature has no
tricks?"

"Bless you, sir!" Mr. Hockle replied, "you might ride her
with a thread of tailor's twist."

During this conversation in the front parlour of my lodging
on the Museum Parade, I got the notion that the Flyman was
a full bodied person, up in years; for I had not noticed that
his box-coat was too big for him, and that the tops of his
boots were not particularly well filled out. When, therefore,
I entered his stable-yard, and beheld a well-knit, middle-aged
man in a close short-tailed under-coat, drawing on a pair of
doeskin gloves, a switch-whip under his arm, his top-boots
pulled neatly up over his leathers, his hat jauntily cocked to
one side, and a lock of hair combed sprucely forward to the
edge of each eye, I attributed the illusion respecting him to
my timorous sensations on seeing the mare and pony ready
saddled and bridled, and overhearing him tell his men (adroitly
speaking with the near side of his mouth, without shaking a
sprig of the woodbine that sprouted out from the off side) "to
take up another link of old Rufa's curb, in case she offered to
bolt with the gent." But, having shut my eyes and desperately
mounted without detecting the trace of a smile on the coun-
nances of either of the spectators, my senses were sufficiently
restored to perceive that the Flyman and the Riding-master

was the same person, wholly changed in appearance by change of dress.

As we paced along, side by side—he on his low pony, I on the tall mare—past the High Tor, over Matlock-bridge, and round the Church Rocks, Mr. Hockle alternated his instructions in riding with descriptions of the scenery. "He was very fond of this country," he said, "for he was born at Crookston-Withers; and, having left home when a lad, only lately returned to the neighbourhood. The absence had made him like it all the more. That's Crookston Hall!" he said, pointing with his whip. "Sit more upright, sir!"

"You mean the stiff, ugly, red-brick house with stone dressings?" I asked, angry with the square edifice that obtruded itself, a prim impertinence, in the open and varied landscape.

"Well, I can't say much for the house," was the answer, "but it stands—Sink your heels, sir!—it stands on the prettiest spot hereabouts. We shall skirt the grounds presently. Out of the drawing-room window, you can see straight over the flower-garden, into this dingle. Pull up, sir—gradually; don't jerk her, for she's apt to rear."

We had arrived on the rising ground beside Crookston Hall, and stopped to look between the trees over the shrubs and saplings, into a trough-like dell that lay between the garden of Crookston Hall and the Derwent, smoothly curved with the brightest and greenest grass. From each side shot up straight and stately firs tipped with evergreen foliage.

"You see that oak on the other bank, where the beeches are?"

After some little difficulty, I made it out.

"Well," continued the Flyman, "when I was a youngster, I went up that tree once too often."

"Birds'-nesting?"

"No, I had a right to be there; but I overheard things that have lasted me for life. Turn in your knees, sir!" We were ambling along again.

"Family secrets, perhaps," I hazarded, to take off Mr. Hockle's attention from the awkward figure I was making.

"Well, perhaps they were."

After some persuasion, Mr. Hockle consented to gratify my curiosity.

"You see I was stable-boy at the Hall at first; afterwards, Mr. George Dornley, the eldest son, took me to be his groom. That was in the old Squire's time. Ah! things were very different then to what they are now. No flint-skinning; no selling of skim-milk, and cabbages, and fruit.—Shorten the right hand. bridle! You've drawn the snaffle right out of her mouth on t'other side!—No hounding of beggars; no stopping up of footpaths across the park; lots of horses in the stable; and some sort of jollification always going on in the house.—You'll do no good unless you sink your heels!"

"The present proprietor is not very liberal then?" I said.

"Liberal?" Mr. Hockle looked up at me quick and savage, as if I were the miser he had in his mind. "Liberal! I should say not. A cold-blooded, close-fisted, stingy tyke, with only one horse in his stable; a mangy gelding, as lank as a hound, only not half so well fed.—Turn in your knees more, and keep your elbows closer to your side!"

"But what about the tree?" We were now ambling under the deep shadows of Arch-lane.

"Well, I'll tell you." Mr. Hockle looked very serious.

"It's more than a few years ago now. There was a good deal of distress about that time. Oats was sixty shillings a quarter: work was scarce, and too many to do what little there was; so there was rioting and rick-burning; though not half so much as the government and the government spies made out. The gentry were dead frightened of being burned in their beds.—Sit more over your legs!—Yet the good jolly old Squire went on just the same. Although the common people grumbled at the extravagance of the rich, never thinking how good it was for trade, he did not bate a single hunt-breakfast, or dinner, or jollification of any sort; and when his second son (he had two, George and Calder) was going to be married, there never had been such goings on. I heard tell, at the time, that that wedding cost the old man more than a thousand pound. Everybody, high and low, rich and poor, was invited; the dingle was half covered with tents for stabling, to accommodate the visitors' cattle; and there was a marquee on the lawn, because the wedding breakfast had to be set out in the regular ball-room: four men from London were had down to cook, and two to let off fireworks; all the labourers in the parish had a day's pay; and they and their wives and young 'uns had as much beef and beer as they could eat and drink. If the rioters themselves had come that way, I do believe the old Squire would have found feed and liquor for every one of 'em.—Don't hang on her bit so; give and take!"

"But you are a long while getting up that tree," I remarked, as a diversion.

"All in good time. You see the bride was a heiress, and there was a queer story about her and my master. The old Squire had, once, set his heart upon Master George having her; he being the heir to Crookston. And Master George jilted her—he was wrong, I own; but he was my gov'ner, and a better master never sat in pig-skin. You should have seen how *he* sat a horse!" As Mr. Hockle emphasised this expression, he turned a glance at me out of the corner of his eye that had, I thought, a dash of contempt in it. "Well," he continued, "it was a settled thing, though *I* never thought it would come to anything; for it was a precious lazy pace we went at, whenever we were bound for Stonard Abbey (it lies behind us; about two miles); and, when we got there, Mr. George never kept me long a leading the horses about; but back he came very soon, and sprang into the saddle smiling because the visit was over, and always bucketed off back, at a hand gallop. I am sure courting at the Abbey must have been a cold job for him; for nobody—not even Miss Stonard, that I saw—ever came to the door, to wave him a good-by as he mounted. Sometimes we met Mr. Calder on his iron-grey, going to where we had come from: that was when we came home over the moor a mile or two round, through the village. There, I always had a long waiting job; for Mr. George never called on Mrs. Levine without having a long spell of talk with her and her daughter.—Give her her head more. Don't bore at her so!—Mrs. Levine was the widow of the last Crookston-Withers rector, and lived in a cottage at one corner of the churchyard: Corner Cottage they call it."

"Was this Miss Stonard of the Abbey handsome?" I asked.

"She wasn't bad-looking," Mr. Hockle replied. "She had good clean limbs; and her short petticoats (no offence meant) showed 'em. She was tall—seventeen hands I should say—and wore her hair cropped and curled all round: for docking

17

was quite the go for manes as well as tails at that time. She had good points in her face, too. Bright black eyes, white skin, a straight nose, broad nostrils, and wide jowls."

"Jowls, Mr. Hockle?"

"Well, jaws then—all good points whether in a horse or a woman, mind you. But I didn't like her countenance. Her eyes were too clear and cold for my money. She could look at you as hard as nails, and petrify you a'most.—That's better! only close your fingers tighter upon the reins, and make a good fist of 'em!—Mr. George and his father never got on well together. The old Squire was high Tory, and his son was all for the rights of the people, and *would* wear a white hat (regular Radical, you know), and would make speeches at torchlight meetings, that his brother Calder, and his father, and Sir Bayle Stonard called treasonable. Well, one day he had been letting out furiously at a great meeting at Wallsend, about the rascally goings on of the government, and about the nobs calling the people, ' A swinish multitude :' so, when he came back to Crookston Hall there was terrible high words between him and his father. They got from politics to matrimony; till at last, Mr. George, in a passion, told the old gent that when he married, he would marry to please himself, and that it didn't please him to marry Miss Stonard. The old man burst out of the room in a tremendous rage, nearly broke a blood-vessel in putting on his boots, and galloped over to the Abbey, like split.—Shake her bridle, and wake her up a bit, sir! She is getting lazy.—As for Mr. George, he went to London on Parliament business, and I went with him."

"But we are still a long way from the tree."

"Not so far as you think," continued Mr. Hockle. "To the old Squire's astonishment, things were taken very coolly at Stonard Abbey; and it was settled, after a while, that George should be cut by his father; and that the young lady —nothing loth, they used to say—should take up with t'other brother. They were better matched; for their sly determined tempers suited one another; and she and Mr. George, with his straightforward, open, honest disposition, would never have run in a curricle together. However, before the wedding-day, and just before Mr. George went abroad, there was a reconciliation, and he came home, and brought me with him. Then came the wonderful preparations. All of us had been up for two nights; and, the evening before the wedding, I was helping to put up the last stable tent in the dingle, when one of the men asked me to get into the oak I showed you, with a line that was to steady the centre tent-pole. I was to hold it there till he told me to fasten it; but I was so dead beat, that I hardly had strength. However, I scrambled up by the garden-seat, and perched myself comfortably upon the lowermost branch, with my back against the trunk. If you'll believe me, I fell fast asleep in no time, with the line in my hand.

"I don't know whether I was left there for a lark, or whether I was forgot; but it was staring moonlight when I woke. I heard voices close under me: one was my master's. There he sat upon the garden-seat that went round the trunk of the tree, pressing something taper and white in his arm; and there was an uncommon pretty little hand clasping his shoulder. I can remember every word they spoke as well as if I was hearing them now."

"You had reason to remember, perhaps," I remarked.

"You'll see. The little hand pressed itself tighter and tighter, and the little arm trembled a good deal. The full moon made it light as day. I could see tears falling upon Mr. George's shoulder. He asked if she was so frightened and sad on account of ——, and he whispered something in her ear; but she turned away, letting the tears drop into her lap, and said No; she could afford to be blamed and gossiped about, and even persecuted, without a murmur; for she felt within her that both of them had no guilt to answer for. No; it was not that. She was frightened about him; and she looked piteously into Mr. George's face. He tried to laugh her out of her fears, and spoke of everything coming right by his next birthday, the ninth of June, when, please God, he should return from Italy. After a minute or two, she said she dreaded what might happen between then, and that day. She knew what the bride was; she knew that she would do anything for spite; and it was not in her nature to forgive him for refusing to marry her. 'Then,' and she trembled worse than ever, 'when she finds out who her rival has been, she will not rest until she has ruined us both.' Mr. George said he thought it was his brother who would be most to be feared, when he and all the world came to know—here he whispered again, and she looked down once more; but there were no tears this time. He kissed her; and she, coaxing and caressing him, entreated him not to go to any more dangerous political meetings. She was proud of his fame, and loved him with all her heart because he manfully helped in the cause of the poor man; but her mother had told her, over and over again, that Mr. Calder, in his cold-hearted way, was trying to make the old Squire believe that he would come to be hanged, and that he was already an outcast from what they called society. For the old Squire often dropped in at Corner Cottage to have a gossip with her mother, when she was able to sit up.

"I had been in the tree for so many hours, that at last I got cramped with the cold, and tried to alter my position. Forgetting I had the cord in my hand, I let the end of it fall. It came right down upon Mr. George's hat. They both started up; he still holding the young lady round the waist, to protect her. Of course I got down.

"'You rascal, you have been listening!' he said.

"I owned I had.

"'Who set you to be a spy upon me?' he halloed out. 'Don't you eat my bread? Who set you to do this?' He was very quick-tempered, Mr. George was.

"I told him nobody had set me on. I told him how it happened. I told him I could not help hearing what I had heard; but I told him, too, that he had been a good master to me, and that all that I could understand of what I had heard I would solemnly swear should never pass my lips to any living soul. I meant what I said, and said it as if I meant it, The young lady looked at me all the time, and took my part, and whispered, in a low, tender voice, 'I think you may trust him;' and she left off struggling out of his arms, as if she was not afraid of my knowing everything that there was between them. I shall never forget her—never!"

Here the ex-groom fell into a reverie and walked his pony on in silence for several minutes; breaking, occasionally, into a market trot, to keep up with the striding mare. Lost in the contemplation of the leading remembrance of his early life, he had, for the last half-hour, allowed me to commit every sort of equestrian misdemeanour; until, at last, something dreadful

he caught me doing, with my toes and knees, awakened him
to a sense of duty; and, after mildly rebuking me, proposed a
canter. "Shorten your left curb bridle, and give her a touch
with your left heel," he said. "There! she springs off into a
canter as easy as a rocking-horse; doesn't she?"

We had, by this time, turned our face homeward; having
skirted the Moor, and reached Crookston-Withers, after a
good ten-mile circuit. I asked my excellent reminiscent to
show me the cottage at which his master used to keep him
waiting so long after his visits to Stonard Abbey.

"You're right!" he remarked, looking up at me from under
his hat. "The young lady under the tree, with my master,
was Miss Levine. That's Corner Cottage!"

He pointed to an ivy-grown cottage at the junction of three
roads; the main road from Matlock and Nottingham coming
straight up to it, and then branching off under its triangular
garden; the right branch leading past Stonard Abbey over
the Moor. A pretty hatch covered with a penthouse opened,
through the churchyard, to the church; which was only separated from the cottage by the left-hand road.

"But you have not told me how the younger Mr. Calder's
wedding went off," I remarked, as we were about to ascend
the Crookston side of Linney Hill.

Mr. Hockle's answer was: "Keep her bit level in her
mouth, sink your heels, and keep the stirrup-irons under the
joints of your feet."

"But about the wedding?"

"Well, it was the grandest thing ever seen in this county:
eighty horsemen and horsewomen, besides carriages. The
ball and fireworks at night were wonderful. As for the sup——
Well sat, sir!"

It was a miracle that I had not tumbled off; for old Rufa,
without the faintest warning, shied right across the road, a
man on horseback having suddenly leaped, through a gap in
the hedge, close before her nose. The unexpected horseman
trotted up the hill a few paces; then turned, and slowly came
back. His nag was lean and meagre; but well-grown and
strong-limbed. The rider sat bolt upright. His hat intensely
brushed, and narrow-brimmed; his trousers pulled tightly
down with a thin strap; his straight, brown surtout, buttoned

to the throat; his neat collar-band turned over evenly all round the cravat, gave to his figure a slim and youthful appearance. But, as he approached, I perceived, by the strong furrows in his face, that he was much above the middle age.

"What is your friend?" I asked, when he had ridden out of hearing. "A Jesuit or a horse-dealer?"

I dare not repeat the expletive with which my instructor prefaced his information. "What is he? He is, or pretends to be, the Squire of Crookston." Hockle switched his whip over his poney's mane, savagely, as if he were cutting down imaginary enemies with a broad-sword. Pulling his hat over his brow, he said, "Let us push on. I daren't think of the villain!"

We trotted into Mr. Hockle's yard in silence; for, from that moment, no expostulation, no entreaty, could induce him to utter one syllable in continuation of the story. At last he said, musingly:

"No, no. I've told you quite enough of other people's secrets: for," he continued, as we dismounted, looking me almost sternly in the face, "we're a'most strangers, as yet."

"Not to remain strangers long, I hope, Mr. Hockle. Give me another call." I stalked stiffly and painfully away, to my lodging.

CHAPTER THE SECOND.

GENTLEMEN, even in good health, who are as little used to the saddle as I am, will readily understand why I was unable to take exercise of any sort next day. About noon, the tedium of my imprisonment was relieved by Mr. Hockle, who came to give the homœopathic advice of curing my complaint with its cause, by taking another ride with him. I declined very decidedly.

" The fact is, sir," he said, abruptly, and without any sort of context, as he stepped up close to the sofa I was lying upon, " when things were as bad with him as they could be——"

" With whom?"

" With my master, Mr. George Dornley," he answered.

" Oh, then you *will* do me the favour of finishing the story!" I interrupted.

" Yes, I will," he rejoined, frankly. " There are some people we draw to at first sight, and there are some people we want to run away from at first sight. Well, you put me a good deal in mind of Mr. George, and I feel somehow a sort of call for to let you know all about him."

" Pray sit down," I said.

The accomplished rider did sit down (how I envied him !). He sat on the edge of the chair, with his hand placed on a bundle of papers tied up in a pocket-handkerchief, to secure it upon his knee. " When things were as bad with him as they could be," he added, " he gave me these papers. They will tell you the rest of the story better than I can."

Mr. Hockle having left me in solemn charge of the bundle, took his leave.

I never robbed a house or poached over a manor; but I think my conscience, when I opened the first letter in the bundle, acquainted me with some of a rogue's sensations. However, curiosity and Mr. Hockle's leave and license prevailed; and I boldly plunged into the inmost recesses of private affairs which I had no earthly right to know.

I was naturally first attracted to a packet of letters in a lady's hand. They were all deeply bordered with black; all addressed to George Dornley, Esq.; and all, except two, were covered with foreign post-marks. They were love-letters; and I deferred exploring a daily newspaper, published in November, eighteen hundred and seventeen and the other epistles— some in the cramped hand of a lawyer—to devour the lady's letters first. Having arranged them according to date, I found the first was written about a month after the interview described by Mr. Hockle in the dingle. It seems to have found young Dr. Dornley at Florence, and announced the unexpected demise of the writer's mother in terms of passionate grief. There was a long interval between that and the others; which were all directed to various places on the road from Florence to England, down to the last letter, sent to the Royal George, Nottingham, " to be left till called for." The second letter ran thus:

" The shock is passing away; for I feel it a duty to you, my dearest, to master my grief. I shut out the past. I look to the future. Only one little month, and then what a change! More happiness than I shall be able to bear! My whole life seems to flow in small slow drops into the current of time which glides towards the ninth of June. Yes, you must not scold me, as you did in your last dear letter, for being too excitable; nor hint that I do not try all my might to command myself; for I have been as calm and as *sane* one day with another as Miss Pim our Quaker postmistress is. But I must describe my remedy. Dr. Bole said last week, that my mind was fixed too constantly upon some one idea. He recommended immediate travel and change, and I have taken his advice without stirring out of the house.

"Dearest, I travel with you here, at home. I trace your journey in poor papa's journal of *his* journey from Florence, which he kept when he was travelling tutor to your, as well as his staunch friend, Lord Wordley. I put myself day by day into the carriage, and am rolled hour by hour from one place to another with you; and see vineyards, and palaces, and peasants, and priests, and wayside chapels, and mountains, and lakes, and valleys, and villages: and change horses with you, and dine with you; and start afresh with you. It is now Tuesday afternoon, a quarter past four, and I am entering Nice with you. I know I am; because I alighted at Genoa yesterday fortnight, at the same hour that your letter, which came to-day, tells me you stopped at that place. I shall go on travelling with you, dear George, day and night, until I hear you hastening down Linney Hill upon Black Nan on the blessed ninth of June."

After the lapse of three days, the next letter began:

"Mrs. Calder is now permanently established at Crookston Hall, and I am extremely uneasy at the frequency of her visits to me. They look like persecution. They talk of sending your father to Bath—for change, they say; but Dr. Bole hints to me that it is to get him out of the way before your arrival. Whenever he is able to speak he asks for you; and I know when you return he would receive you with open arms, if they would only let him. Symptoms of immediate danger from the stroke have subsided; but he is still helpless. Our secret appears to be safe; but I dread Mrs. Calder's search-

ing eyes and calculating visits. Where are we now? Still
at Nice?

"Here is our faithful ally, Tom, with the pony-chase, so I
must conclude, dearest. Take my whole heart.

"Your own EUSTA."

The date of the next letter was a week later:

"Mrs. Calder is always saying that before poor Mr. Dornley was struck with paralysis, he was continually bewailing
that all the influence and consequence of the Crookston patrimony should, at his death, descend to a Radical, who would
use them, as they wickedly say, for base purposes. Dr. Bole
tells me another story. The dear old man, he says, sometimes squeezes the doctor's hand, and tries to say 'George!'
as if he longed to see you. If you could only see him, I am
sure you might safely tell him of our marriage.

"I begin to dread that Mrs. Calder suspects something; because when she speaks of my being dull and wretched—as I
am sometimes—she says very cruelly that it is lucky poor
mamma passed away when she did; and while pretending that
no amount of contumely she heaps upon you can matter to me,
feels all the while that she is putting me upon the rack. One
day she said that your father's greatest consolation, before his
illness, had been that you were not married; for if he saw a
prospect of the property going in succession to any child of
yours, it would kill him. I thank Heaven that I had strength
to bear this, and that I did not betray myself while she remained; but, when she was gone, I had a severe hysterical
attack, and Dr. Bole was obliged to be sent for. He always
looks grave when he speaks of Mr. and Mrs. Calder; and once
hinted, that he thought they would stop short of nothing to
set you and yours aside. Mrs. Calder's pride is inflexible, and
she seems to feel, like the wife of a second son, like a person
labouring under some indelible disgrace. Oh, if she could only
know how, in my utter loneliness, I yearn for some sisterly
affection; how I could take even her to my heart; how I
should bless God, while you are away, if I had one kind and
sympathising friend!

"Still, dearest, I go on counting the hours and minutes of
that narrow gulf which separates us from the ninth of June.

17*

You and I have been jogging on gaily together since my last, and we are now starting from Dijon. I see your dear eager eyes straining out of the carriage window, and hear your big round voice urging the postilion forward. Only three weeks! Oh, that it were only a week, a day, an hour, a minute !"

A few days later:

"They have just heard that your visit to Lord Wordley in Florence has made your election for Shutbury certain, dearest; and nothing can exceed their disappointment. They *will* speak of you, however much I try to turn off the conversation. Yesterday I said to Mr. Calder (who now comes oftener than ever—sometimes they both come together) that the newspapers appeared to say that the country was getting quiet. 'It will never be quiet,' he exclaimed, ' while such treason-hatchers as George Dornley are allowed to be at large!' and a great deal more in that strain; also, that it was the ruin of the country, for such people as you to be allowed to succeed to powerful inheritances. He does not speak passionately; but in a dry way; between his teeth, as if he were grinding his words. Mrs. Calder was more spiteful than ever. When she spoke of the sin of clandestine marriages, and said they ought to be made illegal: that her children would be beggars, compared with your children, she looked at me from head to foot with a malicious look that made me tremble. I felt almost convinced that she knew all, and said it to wound me; yet I always sit in the great chair with my back to the light, and never leave off my pillow-lace-making; but she has such piercing eyes that she can, I am sure, see in the dark. Both of them harp upon your father's illness; not pitying him, but regretting that it is impossible, in his wretched condition, to get the entail of the Crookston estates cut off.

"In spite of all, my dearest, I go on travelling with you as I sit at work (I have made lace enough for six sweet little caps; and *such* a long robe!). · I hear the horses' bells, and the postilion's whip, and feel a jolt now and then, and somebody gets very angry with postmasters, and uses dreadfully strong words. We are now starting from Paris, are we not, darling?"

The next letter was dated a week later:

"Dear old Mr. Dornley was taken to Bath yesterday, and I feel, though I have never seen him since you left, more lonely than ever. Now that the truth will not worry you, my dear husband, I can tell you that I have not related a tenth part of the persecution I have endured from your brother and his wife; although I always wish to think of them with affection and even love, as your relations. Indeed, Dr. Bole has been afraid of something happening before its time in consequence of it : but he does not know what a strong-minded little woman I am.

"This will reach you at Dover; and we are jogging on merrily to London. Your letter to me appears to have been delayed by the post-office. I am delighted with the arrangements of your London friend, and lost no time in obeying your instructions. I learn that the cottage he has chosen for us at Hampstead is quite in the country, yet not a very long drive from the House of Commons, where so much of your time will be passed. But, darling, you must not be angry if I disobey you in not leaving our dear home for the new one, until after your return. Had your letter arrived when it ought, I might perhaps have been glad to get away from (must I call them?) my enemies; but now, as a week has gone by, and as, from the moment we separated, every faculty I have has been strained to picturing our next meeting *here*—in the beloved home which is associated with every particle of the happiness I owe you, I would rather bear my troubles for a few days longer than go to London to meet you there. Besides, Dr. Bole says it may not be safe for me to travel just now. You must, you say, visit Shutbury the moment you land. Now, that town being in the way to Crookston, if your plan were adopted there would be a day's delay, and your birthday—the longed-for ninth—would pass away, and be no more to me than any other day.

"No one except your brother and his wife call upon me. I have had what dear papa used to call parochial visits from the rector; but Mrs. Drawley and her daughters never come, and scarcely speak when we meet in the road. Even good Miss Pim, the Quakeress of the post-office, has been of late very sparing of her conversation when I go to her shop, and has twice hinted that injurious reports are afloat respecting me, and which have, I shudder when I reflect, strong appearances to favour them. But, darling, next Monday week is the bright golden ninth; and you will come; and all the world will know that I——O, I am getting crazy with joy!"

The last letter was that sent to meet the recipient at the Nottingham inn:

"Darling, I send this, as you requested, to the Royal George. Pray, give my best remembrances to the good landlady, who was so kind to me when we stopped there on the day of our stolen journey; and to my beautiful little handmaid, her daughter. How well they have kept our secret!

"We are starting by the night coach from London, and are outside, I fear. Pray, let us wrap up warm; for these June nights are treacherous. I never knew such a cold summer.

"Black Nan was sent away yesterday by Farmer Thorn, who, having business at Shutbury, was glad to ride her there. I know you will be pleased with her condition. Be sure and praise her condition to Thomas when you meet him at Alfreton; for he is excessively proud of it; and has been altogether an excellent and discreet lad from the moment you left. I will not fail to send him to meet you with the old grey, at Alfreton, that you may have a fresh horse to gallop you home. I hope you will gallop all the way—home—to me! The ecstacy of that thought is too great. . . . .

"O my adored husband! as Monday approaches my happiness is scarcely endurable! If my old cloudy fits did not now and then damp it, I believe it would drive me crazy. Sometimes I fancy something *might* happen to prevent or delay our meeting; sometimes I believe that nothing *could* prevent it, and there is no cruelty so terrible upon earth, much less in heaven, to destroy the world of happiness that awaits me. A thousand blessings my beloved!

"P.S.—I open my letter to say that Dr. Bole has been suddenly sent for to go to Bath, to put the Bath doctors in the right way of treating your father."

The rest of the story—learnt from Hockle's packet, from

himself, and from persons whose acquaintance I afterwards made—I must tell in my own way.

CHAPTER THE THIRD.

A THICK Scotch mist fell upon the town of Nottingham on that ninth of June, when the present century was far on in its teens, which fell upon a Monday. A stout, middle-aged man had arrived overnight at the Royal George on a thorough-bred hunter; and, having, in the morning, received a letter directed to the name of Nobble, left a part of his breakfast and hastily went out, and was traced to another inn, the Green Boar.

On his return to the Royal George in the afternoon, he was standing near the bar, when a younger traveller dismounted from a black mare, threw off his dripping white upper-coat, ordered it to be quickly dried, and, knocking at a little bar-window, asked if any letters had been left there for him. A lovely little barmaid threw up the sash, and gleefully shook her clustering curls as she handed him two letters, and hoped he was quite well. (Hearts have been lost to that now more than matured beauty within the last ten years, to my certain knowledge.) He did not answer the question with his usual affability; for the first letter which he opened vexed him. It bore no post-mark, and he asked who left it? The answer was—"Please, sir, the Green Boar's boots left it." While he was reading it, Mr. Nobble, standing on the mat pretending to pare his nails with a large pocket-knife, did not look up; but, covering his eyes with their lids, "took stock" of the visitor (as he would have expressed himself) from under them. The new guest, having ordered dinner, entered a private parlour. Mr. Nobble adjourned to the coffee-room to dine. Looking back, a broad grin spread itself over his broad countenance; for the other gentleman raised the black-bordered letter that had come by post to his lips too soon—before he had quite closed the parlour door.

It was remarkable that exactly one hour afterwards, the same persons, having separately dined, appeared on the same mat at the same instant. Both had ordered their horses round at the same minute, and both were going the same road.

" Shall we jog on together ?" asked Mr. Nobble.

"Thank you," answered the more reserved traveller, " I have business at Alfreton, and shall outstrip you."

"Curious! *I* have business at Alfreton. I want to catch the Chesterfield mail at Alfreton—the up-mail; and I've got a capital mount," returned the other. The person addressed did not answer; but went on reading the bills tacked against the passage wall, which were headed "Riot," "Rick Burning," "Treason," "Seditious Meetings," and so on; and offering five hundred pounds reward for the apprehension of this person, and two hundred pounds for the capture of that.

"Jolly times these!" Mr. Nobble said, quite boldly. The gentleman turned his head quickly round from his broadside studies, and confronted Mr. Nobble with a look of surprise; but was still silent. He knew well enough that, with habeas corpus suspended; with imprisonment, without cause assigned, or regular commitment, or even the pretence of trial, pretty frequent, and with a noisome cloud of spies permeating all the stormy and starving parts of the country, any freeborn Englishman who was not gifted with an independent five hundred a year (as the Reverend Sydney Smith observed at the time) had to be very cautious what sort of politics he talked to a stranger. Perhaps Mr. Nobble *had* five hundred a year: his new blue coat and gilt buttons, his top-boots, his thoroughbred hunter, and his unstinted denunciations of the government when the two had mounted and were trotting out of the town together (there was no shaking him off), would have confirmed that idea, but for a certain familiarity and swagger which Mr. Nobble was unable, though he tried, to suppress.

His topic, dangerous enough, was evidently a congenial one to his companion; who, although the drizzle fell thickly, slackened rein to continue the conversation. But, by the time he had buttoned up his white top-coat, and tucked in the tassels of his hessian boots, he had thought better of it; and, having got clear of the crowds of factory girls who were picking their muddy way home to tea, he broke forward into a canter with a curt "Good afternoon," and was soon beyond the sound of the politician's voice, and of the clicking of pattens.

Mr. Nobble gave him his own way as far as Eastwood, over

Cinder Hill and Moorgreen, to Selstone; but there he over-took him. Even then, attempts at conversation failed; and he was too civil to persevere. Another Good evening; another canter; and, at about three miles further on, the black mare was pulled up at a cross corner, and a young groom appeared from under a hedge, with a dry dark coat and a grey horse. His master changed both in no time; for, he did not wish to be observed, and had passed several stragglers. While thus employed, he asked his servant what orders he had received from his mistress?

"I'm to ride Black Nan into Darby, and put her up at the King's Head; then take the mail for London," was the an-swer.

" Well ?"

" When I get to London, I'm to make the best of my way to Chalcot Cottage, close to Hampstead, and tell the landlady that you and my mistress are to be there on Thursday. And on Thursday I'm to be at the Peacock at Islington with a fly to meet you."

"Right. But my plans are changed. You must go back to Corner Cottage as fast as the mare will carry you (ride her carefully, for she's tired), and tell your mistress that I shall not be with her for some hours later than I expected. You can then catch the Sheffield coach when it passes through Crookston-Withers, go to London by it, and do all you were at first ordered to do."

The master galloped one way, his man trotting gently an-other, down the cross lane; and, several minutes before Mr. Nobble unsuspiciously passed the tryst, the gentleman had drawn bit at the Fox at Alfreton.

"Won't you get off, sir," inquired the landlord, "and tak a fettle o' soommut warm?"

"Thank you—no. Have you seen a groom pass this way lately, towards the Smithy Houses?" He wished to ascertain whether his servant had, before they met, been hanging about needlessly.

The landlord, not best pleased at the traveller's haste, an-swered that he had seen a sight o' stragglers pass towards the Smithy Houses that day; but couldn't tell which on um was grooms, and which on um wasn't. The gentleman said no more, but rode leisurely off.

In a few minutes the other horseman approached the Fox, and the landlord stepped into the road ready to hold his bridle. But he trotted by also, without asking one word about the Chesterfield mail—up or down.

"Oi wonder what's oop, doon by Pentridge and the Smithy Houses to-night, lass?—some devilment of the Captain's, it's loikely," he said to his wife, when he returned in doors. "There was foot stragglers in the road all t' morn, and now, i' t' even, they're coming a horseback." The wife was sure Mr. Flip would tell them all about it when he drove up the mail in a few minutes : "that is, if he isn't in a mortal hurry to get to the Nottin'am Royal George," she added, beginning to warm the ale for Mr. Flip's purl.

"Ah," rejoined the goodman, "Widow Tuckey maun do worse than tak him."

Meantime, when the old grey had put a couple of miles behind him, his rider heard that he was being overtaken once more ; and, looking back, saw his old companion cantering his capital hunter apace.

"A grey horse and a dark coat !" ejaculated Mr. Nobble to himself, as he came up. "Curse my luck ! I've lost the trail of him. Yet," and he brightened up, "he may have changed coats and horses at the Fox." To solve his doubts, he brought his own horse's nose, for the third time, in a line with that of the stranger's, and one glance put him in spirits. "By George !" he exclaimed, "how delighted I am to see you again—de-lighted !" The gentleman did not return the compliment. He simply surmised that Mr. Nobble had changed his mind about taking a place in the mail.

"Yes, I have. I'm not going by the mail." Then he paused a minute. "I'll tell you plump and plain where I am going to. I'm going to the White Horse at Pentridge to meet the Captain, I am."

The stranger was surprised, alarmed, perhaps.

"Come, come," said Nobble; "you needn't be frightened ; one little word will put you and me quite upon the square. But here comes the mail; wait till she passes, and then I'll mention it." In another minute Mr. Flip had parted the

speakers with his team at a canter ; his coach-lamps glimmering in the damp, commencing twilight. When the equestrians
joined again in the wake of the mail, Nobble leant to one
side of his saddle confidingly, and whispered, "Rivets!"

His companion hesitated before he gave the countersign.

"The truth is," he said, "I belong to no society, and have
no secrets. What I do politically, I do from motives quite
independent of any man——"

"Except Lord Wordley," interrupted the other, sneer-
ingly ; "I know all about you ; though you may believe that
I don't. You are the gentleman they call the Young Squire.
You *were* going straight home to Crookston ; but one of the
letters you received at the bar of the Royal George gave you
our countersign; and persuaded you to go to the Pentridge
meeting instead."

"You are a delegate, perhaps," replied the person addressed.

"Yes, I am. An Eastern delegate, and I say again—
Rivets!"

"Double-headed!" was the answer.

After a pause—during which each was considering what
direction the conversation should take, now that their relations were necessarily more confidential—Nobble, attributing
his companion's silence to mistrust, said fiercely, "I tell you
what : I don't hold with the snivelling of you Nobs on our
side, one bit : it's rank cowardice. It's my belief that you're
going to persuade the Nottingham Captain to turn tail."

"I am not accountable to you sir, for my intentions," said
the so-called Young Squire.

"Perhaps not." Mr. Nobble added, "I did not see you at
the Nottingham meeting last night."

"I was not there," was the answer. Mr. Nobble smiled.
"But I know exactly what was done." Mr. Nobble frowned
and growled.

He passed a minute moodily and in silence ; then broke out
with :

"Well, it's of no use your coming into these parts to pour
cold water upon a good cause. The Captain has got his men
together, up to the mark. Well armed, mind you, and he
means to do it. We mean to do it to-night. You're too late

down here—you or any of your Nobs either—with hang-back speeches about patience, and constitutional proceedings."

" We try to convince the people of the Truth : to undo the monstrous deceptions some of their leaders are palming upon them," said the Young Squire ; "and, although I have taken no part in politics lately—having been abroad—I shall go on trying."

"Don't try that game on with the Captain, or you'll get the worst of it," rejoined Nobble, hoarsely. " The blood of his people is up—boiling over; and you'd better not cool it down, I can tell you."

" Whether you mean that as a menace or a warning," returned the gentleman, firmly, " is of no consequence. I am not here to quarrel with any man."

"Perhaps you're afraid," growled Nobble.

The Young Squire was not bound to hear this insult, for they had overtaken groups of working men and boys; some talking earnestly as they walked ; some clashing pikes awkwardly over their shoulders. Others carried long black links as big as bludgeons, to be lighted up by-and-by as torches. A few were snapping the locks of muskets and pistols, to try them. There was noise enough to drown a louder growl than Mr. Nobble's.

They both dismounted at the White House at Pentridge. An ostler took charge of the thorough-bred, and led it to the stable; but the young Squire said he was going on immediately, and had his old grey tied to a ring in the horse-trough; for which purpose, way was made for it by the loiterers that hung about the house, and were fast augmenting. Each new comer inquired if anything had been done ; or, if not, if anything was to be done, and was answered that the Captain and the tithing-men were still deliberating in the parlour. Perhaps the gentlemen on horseback had brought the word they were waiting for.

When Nobble entered the inn parlour, the Nottingham Captain was studying, by the light of a single candle, a map, which had displaced beer-jugs and pipes upon the slopped and gritty table.

" Yes," he said to the men standing round, as he traced a route with his finger. "We must sweep the villages round, first. From every house one man and one gun, and no less. At Lane End, the Wingfield men will meet us. Then, on to the Butterley Iron Works for cannon, and as many men as we can get: then to Topham's Close, through Ripley and Condor to pick up the Swanwick men. After that, in a body through Alfreton, Somercotes, over Pye Bridge, to Eastwood. There, in Nottingham Forest, all the Nottingham boys are assembled —thousands. The town will be ours in half an hour."

"What are you waiting for?" asked one of the men at the table, impatiently.

"I am waiting for the Norwich delegate: he is to bring us word of the exact time of the other risings," replied the Captain.

"Here he is!" said a voice at the door; and Nobble came forward. The Captain started up. "Well," he said, abruptly, "what's the hour to be?"

"Ten o'clock," said Nobble.

"Everywhere?"

"Everywhere. Are you ready?"

"To a man," replied the Captain. "It's nigh nine, now." Rolling up the map and grasping it like a truncheon, he went to the door. A moment or two was spent in earnest conversation with Mr. Nobble; whose travelling-companion overheard a portion of his statements, and knew them to be either exaggerations or untruths. The Nottingham Captain, fired and excited by them, tightened his apron—already twisted up at the waist over his grey kerseys and brown great-coat (the Captain, when at home, was a framework knitter), waved his paper truncheon, and proceeded to address the scarcely distinguishable groups that buzzed and clattered their pikes before the alehouse, in the thickening twilight, made darker by close, ceaseless rain. Silence having been called, he told them that, at ten o'clock that night, the whole country—England, Ireland, Scotland, "and France"—was to rise; that their job was merely to besiege Nottingham, and to take it; that the soldiers in Nottingham barracks were all on their side; that the great Nottingham meeting, the night before, was crowded with red-coats, who sided with the people; that the people had turned out armed to the teeth, awaiting their own arrival in Nottingham forest; that the northern clouds were drifting

down to sweep all before them in other places; and that, each
man would have a hundred guineas and plenty of rum as soon
as the town was taken. That seventy-five thousand men were
at that moment marching into London from the west; and
seventy-five thousand more from the east; that the keys of
the Tower of London were already in the hands of the Hampden
Club; that the Mint, the Mansion House, Carlton Palace, the
Bank of England, and the City of Westminster, would be in possession of their friends and allies by the morning. He ended
with some doggrel verses; which he repeated with the fervour
of an inspired poet invoking the sublimest images. The auditory greeted him with cries of Down with the borough-mongers!
Down with the tax-eaters! Liberty and Parliamentary Reform!
The men cheering and shouting while the boys danced about
and fired pistols in the air: all entreating to be led to Victory
or Death.

The Young Squire, hitherto an unnoticed spectator, now
stepped forward; and, in that strong and musical voice which
had influenced many a larger and rougher auditory, besought
a hearing. "Who was he?" some asked. "The gentleman
they call t' Young Squire," others answered. "O, t' Young
Squire, was he? Well, we've heered nout but what's good
o' t' Young Squire, and we'll heer him now." The Young
Squire then boldly declared that the information brought to
them was false. The northern clouds (meaning the Yorkshire
delegates and their followers) had dispersed, and the Nottingham men had passed resolutions at the meeting on Saturday
night, in favour of peaceful measures; not a soldier appeared
among them.

An exasperated voice near the horse-trough, "That's a
lie!"

And they might look, the speaker continued, for a tent or a
dozen armed reformers in Nottingham forest in vain. (General cries of "You know nout about it!") As to a general
rising, he could state of his own knowledge that such a measure had never been so much as proposed either in London
or elsewhere. He implored them vehemently, even passionately, to refrain from playing into the hands of the government, by giving it excuses for inflicting tyrannical measures
on the country, under pretence of putting down rebellion.

He assured them that every step which they ventured to take
from that spot with the objects they had in view, would be a
step towards their own destruction.

There was a murmur amongst the crowd, a low deliberate hum, as if discussing what had been heard. It wa-
vered. This was quickly noticed by the leaders, and the
Nottingham Captain rushed forward, before the Squire could
utter another word. Speaking loudly and significantly, he
said :

"Let me ask this wonderful Young Squire one question:
Are you," he continued, turning to that gentleman, "or are
you not, putting up for Shutbury, Lord Wordley's rotten
borough ?"

The Young Squire promptly answered that he was the un-
opposed candidate for that borough ; and, was proceeding to
state that he should go into Parliament for the single purpose
of advocating the rights of the people, when a storm of groans
and hisses stopped him. He was denounced by turns as one
of the borough-mongering crew; as a traitor ; and as having
sold himself to the aristocracy. There was a pressure against
the doorway of the inn where he stood ; and he would have
been roughly handled if, in the thick twilight, he could have
been distinguished from those who surrounded him. But Mr.
Nobble stepped forward ; and, under pretence of fair play,
proposed that, as the Young Squire had cast a doubt upon
the staunchness of the Nottingham men, somebody should go
forward to the forest and bring back word whether any of
them were encamped there or not. The son of the host of
the White Horse, young Tanner, who was at his elbow, cocked
a pistol, and ground out between his teeth:

"If he has lied, we'll shoot him !"

The Captain clapped the lad on the shoulder, and said he
was the very boy for the job.

"Take the Young Squire's horse," he said, "and gallop to
Eastwood and back, as fast you can make it go."

The owner protested strongly against this arrangement, and
darted towards the horse to prevent its being untied ; but was
held back in the iron grasp of the Captain, who said:

"No, no ; we mustn't trust turncoats out o' sight !"

In spite of sturdy resistance, the gentleman was overpowered by numbers. The Captain did not lose another minute, and ordered the tithing-men to tell off their gangs; for it was getting near the appointed hour.

"Now's your time, or never!" he exclaimed. "Light up!"

A blazing furze branch was brought from the kitchen-hearth. Each leader of ten men lit his pitch and oakum torch, and moved luridly amongst the crowd to pick out his own followers. The gleaming banners spat and crackled in the rain, shedding foggy rings of light that hardly lessened the gloom. The messenger, as he mounted the Squire's horse, could not distinguish the van from the rear of the little army; nor see in which direction they were turning their faces. Above the buzz of excitement and plashing of feet, he heard the voice of the Nottingham Captain:

"To the iron-works first; and then a man and a gun from every house between this and Nottingham! Look to your prisoner!"

"Prisoner," repeated the scout, as he dug his heels into the flanks of the grey gelding, and galloped away through the murk. "Ah, t' Young Squire 'll have many a fellow-prisoner to keep company wi' him afore it's long. Them that can fight, and won't fight, ought to be made to fight."

CHAPTER THE FOURTH.

THE spongy Scotch mist that dimmed Mr. Nobble's buttons, darkened his blue coat, and made a change of garments necessary to his companion on the road between Nottingham and Pentridge, soddened the roads and flooded the meadows of the village I have called Crookston-Withers; hedges trickled a constant drain into the ditches; cattle, having tried for shelter under trees, returned to the open fields; the stuccoed church-tower, patched with rain, cast a sharp reflection on the shining slate roof; the cottage-eaves constantly dripping, dug pebbly gutters before the doors, making the children duck their heads every time they stepped out or stepped in; the grey kitten from the post-office tripped lightly across the road, on the tops of the stones, to visit a relative at Mary Garstang's; and the postman's terrier slunk heavily along, with his tail jammed between his legs, and his spirits too depressed to bark at the broods of dirty and ruffled chickens hopping and pecking in his way, or fluttering noisily out of it. Very few of the human species had that afternoon passed through the village, except the groom from Corner Cottage, who had been met on the grey horse going towards Alfreton, and the post-office runner. The wheels of the Nottingham waggon, which left a couple of running gutters along the whole of its track, were brought to a stand opposite the Bull and Horns, the steaming horses unwilling to give them one other turn. The waggoner's Welsh pony—its head, its tail, and its mane drooping and dripping—stood in the middle of the road immoveable and stupified. It did not wag so much as a hair of its ear, even when the waggon-horses, tossing up their nosebags and savagely shaking their necks, jangled their bells with a crash "enough," the ostler remarked, as he wantonly dashed the dregs of a pail of water over the wheeler's legs, "to wake a dead donkey!" The waggoner himself leant listlessly against one of the posts of the inn-porch, staring into the blank and draggled prospect; staring even while he covered his countenance with a mug of ale; staring into the dense mist while asking the ostler if he thought it was ever going to leave off; staring while telling the boy to take the band-box out of the forewain into the post-office, and to be sure and bring back the eightpence.

The boy was leaving the little shop with the money in his hand, when it was knocked out of it by the maid-servant from Corner Cottage, who had rushed across the road—blindly, with her apron thrown over her head—to know if the "things" had come. The postmistress replied, in her formal manner, that they had come, and that the whole of the work would be ready in time to go away to London with the rest of Miss Levine's luggage on the following morning. Whereupon the damsel disappeared; expressing her delight by slamming the glass door so violently that she knocked from one of the panes the inscription of painted tin which informed the nobility, gentry, and public in general, that Miss Pim made up ladies' own material on the most reasonable terms.

Having replaced her advertisement as quietly as if the act were a part of her day's routine, Miss Pim produced from the bandbox a little hat, a fold of net, a packet of white Persian,

a strip of dove-coloured cloth, and several yards of the finest
calico. She then cut out the net for half a dozen caps, to
draw them up and trim them with some pillow lace; her customer's own material.

Miss Pim was very thoughtful and very sad. She could not
work with her usual diligence; although she was working
against time. She sighed much, and tears filled her eyes; so
that she was obliged to leave off sewing. Was she committing a sin? Was she wrong in undertaking, upon urgent
entreaty, to assist a single young woman whom the world
called unfortunate? Could it be a crime to help a victim of
misfortune? Yet, when it came to be known that she had
thus secretly assisted Miss Levine, would not ladies take away
their work from her? Perhaps. She knew Mrs. Calder
Dornley would. But right is right; and loss of work she
would not repent, if she could only be sure that she *was* right.
Then a glance at the great square parlour window of Corner
Cottage opposite; and, occasionally, the sight of a pale eager
face, with eyes enlarged, darkly bordered, and straining into
the misty road whenever the faintest sound of horses' hoofs
could be heard, banished irresolution, and the needle was
plied more rapidly than ever.

Besides, continued the conscientious reasoner, "Miss Levine
herself, her mother so lately dead, and her father the late
rector—wise and pious—never made sin a ground for with-
holding help. There was hardly a family in the parish, whatever their creed or condition, who had not to thank them for
some benefit; from simple words of comfort and stealthy acts
of charity, up to salvation from ruin. When her own mother
lay helpless for two years up-stairs, and herself was brought to
actual want, either Parson Levine, or Mrs. Levine, or Miss
Levine, came once a day to the bedside; seldom empty-handed.
It was Parson Levine who spoke to the county member to get
her to be made postmistress—and she and all her family dis-
senters. Then, again, Miss Levine may not have sinned. She
may be married, and be bound down to secrecy.

The shadow of the waggon, slowly grinding the road towards Matlock, darkened the window for an instant; and Miss
Pim once more ceased working. Her head ached. She was
not equal to all the doleful surmises that entered her mind

respecting Miss Levine. She was haunted, too, by the shadow of Mrs. Calder Dornley, that had often clouded her house of late; silently opening her door; sitting down stiffly in her room, and asking spy questions about Corner Cottage: if Miss Pim had noticed anybody go in or come out lately; what letters had arrived, and what letters had been sent away; speaking (even to Miss Pim's meek apprehension) unimpassioned venom; darting, from her sloe-like eyes, sharp rays of anger, when she mentioned how distinguished families may be disgraced by the vices of low-born girls; always applying her censures to the " young person opposite," and ending her visits by threatening, in measured sentences, ruin and disgrace to any person living on the Crookston property, who presumed to further or conceal any family ignominy that may be brewing against the Dornleys or Stonards, whether it related to birth or marriage. Yet it was clear that these objections did not proceed from rooted principle; for Mrs. Calder was continually showing kindness to that pert and improper young woman, Mary Garstang, and *her* ill-starred baby.

The troubled Quakeress looked again for relief from her thoughts, towards the window of the cottage across the way. The same face presented itself—the same large eager eyes, straining towards the Nottingham road. Miss Pim knew that Mr. George Dornley was expected back to take Miss Levine with him to London, on his birthday. This was it—the ninth of June. Miss Levine was watching for him, no doubt. But if he should not come?

This brought into her mind the fact that sudden grief, or even joy, sometimes hastens nature; and she once more set to work, determined to complete the order in hand before bedtime.

Eusta Levine had been equally busy in the parlour of Corner Cottage. After breakfast she had to pack for the journey to London; but without disturbing those pretty ornaments about her rooms which The Expected loved to see. In the intervals of activity she continued her imaginary journey with him, as long as imagination was under control. It had taken her from Dover to London, from London to Shutbury, and from Shutbury to Nottingham; and now brought her to the very inn in which she had spent, the year before, the one supremely happy

18

day of her existence. She saw him in her mind's eye mount
Black Nan at the inn door to come to her, and felt that only
a few diminishing hours divided them.

She watched the clock incessantly, hoping he might intend
to surprise her by arriving earlier than he had promised to
come ; and, knowing every turn of the road, she traced him
accurately through each stride of it, to his meeting-place with
his groom, and thence to her own door, and into her own
arms. Then, Fancy being at fault with Reality, she tried
back and went over the ground again ; but, when imagination
brought him again to the door, and Reality denied his presence, it was not with the full bitterness of disappointment ;
for, although every faculty of her mind strained itself towards
the one absorbing expectation, desire for his arrival was not
unmixed with a wayward dread of its realisation. The ecstacy
of the meeting would be insupportable ; and, whenever it
seemed to be imminent, she felt herself too weak to bear
it. Every successive disappointment when she heard, or fan-
cied she heard, a horse approaching, and when the sound
died away, was, therefore, tempered with a sensation of relief.

The acuteness of Eusta's sufferings would have been much
lessened had there been any one to confide in ; any one to
speak to. But she was isolated : even those who had come
near her seemed to have entered into a league either to preserve an ominous reserve, or to torture her with inuendoes.

To banish such recollections, she gave up her imagination
once more to picturing the coming meeting. She went on
acting over again the minutest incident. She imagined George
Dornley gaining the top of the hill ; she heard him cantering
down towards her, on the brave old grey. She was at the door
to receive him ; she was in his strong embrace ; she felt upon
her cheek, the breath of his deep noble voice softened by murmurs of passionate tenderness and love. . . . . Her head
swam.

Dr. Bole knowing better than any one how very critical her
condition was at this time, would, had he been present, have
reckoned the noiseless entrance of Mrs. Calder Dornley into
the room (which happened at that moment) a very fortunate
intrusion. That lady, having been set down from the carriage

by her husband at the church, had walked across the church-yard, had entered the cottage, and deposited her wet bonnet and cloak in the passage, unheard and unobserved. She appeared—her countenance so frigid and dry, and her short thick curls as crisp as if she had stepped out of a frost—exactly in time to change the current of Eusta's blood and to preserve her from fainting. Eusta experienced so complete a reaction, on seeing Mrs. Calder Dornley, that she soon recovered sufficient composure to speak. It was her nature to be timid; but now, hope so near realisation gave her courage and strength, beset and helpless as she was. She ventured to say that her visitor's presence was, at that time, very undesirable.

Mrs. Calder Dornley established herself on the hardest and straightest chair, and deliberately produced from her pocket some muslin-work with a stiff geometrical pattern—a proceeding which denoted that she did not intend to go, and that her stay would not be short. "This is a visit of duty," she said, "and I have arranged with my husband to remain here, until he fetches me, on his return in the carriage from Matlock. However disagreeable to you and to me, Miss Levine, I must perform the duty which is imposed upon me."

"Imposed upon you by whom?" Eusta innocently asked.

"By my husband and my own conscience," was the answer. "There is no time to be lost; for we half expect my brother-in-law to arrive to-day, this being his birthday; when he arranged to come home, and——"

"Half expect?" Eusta interrupted, dreading the news implying delay had transpired. "Are you not sure he will come?"

Mrs. Calder Dornley was always so indisputably right in her statements and surmises that she never noticed interruptions. "And," she went on, with the same breath she had begun with, "as my husband thinks it is imperative that I should ascertain from you facts which are important to our family to be known, I am here to ascertain them." She then pointed out, in the clearest and most convincing manner, the county, the national importance of the Crookston property and the Crookston lineage; contrasting it with the meanness of Miss Levine's own origin; for, although her late mother was the. daughter of a bishop, that bishop's father had been a brewer, and Miss Levine's paternal grandfather was a very small farmer. Any thought of an alliance between two such families, therefore, would excite a fever of indignation from one end of the county to the other; putting any additionally discreditable circumstances out of the question.

It was Mrs. Dornley's habit not to look people in the face while speaking to them; least of all, persons she disliked. She did not, therefore, notice that Eusta—tortured by the doubts dropped into her mind one minute, and the next persuading herself that George was galloping towards her only a few miles off—paid no attention to what was said. Restless and impatient, she moved about the room, distraught, but silent.

The persecutor bore this silence very stoically. Never ceasing to draw out her needle and thread with vicious regularity; never once looking up; patiently waiting until Eusta returned to the sofa.

And when Eusta seated herself, Mrs. Calder said in hard cold accents, "I really must obtain some satisfactory explanation for my husband. It is now nine o'clock, and he agreed to be here at a quarter past nine. Before he comes, and before his brother returns (if he do return), I must know whether you are married or whether you are not married; the more so as, in two months at least I judge, you will be a mother." She had never before spoken so plainly, and her words gradually recalled Eusta's attention.

Eusta's words swelled her throat, and she could not speak. She looked imploringly toward her questioner and sobbed. Without avail; for Mrs. Calder did not move her eyes from her work, and showed no sort of impatience to hear the required confession. She preferred the sound of the sobs; and, when these grew louder and stronger, she expressed a hope that Miss Levine would not, like most vulgar young women, seek shelter from discussion in hysterics. Poor Eusta! it was her struggle to speak that made hysterics so hard to be suppressed. But the recollection that her husband's interests and wishes were at stake restored her, and she said, in half-choked accents:

"I have told you frequently that my word and honour are pledged not to reveal to any one, the nature of my engagement with Mr. George Dornley. O, do have pity on me! Do not seek to make me break my word! Do not tempt me! I have borne your scorn and your husband's anger. I have heard you accuse him, whom I love better than life, of being a libertine and a traitor. This has been going on for months, and will you not wait an hour longer? Will you not wait until Mr. Dornley comes to answer for me and for himself?"

"It is not certain that he will come. My expectation is that he will be prevented from coming. The government——"

"I am as sure he will come as that there is a Providence now watching over me!" Eusta exclaimed, fervently. "He *must* come. What do I live for, but for him to come?" She said this almost fiercely.

"The government," continued placid Mrs. Calder, "may find occasion to enforce his presence elsewhere; in some secure place where the seditious practices he was guilty of before he went abroad, cannot be repeated."

"But he will come: here: to me. Stone walls will not keep him from me: hosts of enemies will not keep him from me. I feel it to be as impossible for him not to come, as it will be impossible for me to live, if he does not come."

"In either case," said Mrs. Calder, making an eyelet-hole, "my question must be answered. You need not hesitate; for, whether you are married or whether you are not, your lot in life will be wretched enough. If you are not a wife, you will have to endure the disgust which all right-minded persons——" She did not finish the sentence; but complained that it was too dark to work. "If you are married," she continued, "your child will be a beggar; born without inheritance.

Eusta's mind had again shut out everything except the devouring desire for George Dornley's approach. She was once more studying the clock, and computing time against distance; reckoning that, at about this moment he ought certainly to be within hearing; for the appointed time had nearly arrived. The servant, who had entered with lights, aroused her, by attempting to close the shutters. "They must not be shut!" Eusta hastily said. "They would deaden the sounds from the road."

When the girl had left the room, Mrs. Calder resumed her

sewing. "Dr. Bole," she said, "and Mr. Bearshaw, the family lawyer, have both pronounced old Mr. Dornley so much better since his sojourn at Bath, that he will soon be capable of transacting business; and should his eldest son have married a person without family or fortune, the first use of his recovery will be to cut off the entail of the Crookston estates." Mrs. Calder stopped to watch the effect of this announcement, and looked up. She found Eusta panting with expectation close to the window, every faculty absorbed in listening. Perceiving that all that had been said went for nothing, the rigid moralist felt it to be her duty to put the case somewhat stronger. "I was saying, Miss Levine, that positive beggary ——"

"Hush!" exclaimed Eusta, raising her finger. "I hear a sound;" she paused, "yes, it is the tramp of a horse." She listened again, her face flushed, the veins starting in her forehead.

"I really must claim your attention," Mrs. Calder persevered, "to the disreputable——"

"No," Eusta said, sinking into a chair. "There are two horses. It cannot be he!" Then, willing to mitigate one agony by courting another, she gave attention to her lecturer.

Mrs. Calder described, in a few more acrid words, the probable destitution that awaited George Dornley; and Eusta, never having before contemplated the possibility of her husband's ruin, and attributing it, if it happened, to herself, felt her head burn, and her eyes swim; but was relieved by tears. Her companion went on sawing the air with her needle and thread, as mechanically and regularly as the clock ticked. The Crookston carriage was now heard driving towards the door, and Eusta dreading the entrance of Calder Dornley, determined to make a last appeal to his wife.

"You hate me, I know," she said, looking at her through her tears. "You hate him—George—the more that you once loved him." Mrs. Calder bit her thin lip, and her thread, hitherto pulled out firm and straight, trembled in the air; "but as one woman appealing to another, I implore you to have some tenderness for me. I have no thought of unkindness towards you. I could be as a sister to you. Utterly bereft and alone, I have yearned for sisterly sympathy and compassion. I have not one friend in the world, except him whose love for me is, you say, to be his destruction. Give me but one kind word," she sobbed piteously. "Give me such a look as you would cast upon a dying beggar." She drew herself nearer. "If," she continued, passionately, " you hate me because I have kept my secret from you, if breaking my solemn pledge will save him from ruin——"

"Well," said the sister-in-law, looking down grimly but eagerly upon the suppliant.

Eusta threw herself at Mrs. Calder's feet :

"I confess. We *are* married."

Mrs. Calder thrust herself suddenly back, as if Eusta had stung her. Married! The coming child legitimate, and herself childless! If George Dornley do not forfeit his inheritance by sedition and treason, the estates will still revert to his lawful heirs, and pass away from her husband! O, that old Mr. Dornley were in a condition to cut off the entail!

Eusta was not conscious of being so hatefully spurned as she really was; for her attention was acutely averted. Mr. Calder's carriage had stopped and its occupant had alighted : but there came a new sound from the road, and Eusta started to her feet and exclaimed,

"I hear him !"

She flew to the window and looked wildly through it into the thick small rain.

"It is Black Nan," she said, listening intently. "I know the sound of her canter as well as I know *his* footfall."

She paused and reflected.

"Yes, George has missed the groom, could not change horses, and has ridden the poor staunch creature all the way. That is why he is so late. At last ! at last !"

She fixed her eyes on Mrs. Calder when a horse rattled past the window and suddenly stopped.

"You hear ? He is at the door. He dismounts ! George, George, come to me !"

She threw up her arms ready for George Dornley to fall into them. Thomas Hockle presented himself.

A shrill unearthly laugh pierced the gloom in the road, shot through the village, frightened the horses standing at the cottage door, and made them so restive that the grooms could scarcely hold them. Miss Pim, stamping letters for the night post, drew aside her curtains, looked through her own windows into the window of Corner Cottage, and observed some one supporting a lifeless woman towards a sofa, and another woman hastily closing the shutters. Perceiving a carriage and pair, and a saddle-horse at the door, she thought Mr. George Dornley had arrived, and ejaculated as she returned to her duty: "Poor thing! Joy has overpowered her."

In the postmistress's excitement, her hand strayed from the letters to one of the little night-gowns which lay folded beside them, and she stamped upon it the words, "Crookston-Withers, June nine," with, to her extreme mortification, indelible ink.

There was a hurried but subdued talking in the road close to the door.

It was the voice of Mrs. Calder speaking to her husband: "Yes, that must be done—at once."

The Corner Cottage servant burst into the post-office, breathlessly demanding, "The things!" and Miss Pim, anticipating why they were wanted, did not ask a single question, but quietly packed them so that the rain should not damp them in their short transit.

The servant had not departed two minutes before she again appeared. "Missus is very ill," she said, "and they have sent Tom Hockle (who has only just come back from Alfreton) upon Black Nan, off to Matlock on some errand or another; though the mare's so tired he thinks he'll never get there. They, the Dornley folk, say that I am in the way, and they have turned me out too. I'm to sleep with mother to-night. They're opening the boxes Missus had packed up to take to London with her, and they've ordered the carriage not to stir from the door, if it waits there all night. For my part I'm most mazed with it all; but I must be off to fetch Molly Garstang."

When Miss Pim went outside to shut her shutters, before going to bed (her hour was ten o'clock), she saw the nurse hurrying towards Corner Cottage.

CHAPTER THE FIFTH.

ALTHOUGH the dawn which rose when the ninth of June had died away, began to brighten the brow of Linney Hill and the first beams of the morning sun faintly glistened upon the mountings of a carriage rolling rapidly over it from Corner Cottage towards Matlock, yet Arch-lane, with its overhanging trees, continued as dark and silent as a cavern. The birds silently fluttered round the outer branches, and there was not a breath of air to rustle a leaf. The stillness was broken by a tall man—his dress torn, and his Hessian boots muddy to the tassels—who entered the lane to make his way towards Crookston. He had escaped from the rioters, and now nothing, he thought, lay between him and the joy of his life.

He had not, however, penetrated far into the lane, before he distinguished a whispering amongst some persons concealed in the hedge. Then came a clattering of sabres and a cocking of carbines. Then a couple of dismounted hussars rushed upon him, and, after a struggle, secured him. There was so little light, that had not a corporal-major (looking grimly on, guarding another prisoner—a portly person in a blue coat) called out to the combatants to stand clear, they would have been ridden over by a carriage as it came dashing through the dark and rugged avenue. It was obliged to stop. A window was let down; a man thrust out his head, and ordered the postilion to go on for his life; or, if he didn't (an oath darted out between the teeth like a bullet), he would shoot him!

The prisoner had not noticed this, for, having temporarily released himself, he was busy felling his fellow-captive—who had, he found, betrayed him—to the earth. But, he was soon secured again, and dragged to the gate to which the troop horses were tied. The road being clear, the carriage dashed onward; and, one glance towards the gate as they passed, showed to two of its occupants, Mr. and Mrs. Calder Dornley, who the newly taken prisoner was. A short sharp glance passed between the husband and wife. Mrs. Dornley would have spoken but for an interruption which came from the op-

18*

posite seat—the cry of a newly-born infant laying upon Mary
Garstang's lap.

CHAPTER THE SIXTH.

THE good town of Nottingham, not having the remotest
suspicion that a besieging force was in motion to sack it, slept
soundly on the night of the ninth of June. But, towards the
morning of the tenth, it woke in a fright. Very early, its
great triangular market-place resounded with the tramp of
infantry, the grounding of muskets, and the clattering of
cavalry hoofs. The mayor and municipal officers were knocked
untimely out of their beds, and appeared in the town-hall with
their robes of office awry, and their countenances bewildered
and dazed. As the morning advanced, fasting county magistrates galloped in from their distant homes, and made straight
for the Royal George; where, in petty sessions assembled,
they communicated with the barracks, by means of special constables and orderlies, between hastily-snatched cups of tea
and half-eaten eggs. Expresses were sent off for the high-
sheriff and deputy-lieutenant, and Mr. Vollum, the town-clerk,
chief legal functionary of the town (of the firm of Vollum
and Knoll), sent his partner post to London to confer with
the solicitor of his majesty's treasury. The tradespeople under the arcades, would not open their shops; but wandered
between the Royal George, the town-hall, and the newspaper
offices, asking what was the matter, and getting for answer
wild and alarming information. The panic was not allayed
by the frequent arrival of prisoners, guarded by constables or
escorted by hussars, on the tops of through-coaches, or in the
bottoms of farmers' carts.

By noon, the prevalent horrors had evaporated sufficiently
to leave a residum of truth; and this was published in a supplement of the local journal. The Pentridge rioters had
attacked the Butterley iron-works without success, but had
proceeded to rifle the cottages along the road of guns and
ammunition, and to pull unwilling men out of their beds to
join in the intended capture of Nottingham, on pain of being
pistolled. One man at Topham's Close farm, who did not lace
his boots quite quickly enough to please the Nottingham
Captain, was shot dead on the spot. The rioters actually

advanced as far as Eastwood, about six miles from the town ; but were met there by a county Squire who was riding home from a late sitting of the House of Lords—a club of that distinguished name which was held at the Green Boar; and he cantered back to mention the circumstance to the officer on duty at the cavalry barracks. Eighteen troopers, who happened to have been kept under arms all night, were instantly led, by a captain and a cornet, to the scene of action ; and, in five minutes, they captured forty stand of the rioters' arms and several prisoners. A detachment of troopers at Matlock also had got the alarm ; had scoured that part of the country, arresting as many of the mob as had not straggled away during their previous march.

This was the true account. But the true account did not suit the views either of the imperial government or of the London newspapers in government pay. When *their* description came out, it was the description of a wide-spread rebellion. It was produced piecemeal, in first, second, third, fourth, and fifth editions, all bristling with prodigious notes of admiration, and headed with appalling capitals.

Towards evening, the bewitching curls of the engaging little barmaid at the Royal George again shook like hanging fruit; but, this time, they shook with grief. Her friend the Young Squire had been marched up-stairs by a guard of hussars, hand-cuffed to the " party" who had got away a letter yesterday morning in the name of Nobble.

Mrs. Tuckey, the landlady, was hardly less affected than her daughter, and had her reasons for entreating Mr. Vollum to look over his papers in the bar-parlour. The prisoners had just been searched, and the Bench had ordered their clerk to retire for the purpose of perusing, in calm privacy, the documents found upon their persons, and then to discharge himself in open Court, of all the treason he could pick out.

The hostess was determined that Mr. Vollum—a rival of Mr. Flip—should have his task made as pleasant to him as possible ; and sat him down at a table near an open window behind the screen, to a delicious anchovy toast and a tumbler of diluted sherry sprinkled with a generous surface of nutmeg —a cool drink which was, next to the landlady herself, Mr. Vollum's special weakness.

The personal effects found on Mr. Nobble were few ; and denoted a leaning more to order's than to-treason's side. They consisted of six one-pound notes, a short letter, and a pic-nic knife. This knife, besides being a horse-pick, a toothpick, a gimblet, a corkscrew, a punch, a tweezer, a file, a wrench, and a screw-driver, was knobbed at the end with a silver crown, which made it also a clandestine constable's staff. The letter ran thus :

"I now learn that he intends to ride across country from Shutbury to Nottingham; where he may arrive on Monday afternoon. He is certain to stop at the Royal George. He is easily wrought upon, and something must be done to induce him to push on at once to the Pentridge meeting on pretence that his influence alone can turn the Nottingham Captain and his crew from their fanatical purpose. The meeting is sure to be a seditious one ; and, if we can fix him with taking *any* part in it, we are safe. His intention is to come straight home from the Royal George, where this awaits you. He must *not* come home."

This epistle had no signature, although Mr. Vollum happened to know the handwriting, and was addressed to Mr. Nolliver, under cover to K. N. Nobble, Esq., Royal George, Nottingham, to be left till called for. "The only suspicious circumstance against the man," said Mr Vollum, is this going about with an alias." The letter bore the Crookston-Withers postmark.

And, to Mr. Vollum's astonishment, so did all the letters found on the other prisoner ; except one, and this had no postmark at all. It purported to be written by a political friend of Lord Wordley, but the writing was very like that of the prisoner, Nobble. It entreated the recipient to go to Pentridge, and use all his eloquence and influence with the assembly to abandon its hopeless purpose, and contained the secret pass-words, by the mention of which he would be known as one of the initiated. All the other letters were deeply black-bordered and were from the same writer—a lady. Although Mr. Vollum divined at a glance the tender nature of this correspondence, he sorted it according to dates, and went through it as methodically as if it had consisted of indictments or leases. When he had finished this part of his task, Mr. Vollum observed, speaking to himself (a habit he had), " No treason here, worse than domestic treason. Well, when one brother does hate another, the case—especially if the hate of a soured woman is thrown into the bargain—always turns out to be a case of Cain and Abel."

He had been occupied in his scrutiny for nearly an hour, when, overhead—where all had been hitherto deadly quiet—there was a sudden moving of chairs, and scuffling of feet. The court was being broken up abruptly. A constable (Mr. Frontis, in fact, the ladies' hairdresser) ran down stairs, rang the ostler's bell, and ordered, in the highest pitch of his treble voice, " A po-shay and pair immejently !" He then satisfied the curiosity that bloomed in the landlady's face, by squeaking, " Why, mem, we're in the wrong county. The prisoners is remanded to Derby."

CHAPTER THE SEVENTH.

FOUR months had passed away. Four months of lonely agony for the untried prisoners in Derby gaol; four months of unwearied machination against them from their enemies. In this time Mr. Flip, of the Royal Chesterfield Mail, had resigned his Majesty's service, and accepted office under the proprietary of the Derby Swiftsure; some said to be oftener in the bar of the Royal George.

Considering that it was his pride always to change horses, even at those attractive stables, in one minute and three-quarters, the accomplished whip kept his foot unconscionably long on the roller-bolt, and took an aggravating time to divide the reins between his fingers, on the open sunshiny day which preceded the trial of George Dornley for high treason at Derby; yet he could not ascend to his seat without a full and satisfying view of the gorgeous apparition at the bar of the Royal George. He would not say how many years he had known and loved the landlady in her bar-dress (he had never seen her in any other), and had gone on driving through life in hope; but now, the high-waisted satin pelisse with dangling buttons, and broad fur edging grandly displayed on her magnificent figure; dashing Legborn bonnet with the fluttering cherry-coloured ribbons; her smart reticule, and her green Limerick gloves daintily confining a sprig of rosemary between her fingers, struck him with an awful sensation that he had lived a life of presumption. When he saw his rival, Mr. Vollum, handing her into an inside place, he mounted his box moodily, and drove to within one stage of Derby without opening his mouth either to speak to the " box-seat," to drink, or indeed, to disentomb it once from its shawl sepulchre.

The merry little daughter and barmaid preferred to travel outside in the sunshine with her good friend the guard, and Mr. Vollum deposited her mother fussily in an inside seat; but, in his overwhelming desire to secure a place next to that lady he tumbled over the top-boots of one of the passengers.

"I suppose he's mad!" exclaimed a young man who sat opposite. Mr. Vollum frowned, and considered whether these words were indictable or not; but the speaker escaped prosecution by continuing the talk, which the change of horses had not interrupted:

"Nobody but a maniac could have believed himself able to sack Nottingham with a handful of rabble; and, as to his punishment, surely it is not humane to hang poor wretches because they are mad."

"Ecod! if that were the law," said the old gentleman in the corner, chuckling till he shook a sleet of hair powder over the collar of his coat, "I, being a physician, should be hanging people every day."

The country gentleman rapped out an oath. "Rot it, sir! rebellion's a madness that deserves hanging; and, by the blessing of Heaven, while England remains a free and happy country, rioters will always be hanged. But I don't believe any of 'em are mad; neither the Nottingham Captain, nor any of his crew; including your learned friend the Young Squire, who's to be tried to-morrow. They are sane enough, every man Jack of 'em."

"A man may be sane on every subject except one. He may be a monomaniac," returned the young man.

"Stuff!" was the reply. "I've been a visiting justice for a quarter of a century, and I think I ought to know something about lunatics. New-fangled nonsense! A man's mad, or he isn't mad. He can't be a quarter mad, or half mad, or three parts mad, can he? As for mono-what-d'ye-call it, nobody ever heard of such a thing when I was a boy."

"Nevertheless," said the physician, "it is very common. Why, there is a patient of mine, a lady (of course, I don't mention names), who is as rational, and patient, and clear-headed as the best of us—more so than the best of us would be, perhaps, if we were in as much trouble as she is—but who as thoroughly believes that she saw and conversed with a certain person, at a time when that certain person was ten miles away, as I believe you sit there."

Vollum pricked up his ears, and looked very hard at the doctor above his spectacles. The hanging philosopher, tired of the subject, asked, "When is this Nottingham Captain fellow to be hung? On Monday?"

"I think not," answered the younger traveller, "not until the trial of my friend as you call him, the Young Squire, Mr. Dornley, is over; and that comes on, as you observed, to-morrow."

"Well, *he's* sure to swing for it; that's one comfort," rejoined Rustic Humanity.

The younger man protested against such comfort, and the two kept up the dispute between them.

"As for young Dornley," roared the boisterous disputant, "hanging 's too good for him. A fellow of good blood leading poor ignorant devils into trouble, and then——"

"Stop!" said his opponent, warmly. "You are sentencing the man before he is tried. How do you know what he deserves? Perhaps he is innocent."

"Nobody would talk in that way but a radical, and a radical in disguise," exclaimed the other. "Where's your white hat?"

"I do not care who hears me," continued the person, not heeding the vulgar question, "and I say that I would not hang a dog upon such evidence as that which is to be brought against Young Dornley. If a certain amount of hanging be necessary for public tranquility—a notion not too ridiculous to be entertained in high quarters—I would feed the gallows with the witnesses: not with the prisoners, but with the paid spies and suborned treason-mongers." The county magistrate, in pulling his hat over his eyes, disturbed his flaxen wig. " Nolliver, the arch-spy, was afraid to show himself at the recent trials.; but he is the principal witness against Young Dornley, and they cannot do without him. If the Derby people catch him, they threaten, I'm told, to tear him limb from limb."

" It's infernal hot ! Wouldn't you like the window down, ma'am ?" the country squire asked, without looking round.

Mrs. Tuckey complacently assented ; remarking that it was more like June than October. From this minute the leather-lunged champion of the gallows deprived his fellow-travellers of the light of his countenance (a very red light, fed with ardent spirits) by looking out of window ; Mr. Vollum went on talking to himself and gazing at Mrs. Tuckey over his spectacles in a tender and abstracted manner ; but presently proved that she alone did not occupy his thoughts, by turning to the doctor, and saying, in an earnest under tone, " You, of your own actual knowledge, could not say that that gentle-man was not with the lady you have mentioned at the precise time she is so sure he was, could you ?"

" No, I could not. Because I was at Bath on the ninth of last June," the physician answered ; " you seem to know the lady."

" Perhaps I do."

Mrs. Tuckey experienced very few of the attorney's atten-tions from that moment ; for he was plunged into a whispered conversation with the doctor, whom he rightly guessed to be Dr. Bole. He stated that he was the attorney for George Dornley's defence. The crown had got nothing by using him —the town-clerk—shabbily, and giving the case for the pro-secution to Battam and Ball, of Derby, his rivals, as they would see ; for, having, as public officer of Nottingham, got hold of certain documents at the preliminary examination, he could impede, if not overthrow, the prosecution. But there were still certain facts which he wanted to know. He could not account, for instance, for the taciturnity and utter indif-ference of George Dornley to the result of his trial. Dr. Bole could. Mr. and Mrs. Calder Dornley had estranged him from his young and suffering wife by getting him tortured with all sorts of unfounded suspicions of her honour. They had also estranged him from Lord Wordley, and irreparably from his father.

"You have not received a subpœna, have you?" Vollum asked.

"No. What do I know of the matter?"

"Enough," said Vollum to himself, "to upset my defence: and" (aloud) "you won't be, perhaps?"

"Not if I can help it. Indeed I expect to meet the Crookston Hall travelling-carriage at Ripley to take me on to Bath; for, while visiting a patient at Nottingham, I got a summons informing me of old Mr. Dornley being *in extremis.*"

The attorney rubbed his hands, and stared over his spectacles at Mrs. Tuckey more abstractedly than ever. Then he talked to himself more than ever, and took notes of his own conversation with a pencil upon a card.

The talk was, after a pause, taken up by the barrister, who began describing a case in which he had got off a poacher by evidence that turned out to be false. The physician exclaimed, "Surely *that* passed the bounds of professional morality!"

"Not at all," volunteered the attorney, waking up to discuss "a point;" "you must remember that a barrister is bound to do the best he can for his client; and we must also remember that the barrister is not the judge. It is not for him to pronounce upon the likelihood or falsehood of the statements in his brief: all that he has got to do is to stick them into the jury as hard as he can. The great use of the go-between, an attorney, is to select what facts to lay before counsel, and what facts to conceal from him."

"Then the attorney is the culprit," the old gentleman persisted.

"Nothing of the sort. The attorney won't learn too much, if he knows his business. Supposing a person thinks himself (many a person does) more a culprit than he is?"

"Surely, I should know if I had committed murder or not," replied the doctor.

"No, you might not," Vollum answered quickly. "You would, of course, know whether you had killed any one or not; but you may not know whether you killed him with all the circumstances which, in the eye of the law, go to make a murder. In civil cases it constantly happens that people believe themselves to be in the wrong when they are in the right, Everything depends upon counsel."

"I only hope Mr. Dornley will be fortunate in his counsel," said the doctor.

Mr. Vollum feared not. Sergeant Penett having been suddenly taken ill, the weight of the defence would fall on the junior, Mr. Marsden, who was coming down special. Here an extraordinary phenomenon occurred—the barrister in the corner seat blushed to the ears.

"I have been," continued the attorney, "back to Nottingham to see what I could get out of the witnesses for the prosecution (I'm for the defence) that might tell in our favour. This lady's daughter is one of them." Mrs. Tuckey now blushed also—a deeper colour than her ribbons. The county magistrate, still with his face out of window, turned up the collar of his coat to the very corners of his eyes.

Here the coach stopped, and the guard opened the door to announce their arrival at Ripley.

"O, Ripley, is it!" was ejaculated through the edges of the coat-collar. "Don't shut the door. I'll get out here. Good day, gentlemen! Good day, ma'am?" Tightening his hat, and bringing the flaxen wig down over his forehead the Squire alighted, and strode into the inn without looking round.

"Well, but," intercepted the guard, showing his way-bill, "you're booked for Darby, sir."

"Very true, but I don't want to be in Darby till to-morrow. Hy there! Take my portmanteau out of the fore-boot!" The traveller then disappeared in the shadow of the inn-porch, without bestowing one instant on the extrication of his luggage from the boot, or on the guard's expected half-crown from his pocket.

That sum was, however, adroitly administered by another hand. "I want," insinuated Mr. Vollum, to have one look at your way-bill: only to know the names of the passengers.

"O, you needn't look. The big fellow just got out calls himself Robert Bumpton, Esquire; booked in London. The old gentleman in black is Dr. Bole of Matlock; and the tall chap is Mr. Marsden, a counsellor. The box-seat is Bantam's clerk from Darby, in charge of witnesses for to-morrow's trial."

Before Mr. Vollum could finish the prolonged whistle this news had prompted, a carriage and four dashed up, too fast and too close to the stage-coach to please the near leader, which reared and plunged in an ungovernable manner. Mr. Flip burned to add his shot to the volley of oaths discharged by the postboys, horse-keepers, and stable-idlers; but the melancholy state of his mind, and respect for the satin and fur inside, restrained him. At last the rackety leader was restrained also; and the coach would have started, if it had not been hailed by a servant in the private carriage, asking loudly for Dr. Bole. The guard, Mr. Flip's sworn friend, apprised the doctor of this summons, and then persuaded Mrs. Tuckey to join her daughter on the outside, Mr. Vollum being engaged in copying names from the way-bill. Dr. Bole was not long in getting out, and making his deferential bow at the carriage-door to the occupant inside.

"The crisis is so imminent, that I have come myself," said Mrs. Calder Dornley. "We cannot expect to find old Mr. Dornley alive when we get to Bath. I wish Bath were not so far off." The lady leaned very far back in her carriage to escape public observation; to which the coming trial of George Dornley had greatly subjected the family.

"You see, Dr. Bole," she remarked, when the doctor had transferred his luggage from the stage-coach to the carriage, "the death of Mr. Dornley would be very inconvenient to us were it to happen before the trial is over. If the wretched young man is found guilty before the entail can be cut off, and while he is even in nominal possession, the property would be forfeited to the crown, and go quite out of the family." Mrs. Calder Dornley said this very calmly: not in the least like a person in dread of a near relative being hanged next week.

The good old physician looked steadfastly into Mrs. Calder's face. "His son and heir might possibly recover it upon petition," he said. The lady's round black eyes flashed; but she divided the words of her reply with her usual deliberation. "Just so—if he had a son."

The change of horses having been made, the carriage rolled away towards Bath, taking the doctor with it.

Meanwhile, what with the delay, and the successes of his rival achieved in his own coach, Mr. Flip was in a state of mind to drive like a desperado. If the mere upsetting of the Swiftsure could bring mortal injury upon the lawyer without crumbling so much as a ribbon-end of Mrs. Tuckey's bonnet, there is no knowing what might happen; but, when Mr. Flip found that by the guard's good offices his resplendent "inside" had been induced to change her place for one outside next to him, and that her blithe little daughter was merrily shaking her curls on the roof beside the deposed " box-seat," he became another man, and was so merciful to his beasts that, when he dawdled into the yard of the King's Arms at Derby, he was fined eleven half-crowns for being eleven minutes behind time. Nor did Mr. Vollum take the absence of his beloved landlady much to heart; for he had a vast deal to cram Mr. Marsden with, now he knew him to be the junior who was to bear the whole brunt of Dornley's defence.

He was, however, much chagrined to find—while delicately helping the lady down the ladder at the journey's end—that her sprig of roemary had been transferred to the button-hole of his jolly rival.

CHAPTER THE EIGHTH.

It required all Mr. Flip's strength of limb and voice and all his good-nature to work his way with the blooming mother and daughter, next morning, through the surging multitude that choked up St. Mary's gate, before the Derby County Hall. Half an hour's labour had brought the little party no further than the door of the edifice; and they would not have got even into the outer hall, but for the chance assistance of Mr. Frontis, the Nottingham constable, who used his staff and his treble voice (too weak to disturb the proceedings within) so adroitly, that his friends managed to struggle into the court time enough to hear part of the opening of the prosecuting counsel's speech. The landlady had been greatly mortified that Mr. Vollum, after promising to obtain a good place for her in the great range of temporary seats (that her daughter, being the first witness to be called, might be saved from herding with the other witnesses), had not appeared at all. The effect of this lapse on Mr. Flip's mind was, on the contrary, quite exhilarating.

Mrs. Tuckey's ribbons and furs and satins, did everything, however, to get good places. Room was involuntarily made for her and her daughter on the front seat, Flip standing respectfully beside them in the crowd. Mrs. Tuckey was extraordinarily confused; not so much by the sharp artillery of eyes discharged at her pictorial attire from every corner of the court, as from the frequent reference then being made by Serjeant Moss to her establishment in Nottingham. At first, her daughter was too much amazed and absorbed to mind being constantly mentioned. The brown parched faces, the white wigs, and the purple vestments of the judges, amused her; the expansive presence and deep-voiced "Silence!" of the crier of the court, awed her; the haggard, callous look of her friend the prisoner, pained her; and the constant glances of his counsel (her mother's fellow-traveller) towards the door, whenever it opened, puzzled her. But presently she too was covered with blushes; for Serjeant Moss was again mentioning her in his smoothest tones. "I shall bring the barmaid before you," he was saying, wiping his forehead and balancing his bulging figure between the seat of the inner bar and the edge of the table, "to prove that the prisoner arrived at the Royal George at Nottingham on the afternoon of the day laid in the indictment—namely, the ninth day of June last past; that that young person gave him two letters, one of which, as I am advised, contained the secret password by which the conspirators made themselves known to one another. I shall produce another witness, by the aid of whose testimony you will trace him from Nottingham, to the White Horse at Pentridge, and thence to the actual scene of the riot. I must, however, inform you that there was an interval of ten minutes, during which the witness I am now alluding to lost sight of the prisoner: that hiatus will be partly filled up by the landlord of the Fox at Alfreton, at whose inn the prisoner drew rein, and inquired respecting a groom. Thus, then, gentlemen of the jury, we trace him to Pentridge, where his co-conspirators had already assembled. The defense may probably take advantage of the missing link I have mentioned in the chain of evidence, and of the mistiness of that evening. It may make much of the fact that the unhappy persons best able to identify the prisoner at the bar, are now lying under their respective sentences, and cannot with propriety be dragged into court to give evidence. But, gentlemen, in the face of such convincing testimony as that which I shall have the honour of bringing before you; in the face of the tumultuous transactions at the Butterley Iron Works; the shooting of the farm-servant at Topham's Close; and the capture of the prisoner early the next morning, when he had almost effected his escape; in the face of such an accumulation of proof, it will be impossible to dispute the facts of this distressing case." Here the learned gentleman looked at his brief. "These will not perhaps be denied; but 'motives' may be urged upon you. You may be told that this misguided and misguiding young gentleman presented himself amongst the rioters to warn and to dissuade; that he went to them in the cause of law and order. But, men in possession of passwords; men so well known to a seditious fraternity as to have cant designations conferred upon them—the Young Squire, to wit—men actually caught in the fact of rebellion, which is the most heinous form of peace-breaking, do not usually range themselves on the side of peace-making. Besides, gentlemen of the jury, motives, whether of the purest or of the basest kind, must be discarded altogether. The law says that mere presence at a riot is participation in it. The prisoner was there: present with the rebels. That is enough. I feel most sensibly, gentlemen," continued Serjeant Moss, with oily solemnity, "the dreadful position in which you are placed. I appreciate the awful responsibility which may demand the condemnation of a fellow-creature—one of your own order—to the appalling expiation of the crime of high treason. But you must not shrink from that responsibility; this august bench must not shrink from that responsibility; I, the humble individual whose painful task it is now to address you, must not shrink from that responsibility." The learned serjeant then sat down, having wiped out, with his cambric pocket-handkerchief, the unctuous smile with which his last words to a county jury were always accompanied.

If Mrs. Tuckey had not given her daughter's skirt a parting pull to take a pucker out of the skirt, as the damsel left her seat to ascend the witness-box, and if the maiden's dangling curls—hardly confined by her bonnet—had not obscured her face whenever she was asked a question, there would not have been so much tittering in the court as there was; even although she would persist in prefacing each answer with "Please, sir." She felt very unhappy when, after having told the whole truth to the first gentleman, the second gentleman—who she thought would be very kind indeed to her, as he was on her friend's side—appeared not to believe one word she had uttered. She was ready to cry when Counsellor Marsden asked her, severely, whether she was quite sure that the gentleman she gave two of the letters to, and the prisoner at the bar, was the same person.

Nothing could be more certain. Her answer was confirmed by the prisoner himself; who, roused from his callousness to the proceedings, gave her a smile; and it was a smile of recognition. Mr. Marsden bit his lip, but went on, after a pause. The prisoner had arrived on horseback, had he: of what colour was the horse?

"Please, sir, it was a black horse?"

A black horse. Well, about the letters? "Why, please sir, I handed over two letters in the name of Dornley, and one letter in the name of Nobble."—Would she know Mr. Nobble again if she saw him? "Please, sir, yes, in a minute."—Could she remember how Mr. Dornley was dressed? "Please, sir, he had on a white great coat and a white hat."

A pause. While the witness was "standing down," the prisoner leant over to whisper a word into the ear of his counsel, which sounded like a word of remonstrance; but his counsel looked towards the door, and took not the slighest notice of it.

The next witness was a long time in appearing. He had to be fetched from a hiding-place somewhere under the building. Why he was afraid of being seen in public, the hiss of execration, too spontaneous to be suppressed, which greeted him when he answered to the name of Nolliver, sufficiently explained. Although he squared his shoulders and looked boldly round the court, the tight grasp with which he held on to the rail of the witness-box, and the twitching of his nether lip, showed that he was not so much at ease as he wished it to be supposed he was. He proved, however, what lawyers call a good witness; for practice had made perfect. Nothing could be clearer than his narrative of the ride with the prisoner from Nottingham to Pentridge; nothing more exact than his recollection of the precise minute at which each incident of the journey took place. He detailed with studied accuracy what passed at the White Horse; what happened afterwards; how the farm-servant was murdered at Topham's Close, the prisoner being present; how he himself was captured by horse soldiers; the same squadron took him on to capture the prisoner; how the latter was arrested in Arch-lane; and how himself was ultimately released on turning approver.

The heavy despairing look which Marsden constantly cast towards the door, left him when he began to cross-examine Mr. Nolliver. The legal mind lighted up at the prospect of reducing this burley witness to the smallest dimensions. It delighted to extract confessions of his various disguises and aliases; of having taken the name of Nobble, and the character of an Eastern Delegate; of having spoken frequently at seditious meetings; of having also made himself known, on the road, as Squire Bumpton, a visiting justice of twenty years' standing.—What was his profession? Nothing particular.—Was he in the pay of Government? No.—Had he ever been in the pay of the Government? Never—that is, no more than a councillor might be, when he received a Government fee.—Had he ever worn a red waistcoat? Perhaps he had, when it was the fashion to wear red waistcoats.—But are not red waistcoats the uniform of Bow-street officers? He believed they were.—In one word, sir, are you not a paid Government spy?

The Other Side interfered. The question was in outrageous excess of forensic licence; and the Court concurred. Marsden bowed and resumed—

"Now, sir, on the word of a man who may, or may not be a Government spy, was the horseman, with whom you parted before you entered Alfreton, and the horseman whom you overtook after having passed through Alfreton, one and the same person?"

"He was."

"Take care, sir! You swear that?"

" I swear it, if it was the last words I have to speak."

Re-examined by Serjeant Moss: "Is that man the prisoner at the bar?"

Witness : " He is."

The prisoner uttered an involuntary expression of assent; and his counsel, seeing that it had been noted by the jury, occupied himself, while one of the judges asked Mr. Nolliver a few questions, in writing on a scrap of paper which ho handed to the prisoner, these words: "If you do not leave your case entirely in my hands, I will throw up my brief."

Dornley's answer pencilled on the same paper was: " I will *not* be defended by the help of a lie."

Mr. Marsden tore up the memorandum, and said partly to himself and partly to the young coadjutor who was taking notes for him, " I *can* put a stop to this, and I will." He then examined the informer relative to the letter he had received at the bar of the Royal George; but no sort of tortuous interrogating could extract from him the writer's name. The court ruled that he was not bound to reveal it. Then came a rack of questions about the letter sent in to the prisoner from the Green Boar. Had not the prisoner gone from the Royal George to that Inn ? He had: to see a friend.—Had he not written a letter there ? He had, to his wife.—In short, was not the letter which enticed the prisoner to the Pentridge meeting, written by himself, the witness ? The baffled witness said, " I decline to answer that question," with such a mixture of hesitation and shamelessness, that he might as well have answered it in the affirmative.

The prisoner had relapsed into his old abstraction ; but Mr. Marsden roused him from it during the change of witnesses, by handing him another letter—that which had been directed to Mr. Nobble, and which Vollum got possession of at his preliminary examination of both prisoner's personal effects, and had never given up. He wrote on the back of it, "Here is the letter. Shall I call witnesses to prove the handwriting ?"

George Dornley read these words, and saw that the letter of instruction addressed to Nobble at the Green Boar, to which alone he owed his present position, was in the handwriting of his own brother. Trembling, he pressed his hand over his eyes as if to hide from himself this hideous revelation. His agitation was so manifest that one of the judges ordered him the indulgence of a chair. For some time he seemed to take no interest in the trial.

19

The witness then in the box was the landlord of the Fox, at Alfreton. He swore that a gentleman came past his house on horseback and asked about a groom. Serjeant Moss's junior (a gentleman about sixty, named Baldy) worked very hard at this last question; but the witness had never seen a groom; nobody, as he had heard of, had seen a groom at Alfreton, about nine o'clock at night, on the ninth of June.

This was the weak point—perhaps the only weak point—of the prosecution; for it had failed, after spending hundreds of pounds, to find the servant with whom the prisoner had changed coats and horses. It failed, because none of its myrmidons had thought of seeking a soldier instead of a groom. If they had, they need have gone no further than Nottingham Barracks; where, by looking up the C troop of the Twelfth Hussars, they would have found Thomas Hockle occupying the rank and title of Lance-Corporal Haimes. Disgusted with the world, he had enlisted on the day after his master's incarceration.

Examination of the landlord continued: Could not swear that the gentleman witness spoke to was the prisoner, though witness thought he was. It was getting dark.

"Was there," asked Marsden, in cross-examination, "light enough to see the colour of the traveller's horse?"

"Oi, there war that. It war a grey horse—a'most white."

"Could you distinguish the colour of the gentleman's coat?"

"Well, no. But it was a darkish coat."

"Was it a white coat."

"No."

Here the aspect of the jury-box changed. Instead of two rows of motionless faces, it suddenly presented several knots of shoulders and heads, that gave forth a confused buzz, in which the barmaid's evidence, thus flatly contradicted, was often mentioned. The Other Side bent down the corners of its mouth, and leaned back, throwing its pen upon the table contemptuously. Then its senior rose, and, in a confident tone, called Thomas Tanner.

Thomas Tanner swore that it was he who rode the old grey horse from Pentridge to Eastwood. It was the prisoner's horse. The prisoner, dressed in a dark coat, was the person called the Young Squire, who appeared at the meeting. He had no doubt of his identity. He'd swear to him amongst a thousand. Serjeant Moss gave the jury a sharp nod, which implied, "*that* point is settled;" whereupon the knots in the jury-box relaxed again into two rows of calm, convinced faces.

The defence put one last question to Thomas Tanner:

"You turned approver at the recent trial of the so-called Nottingham Captain, did you not?" And it got a reluctant affirmative. The jury again consulted busily amongst themselves. This closed the case for the prosecution.

Marsden's lip quivered and his hand shook when, standing up to commence the defence, he looked round for Vollum. Should he ask for time, or should he go on, now that the jury seemed on the whole generously disposed? He determined to proceed. He would talk on and gain time until the witness upon whose testimony the entire defence rested, should arrive; if indeed Vollum could succeed in bringing her. He plunged into his exordium almost recklessly. He pointed out the extraordinary disadvantages under which the defence laboured; the absence of his own leader, and the consequent loss to the prisoner of the two addresses to the jury which the law mercifully allowed to persons accused of high treason. When he alluded to certain distressing passages of his client's private life; when he revealed that the gentleman at the bar had, within scarcely a year, become a husband and a bereft father; when he pictured the desolation of her who was nearest and dearest to him, the jury showed signs of emotion. He would not, Marsden continued to say, dispute the law of the case as laid down by his learned friend the counsel for the crown; but would address himself wholly to the facts. Could they believe the oath of the witness Nolliver? Could they believe a man who assumed a variety of aliases, and whom he would prove to be a traitor and a spy? (The county gentlemen in the jury-box shook their heads and moved uneasily.) Could they believe the witness Tanner, who had turned king's evidence against the wretched persons now awaiting the execution of their dreadful sentence? And upon whose evidence did the accusation rest? Why, upon those men, and those only. Even if they could be believed, they had not said enough to establish the identity of the prisoner in connecting him with the transactions of the ninth of June. Could it be credited that a man who appeared in the public road on a black mare in a white coat, could be the same individual, who after an incredibly short interval of time, was seen on the same public road, on a white gelding in a dark coat? Could he have changed his horse and his clothes by magic?

Here the prisoner, roused by the fervour of Marsden's appeal, rose and uttered what appeared to be a protest. But the Chief Justice, leaning very far over his desk, told him, that he must either leave his case wholly in the hands of the barrister, or wholly take it out of them.

"Meantime let me ask you, Mr. Marsden," said another of the judges, "what you are going upon? Do you, or do you not, intend to set up an alibi?" His lordship merely asked the question to save the time of the court.

This was an anxious moment. Marsden must now elect either to set up a defence for the support of which the direct evidence he was waiting for had not arrived—would, perhaps, never arrive—or he must simply abandon the case to mere conjectures and probabilities. He stood nervously clenching his brief with one hand, his face turned full towards the door.

But it opened. Mr. Vollum dragged, rather than supported, a lady through the crowded passage into the body of the court. Marsden fetched a long deep breath, as if an incubus had been removed from him. But the new presence in the court had an opposite effect upon the prisoner. A single shadow manifested his astonishment and despair. He exclaimed, "My God!" and, sinking into the chair, buried his face within his hands, like one stricken. Mrs. Tuckey gave up her seat to the trembling lady; who could not once raise her eyes from the ground to look at the prisoner.

"Yes, my lord, and gentlemen of the jury," Marsden continued, in a clear, full, almost cheerful voice, "that *is* our defence. We plead alibi. I have nothing more to say. Our witnesses will do the rest."

Serjeant Moss looked up at Marsden, and whispered, "Now really this is too——Well, we shall see."

The witness was in the box, with her head averted from the prisoner.

The words, "Speak up!" which ended the form of oath as administered by the swearing officer, seemed to be a necessary adjuration to this witness; for, surely from so fragile and trembling a form; from so pale a face, with its large, rimmed, wan eyes; from such parched, colourless lips, the sounds that were to come would be very faint and low. Yet, the first answer startled the whole assembly by its distinctness and clearness. The prisoner, when it struck upon his ear, uttered a deep despairing sigh.

Her testimony was to the effect that, at the very time his presence at Pentridge had been sworn to on the night of the ninth of June, George Dornley, "my husband" (spoken in a louder and prouder tone), arrived at the cottage at Crookston-Withers. Then the witness faltered. She was very ill at that time, but not too ill to recollect that he came; that she spoke to him, as he sat or stood beside her couch. She remembered what she said to him.

"And what," Serjeant Moss interrogated, "did he say to you?"

She paused, and moved her eyes quickly to and fro, as if making a strong effort of memory. The question was repeated. She could not answer it, and it was not pressed; but she responded to succeeding questions readily. He was present beside her from long after ten o'clock, until—until—— Her eyes, gradually turning, as if by slow but irresistible fascination towards her husband, at length rested upon him crouching, prostrate, overwhelmed; and stretching out her arms towards him, she exclaimed, "George!" and swooning, fell forward upon the rail of the witness-box.

The commotion occasioned by her removal from the court drowned the commencement of the prosecuting counsel's reply; which was, however, short, and not very lucid; for the last witness had overthrown all his calculations, and neutralised all his well-studied arguments.

The presiding judge, in summing up, balanced the extraordinary contradictions in the evidence without professing to reconcile them. "You may find it difficult," he said to the jury, "to unite, out of the evidence I have just read to you, the rider of the two horses and the wearer of the two coats in one person, and that person the prisoner; but it will be for you to say whether you can do so with sufficient accuracy to fix his identity. I frankly confess to you, that the evidence of the lady who was last examined (who, I am bound to say, gave it with remarkable clearness so long as she could control her feelings) appears to me to render the conflict of testimony explicable upon no other ground than that of the witness labouring under some hallucination respecting the arrival of her husband at her house, and his presence at the time and during all the time, which other witnesses have sworn that he was present elsewhere. Still, there being no evidence before us as to the state of the lady's mind at that time, no supposition must for one moment weigh in your minds against positive evidence."

During the partial silence which reigned in the court while the jury were absent considering their verdict, the little barmaid wept in her mother's lap, and the landlady wept too; for hysterical shrieks pierced the court from the witness's room; into which the witness for the defence, Eusta Dornley, had been assisted.

But there was a dead silence when the jury reappeared, and the crier put the question—

"How say you, gentlemen of the jury, guilty or not guilty?"

Not a breath was drawn until the foreman had pronounced the words: "Not guilty!"

CHAPTER THE NINTH.

THE morning after George Dornley's trial was not a very gloomy time in Derby, although a public execution had taken place in the town. The Nottingham Captain and some of his tithing-men had paid the terrible penalty of their belief in the glowing statements of Mr. Nolliver, and in their own ability to put down borough-mongering by force of arms, to improve trade and to repeal taxation. So far, the plans of his majesty's ministers prospered. The dreadful lesson would, they believed, spread terror and obedience throughout the land. But George Dornley's acquittal was an untoward event. His conviction would have favoured the notion that the Strong Government of that day exercised no class favouritism, and that gentle and simple were made equally to feel the weight of its iron authority. Although the Young Squire was a local political idol, his escape from the fate which that morning overtook his fellow-prisoners, did not improve public faith in even-handed justice. Everybody knew, it was argued, that Mr. George Dornley appeared at the Pentridge meeting; the jury must have known he was there; his own counsel knew it; the judges knew it; and if his wife had been the wife of a hammerman or frame-work knitter, d'ye think she would have been believed? But, poor soul! what she did, she did for the best; and the best came of it: for Young Dornley was a good lad—they all knew that—and nobody could say they were not glad he was let free.

This was the general turn of talk at the bars and in the tap-rooms of the Derby public-houses; over the counters of most of the shops; in the mills and factories where holiday had not been made; and in the market-place—for the great Gallows Instructor always taught its egregious lessons on market days, when the largest number of pupils could be assembled—yet, no stranger entering the town during that day could have distinguished it from a day of pleasure. It was not extraordinary, therefore, that the landlord of the Angel and Bells close to the County Hall was embarrassed with too great a crowd of customers. He gave up serving in despair, and went on arguing vehemently about the acquitted prisoner. The claims of Lance-Corporal Haimes, of the Twelfth Hussars, with a billet for himself and four comrades, were, of course, utterly disregarded. The dispute waxed warm. The landlord thumped the bar with his fist. "Wasn't I," he angrily asked, "at the trial, looking at him all the time? D'ye think I didn't know him directly he walked into this very passage?"

"Don't tell me!" answered Mr. Frontis, as he dug a sixpennyworth of lunch out of a double Gloucester cheese. "I don't mean to believe that a gentleman so well known about here—he and his ancestors for centuries—has got no other place to put his head into than this? Here! a nip of Burton!"

"I say it 's him and nobody else!" The landlord was growing irate: "why, I'm not such a fool as not to know a man again that I'd been looking at all the morning, just because he had got a hat on. I tell you he walked in by himself, and asked, in a mournful sort of voice, if he could have a private sitting-room and a bed. You might have knocked me down with a pipe-stalk!"

"Then do you mean to say he has been here all night?"

"Yes, I do, and as solitary as ever he was in gaol. There's been his lawyer and his lady here to see him a dozen times; but he won't see a soul," replied the landlord, whose ruffled veracity was now sufficiently calmed to enable him to serve his most clamourous customers.

Meanwhile, some of them were helping themselves; for the lance-corporal knew of no other way to attract attention, than to order his men to draw what beer they wanted, to drink it, and not to pay for it. While these words of command were being implicitly obeyed, the lance-corporal marched up-stairs; having already heard enough from the landlord to induce him to enter the first-floor sitting-room without knocking. The occupant was writing; and, having started up menacingly to resent the intrusion, found the corporal standing straight against the open door, performing a military salute; but sat down quietly when he recognised Thomas Hockle, in spite of his regimentals.

The interviw was so painful that even in trying to describe it to me, the riding-master was too much affected to give a clear idea of what passed. George Dornley, utterly forsaken and hopeless, was arranging his papers. He was totally changed. Although touched by the interest which his former groom took in him, he was almost sullen. He tried every practical method to rid himself of Tom's presence. Tom, however, said frankly, that Mr. George was not in a state to be left to himself, and that it was his intention to keep guard over him. After a minute or two passed in deep thought, Dornley determined to confide in the man thus far:—as he intended to go abroad, he would give his papers into Hockle's charge.

"But," said the lance-corporal, "I am going abroad myself—to India. We have got our route, and sail next Thursday."

That was of no consequence. Wherever he went he could take the papers with him.

The document had scarcely been tied up securely, before the door opened again, and Mr. Vollum presented himself with a lady. Hockle described her as thin and pale; but upright, undaunted; an unnatural brightness flashing from her eye. She cast herself towards Dornley; but he stood aloof. She trembled; and, during that short spasm, seized the back of a chair for support; for Vollum, having introduced her into the room, retired as quickly and timidly as if he had set light to a powder magazine. Hockle would also have left the room, but Dornley desired—commanded him—to remain.

"I will not be alone," he said, partly aloud, "with, with—" he hesitated, mentioned no name; did not even look at his wife. "There can," he said louder, "be nothing for us to speak about which any person may not hear."

"Upon this," Hockle said, in telling me this part of the story—"Mrs. George looked at me in a way that went to my very heart. It was the old look that she gave me in the dingle, when she said, 'I think we may trust him, dear George.' I guessed why Mr. George was so deadly against her:—no honest man would have liked his wife any the better for perjuring herself, even to save him. But my blood boiled against Mr. George for being so cold—so different from what he used to be. As for me, I could at that moment have laid down my life for her; perjury, or no perjury."

She spoke first; but she said very little. She said simply, that her enemies had prevailed; that she and Mr. George were separated for ever; but that before she died (Mr. George shuddered), she *would* set herself right with him. She had done nothing—nothing (she thought a moment), no nothing which she could repent of—"I solemnly swear it!"

Mr. George saw her standing before him, erect, brave, but not bold, looking straight upon him. Their eyes were fixed upon each other; they did not seem to breathe. She did not take her eyes from him even when she added, "I will go now." And she would have gone; but I placed a chair in her way, so that I could gently sink her into it.

Mr. George waited a little while, and then said, "I hoped that this would not have been—I am not adamant; although trouble and desolation have driven me——" He checked himself; for tears were welling up into his wife's eyes, and tears were then to be very much dreaded. "I know that I have

escaped ignominy, and that you have saved me. But an ignominious death is better than an ignominious life."

It was terrible to see her eyes move from side to side like
lightning, as if thought and recollection and perplexed ideas
were all battling together in her brain. Mr. George looked
frightened. "I never saw a mad person," Hockle remarked
to me, "but I am sure that the way she looked about—so
quick and wild, and yet without seeing anything except what
was going on in her mind—must be just the way people look
who are not in their senses. It was awful."

Presently she spoke in an unearthly whisper. Hockle could
not distinguish what she uttered; but the words conveyed to
Dornley something that changed—roused him. He rose and
clutched the front of his hair fiercely, as if trying to crush in
his forehead. He kept on repeating the words which his wife
had, I suppose, whispered: "Not dead of neglect, but stolen!"
"Not dead of neglect, but stolen!" With this he took her
hand tenderly; but she, who coming into the room, seemed
ready to fall into his arms and pour out a torrent of love that
would have swept away every trace of past grief—did not return the pressure of his hand. She smiled on him, but without recognition; the power of distinguishing him as her husband seemed to have left her.

How Dr. Bole came upon the scene at this crisis, Hockle's
narrative was too confused for me to understand. Perhaps,
having travelled back post from Bath, with the news of old
Mr. Dornley's death after having cut off the entail of the
Crookston estates (the doctor thought illegally), Vollum had
met him in the street and told him where the disinherited
gentleman was to be found. His whole attention was, however, absorbed by his patient. She smiled on him too; calmly,
mechanically, but did not speak a word. The doctor gave
me a look which told me to watch her while he took Mr.
Dornley to the window.

"I have heard the manner of your acquittal," he said, in a
lone tone, "and can thoroughly reconcile it with your wife's
truthfulness."

"God bless you, doctor!" Dornley took Bole's hand in
both his own, and listened with even more eagerness than he
showed when waiting the verdict of the jury.

"You know," pursued the physician, "how her whole mind and soul were set upon your returning to her from Italy on the ninth of June. You know also her delicate condition at that time; but you do not know that, after she recovered from the shock of your non-appearance, and the event it brought on, she continued under the delusion—one of those delusions not uncommon to young mothers—that you were present, and she talked to the air as if she were talking to you; conscious of no other person's presence, not even the presence of her baby."

"How do you know all this? you—you were not present."

"No; but, as the delusion remained—lasts, indeed, to this moment—I took pains to trace its origin. Your wife is sound and sensible on every subject, except that one conviction of your presence on the ninth of June; and I, as her medical adviser, always enjoined her never to speak of the circumstance, lest her enemies should get her pronounced insane. She as firmly believes in the truth of what she swore to, as that I know it is a delusion."

When the husband, on hearing this, clasped his wife in his arms, kissed her, called her by every endearing name; and when Hockle saw that it was too late, and that she was insensible to his caresses, it was more, he said, than he could bear.

That night stern military duty obliged Lance-Corporal Haimes to leave Derby; and, in less than a week, he was on the sea bound for Bombay. Another ship from another port was at the same time bearing George Dornley, alone, broken-down and broken-hearted, to the West Indies, where Lord Wordley had kindly provided him with honourable banishment, on an estate of his own. Dr. Bole had strongly advised the separation from his wife, as best calculated to promote her eventual recovery; of which he spoke very confidently. She was placed in the best private asylum in the county.

CHAPTER THE TENTH.

On taking possession of the Crookston Hall estate, Calder Dornley found that his late father's profusion had considerably embarrassed it, and the first year was passed by him and his wife in schemes of parsimony for emancipating it from debt. In the second year they were rich; for Sir Bayle Stonard had died, and Stonard Abbey, with an enormous hoard of personal wealth, came into their possession. But—being rich, and feeling that all in the world they had ever hoped for was theirs; shunning society; owning no ties; enjoying no resources or occupations beyond those afforded by the practice of parsimony; having no future, life became to them a dreary penance. To each other they were indeed all in all; but the bond was rather that of partners in guilt than of partners in affection. It was less love, than a worrying discomfort when apart.

At length this sort of life became insupportable. The only mitigation of it was derived from any little good they had done, or could do. It got to be a great relief to them, that having basely intended to conceal their brother's child, they had written to George to apprise him of its existence, and to assure him that every care should be taken of it. They also administered to the wife as frequently and liberally as her unhappy state would permit.

It was not, however, until Mrs. Calder Dornley had herself lingered and sunk under an hereditary disease which had already extinguished the Stonard baronetcy, that the widower, now reduced to the condition of a second Cain—doubting the legality of his father's proceedings in barring the entail—deriving no moment of pleasure from his wealth, and hating his position—determined to repair the wrong he had done. By this time Eusta had so far recovered that, under the advice of the good old Dr. Bole, an experiment could be safely tried for her return to the world. It was at the time when emancipation was granted to the West India slaves, and George's services on Lord Wordley's plantations were no longer needed. He was, in fact, on his way to England.

Miss Pim, the latest object of Mrs. Calder's relenting good deeds, had been granted free residence in Corner Cottage. She had scrupulously preserved, not only every article of furniture, but the arrangement of it. Eusta was successfully removed from the asylum; and, for several days, fell into the routine of home duties she had been accustomed to, before the fatal ninth of June.

Dr. Bole had always dreaded the first meeting of Eusta with her son; but when, on her return to the cottage, she beheld a fine, frank-looking boy reading at the parlour table, she at once accepted him as her son; kissing him affectionately, as if she and he had not been parted. It would appear that she had never doubted his having been preserved to her, and her facility of creating mind-pictures, had followed him in imagination from infancy to his present stature and appearance, during the whole of her seclusion.

Years had set no mark upon her; for her malady had left her mind calm and unexcited. Except that her figure was rounder and her manner more reserved and grave, she appeared to be as young, and was, in reality, handsomer than formerly. She spoke of her husband's absence, as of something neither strange nor inexplicable. Only she was apt to confound Italy with the West Indies.

At length Dr. Bole had the courage to allude to the events of the terrible Ninth of June. To his mortification, he found that the impression that her husband had stood beside her on that unfortunate night, seemed ineffaceable. It happened that, unless the ship was delayed, her husband would arrive very near its anniversary; and the good old physician determined to turn the coincidence to account. He wrote a letter to George Dornley, which reached him on landing; giving a full and cheerful account of his wife's health, and detailing his plan for completing her cure.

On this later Ninth of June, Crookston-Withers glowed with sunshine. Eusta sat at her parlour-window. The palace of the Sleeping Beauty could not have remained so exactly the same as of old, as Corner Cottage did. Eusta was again engaged in lace-making. Her longing heart again bounded with the old hope that The Expected was coming before his time; then sank with disappointment when some strange horseman passed. Dr. Bole had arranged that her son should spend that day at Crookston Hall; but that his uncle (who had, at the doctor's earnest entreaty hitherto kept from Mrs. George's sight) should call towards the end of the day. The death of Mrs. Calder had left out one character of the former dramatis personæ.

Eusta received Mr. Calder Dornley as she had received her son; precisely as if their intercourse had never been broken off; but impatiently. She tacitly expressed that his presence was an intrusion. Nine o'clock approached. Dr. Bole, in the little kitchen—the temporary guest of dear old Miss Pim— watched the crisis with an anxiety almost insupportable. Presently a horse's canter was heard. It ceased. The door opened suddenly; some one rushed into the little parlour; there was an hysterical scream of joy; George Dornley and his wife were locked in a close embrace.

"I cannot describe to you" (it was the good old physician himself who told me this part of the story), "the anguish of dread which I felt to hear what words Mrs. George would first speak, after her emotions had subsided. It was worse than waiting to hear a sentence of life or death. Thank God, what she did say proved that the experiment had succeeded?"

"Was the old delusion thoroughly expelled?"

"Yes; or rather, it is now confused with the real meeting on the last ninth of June. George Dornley, his wife, and their son, are now travelling in Italy."

"But how comes it that Mr. Calder is still in possession of the Crookston estate?"

"George Dornley would not dispossess his brother, and Calder now acts as his steward. When the latter nearly knocked you off Tom Hockle's horse, he was looking after some improvements he was carrying out in the estate for his brother's benefit."

XXXV.

THE LAMBETH-MARSH MULCIBERS.

JANUARY 10, 1857.

WHEN I looked down, down, down into the crater of her Majesty's screw steamship Volcano (eight hundred horse-power), and pondered breathlessly on the distracting maze of shafts, beams, cranks, wheels, and cylinders; when I was told that a single finger pressing down a certain small lever can set the whole mass in ruthless motion; driving the Volcano her-

self through the water at the rate of fourteen miles an hour,
—I wondered where the present race of Vulcans and Cyclops
(born with more eyes than one) were bred, and under what
Memnonian roof the bewildering engines were brought into
existence. Surely, I reflected, the blacksmiths of Etna and
Lemnos must have been pigmies compared with the giants of
these later days; and their forges mere village smithies. Else
how could those shafts, each a single mass of wrought iron,
some sixteen tons in weight, be formed, and polished, and adjusted to a hair's breadth; how could the two-bladed brass
fan, or screw-propeller, weighing eleven tons or so, be cast
and fitted, carried from the factory to the ship, and put into
its place under water, with all the accuracy and some of the
ease with which the mainspring fixed to a lady's watch?

This tremendous work is done, I afterwards learnt, by modern, but not wholly by human, giants. Even when Vulcan
forged the bolts of Jove, he found flesh and muscle journeymen not strong enough for his place; and—if Hesiod may be
trusted—contrived automaton statues, by whose help alone he
was able to turn out the heaviest government orders for thunderbolts. Vulcan's plan has been followed by our British
Vulcans, the Nasmyths, Whitworths, Fairbairns, Penns, and
by the parents and teachers of some of those eminent machin-
ists, the Maudslays; their automata being steam-hammers, and
cutting, planing, punching, slotting, and riveting machines:
giants all, capable of making any sort of ironmongery, from
thunderbolts of fifty Jupiter-power (should such classical hard-
ware ever come into demand), down to fish-hooks and cambric
needles. The entire plant of Vulcan, Polyphemus and Company,
with supernatural improvements must, I considered, have been
removed from Sicily and the Euxine, to Manchester, Leeds,
Birmingham, Wolverhampton, Millwall, and Lambeth Marsh;
and gigantic intellect must have succeeded gigantic stature in
the good-will and management of the business.

Growing still more dizzy, yet still more curious in contemplating the complex abyss of the Volcano's machinery, I conceived the wild wish of seeing Titanic engines like hers in the
home of their birth; where, perhaps, they are made, and kept
—wholesale, retail, and for exportation—in rows, like time-
pieces in a French clock-shop. In satisfaction of this desire

I was directed to the great factory of Messrs. Maudslay and Field.

This establishment spreads itself over about five acres of Lambeth Marsh, now a densely peopled district of South London, and only a marsh by tradition ; but, being built in floors, would, if all were on the ground, cover some dozen acres. It gives employment to fifteen hundred Mulcibers, who are chiefly employed in feeding and attending upon the iron giants that execute most of the work.

O, the grim, rigid, relentless power, with which they shaved, and shared, and cut, and bored blocks and pillars of iron, tons in weight! They cut out and put together a huge steam-boiler with an inevitable directness of purpose that is simply awful, and with much less fuss than a seamstress makes to complete a calico-bolster. A broad plank of iron, nearly an inch thick and as large as a long dining-table, is laid on an automaton's flat lap, and is cut by a scissor-like chisel moving up and down at its edge, into any shape the superintending Mulciber wills. It can be sewn to other iron sheets by an inexorable seamstress—a giant twin of her planing and cutting sisters,—that punches rows of holes all round the edges of the plate, with less effort than I could bore card-board. Her coadjutor, a thick-set, determined steam workman, then fastens the edges of the plates together by crushing rivet-bolts into the holes at each edge and instantly riveting them to one another with a cold-blooded, terrifying force. Compare these operations with the tinkering of the Vulcans of old! who had to use niggling centrebits, and to rivet their work with noisy hammers; and took a longer time to turn out the tip of an arrow or the crest of a helmet, than their powerful progeny require to twist a score of gun-barrels, or to complete a locomotive engine.

"Take care! The forge hammer is not quite obsolete." I should have known this to my cost if a stalwart arm had not dragged me out of the swing of a double-handed hammer then being wielded by a flesh and blood blacksmith, to form rods for rivet-bolts. In watching this man, the impression that the mechanical arts do not promote the picturesque or help to inspire the artist, was forcibly revived. The graceful elasticity of his motions was a delightful contrast to the hard, undeviating routine of his automaton shopmates. The highest models of Grecian art, were not more graceful than the unconscious attitudes of this smith, while swinging his hammer over his head to bring it tremendously down upon the glowing metal. Rooting his feet apart upon the ground while stooping to raise the hammer, and drawing them together when swinging it to deliver the blow, every limb fell, in its turn, into harmony with the rest of the figure, and expressed muscular strength and elasticity perfectly. I once saw even greater elegance of motion displayed in connexion with boiler plates. It was in Lancashire, where they made them in an enormous smithy surrounded by furnaces; an overpowering steam hammer standing in the midst. The men, having drawn out a big, shapeless lump of metal white hot from the fire, and having dragged it along the sheet-iron floor to the hammer, escaped myriads of sparks by holding their leather aprons at one corner, up to their faces, and turning elegant pirouettes, to present their backs as targets for the showers of shooting sparks. Nothing at the opera could be more graceful. Then—when they dragged the still red mass to the rolling mills, through which it was to be passed, from wider to narrower, until pressed into such plates as I had just seen sewn together by the iron stitchers—the attitudes of the men, swaying their bodies back to receive the red-hot sheet from one roller and to return it through another, were quite picturesque.

The grotesque diablerie, of iron-working, is practised in the Lambeth Marsh casting-shop on the first floor : an enormous apartment, roofed chiefly with skylights, and floored with sand and earth, very like the carpet trod by the horses at the Royal Equestrian Amphitheatre close by. Underneath a part of it, are the loam and masonry of which the form of the article to be cast is made ; and, into which, the molten metal is now being poured from a prodigious lipped basin. This form, besides earth, sand, and bricks, is composed of hay, dung, and other combustibles ; which, when the molten metal is run into it, generates a gas that would inevitably blow the mould and the men through the roof, if it had no vent. Tubes, therefore, convey it to the surface, where it is lighted ; burning in strong, blue, unearthly jets that dim the other lights, and cast a diabolical hue upon the faces of the Mulcibers and upon the gaunt file of travelling cranes which pass the cauldron from the cylindrical melting furnaces to the mould; and, if needed, from one end of the shop to the other. Lively sparks occasionally fly off from the mouth of the mould with a force and profusion that no display of fire-works could surpass. The whole scene is so grim, and hot, and lurid, that a stranger, suddenly coming on it from the outer world, could hardly help inquiring, of the dark, perspiring artisans puddling down the molten metal at various openings of the mould—

"Ye black and midnight hags! What is't ye do?"

The answer to that question would be, "Casting a ten-ton steam cylinder for one of her Majesty's marine engines;" or —if the flaming cauldron gave forth a more ghastly illumination of green, and yellow, and purple, with gaseous exhalations hotter, drier, and more suffocating—"Running eleven tons of brass into the form of a screw propeller." Whereupon Macbeth would fall—after the manner of his countrymen —into an arithmetical reverie, and reckon that eleven tons of brass at a shilling a pound comes to nearly twelve hundred pounds sterling, for material alone; then, indulging in a playful application of the rule of three, he would compute that if the screw propeller costs the nation twelve hundred pounds, the entire cost of a pair of marine engines with extras and accessories would be from thirty-five to forty thousand pounds; and he would be right. Whence he would infer the origin of the term "putting on the screw," in reference to double income-tax; from which, indirectly the Lambeth-Marsh Mulcibers derive their profits, and the auxiliary Cyclops their wages.

It is vain to hint that attention is exhausted and limbs are tired. Before a notion can be formed of how the volcano's engines were constructed, acres of smiths'-shop, turning-shop, planing-shop, finishing-shop, and fitting-shop, have yet to be inspected; even if more acres of model-shop up-stairs are to be shirked; where carpenters make wooden models to be cast from, of the smaller parts of the steam-engine. More automata hugging tremendous cranks in staunch embraces; cutting them to fit hair's-breadths; polishing them to rival mirrors; worming pillars of iron through screw-plates; all cutting, planing, crunching, grinding the stubborn metal; themselves under the indomitable sway of the parent steam-automata in the engine-houses that give life and motion to the whole; never lying idle; untiring, incessant, inexhaustible; plodding on from Monday morning till Saturday night; working, working, working, here, on the banks of the Thames, the Clyde, the Tay, and the Humber; at the feet of Welsh mountains, upon the plains of Lancashire, and in the vales of Staffordshire, to fulfil the destiny that makes Britain the master manufacturer of the world, the British navy mistress of the seas, and the British subject the most boastful traveller and the patientest tax-payer under the sun.

I was delighted to discover that iron does not enter alone into the souls and composition of the Lambeth-Marsh Mulcibers. The softer influences of kindness, brotherhood, and hearty good fellowship reign amongst them. Their hearts, and their rough hands, are open when Charity makes her appeal. Not long before my visit, there had been a public meeting held in the fitting-shop, the occasion of which arose out of one such appeal; indirectly, but silently and spontaneously, made. A subscription had been entered into, and there was to be a presentation; not one of those fulsome ceremonies at which the donors flatter and soap and puff the recipient, that the recipient may return money's worth in more flattery and puffery and soft sawder, to the donors; but a hearty, unstudied tribute to worth in misfortune. The gift was neither a silver épergne servilely laid at the feet of a partner (the heads of the firm were ignorant of the proceedings until after they had taken place); nor a gold watch and appendages given to a popular foreman, nor any such compliment. It was a sensible live present, with long ears and four legs. It was a Donkey.

A poor old man and his ass, I learned from a well written account of the transaction by one of its promoters, had been in the habit of supplying the factory with chisel-rods and birch-brooms for the last two-and-thirty years. The respected quadruped and his master had gone on together in harmony and companionship for a quarter of a century, when the donkey died. The master was inconsolable and ruined; for,

in addition to this great affliction, another partner—his wife—
was on the point of following his other and equally faithful
friend graveward. A subscription was organised; not so
much to commemorate the startling fact coming within the
knowledge of fifteen hundred credible witnesses, of a donkey
actually dying, as to help the poor man in his distress. A
new ass for the husband, and every sort of comfort for the
wife, were speedily bought; and were presented at the meeting convened for the purpose. "Gentlemen," said the chairman, at the moment of actual presentation, "the art of engineering has arrived at a point of great perfection, and I
think I may assert, without fear of contradiction, that this is
the first instance that a piece of machinery of this description" (pointing to the donkey) "has been turned out from an
engine factory." The testimonial was then trotted over to
the hero of the evening, and a document was handed to him,
inscribed thus: "We hereby present you with this donkey,
harness, cart, and other articles. The animal being of the
feminine gender, we have designated Susan, after the name of
your wife, and we hope that you and she, and the Susan now
before us, may live long in health and happiness." When the
presentee marched off with his prize (which was gaily ornamented with ribbons and rosettes), he was received by the
outer populace of Lambeth-Marsh with deafening cheers.

XXXVI.

THE MANCHESTER SCHOOL OF ART.

OCTOBER 10, 1857.

No longer ago than when Hazlitt wrote, English connoisseurs
were stigmatised as a selfish class, who chiefly valued their
treasures because nobody else could derive pleasure from
them. They played the Blue Beard with all the beauty they
could get into their possession. They locked it up; would
admit only a chosen few to a share of their enjoyment, and
even those under stringent conditions and vigilant surveillance.
Frequent exposure to the basilisk eyes of the vulgar world
would, they believed, strike it dead. Of the hands of the

vulgar they had a not unreasonable horror also; for, it was then alleged, that the uneducated would resent the rarity of such opportunities, by carving their names on statues and defacing pictures, the beauties of which a "swinish multitude" could never recognise.

Times have changed. Great Exhibitions have come into vogue since eighteen hundred and fifty-one, and have induced many of the wealthy cheerfully to commit their most cherished Art-objects to the risks of packing and rough handling in transit, for the very purpose of disseminating the enjoyment, which is, by strict but churlish right, solely their own. In the belief—contrary to that of their fathers—that the value of their Art-possessions is increased rather than diminished by wide appreciation, they feel a pride in extending, instead of confining, the bounds of sympathy with their own tastes. The judgment which is extensively sympathised with, is flattered; for the more persons who admire any work of art, the more admire the taste of its possessor, that made the objects of it their property.

Limits, however, ought to be set to borrowing by the promoters of Great Exhibitions; otherwise, the generosity of lenders may be greatly abused by the application of an unwarrantable sort of pressure. Will you incur the odium of refusing your countenance, and your cherished valuables, to a glorious enterprise that is to awaken the million to a sense of the beautiful in Art? Will you refuse what Royalty itself has readily granted? Have you the courage to despise the noble example of His Grace of this, or of My Lord That? Queries of this kind have, we believe, forced valuable loans from unwilling but facile collectors, which their owners had strong and legitimate private reasons for wishing to keep readily at home: reasons quite independent of a want of confidence in the million-fingered public; the old theories concerning whom, experience has most satisfactorily reversed. Despite the extravagant predictions of ruin and devastation that were vented when the national galleries and parks were unrestrictedly thrown open to the people, no grave abuse of the privilege has been detected: the maniacal destruction of the Portland vase in the British Museum alone excepted; a single exception which proves the rule. The reports of the Minister

of Public Works show, that nearly every wilful act of wan-
tonness in public places and in public galleries has been
perpetrated, not by the uneducated throng, but by the so-
called respectable: not by the suspected poor, but by the
vulgar rich.

The metropolitan lieges having come out of such ordeals
with honour, a new and provincial instance of the respect
which large numbers of people show for works of Art has
been furnished by the Exhibition of Art-Treasures at Manchester. This well-fulfilled project has proved, that the
country public do not, as their enemies asserted they would
do, misbehave themselves while partaking of a tempting Art-
banquet, any more than the London public does; and, although
fewer of the poor class have partaken of it than were bidden
to the feast (at, be it remembered a shilling per head), yet
it is no light additional contradiction of the old slander about
the destructive propensities of the English mob, that nearly
one million individuals of all classes have passed through the
Manchester building, without any perceptible damage having
been done to any one of the ten thousand Art-objects of various descriptions that have been, for six months, placed within
their reach.

Although the originators of the great Art-Exhibition cannot
have been disappointed at the general results of their scheme,
it is notorious that the hope of its attracting the humbler classes
in sufficient numbers to occasion a great impulse to their sluggish appreciation of the Fine Arts, has nearly failed. The
working man has not come forward eagerly, neither with his
shilling, nor with that glow of enthusiasm for the thing of
beauty, which, it was promised him, would be a joy to him for
ever. Even when he has been admitted gratis, the attractions
of Knott-Mill Fair and Belle Vue Gardens have beaten the
Art-Treasures hollow. Many of the large manufacturers in
the north—to their honour be it spoken—paid, not only the
admission fees, but the railway fares, for the workpeople and
their families. One gentleman gave each man, in addition, a
neat little manual of his own composition to guide him to the
subjects to be selected for especial notice, from the gorgeous
array of colour and canvas. Another manufacturer provided
more materially. Having franked fourteen hundred of his

men and their relatives from Sheffield, he calculated that
the odd four hundred would, perhaps, after a hasty glance,
wander away, and not present themselves at dinner-time. He
therefore prudently ordered dinner in the refreshment department of the building, for no more than the remaining
thousand. But, when the hour of repast arrived, only two
hundred had stayed to dine. It was Whit-Monday, and more
congenial diversions had abstracted the great majority of his
guests.

It is not difficult to perceive why the Manchester Exhibition
has not proved such a propaganda of Art as its promoters
foretold. The plain fact is, that a collection of pictures of
various "schools" excites no interest, and affords but little
pleasure to the uninstructed eye. The ancient way of imitating
Nature, or the manner of copying her in various countries, is,
to the factory-worker or farm-labourer, simply unintelligible.
The only school he has the wit to recognise, is the school of
Nature; and that era or that nation in which Nature is imitated with the greatest truth, fitness, and beauty, presents the
only school which his unlearned taste can appreciate. The
touch of the Italian painter or of the Flemish painter, of the
German, French, or English painter, offers to him no subject
for discrimination. It is the one touch of Nature which
makes the whole world kin to him. Even that touch must be
distinct: must appeal at once to his apprehension. If he could
pick out from amidst a tangle of grotesque forms, in some of
the examples of early Christian art, one of those faces which
abound in them, faithfully expressing suffering, or adoration,
or intense piety, no doubt even *his* emotions would be excited.
But he cannot. He sees groups of figures in hard and falsely-
contrasted colours, with hands like gloves, arms growing an-
gularly out of trunks like ill-grafted branches, and he looks no
longer and no further. Not having the gift of connoisseurship,
he would not forgive what he knows to be gross departures
from real forms in one part of a figure, for the sake of the
exquisite pathos and passion expressed in another part of it.
Nor is he blessed with the power of finding sources of inspiration in distorted anatomy and distracting perspective. If he
were, he would probably leave the plough or the loom and
take to lecturing young painters; trying to teach them to

imitate the defects, as a means of emulating the genius, of the pre-Raphaelite masters.

Precisely the same case holds with modern pictures. The general public—especially the humbler sections of it—being happily uninformed on the subject of technicalities, take not the faintest interest in it. Their ignorance is their bliss. They concern themselves solely with results, and they refer those results to the test of those natural objects with which they are most familiar. The picture which delights them most, is that which most vividly recals familiar scenes or familiar faces to their imagination.

Small blame, therefore, to the Lancashire folk for not fulfilling the flattering predictions respecting their supposed desire to be made acquainted with Art. The gigantic Art-Treasury at Manchester can only be enjoyed to the full by persons who have habitually seen pictures, and who have acquired a knowledge of the painters. Such spectators are few in every station of life. The experience of the habitué of the Manchester galleries was, that the majority of the well-dressed crowd gossiped and grouped round the music, promenaded and looked at and admired each other—did everything except examine the pictures. Those who did vary their amusements by glancing at the walls, were generally found studying the portraits. The experience of the true amateur was no less curious. Amongst the lounging, promenading, over-dressed, and flirting many, he scarcely could distinguish the same face twice; but, after a few visits, he got to know by sight, the picture-loving few, by meeting them frequently lingering as he lingered, at the most notable masterpieces.

To such visitors, their trip to the Manchester Exhibition of Art-Treasures will hereafter be remembered as an era in their lives. It is scarcely possible that such an assemblage of all they most desired to see, can ever again be brought together. Certainly no such collection will ever be better arranged. The chronological plan was the only one capable of evolving order out of chaos; and great clearness was attained in this object by Mr. Scharf the younger, who hung the ancient works; and by Mr. Egg, who arranged the modern pictures. Mr. Peter Cunningham's mode of placing the portraits, affords, by the aid of his catalogue, a biographical History of England, much more striking and instructive than that by Granger and Noble. In truth, the whole Exhibition is, in itself, a history. The annals of Historic Art are so distinctly written on its walls, that those who are not wholly uninstructed in Art literature may easily read them.

At the same time, it is not difficult to define the popular attractions of the show, apart from the paintings. They are numerous and captivating. Three long, well-proportioned galleries; cases filled with priceless Art-objects in the precious metals, in ivory and in wood, besides jewels, bijouterie, and rare carvings: trophies of warlike Art composed of arms and armour; an admirable orchestra discoursing most excellent music; and, lastly, the moving spectacle of well-dressed, ever-changing company, always delightfully sprinkled with Lancashire witchcraft, which spreads its incantations (and its drapery) broad-cast over the scene.

Few can estimate the energy and perseverance, the administrative and executive skill, which, in no more time than palaces are built in story-books, converted a cricket-ground into this enormous and unsurpassed casket of gems. On the tenth of June eighteen hundred and fifty-six, the two elevens of a Manchester cricket club played a match in their own field at Old Trafford, a couple of miles west of Manchester. Before the first anniversary of that game was completed, the ground was not only occupied by an edifice that would have covered every one of the twenty-two at his post, including longstop and field-scout; but it had been made the terminus of a railway communicating with every part of Great Britain, and by which it was already filled with works of Art. How, by the first of May in the present year, these were conveyed and unpacked without a scratch; how arranged in their proper places,—the tiniest miniature and the grandest historical picture, the smallest signet ring and the hugest suit of armour, —how registered, ticketed, catalogued and placed, the executive committee, and Mr. John Deane, the general commissioner, can only tell.

The modest assurance essential to solicit, from the least accessible people in this land, the loan of objects they cherish more tenderly and guarded more jealously than most of their material possessions; the thousand and one well-considered details necessary to the packing and conveyance of these priceless loans; the precautions for their safe custody and preservation; the contrivances for admitting vast crowds of entrants, for feeding them when hungry, and seating them when tired; the arrangements for bringing them not only from Manchester and all Lancashire, but from every corner of this island, are seldom thought of, even by the most inquisitive visitor. He hardly suspects that he treads over an arterial system of water-supply, capable of quenching an outburst of fire in one moment in any part of the building, at any height, and no fire-engine required. Although he dines in the refreshment-room, he little wots of the kitchen, and the cooks, and the bewildering apparatus capable of producing a dinner of any reasonable number of courses, for ten thousand guests. He does not suspect the near neighbourhood of a police barrack, or imagine the acres of shed, and pyramids of packing-cases so arranged, that each case shall be promptly mated with its containee, when the great day of restitution arrives. In short, he does not realise a tithe of the clever and untiring pre-arrangement by which the great Art-Treasures' feat has been accomplished. Then the expense! In no other place, could seventy gentlemen be found to guarantee one thousand pounds each to carry out an undertaking promising no hope of profit, but every prospect of loss. Unhappily, that prospect will be fulfilled, and these gentlemen will be losers in money, in consequence of their miscalculation of support from the working classes; but they have conferred a distinction on their city which no money could buy.* They have shown themselves to be true patrons of art. The methodical, business-like, energetic manner in which their money has been spent and their original intentions realised, affords a profitable lesson to the bungling incapability with which the simplest State transaction is mismanaged at head-quarters. The first idea of the Exhibition was conceived by Mr. Deane in conjunction with Mr. Peter Cunningham, and the general details of its management have been thoroughly superintended (under the direction of the executive committee, headed by Mr. Thomas Fairbairn, junior) by Mr. Deane; who presents a rare

---

* Happily, the final result arrived at when the accounts were closed (after this paper was written), showed, it is believed, a small surplus.

instance of the union in one person, of a bold and comprehensive projector with an exact and able executant.

In five days from the date of the present number of Household Words, this grand treasury of art will be closed. In due time its treasures will be dispersed; the building, like its predecessors in London and Dublin, removed, and the cricketers put in possession of their cricket-ground again as quietly as if they had awoke from a bright and sparkling dream after that excellent supper which usually follows a well-played game. The effects of the short-lived enterprise will, however, be permanent; for some of the seed it has sown will assuredly bear fruit. Setting aside the sight of so many beautiful objects enjoyed by a million pair of eyes, the mere talk and discussion about art which it occasions would materially conduce to the spread of a taste for and appreciation of Art, among persons over whom Art always exercises a good influence.

XXXVII.

MY ANNULAR ECLIPSE.

APRIL 24, 1858.

ON Monday, the fifteenth of March last, I rose soon after daylight to study two interesting documents: one, a map of England, which Mr. Warren De la Rue had intersected with three straight lines, to show the direct path, across this island, to be traversed that morning by the Solar Eclipse: the other, a hand-bill invitation to the public generally from the Great Western Railway Company, to an excursion to Swindon; for, at Swindon, according to the astronomers, the darkness which was to prevail at mid-day, would be most visible. To these aids to reflection were added a few personal observations of the state of the weather: which, as the morning advanced, was very encouraging.

The result of this my first lesson in astronomical and meteorological science, was a rapid toilette, a cold breakfast (I am a bachelor), a sharp walk, and a seat in a railway carriage. Of this carriage I and my friend The Count, whom I had picked up on the platform, were the earliest occupants.

"It is a singular fact," observed this friend of mine—a

Scotch schoolfellow—who was looking out of the window, and filling it up with his broad shoulders to prevent the intrusion of strangers; "that, of the crowd of passengers now struggling for places, at least fifty per cent. wear spectacles; and, of these, twenty-five per cent. are adorned with white cravats." It was his passion for arithmetic (termed "counting" in Scotch schools), that gave him his title; he being plain Mr. MacAli quot. "The luggage, too, is exceptional," he went on to observe. "It is all mahogany, bound at the edges with brass, if you notice. And——" here The Count, suddenly seeing some one he knew, waved his arm frantically, exclaiming: "Hi! hi! Sidery! Professor! There's plenty of room here! Come in." The signal was answered. "Capital fellow!" he said to me, as he gathered up his coat, his newspaper, his hat, and his gloves from five of the seats, which he had appropriated. "Formerly Professor of Conic Sections at Saint Cwrg's College, South Wales: and no mean astronomer, I can tell you. See what a lot of apparatus he has brought!"

"Do you include in that expression the lovely young woman clinging so gracefully about him, amidst the unwieldy pile of things at his feet; and the three young men looking on?" I asked.

"Well, yes," said The Count, who was always as literal as an Arabic numeral. "You will see: Sidery will utilise even his daughter and sons somehow for eclipse purposes; as he will me, and you, too, if you don't mind."

"Have you room for five?" the astronomer asked, with timidity.

"For *any* number," I answered fervently, while making room for Miss Sidery, who passed me with a gracious bend, and the sweetest unspoken "Thank you!" She was followed by her brothers, to whom the Professor handed in, tenderly—as if it were a well-packed baby—a great mahogany box containing his telescope. Then he delivered through the open door, several thermometers, pronouncing with each a verbal label: "dry bulb;" "wet bulb;" "red bulb;" "black bulb." Then a barometer; then a sextant boxed up in a mahogany cocked-hat; then a couple of lorgnettes; then a pair of clouded goggles; then some packets of stained glass. I felt dreadfully afraid of the Professor and of all these instruments. My ignorance of every kind of heavenly body was now to be punished by seventy-seven miles of humiliation; and, I should have hated The Count for bringing it upon me, if any sort of harsh sentiment could have been possible in the benign presence of the pair of day-stars that shone full upon me from the opposite seat. Still the Professor went on shipping apparatus with all the perseverance and with something of the manner of a wharf-clerk; calling out the names of the objects as they were taken from him; a box of lucifers; a candle; a Welsh testament, large print; a Greek testament, small print; a copy of Jones's Diamond Classics; a roll of photographic paper; a burning glass; two ounces of gunpowder; a pot of crocuses in full bloom; a pot of violets; a bundle of camp-stools; three umbrellas, several papers of sandwiches, and two full flasks; "for," Mr. Sidery observed, in allusion to the latter miscellanea, as he entered the carriage with the train already in motion, "Science must be fed."

Surely they were not going to eat the candle, or the crocuses, or the gunpowder! Could those strange appliances be wanted to observe the phenomena of an eclipse with? Not liking to show my ignorance too soon, I suppressed inquiry for the present.

By dint of packing this medley underneath the seats, and overhead in the netting, the Professor eventually found a seat for himself while we were passing Hanwell.

"We must now distribute our parts," he said when fairly settled. "There are so many phenomena to note while the Eclipse lasts, and so little time to note them in, that each of us must undertake to observe one, or one class of them. What will your friend be responsible for?" he asked of MacAliquot. "The time of occultation, the barometer, or Bailey's beads?"

I blushed to the ears; for the day-stars beamed an effulgent curiosity upon me; but The Count interrupted, to my great relief, with, "We had better leave him out. He is not scientific."

"Not scientific!" exclaimed the bright particular star gleefully. "I am so glad! There will be somebody to sympathise with me."

I should not like to describe—even if I could—the effect of this little remark upon my sensations. Fortunately, I kept them so strictly to myself, that I did not do anything ridiculous. "The sun is to be darkened," she continued, glancing charitably at me, "I know. But I really do not know how or why."

The Professor seemed delighted to have, or to pretend to have, somebody to teach. In a minute he had out two pocket-handkerchiefs; one white, the other snuff-colour. He rolled them up into balls, tight enough to play at tennis with. He suspended one between each finger and thumb. He declared that the globular lamp in the roof of the carriage was the sun, that the bandana handkerchief was the earth, and the cambric handkerchief the moon. He then imitated an orrery, with the earth moving round the sun (as far as the roof of the carriage would permit), and the moon revolving round the earth. "That being so" (he always addressed me), "a time comes when the three spheres must, for a few moments, travel into one line; the moon getting between the earth and the sun, thus: you don't see the sun now," he continued, as if speaking to his daughter, but still looking my way.

"How can I, while you put your linen moon between it and my eyes?" said the young lady. "But I can see part of it."

"Of course you can; because the moon is smaller than the sun, and nearer to you," was the reply. "You see the outer rim of the lamp in the form of a ring, don't you? Well, that's an annular eclipse."

"From annulus, a ring," whispered Sidery Tertius, popping in a quotation from his Latin dictionary.

"May I ask" (I thought I was bound not to be absolutely dumb) "why it is that the moon, being the smaller body as you say it is, will obscure so much of the sun as to leave, when the eclipse is at its height, no more than a narrow rim of the sun visible?"

Mr. Sidery and MacAliquot were both eager to let off an answer upon me; but Sidery conquered, by generously offering to lend me a fourpenny-piece. "Place it before one eye; shut the other, and look at the sun—no, not at the lamp, but the real sun; which is now fortunately just enough obscured by thin clouds not to blind you. That very small disc completely obscures the sun, does it not?"

"Yes."

"Hold it further from your eye, at arm's length. Does it still hide the sun from you?"

"It does."

"Ay; but if held nearer by three or four yards, your little silver moon would cover no more of the sun than would produce an annular eclipse."

The Count could hold out no longer. "The distance of the sun from the fourpenny-piece, when close to the eye, is about ninety-five millions of miles, and the eclipse is total; but reduce the distance to ninety-five millions of miles, less half a dozen yards, and the eclipse becomes annular so long as you keep your eye and the two bodies in a straight line with one another. Now, the moon——"

"Very true," interrupted the lecturer, impatiently, "the further you remove the coin from your eye, the less of the sun will be eclipsed. You see, now, how it is that a small body can eclipse a large one."

"Therefore," (MacAliquot was not to be beaten), "the moon, although one quarter the size of the sun, being also only a four-hundredth part of his distance from the earth, naturally eclipses a large portion of that luminary when it passes between him and us."

"Bless me, here's Reading!" exclaimed the Professor, "and we have not appointed our observing officers yet. As, ladies," he continued, addressing his daughter with the mild rudiments of a joke twinkling in his eye, "are said to be particularly astute wherever rings are concerned; you shall watch the annulus. It will be perfect at two minutes past one o'clock, when it will be half a digit broad."

"But I don't know what a digit is, papa," murmured Bright-Eyes, looking down. "Is it the ring finger?"

Everybody laughed except MacAliquot; who gravely informed us that a digit is the twelfth part of the circumference of the sun and moon. His friend the scientific stage-manager went on casting the parts:

"You, Charles" (his eldest son), "will fix your attention on Bailey's beads. Bailey's beads, my dear," he looked at Stella, but he meant the enlightenment he was going to administer for me, "are curious and unaccountable appearances that were first accurately noted by Mr. Bailey. During that stage of an

annular eclipse when it is complete and the ring is about to
be put out of shape, a number of long black parallel lines are
drawn out by the moon, as if some glutinous substance had
stuck to the edge of the sun, and was being pulled out in
strings (the light between them giving an appearance like
beads), until they break and wholly disappear. This phenomenon has been observed during every eclipse."

"May I have the job of letting off the gunpowder?" asked
Sidery the Third, flourishing the burning-glass.

"Yes; but George" (Sidery Secundus) "must stand by
with the watch, and register the power of the sun by noting
the time its rays, concentrated by the burning-glass, take to
explode the gunpowder."

"I fear there will be no rays to catch. Look at those provoking clouds!" Miss Sidery pointed to windward.

The astronomer nervously surveyed first the weather, then
his elaborate preparations; but was too hopeful to encourage
a doubt that the eclipse would be an entire success. Before
we arrived at Swindon, he had distributed all his offices. I
was to observe that the beasts of the field knelt down to
rest; that the birds in the air fluttered back to their nests. I
was to watch the crocuses in the flower-pot, that they duly
partook in the universal deception as to the time of day, and
closed themselves; I was to perceive that the violets gave
out their more powerful night-scent. These duties were imparted to me in a tone which conveyed a threat that I should
be held responsible if Nature did not behave precisely as philosophy had foretold. Charles was to hold the lighted candle
between the sun and his eye, to testify at how many sun's
breadths' distance from the sun the flame could be seen.
MacAliquot undertook the Welsh Scriptures and the Diamond Classics, to ascertain the different degrees of darkness,
by his ability to read the three sizes of print. He was also
to be general timekeeper; to check off the punctuality of the
eclipse in keeping the appointment astronomers had made
for it, both in its first appearance, its greatest magnitude,
and its exit over the face of the sun. The Professor took to
the telescope. He was, besides, to keep everybody at his
post, and to maintain a thorough discipline amongst his corps
of observation.

Swindon refreshment-room, ten fifty-five. Coffee, sandwiches, tea, sausage-rolls, bread-and-butter, Banbury cakes, buns, soda, brandy, bottled porter, pork-pies for everybody (about two hundred) immediately! The young ladies at the counters conduct themselves with that deliberate self-possession which is characteristic of great minds under the pressure of emergencies. They move like duchesses. The Sidery flask and sandwiches, however, make us independent of them. Meanwhile the male branches of the Sidery family have unloaded all the apparatus upon the south platform; and, being persons of great constructive abilities, have fitted up an observatory in defiance of every railway regulation, and even of a train, which is ready to run away from the Eclipse, to Gloucester. They construct it of chairs purloined from the offices, wheel-barrows, their own camp-stools, umbrellas, and other impromptu materials. Even the telescope finds a station of its own in the same precincts.

The two hundred orders for refreshment have at length been executed, and some of the excursionists post themselves on a rising ground to the left; others climb the hill into the town; but the knowing ones make for the old churchyard. So many are, however, of one way of thinking, that every foot of the station is very soon occupied. Sofas are brought out, and ladies gracefully recline upon them, opera-glasses in hand, precisely as if they were waiting to scrutinise the luminaries of Her Majesty's Theatre.

Eleven thirty. Clouds pass rapidly over the sun. Some obscure him altogether; others supersede coloured glasses. Mr. Sidery looks vexed and disappointed. Little Sidery lets off his "poofs!" of gunpowder with the rays from the burning-glass; now in one minute; now in seven. MacAliquot, watch in hand, looks official and important. Miss Sidery, having as yet nothing celestial to observe, makes delightful observations to me on subjects I am better acquainted with, than the firmament; such as pictures, music, pic-nics, and light literature. I am occasionally called to a sense of duty by our chief, who points out a cow in the meadow and a particularly spruce sparrow perched upon the wires of the telegraph. More clouds.

Eleven thirty-five. Intense excitement. Clouds too thin to

20*

obscure the sun. Every bit of coloured glass patching every
eye. Yet the eclipse must have come upon some of the spectators as an unexpected accident; for they have brought nothing wherewith to see the garish orb of day as in a glass,
darkly. Whereupon railway workmen suddenly ascend from
unexplained lower regions with bits of smoked glass, for which,
people, who have not courage to borrow of the better provided
distractedly bargain. One slender gentleman seizes a huge
red danger signal-lamp, and lifts it up before his face; but being unable to maintain it in that position long enough even for
a glimpse of the sun, restores it to its rack.

Eleven forty. The right-hand lower edge of the sun begins
to flatten. The watch trembles in MacAliquot's hand as he
exclaims, " Wonderful!" The dark segment increases in size.
" What a testimony is this to the power of the science of as-
tronomy and the powers of arithmetic." The Count continues. " As we have always known that eleven digits and a
half of the sun will be eclipsed exactly at one o'clock to-day;
we also as certainly know that on the nineteenth of August
eighteen hundred and eighty-seven, at three o'clock in the
afternoon precisely, the next great eclipse will occur; leaving
only the small fraction of a digit of the sun unobscured."

A woful disappointment! A total eclipse by clouds. No
annulus, no flames, no Bailey's beads; very little darkness,
even at the moment (two minutes past one) of the greatest ob-
scuration. Bright-Eyes, in admiration of whom I had been
again lost, woke me up by observing that the atmosphere
(Miss Sidery is a distinguished amateur in water-colours)
seemed to be tinted with a weak wash of Indian ink. The air
was perceptibly colder, all the thermometers having fallen at
a mean rate of three degrees. I am bound, however, to state
that the cow in the meadow, the crocuses, the violets, and the
other natural objects that came under my ken, treated the
eclipse with provoking unconcern. The spruce sparrow flew
away from the wires, leisurely and playfully, over the station
roof; the country people going along the road, did not even
look up; and everything else in the surrounding landscape
conducted itself very much as usual; but a despondent astronomer, coming back from the churchyard under a load of unused instruments, assured us that he saw a flight of rooks

return to their nests; and Mr. Charles Sidery—who having given up the annular eclipse in despair, had strolled into the village—testified to the jackdaw belonging to the Odd Fellows' Arms going to roost, and to a horse having been so frightened (perhaps by the darkness) that he threw his rider and ran away. We ourselves witnessed an unpleasant phenomenon. A good-looking young country squire had mistaken mid-day for dinner-time, had drunk accordingly, and created great consternation at the station by banging everybody and everything about, in a state of distressing post-prandial excitement. He was speedily eclipsed by the police.

I asked my friend The Count to describe the journey back to London; as I found that task impossible, for reasons which need not be explained; but, as his manuscript is arranged in columns in the manner of Bradshaw's Guide, and consists of a record of the times of our passing places of note, of our arrival and departure at each station, of the number of successful puns he made, and of the number which all the rest of us failed in, I shall make no further mention of it.

It is now five weeks since the Great Solar Eclipse happened. I have been observing the stars, as much as possible, ever since; having become Mr. Sidery's pupil. Every evening, clear or cloudy, I have spent at his villa at Dulwich. I find in him a friend and a confidant. Last night, during an occultation of Venus (she had hastily retired to her mamma's room after an embarrassing interview with me), I laid before the kind astronomer, while standing at the end of his telescope in the garden, a statement of my private circumstances and prospects.

MacAliquot has since made his calculations, and confidently predicts that the Annular Eclipse of my bachelorhood will take place on an early day in the August of the present year

THE END.

☞ Every Number of Harper's Magazine contains from 20 to 50 pages—and from one third to one half more reading—than any other in the country.

HARPER'S MAGAZINE.

THE Publishers believe that the Nineteen Volumes of HARPER'S MAGAZINE now issued contain a larger amount of valuable and attractive reading than will be found in any other periodical of the day. The best Serial Tales of the foremost Novelists of the time: LEVERS' "Maurice Tiernay," BULWER LYTTON'S "My Novel," DICKENS'S "Bleak House" and "Little Dorrit," THACKERAY'S "Newcomes" aud "Virginians," have successively appeared in the Magazine simultaneously with their publication in England. The best Tales and Sketches from the Foreign Magazines have been carefully selected, and original contributions have been furnished by CHARLES READE, WILKIE COLLINS, Mrs. GASKELL, Miss MULOCH, and other prominent English writers.

The larger portion of the Magazine has, however, been devoted to articles upon American topics, furnished by American writers. Contributions have been welcomed from every section of the country; and in deciding upon their acceptance the Editors have aimed to be governed solely by the intrinsic merits of the articles, irrespective of their authorship. Care has been taken that the Magazine should never become the organ of any local clique in literature, or of any sectional party in politics.

At no period since the commencement of the Magazine have its literary and artistic resources been more ample and varied; and the Publishers refer to the contents of the Periodical for the past as the best guarantee for its future claims upon the patronage of the American public.

TERMS.—One Copy for One Year, $3 00; Two Copies for One Year, $5 00; Three or more Copies for One Year (each), $2 00; "Harper's Magazine" and "Harper's Weekly," One Year, $4 00. And an Extra Copy, gratis, for every Club of TEN SUBSCRIBERS.

Clergymen and Teachers supplied at Two DOLLARS a year. The Semi-Annual Volumes bound in Cloth, $2 50 each. Muslin Covers, 25 cents each. The Postage upon HARPER'S MAGAZINE must be paid at the Office where it is received. The Postage is Thirty-six Cents a year.

HARPER & BROTHERS, Publishers, Franklin Square, New York.

HARPER'S WEEKLY.

A JOURNAL OF CIVILIZATION.

A First-class Illustrated Family Newspaper.

PRICE FIVE CENTS.

HARPER'S WEEKLY has now been in existence three years. During that period no effort has been spared to make it the best possible Family Paper for the American People, and it is the belief of the Proprietors that, in the peculiar field which it occupies, no existing Periodical can compare with it.

Every Number of HARPER'S WEEKLY contains all the News of the week, Domestic and Foreign. The completeness of this department is, it is believed, unrivaled in any other weekly publication. Every noteworthy event is profusely and accurately illustrated at the time of its occurrence. And while no expense is spared to procure Original Illustrations, care is taken to lay before the reader every foreign picture which appears to possess general interest. In a word, the Subscriber to HARPER'S WEEKLY may rely upon obtaining a Pictorial History of the times in which we live, compiled and illustrated in the most perfect and complete manner possible. It is believed that the Illustrated Biographies alone—of which about one hundred and fifty have already been published—are worth far more to the reader than the whole cost of his subscription.

The literary matter of HARPER'S WEEKLY is supplied by some of the ablest writers in the English language. Every Number contains an installment of a serial story by a first-class author—BULWER'S "*What will he do with It?*" has appeared entire in its columns; one or more short Stories, the best that can be purchased at home or abroad; the best Poetry of the day; instructive Essays on topics of general interest; Comments on the Events of the time, in the shape of Editorials and the Lounger's philosophic and amusing Gossip; searching but generous Literary Criticisms; a Chess Chronicle; and full and careful reports of the Money, Merchandise, and Produce Markets.

In fixing at so low a price as Five Cents the price of their paper, the Publishers were aware that nothing but an enormous sale could remunerate them. They are happy to say that the receipts have already realized their anticipations, and justify still further efforts to make HARPER'S WEEKLY an indispensable guest in every home throughout the country.

TERMS.—One Copy for Twenty Weeks, $1 00; One Copy for One Year, $2 50; One Copy for Two Years, $4 00; Five Copies for One Year, $9 00; Twelve Copies for One Year, $20 00; Twenty-five Copies for One Year, $40 00. *An Extra Copy will be allowed for every Club of* TWELVE *or* TWENTY-FIVE SUBSCRIBERS.

THE

LAND · AND THE BOOK;

OR,

BIBLICAL ILLUSTRATIONS DRAWN FROM THE MANNERS
AND CUSTOMS, THE SCENES AND SCENERY OF
THE HOLY LAND.

By W. M. THOMSON, D.D.,

Twenty-five Years a Missionary of the A.B.C.F.M. in Syria and Palestine.

With two elaborate Maps of Palestine, an accurate Plan of Jeru-
salem, and *several hundred Engravings* representing the Scenery,
Topography, and Productions of the Holy Land, and the Cos-
tumes, Manners, and Habits of the People. Two elegant Large
12mo Volumes, Muslin, $3 50; Half Calf, $5 20.

The Land of the Bible is part of the Divine Revelation. It bears
testimony essential to faith, and gives *lessons* invaluable in exposition. Both have been written all over the fair face of Palestine,
and deeply graven there by the finger of God in characters of living
light. To collect this testimony and popularize these lessons for
the biblical student of every age and class is the prominent design
of this work. For *twenty-five years* the Author has been permitted
to read the Book by the light which the Land sheds upon it; and
he now hands over this friendly torch to those who have not been
thus favored. In this attempt the pencil has been employed to aid
the pen. A large number of pictorial illustrations are introduced,
many of them original, and all giving a genuine and true representation of things in the actual Holy Land of the present day. They
are not fancy sketches of imaginary scenes thrown in to embellish
the page, but pictures of living manners, studies of sacred topography, or exponents of interesting biblical allusions, which will add
greatly to the value of the work.

Published by HARPER & BROTHERS,
Franklin Square, New York.

HARPER & BROTHERS will send the above Work by Mail, postage paid, to any
part of the United States, on receipt of the Money.

MISS MULOCH'S NOVELS.

The Novels, of which a reprint is now presented to the public, form one of the most admirable series of popular fiction that has recently been issued from the London press. They are marked by their faithful delineation of character, their naturalness and purity of sentiment, the dramatic interest of their plots, their beauty and force of expression, and their elevated moral tone. No current Novels can be more highly recommended for the family library, while their brilliancy and vivacity will make them welcome to every reader of cultivated taste.

John Halifax, Gentleman. 8vo, Paper, 50 cents.

The Head of the Family. 8vo, Paper, 37½ cents.

Olive. 8vo, Paper, 25 cents.

Agatha's Husband. 8vo, Paper, 37½ cents.

Avillion, and other Tales. 8vo, Paper, 50 cents.

A Hero, and other Tales. 12mo, Muslin, 75 cents.

The Ogilvies. 8vo, Paper, 25 cents.

Nothing New. Tales. 8vo, Paper, 50 cents.

Published by HARPER & BROTHERS,
Franklin Square, New York.

HARPER & BROTHERS will send the following Works by Mail, postage paid (for any distance in the United States under 3000 miles), on receipt of the Money.

THE BRONTÉ NOVELS.

THE PROFESSOR. By CURRER BELL (Charlotte Brontë). 12mo, Paper, 60 cents; Muslin, 75 cents.

JANE EYRE. An Autobiography. Edited by CURRER BELL (Charlotte Brontë). Library Edition. 12mo, Muslin, 75 cents.—Cheap Edition. 8vo, Paper 37½ cents.

SHIRLEY. A Tale. By the Author of "Jane Eyre." Library Edition. 12mo, Muslin, 75 cents.—Cheap Edition. 8vo, Paper, 37½ cents.

VILLETTE. By the Author of "Jane Eyre," and "Shirley." Library Edition. 12mo, Muslin, 75 cents.—Cheap Edition. 8vo, Paper, 50 cents

WUTHERING HEIGHTS. By ELLIS BELL (Emily Brontë). 12mo, Muslin, 75 cents.

THE TENANT OF WILDFELL HALL. By ACTON BELL (Anna Brontë.) 12mo, Muslin, 75 cents

The wondrous power of Currer Bell's stories consists in their fiery insight into the human heart, their merciless dissection of passion, and their stern analysis of character and motive. The style of these productions possesses incredible force—sometimes almost grim in its bare severity—then relapsing into passages of melting pathos—always direct, natural, and effective in its unpretending strength. They exhibit the identity which always belongs to works of genius by the same author, though without the slightest approach to monotony. The characters portrayed by Currer Bell all have a strongly-marked individuality. Once brought before the imagination, they haunt the memory like a strange dream. The sinewy, muscular strength of her writings guarantees their permanent duration, and thus far they have lost nothing of their intensity of interest since the period of their composition.

Published by HARPER & BROTHERS, Franklin Square, N. Y.

A HISTORY OF GREECE,

FROM THE EARLIEST PERIOD TO THE CLOSE OF THE GENERA-
TION CONTEMPORARY WITH ALEXANDER THE GREAT.

BY GEORGE GROTE, ESQ.

Vol. XII. contains Portrait, Maps, and Index.   Complete in 12 vols. 12mo,
Muslin, $9 00 ; Sheep, $12 00 ; Half Calf, $15 00.

It is not often that a work of such magnitude is undertaken ; more seldom still
is such a work so perseveringly carried on, and so soon and yet so worthily accomplished. Mr. Grote has illustrated and invested with an entirely new significance a portion of the past history of humanity, which he, perhaps, thinks the most
splendid that has been, and which all allow to have been very splendid. He has made
great Greeks live again before us, and has enabled us to realize Greek modes of thinking. He has added a great historical work to the language, taking its place with
other great histories, and yet not like any of them in the special combination of
merits which it exhibits : scholarship and learning such as we have been accustomed to demand only in Germans ; an art of grouping and narration different
from that of Hume, different from that of Gibbon, and yet producing the effect of
sustained charm and pleasure ; a peculiarly keen interest in events of the political
order, and a wide knowledge of the business of politics ; and, finally, harmonizing
all, a spirit of sober philosophical generalization always tending to view facts
collectively in their speculative bearing as well as to record them individually.
It is at once an ample and detailed narrative of the history of Greece, and a lucid
philosophy of Grecian history.— *London Athenæum, March 8, 1856.*

Mr. Grote will be emphatically *the* historian of the people of Greece.—*Dublin
University Magazine.*

The acute intelligence, the discipline, faculty of intellect, and the excellent erudition every one would look for from Mr. Grote ; but they will here also find the
element which harmonizes these, and without which, on such a theme, an orderly
and solid work could not have been written.—*Examiner.*

A work second to that of Gibbon alone in English historical literature. Mr.
Grote gives the philosophy as well as the facts of history, and it would be difficult
to find an author combining in the same degree the accurate learning of the scholar with the experience of a practical statesman. The completion of this great
work may well be hailed with some degree of national pride and satisfaction.—
Literary Gazette, March 8, 1856.

The better acquainted any one is with Grecian history, and with the manner in
which that history has heretofore been written, the higher will be his estimation
of this work. Mr. Grote's familiarity both with the great highways and the ob-
scurest by-paths of Grecian literature and antiquity has seldom been equaled, and
not often approached, in unlearned England ; while those Germans who have ri-
valed it have seldom possessed the quality which eminently characterizes Mr.
Grote, of keeping historical imagination severely under the restraints of evidence.
The great charm of Mr. Grote's history has been throughout the cordial admiration he feels for the people whose acts and fortunes he has to relate. * * We bid
Mr. Grote farewell ; heartily congratulating him on the conclusion of a work which
is a monument of English learning, of English clear-sightedness, and of English
love of freedom and the characters it produces.—*Spectator.*

Endeavor to become acquainted with Mr. Grote, who is engaged on a Greek
History. I expect a great deal from this production.—NIEBUHR, *the Historian,
to Professor* LIEBER.

The author has now incontestably won for himself the title, not merely of *a*
historian, but of *the* historian of Greece.—*Quarterly Review.*

Mr. Grote is, beyond all question, *the* historian of Greece, unrivaled, so far as
we know, in the erudition and genius with which he has revived the picture of a
distant past, and brought home every part and feature of its history to our intellects and our hearts.—*London Times.*

For becoming dignity of style, unforced adaptation of results to principles, careful verification of theory by fact, and impregnation of fact by theory—for extensive
and well-weighed learning, employed with intelligence and taste, we have seen no
historical work of modern times which we would place above Mr. Grote's history.—*Morning Chronicle.*

HARPER & BROTHERS, PUBLISHERS, FRANKLIN SQUARE, N. Y.

THE RISE OF
THE DUTCH REPUBLIC.

A History.

By JOHN LOTHROP MOTLEY.

New Edition. With a Portrait of WILLIAM OF ORANGE. 3 vols. 8vo, Muslin, $6 00; Sheep, $6 75; Half Calf antique, $9 00; Half Calf, extra gilt, $10 50.

We regard this work as the best contribution to modern history that has yet been made by an American.—*Methodist Quarterly Review.*

The "History of the Dutch Republic" is a great gift to us; but the heart and earnestness that beat through all its pages are greater, for they give us most timely inspiration to vindicate the true ideas of our country, and to compose an able history of our own.—*Christian Examiner* (Boston).

This work bears on its face the evidences of scholarship and research. The arrangement is clear and effective; the style energetic, lively, and often brilliant. * * * Mr. Motley's instructive volumes will, we trust, have a circulation commensurate with their interest and value.—*Protestant Episcopal Quarterly Review.*

To the illustration of this most interesting period Mr. Motley has brought the matured powers of a vigorous and brilliant mind, and the abundant fruits of patient and judicious study and deep reflection. The result is, one of the most important contributions to historical literature that have been made in this country.—*North American Review.*

We would conclude this notice by earnestly recommending our readers to procure for themselves this truly great and admirable work, by the production of which the author has conferred no less honor upon his country than he has won praise and fame for himself, and than which, we can assure them, they can find nothing more attractive or interesting within the compass of modern literature. —*Evangelical Review.*

It is not often that we have the pleasure of commending to the attention of the lover of books a work of such extraordinary and unexceptionable excellence as this one.—*Universalist Quarterly Review.*

There are an elevation and a classic polish in these volumes, and a felicity of grouping and of portraiture, which invest the subject with the attractions of a living and stirring episode in the grand historic drama.—*Southern Methodist Quarterly Review.*

The author writes with a genial glow and love of his subject.—*Presbyterian Quarterly Review.*

Mr. Motley is a sturdy Republican and a hearty Protestant. His style is lively and picturesque, and his work is an honor and an important accession to our national literature.—*Church Review.*

Mr. Motley's work is an important one, the result of profound research, sincere convictions, sound principles, and manly sentiments; and even those who are most familiar with the history of the period will find in it a fresh and vivid addition to their previous knowledge. It does honor to American literature, and would do honor to the literature of any country in the world.—*Edinburgh Review.*

A serious chasm in English historical literature has been (by this book) very remarkably filled. * * * A history as complete as industry and genius can make it now lies before us, of the first twenty years of the revolt of the United Provinces. * * * All the essentials of a great writer Mr. Motley eminently possesses. His mind is broad, his industry unwearied. In power of dramatic description no modern historian, except, perhaps, Mr. Carlyle, surpasses him, and in analysis of character he is elaborate and distinct.—*Westminster Review.*

It is a work of real historical value, the result of accurate criticism, written in a liberal spirit, and from first to last deeply interesting.—*Athenæum.*

The style is excellent, clear, vivid, eloquent; and the industry with which original sources have been investigated, and through which new light has been shed over perplexed incidents and characters, entitles Mr. Motley to a high rank in the literature of an age peculiarly rich in history.—*North British Review.*

It abounds in new information, and, as a first work, commands a very cordial recognition, not merely of the promise it gives, but of the extent and importance of the labor actually performed on it.—*London Examiner.*

Mr. Motley's "History" is a work of which any country might be proud.—*Press* (London).

Mr. Motley's History will be a standard book of reference in historical literature.—*London Literary Gazette.*

Mr. Motley has searched the whole range of historical documents necessary to the composition of his work.—*London Leader.*

This is really a great work. It belongs to the class of books in which we range our Grotes, Milmans, Merivales, and Macaulays, as the glories of English literature in the department of history. * * * Mr. Motley's gifts as a historical writer are among the highest and rarest.—*Nonconformist* (London).

Mr. Motley's volumes will well repay perusal. * * * For his learning, his liberal tone, and his generous enthusiasm, we heartily commend him, and bid him good speed for the remainer of his interesting and heroic narrative.—*Saturday Review.*

The story is a noble one, and is worthily treated. * * * Mr. Motley has had the patience to unravel, with unfailing perseverance, the thousand intricate plots of the adversaries of the Prince of Orange; but the details and the literal extracts which he has derived from original documents, and transferred to his pages, give a truthful color and a picturesque effect, which are especially charming.—*London Daily News.*

M. Lothrop Motley dans son magnifique tableau de la formation de notre Ré-publique.—*G. GROEN VAN PRINSTERER.*

Our accomplished countryman, Mr. J. Lothrop Motley, who, during the last five years, for the better prosecution of his labors, has established his residence in the neighborhood of the scenes of his narrative. No one acquainted with the fine powers of mind possessed by this scholar, and the earnestness with which he has devoted himself to the task, can doubt that he will do full justice to his important but difficult subject.—*W. H. PRESCOTT.*

The production of such a work as this astonishes, while it gratifies the pride of the American reader.—*N. Y. Observer.*

The "Rise of the Dutch Republic" at once, and by acclamation, takes its place by the "Decline and Fall of the Roman Empire," as a work which, whether for research, substance, or style, will never be superseded.—*N. Y. Albion.*

A work upon which all who read the English language may congratulate themselves.—*New Yorker Handels Zeitung.*

Mr. Motley's place is now (alluding to this book) with Hallam and Lord Mahon, Alison and Macaulay in the Old Country, and with Washington Irving, Prescott, and Bancroft in this.—*N. Y. Times.*

THE authority, in the English tongue, for the history of the period and people to which it refers.—*N. Y. Courier and Enquirer.*

This work at once places the author on the list of American historians which has been so signally illustrated by the names of Irving, Prescott, Bancroft, and Hildreth.—*Boston Times.*

The work is a noble one, and a most desirable acquisition to our historical literature.—*Mobile Advertiser.*

Such a work is an honor to its author, to his country, and to the age in which it was written.—*Ohio Farmer.*

Published by HARPER & BROTHERS,
Franklin Square, New York.

HARPER & BROTHERS will send the above Work by Mail (postage paid (for any distance in the United States under 8000 miles), on receipt of the Money.

CURTIS'S HISTORY

OF THE

CONSTITUTION.

HISTORY OF THE ORIGIN, FORMATION, AND ADOP-
TION OF THE CONSTITUTION OF THE UNITED
STATES. By GEORGE TICKNOR CURTIS. Complete in 2 vols.
8vo, Muslin, $4 00 ; Law Sheep, $5 00 ; Half Calf, $6 00.

A book so thorough as this in the comprehension of its subject, so impartial
in the summing up of its judgments, so well considered in its method, and so
truthful in its matter, may safely challenge the most exhaustive criticism. The
Constitutional History of our country has not before been made the subject of a
special treatise. We may congratulate ourselves that an author has been found
so capable to do full justice to it; for that the work will take its rank among the
received text-books of our political literature will be questioned by no one who
has given it a careful perusal.—*National Intelligencer.*

We know of no person who is better qualified (now that the late Daniel Web-
ster is no more), to undertake this important history.—*Boston Journal.*

It will take its place among the classics of American literature.—*Boston Courier.*

The author has given years to the preliminary studies, and nothing has escaped him in the patient and conscientious researches to which he has devoted
so ample a portion of time. Indeed, the work has been so thoroughly performed
that it will never need to be done over again; for the sources have been exhausted, and the materials put together with so much judgment and artistic skill that
taste and the sense of completeness are entirely satisfied.—*N. Y. Daily Times.*

A most important and valuable contribution to the historical and political literature of the United States. All publicists and students of public law will be
grateful to Mr. Curtis for the diligence and assiduity with which he has wrought
out the great mine of diplomatic lore in which the foundations of the American
Constitution are laid, and for the light he has thrown on his wide and arduous
subject.—*London Morning Chronicle.*

To trace the history of the formation of the Constitution, and explain the circumstances of the time and country out of which its various provisions grew, is a
task worthy of the highest talent. To have performed that task in a satisfactory manner is an achievement with which an honorable ambition may well be
gratified. We can honestly say that in our opinion Mr. Curtis has fairly won
this distinction.—*N. Y. Courier and Enquirer.*

We have seen no history which surpasses it in the essential qualities of a
standard work destined to hold a permanent place in the impartial judgment of
future generations.—*Boston Traveler.*

Should the second volume sustain the character of the first, we hazard nothing
in claiming for the entire publication the character of a standard work. It will
furnish the only sure guide to the interpretation of the Constitution, by unfolding
historically the wants it was intended to supply, and the evils which it was intended to remedy.—*Boston Daily Advertiser.*

This volume is an important contribution to our constitutional and historical
literature. * * * Every true friend of the Constitution will gladly welcome it.
The author has presented a narrative clear and interesting. It evinces careful
research, skillful handling of material, lucid statement, and a desire to write in
a tone and manner worthy of the great theme.—*Boston Post.*

Published by HARPER & BROTHERS,
Franklin Square, New York.

HISTORY

OF THE

UNITED STATES OF AMERICA.

By RICHARD HILDRETH.

FIRST SERIES.—From the First Settlement of the Country to the Adoption of the Federal Constitution. 3 vols. 8vo, Muslin, $6 00; Sheep, $6 75; Half Calf, $7 50.

SECOND SERIES.—From the Adoption of the Federal Constitution to the End of the Sixteenth Congress. 3 vols. 8vo, Muslin, $6 00; Sheep, $6 75; Half Calf, $7 50.

HILDRETH'S HISTORY OF THE UNITED STATES.

Written with candor, brevity, fidelity to facts, and simplicity of style and manner, and forms a welcome addition to the library of the nation.—*Prot. Churchman.*

Mr. Hildreth is a bold and copious writer. His work is valuable for the immense amount of material it embodies.—*De Bow's Review of the Southern and Western States.*

We may safely commend Mr. Hildreth's work as written in an excellent style, and containing a vast amount of valuable information.—*Albany Argus.*

His style is vigorously simple. It has the virtue of perspicuity. — *Zion's Herald.*

We value it on account of its impartiality. We have found nothing to indicate the least desire on the part of the author to exalt or debase any man or any party. His very patriotism, though high-principled and sincere, is sober and discriminate, and appears to be held in strong check by the controlling recollection that he is writing for posterity, and that if the facts which he publishes will not honor his country and his countrymen, fulsome adulation will not add to their glory.—*N. Y. Commercial Advertiser.*

We are confident that when the merits of this history come to be known and appreciated, it will be extensively regarded as decidedly superior to any thing that before existed on American history, and as a valuable contribution to American authorship. These stately volumes will be an ornament to any library, and no intelligent American can afford to be without the work. We have nobly patronized the great English history of the age, let us not fail to appreciate and patronize an American history so respectable and valuable as this certainly is.—*Biblical Repository (Bibliotheca Sacra).*

This work professes only to deal in *facts;* it is a book of *records;* it puts together clearly, consecutively, and, we believe, with strict impartiality, the events of American history. The work indicates patient, honest, and careful research, systematic arrangement, and lucid exposition.—*Home Journal.*

To exhibit the progress of the country from infancy to maturity; to show the actual state of the people, the real character of their laws and institutions, and the true designs of their leading men, at different periods, and to relate a sound, unvarnished tale of our early history, has been his design; and we are free to acknowledge that it has been executed with marked ability and triumphant success. Every lover of impartial history will accord to Mr. Hildreth his due meed of praise for the able and honest manner in which he has given the true history of the United States.—*Pennsylvanian.*

This work is full of detail, bears marks of care and research, and is written under the guidance of clear sight and good judgment rather than of theory, philosophical or historical, or of prejudice of any sort whatever. We trust that it will be widely read.—*N. Y. Courier and Enquirer.*

We pronounce it unsurpassed as a full, clear, and truthful history of our country so far. We rejoice that a work so important to our nation has been so ably performed.—*Literary American.*

Interesting, valuable, and very attractive. It is written in a style eminently clear and attractive, and presents the remarkable history which it records in a form of great simplicity and with graphic force. There is in it no attempt to palliate what is wrong, or to conceal what is true. It is a life-like and reliable history of the most remarkable series of events in the annals of the world.—*N. Y. Journal of Commerce.*

It is a valuable acquisition to American literature.—*Baltimore American.*

The history of our country with a scrupulous regard to truth.—*Buffalo Courier.*

We believe this to be a truthful, judicious, and valuable history, worthy of general acceptation.—*Philadelphia North American.*

The first complete history of our country.—*Chronotype.*

Published by *HARPER & BROTHERS,*
Franklin Square, New York.

*** HARPER & BROTHERS will send the above Work by Mail, postage paid (for any distance in the United States under 3000 miles), on receipt of the Money.

Harper's Catalogue.

A New Descriptive Catalogue, Harper & Brothers' Publications, with an Index and Classified Table of Contents, is now ready for Distribution, and may be obtained gratuitously on application to the Publishers personally, or by letter inclosing Six Cents in Postage Stamps.

The attention of gentlemen, in town or country, designing to form Libraries or enrich their Literary Collections, is respectfully invited to this Catalogue, which will be found to comprise a large proportion of the standard and most esteemed works in English Literature —COMPREHENDING MORE THAN TWO THOUSAND VOLUMES — which are offered, in most instances, at less than one half the cost of similar productions in England.

To Librarians and others connected with Colleges, Schools, &c., who may not have access to a reliable guide in forming the true estimate of literary productions, it is believed this Catalogue will prove especially valuable as a manual of reference.

To prevent disappointment, it is suggested that, whenever books can not be obtained through any bookseller or local agent, applications with remittance should be addressed direct to the Publishers, which will be promptly attended to.

www.ingramcontent.com/pod-product-compliance
Lightning Source LLC
Chambersburg PA
CBHW052340110726
47901CB00005B/1301